HARLAN COBEN
Three Great Novels

D1342325

Harlan Coben is widely recognized as one of the most exciting talents in American crime writing. He was the first ever author to win all three major crime awards in the US, and has established a bestselling series of crime novels starring his powerful creation, Myron Bolitar. He currently lives in New Jersey with his wife and four children.

Also by Harlan Coben

Deal Breaker
Drop Shot
Fade Away
Back Spin
One False Move
The Final Detail
No Second Chance
Just One Look

Harlan Coben

Three Great Novels

Darkest Fear
Tell No One
Gone For Good

ORION

Darkest Fear Copyright © 2000 Harlan Coben
Tell No One Copyright © 2001 Harlan Coben
Gone For Good Copyright © 2002 Harlan Coben

All rights reserved

The right of Harlan Coben to be identified as the author of this work has been asserted by him in accordance with the Copyright, Designs and Patents Act 1988.

First published in Great Britain in 2004 by
Orion
An imprint of Orion Books Ltd
Orion House, 5 Upper St Martin's Lane, London WC2H 9EA

ISBN 0 75286 735 0

A CIP catalogue record for this book is available from the British Library

Printed and bound in Great Britain by
Clays Ltd, St Ives plc

www.orionbooks.co.uk

Contents

Darkest Fear

When a father gives to his son, they both laugh.
When a son gives to his father, they both cry.
—Yiddish proverb

This one is for your father and mine

"What is your darkest fear?" the voice whispers. "Close your eyes now and picture it. Can you see it? Do you have it yet? The very worst agony you can imagine?"

After a long pause, I say, "Yes."

"Good. Now imagine something worse, something far, far worse . . ."

—"The Mind of Terror" by Stan Gibbs,
column in the *New York Herald*, January 16

The author wishes to thank Sujit Sheth, M.D., Department of Pediatrics, Babies and Children's Hospital in New York, Anne Armstrong-Coben, M.D., Department of Pediatrics, Babies and Children's Hospital (and my love monkey), and Joachim Schulz, Executive Director, Fanconi Anemia Research Fund, all of whom offered up wonderful medical insights and then watched me take liberties with them; two fellow scribes, friends, and experts in their fields, Linda Fairstein and Laura Lippman; Larry Gerson, the inspiration; Nils Lofgren, for rocking me over the last hurdle; early reader and long-time bud Maggie Griffin; Lisa Erbach Vance and Aaron Priest for another job well done; Jeffrey Bedford, FBI Special Agent (and not a bad freshman dorm counselor); as always, Dave Bolt; and mostly, Jacob Hoye, my editor for all the Myron Bolitar books—and now a father. That dedication is for you, too, Jake. Thanks, dude.

For those interested in becoming a bone marrow donor and perhaps saving a life, I urge you to contact the Anthony Nolan Trust at

www.anthonynolan.org.uk
or 020 7284 1234

For more information on Fanconi anemia, check out

www.fanconi.org

This book is a work of fiction. That means I make stuff up.

1

An hour before his world exploded like a ripe tomato under a stiletto heel, Myron bit into a fresh pastry that tasted suspiciously like a urinal cake.

"Well?" Mom prompted.

Myron battled his throat, won a costly victory, swallowed. "Not bad."

Mom shook her head, disappointed.

"What?"

"I'm a lawyer," Mom said. "You'd think I'd have raised a better liar."

"You did the best you could," Myron said.

She shrugged and waved a hand at the, uh, pastry. "It's my first time baking, *bubbe.* It's okay to tell me the truth."

"It's like biting into a urinal cake," Myron said.

"A what?"

"In men's public bathrooms. In the urinals. They put them there for the smell or something."

"And you eat them?"

"No—"

"Is that why your father takes so long in there? He's having a little Tastykake? And here I thought his prostate was acting up."

"I'm joking, Mom."

She smiled through blue eyes tinged with a red that Visine could never hope to get out, the red you can only get through slow, steady tears. Normally Mom was heavily into histrionics. Slow, steady tears were not her style. "So am I, Mr. Smarty Pants. You think you're the only one in this family with a sense of humor?"

Myron said nothing. He looked down at the, uh, pastry, fearing or perhaps hoping it might crawl away. In the thirty-plus years his mother had lived in this house, she had never baked—not from a recipe, not from scratch, not even from one of those Pillsbury morning croissant thingies that came in small mailing tubes. She could barely boil water without strict instructions and pretty much never cooked, though she could whip up a mean Celeste frozen pizza in the microwave, her agile fingers dancing across the numerical keypad in the vein of Nureyev at Lincoln Center. No, in the Bolitar household, the kitchen was more a gathering place—a Family Room Lite, if you will—than anything related to even the basest of the culinary arts. The round table held magazines and catalogs and congealing white boxes of Chinese takeout. The stovetop saw less action than a Merchant-Ivory production. The oven was a prop, strictly for show, like a politician's Bible.

Something was definitely amiss.

They were sitting in the living room with the dated pseudo-leather white modular couch and aqua-tinged rug whose shagginess reminded Myron of a toilet-seat cover. Grown-up Greg Brady. Myron kept stealing glances out the picture window at the For Sale sign in the front yard as though it were a spaceship that had just landed and something sinister was about to step out.

"Where's Dad?"

Mom gave a weary wave toward the door. "He's in the basement."

"In my room?"

"Your *old* room, yes. You moved out, remember?"

He did—at the tender age of thirty-four no less. Childcare experts would salivate and tsk-tsk over that one—the prodigal son choosing to remain in his split-level cocoon long after the deemed appropriate deadline for the butterfly to break free. But Myron might argue the opposite. He might bring up the fact that for generations and in most cultures, offspring lived in the familial home until a ripe old age, that adopting such a philosophy could indeed be a societal boom, helping people stay rooted to something tangible in this era of the disintegrating nuclear family. Or, if that rationale didn't float your boat, Myron could try another. He had a million.

But the truth of the matter was far simpler: He liked hanging out in the burbs with Mom and Dad—even if confessing such a sentiment was about as hip as an Air Supply eight track.

"So what's going on?" he asked.

"Your father doesn't know you're here yet," she said. "He thinks you're not coming for another hour."

Myron nodded, puzzled. "What's he doing in the basement?"

"He bought a computer. Your father plays with it down there."

"Dad?"

"My point exactly. The man can't change a lightbulb without a manual—all of a sudden he's Bill Gates. Always on the nest."

"The Net," Myron corrected.

"The what?"

"It's called the Net, Mom."

"I thought it was nest. The bird's nest or something."

"No, it's Net."

"Are you sure? I know there's a bird in there somewhere."

"The Web maybe," Myron tried. "Like with a spider."

She snapped her fingers. "That's it. Anyway your father is on there all the time, weaving the Web or whatever. He chats with people, Myron. That's what he tells me. He chats with complete strangers. Like he used to do with the CB radio, remember?"

Myron remembered. Circa 1976. Jewish Dads in the suburbs checking for "smokeys" on the way to the delicatessen. Mighty convoy of Cadillac Sevilles. Ten-four, good buddy.

"And that's not all," she went on. "He's typing his memoirs. A man who can't scribble down a grocery list without consulting Strunk and White suddenly thinks he's an ex-president."

They were selling the house. Myron still could not believe it. His eyes wandered about the overly familiar surroundings, his gaze getting snagged on the photographs running up the stairwell. He saw his family mature via fashion—the skirts and sideburns lengthening and shortening, the quasi-hippie fringes and suede and tie-dyes, the leisure suits and bell-bottoms, the frilly tuxedos that would be too tacky for a Vegas casino—the years flying by frame by frame like one of those depressing life insurance commercials. He spotted the poses from his basketball days—a sixth-grade suburban-league foul shot, an eighth-grade drive to the hoop, a high school slam dunk—the row ending with *Sports Illustrated* cover shots, two from his days at Duke and one with his leg in a cast and a large-fonted IS HE FINISHED? emblazoned across his knee-cast image (the answer in the mind's eye being an equally large-fonted YES!).

"So what's wrong?" he asked.

"I didn't say anything was wrong."

Myron shook his head, disappointed. "And you a lawyer."

"Setting a bad example?"

"It's no wonder I never ran for higher office."

She folded her hands on her lap. "We need to chat."

Myron didn't like the tone.

"But not here," she added. "Let's take a walk around the block."

Myron nodded and they rose. Before they reached the door, his cell phone rang. Myron snatched it up with a speed that would have made Wyatt Earp step back. He put the phone to his ear and cleared his throat.

"MB SportsReps," he said, silky-smooth, professional-like. "This is Myron Bolitar speaking."

"Nice phone voice," Esperanza said. "You sound like Billy Dee ordering two Colt 45s."

Esperanza Diaz was his longtime assistant and now sports-agent partner at MB SportsReps (M for Myron, the B for Bolitar—for those keeping score).

"I was hoping you were Lamar," he said.

"He hasn't called yet?"

"Nope."

He could almost see Esperanza frown. "We're in deep doo-doo here," she said.

"We're not in deep doo-doo. We're just sucking a little wind, that's all."

"Sucking a little wind," Esperanza repeated. "Like Pavarotti running the Boston Marathon."

"Good one," Myron said.

"Thanks."

Lamar Richardson was a power-hitting Golden Glove shortstop who'd just become a free agent—"free agent" being a phrase agents whisper in the same way a mufti might whisper "Praise Allah." Lamar was shopping for new representation and had whittled his final list down to three agencies: two supersized conglomerates with enough office space to house a Price Club and the aforementioned pimple-on-the-buttocks but oh-so-personal MB SportsReps. Go, pimple-butt!

Myron watched his mother standing by the door. He switched ears and said, "Anything else?"

"You'll never guess who called," Esperanza said.

"Elle and Claudia demanding another ménage à trois?"

"Oooo, close."

She would never just tell him. With his friends, everything was a TV game show. "How about a hint?" he said.

"One of your ex-lovers."

He felt a jolt. "Jessica."

Esperanza made a buzzing noise. "Sorry, wrong bitch."

Myron was puzzled. He'd only had two long-term relationships in his life: Jessica on and off for the past thirteen years (now very off). And before that, well, you'd have to go back to . . .

"Emily Downing?"

Esperanza made a *ding-ding* noise.

A sudden image pierced his heart like a straight-blade. He saw Emily sitting on that threadbare couch in the frat basement, smiling that smile at him, her legs bent and tucked under her, wearing his high school varsity jacket that was several sizes too big, her gesturing hands slipping down and disappearing into the sleeves.

His mouth went dry. "What did she want?"

"Don't know. But she said that she simply *had* to talk to you. She's very breathy, you know. Like everything she says is a double entendre."

With Emily, everything was.

"She good in the sack?" Esperanza asked.

Being an overly attractive bisexual, Esperanza viewed everyone as a potential sex partner. Myron wondered what that must be like, to have and thus weigh so many options, and then he decided to leave that road untraveled. Wise man.

"What did Emily say exactly?" Myron said.

"Nothing specific. She just spewed out a colorful assortment of breathy teasers: urgent, life-and-death, grave matters, etceteras, etceteras."

"I don't want to talk to her."

"I didn't think so. If she calls back, you want me to give her the runaround?"

"Please."

"*Más tarde* then."

He hung up as a second image whacked him like a surprise wave at the beach. Senior year at Duke. Emily so composed as she dumped the varsity jacket onto his bed and walked out. Not long after that, she married the man who'd ruin Myron's life.

Deep breaths, he told himself. In and out. That's it.

"Everything okay?" Mom asked.

"Fine."

Mom shook her head again, disappointed.

"I'm not lying," he said.

"Fine, right, sure, you always breathe like an obscene phone call. Listen, if you don't want to tell your mother—"

"I don't want to tell my mother."

"Who raised you and . . ."

Myron tuned her out, as was his custom. She was digressing again, taking on a past life or something. It was something she did a lot. One minute she was thoroughly modern, an early feminist who marched alongside Gloria Steinem and became proof that—to quote her old T-shirt—A Woman's Place Is in the House . . . and Senate. But at the sight of her son, her progressive attire slid to the floor and revealed the babushka-clad yenta beneath the burned bra. It made for an interesting childhood.

They headed out the front door. Myron kept his eyes on the For Sale sign as though it might suddenly brandish a gun. His mind flashed onto something he had never actually seen—the sunny day when Mom and Dad had arrived here for the first time, hand in hand, Mom's belly swelling with child, both of them scared and exhilarated realizing that this cookie-cut three-bedroom split-level would be their life vessel, their SS *American Dream.* Now, like it or not, that journey was coming to an end. Forget that "close one door, open another" crap. That For Sale sign marked the end—the end of youth, of middle age, of a family, the universe of two people who'd started here and fought here and raised kids here and worked and carpooled and lived their lives here.

They walked up the street. Leaves were piled along the curb, the surest sign of suburban autumn, while leaf blowers shattered the still air like helicopters over Saigon. Myron took the inside track so his path would skim the piles' edges. The dead leaves crackled under his sneakers and he liked that. He wasn't sure why.

"Your father spoke to you," Mom said, half-question. "About what happened to him."

Myron felt his stomach tense up. He veered deeper into the leaves, lifting his legs high and crunching louder. "Yes."

"What did he say exactly?" Mom asked.

"That he'd had chest pains while I was in the Caribbean."

The Kaufman house had always been yellow, but the new family had painted it white. It looked wrong with the new color, out of place. Some homes had gone the aluminum-siding route, while others had built on additions, bumping out the kitchens and master bedrooms. The young family who'd moved into the Miller home had gotten rid of the Millers' trademark overflowing flower boxes. The new owners of the Davis place had ripped out those wonderful shrubs Bob Davis had worked on every weekend. It all reminded Myron of an invading army ripping down the flags of the conquered.

"He didn't want to tell you," Mom said. "You know your father. He still feels he has to protect you."

Myron nodded, stayed in the leaves.

Then she said, "It was more than chest pains."

Myron stopped.

"It was a full-blown coronary," she went on, not meeting his eyes. "He was in intensive care for three days." She started blinking. "The artery was almost entirely blocked."

Myron felt his throat close.

"It's changed him. I know how much you love him, but you have to accept that."

"Accept what?"

Her voice was gentle and firm. "That your father is getting older. That I'm getting older."

He thought about it. "I'm trying," he said.

"But?"

"But I see that For Sale sign—"

"Wood and bricks and nails, Myron."

"What?"

She waded through the leaves and took hold of his elbow. "Listen to me. You mope around here like we're sitting shiva, but that house is not your childhood. It isn't a part of your family. It doesn't breathe or think or care. It's just wood and bricks and nails."

"You've lived there for almost thirty-five years."

"So?"

He turned away, kept walking.

"Your father wants to be honest with you," she said, "but you're not making it any easier."

"Why? What did I do?"

She shook her head, looked up into the sky as though willing divine inspiration, continued walking. Myron stayed by her side. She snaked her arm under his elbow and leaned against him.

"You were always a terrific athlete," she said. "Not like your father. Truth be told, your father was a spaz."

"I know this," Myron said.

"Right. You know this because your father never pretended to be something he wasn't. He let you see him as human—vulnerable even. And it had a strange effect on you. You worshipped him all the more. You turned him into something almost mythical."

Myron thought about it, didn't argue. He shrugged and said, "I love him."

"I know, sweetheart. But he's just a man. A good man. But now he's getting old and he's scared. Your father always wanted you to see him as human. But he doesn't want you to see him scared."

Myron kept his head down. There are certain things you cannot picture your parents doing—having sex being the classic example. Most people cannot—probably should not even try to—picture their parents in flagrante delicto. But right now Myron was trying to conjure up another taboo image, one of his father sitting alone in the dark, hand on his chest, scared, and the sight, while achievable, was aching, unbearable. When he spoke again, his voice was thick. "So what should I do?"

"Accept the changes. Your father is retiring. He's worked his whole life and like most moronically macho men of his era, his self-worth is wrapped up in his job. So he's having a tough time. He's not the same. You're not the same. Your relationship is shifting and neither one of you likes change."

Myron stayed silent, waiting for more.

"Reach out to him a little," Mom said. "He's carried you your whole life. He won't ask, but now it's his turn."

When they turned the final corner, Myron saw the Mercedes parked in front of the For Sale sign. He wondered for a moment if it was a Realtor showing the house. His father stood in the front yard chatting with a woman. Dad was gesturing wildly and smiling. Looking at his father's face—the rough skin that always seemed in need of a shave, the prominent nose Dad used to "nose punch" him during their giggling fun-fights, the heavy-lidded eyes à la Victor Mature and Dean Martin, the wispy hairs of gray that held on stubbornly after the thick black had fled—Myron felt a hand reach in and tweak his heart.

Dad caught his eye and waved. "Look who stopped by!" he shouted.

Emily Downing turned around and gave him a tight smile. Myron looked back at her and said nothing. Fifty minutes had passed. Ten more until the heel crushed the tomato.

2

Too much history.

His parents made themselves scarce. For all their almost legendary butting in, they both had the uncanny ability to trample full tilt through the Isle of Nosiness without tripping any gone-too-far mines. They quietly disappeared into the house.

Emily tried a smile, but it just wasn't happening. "Well, well, well," she said when they were alone. "If it isn't the good one I let get away."

"You used that line last time I saw you."

"Did I?"

They had met in the library freshman year at Duke. Emily had been bigger then, a bit fleshier, though not in a bad way, and the years had definitely slimmed her down and toned her up, though again not in a bad way. But the visual whammy was still there. Emily wasn't so much pretty as, to quote *SuperFly*, foxy. Hot. Sizzlingly so. As a young coed, she'd had long, kinky hair that always had that just-did-the-nasty muss to it, a crooked smile that could knock a movie up a rating, and a subconsciously undulating body that continuously flickered out the word *sex* like an old movie projector. It didn't matter that she wasn't beautiful; beauty had little to do with it, in fact. This was an innate thing; Emily couldn't turn it off if she donned a muumuu and put roadkill on her head.

The weird thing was, they were both virgins when they met, somehow missing the perhaps overblown sexual revolution of the seventies and early eighties. Myron always believed that the revolution was mostly hype or, at the very least, that it didn't seep past the brick façades of suburban high schools. But then again, he was pretty good at self-rationalization. More likely, it was his fault—if you could consider not being promiscuous a fault. He'd always been attracted to the "nice" girls, even in high school. Casual affairs never interested him. Every girl he met was gauged as a potential life partner, a soul mate, an undying love, as though every relationship should be a Carpenters song.

But with Emily it had been complete sexual exploration and discovery. They learned from each other in stuttering, though achingly blissful, steps. Even now, as much as he detested her very being, he could still feel the tightening, could still recall the way his nerve endings would sing and surge when they were in bed. Or the back of a car. Or a movie theater or a library or once even during a poly sci lecture on Hobbes's *Leviathan*. While he may have yearned to be a Carpenters man, his first long-term relationship had ended up more like something off Meat Loaf's *Bat Out of Hell* album—hot, heavy, sweaty, fast, the whole "Paradise by the Dashboard Light."

Still, there had to have been more to it. He and Emily had lasted three years. He had loved her, and she'd been the first to break his heart.

"There a coffee bar near here?" she asked.

"A Starbucks," Myron said.

"I'll drive."

"I don't want to go with you, Emily."

She gave him the smile. "Lost my charms, have I?"

"They lost their effect on me a long time ago." Half lie.

She shifted her hips. Myron watched, thinking about what Esperanza had said. It wasn't just her voice or her words—even her movements ended up a double entendre. "It's important, Myron."

"Not to me."

"You don't even know—"

"It doesn't matter, Emily. You're the past. So is your husband—"

"My *ex*-husband. I divorced him, remember? And I never knew what he did to you."

"Right," Myron said. "You were just the cause."

She looked at him. "It's not that simple. You know that."

He nodded. She was right, of course. "I always knew why I did it," Myron said. "I was being a competitive dumbass who wanted to get one up on Greg. But why you?"

Emily shook her head. The old hair would have flown side to side, ending up half covering her face. Her new coif was shorter and more stylized, but his mind's eye still saw the kinky flow. "It doesn't matter anymore," she said.

"Guess not," he said, "but I've always been curious."

"We both had too much to drink."

"Simple as that?"

"Yes."

Myron made a face. "Lame," he said.

"Maybe it was just about sex," she said.

"A purely physical act?"

"Maybe."

"The night before you married someone else?"

She looked at him. "It was dumb, okay?"

"You say so."

"And maybe I was scared," she said.

"Of getting married?"

"Of marrying the wrong man."

Myron shook his head. "Jesus, you're shameless."

Emily was about to say more, but she stopped as though her last reserves had suddenly been zapped away. He wanted her gone, but with ex-loves there is also a pulling sadness. There before you stands the true road untraveled, the lifetime what-if, the embodiment of a totally alternate life if things had gone a little different. He had absolutely no interest in her anymore, yet her words still drew out his old self, wounds and all.

"It was fourteen years ago," she said softly. "Don't you think it's time we moved on?"

He thought about what that "purely physical" night had cost him. Everything, maybe. His lifelong dream, for sure. "You're right," he said, turning away. "Please leave."

"I need your help."

He shook his head. "As you said, time to move on."

"Just have coffee with me. With an old friend."

He wanted to say no, but the past had too strong a pull. He nodded, afraid to speak. They drove in silence to Starbucks and ordered their complicated coffees from an artist-wannabe *barista* with more attitude than the guy who works at the local record store. They added whatever condiments at the little stand, playing a game of Twister by reaching across one another for the nonfat milk or Equal. They sat down in metal chairs with too-low backs. The sound system was playing reggae music, a CD entitled *Jamaican Me Crazy.*

Emily crossed her legs and took a sip. "Have you ever heard of Fanconi anemia?"

Interesting opening gambit. "No."

"It's an inherited anemia that leads to bone marrow failure. It weakens your chromosomes."

Myron waited.

"Are you familiar with bone marrow transplants?"

Strange line of questioning, but he decided to play it straight. "A little. A friend of mine had leukemia and needed a transplant. They had a marrow drive at the temple. We all went down and got tested."

"When you say 'we all'—"

"Mom, Dad, my whole family. I think Win went too."

She tilted her head. "How is Win?"

"The same."

"Sorry to hear that," she said. "When we were at Duke, he used to listen to us making love, didn't he?"

"Only when we pulled down the shade so he couldn't watch."

She laughed. "He never liked me."

"You were his favorite."

"Really?"

"That's not saying much," Myron said.

"He hates women, doesn't he?"

Myron thought about it. "As sex objects, they're fine. But in terms of relationships . . ."

"An odd duck."

She should only know.

Emily took a sip. "I'm stalling," she said.

"I sorta figured that."

"What happened to your friend with leukemia?"

"He died."

Her face went white. "I'm sorry. How old was he?"

"Thirty-four."

Emily took another sip, cradling the mug with both hands. "So you're listed with the bone marrow national registry?"

"I guess. I gave blood and they gave me a donor card."

She closed her eyes.

"What?" he asked.

"Fanconi anemia is fatal. You can treat it for a while with blood transfusions and hormones, but the only cure is a bone marrow transplant."

"I don't understand, Emily. Do you have this disease?"

"It doesn't hit adults." She put down her coffee and looked up. He was not big on reading eyes, but the pain was neon-obvious. "It hits children."

As though on cue, the Starbucks soundtrack changed to something instrumental and somber. Myron waited. It didn't take her long.

"My son has it," she said.

Myron remembered visiting the house in Franklin Lakes when Greg disappeared, the boy playing in the backyard with his sister. Must have been, what, two, three years ago. The boy was about ten, his sister maybe eight. Greg and Emily were in the midst of a bloody take-no-prisoners custody battle, the two children pinned down in the crossfire, the kind no one walks away from without a serious hit.

"I'm sorry," he said.

"We need to find a bone marrow match."

"I thought siblings were an almost automatic match."

Her eyes flicked around the room. "One-in-four chance," she said, stopping abruptly.

"Oh."

"The national registry found only three potential donors. By potential I mean that the initial HLA tests showed them as possibilities. The A and B match, but then they have to do a full blood and tissue workup to see—" She stopped again. "I'm getting technical. I don't mean to. But when your kid is sick like this, it's like you live in a snow globe of medical jargon."

"I understand."

"Anyway, getting past the initial screening is like winning a second-tier lottery ticket. The chance of a match is still slim. The blood center calls in the potential donors and runs a battery of tests, but the odds they'll be a close enough match to go through with the transplant are pretty low, especially with only three potential donors."

Myron nodded, still having no idea why she was telling him any of this.

"We got lucky," she said. "One of the three was a match with Jeremy."

"Great."

"There's a problem," she said. Again the crooked smile. "The donor is missing."

"What do you mean, missing?"

"I don't have the details. The registry is confidential. No one will tell me what's going on. We seemed to be on the right track, and then all of a sudden, the donor just pulled out. My doctor can't say anything—like I said, it's protected."

"Maybe the donor just changed his mind."

"Then we better change it back," she said, "or Jeremy dies."

The statement was plain enough.

"So what do you think happened?" Myron asked. "You think he's missing or something?"

"He or she," Emily said. "Yes."

"He or she?"

"I don't know anything about the donor—age, sex, where they live, nothing. But Jeremy isn't getting any better and the odds of finding another donor in time are, well, almost nonexistent." She kept the face tight, but Myron could see the foundation starting to crack a bit. "We have to find this donor."

"And that's why you've come to me? To find him?"

"You and Win found Greg when no one else could. When he disappeared, Clip went to you first. Why?"

"That's a long story."

"Not so long, Myron. You and Win are trained in this sort of thing. You're good at it."

"Not in a case like this," Myron said. "Greg is a high-profile athlete. He can take to the airwaves, offer rewards. He can buy private detectives."

"We're already doing that. Greg has a press conference set up for tomorrow."

"So?"

"So it won't work. I told Jeremy's doctor we would pay anything to the donor, even though it's illegal. But something else is wrong here. I'm afraid all the publicity might even backfire—that it may send the donor deeper into hiding or something, I don't know."

"What does Greg say to that?"

"We don't talk much, Myron. And when we do, it's usually not very pretty."

"Does Greg know you're talking to me now?"

She looked at him. "He hates you as much as you hate him. Maybe more so."

Myron decided to take that as a no. Emily kept her eyes on him, searching his face as though there were an answer there.

"I can't help you, Emily."

She looked like she'd just been slapped.

"I sympathize," he went on, "but I'm just getting over some major problems of my own."

"Are you saying you don't have time?"

"It's not that. A private detective would have a better chance—"

"Greg's hired four already. They can't even find out the donor's name."

"I doubt I can do any better."

"This is my son's life, Myron."

"I understand, Emily."

"Can't you put aside your animosity for me and Greg?"

He wasn't sure that he could. "That's not the issue. I'm a sports agent, not a detective."

"That didn't stop you before."

"And look how things ended up. Every time I meddle, it leads to disaster."

"My son is thirteen years old, Myron."

"I'm sorry—"

"I don't want your sympathy, dammit." Her eyes were smaller now, black. She leaned toward him until her face was scant inches from his. "I want you to do the math."

He looked puzzled. "What?"

"You're an agent. You know all about numbers, right? So do the math."

Myron tilted back, giving himself a little distance. "What the hell are you talking about?"

"Jeremy's birthday is July eighteenth," she said. "Do the math."

"What math?"

"One more time: He's thirteen years old. He was born July the eighteenth. I was married October tenth."

Nothing. For several seconds, he heard the mothers chatting over one another, one baby cry, one *barista* call out an order to another, and then it happened. A cold gust blew across Myron's heart. Steel bands wrapped around his chest, making it almost impossible to breathe. He opened his mouth but nothing came out. It was like someone had whacked his solar plexus with a baseball bat. Emily watched him and nodded.

"That's right," she said. "He's your son."

3

You can't know that for sure," Myron said.

Emily's whole persona screamed exhaustion. "I do."

"You were sleeping with Greg too, right?"

"Yes."

"And we only had that one night during that time. You probably had a whole bunch with Greg."

"True."

"So how can you possibly know—?"

"Denial," she interjected with a sigh. "The first step."

He pointed a finger at her. "Don't hand me that psychology-major crap, Emily."

"Moving quickly to anger," she continued.

"You can't know—"

"I've always known," she interrupted.

Myron sat back. He stayed composed but underneath he could almost feel the fissure widening, his foundation starting to shift.

"When I first got pregnant, I figured like you: I'd slept with Greg more, so it was probably his baby. At least, that's what I told myself." She closed her eyes. Myron stayed very still, the knot in his stomach tightening. "And when Jeremy was born, he favored me, so who was to say? But—and this is going to sound so goddamn stupid—a mother knows. I can't tell you how. But I knew. I tried to deny it too. I told myself I was just feeling guilty over what we'd done, and that this was God's way of punishing me."

"How Old Testament of you," Myron said.

"Sarcasm," she said with almost a smile. "Your favorite defense."

"Your maternal intuition hardly counts as evidence, Emily."

"You asked before about Sara."

"Sara?"

"Jeremy's sister. You wondered about her matching as a donor. She didn't."

"Right, but you said there was only a one-in-four chance with siblings."

"For *full* siblings, yes. But the match wasn't even close. Because she's only Jeremy's half sister."

"The doctor told you this?"

"Yes."

Myron felt the stone footing beneath his feet give way. "So . . . Greg knows?"

Emily shook her head. "The doctor pulled me aside. Because of the divorce, I'm Jeremy's primary custodian. Greg has custody too, but the children live with me. I'm in charge of the medical decisions."

"So Greg still believes . . . ?"

"That Jeremy is his, yes."

Myron was floundering in deep water with no land in sight. "But you said you've always known."

"Yes."

"Why didn't you tell me?"

"Are you kidding? I was married to Greg. I loved him. We were starting our life together."

"You still should have told me."

"When, Myron? When should I have told you?"

"As soon as the baby was born."

"Aren't you listening? I just told you I wasn't sure."

"A mother knows, you said."

"Come on, Myron. I was in love with Greg, not you. You with your corny sense of morality—you would have insisted I divorce Greg and marry you and live some suburban fairy tale."

"So instead you chose to live a lie?"

"It was the right decision based on what I knew then. With hindsight"—she stopped, took a deep sip—"I probably would have done a lot of things differently."

He tried to let some of it sink in, but it was a no-go. Another group of stroller-laced soccer moms entered the coffee shop. They took a corner table and started jabbering about little Brittany and Kyle and Morgan.

"How long have you and Greg been separated?" Myron's voice sounded sharper than he intended. Or maybe not.

"Four years now."

"And you were no longer in love with him, right? Four years ago?"

"Right."

"Earlier even," he went on. "I mean, you probably fell out of love with him a long time ago, right?"

She looked confused. "Right."

"So you could have told me then. At least four years ago. Why didn't you?"

"Stop cross-examining me."

"You're the one who dropped this bombshell," he said. "How do you expect me to react?"

"Like a man."

"What the hell does that mean?"

"I need your help. Jeremy needs your help. That's what we should be concentrating on."

"I want some answers first. I'm entitled to that much."

She hesitated, looked like she might argue, then nodded wearily. "If it'll help you get past this—"

"Get past this? Like it's a kidney stone or something?"

"I'm too tired to fight with you," she said. "Just go on. Ask your questions."

"Why didn't you tell me before now."

Her eyes drifted over his shoulder. "I almost did," she said. "Once."

"When?"

"Do you remember when you came to the house? When Greg first vanished?"

He nodded. He had just been thinking about that day.

"You were looking out the window at him. He was in the yard with his sister."

"I remember," Myron said.

"Greg and I were going through that nasty custody battle."

"You accused him of abusing the children."

"It wasn't true. You realized that right away. It was just a legal ploy."

"Some ploy," Myron said. "Next time accuse him of war atrocities."

"Who are you to judge me?"

"Actually," Myron said, "I think I'm just the person."

Emily pinned him with her eyes. "Custody battles are war without the Geneva Accords," she said. "Greg got nasty. I got nasty back. You do whatever you have to in order to win."

"And that includes revealing that Greg wasn't Jeremy's father?"

"No."

"Why not?"

"Because I won custody anyway."

"That's not an answer. You hated Greg."

"Yes."

"Still do?" he asked.

"Yes." No hesitation.

"So why didn't you tell him?"

"Because as much as I loathe Greg," she said, "I love Jeremy more. I could hurt Greg. I'd probably enjoy it. But I couldn't do that to my son—take away his father like that."

"I thought you'd do anything to win."

"I'd do anything to Greg," she said, "not Jeremy."

It made sense, he guessed, but he suspected she was holding something back. "So you kept this secret for thirteen years."

"Yes."

"Do your parents know?"

"No."

"You never told anyone?"

"Never."

"So why are you telling me now?"

Emily shook her head. "Are you being purposely dense, Myron?"

He put his hands on the table. They weren't shaking. Somehow he understood that these questions came from more than mere curiosity; they were part of the defense mechanism, the internal barbed wire and moat he'd lavishly built to keep Emily's revelation from reaching him. He knew that what she was telling him was life altering in a way nothing he'd ever heard before was. The words *my son* kept floating through his subconscious. But they were just words right now. They'd get through eventually, he guessed, but for now the barbed wire and moat were holding.

"You think I wanted to tell you? I practically begged you to help, but you wouldn't listen. I'm desperate here."

"Desperate enough to lie?"

"Yes," she said, again with no hesitation. "But I'm not, Myron. You have to believe that."

He shrugged. "Maybe someone else is Jeremy's father."

"Excuse me?"

"A third party," he said. "You slept with me the night before your wedding. I doubt I was the only one. Could be one of a dozen guys."

She looked at him. "You want your pound of flesh, Myron? Go ahead, I can take it. But this isn't like you."

"You know me that well, huh?"

"Even when you got angry—even when you had every right to hate me—you've never been cruel. It's not your way."

"We're in uncharted waters here, Emily."

"Doesn't matter," she said.

He felt something well up, making it hard to breathe. He grabbed his mug, looked into it as though it might have an answer on the bottom, put it back down. He couldn't look at her. "How could you do this to me?"

Emily reached across the table and put her hand on his forearm. "I'm sorry," she said.

He pulled away.

"I don't know what else to say. You asked before why I never told you. My main concern was always Jeremy's welfare, but you were a consideration too."

"Bull."

"I know how you are, Myron. I know you can't just shrug this off. But for now you have to. You have to find the donor and save Jeremy's life. We can worry about the rest after that."

"How long has"—he almost said *my son*—"Jeremy been ill?"

"We learned about it six months ago. When he was playing basketball. He started getting bruised too easily. Then he was short of breath for no reason. He started falling down . . ." Her voice tailed off.

"Is he in the hospital?"

"No. He lives at home and goes to school and he looks fine, just a little pale. But he can't play competitive sports or anything like that. He seems to be doing well, but . . . it's just a matter of time. He's so anemic and his marrow cells are so weak that something will get him. Either he'll contract a life-threatening infection or if he manages to get past that, malignancies will eventually develop. We treat him with hormones. That helps, but it's a temporary treatment, not a cure."

"And a bone marrow transplant would be a cure?"

"Yes." Her face brightened with an almost religious fervor. "If the transplant takes, he can be completely cured. I've seen it happen with other kids."

Myron nodded, sat back, crossed his legs, uncrossed them. "Can I meet him?"

She looked down. The sound of the blender, probably making a frappuccino, exploded while the espresso maker shrieked its familiar mating call to the various lattes. Emily waited for the noise to die down. "I can't stop you. But I'm hoping you'll do the right thing here."

"That being?"

"It's hard enough being thirteen years old and almost terminally ill. Do you really want to take away his father too?"

Myron said nothing.

"I know you're in shock right now. And I know you have a million more questions. But you have to forget that for now. You have to work through your confusion, your anger, everything. The life of a thirteen-year-old boy—our son—is at stake. Concentrate on that, Myron. Find the donor, okay?"

He looked back toward the soccer moms, still cooing about their children. Listening to them, he felt an overwhelming pang.

"Where can I find Jeremy's doctor?" he asked.

4

When the elevator doors opened into the reception area of MB SportsReps, Big Cyndi reached out to Myron with two arms the approximate circumference of the marble columns at the Acropolis. Myron almost leaped out of the way—involuntary survival reflex and all—but he stayed still and closed his eyes. Big Cyndi embraced him, which was like being wrapped in wet attic insulation, and lifted him into the air.

"Oh, Mr. Bolitar!" she cried.

He grimaced and rode it out. Eventually she put him back down as though he were a porcelain doll she was returning to a shelf. Big Cyndi is six-six and on the planetoid side of three hundred pounds, the former intercontinental tag-team wrestling champion with Esperanza, aka Big Chief Mama to Esperanza's Little Pocahontas. Her head was cube shaped and topped with hair spiked to look like the Statue of Liberty on a bad acid trip. She wore more makeup than the cast of *Cats*, her clothing form-fitted like sausage casing, her scowl the stuff of sumos.

"Uh, everything okay?" Myron ventured.

"Oh, Mr. Bolitar!"

Big Cyndi looked like she was about to hug him again, but something stopped her, perhaps the stark terror in Myron's eyes. She picked up luggage that in her manhole-paw resembled a Close'N Play phonograph from the early seventies. She was that kind of big, the kind of big where the world around her always looked like a bad B-monster movie set and she was walking through a miniature Tokyo, knocking over power lines and swatting at buzzing fighter planes.

Esperanza appeared in her office doorway. She folded her arms and rested against the frame. Even after her recent ordeal, Esperanza still looked immensely beautiful, the shiny black ringlets still falling over her forehead just so, the dark olive skin still radiant—the whole image a sort of gypsy, peasant-blouse fantasy. But he could see some new lines around the eyes and a slight slouch in the perfect posture. He'd wanted her to take time off after her release, but he knew she wouldn't. Esperanza loved MB SportsReps. She wanted to save it.

"What's going on?" Myron asked.

"It's all in the letter, Mr. Bolitar," Big Cyndi said.

"What letter?"

"Oh, Mr. Bolitar!" she cried again.

"What?"

But she didn't respond, hiding her face in her hands and ducking into the elevator as though entering a tepee. The elevator doors slid closed, and she was gone.

Myron waited a beat and then turned to Esperanza. "Explanation?"

"She's taking a leave of absence," Esperanza said.

"Why?"

"Big Cyndi isn't stupid, Myron."

"I didn't say she was."

"She sees what's going on here."

"It's only temporary," Myron said. "We'll snap back."

"And when we do, Big Cyndi will come back. In the meantime she got a good job offer."

"With Leather-N-Lust?" Big Cyndi worked nights as a bouncer at an S&M bar called Leather-N-Lust. Motto: Hurt the ones you love. Sometimes—or so he had heard—Big Cyndi was part of the stage show. What part she played Myron had no idea nor had he worked up the courage to ask—another taboo abyss his mind did its best to circumvent.

"No," Esperanza said. "She's returning to FLOW."

For the wrestling uninitiated, FLOW is the acronym for the Fabulous Ladies of Wrestling.

"Big Cyndi is going to wrestle again?"

Esperanza nodded. "On the senior circuit."

"Excuse me?"

"FLOW wanted to expand its product. They did some research, saw how well the PGA is doing with the senior golf tour and . . ." She shrugged.

"A senior ladies' wrestling tour?"

"More like retired," Esperanza said. "I mean, Big Cyndi is only thirty-eight. They're bringing back a lot of the old favorites: Queen Qaddafi, Cold War Connie, Brezhnev Babe, Cellblock Celia, Black Widow—"

"I don't remember the Black Widow."

"Before our time. Hell, before our parents' time. She must be in her seventies."

Myron tried not to make a face. "And people are going to pay money to see a seventy-year-old woman wrestle?"

"You shouldn't discriminate on the basis of age."

"Right, sorry." Myron rubbed his eyes.

"And professional women's wrestling is struggling right now, what with the competition from Jerry Springer and Ricki Lake. They need to do something."

"And grappling old ladies is the answer?"

"I think they're aiming more for nostalgia."

"A chance to cheer on the wrestler of your youth?"

"Didn't you go see Steely Dan in concert a couple of years ago?"

"That's different, don't you think?"

She shrugged. "Both past their prime. Both mining more on what you remember than what you see or hear."

It made sense. Scary sense maybe. But sense. "How about you?" Myron asked.

"What about me?"

"Didn't they want Little Pocahontas to return?"

"Yep."

"Were you tempted?"

"To what? Return to the ring?"

"Yes."

"Oh, sure," Esperanza said. "I busted my shapely ass working full-time while getting my law degree, so I could once again don a suede bikini and grope aging nymphs in front of drooling trailer trash." She paused. "Still, it is a step above being a sports agent."

"Ha-ha." Myron walked over to Big Cyndi's desk. There was an envelope with his name scrawled across the top in glow-in-the-dark orange.

"She wrote it in crayon?" Myron said.

"Eye shadow."

"I see."

"So are you going to tell me what's wrong?" she asked.

"Nothing," Myron said.

"Bullshit," she said. "You look like you just heard Wham split up."

"Don't bring that up," Myron said. "Sometimes, late at night, I still suffer flashbacks."

Esperanza studied his face a few more seconds. "This have something to do with your college sweetheart?"

"Sort of."

"Oh Christ."

"What?"

"How do I say this nicely, Myron? You are beyond moronic in the ways of women. Exhibits A and B are Jessica and Emily."

"You don't even know Emily."

"I know enough," she said. "I thought you didn't want to talk to her."

"I didn't. She found me at my parents' place."

"She just showed up there?"

"Yep."

"What did she want?"

He shook his head. He still wasn't ready to talk about it yet. "Any messages?"

"Not as many as we'd like."

"Win upstairs?"

"I think he went home already." She picked up her coat. "I think I'll do likewise."

"Good night."

"If you hear anything from Lamar—"

"I'll call you."

Esperanza put on her coat, flipping the glistening black flow out of the collar. Myron headed into his office and made a few phone calls, mostly of a recruiting nature. It was not going well.

Several months ago, a friend's death had sent Myron into a tail-spin, causing him to—and we're using complex psychiatric jargon here—wig out. Nothing overly drastic, no nervous breakdown or institutional commitment. He had instead fled to a deserted Caribbean island with Terese

Collins, a beautiful TV anchorwoman he didn't know. He had told no one—not Win, not Esperanza, not even Mom and Dad—where he was going or when he'd be back.

As Win put it, when he wigged out, he wigged out in style.

By the time Myron was forced to return, their clients were scattering into the night like kitchen help during an immigration bust. Now Myron and Esperanza were back, attempting to revive the comatose and perhaps dying MB SportsReps. This was no easy task. The competition in this business was a dozen starving lions, and Myron was one heavily limping Christian.

The MB SportsReps office was nicely situated on Park Avenue and Forty-sixth Street in the Lock-Horne Building, owned by the family of Myron's college-and-current roommate, Win. The building was in primo midtown location and offered up some semi-dazzling views of the Manhattan skyline. Myron soaked it in for a moment and then looked down at the suits speeding below. The sight of the working ants always depressed him, a chorus of "Is That All There Is?" playing in his head.

He turned now toward his Client Wall, the one with action shots of all the athletes represented by MB SportsReps, which now looked as spotty and sparse as a bad hair transplant. He wanted to care, but unfair as it was to Esperanza, his heart wasn't really in it. He wanted to go back, to love MB and have that old hunger, but no matter how much he tried to stoke the old fire, it wouldn't flame up.

Emily called about an hour later.

"Dr. Singh doesn't have office hours tomorrow," Emily said. "But you can hook up during rounds tomorrow morning."

"Where?"

"Babies and Children's Hospital. It's part of Columbia Presbyterian on 167th Street. Tenth floor, south."

"What time?"

"Rounds start at eight," Emily said.

"Okay."

Brief silence.

"You okay, Myron?"

"I want to see him."

It took her a few seconds. "Like I said before, I can't stop you. But sleep on it, okay?"

"I just want to see him," Myron said. "I won't say anything. Not yet, at least."

"Can we talk about this tomorrow?" Emily asked.

"Yeah, sure."

She hesitated again. "Do you have Web access, Myron?"

"Yes."

"We have a private URL."

"What?"

"A private Web address. I take photos with the digital camera and post them there. For my parents. They moved to Miami last year. They check it out every week. Get to see new pictures of the grandkids. So if you want to see what Jeremy looks like . . ."

"What's the address?"

She gave it to him and Myron typed it in. He hung up before hitting the return button. The images came up slowly. He drummed his fingers on the desk. On top of the screen was a banner saying HI, NANA AND POP-POP. Myron thought about his parents and shook it off.

There were four photographs of Jeremy and Sara. Myron swallowed. He placed the arrow on Jeremy's image and clicked the mouse, zooming in closer, enlarging the boy's face. He tried to keep his breathing steady. He stared at the boy's face for a long time without really registering anything. Eventually his vision blurred, his own face reflecting on the monitor over the boy's, blending the images together, creating a visual echo of he knew not what.

5

Myron heard the cries of ecstasy through the door.

Win—real name: Windsor Horne Lockwood III—was letting Myron temporarily crash at his apartment in the Dakota on Seventy-second Street and Central Park West. The Dakota was an old New York landmark whose rich and lush history had been totally eclipsed by the murder of John Lennon twenty-some-odd years ago. Entering meant crossing over the spot where Lennon had bled to death, the feeling not unlike trampling over a grave. Myron was finally getting used to it.

From the outside, the Dakota was beautiful and dark and resembled a haunted house on steroids. Most apartments, including Win's, had more square footage than a European principality. Last year, after a lifetime of living in Mom and Dad's suburban sprawl, Myron had finally moved out of the basement and into a SoHo loft with his ladylove, Jessica. It was a huge step, the first sign that after more than a decade, Jessica was ready to—gasp!—commit. So the two lovers clasped hands and took the live-together plunge. And like so many plunges in life, it ended in an ugly splat.

More cries of ecstasy.

Myron pressed his ear against the door. Cries, yes, and a soundtrack. Not live action, he decided. He used his key and pushed open the door. The cries were coming from the TV room. Win never used that room for, uh, filming. Myron sighed and stepped through the portal.

Win wore his casual WASP uniform: khakis, shirt with a color so loud you couldn't look at it straight on except through a pinhole, loafers, no socks. His blond locks had been parted with the precision of old ladies dividing up a lunch check; his skin was the color of white china with dabs of golf-ruddy red on both cheeks. He sat yoga-lotus-style, his legs pretzeled to a point man was never supposed to achieve. His index fingers and thumbs formed two circles, the hands resting against the knees. Yuppie Zen. Old World European clashing heads with Ancient Oriental. The sweet smell of Main Line mixed with the heavy Asian incense.

Win breathed in for a twenty count, held it, breathed out for a twenty count. He was meditating, of course, but with a Win-like twist. He did not, for example, listen to soothing nature sounds or chimes; no, he preferred meditating to the sound tracks of, uh, skin flicks from the seventies, which basically sounded like a bad Jimi Hendrix impersonator making wah-wah-wah noises on an electric kazoo. Just listening to it was enough to make you rush out for a shot of antibiotics.

Win did not close his eyes either. He did not visualize a deer sipping water by a lapping stream or a gentle waterfall against green foliage or any of that. His gaze remained fixed on the television screen; more specifically, on homemade videotapes of himself and a potpourri of females in the throes of passion.

Myron stepped fully into the room. Win turned one of his finger-Os into a flat-palm stop sign, then lifted the index finger up to indicate he wanted another moment. Myron risked a glance at the screen, saw the writhing flesh, turned away.

A few seconds later, Win said, "Hello."

"I'd like my disgust noted for the record," Myron said.

"So noted."

Win moved fluidly from the lotus position to a full stand. He popped out the tape and put it in a box. The box was labeled *Anon 11. Anon*, Myron knew, stood for *Anonymous.* It meant Win had either forgotten her name or never learned it.

"I can't believe you still do this," Myron said.

"Are we moralizing again?" Win asked with a smile. "How nice for us."

"Let me ask you something."

"Oh, please do."

"Something I always wanted to know."

"My ears are all atwitter."

"Putting aside my repugnancy for a moment—"

"Not on my account," Win said. "I so enjoy when you're superior."

"You claim this"—Myron motioned vaguely at the videotape and then the TV screen—"relaxes you."

"Yes."

"But doesn't it also . . . I mean, sick as it is . . . doesn't it also arouse you?"

"Not at all," Win replied.

"That's the part I don't understand."

"Viewing the act does not arouse me," Win explained. "Thinking about the act does not arouse me. Videos, dirty magazines, *Penthouse Forum*, cyberporn—none of them arouse me. For me, there is no substitute for the real thing. A partner must be present. The rest has the same effect as tickling myself. It's why I never masturbate."

Myron said nothing.

"Problem?" Win asked.

"I'm just wondering what possessed me to ask," Myron said.

Win opened a Ming dynasty cabinet that had been converted into a small fridge and tossed Myron a Yoo-Hoo. He poured himself a snifter of cognac. The room was lush antiques and rich tapestries and Oriental carpets and busts of men with long, curly hair. If not for the state-of-the-art home entertainment system, the room could have been something you'd stumble across on a tour of a Medici palace.

They grabbed their usual seats.

Win said, "You look troubled."

"I have a case for us."

"Ah."

"I know I said we weren't going to do this anymore. But this is sort of a special circumstance."

"I see," Win said.

"Do you remember Emily?"

Win did that swirl thing with his snifter. "College girlfriend. Used to make monkey noises during sex. Dumped you in the beginning of our senior year. Married your archenemy Greg Downing. Dumped him too. Probably still makes monkey noises."

"She has a son," Myron said. "He's sick." He quickly explained the situation, leaving out the part about possibly being the kid's father. If he couldn't talk about it with Esperanza, there was no way he could raise the subject with Win.

When he finished, Win said, "It shouldn't be too difficult. You're going to talk to the doctor tomorrow?"

"Yes."

"Find out what you can about who handles the records."

Win picked up the remote and flicked on the television. He flipped the channels because there were a lot of commercials on and because he was male. He stopped at CNN. Terese Collins was anchoring the news.

"Is the lovely Ms. Collins visiting us tomorrow?" Win asked.

Myron nodded. "Her flight comes in at ten."

"She's been visiting quite a bit."

"Yep."

"Are you two"—Win crinkled his face as if someone had just flashed him a particularly nasty case of jock rot— "getting serious?"

Myron looked at Terese on the screen. "Still too new," he said.

There was an *All in the Family* marathon on cable, so Win flipped to it. They ordered in some Chinese food and watched two episodes. Myron tried to get lost in the bliss of Archie and Edith, but it wasn't happening. His thoughts naturally kept returning to Jeremy. He managed to deflect the paternity issue, concentrating, as Emily had asked, on the disease and task at hand. Fanconi anemia. That was what she said the boy had. Myron wondered if they had anything about it on the Web.

"I'll be back in a little while," Myron said.

Win looked at him. "The Stretch Cunningham funeral episode is up next."

"I want to check something on the Web."

"The episode where Archie gives the eulogy."

"I know."

"Where he comments that he never thought Stretch Cunningham was Jewish because of the 'ham' in his last name."

"I know the episode, Win."

"And you're willing to miss it for the sake of the Web?"

"You have it on tape."

"That's not the point."

The two men looked at each other, comfortable in the silence. After some time passed, Win said, "Tell me."

He barely hesitated. "Emily said I'm the boy's father."

Win nodded and said, "Ah."

"You don't sound surprised."

Win used the chopsticks to grab another shrimp. "You believe her?"

"Yes."

"Why?"

"For one thing, it's a hell of a thing to lie about it."

"But Emily is good at lying, Myron. She's always lied to you. She lied to you in college. She lied to you when Greg disappeared. She lied in court about Greg's behavior with the children. She betrayed Greg the night before their wedding by sleeping with you. And, if you will, if she is telling the truth now, she lied to you for the better part of thirteen years."

Myron thought about it. "I think she's telling the truth about this."

"You *think*, Myron."

"I'm going to take a blood test."

Win shrugged. "If you must."

"What does that mean?"

"I'll let the statement speak for itself."

Myron made a face. "Didn't you just say I should find out for sure?"

"Not at all," Win said. "I was merely pointing out the obvious. I didn't say it made a difference."

Myron thought about it. "You're confusing me."

"Simply put," Win said, "so what if you are the boy's biological father? What difference does it make?"

"Come on, Win. Not even you can be that cold."

"Quite the opposite. As strange as this might sound, I am using my heart on this one."

"How do you figure?"

Win swirled the liquid again, studied the amber, took a sip. It colored his cheeks a bit. "Again I'll put it simply: No matter what a blood test might indicate, you are not Jeremy Downing's father. Greg is. You may be a sperm donor. You may be an accident of lust and biology. You may have provided a simple microscopic cell structure that combined with one slightly more complex. But you are not this boy's father."

"It's not that simple, Win."

"It is that simple, my friend. The fact that you insipidly choose to confuse the issue does not change the fact. I'll demonstrate, if you'd like."

"I'm listening."

"You love your father, correct?"

"You know the answer to that."

"I do," Win said. "But what makes him your father? The fact that he once grunted on top of Mommy after a few drinks—or the way he has cared for you and loved you for the past thirty-five years?"

Myron looked down at the can of Yoo-Hoo.

"You owe this boy nothing," Win continued, "and equally important, he owes you nothing. We will try to save his life, if that is what you wish, but that should be where it ends."

Myron thought about it. The only thing scarier than Win irrational was when Win made sense. "Maybe you're right."

"But you still don't think it's that simple."

"I don't know."

On the television, Archie approached the pulpit, a yarmulke on his head. "It's a start," Win said.

6

Myron mixed childlike Froot Loops and very adult All-Bran into a bowl and poured on skim milk. For those not reading the Cliffs Notes, this act denotes that there is still a great deal of boy in the man. Heavy symbolism. How poignant.

The Number 1 train took Myron to a platform on 168th Street so far below ground that commuters had to take a urine-encapsulated elevator to reach the surface. The elevator was big and dark and shaky and brought on images of a PBS documentary on coal mining.

Located in Washington Heights, a quick stone's toss from Harlem and directly across Broadway from the Audubon Ballroom where Malcolm X was gunned down, Columbia Presbyterian Medical Center's famed pediatric building was called Babies and Children's Hospital. It used to be called just Babies Hospital, but a committee of learned medical experts was formed and after hours of intense study, they decided to change the name from Babies Hospital to Babies and Children's Hospital. Moral of the story: Committees are really, really important.

But the name, while not exactly Madison Avenue, does adequately reflect the reality of the situation—the hospital is strictly pediatric and deliveries, a well-worn twelve-floor edifice with eleven of them devoted to sick children. There was something very wrong with that, but probably nothing beyond the theologically obvious.

Myron stopped before the entranceway and looked up at the pollution-brown brick. Lots of misery in the city and much of it ended up here. He ducked inside and checked in at the security desk. He gave his name to a guard. The guard tossed him a pass, almost glancing up from his *TV Guide* in the process. Myron waited a long time for the elevator, reading the Patient's Bill of Rights, which was printed in both English and Spanish. There was a sign for the Sol Goldman Heart Center right next to a sign for the hospital's Burger King. Mixed messages or assuring future business—Myron wasn't sure which.

The elevator opened on the tenth floor. Directly in front of him, there was a rainbow-hued "Save the Rain Forest" mural, painted, according to the sign, by the "pediatric patients" of the hospital. Save the Rain Forest. Oh, like these kids didn't have enough on their plate, right?

Myron asked a nurse where he might find Dr. Singh. The nurse pointed to a woman leading a dozen interns through the corridor. Myron was a little surprised to see that Dr. Singh was of the female persuasion, mostly because he had somehow imagined her being a man. Terribly sexist, but there you go.

Dr. Singh was, as her name strongly implied, Indian, from-India Indian as opposed to Native American Indian. Mid-thirties, he figured, her hair a lighter brown than what he was used to seeing on India Indians. She wore a white doctor coat, of course. So did all the interns, most of them appearing to be about fourteen years of age, their white coats more like smocks, like they were about to finger-paint or maybe dissect a frog in a junior high biology class. Some wore grave expressions that were almost laughable on their cherubic faces, but most emanated that medical-intern exhaustion from too many nights on call.

Only two of the interns were men—boys really—both sporting blue jeans, colorful ties, and white sneakers like waiters at Bennigan's. The women—to call them girls would use up Myron's anti-PC quota for the week—favored hospital scrubs. So young. Babies taking care of babies.

Myron followed the group at a semi-discreet distance. Every once in a while he glanced in a room and immediately regretted it. The corridor walls were festive and brightly painted, jammed with Disney/Nick Junior/PBS kiddie images and collages and mobiles, but Myron only saw black. A floor filled with dying children. Bald little boys and girls in pain, their veins blackened by toxins and poisons. Most of the children looked so calm and unafraid and unnaturally brave. If you wanted to see the stark terror, you had to look in the eyes of the parents, as though Mom and Dad were sucking the horror toward them, taking it on so that their child wouldn't have to.

"Mr. Bolitar?"

Dr. Singh met his eye and held out her hand. "I'm Karen Singh."

Myron almost asked her how she did this, how she stayed on this floor day in and day out, watching children die. But he didn't. They exchanged the usual pleasantries. Myron had expected an Indian accent, but the only thing he picked up was a little Bronx.

"We can talk in here," she said.

She pushed open one of the superheavy, superwide doors endemic to hospitals and nursing homes, and they stepped into an empty room with stripped beds. The barrenness ignited Myron's imagination. He could almost see a loved one rushing into the hospital, repeatedly pushing the elevator call button, diving inside, pushing more buttons, sprinting down the corridor into this silent room, the bed being stripped by a nurse, then the sudden cry of anguish . . .

Myron shook his head. He watched too much TV.

Karen Singh sat on the corner of the mattress, and Myron studied her face for a moment. She had long sharp features. Everything pointed down—her nose, her chin, her eyebrows. Sort of harsh.

"You're staring," she said.

"I don't mean to."

She pointed to her forehead. "You were maybe expecting a dot?"

"Er, no."

"Very good, then let's get to it, shall we?"

"Okay."

"Mrs. Downing wants me to tell you whatever you want to know."

"I appreciate your taking the time."

"Are you a private investigator?" she asked.

"More like a family friend."

"Did you play basketball with Greg Downing?"

Myron was always surprised by the memory of the public. After all these years, people could still recall his big games, his big shots, sometimes with more clarity than Myron could. "You're a fan?"

"Nope," she said. "Can't stand sports actually."

"So how did you—"

"Just a deduction. You're tall and about the right age and you said you were a family friend. So . . ." She shrugged.

"Nice deduction."

"It's what we do here when you think about it. Deduce. Some diagnoses are easy. Others must be deduced from the evidence. You ever read Sherlock Holmes?"

"Sure."

"Sherlock said that you should never theorize before you have facts—because then you twist facts to suit theories rather than twisting theories to suit facts. If you see a misdiagnosis, nine times out of ten they ignored Sherlock's axiom."

"Did that happen with Jeremy Downing?"

"As a matter of fact," she said, "it did."

Somewhere down the hall, a machine started beeping. The sound hit the nerves like a police taser.

"So his first doctor screwed up?"

"I won't get into that. But Fanconi anemia isn't common. And because it looks like other things, it's often misdiagnosed."

"So tell me about Jeremy."

"What's to tell? He has it. Fanconi anemia, that is. In simple terms, his bone marrow is corrupted."

"Corrupted?"

"In layman's term, it's shit. It makes him susceptible to a host of infections and even cancers. It commonly turns into AML." She saw the puzzled look on his face and added, "That's acute myelogenous leukemia."

"But you can cure him?"

" 'Cure' is an optimistic word," she said. "But with a bone marrow transplant and treatments with a new fludarabine compound, yes, I believe his prognosis is excellent."

"Fluda-what?"

"Not important. We need a bone marrow donor that matches Jeremy. That's what counts here."

"And you don't have one."

Dr. Singh shifted on the mattress. "That's correct."

Myron felt the resistance. He decided to back off, test another flank. "Could you take me through the transplant process?"

"Step by step?"

"If it's not too much trouble."

She shrugged. "First step: find a donor."

"How do you go about that?"

"You try family members, of course. Siblings have the best chance of matching. Then parents. Then people of similar background."

"When you say people of similar background—"

"Blacks with blacks, Jews with Jews, Latino descent with Latino descent. You'll see that quite often in marrow drives. If the patient is, for example, a Hasidic Jew, the donation drives will take place within their shuls. Mixed blood is usually the hardest to match."

"And Jeremy's blood or whatever you need to match—it's fairly rare?"

"Yes."

Emily and Greg were both of Irish descent. Myron's family came from the usual potpourri of old Russia and Poland and even a little Palestine thrown in. Mixed blood. He thought about the paternity implications.

"So after you exhausted the family, how do you search for the match?"

"You go to the national registry."

"Where are they located?"

"In Washington. You listed?"

Myron nodded.

"They keep computer records there. We search for a preliminary match in their banks."

"Okay, now assuming you find a match in the computer—"

"A *preliminary* match," she corrected. "The local center calls the potential donor and asks them to come in. They run a battery of tests. But the odds of matching are still fairly slim."

Myron could see that Karen Singh was relaxing, comfortable with the familiar subject matter, which was exactly what he wanted. Interrogations are a funny thing. Sometimes you go for the full frontal attack, and sometimes you sidle up, friendly-like, and sneak in the back. Win put it simpler: Sometimes you get more ants with honey, but you should always pack a can of Raid.

"Let's suppose you find a full-fledged donor," Myron said. "What then?"

"The center acquires the donor's permission."

"When you say 'center,' do you mean the national registry in Washington?"

"No, I mean the local center. Do you have your donor card in your wallet?"

"Yes."

"Let me see it."

Myron took out his wallet, flipped through about a dozen supermarket discount cards, three video club memberships, a couple of those buy-a-hundred-coffees-get-ten-cents-off-the-hundredth coupon, that sort of thing. He found the donor card and handed it to her.

"See here," she said, pointing to the back. "Your local center is in East Orange, New Jersey."

"So if I was a preliminary match, the East Orange center would call me?"

"Yes."

"And if I ended up being a full match?"

"You'd sign some papers and donate marrow."

"Is that like donating blood?"

Karen Singh handed the card back to him and shifted again. "Harvesting bone marrow is a more invasive procedure."

Invasive. Every profession has its own buzzwords. "How so?"

"For one thing, you have to be put under."

"Anesthesia?"

"Yes."

"And then what do they do?"

"A doctor sticks a needle through the bone and sucks the marrow out with a syringe."

Myron said, "Eeuw."

"As I just explained, you're not awake during the procedure."

"Still," Myron said, "it sounds much more complicated than giving blood."

"It is," she said. "But the procedure is safe and relatively painless."

"But people must balk. I mean, most probably signed up the same way I did: They had a friend who was sick and ran a drive. For someone you know and care about, sure, you're willing to make a sacrifice. But for a stranger?"

Karen Singh's eyes found his and settled in hard. "You are saving a life, Mr. Bolitar. Think about that. How many opportunities do you get to save a fellow human being's life?"

He had hit a nerve. Good. "Are you saying people don't balk?"

"I'm not saying it never happens," she said, "but most people do the right thing."

"Does the donor get to meet the person he or she is saving?"

"No. It's totally anonymous. Confidentiality is very important here. Everything is held in the utmost secrecy."

They were getting to it now, and Myron could sense that her defenses were starting to slide back up like a car window. He decided to pull back again, let her resettle on comfy ground. "What's the patient going through during all this?" he asked.

"At what point?"

"While the marrow is being harvested. How do you prep the patient?" Prep. Myron had said "prep." Like a real doctor. Who said watching *St. Elsewhere* was a waste of time?

"It depends on what you're treating," Dr. Singh said. "But for most diseases, the recipient goes through about a week's worth of chemotherapy."

Chemotherapy. One of those words that hush a room like a nun's scowl. "They get chemo before the transplant?"

"Yes."

"I would think that would weaken them," Myron said.

"To some degree, yes."

"Why would you do it, then?"

"You have to. You're giving the recipient new bone marrow. Before you do that, you have to kill the old marrow. With leukemia, for example, the amount of chemo is high because you have to kill off all the living marrow. In the case of Fanconi anemia, you can be less aggressive because the marrow is already very weak."

"So you kill off all the bone marrow?"

"Yes."

"Isn't that dangerous?"

Dr. Singh gave him the steady eyes again. "This is a dangerous procedure, Mr. Bolitar. You are in effect replacing a person's bone marrow."

"And then?"

"And then the patient is infused with new marrow through an IV. He or she is kept isolated in a sterile environment for the first two weeks."

"Quarantined?"

"In effect. Do you remember the old TV movie *The Boy in the Plastic Bubble*?"

"Who doesn't?"

Dr. Singh smiled.

"Is that what the patient lives in?" Myron asked.

"A bubble chamber of sorts, yes."

"I had no idea," Myron said. "And this works?"

"Rejection is always a possibility, of course. But our success rate is quite high. In the case of Jeremy Downing, he can live a normal, active life with the transplant."

"And without it?"

"We can keep treating him with male hormones and growth factors, but his premature death is inevitable."

Silence. Except for that steady mechanical beep coming from down the hall.

Myron cleared his throat. "When you said that everything involving the donor is confidential—"

"I meant totally."

Enough wading. "How does that sit with you, Dr. Singh?"

"What do you mean?"

"The national registry located a donor who matched Jeremy, didn't they?"

"I believe so, yes."

"So what happened?"

She tapped her chin with her index finger. "May I speak candidly?"

"Please."

"I believe in the need for secrecy and confidentiality. Most people don't understand how easy, painless, and important it is to put their name in the registry. All they have to do is give a little blood. Just a little tube of the stuff, less than you would for any blood donation. Do that simple act—and you can save a life. Do you understand the significance of that?"

"I think so."

"We in the medical community must do all we can to encourage people to join the bone marrow registry. Education, of course, is important. So, too, is confidentiality. It has to be honored. The donors have to trust us."

She stopped, crossed her legs, leaned back on her hands. "But in this case, something of a quandary has developed. The importance of confidentiality is bumping up against the welfare of my patient. For me, the quandary is easy to resolve. The Hippocratic oath trumps all. I'm not a lawyer or a priest. My priority must be to save the life, not protect confidences. My guess is that I'm not the only doctor that feels that way. Perhaps that's why we have no contact with the donors. The blood center—in your case, the one in East Orange—does everything. They harvest the marrow and ship it to us."

"Are you saying that you don't know who the donor is?"

"That's right."

"Or if it's a he or she or where they live or anything?"

Karen Singh nodded. "I can only tell you that the national registry found a match. They called and told me so. I later received a call telling me that the donor was no longer available."

"What does that mean?"

"My question exactly."

"Did they give you an answer?"

"No," she said. "And while I see things on the micro level, the national registry has to remain macro. I respect that."

"You just gave up?"

She stiffened at his words. Her eyes went small and black. "No, Mr. Bolitar, I did not give up. I raged against the machine. But the people at the national registry are not ogres. They understand that this is a life-or-death situation. If a donor backs out, they try their best to bring them back into the fold. They do everything I would do to convince the donor to go through with it."

"But nothing worked here?"

"That seems to be the case."

"The donor would be told that he's sentencing a thirteen-year-old boy to death?"

She didn't hesitate. "Yes."

Myron threw up his hands. "So what do we conclude here, Doctor? That the donor is a selfish monster?"

Karen Singh chewed on that one for a moment. "Perhaps," she said. "Or perhaps the answer is simpler."

"For example?"

"For example," she said, "maybe the center can't find the donor."

Hello. Myron sat up a bit. "What do you mean, 'can't find'?"

"I don't know what happened here. The center won't tell me, and that's probably how it should be. I'm the patient's advocate. It's their job to deal with the donors. But I believe they were"—she stopped, searching for the right word—"perplexed."

"What makes you say that?"

"Nothing concrete. Just a feeling that this might be more than a donor with cold feet."

"How do we find out?"

"I don't know."

"How do we find the donor's name?"

"We can't."

"There has to be a way," Myron said. "Play pretend with me. How could I do it?"

She shrugged. "Break into the computer system. That's the only way I know."

"The computer in Washington?"

"They network with the local centers. But you'd have to know codes and passwords. Maybe a good hacker could get through, I don't know."

Hackers, Myron knew, worked better in the movies than in real life. A few years ago, maybe—but most computer systems nowadays were secure against such invasions.

"How long do we have here, Doctor?"

"There's no way of telling. Jeremy is reacting well to the hormones and growth factors. But it's only a question of time."

"So we have to find a donor."

"Yes." Karen Singh stopped, looked at Myron, looked away.

"Is there something else?" Myron asked.

She did not face him. "There is one other remote possibility," she said.

"What?" Myron asked.

"Keep in mind what I said before. I'm the patient's advocate. It's my job to explore every possible avenue to save him."

Her voice was funny now.

"I'm listening," Myron said.

Karen Singh rubbed her palms on her pant legs. "If Jeremy's biological parents were to conceive again, there is a twenty-five percent chance that the offspring would be a match."

She looked at Myron.

"I don't think that's a possibility," he said.

"Even if it's the only way to save Jeremy's life?"

Myron had no reply. An orderly walked by, looked in the room, mumbled an apology, left. Myron stood and thanked her.

"I'll show you to the elevator," Dr. Singh said.

"Thank you."

"There's a lab on the first floor in the Harkness Pavilion." She handed him a slip of paper. Myron looked at it. It was an order form. "I understand you might want to take a certain confidential blood test."

Neither of them said anything else as they walked toward the elevators. There were several children being wheeled through the corridor. Dr. Singh smiled at them, the pointed features softening into something almost celestial. Again the children looked unafraid. Myron wondered if the calmness spawned from ignorance or acceptance. He wondered if the children did not understand the gravity of what was happening to them or if they possessed a quiet clarity their parents would never know. Such philosophical queries, Myron knew, were best left to those more learned. But maybe the answer was simpler than he imagined: The children's suffering would be relatively short; their parents' would be eternal.

When they reached the elevator, Myron said, "How do you do it?"

She knew what he meant. "I could say something fancy about finding solace in helping, but the truth is, I block and I compartmentalize. It's the only way."

The elevator door opened, but before Myron could move he heard a familiar voice say, "What the hell are you doing here?"

Greg Downing stepped toward him.

7

Too much history. Again.

The last time the two men had been in the same room, Myron was straddled over Greg's chest, trying to kill him, punching him repeatedly in the face until Win—Win of all people—pulled him off. Three years ago. Myron hadn't seen him since, except on highlight films during the evening news.

Greg Downing glared at Myron, then at Karen Singh, then back at Myron as though he expected him to have evaporated by then.

"What the hell are you doing here?" he asked again.

Greg was clad in a flannel shirt over some waffle knit you'd buy at Baby Gap, faded jeans, and preternaturally scuffed work boots. The Suburban Lumberjack.

Something sparked hot in Myron's chest, ignited, took flight.

From the day they first battled for a rebound in the sixth grade, Greg and Myron were the pure definition of cross-town rivals. In high school, where their competitive cup truly runneth over, Greg and Myron met up eight times, splitting the games evenly. Rumor had it that there was bad blood between the budding superstars, but that was just standard sports hyperbole. The truth was, Myron barely knew Greg off the court. They were killer competitors, sure, willing to do just about anything to win, but once the final buzzer sounded, the two boys shook hands and the rivalry hibernated until the next opening tap.

Or so Myron had always thought.

When he accepted a scholarship at Duke and Greg chose the University of North Carolina, basketball fans rejoiced. Their seemingly innocent rivalry was ready for ACC prime time. Myron and Greg did not disappoint. The Duke-UNC matchups drew fantastic television ratings, no game decided by more than three points. Both had spectacular college careers. Both were named first-team All-Americans. Both were on covers of *Sports Illustrated*, once even sharing it. But the rivalry stayed on the court. They would do battle until bloody, but the competition never overlapped into their personal arenas.

Until Emily.

Before the start of senior year, Myron broached the subject of marriage with Emily. The next day she came to him, held his hands, looked into his eyes, and said, "I'm not sure I love you." Bam, like that. He still wondered what happened. Too much too soon, he guessed. A need to spread the proverbial wings a bit, play the proverbial field, what have you. Time passed. Three months, by Myron's count. Then Emily took up with Greg.

Myron publicly shrugged it off—even when Greg and Emily got engaged just before graduation. The NBA draft took place right about then too. Both went in the first round, though Greg was surprisingly picked before Myron.

That was when it all unraveled.

The end result?

Almost a decade and a half later, Greg Downing was winding down an All-Star pro basketball career. People cheered him. He made millions and was famous. He played the game he loved. For Myron, his lifelong dream had ended before it had begun. During his first preseason game with the Celtics, Big Burt Wesson had slammed into him, sandwiching Myron's knee between himself and another player. There was a snap, crackle, pop—and then a hot, ripping pain, as though metal talons were shredding his kneecap into thin strips.

His knee never recovered.

A freak accident. Or so everyone thought. Including Myron. For more than ten years, he'd believed that the injury was merely a fluke, the fickle work of the Fates. But now he knew better. Now he knew the man who stood in front of him had been the cause. Now he knew that their seemingly innocent childhood rivalry had grown monstrous, had feasted upon his dream, had slaughtered Greg and Emily's marriage, and had in all probability led to the birth of Jeremy Downing.

He felt his hands tighten into fists. "I was just leaving."

Greg put a hand on Myron's chest. "I asked you a question."

Myron stared at the hand. "One good thing," he said.

"What?"

"No transportation time," Myron said. "We're already at the hospital."

Greg sneered. "You sucker-punched me last time."

"You want to go again?"

"Pardon me," Karen Singh said. "But are you guys for real?"

Greg kept glaring at Myron.

"Stop it," Myron said, "or I'll wet myself."

"You're a son of a bitch."

"And you're not on my Christmas card list either, Greggy-poo." Greggy-poo. Very mature.

Greg leaned closer. "You know what I'd like to do to you, Bolitar?"

"Kiss me on the lips? Buy me flowers?"

"Flowers for your grave maybe."

Myron nodded. "Good one, Greg. I mean, ouch, I'm wounded."

Karen Singh said, "Just because this is a children's floor doesn't mean you two have to act like ones."

Greg took a step back, his eyes never leaving Myron. "Emily," he spat suddenly. "She called you, right?"

"I have nothing to say to you, Greg."

"She asked you to find the donor. Like you found me."

"You always were a bright boy."

"I'm calling a press conference today. I'm going to make a direct appeal to the donor. Offer a reward."

"Good."

"So we don't need you, Bolitar."

Myron looked at Greg, and for a moment they were back on the court, faces drenched with sweat, the crowd cheering, the clock ticking down, the ball bouncing. Nirvana. Gone forever. Snatched away by Greg. And by Emily. And maybe most of all, when he looked at it honestly, by Myron's own stupidity.

"I've got to go," Myron said.

Greg took a step back. Myron moved past him and pressed the elevator button.

"Hey, Bolitar."

He faced Greg.

"I came here to talk to the doc about my son," Greg said, "not rehash our past."

Myron said nothing. He turned back to the elevator.

"You think you can help save my boy?" Greg asked.

Myron's mouth went dry. "I don't know."

The elevator dinged and opened. There were no good-byes, no nods, no further communication of any sort. Myron stepped inside and let the doors close. When he reached the first level, he went to the lab. He rolled up his sleeve. A woman drew his blood, untied the tourniquet, and said, "Your doctor will be in touch with you about the results."

8

Win was bored, so he drove Myron to the airport to pick up Terese. His foot pushed down on the gas pedal as though it had offended him. The Jag flew. As was his custom when driving with Win, Myron kept his eyes averted.

"It would appear," Win began, "that our best option would be to locate a satellite marrow clinic in a somewhat remote area. Upstate maybe or in western Jersey. We would then break in at night with a computer expert."

"Won't work," Myron said.

"Por qua?"

"The Washington center shuts down the computer network at six o'clock. Even if we were to break in, we couldn't bring up the mainframe."

Win said, "Hmm."

"Don't fret," Myron said. "I have a plan."

"When you talk like that," Win said, "my nipples harden."

"I thought only the real thing aroused you."

"This isn't the real thing?"

They parked in JFK Airport's short-term parking and reached the Continental Airlines gate ten minutes before the flight touched down. When the passengers began to appear, Win said, "I'll stand over in the corner."

"Why?"

"I wouldn't want to cast a shadow on your greeting," he said. "And standing over there affords me a better view of Ms. Collins's derriere."

Ah, Win.

Two minutes later, Terese Collins—to use a purely transportational term—disembarked. She was casually decked out in a white blouse and green slacks. Her brown hair was up in a ponytail. People lightly elbowed one another, whispering and subtly gesturing, giving her that surreptitious glance, the one that says "I recognize you but don't want to appear fawning."

Terese approached Myron and offered up her breaking-to-commercial smile. It was small and tight, trying to be friendly but reminding viewers that she was telling them about war and pestilence and tragedy and that maybe a big happy smile would be somewhat obscene. They hugged a little too tightly, and Myron felt the familiar sadness overwhelm him. It happened to him every time they hugged—a sense that something inside of him was crumbling anew. He sensed that the same thing happened to her.

Win came over.

"Hello, Win," she said.

"Hello, Terese."

"Checking out my ass again?"

"I prefer the term 'derriere.' And yes."

"Still choice?"

"Grade A."

"Ahem," Myron said. "Please wait for the meat inspector."

Win and Terese looked at each other and rolled their eyes.

Myron had been wrong before. Emily was not Win's favorite. Terese was—though it was strictly because she lived far away. "You are the pitiful, needy type who feels incomplete without a steady girlfriend," Win had told him. "Who better than a career woman who lives a thousand miles away?"

Win headed for his Jag while they waited for her luggage. Terese watched Win walk away.

Myron said, "Is his ass better than mine?"

"No ass is better than yours," she said.

"I know that. I was just testing you."

Terese kept looking. "Win is an interesting fellow," she said.

"Oh yeah," Myron agreed.

"On the outside, he's all cold and detached," she said. "But underneath that—way down deep inside—he's all cold and detached."

"You read people well, Terese."

Win dropped them off at the Dakota and returned to the office. When Myron and Terese got inside the apartment, she kissed him hard. Always an urgency with Terese. A desperation in their lovemaking. Pleasant, sure. Awesome even. But there was still the aura of sadness. The sadness didn't go away when they made love, but for a little while it lifted like cloud cover, hovering above instead of weighing them down.

They had hooked up at a charity function a few months back, both dragged there by well-meaning friends. It was their mutual misery that drew them, as though it were one of those psychic crowns only they could spot on each other. They met and ran away that very night to the Caribbean on a let's-just-flee dare. For the usually predictable Myron, the spontaneous act felt surprisingly right. They spent a numbingly blissful three weeks alone on a private island, trying to stave off the flow of pain. When Myron was finally forced to return home, they'd both assumed it was over. They'd assumed wrong. At least, it appeared that way.

Myron recognized that his own healing was finally under way. He wasn't back to full strength or normal or any of that. He doubted he ever would be. Or even wanted to be. Giant hands had twisted him and then let go, and while his world was slowly untwisting, he knew that it would never fully return to its original position.

Again with the poignant.

But whatever had happened to Terese—whatever had brought on the sadness and twisted her world, if you will—still held firm, refusing to let go.

Terese's head lay on his chest, her arms wrapped around him. He could not see her face. She never showed him her face when they finished.

"You want to talk about it?" he asked.

She still hadn't told him, and Myron rarely asked. Doing so, he knew, was breaking an unspoken though cardinal rule.

"No."

"I'm not pushing," he said. "I just wanted you to know that if you're ever ready, I'm here."

"I know," she said.

He wanted to say something more, but she was still at a place where words were either superfluous or they stung. He stayed quiet and stroked her hair.

"This relationship," Terese said. "It's bizarre."

"I guess."

"Someone told me you're dating Jessica Culver, the writer."

"We broke up," he said.

"Oh." She did not move, still holding him a little too tightly. "Can I ask when?"

"A month before we met."

"And how long were you two together?"

"Thirteen years, on and off."

"I see," she said. "Am I the recovery?"

"Am I yours?"

"Maybe," she said.

"Same answer."

She thought about that a little. "But Jessica Culver is not the reason you ran away with me."

He remembered the cemetery overlooking the school yard. "No," he said, "she's not the reason."

Terese finally turned to him. "We have no chance. You know that, right?"

Myron said nothing.

"That's not unusual," she went on. "Plenty of relationships have no chance. But people stay in them because it's fun. This isn't fun either."

"Speak for yourself."

"Don't get me wrong, Myron. You're a hell of a lay."

"Could you put that in a sworn affidavit?"

She smiled but there was still no joy. "So what do we have here?"

"Truth?"

"Preferably."

"I always overanalyze," Myron said. "It's my nature. I meet a woman, and I immediately picture the house in the burbs and the white picket fence and the two-point-five kids. But for once I'm not doing that. I'm just letting it happen. So, to answer your question, I don't know. And I'm not sure I care."

She lowered her head. "You realize that I'm pretty damaged."

"I guess."

"I have more baggage than most."

"We all have baggage," Myron said. "The question is, does your baggage go with mine?"

"Who said that?"

"I'm paraphrasing from a Broadway musical."

"Which one?"

"*Rent.*"

She frowned. "I don't like musicals."

"Sorry to hear that," Myron said.

"You do?"

"Oh yeah."

"You're in your mid-thirties, single, sensitive, and you like show tunes," she said. "If you were a better dresser, I'd say you were gay."

She pressed a hard, quick kiss to his lips, and then they held each other a little more. Once again he wanted to ask her what had happened to her, but he wouldn't. She would tell him one day. Or she wouldn't. He decided to change subjects.

"I need your help with something," Myron said.

She looked at him.

"I need to break into a bone marrow center's computer system," he said. "And I think you can help."

"Me?"

"Yup."

"You got the wrong technophobe," she said.

"I don't need a technophobe. I need a famous anchorwoman."

"I see. And you're asking for this favor postcoital?"

"Part of my plan," Myron said. "I've weakened your will. You cannot refuse me."

"Diabolical."

"Indeed."

"And if I refuse?"

Myron wiggled his eyebrows. "I'll once again use my brawny body and patented lovemaking technique to make you succumb."

" 'Succumb,' " she repeated, pulling him closer. "Is that one word or two?"

9

It took a shockingly short time to set up.

Myron told Terese his plan. She listened without interruption. When he finished, she started placing calls. She never asked why he was looking for the donor or how he and the donor were connected. The unspoken rule again, he guessed.

Within the hour a news van complete with a handheld television camera was delivered to the Dakota. The director of the Bergen County Blood Center—a nearby New Jersey bone marrow center—had agreed to drop everything for an immediate interview with Terese Collins, anchorwoman extraordinaire. The power of the idiot box.

They took the Harlem River Drive up to the George Washington Bridge, crossing the Hudson and exiting onto Jones Road in Englewood, New Jersey. After they parked, Myron hoisted up the camera. Heavier than he thought. Terese showed him how to hold it, how to lean it against his shoulder and aim. There was something bazooka-like about the whole thing.

"Do you think I should wear a disguise?" Myron asked.

"Why?"

"People still recognize me from my playing days."

She made a face.

"I'm rather famous in certain circles."

"Get real, Myron. You're an ex-jock. If someone by some miracle recognizes you, they'll think you got lucky and didn't end up in a gutter like most ex-jocks."

He thought about it. "Fair enough."

"One other thing," she said. "And this will be nearly impossible for you."

"What?"

"You have to keep your big mouth shut," Terese said.

"Egads."

"You're just the cameraman here."

"We prefer to be called 'photographic artists.' "

"Just play your part. Trust me to handle him."

"Can I at least use a pseudonym?" He put the camera to his eye. "You can call me Lens. Or Scoop."

"How about Bozo? No, wait, that would be a synonym."

Everyone's a wise guy.

When they entered the clinic's lobby, people turned toward Terese and did that surreptitious stare again. Myron realized that today was the first time he had been with her in public. He had never quite thought about how famous she was.

"You get these stares wherever you go?" he whispered.

"Pretty much."

"Does it bother you?"

She shook her head. "That's horseshit."

"What is?"

"Celebrities who complain about people staring at them. Want to really piss off a celebrity? Let him go someplace and not be recognized."

Myron smiled. "You're so self-realized."

"That a new way of saying cynical?"

The receptionist said, "Mr. Englehardt will see you now."

She led them down a corridor with thin plaster walls and a bad paint job. Englehardt sat behind a plastic-wood desk. He was probably late twenties with a slight build and a chin weaker than machine-dispensed coffee.

Myron quickly noted the computer setup. Two of them. One on his desk. One on the credenza. Hmm.

Englehardt jumped up as though he'd just been passed a note that his chair had cooties. His eyes were wide and fixed on Terese. Myron was ignored and felt like, well, the cameraman. Terese smiled brightly at Englehardt, and he was lost.

"I'm Terese Collins," she said, extending her hand. Englehardt did everything but take a knee and kiss it. "This is my cameraman, Malachy Throne."

Myron sort of smiled. After the Broadway-musical debacle, he had worried. But Malachy Throne? Genius. Pure genius.

They all exchanged quick pleasantries. Englehardt kept touching his hair, trying very hard to look subtle about it and not like he was prepping for the camera. Not happening, bub. Finally Terese signaled that they were ready to begin.

"Where would you like me to sit?" Englehardt asked.

"Behind the desk would be nice," she said. "Don't you agree, Malachy?"

"Behind the desk," Myron said. "Yeah, that's the ticket."

The interview began. Terese kept her gaze on her subject; Englehardt, trapped in the beam, could look nowhere else. Myron put his eye to the camera. The consummate professional. Very Richard Avedon.

Terese asked Englehardt how he'd gotten started in this business, his background, general crap, relaxing him, putting him on that comfy ground, not all that different from the technique Myron had used with Dr. Singh. She was in on-air mode now. Her voice was different, her eyes steadier.

"So the national registry in Washington keeps track of all donors?" Terese asked.

"That's correct."

"But you can access the records?"

Englehardt tapped the computer on his desk. The screen faced him, the back of the monitor toward them. Okay, Myron thought, so it was the one on his desk. That would make it more difficult, but not impossible.

Terese looked at Myron. "Why don't you get a back shot, Malachy?" Then turning to Englehardt, "If that's okay with you."

"No problem at all," Englehardt said.

Myron started moving into position. The monitor was off. No surprise.

Terese continued to hold Englehardt's gaze. "Does everyone in the office have access to the national registry's computer?"

Englehardt shook his head firmly. "I'm the only one."

"Why's that?"

"The information is confidential. We don't breach the secrecy under any circumstance."

"I see," she said. Myron was in place now. "But what's to stop someone from coming in here when you're not around?"

"I always lock my office door," Englehardt said, up on his haunches and eager to please. "And you can only access the network with a password."

"You're the only one who knows the password?"

Englehardt tried not to preen, but he didn't try too hard. "That's correct."

Ever see those hidden-camera stories on *Dateline* or *20/20*? They always shoot from some strange angle and in black-and-white. Truth is, it's easy for any layperson to buy one and it's even easy to get one that films in color. There are stores that sell them right in Manhattan, or you can go online and search under "spy stores." You'll see hidden cameras in clocks, pens, briefcases and, most common of all, smoke detectors—available to anyone with the proper buckage. Myron had one that looked like a film case. He dropped it now on the window ledge with the lens pointing toward the computer monitor.

When it was in place, Myron tapped his nose with his finger, à la Redford in *The Sting*. Their signal. *Bolitar. Myron Bolitar. A Yoo-Hoo. Shaken not stirred.* Terese picked up her cue. The smile dropped off her face like an anvil.

Englehardt looked startled. "Ms. Collins? Are you okay?"

For a moment she could not bear to face him. Then: "Mr. Englehardt," Terese said, her voice Gulf War-grave, "I must confess something."

"I'm sorry?"

"I am here under somewhat false pretenses."

Englehardt looked confused. Terese was so good, Myron almost looked confused.

"I sincerely believe you are doing important work here," she continued. "But others are not so sure."

Englehardt's eyes were widening. "I don't understand."

"I need your help, Mr. Englehardt."

"Billy," he corrected.

Myron made a face. Billy?

Terese didn't miss a beat. "Someone is trying to disrupt your work, Billy."

"My work?"

"The national registry's work."

"I'm still not sure what you—"

"Are you familiar with the case of Jeremy Downing?"

Englehardt shook his head. "I never know the names of patients."

"He's the son of Greg Downing, the basketball star."

"Oh, wait, yes, I heard about this. His son has Fanconi anemia."

Terese nodded. "That's correct."

"Isn't Mr. Downing supposed to hold a press conference today? To track down a donor?"

"Exactly, Billy. And that's the problem."

"What is?"

"Mr. Downing has found the donor."

Still confused. "That's a problem?"

"No, of course not. If the person is the donor. And if the person is telling the truth."

Englehardt looked at Myron. Myron shrugged and moved back to the front of the desk. He left the film case on the windowsill.

"I'm not following you, Ms. Collins."

"Terese," she said. "A man has come forward. He claims that he is the matching donor."

"And you think he's lying?"

"Let me finish. He not only claims he's the donor, but he says that the reason he refused to donate his marrow was because of the terrible treatment he received from this center."

Englehardt nearly tipped back. "What?"

"He claims he was treated shabbily, that your staff was rude, and that he's even debating leveling a lawsuit."

"That's ridiculous."

"Probably."

"He's lying."

"Probably," she said again.

"And he'll be found out," Englehardt continued. "They'll test his blood and see he's a phony."

"But when, Billy?"

"What?"

"When will they do that? A day from now? A week from now? A month? But by then the damage is done. He's going to appear at the press conference today with Greg Downing. The media will be there in force. Even if it ends up being false, no one remembers the retraction. They just remember the allegation."

Englehardt sat back. "Jesus."

"Let me be frank, Billy. A number of my colleagues believe him. I don't. I smell a publicity hound. I'm having some of my best investigators dig into this man's past. So far they've come up with nothing, and time is running short."

"So what can I do?"

"I need to *know* it's not true. I can't stop it merely because I *believe* it's not true. I have to know for certain."

"How?"

Terese chewed on her lower lip. Deep thought. "Your computer network."

Englehardt shook his head. "The information in here is confidential. I explained that before. I can't tell you—"

"I don't need to know the name of the donor." She leaned forward.

Myron moved as far away from the action as possible, trying to be no threat whatsoever. "I need to know what's *not* the name."

Englehardt looked hesistant.

"I'm sitting over here," she said. "I can't see the monitor. Malachy is by the door." She turned to Myron. "Your camera is off, Malachy?"

"Yes, Terese," Myron said. He put it down for emphasis.

"So here is what I suggest," Terese said. "You look up Jeremy Downing in your computer. It will list a donor. I give you a name. You tell me if the name matches. Simple?"

Englehardt still looked hesitant.

"You wouldn't be violating anyone's confidentiality," she said. "We can't see your screen. We can even leave the room while you look it up, if you'd like."

Englehardt said nothing. Terese said nothing either. Waiting him out. The perfect interviewer. She finally turned to Myron. "Grab your stuff," she said to him.

"Wait." Englehardt's eyes slid left, then right, up then down. "Jeremy Downing, you say?"

"Yes."

He did another quick series of eye-slides. When he saw that the coast was clear, he hunched over the keyboard and typed quickly. A few seconds later, he asked, "What's the name of this supposed donor?"

"Victor Johnson."

Englehardt looked at the monitor and smiled. "That's not him."

"You're sure?"

"Absolutely."

Terese matched the smile. "That's all we needed to know."

"You'll stop him?"

"He won't even get to the press conference."

Myron grabbed the film case and camera, and they hurried down the corridor. Once outside he turned to her and said, "Malachy Throne?"

"You know who he is?"

"He played False Face on *Batman*."

Terese smiled and nodded. "Very good."

"Can I tell you something?"

"What?"

"It turns me on when you talk *Batman*," he said.

"And even when I don't."

"Are you trying to make a point?"

Five minutes later they were watching the tape in the van.

10

Mr. Davis Taylor
221 North End Ave
Waterbury, Connecticut

The social security and phone numbers were there too. Myron took out his cell phone and dialed. After two rings, a machine picked up and a robotic voice, the default greeting, asked him to leave a message at the tone. He left his name and mobile number and asked Mr. Taylor to return his call.

"So what are you going to do?" Terese asked.

"I guess I'll drive up and try to talk to Mr. Davis Taylor."

"Hasn't the clinic already tried that?"

"Probably."

"But you're more persuasive?"

"Questionable."

"I have to cover the Waldorf tonight," she said.

"I know. I'll go alone. Or maybe I'll bring Win."

She still would not face him. "This boy who needs the transplant," she said. "He's not a stranger, is he?"

Myron was not sure how to answer that. "I guess not."

Terese nodded in a way that told him not to say any more. He didn't. He picked up the phone and called Emily. She answered halfway through the first ring.

"Hello?"

"When is Greg doing the news conference?" he asked.

"In two hours," Emily said.

"I need to reach him."

He heard a hopeful gasp. "Did you find the donor for Jeremy?"

"Not yet."

"But you have something."

"We'll see."

"Don't patronize me, Myron."

"I'm not patronizing you."

"This is my son's life we're talking about here."

And mine? "I have a lead, Emily. That's all."

She gave him the number. "Myron, please call me if—"

"The moment I know something."

He hung up and called Greg.

"I need you to put off the press conference," Myron said.

"Why?" Greg asked.

"Just give me till tomorrow."

"You have something?"

"Maybe," Myron said.

"Maybe nothing," Greg said. "Do you have something or not?"

"I have a name and address. It might be our man. I want to check it out before you make a public plea."

"Where does he live?" Greg asked.

"Connecticut."

"You driving up?"

"Yes."

"Right now?"

"Pretty much."

"I want to go with you," Greg said.

"That's not a good idea."

"He's my kid, dammit."

Myron closed his eyes. "I understand that."

"So then you'll understand this: I'm not asking your permission. I'm going. So stop dicking around and tell me where you want me to pick you up."

Greg drove. He had one of those fancy SUV four-by-fours that are all the rage with New Jersey suburbanites whose idea of "off-road" is a speed bump at the mall. Très truck chic. For a long while neither man spoke. The tension in the air was more than the cut-with-a-knife variety; it pressed against the car windows, weighed Myron down, made him tired and gloomy.

"How did you get this name?" Greg asked.

"It's not important."

Greg left it alone. They drove some more. On the radio, Jewel earnestly insisted that her hands were small, she knew, but they were hers and not someone else's. Myron frowned. Not exactly "Blowing in the Wind," was it?

"You broke my nose, you know," Greg said.

Myron kept quiet.

"And my vision hasn't been the same. I'm having trouble focusing on the basket."

Myron could not believe what he was hearing. "You blaming me for your crappy season, Greg?"

"I'm just saying—"

"You're getting old, Greg. You've played fourteen seasons, and sitting out the strike didn't help you."

Greg waved a hand. "You wouldn't understand."

"You're right." Myron's knob turned from Simmer to Boil. "I never got to play pro ball."

"Right, and I never fucked my friend's wife."

"She wasn't your wife," Myron said. "And we weren't friends."

They both stopped then. Greg kept his eyes on the road. Myron turned away and stared out the passenger window.

Waterbury is one of those cities you bypass to reach another city. Myron had probably taken this stretch of 84 a hundred times, always remarking that at a distance Waterbury was a butt-ugly city. But now that he had the opportunity to see the city up close, he realized that he had underestimated the city's offensiveness to the eyes, that indeed the city had a butt-ugly quality to it that you just couldn't appreciate from afar. He shook his head. And people make fun of New Jersey?

Myron had gotten directions from the MapQuest Web site. He read them off to Greg in a voice he barely recognized as his own. Greg followed them in silence. Five minutes later, they pulled up to a dilapidated clapboard house in the middle of a street of dilapidated clapboards. The houses were uneven and crammed so close together, they looked like a set of teeth needing extensive orthodontic work.

They got out of the car. Myron wanted to tell Greg to stay back, but that would be pointless. He knocked on the door and almost immediately a gruff voice said, "Daniel? That you, Daniel?"

Myron said, "I'm looking for Davis Taylor."

"Daniel?"

"No," Myron said, yelling through the door. "Davis Taylor. But maybe he calls himself Daniel."

"What are you talking about?" An old man opened the door, already in full-suspicious squint. He wore glasses too small for his face, so that the metal earpieces were embedded into the folds of skin beneath both temples, and a bad yellow wig, like something Carol Channing wore once too often, adorned his crown. He had on one slipper and one shoe, and his bathrobe looked as if it'd been trampled over during the Boer War.

"I thought you was Daniel," the old man said. He tried to readjust the glasses, but they wouldn't move. He squinted again. "You look like Daniel."

"Must be the clouds in your eyes," Myron said.

"What?"

"Never mind. Are you Davis Taylor?"

"What do you want?"

"We're looking for Davis Taylor."

"Don't know no Davis Taylor."

"This is 221 North End Drive?"

"That's right."

"And there's no Davis Taylor living here?"

"Just me and my boy Daniel. But he's been away. Overseas."

"Spain?" Myron asked. He pronounced it Spahhheeeeen. Elton would have been proud.

"What?"

"Never mind." The old man turned to Greg, tried again to readjust the glasses, gave another squint. "I know you. You play basketball, right?"

Greg gave the old man a gentle if not superior smile—Moses gazing down at a skeptic after the Red Sea parted. "That's right."

"You're Dolph Schayes."

"No."

"You look like Dolph. Helluva shooter. Saw him play in St. Louis last year. What a touch."

Myron and Greg exchanged a glance. Dolph Schayes had retired in 1964.

"I'm sorry," Myron said. "We didn't catch your name."

"You're not wearing uniforms," the old man said.

"No, sir, he only wears it on the court."

"Not that kind of uniform."

"Oh," Myron said, though he had no idea why.

"So you can't be here about Daniel. That's what I mean. I was afraid you were with the army and . . ." His voice drifted off then.

Myron saw where this was going. "Your son is stationed overseas?"

The old man nodded. "Nam."

Myron nodded, feeling bad now about the Elton John teasing. "We still didn't catch your name."

"Nathan. Nathan Mostoni."

"Mr. Mostoni, we're looking for someone named Davis Taylor. It's very important we find him."

"Don't know no Davis Taylor. He a friend of Daniel's?"

"Might be."

The old man thought about it. "Nope, don't know him."

"Who else lives here?"

"Just me and my boy."

"And it's just the two of you?"

"Yep. But my boy is overseas."

"So right now you live here alone?"

"How many different ways you gonna ask that question, boy?"

"It's just that it's a pretty big house," Myron said.

"So?"

"Ever take in any boarders?"

"Sure. Had a college girl just moved out of here."

"What was her name?"

"Stacy something. I don't remember."

"How long did she live here?"

"About six months."

"And before that?"

That one took some thought. Nathan Mostoni scratched his face like a dog going after his own belly. "A guy named Ken."

"Did you ever have a tenant named Davis Taylor?" Myron asked. "Or something like that?"

"Nope. Never."

"Did this Stacy have a boyfriend?"

"I don't think so."

"Do you know her last name?"

"My memory ain't so good. But she's at the college."

"Which college?"

"Waterbury State."

Myron turned to Greg and another thought hit him. "Mr. Mostoni, have you heard the name Davis Taylor before today?"

Another squint. "What do you mean?"

"Has anybody else visited you or called you and asked about Davis

Taylor?"

"No, sir. Never heard the name before."

Myron looked at Greg again, then turned back to the old man. "So no one from the bone marrow center has been in touch with you?"

The old man cocked his head and put a hand to his ear. "The bone what?"

Myron asked a few more questions, but Nathan Mostoni started time-traveling again. There was nothing more to get here. Myron and Greg thanked him and headed back down the cracked pathway.

When they were back in the car, Greg asked, "Why didn't the bone marrow center contact this guy?"

"Maybe they did," Myron said. "Maybe he just forgot."

Greg didn't like it. Neither did Myron. "So what's next?" Greg asked.

"We run a background check on Davis Taylor. Find out everything we can about him."

"How?

"It's easy nowadays. Just a few keystrokes and my partner will know it all."

"Your partner? You mean that violent wacko you used to room with in college?"

"A, it is unhealthy to refer to Win as a violent wacko, even when he appears not to be in the vicinity. B, no, I mean my partner at MB SportsReps, Esperanza Diaz."

Greg looked back at the house. "What do I do?"

"Go home," Myron said.

"And?"

"And be with your son."

Greg shook his head. "I don't get to see him until the weekend."

"I'm sure Emily wouldn't mind."

"Yeah, right." Greg smirked, shook his head. "You don't know her too well anymore, do you, Myron?"

"I guess not, no."

"If she had her way, I'd never get to see Jeremy again."

"That's a bit harsh, Greg."

"No, Myron. If anything, it's being generous."

"Emily told me that you're a good father."

"Did she also tell you what she charged in our custody battle?"

Myron nodded. "That you abused the kids."

"Not just abused them, Myron. *Sexually* abused them."

"She wanted to win."

"And that's an excuse?"

"No," Myron said. "It's deplorable."

"More than that," Greg said. "It's sick. You have no idea what Emily's capable of doing to get her way."

"For example?"

But Greg just shook his head and started up the car. "I'll ask you again: What can I do to help?"

"Nothing, Greg."

"No good. I'm not sitting around while my kid is dying, you understand?"

"I do."

"You have anything besides this name and address?"

"Nope."

"Fine," Greg said. "I'll drop you off at the train station. I'm staying up here and watching the house."

"You think the old man is lying?"

Greg shrugged. "Maybe he's just confused and forgot. Or maybe I'm wasting my time. But I got to do something."

Myron said nothing. Greg continued to drive.

"You'll call me if you hear something?" Greg asked.

"Sure."

During the train ride back to Manhattan, Myron thought about what Greg had said. About Emily. And about what she'd done—and what she'd do—to save her son.

11

Myron and Terese started out the next morning showering together. Myron controlled the temperature and kept the water hot. Prevents, er, shrinkage.

When they stepped out of the steamy stall, he helped Terese towel off.

"Thorough," she said.

"We're a full-service operation, ma'am." He toweled her off some more.

"One thing I notice when I shower with a man," Terese said.

"What's that?"

"My breasts always end up squeaky clean."

Win had left several hours ago. Lately he liked to get to the office by six. Overseas markets or something. Terese toasted a bagel while Myron fixed himself a bowl of cereal. Quisp cereal. They didn't have it in New York anymore, but Win had it shipped in from a place called Woodsman's in Wisconsin. Myron downed an industrial-size spoonful; the sugar rush came at him so fast he nearly ducked.

Terese said, "I have to go back tomorrow morning."

"I know."

He took another spoonful, feeling her eyes on him.

"Run away with me again," Terese said.

He glanced up at her. She looked smaller, farther away.

"I can get us the same house on the island. We can just hop on a plane and—"

"I can't," he interrupted.

"Oh," she said. Then: "You need to find this Davis Taylor?"

"Yes."

"I see. And after that . . . ?"

Myron shook his head. They ate some more in silence.

"I'm sorry," Myron said.

She nodded.

"Running away isn't always the answer, Terese."

"Myron?"

"What?"

"Do I look in the mood for platitudes?"

"I'm sorry."

"Yeah, you said that already."

"I'm just trying to help."

"Sometimes you can't help," she said. "Sometimes all that's left is running away."

"Not for me," he said.

"No," she agreed. "Not for you."

She wasn't angry or upset, just flat and resigned, and that scared him all the more.

An hour later Esperanza came into Myron's office without knocking.

"Okay," she began, grabbing a seat, "here's what we've got on Davis Taylor."

Myron leaned back and put his hands behind his head.

"One, he's never filed a tax return with the IRS."

"Never?"

"Glad you're paying attention," Esperanza said.

"Are you saying he's never shown any income?"

"Will you let me finish?"

"Sorry."

"Two, he has virtually no paperwork. No driver's license. One credit card, a Visa recently issued by his bank. It has very little activity. Only one bank account, with a current balance of under two hundred dollars."

"Suspicious," Myron said.

"Yes."

"When did he open the account?"

"Three months ago."

"And before that?"

"Nada. At least nada that I've been able to come up with so far."

Myron stroked his chin. "No one flies that far below the radar screen," he said. "It has to be an alias."

"I thought the same thing," Esperanza said.

"And?"

"The answer is yes and no." Myron waited for the explanation. Esperanza tucked some loose tresses behind both ears. "It appears to be a name change."

Myron frowned. "But we got his social security number, right?"

"Right."

"And most records are kept by social security number, not name, right?"

"Another right."

"So I don't get it," Myron said. "You can't change your social security number. A name change might make you harder to find, but it wouldn't wipe out your past. You'd still have tax returns and stuff like that."

Esperanza turned both palms upward. "That's what I mean by yes and no."

"There's no paperwork under the social security number either?"

"That's correct," Esperanza said.

Myron tried to digest this. "So what's Davis Taylor's real name?"

"I don't have it yet."

"I would have thought it'd be easy to locate."

"It would," she said, "if he had any records at all. But he doesn't. The social security number has no hits. It's as though this person hasn't done a thing in his whole life."

Myron thought about it. "Only one explanation," he said.

"That being?"

"A fake ID."

Esperanza shook her head. "The social security number exists."

"I don't doubt that. But I think someone pulled the classic tombstone-fake-ID trick."

"That being?"

"You go to a graveyard and find the tombstone of a dead child," Myron said. "Someone who would be about your age if he'd lived. Then you write and request his birth certificate and paperwork and *voilà*, you've set up the perfect fake ID. Oldest trick in the book."

Esperanza gave him the look she saved for his most idiotic moments. "No," she said.

"No?"

"You think the police don't watch TV, Myron? That doesn't work anymore. Hasn't worked in years, except maybe on cop shows. But just to make sure, I double-checked."

"How?"

"Death records," she said. "There's a Web site that has the social security numbers of all the deceased."

"And the number isn't there."

"Ding, ding, ding," Esperanza said.

Myron leaned forward. "This makes absolutely no sense," he said. "Our phony Davis Taylor has gone to a great deal of trouble to create this phony ID—or at least to fly below the radar, right?"

"Right."

"He wants no records, no paperwork, nothing."

"Right again."

"Even changes his name."

"You go, boy."

Myron put his arms out. "Then why would he sign up to be a bone marrow donor?"

"Myron?"

"Yeah."

"I don't know what you're talking about," Esperanza said.

True enough. He'd called last night and asked her to check out Davis Taylor. He had not yet told her why.

"I guess I owe you an explanation," he said.

She shrugged.

"I sort of promised you I wouldn't be doing this anymore," he said.

"Investigating," she said.

"Right. And I meant it. I wanted this to be a straight agency from now on."

She didn't respond. Myron glanced at the wall behind her. The sparse Client Wall again reminded him of a hair transplant that hadn't taken. Maybe he should paint on a couple of coats of Rogaine.

"You remember Emily's call?" he said.

"It was yesterday, Myron. My memory can sometimes go back a whole week."

He explained it all. Some men—men Myron grudgingly admired—keep it all inside, bury their secrets, hide the pain, the whole cliché. Myron rarely did. He was not one to walk down the mean streets alone—he liked Win to be his backup. He didn't grab a bottle of whiskey and drown his sorrows—he discussed them with Esperanza. Not very macho, but there you have it.

Esperanza stayed silent as he spoke. When he got to the part about being Jeremy's father, she let out a small groan and closed her eyes and kept them shut for a very long time. When she finally opened them, she asked, "So what are you going to do?"

"I'm going to find the donor."

"That's not what I meant."

He knew that. "I don't know," he said.

She thought about it, shook her head in disbelief. "You have a son."

"Seems so."

"And you don't know what you're going to do about it?"

"That's right."

"But you're leaning," she said.

"Win made a pretty good case for not saying anything."

She made a sound. "Win would."

"Actually he claims to be using his heart."

"If only he had one."

"You don't agree?"

"No," she said. "I don't agree."

"You think I should tell Jeremy?"

"I think first and foremost you should put aside your Batman complex," she said.

"What the hell does that mean?"

"It means you always try a little too hard to be heroic."

"And that's bad?"

"Sometimes it clouds your thinking," she said. "The heroic thing is not always the right thing."

"Jeremy already has a family. He has a mother and a father—"

"He has," Esperanza interrupted, "a lie."

They sat there and stared at each other. The phone, usually so active, was silent, as it had been for too long now. Myron wondered how he could explain it so that she would understand. She stayed still, waiting.

"We were both lucky when it came to parents," Myron said.

"Mine are dead, Myron."

"That's not what I mean," he said. He took a deep breath. "How many days pass that you don't still miss them?"

"None," she said without hesitation.

He nodded. "We were both loved unconditionally and we both loved our parents the same way."

Esperanza's eyes started misting. "So?"

"So—and this was what Win said—isn't that what makes a mother or father? Isn't it about who raised us and loved us and not simply an accident of biology?"

Esperanza leaned back. "Win said that?"

Myron smiled. "He has his moments."

"That he does," she said.

"And think about your father—the one who raised and loved you. What happens to him?"

Her eyes were still misty. "My love for him is strong enough to survive the truth. Isn't yours?"

He tilted back as though the words were jabs at his chin. "Sure," he said. "But it would still hurt him."

"Your father would be hurt?"

"Of course."

"I see," Esperanza said. "So now you're worried about poor Greg Downing?"

"Hardly. You want to hear something awful?"

"Love to."

"When Greg constantly refers to Jeremy as 'my son,' I want to yell out the truth. Right in his smug face. Just to see his reaction. Just to watch his world crumble."

"So much for your Batman complex," Esperanza said.

Myron held out his hands. "I have my moments too," he said.

Esperanza stood and headed for the door.

"Where you going?"

"I don't want to talk about this anymore," she said.

He sat back.

"You're blocking," she said. "You know that?"

He nodded slowly.

"When you move past it—and you will—we'll talk about it again. Otherwise, we're wasting our time here, okay?"

"Okay."

"Just don't be stupid."

" 'Don't be stupid,' " he repeated. "Check."

Her departing smile was brief.

12

Myron spent the rest of the day working the phones. He strapped on his Ultra Slim headset and paced the office. He talked up college coaches, mining for potential free agents. He touched base with his clients and listened to their problems, both real and imagined, therapist-style, which was a large part of his job. He sifted through his Rolodex of companies, trying to conjure up a few endorsement deals.

One serious lead came a-knocking on its own.

"Mr. Bolitar? I'm Ronny Angle from Rack Enterprises. Are you familiar with us?"

"You run a bunch of topless bars, right?"

"We prefer they be called upscale exotic nightclubs."

"And I prefer to be called a well-endowed stallion," Myron said. "What can I do for you, Mr. Angle?"

"Ronny please. Can I call you Myron?"

"Myron please."

"Great, Myron. Rack Enterprises is entering a new venture."

"Uh-huh."

"You've probably read about it. A chain of coffee-houses called La, La, Latte."

"For real?"

"Pardon?"

"Well, I think I did see something about this, but I figured it was a joke."

"It's no joke, Mr. Bolitar."

"So you guys are really going to open up topless coffee bars?"

"We prefer they be called upscale erotic coffee experiences."

"I see. But you're, uh, *baristas* will be topless, correct?"

"Correct."

Myron thought about it. "Makes asking for milk something of a double entendre, don't you think?"

"That's very funny, Myron."

"Thanks, Ronny."

"We're going to open with a big splash."

"That another milk joke, Ronny?"

"No, Myron, but you're a pretty funny guy."

"Thanks, Ronny."

"Let me cut right to it, okay? We like Suzze T." Suzze T was Suzze Tamirino, a journeyman (or is it journeywoman?) on the pro tennis circuit. "We saw her picture in the *Sports Illustrated* swimsuit issue, and, well, we were very impressed. We'd like her to do a cameo for our grand opening."

Myron rubbed the bridge of his nose with his thumb and forefinger. "When you say cameo—"

"A brief performance."

"How brief?"

"No more than five minutes."

"I don't mean brief in terms of time. I mean in terms of clothing."

"We'd require full frontal nudity."

"Well, thanks for thinking of us, Ronny, but I don't think Suzze will be interested."

"We're offering two hundred thousand dollars."

Myron sat up. Easy to hang up, but with this kind of dough, he had a responsibility to follow up. "How about if she wears a small top?"

"No."

"A bikini?"

"No."

"An itsy-bitsy, teeny-weeny bikini?"

"Like in the song?"

"Exactly," Myron said. "Like in the song."

"I'm going to state this as plainly as I can," Ronny said. "There must be nipple visibility."

"Nipple visibility?"

"This point is non-negotiable."

"So to speak."

Myron promised to call him back later in the week. The two men hung up. Negotiating nipple visibility. What a business.

Esperanza came in without knocking. Her eyes were wide and bright.

"Lamar Richardson is on line one," she said.

"Lamar himself?"

She nodded.

"No relative or personal manager or favorite astrologer?"

"Lamar himself," Esperanza repeated.

They both nodded. This was a good thing.

Myron picked up the phone. "Hello."

"Let's meet," Lamar said.

"Sure," Myron said.

"When?"

"You name it."

"When are you free?"

"You name it," Myron said.

"I'm in Detroit right now."

"I'll catch the next plane out."

"Just like that?" Lamar said.

"Yup."

"Shouldn't you pretend you're really busy?"

"We going to date, Lamar?"

Lamar chuckled. "No, I don't think so."

"Then I'll skip the playing-hard-to-get stage. Esperanza and I want you to sign up with MB SportsReps. We'll do a good job. We'll make you a priority. And we won't play mind games with you."

Myron smiled at Esperanza. Was he good or what?

Lamar said he was going to be in Manhattan later in the week and would like to meet then. They set up a time. Myron hung up. He and Esperanza sat there and smiled at each other.

"We have a chance," she said.

"Yep."

"So what's our strategy?"

"I thought I'd impress him with my nimble mind," he said.

"Hmm," Esperanza said. "Maybe I should wear something low cut."

"I was kinda counting on that."

"Hit him with brains and beauty."

"Yes," Myron said. "But which one of us is which?"

When Myron got back to the Dakota, Win was heading out with his leather gym bag and Terese was gone.

"She left a note," Win said, handing it to Myron.

Had to go back early. I'll call.
Terese

Myron read the note again. It didn't change. He folded it up and put it away.

"You going to Master Kwon's?" Myron asked. Master Kwon was their martial arts instructor.

Win nodded. "He's been asking for you."

"What did you tell him?" Myron asked.

"That you wigged out."

"Thanks."

Win gave a slight bow and lifted his gym bag. "May I make a suggestion?"

"Shoot."

"You haven't been to the *dojang* in a long while."

"I know."

"You have a great deal of stress in your life," Win said. "You need an outlet. You need some focus. Some balance. Some structure."

"You're not going to make me snatch a pebble from your hand, are you?"

"Not today, no. But come with me."

Myron shrugged. "I'll grab my stuff."

They were halfway out the door when Esperanza called. He told her they were just on their way out.

"Where?" she asked.

"Master Kwon's."

"I'll meet you there."

"Why? What's up?"

"I got some information on Davis Taylor."

"And?"

"And it's more than a little strange. Is Win going with you?"

"Yes."

"Ask him if he knows anything about Raymond Lex's family."

Silence. "Raymond Lex is dead, Esperanza."

"Duh, Myron. I said *family*."

"This has something to do with Davis Taylor?"

"It'll be easier to explain in person. I'll see you down there in an hour."

She hung up.

One of the doormen had already fetched Win's Jag. It sat waiting for them on Central Park West. The rich. Myron settled into the lush leather. Win hit the accelerator pad. He was big with the accelerator pad; he had a bit more trouble when it came to the brake.

"Do you know Raymond Lex's family?"

"They used to be clients," Win said.

"You're kidding?"

"Oh yes, I'm a regular Red Buttons."

"Were you directly involved in this inheritance squabble?"

"Calling this a squabble would be similar to calling nuclear Armageddon a campfire."

"Hard to divide up billions, huh?"

"Indeed. So why are we discussing the Lex clan?"

"Esperanza is going to meet us down at the *dojang*. She has some information on Davis Taylor. Somehow the Lex family is connected."

Win arched his eyebrow. "The plot doth thicken."

"So tell me a little about them."

"Most of it was in the media. Raymond Lex writes a controversial bestseller called *Midnight Confessions*. Said bestseller becomes an Oscar-winning blockbuster. Suddenly he goes from obscure junior-college instructor to millionaire. Unlike most of his artistic brethren, he understands business. He invests and amasses private holdings with a substantial yet confidential net worth."

"The papers place it in the billions."

"I won't argue."

"That's a lot of money."

"He never wrote another book?"

"No."

"Odd."

"Not really," Win said. "Harper Lee and Margaret Mitchell never wrote another book. And at least Lex kept busy. It's hard to build one of the largest privately held corporations and do book signings."

"So now that he's dead, his family is—how to say it?—nuclear Armageddoning?"

"Close enough."

Master Kwon had moved his headquarters and main *dojang* into the second floor of a building on Twenty-third Street near Broadway. Five rooms—studios really—with hardwood floors, mirrored walls, high-tech sound system, sleek and shiny Nautilus equipment—oh, and some of those rice-paper Oriental scroll-posters. Gave the place a real Old World Asia feel.

Myron and Win slipped into their *dobok*, a white uniform, and tied their black belts. Myron had been studying tae kwon do and *hapkido* since Win had first introduced him to them in college, but he hadn't been to a *dojang* more than five times in the past three years. Win, on the other hand, remained devoutly lethal. Don't tug on Superman's cape, don't spit in the wind, don't pull the mask off the ol' Lone Ranger, and you don't mess around with Win. Bah, bah, dee, dee, dee, dee, dee.

Master Kwon was in his mid-seventies but could easily pass for two decades younger. Win had met him during his Asian travels when he was fifteen. As near as Myron could tell, Master Kwon had been a high priest or some such thing at a small Buddhist monastery straight out of a Hong Kong revenge flick. When Master Kwon emigrated to the United States, he spoke very little English. Now, some twenty years later, he spoke almost none. As soon as the wise master hit our shores, he opened up a chain of state-of-the-art tae kwon do schools—with Win's financial backing, of course. Once he saw the *Karate Kid* movies, Master Kwon started playing the old wise man to the hilt. His English disappeared. He started dressing like the Dalai Lama and began every sentence with the words "Confucius say," ignoring the small fact that he was Korean and Confucius was Chinese.

Win and Myron headed to Master Kwon's office. At the entrance, both men bowed deeply.

"Please in," Master Kwon said.

The desk was fine oak, the chair rich leather and orthopedic looking. Master Kwon was standing near a corner. He held a putter in his hands and wore a splendidly tailored suit. His face brightened when he saw Myron, and the two men embraced.

When they broke apart, Master Kwon said, "You better?"

"Better," Myron agreed.

The old man smiled and grabbed his own lapel. "Armani," he said.

"I thought so," Myron said.

"You like?"

"Very nice."

Satisfied, Master Kwon said, "Go."

Win and Myron bowed deeply. Once in the *dojang*, they fell into their customary roles: Win led and Myron followed. They started with meditation. Win loved meditating, as we already graphically witnessed. He sat in the lotus position, palms tilted up, hands resting on knees, back straight, tongue folded against the upper teeth. He breathed in through his nose, forcing the air down, letting his abdomen do all the work. Myron tried to duplicate—had been trying for years—but he had never quite gotten the hang of it. His mind, even during less chaotic times, wandered. His bad knee tightened. He got fidgety.

They cut down the stretching to only ten minutes. Again Win was effortless, executing splits and toe touches and deep bends with ease, his bones and joints as flexible as a politician's voting record. Myron had never been a naturally limber guy. When he was training seriously, he could touch his toes and complete a hurdle stretch with little problem. But just then, that felt like a long time ago.

"I'm already sore," Myron said through a grunt.

Win tilted his head. "Odd."

"What?"

"That's precisely what my date said last night."

"You weren't kidding before," Myron said. "You really are another Red Buttons."

They did a little sparring, and Myron immediately realized how out of shape he was. Sparring is the most tiring activity in the world. Don't believe it? Find a punching bag and pretend-box with it for one three-minute round. Just a bag that can't fight back. Try it, just one round. You'll see.

When Esperanza came in, the sparring mercifully ceased and Myron grabbed his knees, sucking wind. He bowed to Win, threw a towel over his shoulder, grabbed some Evian. Esperanza folded her arms and waited. A group of students walked past the door, saw Esperanza, did a double take.

Esperanza handed Myron a sheet of paper. "The birth certificate of Davis Taylor né Dennis Lex."

"Lex," Myron repeated. "As in . . . ?"

"Yep."

Myron scanned the photocopy. According to the document, Dennis Lex would be thirty-seven years old. His father was listed as one Raymond Lex, his mother as Maureen Lehman Lex. Born in East Hampton, New York.

Myron handed it to Win.

"They had another child?"

"Apparently so," Esperanza said.

Myron looked at Win. Win shrugged.

"He must have died young," Win said.

"If he did," Esperanza said, "I can't find it anywhere. There's no death certificate."

"No one in the family ever mentioned another child?" Myron asked Win.

"No one," Win said.

He turned back to Esperanza. "What else you got?"

"Not much. Dennis Lex changed his name to Davis Taylor eight months ago. I also found this." She handed him a photocopy of a news clipping. A small birth announcement from the *Hampton Gazette* dated thirty-seven years ago:

> Raymond and Maureen Lex of Wister Drive in East Hampton are delighted to announce the birth of their son, Dennis, six pounds eight ounces on June 18th. Dennis joins his sister Susan and his brother Bronwyn.

Myron shook his head. "How could no one know about this?"

"It's not all that surprising," Win said.

"How do you figure?"

"None of the Lex family holdings are public. They are fiercely protective of their privacy. Security around them is around-the-clock and the best money can buy. Everyone who works with them must sign confidentiality agreements."

"Even you?"

"I don't do confidentiality agreements," Win said. "No matter how much money is involved."

"So they never asked you to sign one?"

"They asked. I refused. We parted ways."

"You gave them up as clients?"

"Yes."

"Why? I mean, what would have been the big deal? You keep everything confidential anyway."

"Exactly. Clients hire me not only because of my brilliance in the ways of finance but because I am the very model of discretion."

"Don't overlook your startling modesty," Myron added.

"I don't need to sign a contract saying I won't reveal anything. It should be a given. It's the equivalent of signing a document saying that I won't burn down their house."

Myron nodded. "Nice analogy," he said.

"Yes, thank you, but I'm trying to illustrate how far this family will go to maintain their privacy. Until this inheritance feud erupted, the media had no idea how extensive Raymond Lex's holdings were."

"But come on, Win. This is Raymond Lex's son. You'd know about a son."

Win pointed to the top of the clipping. "Notice when the child was born—*before* Raymond Lex's book came out, when Lex was just a typical small-town professor. It wouldn't make news."

"You really buy that?"

"Do you have a better explanation?"

"So where is the kid now? How can the son of one of America's wealthiest families have no paperwork? No credit cards, no driver's license, no IRS filings, no trail at all? Why did he change his name?"

"The last one is easy," Win said.

"Oh?"

"He's hiding."

"From?"

"His siblings perhaps," Win said. "As I said before, this inheritance battle is rather nasty."

"That might make sense—and I stress the word 'might'—if he'd been around before. But how can there be no paperwork on him? What is he hiding from? And why on earth would he put his name in the bone marrow registry?"

"Good questions," Win said.

"Very good," Esperanza added.

Myron reread the article and looked at his two friends. "Nice to have a consensus," he said.

13

The mobile phone blew him out of his sleep like a shotgun blast. Myron's hand reached up blindly, his fingers bouncing along the night table until they located the phone.

"Hello?" he croaked.

"Is this Myron Bolitar?"

The voice was a whisper.

"Who is this?" Myron asked.

"You called me."

Still whispering, the sound like leaves skittering across pavement.

Myron sat upright, his heartbeat picking up a little steam. "Davis Taylor?"

"Sow the seeds. Keep sowing. And open the shades. Let the truth come in. Let the secrets finally wither in the daylight."

Ooookay. "I need your help, Mr. Taylor."

"Sow the seeds."

"Yes, of course, we'll sow away." Myron flicked on the light. 2:17 A.M. He checked the LCD display on the phone. The Caller ID was blocked. Damn. "But we have to meet."

"Sow the seeds. It's the only way."

"I understand, Mr. Taylor. Can we meet?"

"Someone must sow the seeds. And someone must unlock the chains."

"I'll bring a key. Just tell me where you are."

"Why do you wish to see me?"

What to say? "It's a matter of life and death."

"Whenever you sow the seeds, it's a matter of life and death."

"You donated blood for a bone marrow drive. You're a match. A young boy will die if you don't help."

Silence.

"Mr. Taylor?"

"Technology cannot help him. I thought you were one of us." Still whispering but sad now.

"I am. Or at least I want to be—"

"I'm hanging up now."

"No, wait—"

"Good-bye."

"Dennis Lex," Myron said.

Silence, except for the sound of breathing. Myron wasn't sure if the sound was coming from him or the caller.

"Please," Myron said. "I'll do whatever you ask. But we have to meet."

"Will you remember to sow the seeds?"

Small chunks of ice dropped down his back.

"Yes," Myron said, "I'll remember."

"Good. Then you know what you must do."

Myron gripped the receiver. "No," he said. "What must I do?"

"The boy," the voice whispered. "Say one last good-bye to the boy."

14

"Sow the seeds?" Esperanza said.

They were in Myron's office. The morning sun striped the floor with Venetian slits, two cutting across Esperanza's face. She didn't seem to mind.

"Right," Myron said. "And something about that phrase keeps gnawing at me."

"It was a Tears for Fears song," Esperanza said.

" 'Sowing the Seeds of Love.' I remember."

"Wasn't that the name of the tour too? We saw them at the Meadowlands in, what, 1988?"

"Eighty-nine."

"What happened to those guys?"

"They broke up," Myron said.

"Why do they all do that?"

"Got me."

"Supertramp, Steely Dan, the Doobie Brothers—"

"Not to mention Wham."

"They break up and then they never make anything decent on their own. They flounder around and end up a segment of VH-1's *Where Are They Now?*"

"We're getting off the subject."

Esperanza handed him a slip of paper. "Here's the office number for Susan Lex, Dennis's older sister."

Myron read the number like it was in code and might mean something. "I had another thought."

"What's that?"

"If Dennis Lex exists, then he had to have gone to school, right?"

"Maybe."

"So let's see if we can find out where the Children Lex schooled—public, private, whatever."

Esperanza frowned. "You mean like college?"

"Start there, yes. Not that siblings go to the same school, but maybe they did. Or maybe they all went to Ivy League schools. Something like that. You might want to start with high school. It's more likely that they all went to the same one."

"And if I don't find any record of him in high school?"

"Go back even further."

She crossed her legs, folded her arms. "How far?"

"As far as you can."

"And what good will this exercise in futility do us?"

"I want to know when Dennis Lex fell off the radar screen. Did people know him in high school? In college? In grad school?"

She did not look impressed. "And assuming I somehow manage to find, say, his elementary school, what exactly is that going to do for us?"

"Damn if I know. I'm grasping at straws here."

"No, you're asking *me* to grasp at straws."

"Then don't do it, Esperanza, okay? It was just a thought."

"Nah," she said with a wave of her hand. "You may be right."

Myron put his palms on his desk, arched his back, looked left, looked right, looked up, looked down.

"What?" she said.

"You said I may be right. I'm waiting for the world as we know it to end."

"Good one," Esperanza said, standing. "I'll see what I can dig up."

She left the room. Myron picked up the telephone and dialed Susan Lex's number. The receptionist transferred the call, and a woman identifying herself as Ms. Lex's secretary picked it up. She had a voice like a steel-wool tire over gravel.

"Ms. Lex does not see people she doesn't know."

"It's a matter of grave importance," Myron said.

"Perhaps you did not hear me the first time." Classic Battle-ax. "Ms. Lex does not see people she doesn't know."

"Tell her it's about Dennis."

"Excuse me?"

"Just tell her that."

Battle-ax put Myron on hold without another word. Myron listened to a Muzak version of Al Stewart's "Time Passages." Myron had thought the original was Muzak-y enough, thank you very much.

The battle-ax came back with a snap. "Ms. Lex does not see people she doesn't know."

"I've been thinking about that, but it doesn't really make sense."

"Excuse me?"

"I mean, at some time she must see people she doesn't know—otherwise she'd never meet anybody new. And if we follow my logic, how did you ever get to see her for the first time? She was willing to see you before she knew you, right?"

"I'm hanging up now, Mr. Bolitar."

"Tell her I know about Dennis."

"I just—"

"Tell her if she doesn't agree to see me, I'll go to the press."

Silence. "Hold." A click and then the Muzak came back on. Time passed. So, mercifully, did "Time Passages," replaced by the Alan Parsons Project's "Time." Myron nearly slipped into a coma.

Battle-ax returned. "Mr. Bolitar?"

"Yes?"

"Ms. Lex will give you five minutes of her time. I have an opening on the fifteenth of next month."

"No good," Myron said. "It has to be today."

"Ms. Lex is a very busy woman."

"Today," Myron said.

"That simply will not be possible."

"At eleven. If I'm not let in, I go immediately to the press."

"You're being terribly rude, Mr. Bolitar."

"To the press," Myron repeated. "Do you understand?"

"Yes."

"Will you be there?"

"What possible difference could that make?"

"All this sexual tension is driving me batty. Maybe afterward we could get together for a nice cool latte."

He heard the phone go click and smiled. The charm, he thought. It's baaaaack.

Esperanza buzzed in. "Topless tennis, anyone?"

"What?"

"I got Suzze T on line one."

He hit a button. "Hey, Suzze."

"Hey, Myron, what's shaking?"

"I got an offer for you to refuse."

"You mean you're going to hit on me?"

The charm suffers a setback. "Where are you going to be this afternoon?"

"Same place as now," she said. "The Morning Mosh. You know it?"

"No."

She gave him the address, and Myron agreed to meet her there in a few hours. He hung up the phone and leaned back.

" 'Sow the seeds,' " he said out loud.

He stared at the wall. An hour to kill before he headed over to the Lex Building on Fifth Avenue. He could sit here and think about life and maybe contemplate his navel. No, too much of that already. He swiveled his seat to the computer, double-clicked the proper icon, connected to the Net. He tried Yahoo first and typed *sow the seeds* into the search field. Only one hit: a Web site for the San Francisco League of Urban Gardeners. They went by the acronym SLUG. Tough guys probably. A gang. Probably wore green bandannas and engaged in drive-by waterings.

He tried Alta Vista's search engine next, but they listed 2,501 Web pages. It was kinda like Goldilocks and the Three Bears. Yahoo's search was toooo small. Alta Vista's was toooo big. They didn't have LEXIS–NEXIS at the office, but Myron tried a less powerful media engine. He typed in the same three words and pressed the return key, and bammo.

http://www.nyherald.com/archives/9800322

Myron hit the link and the article came up:

New York Herald

THE MIND OF TERROR—YOUR DARKEST FEAR

by Stan Gibbs

Whoa, hold the phone. Myron knew the name. Stan Gibbs had been a big-time newspaper columnist, the kind of guy who regularly pontificated (read: pimped) on the cable news talk shows, though he'd been less annoying than most, which is like saying syphilis is less annoying than gonorrhea. But that had all been before the scandal gutted him like Ted Nugent over a fallen moose. Myron read:

> The phone call comes out of the blue.
>
> "What is your darkest fear?" the voice whispers. "Close your eyes now and picture it. Can you see it? Do you have it yet? The very worst agony you can imagine?"
>
> After a long pause, I say, "Yes."
>
> "Good. Now imagine something worse, something far, far worse . . ."

Myron took a deep breath. He remembered the series of articles. Stan Gibbs had broken a story about a bizarre kidnapper. He'd told the heart-wrenching tale of three abductions that the police had supposedly wanted to keep quiet, out of, Stan Gibbs claimed, embarrassment. No names were mentioned. He had spoken with the families under the condition of anonymity. And, the coup de grâce, the kidnapper had granted Gibbs access:

> I ask the kidnapper why he does it. Is it for the ransom?
>
> "I never pick up the ransom money," he says. "I usually leave explosives at the spot and burn it. But sometimes money helps me sow the seeds. That is what I'm trying to do. Sow the seeds."

Myron felt his blood stop.

> "You all think you're safe," he continues, "in your technological cocoon. But you're not. Technology has made us expect easy answers and happy endings. But with me, there is no answer and there is no end."
>
> He has kidnapped at least four people: the father of two young children, age 41; a female college student, age 20; and a young couple, newlyweds ages 28 and 27. All were abducted while in the New York City area.
>
> "The idea," he says, "is to keep the terror going. Let it grow, not with gore or obvious bloodletting, but with your own imagination. Technology is trying to destroy our ability to imagine. But when someone you love is taken away, your mind can conjure up horrors darker than any machine—than anything even I can do. Some minds won't go that far. Some minds stop and put up a barrier. My job is to push them through that barrier."
>
> I ask him how he does that.
>
> "Sow the seeds," he repeats. "You sow the seeds over time."
>
> He explains that sowing the seeds means giving hope and taking it away over a sustained period of time. His first call to the victim's family is naturally devastating, but merely the beginning of a long and torturous ordeal.
>
> He begins the call, he claims, with a normal hello and asks the family member to please hold. After a pause, the family member hears their loved one give a blood-curdling shriek. "Just one," he says, "and it's very short. I

cut them off in mid-scream.

"This is the last they'll ever hear from their loved one," he continues. "Imagine how that scream echoes."

But for the victim's family, it does not end there. He demands a ransom that he has no intention of claiming. He calls after midnight and asks the family to imagine their darkest fear. He convinces them that this time, he will really let their loved one go, but he is only extending hope to those who no longer have it, rekindling their agony.

"Time and hope," he says, "sow the seeds of despair."

The father of two has been missing for three years. The young premed college student has been missing for twenty-seven months. The newlyweds were married almost two years ago this weekend. To date, not a trace of any of them has been found. Rarely does a week pass when the families don't get a call from their tormentor.

When I ask him if his victims are alive or dead, he is coy. "Death is closure," he explains, "and closure stops the sowing."

He wants to talk about society, how computers and technology are doing our thinking for us, how what he does lets us see the power of the human brain.

"That is where God exists," he says. "That is where all things valuable exist. True bliss can only be found inside of you. The meaning of life is not in your new home entertainment system or sports car. People must see their limitless potential. How do you make them see? Right now imagine what these families are going through."

His voice soft, he invites me to try.

"Technology could never conjure up the horrors you are now imagining. Sow the seeds. Sowing the seeds shows us the potential."

Myron's heart pounded in big thuds. He sat back, shook his head, started reading again. The crazed kidnapper ranted on, his theories feverishly demented, sort of Symbionese Liberation Army by way of Ted Kaczynski. Stan Gibbs's column continued into the next day's paper. Myron hit the link and read on. During the second day, Gibbs opened with some heartbreaking quotes from the family of the victims. Then he questioned the kidnapper some more:

I ask him how he has managed to keep these kidnappings out of the media.

"By sowing the seeds," he repeats yet again.

I ask for an example.

"I tell his wife to go to the garage and open the red Stanley toolbox on the third shelf. I tell her to pick out the black pliers with the bubble grip. Then I send her to the basement. I tell her to stand in front of the Mission chair they bought the previous summer at that tag sale on the Cape. Imagine, I say, your husband tied naked to that chair. Imagine those pliers in my hand. And finally, imagine what I'll do if I see anything about him in the newspaper."

But he does not stop there.

"I ask her about the children. I mention their names. I mention their schools and their teachers and their favorite breakfast cereal."

I ask him how he knows these things.

His answer is simple. "Daddy tells me."

Myron fell back. "Jesus," he uttered.

Deep breaths, he told himself again. In and out. That's it. Think it through. Slowly now. Carefully. Okay, first off: Horrible as this is, what does it have to do with Davis Taylor né Dennis Lex? Probably nothing. The worst sort of long shot. And again, horrible as this is, Myron knew that there was more to the story. More—and in a sense, less.

The Gibbs columns drew weeks' worth of nationwide attention and criticism—until, Myron remembered, it all blew up in the most public way possible. What had happened exactly? Myron hit some keys and clicked the mouse. He started a search of articles where Stan Gibbs was the subject. They came up in date order:

FEDS DEMAND GIBBS'S SOURCE

The Federal Bureau of Investigation, which in recent weeks has been denying the allegations listed in Stan Gibbs's columns, took a new tack today. They demanded his notes and information.

Dan Conway, a spokesman for the FBI, began by saying, "We know nothing about these crimes," then added, "But if Mr. Gibbs is being truthful, he has important information on a possible serial kidnapper and killer, perhaps even harboring or aiding him. We have a right to that information."

Stan Gibbs, a popular columnist and television journalist, has refused to reveal his sources. "I'm not protecting a killer here," Mr. Gibbs said. "The families of the victims as well as the perpetrator of the crimes spoke to me under the strict condition of confidentiality. It's a cry as old as our country: I will not reveal my sources."

The *New York Herald* and American Civil Liberties Union have already denounced the FBI and plan on backing Mr. Gibbs. The judge has ordered the case sealed from the public.

Myron read on. The arguments on both sides were pretty standard. Gibbs's attorneys naturally wrapped themselves in the First Amendment, while the feds equally naturally countered that the First Amendment was not an absolute, that you can't yell "Fire!" in a crowded theater, and that freedom of expression does not include protecting possible criminals. The country also argued the issue. It played well on CNBC and MSNBC and CNN and a bunch of other cable letters, lighting up the phone lines like a radio giveaway. The judge was about to render a verdict when the whole story exploded in a way no one expected.

Myron hit the link:

GIBBS FIBS?

Reporter accused of plagiarism

Myron read the endgame shocker: Someone had found a mystery novel published by a tiny press with a minuscule print run in 1978. The novel, *Whisper to a Scream*, by F. K. Armstrong, closely mirrored Gibbs's story. Too closely. Certain snippets of dialogue were pretty much copied verbatim. The crimes in the novel—kidnappings with no resolution—were too similar to what Gibbs had written to be dismissed as coincidence.

The plagiaristic spectres of Mike Barnicle and Patricia Smith and the like rose from the grave and would not disperse. Heads rolled. There were resignations and hand-wringing. For his part, Stan Gibbs refused to comment, which didn't look good. Gibbs ended up "taking a leave of absence," a modern-day euphemism for *getting fired*. The ACLU issued an ambiguous statement and retreated. The *New York Herald* quietly retracted the story, saying that the matter "was under internal review."

After some time passed, Myron reached for the phone and dialed.

"News desk. Bruce Taylor speaking."

"How about meeting me for a drink?"

"I know this is out nowadays, Myron, but I'm strictly hetero."

"I have the ability to change you."

"I don't think so, pal."

"Several women I've dated started out hetero," Myron said. "But one date with me and whammo, they switched teams."

"I love it when you're self-deprecating, Myron. It's just so real."

"So what do you say?"

"I'm on deadline."

"You're always on deadline."

"You buying?"

"To quote my brethren during Passover seders, why should this night be different from any other night?"

"I buy sometimes."

"Do you even own a wallet?"

"Hey, I'm not the one asking for favors," Bruce said. "Four o'clock. The Rusty Umbrella."

15

The Lex Building's wrought-iron gates lined a Fifth Avenue façade with vegetation so dense you wouldn't see light through it if a supernova burst on the other side. The famed edifice was a converted Manhattan mansion with a European courtyard and a regal art deco exterior and enough security to handle a Tyson boxing match. The building had wonderful old lines and detailed Venetian touches, except that for the sake of privacy, the windows had been converted into the smoky-limo variety. It made for a distracting and unnatural mix.

Four blue-blazered, gray-slacked guards stood at the entrance—real guards, Myron noted, with cop eyes and KGB facial tics, not the rent-a-uniforms you saw at department stores or airports. The four of them stood silently, eyeing Myron like he was wearing a tube top in the Vatican.

One of the guards stepped forward. "May I see some ID please?"

Myron took out his wallet and showed him a credit card and driver's license.

"There's no photo on the driver's license," the guard said.

"New Jersey doesn't require them."

"I need a photo ID."

"I have my picture on my health club membership card."

Cop-patient sigh. "That won't do, sir. Do you have a passport?"

"In midtown Manhattan?"

"Yes, sir. For the purposes of ID."

"No," Myron said. "Besides, it's a terrible picture. Doesn't fully capture the radiant blue in my eyes." Myron batted them for emphasis.

"Wait here, sir."

He waited. The other three guards frowned, crossed their arms, studied him as though he might start drinking from a toilet. Myron heard a whirring noise and looked up. A security camera was on him now, focusing in. Myron waved, smiled into the lens, performed a few flexes he had picked up from watching he-man events on ESPN 2. He ended with a pretty dramatic back lat spread and waved to the appreciative crowd. The blue-blazers looked unimpressed.

"All natural," Myron said. "I've never taken steroids."

No replies.

The first guard came back. "Follow me, please."

Stepping into the courtyard was like stepping into C. S. Lewis's wardrobe, another world, the other side of the shrubbery, so to speak. Here in the middle of Manhattan, the street noises were suddenly very far away, muted. The garden was lush, the tile walkways forming a pattern not unlike an Oriental carpet. There was a sprouting fountain in the middle with a statue of a horse rearing back its head.

A new set of blue-blazers greeted him by the ornate front door. This place, Myron thought, must rack up a hell of a dry-cleaning bill. They made him empty his pockets, confiscated his cell phone, frisked him by hand, ran a metal wand over his person so thoroughly he almost asked for a condom, walked him through a metal detector twice, again frisked him with a little too much gusto.

"If you touch my wee-wee one more time," Myron said, "I'm telling my mommy."

More no replies. Maybe the Lexes demanded not only confidentiality but a discriminating sense of humor.

"Follow me, sir," the talking blue-blazer said.

The stillness of the place—a building in the middle of Manhattan, for chrissake—was unnerving, the only sound now the steady echo of their footsteps against the cool marble. It was like walking through an old museum at night, the whole experience like something out of *From the Mixed-up Files of Mrs. Basil E. Frankweiler*. The guards formed a poor man's presidential motorcade—the talking blue-blazer and a buddy three paces in front of him, two other blue-blazers three paces back. Just for fun, Myron would slow down or speed up and watch the guards do likewise. Like a really bad line dance, which was something of a redundancy. At one point he almost did a moonwalk, à la Michael Jackson, but these guys were already viewing him as a potential pedophile.

The mahogany staircase was wide and smelled a bit like lemon Pledge. There were enormous tapestries on the wall, the kind with swords and horses and hedonistic feasts of suckling pig. There were two more blue-blazers on the second floor. Now it was their turn to inspect Myron as though they'd never seen a man before. Myron twirled for their benefit. They too seemed unimpressed.

"You should have seen me flex before," Myron said.

The double doors opened and Myron entered a room slightly larger than a sports arena. Two guards followed him and took up positions in the back corners. There was a big man sitting to the right in a wing chair. At least he looked big in the chair. Or maybe the chair was tiny. The man was probably in his mid-forties. His head and neck formed a near-perfect trapezoid, the top buzzed into a military crew cut. He had a flat nose and ham-hock hands and knockwurst fingers. Ex-boxer or ex-marine or probably both. A man of ninety-degree angles and granite blocks.

Granite Man gave Myron more hard eyes, though his were more relaxed, as though Myron amused him in the way a little kitty nipping at his pant leg might. He didn't stand, choosing instead to stare at Myron and crack his knuckles one at a time.

Myron looked at Granite Man. Granite Man cracked another knuckle.

"Shiver," Myron said.

No one asked him to take a seat. Hell, no one spoke. Myron stood there and waited with the three sets of eyes weighing on him.

"Okay," Myron said. "I'm intimidated. Can we get past this, please?"

Granite Man nodded at the two blazers. They both left. Almost simultaneously, a door on the other side of the room opened and two women appeared. They were pretty far away, but Myron guessed that the first one was Susan Lex. Her hair was done up in an impossibly neat, semi-shellacked bun, and her lips were pursed as if she'd just swallowed a live beetle. The other woman—she looked no more than eighteen or nineteen—had to be her daughter, a carbon copy with the same pursed lips and twenty-five years less wear and tear, not to mention better hair.

Myron started to cross the room with his hand extended, but Susan Lex held up her palm in a stop gesture. Granite Man sat forward, nearly leaning into Myron's path. He gave Myron a small shake of the head, which was no easy task when you have no neck. Myron stayed where he was.

"I don't like being threatened," Susan Lex called from across the room.

"I apologize for that. But I had to see you."

"And that makes it right to threaten and blackmail me?"

Myron had no quick answer to that. "I need to talk to you about your brother Dennis."

"So you said on the phone."

"Where is he?"

Susan Lex looked at Granite Man. Granite Man frowned and cracked his knuckles again. "Just like that, Mr. Bolitar?" Susan Lex said. "You call my office. You threaten me. You insist I alter my schedule to accommodate you. And then you come in here and make demands?"

"I don't mean to be abrupt," Myron said. "But this is a matter of life and death."

Whenever he said "a matter of life and death," he expected to hear that melodramatic *dum-dum-duuuummm* music.

"That's hardly an explanation," Susan Lex said.

"Your brother registered with the national bone marrow center," Myron said. "His marrow matched a sick child's." After the creepy say-good-bye-to-the-boy conversation last night, Myron had decided to stop being gender specific. "Without that transplant, the child will die."

Susan Lex arched an eyebrow. The rich are really good at that, at arching eyebrows without altering anything else on their face. Myron wondered if they learned it at rich-people summer camp. Susan Lex looked at Granite Man again. Granite Man was trying to smile now. "You're mistaken, Mr. Bolitar," she said.

Myron waited for her to say more. When she didn't, he said, "Mistaken how?"

"If you're telling the truth, you've made a mistake. I will say no more."

"With all due deference," Myron said, "that's not good enough."

"It will have to be."

"Where is your brother, Ms. Lex?"

"Please leave, Mr. Bolitar."

"I can still go to the press."

Granite Man crossed his legs and started cracking his knuckles again.

Myron turned to him. "Yes, but can you do this?" Myron patted his head with one hand and rubbed his belly with the other.

Granite Man didn't like that one.

"Look," Myron said, "I don't want to cause any trouble here. You're private people. I understand that. But I need to find this donor."

"It's not my brother," Susan Lex said.

"Then where is he?"

"He's not your donor. More than that is none of your concern."

"Does the name Davis Taylor mean anything to you?"

Susan Lex repursed the lips as though a fresh beetle had sneaked through. She turned and walked out. Her daughter did likewise. Again on cue, the door behind Myron opened and the two blue-blazers filled it. More glares. They stepped fully into the room. Granite Man finally stood, which took some time. He was indeed big. Very big.

The men approached Myron.

"Let's go to the judges," Myron said. "Charles Nelson Reilly, your score?"

Granite Man stepped in front of him, shoulders square, eyes calm.

"The not introducing yourself," Myron said, doing his best Charles Nelson Reilly lisp, which was not very good. "I thought that was really very macho. And that whole silent persona combined with the amused glare. Very nicely done, really. Professional. But—and here's where you kinda lost me—the knuckle cracking, well, Gene, that was overkill, don't you think? Overall score: an 8. Comment: stick with the subtle."

Granite Man said, "You finished?"

"Yes."

"Myron Bolitar. Born in Livingston, New Jersey. Mother Ellen, father Al—"

"They like to be called El-Al," Myron interjected. "Like the Israeli airline."

"Basketball All-American at Duke University. Picked eighth in the NBA draft by the Boston Celtics. Blew out your knee in your first preseason game, ending your career. Currently owns MB SportsReps, a sports representation firm. Dated the novelist Jessica Culver since you graduated college, but you two recently parted ways. Should I go on?"

"You left off the part about my being a snazzy dancer. I can demonstrate if you like."

Granite Man smirked. "You want my score on you now?"

"Suit yourself."

"You wisecrack too much," Granite Man said. "I know you do it to look confident, but you're trying too hard. And since you raised the issue of subtlety, your story about a dying kid needing a bone marrow transplant was touching. The only thing missing was the string quartet."

"You don't believe me?"

"No, I don't believe you."

"So why am I here, then?"

Granite Man spread his satellite-dishes excuse for hands. "That's what I'd like to know."

The three men formed a triangle, Granite in front, the two blue-blazers in back. Granite made a small nod. One of the blazers produced a gun and aimed at Myron's head.

This was not good.

There are ways of disarming a man with a gun, but there's an inherent problem: It might not work. If you miscalculate or if your opponent is better than you think—something not unlikely in an opponent who knows how to handle a gun—you could get shot. That's a serious drawback. And in this particular situation there were two other opponents, both of whom looked good and were probably armed. There is a word expert fighters use for a sudden move at this juncture: *suicide.*

"Whoever did your research on me left something out," Myron said.

"What might that be?"

"My relationship with Win."

Granite Man didn't flinch. "You mean Windsor Horne Lockwood the Third? Family owns Lock-Horne Security and Investments on Park Avenue. Your college roommate from Duke. Since moving out of the Spring Street loft you shared with Jessica Culver, you've been living at his apartment in the Dakota. You have close business and personal ties, might even be called best friends. That relationship?"

"That would be the one," Myron said.

"I am aware of it. I am also aware of Mr. Lockwood's"—he paused, searching for the word—"talents."

"Then you know that if that bozo gets itchy"—Myron head-gestured toward the blazer with the gun—"you die."

Granite Man wrestled with his facial muscles and this time he achieved a smile, though not without effort. Heart's song "Barracuda" played in Myron's head. "I am not without my own, uh, talents, Mr. Bolitar."

"If you really believe that," Myron said, "then you don't know enough about Win's, uh, talents."

"I won't debate the point. But I will point out that he doesn't have an army like this at his disposal. Now, are you going to tell me why you're asking about Dennis Lex?"

"I told you," Myron said.

"You're really going to stick with the dying-child story?"

"It's the truth."

"And how did you get Dennis Lex's name?"

"From the bone marrow center."

"They just gave it to you?"

Myron's turn. "I too am not without my own, uh, talents." It somehow didn't sound right when he said it about himself.

"So you're saying that the bone marrow center told you that Dennis Lex was a donor—that about right?"

"I'm not saying anything," Myron said. "Look, this is a two-way street here. I want some information."

"Wrong," Granite Man said. "It's a one-way street. I'm a Mack truck. You're like an egg in the road."

Myron nodded. "Cutting," he said. "But if you're not going to give me anything, I'm not giving you anything."

The guy with the gun stepped closer.

Myron felt a quiver in his legs, but he didn't blink. Maybe he did overplay the wisecracks, but you don't show fear. Ever. "And let's not pretend you're going to shoot me over this. We both know you won't. You're not that stupid."

Granite Man smiled. "I might beat on you a bit."

"You don't want trouble, I don't want trouble. I don't care about this family or its fortune or any of that. I'm just trying to save a kid's life."

Granite Man played air violin for a moment. Then he said, "Dennis Lex is not your salvation."

"And I'm just supposed to believe you?"

"He's not your donor. That much I personally guarantee."

"Is he dead?"

Granite Man folded his arms across his paddleball-court chest. "If you're telling the truth, the bone marrow people either lied to you or made a mistake."

"Or you're lying to me," Myron said. Then added, "Or you're making a mistake."

"The guards will show you out."

"I can still go to the press."

Granite Man walked away then. "We both know you won't," he said. "You're not that stupid either."

16

Bruce Taylor was in print-journalist garb—like he'd gone to his laundry hamper and dug out whatever was on the bottom. He sat at the bar, scooped up the free pretzels, and pushed them into his mouth as though he were trying to swallow his palm.

"Hate these things," he said to Myron.

"Yeah, I can see that."

"I'm at a bar, for crying out loud. I gotta eat something. But nobody serves peanuts anymore. Too fattening or some such crap. Pretzels instead. And not real pretzels. Little tiny buggers." He held one up for Myron to see. "I mean, what's up with that?"

"And the politicians," Myron said. "They spend all that time on gun control."

"So what do you want to drink? And don't ask for that Yoo-Hoo crap here. It's embarrassing."

"What are you having?"

"The same thing I always have when you pay. Twelve-year-old Scotch."

"I'll just have a club soda with lime."

"Wuss." He ordered it. "What do you want?"

"You know Stan Gibbs?"

Bruce said, "Whoa."

"What whoa?"

"I mean, whoa, you get involved in some hairy-ass shit, Myron. But Stan Gibbs? What the hell could you possibly have to do with him?"

"Probably nothing."

"Uh-huh."

"Just tell me about him, okay?"

Bruce shrugged, took a sip of Scotch. "Ambitious s.o.b. who went too far. What else do you need to know?"

"The whole story."

"Starting with?"

"What exactly did he do?"

"He plagiarized a story, the dumbass. That's not unusual. But to be so stupid about it."

"Too stupid?" Myron asked.

"What do you mean?"

"I mean we both agree that stealing from a published novel is not only unethical but idiotic."

"So?"

"So I'm asking if it's *too* idiotic."

"You think he's innocent, Myron?"

"Do you?"

He chucked down a few more pretzels. "Hell no. Stan Gibbs is guilty as sin. And as stupid as he was, I know plenty stupider. How about Mike Barnicle? The guy steals jokes from a George Carlin book. George Carlin, for chrissake."

"Does seem pretty stupid," Myron agreed.

"And he's not the only one. Look, Myron, every profession's got their dirty laundry, right? The stuff they want swept under the rug. Cops got their blue line when one of them pounds a suspect into the earth. Doctors cover each other's asses when they take out the wrong gallbladder or whatever. Lawyers . . . well, don't even get me started on their dirty little secrets."

"And plagiarism is yours?"

"Not just plagiarism," Bruce said. "Wholesale fabrication. I know reporters who make up sources. I know guys who make up dialogue. I know guys who make up whole conversations. They run stories about crack mothers and inner-city gang leaders who never existed. Ever read those columns? Ever wonder why so many drug addicts, say, sound so friggin' poignant when they can't even watch *Teletubbies* without a tutor?"

"And you're saying this happens a lot?"

"Truth?"

"Preferably."

"It's epidemic," Bruce said. "Some guys are lazy. Some are too ambitious. Some are just pathological liars. You know the type. They'll lie to you about what they had for breakfast just because it comes so naturally."

The drinks came. Bruce pointed at the empty pretzel bowl. The bartender replaced it.

"So if it's so epidemic," Myron said, "how come so few get caught?"

"First off, it's hard to catch. People hide behind anonymous sources and claim people moved, stuff like that. Second, it's like I said before. It's our dirty little secret. We keep it buried."

"I'd think you'd want to clean house."

"Oh, right. Like cops want to. Like doctors want to."

"You're not the same thing, Bruce."

"Let me give you a scenario, Myron, okay?" Bruce finished up his drink, and now he pointed to his glass for a refill. "You're an editor with, say, the *New York Times.* A story is written for you. You print it. Now it's brought to your attention that the story was fabricated or plagiarized or maybe just totally inaccurate, whatever. What do you do?"

"Retract it," Myron said.

"But you're the editor. You're the dumbass responsible for its publication. You're probably the dumbass who hired the writer in the first place. Who do you think the higher-ups are going to blame? And do you think the higher-ups are going to be happy to hear that their paper printed something false? You think the *Times* wants to lose business to the *Herald* or the *Post* or whatever? And hell, the other papers don't even want to hear about it. The public already doesn't trust us as an institution, right? If the truth gets out, who gets hurt? Answer: everyone."

"So you quietly fire the guy," Myron said.

"Maybe. But, again, you're this editor for the *New York Times.* You fire, say, a columnist. Don't you think a higher-up is going to want to know why?"

"So you just let it go?"

"We're like the church used to be with pedophiles. We try to control the problem without hurting ourselves. We transfer the guy to another department. We pass the problem to someone else. Maybe we team him up with another writer. Harder to make shit up with someone looking over your shoulder."

Myron took a sip of his club soda. Flat. "Okay, let me ask the obvious question then. How did Stan Gibbs get caught?"

"He was dumb, dumber and dumbest. It was too high profile a piece to plagiarize like that. Not only that, but Stan rubbed the feds' face in a public crapper and flushed. You don't do that if you don't have the facts, especially to the feds. My guess is he thought he was safe because the novel had a negligible print run from some shitass vanity press in Oregon. I don't think they published more than five hundred copies of the thing, and that was more than twenty years ago. And the author was long dead."

"But someone dug it up."

"Yup."

Myron thought about it. "Strange, don't you think?"

"Most of the time I'd say yes, but not when it's this high-profile. And once the truth was uncovered, boom, Stan was done. Every media outlet got an anonymous press release about it. The feds held a press conference. I mean, there was almost a campaign against him. Someone—probably the feds—were out for their pound of flesh. And they got it."

"So maybe the feds were so pissed they set him up."

"How do you figure?" Bruce countered. "The novel exists. The passages Stan copied exist. There is no way around that."

Myron mulled that one over, looking for a way around it. Nothing came to him. "Did Stan Gibbs ever defend himself?"

"He never commented."

"Why not?"

"The guy's a reporter. He knew better. Look, stories like these become the worst kind of brushfire. Only way to get the fire out is to stop feeding the flame. No matter how bad, if there's nothing new to report—nothing new to feed the flame—it dies out. People always make the mistake of thinking they can douse the flame with their words, that they're so smart, their explanations will work like water or something. It's always a mistake to talk to the press. Everything—even wonderfully worded denials—feed the flames and keep it stoked."

"But doesn't silence make you look guilty?"

"He *is* guilty, Myron. Stan could only get himself in more trouble by talking. And if he hung around and tried to defend himself, someone would dig into his past too. Mainly his old columns. All of them. Every fact, every quote, everything. And if you've plagiarized one story, you've plagiarized others. You don't do it for the first time when you're Stan's age."

"So you think he was trying to minimize the damage?"

Bruce smiled, took a sip. "That Duke education," he said. "It wasn't wasted on you." He grabbed more pretzels. "Mind if I order a sandwich?"

"Suit yourself."

"It'll be worth it," Bruce said with a suddenly big smile. "Because I haven't yet mentioned the last little tidbit that convinced him to keep quiet."

"What's that?"

"It's big, Myron." The smile slid off his face. "Very big."

"Fine, order fries too."

"I don't want this to become public knowledge, you understand?"

"Come on, Bruce. What?"

Bruce turned back to the bar. He picked up a cocktail napkin and tore it in half. "You know the feds took Stan to court to find his sources."

"Yes."

"The court documents were kept sealed, but there was a bit of nastiness. See, they wanted Stan to provide some sort of corroboration. Something to show he didn't totally make the story up. He wouldn't offer any. For a while he claimed that only the families could back him and he wouldn't give them up. But the judge pressed. He finally admitted that there was one other person who could back his story."

"Back up his made-up story?"

"Yes."

"Who?"

"His mistress," Bruce said.

"Stan was married?"

"Guess the word 'mistress' gave it away," Bruce said. "Anyway, he was. Still is, technically, but now they're separated. Naturally Stan was hesitant about naming her—he loved his wife, had two kids, the backyard, whatever—but in the end he gave the judge her name under the condition that it stay sealed."

"Did the mistress back him?"

"Yes. This mistress—one Melina Garston—claimed to have been with him when he met the Sow the Seeds psycho."

Myron's brow creased. "Why does that name ring a bell?"

"Because Melina Garston is dead now. Tied and tortured and you don't want to know what."

"When?"

"Three months ago. Right after the shit hit Stan's fan. Worse, the police think Stan did it."

"To keep her from telling the truth?"

"Again that Duke education."

"But that makes no sense. She was killed after the plagiarism was discovered, right?"

"Right after, yeah."

"So it was too late by then. Everyone thinks he's guilty already. He's lost his job. He's disgraced. If his mistress now comes out and says 'Yeah, I lied,' it wouldn't really change a thing. What would Stan have gained by killing her?"

Bruce shrugged. "Maybe her retraction would have removed any doubt."

"But there's not much doubt there anyway."

The bartender came over. Bruce ordered a sandwich. Myron shook him off. "Can you find out where Stan Gibbs is hiding?"

Bruce waved down the bartender again. "I already know."

"How?"

"He was my friend."

"Was or is?"

"Is, I guess."

"You like him?"

"Yeah," Bruce said. "I like him."

"Yet, you still think he did it."

"Murder, probably not. Plagiarize . . ." He shrugged. "I'm a cynical guy. And just because a guy is a friend of mine doesn't mean he can't do dumb things."

"Will you give me his address?"

"Will you tell me why?"

Myron sipped his flat club soda. "Okay, this is the part where you say you want to know what I have. Then I say I have nothing and when I do, you'll be the first to know. Then you get kinda huffy and say I owe you and that's not good enough, but in the end you take the deal. So why don't we skip all that and just give me the address?"

"Will I still get my sandwich?"

"Sure."

"Fine, then," Bruce said. "Doesn't matter. Stan hasn't talked to anyone since he resigned—not even his close friends. What makes you think he'll talk to you?"

"Because I'm a witty dinner companion and natty dresser?"

"Yeah, that." He turned to Myron and looked at him heavily. "Now, this is the part where I tell you that if you find anything, anything, that suggests that Stan Gibbs is being set up, you tell me because I'm his friend and I'm a reporter hungry for a big story."

"Not to mention a sandwich."

No smile. "You got me?"

"Got you."

"Anything you want to tell me now?"

"Bruce, I got less than nothing. It's just a thread I need to snip away."

"You know Cross River in Englewood?"

"A mid-eighties condo development that looks like something out of *Poltergeist*."

"Twenty-four Acre Drive. Stan just came back to the area. He's renting there."

17

The Morning Mosh was not really the establishment's name. Located in a converted warehouse downtown on the West Side, the Mosh had a neon sign that changed as the day went on. The word *Mosh* stayed lit all the time, but in the morning it blinked *Morning Mosh*, then *Mid-Day Mosh* (as it now read) and later on, *Midnight Mosh*. And that's *Mosh*, not *Nosh*. Myron had expected a bagel store. But the letter was *M*, not *N*, and this place was *Mosh*. As in *Mosh Pit*. As in some retro heavy-metal band minus the talent blaring sounds that could strip paint while kids danced—and we're using that term in its loosest form here—in a pit, careening off one another like a thousand pinballs released into the machine at the same time.

A sign by the front door read FOUR BODY PIERCE MINIMUM TO ENTER (EARS DON'T COUNT).

Myron stayed on the sidewalk and used his cell phone. He called the Mosh's number. A voice answered, "Go for it, dude."

"Suzze T please."

"Dig."

Dig?

Suzze came on two minutes later. "Hello?"

"It's Myron. I'm out on the curb."

"Come in. No one bites. Well, except for that guy who bit the legs off a live frog last night. Man, that was so cool."

"Suzze, please meet me out here, okay?"

"What-ev-er."

Myron hung up, feeling old. Suzze came out less than a minute later. She wore bell-bottom jeans with a gravity-defying waist that stayed up south of her hips. Her top was pink and much too small, revealing not only a flat stomach but a bottom-side hint of what interested the fine folks at Rack Enterprises. Suzze sported only one tattoo (a tennis racket with a snake's head grip) and no piercings, not even her ears.

Myron pointed to the sign. "You don't meet the minimum piercing requirement."

"Yeah, Myron, I do."

Silence. Then Myron said, "Oh."

They started walking down the street. Another strange Manhattan neighborhood. Kids and the homeless hung out together. There were bars and nightclubs alongside daycare centers. The modern city. Myron passed a storefront with a sign: TATTOOS WHILE U WAIT. He reread the sign and frowned. Like how else would you do it?

"We got a weird endorsement offer," Myron said. "You know the Rack Bars?"

Suzze said, "Like, upscale topless, right?"

"Well, topless anyway."

"What about them?"

"They're opening up a chain of topless coffee bars."

Suzze nodded. "Cool," she said. "I mean, taking the popularity of Starbucks and mixing it with Scores and Goldfingers, well, it's totally wise."

"Uh, right. Anyway, they're having this big grand opening and they're trying to generate excitement and media attention and all that. So they want you to make a, uh, guest appearance."

"Topless?"

"Like I said on the phone, I had an offer I wanted you to refuse."

"Totally topless?"

Myron nodded. "They insist on nipple visibility."

"How much they willing to pay?"

"Two hundred thousand dollars."

She stopped. "Are you shitting me?"

"I shit you not."

She whistled. "Lots of cha-ching."

"Yes, but I still think—"

"This was, like, their first offer?"

"Yes."

"Do you think you could get them up?"

"No, that would be your job."

She stopped and looked at him. Myron shrugged his apology.

"Tell them yes," she said.

"Suzze . . ."

"Two hundred grand for flashing a bit of booby? Christ, last night I think I did it in there for free."

"That isn't the same thing."

"Did you see what I wore in *Sports Illustrated?* I might as well have been naked."

"That isn't the same thing either."

"This is Rack, Myron, not some sleazoid place like Buddy's. It's upscale topless."

"Saying 'upscale topless' is like saying 'good toupee,' " Myron said.

"Huh?"

"It might be good," he said, "but it's still a toupee."

She cocked her head. "Myron, I'm twenty-four years old."

"I know that."

"That's like 107 in women-tennis years. I'm ranked thirty-one in the world right now. I haven't made two hundred grand over the past two years on tour. This is a big score, Myron. And man, will it change my image."

"Exactly my point."

"No, listen up, tennis is looking for draws. I'll be controversial. I'll get tons of attention. I'll suddenly be a big name. Admit it, my appearance fees will quadruple."

Appearance fees are the money paid to the big names just to show up, win or lose. Most name players make far more in appearance fees than prize money. It's where the potential major *dinero* is, especially for a player ranked thirty-first.

"Probably," Myron said.

She stopped and grabbed his arm. "I love playing tennis."

"I know that," he said softly.

"Doing this will extend my career. That means a lot to me, okay?"

Christ, she looked so young.

"All of what you're saying may be true," Myron said. "But at the end of the day, you're still appearing at a topless bar. And once it's done, it's done. You will always be remembered as the tennis player who appeared topless."

"There are worse things."

"Yes. But I didn't become an agent to get in the stripping business. I'll do what you want. You're my client. I want what's best for you."

"But you don't think this is best for me?"

"I have trouble advising a young woman to appear topless."

"Even if it makes sense?"

"Even if it makes sense."

She smiled at him. "You know something, Myron? You're cute when you're being a prude."

"Yeah, adorable."

"Tell them yes."

"Think about it for a few days, okay?"

"It's a no-brainer, Myron. Just do what you do best."

"What's that?"

"Get the number up. And tell them yes."

18

Cross River Condos was one of those complexes that looked like a movie façade, like whole buildings might topple over if you pushed against any one wall. The development was sprawlingly cramped, with every building looking exactly the same. Walking through it was like something out of *Alice in Wonderland*, all avenues mirroring the others, until you got dizzy. Have too much drink and you're bound to stick your key in the wrong lock.

Myron parked near the complex pool. The place was nice but too close to Route 80, the major artery that ran from, well, here in New Jersey to California. The traffic sounds sloshed over the fence. Myron located the door to 24 Acre Drive and then tried to figure out which windows belonged to it. If he had it right, the lights were on. So was the television. He knocked on the door. Myron saw a face peer through the window next to the door. The face did not speak.

"Mr. Gibbs?"

Through the glass, the face said, "Who are you?"

"My name is Myron Bolitar."

A brief pause. "The basketball player?"

"At one time, yes."

The face looked through the window for a few more seconds before opening the door. The odor of too many cigarettes wafted through the opening and happily nested inside Myron's nostrils. Not surprisingly, Stan Gibbs had a cigarette in his mouth. He had a gray stubble-to-beard going, too far gone for retro *Miami Vice*. He wore a yellow Bart Simpson sweatshirt, dark green sweatpants, socks, sneakers, and a Colorado Rockies baseball cap—the standard fashion fare shared with equal fervor by joggers and couch potatoes. Myron suspected the latter here.

"How did you find me?" Stan Gibbs asked.

"It wasn't difficult."

"That's not an answer."

Myron shrugged.

"It doesn't matter," Stan said. "I have no comment."

"I'm not a reporter."

"So what are you?"

"A sports agent."

Stan took a puff of the cigarette, didn't remove it from his mouth. "Sorry to disappoint you, but I haven't played competitive football since high school."

"May I come in?"

"No, I don't think so. What do you want?"

"I need to find the kidnapper you wrote about in your article," Myron said.

Stan smiled with very white teeth, especially when you considered the smoking. His skin was sort of clumpy and winter-colorless, his hair thin and tired, but he had those bright eyes, superbright eyes, the kind that look like supernatural beacons are shining out from within. "Don't you read the papers?" he asked. "I made the whole thing up."

"Made it up or copied it from a book?"

"I stand corrected."

"Or maybe you were telling the truth. In fact, maybe the subject of your articles called me on the phone last night."

Stan shook his head, the growing ash on the cigarette holding on like a kid on an amusement park ride. "This is not something I want to revisit."

"Did you plagiarize the story?"

"I already said I wouldn't comment—"

"This isn't for public consumption. If you did—if the story was a fake—just tell me now and I'll go away. I don't have time to waste on false leads."

"Nothing personal," Stan said, "but you're not making a whole lot of sense here."

"Does the name Davis Taylor mean anything to you?"

"No comment."

"How about Dennis Lex?"

That threw him. The dangling cigarette started to slip from Stan's lips, but he caught it with his right hand. He dropped it on the walkway and watched it sizzle for a moment.

"Maybe you better come in."

The condo was a duplex centered with that staple of new American construction, the cathedral ceiling. Plenty of light came in from the big windows, splashing down on a decor straight out of a Sunday circular. A blond-wood entertainment center took up one wall, a matching coffee table not far from it. There was also a white-and-blue-striped couch—Myron would bet his lunch money it was a Serta Sleeper—and matching love seat. The carpeting was the same neutral as the exterior, a sort of inoffensive tan, and the place was clean yet disorderly in a divorcé way, newspapers and magazines and books piled here and there, nothing really put in a specific place.

He had Myron sit on the couch. "Want something to drink?"

"Sure, whatever," Myron said. The coffee table had one photograph on it. A man had his arms around two boys. All three were smiling too hard, like they'd just come in second place and didn't want to appear disappointed. They were standing in a garden of some sort. Behind them loomed a marble statue of a woman with a bow and arrow over her shoulder. Myron picked up the frame and studied it. "This you?"

Gibbs lifted his head while scooping a handful of ice into a glass. "I'm on the right," he said. "With my brother and my father."

"Who's that a statue of?"

"Diana the Huntress. You familiar with her?"

"Didn't she turn into Wonder Woman?"

Stan chuckled. "Sprite okay?"

Myron put the photograph down. "Sure."

Stan Gibbs poured the drink, brought it out to Myron, handed it to him. "What do you know about Dennis Lex?"

"Just that he exists," Myron said.

"So why mention his name to me?"

Myron shrugged. "Why did you react so strongly to hearing it?"

Gibbs took out another cigarette, lit it. "You're the one who came to me."

"True."

"Why?"

No secret. "I'm looking for a man named Davis Taylor. He's a bone marrow donor who matched a kid and then vanished. I traced him to an address in Connecticut, but he's not there. So I dug a little more and found out that Davis Taylor is a name change. His real name is Dennis Lex."

"I still don't see what this has to do with me."

"This might sound a little nutty," Myron said. "But I left a voice mail message for Davis Taylor né Dennis Lex. When he called back, he made little sense. But he kept telling me to 'sow the seeds.' "

A small quake ran through Stan Gibbs. It passed quickly. "What else did he say?"

"That was pretty much it. I should sow the seeds. I should say good-bye to the child. Stuff like that."

"It's probably nothing," Gibbs said. "He probably just read my article and decided to have a little fun at your expense."

"Probably," Myron said. "Except that wouldn't really explain your reaction to Dennis Lex's name."

Stan shrugged, but there wasn't much behind it. "The family is famous."

"If I said Ivana Trump, would you have reacted the same?"

Gibbs stood. "I need some time to think about this."

"Think out loud," Myron said.

Stan just shook his head.

"Did you make up the story, Stan?"

"Another time."

"Not good enough," Myron said. "You owe me something here. Did you plagiarize the story?"

"How do you expect me to answer that?"

"Stan?"

"What?"

"I don't care about your situation. I'm not here to judge you or tell on you. I don't give a rat's ass if you made up the story or not. All I care about is finding the bone marrow donor. Period. End of story. *El Fin.*"

Stan's eyes started to well up. He took another puff of the cigarette. "No," he said. "I never plagiarized. I never saw that book in my life."

It was like the room had been holding its breath and finally let go.

"How do you explain the similarities between your article and that novel?"

He opened his mouth, stopped, shook his head.

"Your silence makes you look guilty."

"I don't have to explain anything to you."

"Yeah, you do. I'm trying to save a kid's life here. You're not that wrapped up in your problems, are you, Stan?"

Stan moved back into the kitchen. Myron stood and followed him. "Talk to me," Myron said. "Maybe I can help."

"No," he said. "You can't."

"How do you explain the similarities, Stan? Just tell me that, okay? You must have thought about it."

"I don't need to think about it."

"Meaning?"

He opened the refrigerator and grabbed another can of Sprite. "Do you think all psychotics are original?"

"I'm not following you."

"You received a call from a guy who told you about sowing the seeds."

"Right."

"There are two possibilities that explain why he did that," Stan said. "One, he is the same killer I wrote about. Or two?" Stan looked at Myron.

"He just repeated what he'd read in the article," Myron said.

Stan snapped and pointed at Myron.

"So you're saying that the kidnapper you interviewed read this novel and it, what, influenced him somehow? That he copied it?"

Stan took a swig from the can. "That's a theory," he said.

And a damn good one, Myron thought. "So why didn't you say that to the press? Why didn't you defend yourself?"

"None of your goddamn business."

"Some people say it's because you were afraid they'd look closer at your work. That they'd find other fabrications."

"And some people are morons," he finished.

"So why didn't you fight?"

"I spent my whole life being a journalist," Stan said. "Do you know what it means for a journalist to be called a plagiarist? It's like a daycare worker being called a child molester. I'm done. No words can change that. I've lost everything to this scandal. My wife, my kids, my job, my reputation—"

"Your mistress?"

He shut his eyes suddenly, tightly, like a child trying to make the bogeyman go away.

"The police think you killed Melina," Myron said.

"I'm well aware of that."

"Tell me what's going on here, Stan."

He opened his eyes and shook his head. "I have to make some calls, check out some leads."

"You can't just cut me loose."

"I have to," he said.

"Let me help."

"I don't need your help."

"But I need yours."

"Not right now," Stan said. "You'll have to trust me on this."

"I'm not big on trust," Myron said.

Stan smiled. "Neither am I," he said. "Neither am I."

19

Myron pulled out. So, too, he noticed, did two men in a black Oldsmobile Ciera. Hmm.

The cell phone rang.

"Have you learned anything?" It was Emily.

"Not really," Myron said.

"Where are you?"

"Englewood."

"Do you have any plans for dinner?" Emily asked.

Myron hesitated. "No."

"I'm a good cook, you know. We dated in college, so I didn't have much chance to demonstrate my culinary skills."

"I remember you cooking for me once," Myron said.

"I did?"

"In my wok."

Emily chuckled. "That's right, you had an electric wok in your dorm, right?"

"Yep."

"I almost forgot about that," Emily said. "Why did you have one, anyway?"

"To impress chicks."

"Really?"

"Sure. I thought I'd invite a girl up to my room, slice up some vegetables, add a little soy sauce—"

"To the vegetables?" she asked.

"For starters."

"So how come you never pulled that one on me?"

"Didn't have to."

"You calling me easy, Myron?"

"How exactly does one answer that," Myron asked, "and maintain possession of both testicles?"

"Come on over," Emily said. "I'll make us some dinner. No soy sauce."

Another hesitation.

"Please don't make me ask again," Emily said.

He wanted very much to say no. "Okay."

"Just take Route 4—"

"I know the way, Emily."

He hung up then and checked the rearview mirror. The black Oldsmobile Ciera was still following. Better safe than sorry. Myron hit the preprogrammed number on his cell phone. After one ring, Win answered.

"Articulate," Win said.

"Got a tail, methinks."

"License plate?"

Myron read it off to him.

"Where should we coordinate?"

"Garden State Plaza mall," Myron said.

"On my way, fair maiden."

Myron stayed on Route 4 until he saw a sign for the Garden State Plaza. He took a rather complicated cloverleaf overpass and veered into the mall's lot. The black Olds followed, dropping back a bit. Stall time. Myron circled a few times before finding a parking space. The Olds kept its distance. He turned off the car and headed for the "Northeast Entrance."

The Garden State Plaza had all the artificial elements endemic in malls—the mall ear-pop when you enter, the stale mall air, the mall hollow acoustics, as though all sound were traveling through a high-volume distorter—the audial equivalent of a shower door, voices somehow rendered both loud and incomprehensible. Too much with the high ceilings and faux marble, nothing soft to cushion the sound.

He strolled through the nouveau riche section of the Garden State Plaza, past several barren shoe stores, the kind that display maybe three pairs of shoes on the ends of what look like deer antlers. He reached a store called Aveda, which sold wildly overpriced cosmetics and lotions. The Aveda saleswoman, a starving young thang in tourniquet-tight black, informed Myron that they were having a sale on face moisturizers. Myron refrained from crying out "Yippee!" and went on his way. Victoria's Secret was next, and Myron did that male surreptitious glance at the lingerie window displays. Most of your more sophisticated heterosexual males are well versed in this art, awarding the racily clad supermodels the most casual of once-overs, feigning a lack of interest in the blown-up, blown-clear images of Stephanie and Frederique in Miracle Bras. Myron, of course, did the same thing—and then he thought, why pretend? He stopped short, squared his shoulders, ogled in earnest. Honesty. Shouldn't a woman respect that in a man too?

He checked his watch. Not yet. More stall. The plan, as it were, was fairly simple. Win drives to the Garden State Plaza. When he arrives, he calls Myron on the cell phone. Myron then goes back to his car. Win looks for the black Olds and follows the followee. Super clever, no?

Myron hit Sharper Image, one of the few places in the world where people use the words *shiatsu* and *ionic* and nobody laughs. He tried out a massage chair (setting: Knead) and debated purchasing a $5,500 life-size statue of a *Star Wars* storm-trooper that had been reduced to a mere $3,499. Talk about redefining nouveau riche. Here's a little tip for you: If you've purchased a Sharper Image life-size *Star Wars* star-trooper, take out your platinum-est charge card, hand it to the nearest cashier, and buy a life.

The cell phone rang. Myron picked it up.

"They're feds," Win said.

"Yikes."

"Yes."

"No reason to follow them, then."

"No."

Myron spotted two men in suits and sunglasses behind him. They were studying the fruit-flavored shampoos in the Garden Botanica store window a little too closely. Two men in suits and sunglasses. Oh, like that happens. "I think they're following me in here too."

"If they arrest you with lingerie," Win said, "tell them it's for your wife."

"That what you do?"

"Keep the phone on," Win said.

Myron did as he asked. An old trick of theirs. Myron kept his cell phone on, thereby freeing Win to listen in. Okay, fine, now what? He kept strolling. Two more men in business suits were window-shopping up ahead. They turned as Myron approached, both staring him down. Some tail. Myron glanced behind him. The first two feds were right there.

The two feds in front of him stepped directly into his path. The other two came up behind him, boxing him in.

Myron stopped, looked at all four feds. "Did you guys check out the facial moisturizer sale at Aveda?"

"Mr. Bolitar?"

"Yes."

One of them, a short guy with a severe haircut, flashed a badge. "I'm Special Agent Fleischer with the Federal Bureau of Investigation. We'd like a word with you, sir."

"What about?"

"Would you mind coming with us?"

They had the standard-issue stone expressions; Myron would get nothing out of them. Probably didn't even know anything themselves. Probably just delivery boys. Myron shrugged and followed them out. Two got into a white Olds Ciera. The other two stayed with Myron. One opened the back door of the black Ciera and head-gestured for Myron to get in. He did so. The interior was very clean. Nice, smooth seats. Myron ran his hand over it.

"Corinthian leather?" he asked.

Special Agent Fleischer turned around. "No, sir, that would be the Ford Granada."

Touché.

No one spoke. No radio played. Myron settled back. He debated calling Emily and postponing their soy-sauce-less encounter, but he didn't want the feds to hear him. He sat tight and kept his mouth shut. He didn't do that often. It felt odd and somehow right.

Thirty minutes later, he was in the basement of a modest high-rise in Newark. He sat at a table with his hands on a semi-sticky table. The room had one barred window and cement walls the color and texture of dried oatmeal. The feds excused themselves and left Myron alone. Myron sighed and sat back. He'd figured that this was the old soften-him-up-by-making-him-wait bit, when the door flew open.

The woman was first. She wore a pumpkin-orange blazer, blue jeans, sneakers, and ball-and-chain earrings. The word that came to mind was *husky*. Not big really. Husky. Everything was husky—even her hair, a sort of canned-corn yellow. The guy riding in on her fumes was geeky thin with a pointy head and a small, greased shock of black hair. He looked like an upside-down pencil. He spoke first.

"Good afternoon, Mr. Bolitar," Pencil said.

"Good afternoon."

"I'm Special Agent Rick Peck," he said. "This is Special Agent Kimberly Green."

The orange-blazered Green did a caged-lion pace. Myron nodded at her. She nodded back but grudgingly, like her teacher had just told her to apologize for something she didn't do.

Pencil Peck continued. "Mr. Bolitar, we'd like to ask you a few questions."

"What about?"

Peck kept his eyes on his notes and spoke like he was reading. "Today you visited one Stan Gibbs at 24 Acre Drive. Is that correct?"

"How do you know I didn't visit two Stan Gibbs?"

Peck and Green exchanged a glance. Then Peck said, "Please, Mr. Bolitar, we'd appreciate your cooperation. Did you visit Mr. Gibbs?"

"You know I did," Myron said.

"Fine, thank you." Peck wrote something down slowly. Then he looked up. "We'd very much like to know the nature of your visit."

"Why?"

"You are the first visitor Mr. Gibbs has had since moving to his current residence."

"No, I mean, why do you want to know?"

Green crossed her arms. She and Peck looked at each other again. Peck said, "Mr. Gibbs is part of an ongoing investigation."

Myron waited. No one said anything. "Well, that pretty much clears it up."

"That's all I can say for the moment."

"Same here."

"Pardon?"

"If you can't say any more, I can't say any more."

Kimberly Green put her hands on the table, gave a toothy grimace—husky teeth?—and leaned down like she might take a bite out of him. The canned-corn hair smelled like Pert Plus. She eyeballed him—must have read a memo on intimidating glares—and then spoke for the first time. "Here's how we're going to play it, asshole. We're going to ask you questions. You're going to listen to them and then you're going to answer them. You got it?"

Myron nodded. "I want to make sure I got this straight," he said to her. "You're playing bad cop, right?"

Peck picked up the ball. "Mr. Bolitar, no one is interested in making trouble here. But we'd very much like your cooperation in this matter."

"Am I under arrest?" Myron asked.

"No."

"Bye then."

He started to stand. Kimberly Green gave him a shove mid-rise and he fell back into the chair. "Sit down, asshole." She looked over at Peck. "Maybe he's part of it."

"You think so?"

"Why else would he be so reluctant to answer questions?"

Peck nodded. "Makes sense. An accomplice."

"We can probably arrest him now," Green said. "Lock him up for the night, maybe leak it to the press."

Myron looked up at her. "Gasp," he said. "Now. I. Am. Really. Scared. Second gasp."

She narrowed her eyes. "What did you say?"

"Don't tell me," Myron said. "Maybe I'm guilty of aiding and abetting. That's my personal favorite. Does anyone actually get prosecuted for that?"

"You think we're playing games here?"

"I do. And by the way, how come you're all called 'special' agent? Doesn't that sound like something someone made up one day? Like a kid's game to raise self-esteem. 'We're promoting you from agent to special agent, Barney,' and then what, super-special agent?"

Green grabbed his lapels and leaned his chair back. "You're not funny."

Myron looked at her hands gripping him. "Are you for real?"

"You want to try me?" she said.

Peck said, "Kim."

She ignored him and kept her glare on Myron. "This is serious," she said.

Her tone aimed for angry but came out more like a frightened plea. Two more agents entered. With the four delivery boys, that made eight. This was something big. What, Myron had no idea. The murder of Melina Garston maybe. But that was doubtful. The locals usually handled murders. You don't call in the feds.

The new guys came at Myron in different ways, but there were only so many routes to travel and Myron knew them all. Threatening, friendly, flattering, insulting, building up, belittling, hard, soft, every sell. They denied him the bathroom, they made excuses to keep him longer, all the while they're working him and he's working them and neither one is giving. Sweat started flowing, mostly from them, the stains and stench filling the air, metastasizing into something Myron could swear was genuine fear.

Kimberly Green came in and out and she kept shaking her head at him. Myron wanted to cooperate, but here's the pertinent cliché: Once the genie is out of the bottle, you can't put it back in. He didn't know what they were investigating. He didn't know if it would benefit Jeremy to talk or hurt him. But once he spoke, once his words were in the public domain, he couldn't take them back. Any leverage he might later be able to apply would be gone. So, for now, even if he might want to help, he wouldn't. Not until he learned more. He had the contacts. He could find out quickly enough, make an informed decision.

Sometimes, negotiating meant shutting up.

When things wound down, Myron got up to leave. Kimberly Green blocked his path. "I'm going to make your life hell," she said.

"That your way of asking me out?"

She leaned back as if he'd slapped her. When she recovered, she shook her head slowly. "You have no idea, do you?"

Shutting up, he reminded himself. Myron pushed past her and headed outside.

20

He called Emily from the car.

"I thought I was being stood up," she said.

Myron checked out the rearview mirror and spotted what might be another fed tail. No matter. "Sorry," he said. "Something came up."

"Involving the donor?"

"I don't think so."

"You still in Jersey?" Emily asked.

"Yes."

"Come on over. I'll reheat dinner."

He wanted to say no. "Okay."

Franklin Lakes was about sprawling. Everything sprawled. The houses were mostly new construction, big brick mansions on eternal cul-de-sacs, little gates at the front of the driveways that opened with push-button or intercom, like that would really protect the owners from what lay outside the lush lawns and pedicure-clipped hedges. The interiors were sprawling too, dining rooms big enough to house helicopters, remote-controlled blinds, Sub-Zero/Viking Stove kitchens with marble islands that overlooked family rooms the size of movie theaters, always with complicated state-of-the-art entertainment centers.

Myron rang the bell and the door opened and for the first time in his life, Myron was face-to-face with his son.

Jeremy smiled at him. "Hi."

Strong, totally alien surges ricocheted haphazardly through Myron, his nervous system melting down and in overdrive all at once. His diaphragm contracted and his lungs stopped. So, he was sure, did his heart. His mouth weakly opened and closed like a dying fish on a boat deck. Tears headed up and pushed toward the eyes.

"You're Myron Bolitar, right?" Jeremy said.

An ocean-shell rushing filled Myron's ears. He managed a nod.

"You played ball against my dad," Jeremy said, still with the smile that ripped at the corners of Myron's heart. "In college, right?"

Myron found his voice. "Yes."

The kid nodded back. "Cool."

"Yeah."

A horn honked. Jeremy leaned to the right and looked behind Myron. "That's my ride. Later."

Jeremy leaped past Myron. Myron numbly turned and watched the boy jog down the driveway. Imagination maybe, but that gait was oh-so-familiar. From Myron's old game films. More surges. *Oh Christ . . .*

Myron felt a hand on his shoulder, but he ignored it and watched the boy. The car door opened and swallowed Jeremy into the darkness. The driver's window slid down and a pretty woman called out, "Sorry I'm late, Em."

From behind him, Emily said, "No problem."

"I'll take them to school in the morning."

"Great."

A wave and the pretty woman's window slid back into place. The car started on its way. Myron watched it disappear down the road. He felt Emily's eyes on him. He slowly turned to her.

"Why did you do that?"

"I thought he'd be gone by now," Emily said.

"Do I really look that stupid?"

She stepped back into the house. "I want to show you something."

Trying to get his legs back, his head wobbly and his internal referee still giving him the eight count, Myron followed her silently up the stairway. She led him down a darkened corridor lined with modern lithographs. She stopped, opened a door, and flipped on the lights. The room was teenage-cluttered, as if someone had put all the belongings in the center of the room and dropped a hand grenade on them. The posters on the walls—Michael Jordan, Keith Van Horn, Greg Downing, Austin Powers, the words *YEAH, BABY!* across his middle in pink tie-dye lettering—had been hung askew, all tattered corners and missing pushpins. There was a Nerf basketball hoop on the closet door. There was a computer on the desk and a baseball cap dangling from a desk lamp. The corkboard had a mix of family snapshots and construction-paper crayons signed by Jeremy's sister, all held up by oversized pushpins. There were footballs and autographed baseballs and cheap trophies and a couple of blue ribbons and three basketballs, one with no air in it. There were stacks of computer-game CD-ROMs and a Game Boy on the unmade bed and a surprising amount of books, several opened and facedown. Clothes littered the floor like war wounded; the drawers were half open, shirts and underwear hanging out like they'd been shot mid-escape. The room had the slight, oddly comforting smell of kids' socks.

"He's a slob," she said. Leaving off the obvious "like you."

Myron stayed still.

"He keeps Oxy 10 in his desk drawer," Emily said. "He thinks I don't know. He's at that age where crushes keep him up all night, but he's never even kissed a girl." She walked over to the corkboard and snatched up a photograph of Jeremy. "He's beautiful, don't you think?"

"This isn't helping, Emily."

"I want you to understand."

"Understand what?"

"He's never been kissed. He is going to die and he's never even kissed a girl."

Myron held up his hands. "I don't know what you want me to say here."

"Try to understand, okay?"

"I don't need melodrama. I understand."

"No, Myron, you don't. You look back at the night and see it as some sort of Gothic blunder. We did something sinful and for that we all paid a heavy price. If we could just go back and erase that tragic mistake, well, it's all so *Hamlet* and *Macbeth*, isn't it? Your ruined basketball career, Greg's future, our marriage—all laid to waste in that one moment of lust."

"It wasn't lust."

"Let's not go through that argument again. I don't care what it was. Lust, stupidity, fear, fate. Call it whatever the hell you want to—but I would never want to go back. That 'mistake' was the best thing that ever happened to me. Jeremy, our son, came out of that mess. Do you hear what I'm saying? I'd destroy a million careers and marriages for him."

She looked at him, challenging. He said nothing.

"I'm not religious and I don't believe in fate or destiny or any of that," she went on. "But maybe, just maybe, there had to be a balance. Maybe the only way to produce something so wonderful was to surround the event with so much destruction."

Myron started backing out of the room. "This isn't helping," he said again.

"Yes," she said, "it is."

"You want me to find the donor. I'm trying to do that. But this kind of distraction doesn't help. I need to stay detached."

"No, Myron, you need attachment. You need to get emotional. You have to understand the stakes—your son, that beautiful boy who opened the door—is going to die before he's even kissed a girl." She moved closer to him and looked into his eyes and Myron thought that her eyes had never looked so clear before.

"I watched you play every game at Duke," she said. "I fell in love with you on that court—not because you were the team star or because you were graceful or athletic. You were so open out there, so raw and emotional. And the more emotional you got, the more pressure there was, the better you played. If the game was a blowout, you lost interest. You needed it to matter. You needed to be double-teamed with only a few seconds on the clock. You needed to lose control a little."

"This isn't a game, Emily."

"Right," she said. "The stakes are higher. The emotion should be higher. I want you desperate, Myron. That's when you're at your best."

He looked at the photograph of Jeremy, and he knew that he was feeling something that he had never felt before. He blinked, caught the expression on his face in the closet-door mirror, and for a moment he saw his own father staring back.

Emily hugged him then. She buried her face in his shoulder and started to cry. Myron held on tight. They stood that way for several minutes before making their way downstairs. Over dinner, Emily told him about Jeremy, and he soaked in every story. They moved to the couch and broke out the photo albums. Emily tucked her legs under her, her elbow on the top of the couch, her head leaning on the heel of her hand, and told him more. It was nearly two in the morning when she walked him to the door. They were holding hands.

"I know you spoke to Dr. Singh," she said in the open door.

"Yes."

She let loose a deep breath. "I'm just going to say this, okay?"

"Okay."

"I've been keeping track. I bought one of those home tests. The, uh, optimum conception day will be Thursday."

He opened his mouth but she stopped him with her hand.

"I know all the arguments against this, but it might be Jeremy's only chance. Don't say anything. Just think about it."

She closed the door. Myron stared at it for a few moments. He tried to conjure up the moment Jeremy had opened it, the crooked smile on the boy's face, but already the image was hazy and fading fast.

21

First thing in the morning, Myron called Terese. Still no answer. He frowned at the phone. "Am I getting the big kiss-off?" he asked Win.

"Doubtful," Win said. He was reading the newspaper and wearing silk pajamas with a matching bathrobe and slippers. Give him a pipe and he could have been something Noël Coward created on an off day.

"What makes you say that?"

"Our Ms. Collins appears to be rather direct," Win said. "If you were being tossed into the dung heap, you'd know the smell."

"And then there's the part about my being irresistible to women," Myron said.

Win turned the page.

"So what's she up to?"

Win tapped his chin with his index finger. "What's the term you relationship people use? Oh, yes. Space. Perhaps she needs some space."

" 'Needing space' is usually a code phrase for the big kiss-off."

"Yes, well, whatever." Win crossed his legs. "You want me to look into it?"

"Into what?"

"What Ms. Collins might be up to."

"No."

"Fine," Win said. "Let's move on, shall we? Tell me about your encounter with the Federal Bureau of Investigation."

Myron recapped the interrogation.

"So we don't know what they wanted," Win said.

"Correct."

"Not a clue?"

"Nothing. Except that they were scared."

"Curious."

Myron nodded.

Win took a sip of tea, pinky up. Oh, the horrors that pinky had witnessed, partaken in, even. They sat in Win's formal dining room and used a silver tea set. Victorian mahogany table with lion-paw feet, silver tea set, silver milk pitcher, boxes of Cap'n Crunch and some new cereal called Oreo, which is exactly what you would imagine. "Theorizing at this juncture is a waste of time. I'll make some calls, see what I can find out."

"Thanks."

"I'm still not sure I see a connection between Stan Gibbs and our blood donor."

"It's a long shot," Myron agreed.

"More than that. A newspaper columnist makes up a story about a serial kidnapper and now—what?—we think the fictional character is the donor?"

"Stan Gibbs claims the story is real."

"Does he now?"

"Yes."

Win rubbed his chin. "Pray tell, why does he not defend himself?"

"No clue."

"Presumably because he is guilty," Win said. "Man is, above all, selfish. He's into self-preservation. It's instinctive. He does not martyr himself. He cares about one thing above all else: saving his hide."

"Assuming I agree with your sunny view of human nature, wouldn't you agree that man would lie to save himself?"

"Of course," Win said.

"So armed with this pretty decent defense—the idea that the serial kidnapper copycatted the novel—why wouldn't Stan use it to defend himself, even if he was guilty of plagiarism?"

Win nodded. "I like the way you're thinking."

"Cynically, yes."

The intercom buzzed. Win pressed the button, and the doorman announced Esperanza. A minute later, she swept into the room, grabbed a chair, and poured herself a bowl of Oreo cereal.

"Why do they always say it's 'part of this complete breakfast'?" Esperanza asked. "Every single time, every single cereal. What's all that about?"

Nobody replied.

Esperanza took a spoonful, looked at Win, head-gestured toward Myron. "I hate it when he's right," she said to Win.

"A bad omen," Win agreed.

Myron said, "I was right?"

She turned her gaze to Myron. "I did that school check on Dennis Lex. I tracked down any and all educational institutions any of his siblings or parents had gone to. Nothing. College, high school, middle school—even grammar school. No trace of Dennis Lex."

"But?" Myron said.

"Preschool."

"You're kidding me."

"Nope."

"You found his preschool?"

"I'm more than just a great piece of ass," Esperanza said.

Win said, "Not to me, my dear."

"You're sweet, Win."

Win bowed his head slightly.

"Miss Peggy Joyce," Esperanza said. "She still teaches and runs the Shady Wells Montessori School for Children in East Hampton."

"And she remembers Dennis Lex?" Myron said. "From thirty years ago?"

"Apparently." Esperanza shoved in another spoonful and tossed Myron a sheet of paper. "This is her address. She's expecting you this morning. Drive safely now, ya hear?"

22

The car phone rang.

"The old man is a lying sack of shit." It was Greg Downing.

"What?"

"The geezer is lying."

"You mean Nathan Mostoni?"

"Jesus Christ, what other old man have I been watching?"

Myron switched ears. "What makes you think he's lying, Greg?"

"Lots of things."

"Like?"

"Like starting with Mostoni never hearing from the bone marrow center. Does that sound logical to you?"

He thought of Karen Singh and her dedication and the stakes. "No," Myron said, "but it's like we said before—he might be confused."

"I don't think so."

"Why not?"

"Nathan Mostoni goes out plenty on his own, for one thing. Sometimes he acts loony, but other times, he seems just fine. He shops himself. He talks to people. He dresses like a normal person."

"That doesn't mean anything," Myron said.

"No? An hour ago he went out, right? So I got close to the house, right up against the back window, and I dialed that number, the one you got for the donor."

"And?"

"And I hear a phone inside the house ringing."

That made Myron pause.

"So what do you think we should do?" Greg asked.

"I'm not sure. Have you seen anybody else at the house?"

"Nobody. Mostoni goes out but nobody's been here. And I tell you something else. He looks younger now. I don't know how else to explain it. It's weird. You making any headway on your end?"

"I'm not sure."

"That's some answer, Myron."

"The only one I got."

"So what do you think we should do about Mostoni?"

"I'll have Esperanza do a background check. In the meantime, stay on him."

"Time's a-ticking away here, Myron."

"I know that. I'll be in touch."

He disconnected the call and flipped on the radio. Chaka Khan was singing "Ain't Nobody Love You Better." If you can listen to that one without moving your feet, you got some serious rhythm issues. He took the Long Island Expressway east, which was shockingly clear today. Usually the road was more or less a parking lot that swayed forward every couple of minutes.

People always tell you that the Hamptons, the swanky Long Island summer spot where Manhattanites get away from it all by being with other Manhattanites, is best in the off season. You always hear that about vacation spots. People, mostly vacationers themselves, whine through the high-season months, waiting to reach this apex of a theoretically swarmless nirvana. But—and this was the part Myron never understood—no one is ever in the Hamptons in the off months. No one. Downtown is dead to the point of craving tumbleweeds. Shop owners sigh and discount nothing. The restaurants are less crowded, sure, but they're also closed. And hey, let's be honest here, the weather and beaches and even the people-watching are big draws here. Who goes to a Long Island beach in the winter?

The school was in a residential neighborhood with older, more modest homes—a place where the true Long Island regulars, none of whom hang out with Alec and Kim at Nick and Toni's, resided. Myron parked in a church lot and followed the signs down the steps into the rectory's basement. A young woman, a hall monitor of sorts, greeted Myron at the landing. He gave her his name and said he was here to see Ms. Joyce. The young woman nodded and told him to follow her.

The corridor was silent. Strange when one considered that this was a preschool. *Preschool.* Another new term. In Myron's day, they had called them nursery schools. Myron wondered when the name had changed and what group had considered the term *nursery school* somehow discriminatory. Professional RNs? Breast-feeding mothers? Bottle-fed infants maybe?

Still silent. Perhaps it was vacation or naptime. Myron was about to ask the young hall monitor when she opened a door. He looked in. Wrong-a-mundo. The room was chock full of small children, probably twenty give or take, and they were all working independently and in total silence. The older teacher smiled at Myron. She whispered to the little boy she was working with—he was doing something with blocks and letters—and stood.

"Hello," she said to Myron, speaking softly.

"Hi," Myron whispered back.

She leaned toward the young monitor. "Miss Simmons, will you help Mrs. McLaughlin?"

"Of course."

Peggy Joyce wore an open yellow sweater over a buttoned-at-the-neck blouse. The collar was frilly. She had half-moon glasses dangling from a chain around her neck. "We can chat in my office."

"Okay." He followed her. The place was silent as, well, a place without children. Myron asked, "Do you give those kids Valium?"

She smiled. "Just a little Montessori."

"A little what?"

"You don't have children, do you?"

The question caused a pang, but he answered in the negative.

"It's a teaching philosophy created by Dr. Maria Montessori, Italy's first female physician."

"It seems to work."

"I suppose."

"Do the children act like this at home?"

"Good Lord, no. Truth be told, it doesn't translate into the real world. But few things do."

They moved into the office, which consisted of a wooden desk, three chairs, one file cabinet.

"How long have you taught here?" Myron asked.

"I'm in my forty-third year."

"Wow."

"Yes."

"I guess you've seen lots of changes?"

"In kids? Almost none. Children don't change, Mr. Bolitar. A five-year-old is still a five-year-old."

"Still innocent."

She cocked her head. " 'Innocent' isn't the word I would use. Children are total id. They are perhaps the most naturally vicious creatures on God's green earth."

"Strange outlook for a preschool teacher."

"Just an honest one."

"So what word would you use?"

She thought about it. "If pressed, I'd say 'unformed.' Or maybe 'undeveloped.' Like a picture you've already taken but haven't processed yet."

Myron nodded, though he had no idea what she meant. There was something about Peggy Joyce that was a little, well, scary.

"Do you remember that book *All I Really Need to Know I Learned in Kindergarten?*" she asked him.

"Yes."

"It's true, but not in the way you think. School removes children from their warm parental cocoon. School teaches them to bully or be bullied. School teaches them how to be cruel to one another. School teaches them that Mommy and Daddy lied to them when they told them that they were special and unique."

Myron said nothing.

"You don't agree?"

"I don't teach preschool."

"That's sidestepping, Mr. Bolitar."

Myron shrugged. "They learn socialization. That's a hard lesson. And like every hard lesson, you have to get it wrong before you can get it right."

"They learn boundaries, in other words?"

"Yes."

"Interesting. And perhaps true. But you remember when I was giving the film-processing example earlier?"

"Yes."

"School only processes the picture. It doesn't snap it."

"Okay," Myron said, not wanting to follow her train of thought.

"What I mean is, everything is pretty much decided by the time these children leave here and enter kindergarten. I can tell who will be successful and who will fail, who will end up happy and who will end up in prison, and ninety percent of the time I'm right. Maybe Hollywood and video games have an influence, I don't know. But I can usually tell which kid will be watching too many violent movies or playing too many violent games."

"You can tell all this by the time they're five years old?"

"Pretty much, yes."

"And you feel that's it? That they don't have the ability to change?"

"The ability? Oh, probably. But they're already on a path, and while they may still be able to change it, the majority do not. Staying on the path is easier."

"So let me ask you the eternal question: Is it nature or nurture?"

She smiled. "I get asked that all the time."

"And?"

"I answer nurture. Know why?"

Myron shook his head.

"Believing in nurture is like believing in God. You might be wrong, but you might as well cover your bases." She folded her hands and leaned forward. "Now, what can I do for you, Mr. Bolitar?"

"Do you remember a student named Dennis Lex?"

"I remember all my students. Does that surprise you?"

Myron didn't want her going off on another tangent. "Did you teach the other Lex children?"

"I taught them all. Their father made a lot of changes after his book became a bestseller. But he kept them here."

"So what can you tell me about Dennis Lex?"

She sat back and regarded him as though seeing him for the first time. "I don't want to be rude, but I'm wondering when you're going to tell me what this is all about. I'm talking to you, Mr. Bolitar—and breaching confidences, I suspect—because I think you're here for a very specific reason."

"What reason is that, Ms. Joyce?"

Her eyes had a steely glint. "Don't play games with me, Mr. Bolitar."

She was right. "I'm trying to find Dennis Lex."

Peggy Joyce kept still.

"I know this sounds weird," he went on. "But as far as I can tell, he fell off the earth after preschool."

She stared straight ahead, though Myron had no idea at what. There were no photographs on the walls, no diplomas, no drawings by little hands. Just cold wall. "Not after," she said finally. "During."

There was a knock on the door. Peggy Joyce said, "Come in." The young hall monitor, Miss Simmons, entered with a little boy. His head was down and he'd been crying. "James needs a little time," Miss Simmons said.

Peggy Joyce nodded. "Let him lie on the mat."

James eyed Myron and left with Miss Simmons.

Myron turned to Peggy Joyce. "What happened to Dennis Lex?"

"It's a question I've been waiting for someone to ask for more than thirty years," she said.

"What's the answer?"

"First, tell me why you're looking for him."

"I'm trying to find a bone marrow donor. I think it might be Dennis Lex." He gave her as few details as he could. When he finished, she put a bony hand to her face.

"I don't think I can help you," she said. "It was so long ago."

"Please, Ms. Joyce. A child will die if I don't find him. You're my only lead."

"You spoke to his family?"

"Only his sister Susan."

"What did she tell you?"

"Nothing."

"I'm not sure what I can add."

"You could start by telling me what Dennis was like."

She sighed and neatly arranged her hands on her thighs. "He was like the other Lex children—very bright, thoughtful, contemplative, perhaps a bit too much so for so young a child. With most students, I try to get them to grow up a bit. With the Lex children, that was never an issue."

Myron nodded, trying to encourage.

"Dennis was the youngest. You probably know that. He was here the same time as his brother Bronwyn. Susan was older." She stopped, looked lost.

"What happened to him?"

"One day he and Bronwyn didn't come to school. I got a call from their father saying that he was taking them on an unplanned vacation."

"Where?"

"He didn't say. He wasn't being very specific."

"Okay, go on."

"That's pretty much it, Mr. Bolitar. Two weeks later, Bronwyn came back to school. I never saw Dennis again."

"You called his father?"

"Of course."

"What did he say?"

"He told me that Dennis wouldn't be coming back."

"Did you ask him why?"

"Of course. But . . . did you ever meet Raymond Lex?"

"No."

"You didn't question a man like that. He mentioned something about home schooling. When I pressed, he made it clear it was none of my concern. Over the years, I've tried to keep track of the family, even when they moved out of the area. But like you, I never heard anything about Dennis."

"What did you think happened?"

She looked at him. "I assumed he was dead."

Her words, though not all that surprising, worked like a vacuum, sucking the room dry, forcing out the air.

"Why?" Myron asked.

"I figured that he was ill, and that was why he was pulled out of school."

"Why would Mr. Lex try to hide something like that?"

"I don't know. After his novel became a bestseller, he became private to the point of paranoia. Are you sure this donor you're looking for is Dennis Lex?"

"Not sure, no."

Peggy Joyce snapped her fingers. "Oh, wait, I have something you may find interesting." She stood and opened a file drawer. She sifted through it, pulled something out, studied it for a moment. Her elbow smacked the drawer closed. "This was taken two months before Dennis left us."

She handed him an old class photograph, the color not so much fading as greening from age. Fifteen kids flanked by two teachers, one a far younger Peggy Joyce. The years had not been unkind to her, but they'd passed anyway. A small black sign with the white lettering read SHADY WELLS MONTESSORI SCHOOL and the year.

"Which one is Dennis?"

She pointed to a boy sitting in the front row. He had a Prince Valiant cut and a face-splitting smile that never quite hit his eyes. "Can I have this?"

"If you think it will help."

"It might."

She nodded. "I better get back to my students."

"Thank you."

"Do you remember your preschool, Mr. Bolitar?"

Myron nodded. "Parkview Nursery School in Livingston, New Jersey."

"How about your teachers? Do you remember them at all?"

Myron thought about it. "No."

She nodded as though he'd answered correctly. "Good luck," she said.

23

AgeComp. Or age-progression software, if you prefer.

Myron had learned a bit about it when searching for a missing woman named Lucy Mayor. The key was in the digital imaging. All Myron had to do—or in the case of their office, all Esperanza had to do—was take the class photograph and scan it into the computer. Then, using common software programs like Photoshop or Picture Publisher, you blow up the face of young Dennis Lex. AgeComp, a software program constantly being retooled and perfected by missing-children organizations, does the rest. Using advanced mathematical algorithms, AgeComp stretches, merges, and blends digital photographs of missing children and produces a color image of what they might look like today.

Naturally, a lot is left to chance. Scarring, facial fractures, facial hair, cosmetic surgery, hairstyle or, in the case of some of the older ones, male pattern baldness. Still, the class photo could be a serious lead.

When he was back in Manhattan, the cell phone rang.

"I spoke to the feds," Win said.

"And?"

"Your impression is correct."

"What impression?"

"They are indeed frightened."

"Did you speak to PT?"

"I did. He put me onto the right person. They requested a face-to-face."

"When?"

"Pretty pronto. We are, in fact, waiting in your office."

"The feds are in my office right now?"

"Affirmative."

"Be there in five."

More like ten. When the elevator opened, Esperanza was sitting at Big Cyndi's desk.

"How many?" he asked.

"Three," Esperanza said. "One blond woman, one extra-strength dork, one nice suit."

"Win's with them?"

"Yep."

He handed her the photograph and pointed to Dennis Lex's face. "How long before we could get an age progression on this?"

"Jesus, when was this taken?"

"Thirty years ago."

Esperanza frowned. "You know anything about age progression?"

"Some."

"It's mostly used to find missing kids," she said. "And it's usually used to age them five, maybe ten years."

"But we can get something, right?"

"Something very rough, yeah maybe." She flicked on the scanner and placed the photo facedown. "If they're in the lab, we'll probably have it by the end of the day. I'll crop it and email it over."

"Do it later," he said, gesturing toward the door. "Mustn't keep the feds waiting. Our tax dollars and all that."

"You want me in there?"

"You're a part of everything that goes on here, Esperanza. Of course I want you in there."

"I see," she said. Then: "Is this the part where I blink back tears because you're making me feel oh-so-special?"

Wiseass.

Myron opened his office door. Esperanza followed. Win sat behind Myron's desk, probably so that none of the feds would. Win could be territorial—just one of the ways he was like a Doberman. Kimberly Green and Rick Peck rose with lack-of-sleep-luggage eyes and squared-off smiles. The third fed stayed in his seat, not moving, not even turning to see who'd entered. Myron saw his face and felt a jolt.

Whoa.

Win watched Myron, an amused smile curling the ends of his mouth. Eric Ford, deputy director of the Federal Bureau of Investigation, was the man in the suit. His presence meant one thing: This was serious big-time.

Kimberly Green pointed at Esperanza. "What's she doing in here?"

"She's my partner," Myron said. "And it's not polite to point."

"Your partner? You think this is a business transaction?"

"She stays," Myron said.

"No," Kimberly Green said. She was still wearing the ball-and-chain earrings, still the jeans and black turtleneck, but the jacket now was spearmint green. "We're not exactly thrilled talking to you and Cheekbones boy over there"—she gestured toward Win—"but at least you have some clearance. We don't know her. She goes."

Win's smile spread and his eyebrows did a quick up-and-down. Cheekbones. He liked that.

"She goes," Green said again.

Esperanza shrugged. "No biggie," she said.

Myron was about to say something, but Win shook his head. He was right. Save it for the important battles.

Esperanza left. Win got up and gave Myron the chair. He stood on Myron's right, arms crossed, totally at ease. Green and Peck fidgeted. Myron turned to Eric Ford. "I don't think we've met."

"But you know who I am," Ford said. He had one of those smooth soft-rock-DJ voices.

"Yes."

"And I know who you are," he said. "So what would be the point?"

Oookay. Myron glanced back at Win. Win shrugged.

Ford nodded at Kimberly Green. She cleared her throat. "For the record," she said, "we don't think we should have to go through this."

"Through what?"

"Telling you about our investigation. Debriefing you. As a good citizen, you should be willing to cooperate with our investigation because it's the right thing to do."

Myron looked at Win and said, "Oh boy."

"Some aspects of an investigation need to be contained," she continued. "You and Mr. Lockwood should understand that better than most. You should be anxious to cooperate with any federal investigation. You should respect what we're trying to do here."

"Right, okay, we respect. Can we skip ahead, please? You looked us up. You know we'll keep our mouths shut. Otherwise none of us would be here."

She folded her hands and put them in her lap. Peck kept his head down and scribbled notes, Lord knew on what. Myron's decor maybe. "What we say here cannot leave this room. It is classified to the highest—"

"Skipping," Myron said with an impatient hand roll. "Skipping."

Green slid her eyes toward Ford. He nodded again. She took a deep breath and said, "We have Stan Gibbs under surveillance."

She stopped, settled back. Myron waited a few seconds and then said, "Label me surprised."

"That information is classified," she said.

"Then I'll leave it out of my diary."

"He isn't supposed to know."

"Well, that's usually implied with words like 'classified' and 'surveillance.' "

"But Gibbs does know. He loses us whenever he really wants. Because when he's out in public, we can't get too close."

"Why can't you get too close?"

"He'll see us."

"But he already knows you're there?"

"Yes."

Myron looked up at Win. "Wasn't there an Abbott and Costello skit that went like this?"

"Marx Brothers," Win said.

"If we were out in the open about tailing him," Green said, "the fact that he's a target could become public knowledge."

"And you're trying to contain that?"

"Yes."

"How long has he been under surveillance?"

"Well, it's not that simple. He's been out of range a lot—"

"How long?"

Again Green looked at Ford. Again Ford nodded. She balled her hands into fists. "Since the first article on the kidnappings appeared."

Myron sat back, feeling something akin to a head rush. He shouldn't have been surprised, but damned if he wasn't. The article came flooding back to him—the sudden disappearances, the awful phone calls, the constant, eternal anguish, the picket-fenced lives suddenly bulldozed over by inexplicable evil.

"My God," Myron said. "Stan Gibbs was telling the truth."

"We never said that," Kimberly Green said.

"I see. So you've been tailing him because you don't like his syntax?"

Silence.

"The articles were true," Myron said. "And you've known it all along."

"What we did or did not know is not your concern."

Myron shook his head. "Unbelievable," he said. "So let me see if I got this straight. You have a serial psycho out there who snatches people out of the blue and torments their families. You want to keep a lid on it because if word got out to the public, you'd have a panic situation. Then the psycho goes directly to Stan Gibbs and suddenly the story is in the public domain . . ." Myron's voice died off, seeing that his logic trail had hit a major pothole. He frowned and forged ahead. "I don't know how that old novel or the plagiarism charges tie in. But either way, you decided to ride it. You let Gibbs get fired and disgraced, probably in part because you were pissed off that he upset your investigation. But mostly"—he spotted what he thought was a clearing—"but mostly you did it so you could watch him. If the psycho contacted him once, you figured, he'd probably do it again—especially if the articles had been discredited."

Kimberly Green said, "Wrong."

"But close."

"No."

"The kidnappings Gibbs wrote about took place, right?"

She hesitated, gave Ford an eye check. "We can't verify all of his facts."

"Jesus, I'm not taking a deposition here," Myron said. "Was his column true, yes or no?"

"We've told you enough," she said. "It's your turn."

"You haven't told me squat."

"And you've told us less."

Negotiating. Life is being a sports agent—constant negotiating. He had learned the importance of leverage, of doling out, of being fair. People forget that last one, and it always costs you in the end. The best negotiator isn't the one who gets the whole pie while leaving scant crumbs behind. The best negotiator is the one who gets what he wants while keeping the other side happy. So normally, Myron would dole out a little something here. Classic give-and-take. But not this time. He knew better. Once he told them the reason for his visit to Stan Gibbs, his leverage would be zippo.

The best negotiator, like the best species, also knows how to adapt.

"First answer my question," Myron said. "Yes or no, was the story Stan Gibbs wrote true?"

"There is no yes-or-no answer to that," she said. "Parts were true. Parts were not true."

"For example?"

"The young couple was from Iowa, not Minnesota. The missing father had three children, not two." She stopped, folded her hands.

"But there have been kidnappings?"

"We knew about those two," she said. "We had no information about the missing college student."

"Probably because the psycho got to her parents. They probably never reported it."

"That's our theory," Kimberly Green said. "But we don't know for sure. Still, there are major discrepancies. The families swear they never spoke to him, for example. Many of the phone calls and events don't match what we know to be true."

Myron saw more clearing. "So you asked Gibbs about it? About his sources?"

"Yes."

"And he refused to tell you anything."

"That's right."

"So you destroyed him."

"No."

"The one part I don't get is the plagiarism," Myron said. "I mean, did you guys somehow set that up? I can't see how. Unless you made up a book and . . . no, that's too far-fetched. So what's the deal with that?"

Kimberly Green leaned forward. "Tell us why you went to his apartment."

"Not until—"

"For several months we couldn't find Stan Gibbs," she interrupted. "We think maybe he left the country. But since he's moved into that condo, he's always alone. As I said before, he loses us sometimes. But he never accepts visitors. Several people have tracked him down. Old friends even. They come to his door or they call on the phone. And you know what always happens, Myron?"

Myron didn't like her tone of voice.

"He sends them away. Every single time. Stan Gibbs sees no one. Except you."

Myron looked up at Win. Win nodded very slowly. Myron took a look at Eric Ford before going back to Kimberly Green. "You think I'm the kidnapper?"

She leaned back with a partial shrug, looking satiated. Turning the tables and all that. "You tell us," she said.

Win started for the door. Myron rose and followed.

"Where the hell are you two going?" Green asked.

Win grabbed the knob. Myron headed around the desk and said, "I'm a suspect. I'm not talking until I have an attorney present. If you'll excuse me."

"Hey, we're just talking here," Kimberly Green said. "I never said I thought you were the kidnapper."

"Sounded that way to me," Myron said. "Win?"

"He snatches hearts," Win told her, "not people."

"You got something to hide?" Green said.

"Just his fondness for cyber pornography," Win said. Then: "Oops."

Kimberly Green stood and blocked Myron's path. "We think we know about the missing college student," she said, her eyes locked hard on his. "Do you want to know how we found out about it?"

Myron kept still.

"Through her father. He got a call from the kidnapper. I don't know what was said. He hasn't said a word since. He's catatonic. Whatever that psycho said to that girl's father put him in a padded room."

Myron felt the room shrink, the walls closing in.

"We haven't found any bodies yet, but we're pretty sure he kills them," she went on. "He kidnaps them, does Lord knows what, and makes the families suffer interminably. And you know he won't stop."

Myron kept his eyes steady. "What's your point?"

"This isn't funny."

"No," he said. "It's not. So stop playing stupid games."

She said nothing.

"I want to hear it from your mouth," Myron said. "Do you think I'm involved in this, yes or no?"

Eric Ford took this one. "No."

Kimberly Green slid back into her chair, her eyes never leaving Myron's. Eric Ford made a big hand gesture. "Please sit down."

Myron and Win moved back to their original positions.

Eric Ford said, "The novel exists. So do the passages Stan Gibbs plagiarized. The book was sent to our office anonymously—more specifically, to Special Agent Green here. We admit that we found that issue confusing at first. On the one hand, Gibbs knows about the kidnappings. On the other hand, he doesn't know everything and he clearly copied excerpts from an old, out-of-print mystery novel."

"There's an explanation," Myron said. "The kidnapper might have read the book. He might have identified with the character, become a copycat of sorts."

"We considered that possibility," Eric Ford said, "but we don't believe that's the case here."

"Why not?"

"It's complicated."

"Does it involve trigonometry?"

"You still think this is a joking manner?"

"You still think it's smart to play games?"

Ford closed his eyes. Green looked on edge. Peck continued scribbling notes. When Ford opened his eyes, he said, "We don't believe Stan Gibbs made up the crimes," he said. "We believe he perpetrated them."

Myron felt a pow. He looked up at Win. Nothing.

"You have some background in the criminal mind, do you not?" Ford asked.

Myron might have nodded.

"Well, here we have an old pattern with a new twist. Arsonists love to watch firemen put out the blaze. Ofttimes they're even the ones who report the fire. They play the good Samaritan. Murderers love to attend the funerals of their victims. We videotape funerals. I'm sure you know this."

Myron nodded again.

"Sometimes killers make themselves part of the story." Eric Ford was gesturing a lot now, his knotted hands rising and falling as though this were a press conference in too big a room. "They claim to be witnesses. They become the innocent bystanders who happened to find the body in the brush. You're familiar with this moth-near-the-flame phenomenon, are you not?"

"Yes."

"So what could be more enticing than being the only columnist to report the story? Can you imagine the high? How mind-bogglingly close to the investigation you'd be. The brilliance of your deception—for a psychotic, it's almost too delicious. And if you are perpetrating these crimes to get attention, then here you get a double dose. Attention as the serial kidnapper, one. Attention as the brilliant reporter with the scoop and possible Pulitzer, two. You even get the bonus attention of a man bravely defending the First Amendment."

Myron was holding his breath. "That's a hell of a theory," he said.

"You want more?"

"Yes."

"Why won't he answer any of our questions?"

"You said it yourself. First Amendment."

"He's not a lawyer or psychiatrist."

"But he is a reporter," Myron said.

"What kind of monster would continue to protect his source in this situation?"

"I know plenty."

"We spoke to the victims' families. They swore they never spoke to him."

"They could be lying. Maybe the kidnapper told them to say that."

"Okay, then why hasn't Gibbs done more to defend himself against the charges of plagiarism? He could have fought them. He could have even provided some detail that would have proved he was telling the truth. But no, instead he goes silent. Why?"

"You think it's because he's the kidnapper? The moth flew too close to the flame and is licking his wounds in darkness?"

"Do you have a better explanation?"

Myron said nothing.

"Lastly, there's the murder of his mistress, Melina Garston."

"What about it?"

"Think it through, Myron. We put the screws to him. Maybe he expected that, maybe he didn't. Either way, the courts don't see everything his way. You don't know about the court findings, do you?"

"Not really, no."

"That's because they were sealed. In part, the judge demanded that Gibbs show some proof he had been in contact with the killer. He finally said that Melina Garston would back him."

"And she did, right?"

"Yes. She claimed to have met the subject of his story."

"I still don't understand. If she backed him up, why would he kill her?"

"The day before Melina Garston died, she called her father. She told him that she lied."

Myron sat back, tried to take it all in.

Eric Ford said, "He's back now, Myron. Stan Gibbs has finally surfaced. While he was gone, the Sow the Seeds kidnapper was gone too. But this brand of psycho never stops on his own. He's going to strike again and soon. So before that happens, you better talk to us. Why were you at his condominium?"

Myron thought about it but not for long. "I was looking for someone."

"Who?"

"A missing bone marrow donor. He could save a child's life."

Ford looked at him steadily. "I assume that Jeremy Downing is the child in question."

So much for being vague, but Myron was not surprised. Phone records probably. Or maybe there had indeed been a tail when he visited Emily's. "Yes. And before I go on, I want your word that you will keep me in the loop."

Kimberly Green said, "You're not a part of this investigation."

"I'm not interested in your kidnapper. I'm interested in my donor. You help me find him, I'll tell you what I know."

"We agree," Ford said, waving Kimberly Green silent. "So how does Stan Gibbs fit in with your donor?"

Myron reviewed it for them. He started with Davis Taylor and then moved on to Dennis Lex and then the cryptic phone call. They kept their faces steady, Green and Peck scratching on their pads, but there was a definite jolt when he mentioned the Lex family.

They asked a few follow-up questions, like why he got involved in the first place. He said that Emily was an old friend. He wasn't about to go into the patrimony issue. Myron could see Green getting antsy. He had served his purpose. She was anxious to get out and start tracking things down.

A few minutes later, the feds snapped their pads closed and rose. "We're on it," Ford said. He looked straight at Myron. "And we'll find your donor. You stay out."

Myron nodded and wondered if he could. After they left, Win took a seat in front of Myron's desk.

"Why do I feel like I was picked up at a bar and now it's the next morning and the guy just handed me the 'I'll call you' line?" Myron asked.

"Because that's precisely what you are," Win said. "Slut."

"Think they're holding something back?"

"Without question."

"Something big?"

"Gargantuan," Win said.

"Not much we can do about it now."

"Nope," Win said. "Nothing at all."

24

Myron's mom met him at the front door.

"I'm picking up the takeout," Mom said.

"You?"

She put her hands on her hips and shot him her best wither. "There a problem with that?"

"No, it's just . . ." He decided to drop it. "Nothing."

Mom kissed his cheek and fished through her purse for the car keys. "I'll be back in a half hour. Your father is in the back." She gave him the imploring eyes. "Alone."

"Okay," he said.

"No one else is here."

"Uh-huh."

"If you catch my drift."

"It's caught."

"You'll be alone."

"Caught, Mom. Caught."

"It'll be an opportunity—"

"Mom."

She put her hands up. "Okay, okay, I'm going."

He walked around the side of the house, past the garbage cans and recycling bins, and found Dad on the deck. The deck was sanded redwood with built-in benches and resin furniture and a Weber 500 barbecue, all brought to being during the famed Kitchen Expansion of 1994. Dad was bent over a railing with a screwdriver in his hand. For a moment, Myron fell back to those "weekend projects" with Dad, some of which lasted almost an entire hour. They would go out with toolbox in tow, Dad bent over like he was now, muttering obscenities under his breath. Myron's sole task consisted of handing Dad tools like a scrub nurse in the operating room, the whole exercise boring as hell, shuffling his feet in the sun, sighing heavily, finding new angles from which to stand.

"Hey," Myron said.

Dad looked up, smiled, put down the tool. "Screw loose," he said. "But let's not talk about your mother."

Myron laughed. They found molded-resin chairs around a table impaled by a blue umbrella. In front of them lay Bolitar Stadium, a small patch of green-to-brown grass that had hosted countless, oft-solo football games, baseball games, soccer games, Wiffle ball games (probably the most popular sport at Bolitar Stadium), rugby scrums, badminton, kickball, and that favorite pastime for the future sadist, bombardment. Myron spotted Mom's former vegetable garden—the word *vegetable* here being used to describe three annual soggy tomatoes and two flaccid zucchinis; it was now slightly more overgrown than a Cambodian rice paddy. To their right were the rusted remnants of their old tetherball pole. Tetherball. Now, there was a really dumb game.

Myron cleared his throat and put his hands on the table. "How you feeling?"

Dad gave a big nod. "Good. You?"

"Good."

The silence floated down, puffy and relaxed. Silence with a father can be like that. You drift back and you're young and you're safe, safe in that all-encompassing way only a child can be with his father. You still see him hovering in your darkened doorway, the silent sentinel to your adolescence, and you sleep the sleep of the naïve, the innocent, the unformed. When you get older, you realize that this safety was just an illusion, another child's perception, like the size of your backyard.

Or maybe, if you're lucky, you don't.

Dad looked older today, the flesh on his face more sagged, the once-knotted biceps spongy under the T-shirt, starting to waste. Myron wondered how to start. Dad closed his eyes for a three count, opened them, and said, "Don't."

"What?"

"Your mother is about as subtle as a White House press release," Dad said. "I mean, when was the last time she picked up the takeout instead of me?"

"Has she ever?"

"Once," Dad said. "When I had a fever of a hundred and four. And even then she whined about it."

"Where's she going?"

"She has me on a special diet now, you know. Because of the chest pains."

Chest pains. Euphemism for *heart attack.*

"Yeah, I figured that."

"She's even tried cooking a little. She told you?"

Myron nodded. "She baked something for me yesterday."

Dad's body went stiff. "By God," he said. "Her own son?"

"It was pretty scary."

"The woman has many, many talents, but they could airdrop that stuff into starving African nations and no one would eat it."

"So where's she going?"

"Your mother is high on some crazy Middle Eastern health food place. Just opened in West Orange. Get this, it's called Ayatollah Granola."

Myron gave him flat eyes.

"Hand to God, that's the name. Food is almost as dry as that Thanksgiving turkey your mother made when you were eight. You remember that?"

"At night," Myron said. "It still haunts my sleep."

Dad looked off again. "She left us alone so we could talk, right?"

"Right."

He made a face. "I hate when she does stuff like that. She means well, your mother. We both know that. But let's not do it, okay?"

Myron shrugged. "You say so."

"She thinks I don't like growing old. News flash: No one does. My friend Herschel Diamond—you remember Heshy?"

"Sure."

"Big guy, right? Played semipro football when we were young. So Heshy, he calls me and he says now that I'm retired, I can do tai chi with him. I mean, tai chi? What the hell is that anyway? If I want to move slowly, I have to drive down to the Y to do it with a bunch of old yentas? I mean, what's that about? I tell him no. So then Heshy, this great athlete, Myron, he could hit a softball a country mile, this marvelous big ox, he tells me we can walk together. Walk. At the mall. Speedwalk, he calls it. At the mall, for chrissake. Heshy always hated the place—now he wants us to trot around like a bunch of jackasses in matching sweatsuits and expensive walking shoes. Pump our arms with these little *faigelah* barbells. Walking shoes, he calls them. What the hell is that anyway? I never had a pair of shoes I couldn't walk in, am I right?"

He waited for an answer. Myron said, "As rain."

Dad stood up. He grabbed a screwdriver and feigned working. "So now, because I don't want to move like an old Chinaman or walk around a god-forsaken mall in overpriced sneakers, your mother thinks I'm not adjusting. You hear what I'm saying?"

"Yes."

Dad stayed bent, fiddling a little more with the railing. In the distance, Myron heard children playing. A bike bell rang. Someone laughed. A lawn mower purred. Dad's voice, when he finally spoke again, was surprisingly soft. "You know what your mother really wants us to do?" he said.

"What?"

"She wants you and I to reverse roles." Dad finally looked up through his heavy-lidded eyes. "I don't want to reverse roles, Myron. I'm the father. I like being the father. Let me stay that, okay?"

Myron found it hard to speak. "Sure, Dad."

His father put his head back down, the gray wisps upright in the humidity, his breathing tool-work heavy, and Myron again felt something open up his chest and grab hold of his heart. He looked at this man he'd loved for so long, who'd gone without complaint to that damn muggy warehouse in Newark for more than thirty years, and Myron realized that he didn't know him. He didn't know what his father dreamed about, what he wanted to be when he was a kid, what he thought about his own life.

Dad kept working on the screw. Myron watched him.

Promise me you won't die, okay? Just promise me that.

He almost said it out loud.

Dad straightened himself out and studied his handiwork. Satisfied, he sat back down. They started talking about the Knicks and the recent Kevin Costner movie and the new Nelson DeMille book. They put away the toolbox. They had some iced tea. They lounged side by side in matching molded-resin chaises. An hour passed. They fell into a comfortable silence. Myron fingered the condensation on his glass. He could hear his father's breathing, moderately wheezy. Dusk had settled in, bruising the sky purple, the trees going a burnt orange.

Myron closed his eyes and said, "I got a hypothetical for you."

"Oh?"

"What would you do if you found out you weren't my real father?"

Dad's eyebrows went skyward. "You trying to tell me something?"

"Just a hypothetical. Suppose you found out right now that I wasn't your biological son. How would you react?"

"Depends," Dad said.

"On?"

"How you reacted."

"It wouldn't make a difference to me," Myron said.

Dad smiled.

"What?" Myron said.

"Easy for both of us to say it wouldn't matter. But news like that is a bombshell. You can't predict what someone will do when a bomb lands. When I was in Korea—" Dad stopped, Myron sat up. "Well, you never knew how someone would react . . ." His voice tailed off. He coughed into his fist and then started up again. "Guys you were sure would be heroes completely lost it—and vice versa. That's why you can't ask stuff like this as a hypothetical."

Myron looked at his father. His father kept his eyes on the grass, taking another deep sip. "You never talk about Korea," Myron said.

"I do," Dad said.

"Not with me."

"No, not with you."

"Why not?"

"It's what I fought for. So we wouldn't have to talk about it."

It didn't make sense and Myron understood.

"There a reason you raised this particular hypothetical?" Dad asked.

"No."

Dad nodded. He knew it was a lie, but he wouldn't push it. They settled back and watched the familiar surroundings.

"Tai chi isn't so bad," Myron said. "It's a martial art. Like tae kwon do. I've been thinking of taking it up myself."

Dad took another sip. Myron sneaked a glance. Something on his father's face began to quiver. Was Dad indeed getting smaller, more fragile—or was it like the backyard and safety, again the shifting perception of a child turned adult?

"Dad . . . ?"

"Let's go inside," his father said, standing. "We stay out much longer, one of us is going to get misty and say, 'Wanna play catch?' "

Myron bit off a laugh and followed him inside. Mom came home not long after that, lugging two bags of food as though they were stone tablets. "Everybody hungry?" she called out.

"Starving," Dad said. "I'm so hungry I could eat a vegetarian."

"Very funny, Al."

"Or even your cooking . . ."

"Ha-ha," Mom said.

". . . though I'd prefer the vegetarian."

"Stop it, Al, I'm going to phlegm up, you keep making me laugh like this." Mom dropped the bags onto the kitchen counter. "See, Myron? It's a good thing your mother is shallow."

"Shallow?" Myron asked.

"If I judged a man on brains or sense of humor," Mom continued, "you'd have never been born."

"Right-o," Dad said with a hearty smile. "But one look at your old man in a bathing suit and whammo—all mine."

"Oh please," Mom said.

"Yes," Myron said. "Please."

They both looked at him. Mom cleared her throat. "So did you two, uh, have a nice talk?"

"We talked," Dad said. "It was very life-affirming. I see the errors of my ways."

"I'm being serious."

"So am I. I see everything differently now."

She put her arms around his waist and nuzzled him. "So you'll call Heshy?"

"I'll call Heshy," he said.

"Promise."

"Yes, Ellen, I promise."

"You'll go to the Y and do jai alai with him?"

"Tai chi," Dad corrected.

"What?"

"It's called tai chi, not jai alai."

"I thought it was jai alai."

"Tai chi. Jai alai is the game with the curved rackets down in Florida."

"That's shuffleboard, Al."

"Not shuffleboard. The other thing with the sticks. And the gambling."

"Tai chi?" Mom said, testing it for sound. "Are you sure?"

"I think so."

"But you're not positive?"

"No, I'm not positive," Dad said. "Maybe you're right. Maybe it is called jai alai."

The name debate continued for a while. Myron didn't bother correcting them. Never cut in on that strange dance known as marital discourse. They ate the health food. It was indeed nasty. They laughed a lot. His parents must have said "You don't know what you're talking about" to each other fifty times; maybe it was a euphemism for "I love you."

Eventually Myron said good night. Mom kissed his cheek and made herself scarce. Dad walked him to the car. The night was silent save a lone dribbling basketball somewhere on Darby Road or maybe Coddington Terrace. A nice sound. When he hugged his father good-bye, Myron again noticed that his father felt smaller, less substantial. Myron held on a little longer than usual. For the first time he felt like the bigger man, the stronger man, and he suddenly remembered what Dad had said about reversing roles. So he held on in the dark. Time passed. Dad patted his back. Myron kept his eyes closed and held on tighter. Dad stroked his hair and shushed him. Just for a little while. Just until the roles reversed themselves again, returning both of them to where they belonged.

25

Granite Man was waiting outside the Dakota.

Myron spotted him from his car. He picked up the cell phone and called Win. "I have company."

"A rather large gentleman, yes," Win said. "Two cohorts are parked across the street in a corporate vehicle owned by the Lex family."

"I'll leave the cell phone on."

"They confiscated it last time," Win said.

"Yes."

"Likely they'll do the same."

"We'll improvise."

"Your funeral," Win said, and hung up.

Myron parked in the lot and approached Granite Man.

"Mrs. Lex would like to see you," Granite Man said.

"Do you know what she wants?" Myron asked.

Granite Man ignored the question.

"Maybe she saw me flexing on the security tape," Myron said. "Wanted to get to know me better."

Granite Man did not laugh. "You ever think about doing this comedy thing professionally?"

"There have been offers."

"I bet. Get in the car."

"Okay, but I have a curfew, you know. And I never French-kiss on the first date. Just so we understand each other."

Granite Man shook his head. "Man, I'd like to waste you."

They got in the car. Two blue-blazers sat in front. The car ride was silent except for Granite Man and His Magic Cracking Knuckles. The Lex building emerged grudgingly through the dark. Myron traveled through the security travail again. As Win predicted, they confiscated his phone. Granite Man and the two blazers turned left this time instead of right. They escorted him into an elevator. It opened into what appeared to be living quarters.

Susan Lex's office had been done sort of Renaissance palatial, but the apartment up here—it looked like an apartment anyway—did a one-eighty. Modern and minimalism were the major themes. The walls were painted stark white and had nothing on them. The floors were a pigeon-gray wood. There were black and white bookshelves made of fiberglass, most empty, some with indistinct figurines. The couch was red and shaped like two lips. There was a well-stocked see-through bar constructed out of Lucite. Two metallic swivel stools were painted red on the base, looking about as inviting as rectal thermometers. A fire danced lazily in the fireplace, fake logs casting an unnatural glow over the black mantel. The whole place had a feel and aura about as warm as a cold sore.

Myron strolled, feigning interest. He stopped at a crystal statue with a marble base. Something modern or cubist or what-have-you. Symmetrical Bowel Movement maybe. Myron put his hand on it. Substantial. He looked out the one-way glass. Too low for much of a view beyond the hedges lining the front gate. Hmm.

The two blue-blazers did the Buckingham Palace Guard thing on either side of the door. Granite Man followed Myron, his hands clasped behind his lower back. A door on the other side of the room opened. Myron was not surprised to see Susan Lex enter, again keeping her distance. There was a man with her this time. Myron did not bother approaching.

"And you are?" he called out.

Susan Lex answered this one. "This is my brother Bronwyn."

"Not the brother I'm interested in," Myron said.

"Yes, I know. Please sit down."

Granite Man gestured toward the lips-couch. Myron sat on the lower lip, waiting to be swallowed. Granite Man sat right next to him. Cozy.

"Bronwyn and I would like you to answer some questions, Mr. Bolitar," Susan Lex said.

"Could you move a little closer?"

She smiled. "I think not."

"I showered."

She ignored the remark. "I understand that you occasionally do some investigative work," Susan Lex said.

Myron did not reply.

"Is that correct?"

"Depends on what you mean by investigative work."

"I'll take that as a yes," Susan Lex said.

Myron gave her a suit-yourself shrug.

"Is that why you're searching for our brother?" she asked.

"I already told you why I was searching for him."

"That bit about him being a bone marrow donor?"

"It's not a bit."

"Please, Mr. Bolitar," Susan Lex said with that rich-people air. "We both know that's a lie."

Myron started to rise. Granite Man put a hand on Myron's knee. It felt like a cinder block. Granite Man shook his head. Myron stayed where he was. "It's not a lie," he said.

"We're wasting time," Susan Lex said. She flicked her eyes at Granite Man. "Show him the pictures, Grover."

Myron turned to him. "Grover is the name of my very favorite *Sesame Street* character. I want you to know that."

"We've been following you, *Myron*." Granite Man handed him a pile of photographs. Myron looked at them. They were eight-by-tens of him at the condo with Stan Gibbs. The first one showed him knocking on the door.

The second one showed Stan sticking his head out. The third one showed them both heading inside the condo.

"Well?"

Myron frowned. "I have no knack for accessorizing."

"We know that you're working for Stan Gibbs," Susan Lex said.

"Doing what exactly?" Myron asked.

"Investigating. As I stated earlier. So now that we understand your true motive, tell me how much it will cost for you to go away."

"I don't know what you're talking about."

"Simply put, how much will it cost to have you cease and desist?" Susan Lex asked. "Or are you going to force us to destroy you too?"

Too?

Brain click.

Myron turned his attention to the silent brother. "Let me ask you something, Bronwyn," he said. "You and Dennis were both going to nursery school. You both disappeared. Two weeks later, only you came back. How come? What happened to your brother?"

Bronwyn's mouth opened and closed, marionette style. He looked to his sister for help.

"It's like he disappeared off the face of the earth after that," Myron went on. "For thirty years, he's totally off the radar. But now, well, it's like he's come back for some reason. He changed his name, opened a small checking account, donated blood to a bone marrow center. So what gives, Bron? You got a clue?"

Bronwyn said, "That simply cannot be!"

His sister silenced him with a look. But Myron felt something in the air. He mulled the feeling over and another thought hit him: Maybe the Lex siblings didn't know the answer themselves. Maybe they were looking for Dennis too.

It was while he was lost in that thought that Granite Man punched him deep in the stomach. The fist followed through to the point where it seemed the knuckles must have reached the fabric of the couch. Myron snapped closed at the waist. He dropped to the floor, struggled to regain a breath, suffocating from within. He lowered his head to his knees, consumed with one thought: air. He needed air.

Susan Lex's voice boomed in his ears. "Stan Gibbs knows the truth. His father is a disgusting liar. His accusations are totally without merit. But I'll defend my family, Mr. Bolitar. You tell Mr. Gibbs he has not yet begun to suffer. What has happened to him so far is nothing compared to what I will do to him—and you—if he doesn't stop. Do you understand?"

Air. Gulps of air. Myron managed not to throw up. He took his time, looked up, met her eye. "Not even a little," he said.

Susan Lex looked at Grover. "Then make him."

With that, she left the room. Her brother took one last look and followed.

Myron gathered his breath a hitch at a time. "Nice sucker punch, Grover," he said.

Grover shrugged. "I went easy on you."

"Next time, go easy when I'm looking, tough guy."

"Won't change the outcome."

"We'll see." Myron sat up. "So what the hell is she talking about?"

"I thought Ms. Lex made herself very clear," he said. "But because you appear to be a little vacant between the ears, I'll restate her position. She doesn't like people interfering with her affairs. Stan Gibbs, for example, interfered. You can see what happened to him. You interfered. You're about to see what's going to happen to you."

Myron struggled to his feet. The blue-blazers stayed by the door. Granite Man started cracking his knuckles again. "Listen closely, please," he said. "I'm going to break your leg. Then you're going to limp your sorry ass out of here and tell Gibbs that if he sniffs around again, I will exterminate you both. Any questions?"

"Just one," Myron said. "Don't you think leg breaking is a tad cliché?"

Grover smiled. "Not the way I do it."

Myron looked around the room.

"Nowhere to run, my friend."

"Who wants to run?" Myron countered.

Without warning, he grabbed the heavy bowel-movement statue. The blue-blazers drew their guns. Granite Man ducked. But Myron wasn't going for them. He heaved the statue, straightened his arms, spun around like a discus thrower, and hurled it marble-base-forward at the plate-glass window. The window exploded.

And that was when the gunfire began.

"Hit the deck!" Myron shouted.

The blue-blazers obeyed. Myron dove. The bullets continued. Sniper fire. One took out the overhead light. One hit the lamp.

Gotta love that Win.

"You want to live," Myron shouted, "stay down."

The bullets stopped. One of the blue-blazers started rising. A bullet sang out, nearly parting the man's hair. The blazer dropped back down, flattening himself into a bearskin rug.

"I'm getting up now," Myron said. "And I'm leaving. I'd advise you guys to stay down. And, Grover?"

"What?"

"Radio downstairs. Tell them not to stop me. I can't be certain but I'm pretty sure my friend will lob in grenades if I'm unduly delayed."

Granite Man made the call. No one moved. Myron stood up. He almost whistled as he walked out.

26

It was midnight when Myron knocked on the door of Stan Gibbs's condo.

"Let's take a walk," Myron said to him.

Stan threw down his cigarette, smothered it with his toe. "A drive might be better," he countered. "The feds use long-range amplifiers."

They got into Myron's Ford Taurus, aka the Chick Trawler. Stan Gibbs flicked on the radio and started playing with the stations. Commercial for Heineken. Does anyone really care that it's imported by Van Munchin and Company?

"Are you wearing a wire, Myron?"

"No."

"But the FBI spoke to you," Stan said. "After you left."

"How did you know?"

"They're watching me," he said with a shrug. "It would only be logical to assume they questioned you."

"Tell me about your connection with Dennis Lex," Myron said.

"I already told you. I don't have one."

"A big guy named Grover picked me up tonight. He and Susan Lex gave me a very stern warning not to play with you anymore. Bronwyn was there too."

Stan Gibbs closed his eyes and rubbed them. "They knew about your visit here."

"Had eight-by-ten glossies."

"And they concluded that you're working for me."

"Bingo."

Stan shook his head. "Get out of this, Myron. You don't want to mess with these people."

"Is that advice you wished someone had given you earlier?"

His smile had nothing behind it. Exhaustion came off him like heat squiggles on a hot sidewalk. "You have no idea," he said.

"Tell me about it."

"No."

"I can help," Myron said.

"Against the Lexes? They're too powerful."

"And being powerful, you wanted to do a story on them, right?"

He said nothing.

"And they didn't like that. In fact, they took exception."

More nothing.

"You started digging where they didn't want you to. You learned that there was another brother named Dennis."

"Yes."

"And that really pissed them off."

Stan started biting a hangnail.

"Come on, Stan. Don't make me drag this out of you."

"You've pretty much got it."

"Then tell me."

"I wanted to do a story on them. An exposé, really. I even had a publisher all lined up for a book deal. But then the Lexes got wind of it. They warned me to stay away. A big man came to my apartment. I didn't catch his name. Looked like Sergeant Rock."

"That would be Grover."

"He told me that I could stop or I could be destroyed."

"And that only made you more curious."

"I guess."

"So you found out about Dennis Lex."

"Just that he existed. And that he vanished into thin air when he was a young child." Stan turned to him. Myron slowed the car and felt something creep along the top of his scalp.

"Like the Sow the Seeds victims," Myron finished.

"No."

"Why not?"

"It's different."

"How?" Myron asked.

"This is going to sound silly," Stan said, "but the family doesn't have that same sense of terror that the other families have."

"The rich are good with façades."

"It's more than that," Stan said. "I can't put my finger on it exactly. But I'm sure Susan and Bronwyn Lex know what happened to their brother."

"But they want to keep it a secret."

"Yes."

"Do you have a guess why?"

"No," Stan said.

Myron glanced back. The feds were following at a discreet enough distance.

"Do you think Susan Lex is responsible for that novel surfacing?"

"The thought has crossed my mind."

"But you never looked into it?"

"I started to. After the scandal hit. But I got a call from the big guy. He told me that it was just the beginning. That he was just flicking his finger and next time he would crush me between both palms."

"He can be a poetic fellow," Myron said.

"Yes."

"But I still don't get something."

"What?"

"You don't scare easily. When they warned you away the first time, you ignored it. After what they did to you, I'd have thought you'd fight back even harder."

"You're forgetting something," Stan said.

"What?"

"Melina Garston."

Silence.

"Think about it," Stan said. "My mistress, the only person who can back up my meeting with the Sow the Seeds kidnapper, ends up dead."

"Her father claims she retracted that."

"Oh, right. In some bizarre before-death confession."

"You think the Lexes arranged that too?"

"Why not? Look at what happened here. Who's the lead suspect in Melina's murder? I am, right? That's what the feds told you. They think I killed her. We know that the Lexes have enough juice to dig up this novel I supposedly plagiarized. Who knows what else they can do?"

"You think they could frame you for the murder?"

"At the very least."

"Are you saying they killed Melina Garston?"

"Maybe. Or it could have been the Sow the Seeds kidnapper. I don't know."

"But you think Melina was a warning."

"She was definitely a warning," Stan Gibbs said. "I just don't know who sent it."

On the radio, Stevie sang out about a landslide coming down. Oh yeah.

"You're leaving something out, Stan."

Stan kept his eyes forward. "What's that?"

"There's a personal connection here," Myron said.

"What do you mean?"

"Susan Lex mentioned your father. She said he was a liar."

Stan shrugged. "She might be right."

"What does he have to do with this?"

"Take me back."

"Don't hold back on me now."

"What do you really want here, Myron?"

"Excuse me?"

"What's your interest here?"

"I told you."

"That boy who needs a bone marrow transplant?"

"He's thirteen years old, Stan. He'll die without it."

"And what if I don't believe you? I did a little research of my own. You used to do government work."

"A long time ago."

"And maybe now you're helping the FBI. Or even the Lex family."

"No."

"I can't take that chance."

"Why not? You're telling me the truth, right? The truth can't hurt you."

He snorted. "You really believe that?"

"Why did Susan Lex mention your father?"

Nothing.

"Where is your father?" Myron said.

"That's just it."

"What?"

Stan looked at him. "He vanished. Eight years ago."

Vanished. That word again.

"I know what you're thinking and you're wrong. My father wasn't a well man. He had been in and out of institutions all his life. We've always assumed he ran off."

"But you never heard from him."

"That's right."

"Dennis Lex vanishes. Your father vanishes—"

"More than twenty years apart," Stan interjected. "It's not connected."

"So I still don't get it," Myron said. "What does your father or his disappearance have to do with the Lexes?"

"They think he's the reason I wanted to do the story. But they're wrong."

"Why would they think that?"

"My father was a student of Raymond Lex's. Before *Midnight Confessions* came out."

"So?"

"So my father claimed the novel was his. He said that Raymond Lex stole it from him."

"Jesus Christ."

"No one believed him," Stan added quickly. "Like I said, he wasn't right in the head."

"Yet you suddenly decided to investigate the family?"

"Yes."

"And you're telling me that's just a coincidence? That your own investigation had nothing to do with your father's accusations?"

Stan leaned his head against the car window like a little kid longing for home. "No one believed my father. That includes me. He was a sick man. Delusional even."

"So?"

"So at the end of the day, he was still my father," Stan said. "Maybe I owed it to him to at least give him the benefit of the doubt."

"Do you think Raymond Lex plagiarized your father?"

"No."

"Do you think your father is still alive?"

"I don't know."

"There has to be a connection here," Myron said. "Your story, the Lex family, your father's accusations—"

Stan closed his eyes. "No more."

Myron switched tracks. "How did the Sow the Seeds kidnapper get in touch with you?"

"I never reveal sources."

"Come on, Stan."

"No," he said firmly. "I may have lost a lot. But not that part of me. You know I can't say anything about my sources."

"You know who it is, don't you?"

"Take me home, Myron."

"Is it Dennis Lex—or did the same kidnapper take Dennis Lex?"

Stan crossed his arms. "Home," he said.

His face closed down. Myron saw it. There would be no more give tonight. He took a right and started heading back. Neither man spoke again until Myron stopped the car in the front of the condominium.

"Are you telling the truth, Myron? About the bone marrow donor?"

"Yes."

"This boy is someone close to you?"

Myron kept both hands on the wheel. "Yes."

"So there's no way you'll walk away from this?"

"None."

Stan nodded, mostly to himself. "I'll do what I can. But you have to trust me."

"What do you mean?"

"Give me a few days."

"To do what?"

"You won't hear from me for a little while. Don't let that shake your faith."

"What are you talking about?"

"You do what you have to," he said. "I'll do the same."

Stan Gibbs stepped out of the car and disappeared into the night.

27

Greg Downing woke Myron early the next morning with a phone call. "Nathan Mostoni left town," he said. "So I came back to New York. I get to pick up my son this afternoon."

Goody-goody for you, Myron thought. But he kept his tongue still.

"I'm going to the Ninety-second Street Y to shoot around," Greg said. "You want to come?"

"No," Myron said.

"Come anyway. Ten o'clock."

"I'll be late." Myron hung up and rolled out of bed. He checked his e-mail and found a JPEG image from Esperanza's contact at AgeComp. He clicked the file and an image slowly appeared on the screen. The possible face of Dennis Lex as a man in his mid to late thirties. Weird. Myron looked at the picture. Not familiar. Not familiar at all. Remarkable work, these age-enhanced images. So lifelike. Except in the eyes. The eyes always looked like the eyes of the dead.

He clicked on the print icon and heard his Hewlett-Packard go to work. Myron checked the clock on the bottom right-hand corner of the screen. Still early in the morning, but he didn't want to wait.

He called Melina Garston's father.

George Garston agreed to meet Myron at his penthouse at Fifth Avenue and Seventy-eighth Street, overlooking Central Park. A dark-haired woman answered the door. She introduced herself as Sandra and led him silently down the corridor. Myron looked out a window. He could see the Gothic outline of the Dakota all the way across the park. He remembered reading somewhere how Woody and Mia would wave towels from their respective apartments on either side of Central Park. Happier days, no doubt.

"I don't understand what you have to do with my daughter," George Garston said to him. Garston wore a collared blue shirt nicely offset by a shock of white neck- to-chest hairs sprouting out like a troll doll's. His bald head was an almost perfect sphere jammed between two boulder-excuses for shoulders. He had the proud, burly build of a successful immigrant, but you could see that he'd taken a hit. There was a slump there now, the stoop of the eternally grieving. Myron had seen it before. Grief like his breaks your back. You go on, but you always stoop. You smile, but it never really reaches the eyes.

"Probably nothing," Myron said. "I'm trying to find someone. He may be connected to your daughter's murder. I don't know."

The study was too-dark cherry-wood with drawn curtains and one lamp giving off a faint yellow glow. George Garston turned to the side, staring at the rich paisley wallpaper, showing Myron his profile. "We've worked together once," he said. "Not us personally. Our companies. Did you know that?"

"Yes," Myron said.

George Garston had made his fortune with a chain of Greek quasi-restaurants, the kind that work best as mall stands in crowded food courts. The chain was called Achilles Meals. For real. Myron had a Greek hockey player who endorsed the chain regionally, in the upper Midwest.

"So a sports agent is interested in my daughter's murder," Garston said.

"It's a long story."

"The police aren't talking. But they think it's her boyfriend. This reporter. Do you agree?"

"I don't know. What do you think?"

He made a scoffing noise. Myron could barely see his face anymore. "What do I think?" he said. "You sound like one of those grief counselors."

"Didn't mean to."

"Spewing all that sensitivity garbage. They're just trying to distract you from reality. They say they want you to face it. But really, it's the opposite. They want you to dig so far into yourself you won't be able to see how terrible your life is now." He grunted and shifted in his chair. "I don't have an opinion on Stan Gibbs. I never met him."

"Did you know he and your daughter were dating?"

In the dark, Myron saw the big head silently go back and forth. "She told me she had a boyfriend," he said. "She didn't tell me his name. Or that he was married."

"You wouldn't have approved?"

"Of course I wouldn't have approved," he said, trying to sound snappish, but he was beyond petty indignation. "Would you approve if it was your daughter?"

"I guess not. So you knew nothing about her relationship with Stan Gibbs?"

"Nothing."

"I understand that you spoke to her not long before she died."

"Four days before."

"Can you tell me about the conversation?"

"Melina had been drinking," he said in that pure monotone you get when the words have been ricocheting around your brain too long. "A lot. She drank too much, my daughter. Got that from her papa—who got it from his papa. The Garston family legacy." He made a chuckling sound that sounded far closer to a sob than anything in the neighborhood of a laugh.

"Melina talked to you about her testimony?"

"Yes."

"Could you tell me what she said exactly?"

" 'I made a mistake, Papa.' That's what she said. She said that she lied."

"What did you say?"

"I didn't even know what she was talking about. It's as I told you before—I didn't know about this boyfriend."

"Did you ask her to explain?"

"Yes."

"And?"

"And she didn't. She said to forget about it. She said she'd take care of it. Then she told me she loved me and hung up."

Silence.

"I had two children, Mr. Bolitar. Did you know that?"

Myron shook his head.

"A plane crash killed my Michael three years ago. Now an animal has tortured and killed my girl. My wife, her name was Melina too, passed away fifteen years ago. There is no one. Forty-eight years ago, I thought I came to this country with nothing. I made a lot of money. And now I truly have nothing. You understand?"

"Yes," Myron said.

"Is that all, then?"

"Your daughter had an apartment on Broadway."

"Yes."

"Are her personal belongings still there?"

"Sandra—that's my daughter-in-law—she's been packing her things. But it's all still there. Why?"

"I'd like to go through them, if it's okay with you."

"The police already did that."

"I know."

"You think you might find something they didn't?"

"I'm almost positive I won't."

"But?"

"But I'm attacking this thing from a different perspective. It gives me a fresh set of eyes."

George Garston flicked on his desk lamp. The yellow from the bulb painted his face a dark jaundice. Myron could see that his eyes were too dry, brittle like fallen acorns in the sun. "If you find whoever killed my Melina, you will tell me first."

"No," Myron said.

"Do you know what he did to her?"

"Yes. And I know what you want to do. But it won't make you feel any better."

"You say this like you know it for a fact."

Myron kept silent.

George Garston flicked off the light and turned away. "Sandra will take you over now."

"He sits in that study all day," Sandra Garston told him, pressing the elevator button. "He won't go out anymore."

"It's still new," Myron said.

She shook her head. Her blue-black hair fell in big, loose curls, like thermal fax paper fresh out of the machine. But despite the hair color, her overall effect was almost Icelandic, the face and build of a world-class speed skater. Her features were sharp and ended rather abruptly. Her skin had the red of raw cold.

"He thinks he has no one," she said.

"He has you."

"I'm a daughter-in-law. He sees me and it's like a tether to Michael. I don't have the heart to tell him I finally started dating."

When they reached the street, Myron asked, "Were you and Melina close?"

"I think so, yes."

"Did you know about her relationship with Stan Gibbs?"

"Yes."

"But she never told her father."

"Oh, she would never. Papa didn't approve of most men. A married one would have sent him off the ledge."

They crossed the street and into the mid-city wonder known as Central Park. The park was packed on this rather spectacular day. Asian sketch artists hustled business. Men jogged by in those shorts that look suspiciously like diapers. Sunbathers lazed around on the grass, crowded together yet totally alone. New York City is like that. E. B. White once said that New York bestows the gift of loneliness and the gift of privacy. Damn straight. It was like everyone was plugged into their own internal Walkman, each playing a different tune, bopping obliviously to his or her own beat.

A yah-dude with a bandanna around his head tossed a Frisbee and yelled "Fetch," but he had no dog. Hard-bodied women skated by in black jogging bras. Lots of men with various builds had their shirts off. Examples: A guy thick with flab that looked like wet Play-Doh jiggled past him. Behind him, a well-built guy skidded to a stop and arrogantly flexed a bicep. Actually flexed. In public. Myron frowned. He didn't know which was worse: guys who shouldn't take their shirts off and do, or guys who should take their shirts off and do.

When they reached Central Park West, Myron asked, "Did you have a problem with her dating a married man?"

Sandra shrugged. "I worried, of course. But he told Melina he would leave his wife."

"Don't they all?"

"Melina believed it. She seemed happy."

"Did you ever meet Stan Gibbs?"

"No. Their relationship was supposed to be a secret."

"Did she ever tell you about lying in court?"

"No," she said. "Never."

Sandra used her key and swung the door open. Myron stepped inside. Colors. Lots of them. Happy colors. The apartment looked like the Magical Mystery Tour meets the Teletubbies, all bright hues, especially greens, with hazy psychedelic splashes. The walls were covered with vivid watercolors of distant lands and ocean voyages. Some surreal stuff too. The effect was like an Enya video.

"I started throwing her stuff in boxes," Sandra said. "But it's hard to pack up a life."

Myron nodded. He started walking around the small apartment, hoping for a psychic revelation or something. None came. He ran his eyes over the artwork.

"She was supposed to have her first show in the Village next month," Sandra said.

Myron studied a painting with white domes and crystal blue water. He recognized the spot in Mykonos. It was wonderfully done. Myron could almost smell the salt of the Mediterranean, taste the grilled fish along the beach, feel the night sand clinging to a lover's skin. No clue here, but he stared another minute or two before turning away.

He started going through the boxes. He found a high school yearbook, class of 1986, and flipped through it until he found Melina's picture. She'd like to paint, it said. He glanced again at the walls. So bright and optimistic, her work. Death, Myron knew, was always ironic. Young death most ironic of all.

He turned his attention back to her photograph. Melina was looking off to the side with the hesitant, unsure smile of high school. Myron knew it well. Don't we all. He closed the book and headed to her closets. Her clothes were neatly arranged, lots of sweaters folded on the top shelf, shoes lined up like tiny soldiers. He moved back to the boxes and found her photographs in a shoebox. A shoebox of all things. Myron shook his head and started going through them. Sandra sat on the floor next to him. "That's her mother," she said.

Myron looked at the photograph of two women, clearly mother and daughter, embracing. There was no sign of the unsure smile this time. This smile—the smile in her mother's arms—soared like an angel's song. Myron stared at the angel-song smile and imagined that celestial mouth crying out in hopeless agony. He thought about George Garston alone in that jaundice-lit study. And he understood.

Myron checked his watch. Time to pick up the pace. He thumbed through pictures of her father, her brother, Sandra, family outings, the norm. No pictures of Stan Gibbs. Nothing helpful.

He found makeup and perfume in another box. In another, he stumbled across a diary, but Melina hadn't written anything in it for two years. He paged through it, but it felt like too much of an unnecessary violation. He found a love letter from an old boyfriend. He found some receipts.

He found copies of Stan's columns.

Hmm.

In her address book. All the columns. There were no markings on them. Just the clippings themselves, held together by a paper clip. So what did that mean? He checked them again. Just clippings. He put them aside and did some more flipping. Something fell out near the back. Myron picked up a piece of cream-colored or aged-white paper torn along the left edge, more a card really, folded in half. The outside was totally blank. He opened it. On the upper half, the words *With Love, Dad* had been written in script. Myron thought again about George Garston sitting alone in that room and felt a deep burn flush his skin.

He sat on the couch now and tried again to conjure up something. That might sound weird—sitting in this too empty room, the sweet smell of a dead woman still hovering, feeling not unlike that tiny old lady in the *Poltergeist* movies—but you never knew. The victims didn't speak to him or anything like that. But sometimes he could imagine what they'd been thinking and feeling and some spark would hit the edges and start to flame. So he tried it again.

Nothing.

He let his eyes wander across the canvases and the burn under his skin started up again. He scanned the bright colors, let them assault him. The brightness should have protected her. Nonsense, but there you have it. She'd had a life. Melina worked and she painted and she loved bright colors and had too many sweaters and stored her precious memories in a shoebox and someone had snuffed that life away because none of that meant anything to him. None of that was important. It made Myron mad.

He closed his eyes and tried to turn the anger down a notch. Anger wasn't good. It clouded reason. He'd let that side of him out before—his Batman complex, as Esperanza had called it—but being a hero seeking justice or vengeance (if they weren't the same thing) was unwise, unhealthy. Eventually you saw things you didn't want to. You learned truths you never should have. It stings and then it deadens. Better to stay away.

But the heat in his blood would not leave him. So he stopped fighting it, let the heat soothe him, relax his muscles, settle gently over him. Maybe the heat wasn't such a bad thing. Maybe the horrors he'd seen and the truths he'd learned hadn't changed him, hadn't deadened him, after all.

Myron closed the boxes, took one last, lingering look at the sunkissed isle of Mykonos, and made a silent vow.

28

Greg and Myron met up on the court. Myron strapped on his knee brace. Greg averted his eyes. The two men shot for half an hour, barely speaking, lost in the pure strokes. People ducked in and pointed at Greg. Several kids came up to him and asked him for autographs. Greg acquiesced, glancing at Myron as he took pen in hand, clearly uncomfortable getting all this attention in front of the man whose career he had ended.

Myron stared back at him, offering no solace.

After some time, Myron said, "There a reason you wanted me here, Greg?"

Greg kept shooting.

"Because I have to get back to the office," Myron said.

Greg grabbed the ball, dribbled twice, took a turn-around jumper. "I saw you and Emily that night. You know that?"

"I know that," Myron said.

Greg grabbed the rebound, took a lazy hook, let the ball hit the floor and slowly bounce toward Myron. "We were getting married the next day. You know that?"

"Know that too."

"And there you were," Greg said, "her old boyfriend, screwing her brains out."

Myron picked up the ball.

"I'm trying to explain here," Greg said.

"I slept with Emily," Myron said. "You saw us. You wanted revenge. You told Big Burt Wesson to hurt me during a preseason game. He did. End of story."

"I wanted him to hurt you, yes. I didn't mean for him to end your career."

"You say tomato, I say tomahto."

"It wasn't intentional."

"Don't take this the wrong way," Myron said in a voice that sounded awfully calm in his own ears, "but I don't give two shits about your intentions. You fired a weapon at me. You might have aimed for a flesh wound, but that didn't happen. You think that makes you blameless?"

"You fucked my fiancée."

"And she fucked me. I didn't owe you anything. She did."

"Are you telling me you don't understand?"

"I understand. It just doesn't absolve you."

"I'm not looking for absolution."

"Then what do you want, Greg? You want us to clasp hands and sing

'Kumbaya'? Do you know what you did to me? Do you know what the one moment cost me?"

"I think maybe I do," Greg said. He swallowed, put out a pleading hand as though he wanted to explain more, and then he let the hand drop to the side. "I'm so sorry."

Myron started shooting but he felt his throat swell.

"You don't know how sorry I am."

Myron said nothing. Greg tried to wait him out. It didn't work.

"What else do you want me to say here, Myron?"

Myron kept shooting.

"How do I tell you I'm sorry?"

"You've already done it," Myron said.

"But you won't accept it."

"No, Greg. I won't. I live without playing pro ball. You live without my accepting your apology. Pretty good deal for you, you ask me."

Myron's cell phone rang. He ran over, picked it up, said hello.

A whisper asked, "Did you do as I instructed?"

His bones turned to solid ice. He swallowed away something thick and said, "As you instructed?"

"The boy," the voice whispered.

The stale air pressed against him, weighed down his lungs. "What about him?"

"Did you say one last good-bye?"

Something inside of Myron withered up and blew away. His knees buckled as the realization seeped into his chest. And the voice came on again:

"Did you say one last good-bye to the boy?"

29

Myron snapped his head toward Greg. "Where's Jeremy?"

"What?"

"Where is he?"

Greg saw whatever it was on Myron's face and dropped the basketball. "He's with Emily, I guess. I don't get him until noon."

"Got a cell phone?"

"Yes."

"Call her."

Greg was already heading toward his gym bag, the athlete with the wonderful reflexes. "What's going on?"

"Probably nothing."

Myron explained about the call. Greg did not slow down to listen. He dialed. Myron started running toward his car. Greg followed, the phone pressed against his ear.

"No answer," Greg said. He left a message on the machine.

"Does she have a cell phone?"

"If she does, I don't have the number."

Myron hit a stored number as they walked. Esperanza picked up.

"I need Emily's cell phone number."

"Give me five," Esperanza said.

Myron hit another stored number. Win answered and said, "Articulate."

"Possible trouble."

"I'm here."

They reached the car. Greg was calm. That surprised Myron. On the court, when the pressure mounted, Greg's modus operandi was to get freaky, start screaming, psych himself into a frenzy. But of course, this was not a game. As his father had recently told him, when real bombs drop, you never know how someone will react.

Myron's phone rang. Esperanza gave him Emily's cell phone number. Myron dialed it. After six rings, Emily's voice mail picked up. Damn. Myron left a message. He turned to Greg.

"Any clue where Jeremy might be?" Myron asked.

"No," Greg said.

"How about a neighbor we can call? Or a friend?"

"When Emily and I were married, we lived in Ridgewood. I don't know the neighbors in Franklin Lakes."

Myron gripped the steering wheel. He hit the accelerator. "Jeremy's probably safe," Myron said, trying to believe it. "I don't even know how this guy would know his name. It's probably a bluff."

Greg started shaking.

"He'll be all right."

"Jesus, Myron, I read those articles. If that guy has my kid . . ."

"We should call the FBI," Myron said. "Just in case."

"You think that's the way to go?" Greg asked.

Myron looked at him. "Why? You don't?"

"I just want to pay the ransom and get my boy back. I don't want anybody screwing it up."

"I think we should call," Myron said. "But it's your decision."

"There's something else we have to consider," Greg said.

"What?"

"There's a good chance this wacko is our donor, right?"

"Yes."

"If the FBI kills him, it's over for Jeremy."

"First things first," Myron said. "We have to find Jeremy. And we have to find this kidnapper."

Greg kept shaking.

"What do you want to do, Greg?"

"You think we should call?"

"Yes."

Greg nodded slowly. "Call," he said.

Myron dialed Kimberly Green's number. He felt waves pounding in his head, the blood flowing to his ears. He tried not to think about Jeremy's face, what his smile had looked like when he opened that door.

Did you say one last good-bye to the boy?

A voice said, "Federal Bureau of Investigation."

"Myron Bolitar calling Kimberly Green."

"Special Agent Green is unavailable."

"The Sow the Seeds kidnapper may have taken somebody else. Put her on."

The hold was longer than Myron expected.

Kimberly Green started with a bark. "What the hell are you ranting about?"

"He just called me." Myron filled her in.

"We're on our way," she said.

They hit a patch of traffic where Route 4 met Route 17, but Myron went up on the grass and knocked over several orange construction buckets. He broke off at Route 208 and exited near the synagogue. Two miles later, they made the final turn onto Emily's street. Myron could see two FBI cars making the turn at the same time.

Greg, who had gone into something of a trance, woke up and pointed. "There she is."

Emily was putting her key in the front door. Myron started honking madly. She looked back confused. He turned the car and skidded. The FBI car followed. Myron and Greg were both out the door almost before the car had stopped.

"Where's Jeremy?" they both said in unison.

Emily had her head tilted to the side. "What?" she called back. "What's going on here?"

Greg took it. "Where is he, Emily?"

"He's with a friend—"

From inside the house, the phone started ringing. Everyone froze. Emily snapped out of it first. She ran inside and picked up the phone. She put the phone to her ear, cleared her throat, and said, "Hello."

Through the receiver, they could all hear Jeremy's scream.

30

There were six federal agents in all. Kimberly Green was the task force leader. They set up with quiet efficiency. Myron sat on one couch, Greg the other. Emily paced between them. There was probably something symbolic in that, but Myron was not sure what. He tried to push himself past the numb so he could get to a place where he could do some good.

The phone call had been brief. After the scream, the whispery voice had said, "We'll call back." That was it. No warnings not to contact the authorities. No telling them to prepare funds. No setting up another time to call. Nothing.

They all sat there, the boy's scream still echoing, mauling, shredding, conjuring up images of what could have made a thirteen-year-old boy scream like that. Myron shut his eyes and pushed hard. That was what the bastard wanted. Unwise to play into that.

Greg had contacted his bank. He was not a risky investor, and so most of his assets were liquid. If ransom money was needed, he'd be ready. The various feds, all male except for Kimberly Green, put traces on all the possible phones, including Myron's. She and her men were doing a lot of sotto voce. Myron hadn't pressed them yet. But that wasn't going to last.

Kimberly caught his eyes and waved him over. He stood and excused himself. Greg and Emily paid no attention, still lost in the vortex of that scream.

"We need to talk," she said.

"Okay," Myron said. "Start by telling me what happened when you checked out Dennis Lex."

"You're not family," she said. "I could throw you out."

"This isn't your house," he said. "What happened with Dennis Lex?"

She put her hands on her hips. "It's a dead end."

"How so?"

"We traced it down. He's not involved in any of this."

"How do you know that?"

"Myron, come on. We're not stupid."

"So where is Dennis Lex?"

"It's not relevant," she said.

"The hell it's not. Even if he's not the kidnapper, we still have him as the bone marrow donor."

"No," she said. "Your donor is Davis Taylor."

"Who changed his name from Dennis Lex."

"We don't know that."

Myron made a face. "What are you talking about?"

"Davis Taylor was an employee in the Lex conglomerate."

"What?"

"You heard me."

"So why did he donate blood for a bone marrow drive?"

"It was a work thing," she said. "The plant boss had a sick nephew. Everyone at the plant gave."

Myron nodded. Something finally made sense. "So if he didn't give a blood sample," he said, "it would have been conspicuous."

"Right."

"You got a description on him?"

"He worked on his own, kept to himself. All anyone remembers is a man with a full beard, glasses, and long blond hair."

"A disguise," Myron said. "And we know Davis Taylor's original name was Dennis Lex. What else?"

Kimberly Green raised her hand. "Enough." She sort of hitched herself up, trying to alter momentum. "Stan Gibbs is still our top suspect here. What did you talk about last night?"

"Dennis Lex," Myron said. "Don't you get it?"

"Get what?"

"Dennis Lex is connected into all this. He's either the kidnapper, or maybe he was the first victim."

"Neither," she said.

"Then where is he?"

She shook it off. "What else did you two talk about?"

"Stan's father."

"Edwin Gibbs?" That got her attention. "What about him?"

"That he vanished eight years ago. But you already know about that, don't you?"

She nodded a little too firmly. "We do," she said.

"So what do you think happened to him?" Myron asked.

She hesitated. "You believe that Dennis Lex may be Sow the Seeds' first victim, correct?"

"I think it's something to look into, yes."

"Our theory," she went on, "is that the first victim may have been Edwin Gibbs."

Myron made a face. "You think Stan kidnapped his own father?"

"Killed him. And the others. We don't believe any of them are still alive."

Myron tried not to let that sink in. "You have any evidence or motive?"

"Sometimes the apple doesn't fall far from the tree."

"Oh, that'll go over big with a jury. Ladies and gentlemen, the apple doesn't fall far from the tree. And you should never put the cart before the horse. Plus every dog has his day." He shook his head. "Are you listening to yourself?"

"On its own, I admit it doesn't make sense. But put it all together. Eight years ago, Stan was starting out on his own. He was twenty-four, his father forty-six. By all accounts, the two men did not get along. Suddenly Edwin Gibbs vanishes. Stan never reports it."

"This is silly."

"Maybe. But then add back everything else we already know. The only columnist to get this scoop. The plagiarism. Melina Garston. Everything that Eric Ford discussed with you yesterday."

"It still doesn't add up."

"Then tell me where Stan Gibbs is."

Myron looked at her. "Isn't he at the condo?"

"Last night, after you two talked, Stan Gibbs slipped surveillance. He's done that before. We usually pick him up a few hours later. But that hasn't happened this time. He's suddenly out of sight—and by coincidence, Jeremy Downing has been snatched by the Sow the Seeds kidnapper. You want to explain that one to me?"

Myron's mouth felt dry. "You're searching for him?"

"We got an APB. But we know he's good at hiding. You got any clue where he went?"

"None."

"He said nothing to you about it?"

"He mentioned that he might go away for a few days. But that I should trust him."

"Bad advice," she said. "Anything else?"

Myron shook his head. "Where is Dennis Lex?" he tried again. "Did you see him?"

"I didn't have to," she said. But her voice had a funny monotone to it. "He's not involved in this."

"You keep saying that," Myron said. "But how do you know?"

She slowed down. "The family."

"You mean Susan and Bronwyn Lex?"

"Yes."

"What about them?"

"They gave us reassurances."

Myron almost stepped back. "You just took their word for it?"

"I didn't say that." She glanced around, let loose a sigh. "And it's not my call."

"What?"

She looked straight through him. "Eric Ford handled it personally."

Myron could not believe what he was hearing.

"He told me to stay away," she said, "that he had it covered."

"Or covered up," Myron said.

"Nothing I can do about it." She looked at him. She had stressed the word *I*. Then she walked away without another word. Myron dialed his cell phone.

"Articulate," Win said.

"We're going to need help," Myron said. "Is Zorra still working free-lance?"

"I'll call her."

"Maybe Big Cyndi too."

"Do you have a plan?"

"No time for a plan," Myron said.

"Ooo," Win said. "Then we're going to get nasty."

"Yes."

"And here I thought you weren't going to break the rules anymore."

"Just this once," Myron said.

"Ah," Win countered. "That's what they all say."

31

Win, Esperanza, Big Cyndi, and Zorra were all in his office.

Zorra wore a yellow monogrammed sweater (the monogram being one letter: Z), large white pearls à la Wilma Flintstone, a plaid skirt, and white bobby socks. Her—or if you want to be anatomically correct, his—wig looked like early Bette Midler or maybe Little Orphan Annie on methadone. Shiny red high-heel shoes like something stolen from a trampy Dorothy in Oz adorned the men's-size-twelve feet.

Zorra smiled at Myron. "Zorra is happy to see you."

"Yeah," Myron said. "And Myron is happy to see you too."

"This time, we're on the same side, yes?"

"Yes."

"Zorra pleased."

Zorra's real name was Shlomo Avrahaim, and she was a former Israeli Mossad agent. The two had had a nasty run-in not long ago. Myron still carried the wound near his rib cage—a scar-shaped Z made by a blade Zorra hid in her heel.

Win said, "The Lex Building is too well guarded."

"So we go with Plan B," Myron said.

"Already in motion," Win said.

Myron looked at Zorra. "You armed?"

Zorra pulled a weapon out from under her skirt. "The Uzi," Zorra said. "Zorra likes the Uzi."

Myron nodded. "Patriotic."

"Question," Esperanza said.

"What?"

Esperanza settled her eyes on his. "What if this guy doesn't cooperate?"

"We don't have time to worry about it," Myron said.

"Meaning?"

"This psycho has Jeremy," Myron said. "You understand that? Jeremy has to be the priority here."

Esperanza shook her head.

"Then stay behind," he said.

"You need me," she said.

"Right. And Jeremy needs *me*." He stood. "Okay, let's go."

Esperanza shook her head again, but she went along. The group—a sort of cut-rate Dirty (One-Third of a) Dozen—broke off when they reached the street. Esperanza and Zorra would walk. Win, Myron, and Big Cyndi headed into a garage three blocks away. Win had a car there. Chevy Nova.

Totally untraceable. Win had a bunch of them. He referred to them as disposable vehicles. Like paper cups or something. The rich. You don't want to know what he does with them.

Win drove, Myron took the front passenger seat, and Big Cyndi squeezed into the back, which was a little like watching a film of childbirth on rewind. Then they were off.

The Stokes, Layton and Grace law firm was one of the most prestigious in New York. Big Cyndi stayed in reception. The receptionist, a skinny skirt-suit of gray, tried not to stare. So Big Cyndi stared at her, daring her not to look. Sometimes Big Cyndi would growl. Like a lion. No reason. She just liked to do it.

Myron and Win were ushered into a conference room that looked like a million other big Manhattan law firm conference rooms. Myron doodled on a yellow legal pad that looked like a million other big Manhattan law firm legal pads, watched through the window the smug, pink, fresh-scrubbed Harvard grads stroll by, again all looking exactly the same as the ones at a million other big Manhattan law firms. Reverse discrimination maybe, but all young white male lawyers looked the same to him.

Then again, Myron was a white Harvard law school graduate. Hmm.

Chase Layton trollied in with his rolly build and well-fed face and chubby hands and gray comb-over, looking like, well, a name partner at a big Manhattan law firm. He wore a gold wedding band on one hand and a Harvard ring on the other. He greeted Win warmly—most wealthy people do—and then gave a firm, I'm-your-guy hand-shake to Myron.

"We're in a rush," Win said.

Chase Layton shoved the big smile out of the room and strapped on his best battle-ready face. Everyone sat. Chase Layton folded his hands in front of him. He leaned forward, putting a bit of a belly push on the vest buttons. "What can I do for you, Windsor?"

Rich people always called him Windsor.

"You've been after my business for a long time," Win said.

"Well, I wouldn't say—"

"I'm here to give it to you. In exchange for a favor."

Chase Layton was too smart to snap-bite at that. He looked at Myron. An underling. Maybe there'd be a clue how to play on this plebeian's face. Myron kept up the neutral. He was getting better at it. Must be from hanging around Win so much.

"We need to see Susan Lex," Win said. "You are her attorney. We'd like you to get her to come here immediately."

"Here?"

"Yes," Win said. "At your office. Immediately."

Chase opened his mouth, closed it, checked on the underling again. Still no clue. "Are you serious, Windsor?"

"You do that, you get the Lock-Horne business. You know how much income that would generate?"

"A great deal," Chase Layton said. "And yet not even a third of what we receive from the Lex family."

Win smiled. "Talk about having your cake and eating it too."

"I don't understand this," Chase said.

"It's pretty straightfoward, Chase."

"Why do you want to see Ms. Lex?"

"We can't divulge that."

"I see." Chase Layton scratched a ham-red cheek with a manicured finger. "Ms. Lex is a very private person."

"Yes, we know."

"She and I are friends."

"I'm sure," Win said.

"Perhaps I can set up an introduction."

"No good. It has to be now."

"Well, she and I usually conduct business at her office—"

"Again no good. It has to be here."

Chase rolled his neck a bit, stalling for time, trying to sort through this, find an angle to play. "She's a very busy woman. I wouldn't even know what to say to get her here."

"You're a good attorney, Chase," Win said, steepling his fingers. "I'm sure you'll come up with something."

Chase nodded, looked down, studied his manicure. "No," he said. He looked back up slowly. "I don't sell out clients, Windsor."

"Even if it meant landing a client as big as Lock-Horne?"

"Even then."

"And you're not doing this just to impress me with your discretion?"

Chase smiled, relieved, as though he finally got the joke. "No," he said. "But wouldn't that be having my cake and eating it too?" He tried to laugh it off. Win didn't join him.

"This isn't a test, Chase. I need you to get her here. I guarantee that she won't find out you helped me."

"Do you think that's all that concerns me here—how it would look?"

Win said nothing.

"If that's the case, you've misread me. The answer is still no, I'm afraid."

"Think about it," Win said.

"Nothing to think about," Chase said. He leaned back, crossing one leg over the other, making sure the crease sat right. "You didn't really think I'd go along with this, did you, Windsor?"

"I hoped."

Chase again looked at Myron, then back at Win. "I'm afraid I can't help you, gentlemen."

"Oh, you'll help us," Win said.

"Pardon me?"

"It's just a matter of what we need to do to get your cooperation."

Chase frowned. "Are you trying to bribe me?"

"No," Win said. "I already did that. By offering you our business."

"Then I don't understand—"

Myron spoke for the first time. "I'm going to make you," he said.

Chase Layton looked at Myron and smiled. Again he said, "Pardon me?"

Myron rose. He kept his expression flat, remembering what he'd learned from Win about intimidation. "I don't want to hurt you," Myron said. "But you will call Susan Lex and get her to come here. And you'll do it now."

Chase folded his arms and sat them atop his belly. "If you wish to discuss this further—"

"I don't," Myron said.

Myron walked around the table. Chase did not back away. "I will not call her," he said firmly. "Windsor, would you tell your friend to sit down?"

Win feigned a helpless shrug.

Myron stood directly over Chase. He looked back at Win. Win said, "Let me handle it."

Myron shook his head. He loomed over Chase and let his gaze fall. "One last chance."

Chase Layton's face was calm, almost amused. He probably saw this as a bizarre put-on—or perhaps he was just certain that Myron would back down. That was how it was with men like Chase Layton. Physical violence was not a part of the Layton equation. Oh, sure, those uneducated animals on the street might engage in it. They might knock him on the head for his wallet. Other people—lesser people, really—yes, they solved problems with physical violence. But that was another planet—one filled with a more primitive species. In Chase Layton's world, a world of status and position and lofty manners, you were untouchable. Men threatened. Men sued. Men cursed. Men schemed behind one another's backs. Men never engaged in face-to-face violence.

That was why Myron knew that no bluff would work here. Men like Chase Layton believed that anything remotely physical was a bluff. Myron could probably point a gun at him, and he wouldn't budge. And in that scenario, Chase Layton would be right.

But not this one.

Myron boxed Chase Layton's ears hard with his palms.

Chase's eyes widened in a way they probably never had before. Myron put his hand over the lawyer's mouth, muffling the scream. He cupped the back of the man's skull and pulled him back, knocking him off his chair and onto the floor.

Chase lay on his back. Myron looked him straight in the eye and saw a tear roll down the man's cheek. Myron felt ill. He thought about Jeremy and that helped keep his face neutral. Myron said, "Call her."

He slowly released his hand.

Chase's breathing was labored. Myron glanced at Win. Win shook his head.

"You," Chase said, spitting out the word, "are going to jail."

Myron closed his eyes, made a fist, and punched the lawyer up and under the ribs, toward the liver. The lawyer's face fell into itself. Myron held the man's mouth again, but this time there was no scream to smother.

Win eased back in his chair. "For the record, I am the sole witness to this event. I'll swear under oath that it was self-defense."

Chase looked lost.

"Call her," Myron said. He tried to keep the pleading out of his voice. He looked down at Chase Layton. Chase's shirttail was out of his pants, his tie askew, his comb-over unraveling, and Myron realized that nothing would ever be the same for this man. Chase Layton had been physically assaulted. He would always walk a little more warily now. He would sleep a little less deeply. He would always be a little different inside.

Maybe so too would Myron.

Myron punched him again. Chase made an *oof* noise. Win stood by the door. Keep your face even, Myron told himself. A man at work. A man who won't stop no matter what. Myron cocked his fist again.

Five minutes later, Chase Layton called Susan Lex.

32

'Would have been better," Win said, "if you let me hurt him."

Myron kept walking. "It would have been the same," he said.

Win shrugged. They had an hour to set up. Big Cyndi was now in the conference room with Chase Layton, supposedly going over her new professional-wrestling contract. When she entered the room, all six-six, three hundred pounds of her wearing her Big Chief Mama costume, Chase Layton barely looked up. The pain from the punches, Myron was sure, was ebbing. He had not struck the man in any place that would do lasting damage, except maybe to the obvious.

Esperanza was set up in the lobby. Myron and Win met Zorra two levels down, on the seventh floor. Zorra had staked out the lower floors and decided that this would be the quietest and easiest to contain. The office suites on the northern side were empty, Zorra noted. Anyone entering or leaving had to do so from the west. Zorra was stationed there with one cell phone. Esperanza had the other one downstairs. Win held the third. They were on a three-way line with one another. Myron and Win were in position. In the last twenty minutes, the elevator had stopped at their floor only twice. Good. Both times the door opened, Myron and Win feigned conversation, just two guys waiting for an elevator heading in the opposite direction. Real undercover commandos.

Myron hoped like hell no one happened upon the scene when it all went down. Zorra would warn them, of course, but once the operation was under way, it couldn't be stopped. They'd have to come up with some excuse, say it was a drill maybe, but Myron was not sure he could stomach hurting any more innocents today. He closed his eyes. Can't back down now. Too far gone.

Win smiled at him. "Wondering yet again if the ends justify the means?"

"Not wondering," Myron said.

"Oh?"

"I know they don't."

"And yet?"

"I'm not in the mood for introspection right now."

"But you're so good at it," Win said.

"Thanks."

"And knowing you as well as I do, you'll save it for later—for when you have more time. You'll gnash your teeth over what you just did. You'll feel ashamed, remorseful, guilty—though you'll also be oddly proud that you didn't have *moi* do your dirty work. You'll end up making a clear declaration that it will never happen again. And perhaps it won't—not, at least, until the stakes are this high."

"So I'm a hypocrite," Myron said. "Happy?"

"But that is my point," Win said.

"What?"

"You're not a hypocrite. You aim toward lofty heights. The fact that your arrow cannot always reach them does not make you a hypocrite."

"So in conclusion," Myron said, "the ends do not justify the means. Except sometimes."

Win spread his hands. "See? I just saved you hours of soul-searching. Perhaps I should consider penning one of those how-to-manage-your-time manuals."

Esperanza broke in through the phone. "They're here," she said.

Win put the phone to his ear. "How many?"

"Three coming in. Susan Lex. That granite guy Myron keeps talking about. Another bodyguard. Two more staying parked outside."

"Zorra," Win said into the phone. "Please keep an eye on the two gentlemen outside."

Zorra said, "And if they move?"

"Detain them."

"With pleasure." Zorra giggled. Win smiled. Welcome to the Psycho Hotline. Only $3.99 per minute. First call is free.

Myron and Win waited now. Two minutes past. Esperanza said, "Middle elevator. All three are inside."

"Anyone else with them?"

"No . . . wait. Damn, two businessmen are going in."

Myron closed his eyes and cursed.

Win looked at him. "Your call."

Panic squeezed Myron's chest. Innocent people in the elevator. There was sure to be violence. Witnesses now.

"Well?"

"Hold the phone." It was Esperanza. "The granite guy blocked their path. Looks like he told them to wait for another elevator."

"Top-notch security," Win said. "Good to see we're not dealing with amateurs."

"Okay," Esperanza said. "Just the three of them are inside now."

The relief in Myron's face was palpable.

Esperanza said, "Elevator closing . . . now."

Myron pressed the Up button. Win took out his forty-four. Myron pulled out a Glock. They waited. Myron kept the gun by his thigh. It felt heavy in a terrible, comforting way. Myron kept glancing down the corridor. No one. He hoped their luck would hold. He felt his pulse start to race. His mouth was dry. The room suddenly felt warmer.

A minute later, the light above the middle elevator dinged.

Win's face was in the zone, semi-euphoric. He wriggled his eyebrows and said, "Showtime."

Myron tensed his muscles, leaned in a bit. The elevator's whirring noise stopped. There was a delay and then the doors started sliding open. Win didn't wait. He was inside before the opening had reached a foot. He found Grover and stuck the gun in the big man's ear. Myron did the same with the other guard.

"Waxy ear buildup a problem, Grover?" Win said in his best voice-over. "Smith and Wesson has the solution!"

Susan Lex started to open her mouth. Win cut her off with a finger against her lip and a gentle "Shh."

Win frisked and disarmed Grover. Myron followed his lead with the second guard. Grover glared daggers at Win. Win took them on and said, "Please—no, pretty please—make a sudden move."

Grover didn't budge.

Win stepped back. The elevator door started closing. Myron stopped it with his foot. He pointed the weapon at Susan Lex. "You're coming with me," Myron said.

"Don't you want revenge first?" Grover said.

Myron looked at him.

"Go ahead." Grover spread his hands. "Hit me in the gut. Go ahead, give it your best shot."

"Pardon *moi*," Win said. "But does that offer apply to me too?"

Grover looked at the smaller man like a tasty leftover. "I heard you're not bad," he said.

Win looked back at Myron. " 'Not bad,' " he repeated. "Monsieur Grover heard I was 'not bad.' "

"Win," Myron said.

Win snapped his knee deep into Grover's groin. He followed through, driving the man's testicles all the way into his stomach. Grover did not make a sound. He simply folded like a bad hand of poker.

"Oh, wait, you said 'gut,' didn't you?" Win looked down at him, frowned. "Must work on my aim. Perhaps you're right. Perhaps I am merely 'not bad.' "

Grover was on his knees, his hands between his legs. Win kicked him in the head with his instep. Grover toppled over like a bowling pin. Win looked over at the other guard, who was putting his hands up and backing quickly into a corner.

"Will you tell your friends I was 'not bad?' " Win asked him.

The guard shook his head.

"Enough," Myron said.

Win picked up the cell phone. "Zorra, report."

"They are not moving, handsome."

"Come back up then. You can help me clean up."

"Clean up? Ooo, Zorra will hurry."

Win laughed.

"No more," Myron said. Win did not reply, but Myron hadn't really expected him to. Myron grabbed Susan Lex's arm. "Let's go."

He pulled her into the stairwell. Zorra bounded into view—on high heels no less. Leaving two unarmed men alone with Win and Zorra. Talk about scary. But he had no choice here. Myron turned to Susan Lex, keeping tight hold of her elbow.

"I need your help," he said to her.

Susan Lex looked at him, head high, not backing off.

"I promise not to say anything," he went on. "I have no interest in hurting you or your family. But you're going to take me to see Dennis."

"And if I say no?"

Myron just looked at her.

"You'd hurt me?" she said.

"I just beat up an innocent man," Myron said.

"And you'd do the same to a woman?"

"I wouldn't want to be accused of sexism."

Her expression remained defiant, but unlike Chase Layton, she seemed to understand how the real world worked. "You know what sort of power I have."

"I do."

"Then you know what I'll do to you when this is all over?"

"I don't much care. A thirteen-year-old boy has been kidnapped."

She almost smiled. "I thought you said he needed a bone marrow transplant."

"I don't have time to explain."

"My brother isn't involved in this."

"I keep hearing that."

"Because it's true."

"Then prove it to me."

Something in her face shifted then, changing her features, relaxing them into something strangely approaching tranquility. "Come," she said. "Let's go."

33

Susan Lex directed him north on the FDR to the Harlem River Drive and then north again to 684. Once they were in Connecticut, the roads grew quieter. Woods thickened. Buildings grew scarce. Traffic was pretty much nonexistent.

"We're almost there," Susan Lex said. "I'd like the truth now."

"I'm telling you the truth."

"Fine," she said. Then: "How do you plan on getting away with this?"

"With what?"

"Are you going to kill me when this is all over?"

"No."

"Then I'll come back after you. I'll press charges, if nothing else."

"I told you before. I don't much care. But I've thought of something."

"Oh?"

"Dennis will save me."

"How?"

"If he is the Sow the Seeds kidnapper—"

"He's not."

"—or somehow involved with him, then what I'm doing here will be small potatoes by comparison."

"And if he's not?"

Myron shrugged. "Either way, I'm going to learn whatever it is you want to hide. We make a deal. I never tell what I saw. In exchange, you leave me alone."

"Or I can simply kill you."

"I don't believe you'd do that."

"No?"

"You're not a killer. And even if you were, it would be too complicated. I'd leave evidence behind. I have Win covering my back. It would be too messy."

"We'll see," she said, but there was no starch there. She pointed up ahead. "Turn off up here."

She pointed to a dirt road that seemed to materialize from nowhere. There was a guardhouse fifty yards down and to the left. Myron pulled up. Susan Lex leaned over and smiled. The guard waved her through. There were no signs, no identification marks, nothing. The whole setup looked like some sort of militia compound.

After the gatehouse, the dirt road stopped and a paved one began. New pavement from the looks of it colored the dark black-gray of heavy rain. Trees crowded the sides like parade watchers. Up ahead, the road narrowed. The trees closed in too. Myron veered the car to the left and passed through wrought-iron gates guarded by two stone falcons.

"What is this?" Myron asked.

Susan Lex did not reply.

A mansion seemed to push out of the green, elbowing its way forward. The exterior was classic off-white Georgian but on an oversized scale. Palladian windows, pilasters, fancy pediments, curved balconies, brick cornering and what looked like real stone masonry were all garnished with hints of green ivy. A set of oversized double doors were dead center, the entire edifice perfectly symmetrical.

"Park in the lot over there," Susan Lex said.

Myron followed her finger. There was indeed a paved lot. Myron figured it contained close to twenty cars. Various makes. A BMW, a couple of Honda Accords, three Mercedes of different lineage, Fords, SUVs, one station wagon. Your basic American melting pot. Myron glanced back at the oversized manor. He noticed ramps now. Lots of them. He checked the cars. Several had MD license plates.

"A hospital," he said.

Susan Lex smiled. "Come along."

They headed up the brick path. Gloved gardeners were on their knees, working on the flower beds. A woman walked by in the opposite direction. She smiled politely but said nothing. They passed through an arched entranceway and into a two-story foyer. A woman seated behind the desk stood, slightly startled.

"We weren't expecting you, ma'am," she said.

"That's fine."

"I don't have security set up."

"That's fine too."

"Yes, ma'am."

Susan Lex barely broke stride. She took the sweeping staircase on her left, staying in the middle, not touching a handrail. Myron followed.

"What did she mean about security?" Myron asked.

"When I visit, they make sure the hallways are kept clear and that no one else is present."

"To keep your secret?"

"Yes," she said. She did not stop moving. "Perhaps you noticed that she called me 'ma'am.' That's part of the discretion here. They never use names."

When they reached the top level, Susan turned to the left. The corridor had raised wallpaper in a classic floral design and nothing else. No small tables, no chairs, no pictures in frames, no Oriental runners. They passed by maybe a dozen rooms, only two with doors open. Myron noticed that the doors were extra wide and he remembered his visit to Babies and Children's Hospital. Extra wide doors there too. For wheelchairs and stretchers and the like.

When they reached the end of the corridor, Susan stopped, took a deep breath, looked back at Myron. "Are you ready?"

He nodded.

She opened the door and stepped inside. Myron followed. A four-poster antique bed, like something you'd see on a tour of Jefferson's Monticello, overwhelmed the room. The walls were warm green with woodwork trim.

There was a small crystal chandelier, a burgundy Victorian couch, a Persian rug with deep scarlets. A Mozart violin concerto was playing a bit too loudly on the stereo. A woman sat in the corner reading a book. She too started upright when she saw who it was.

"It's okay," Susan Lex said. "Would you mind leaving us for a few moments?"

"Yes, ma'am," the woman said. "If you need anything—"

"I'll ring, thank you."

The woman did a semi-curtsy/semi-bow and hurried out. Myron looked at the man in the bed. The resemblance to the computer rendering was uncanny, almost perfect. Even, strangely enough, the dead eyes. Myron moved closer. Dennis Lex followed him with the dead eyes, unfocused, empty, like windows over a vacant lot.

"Mr. Lex?"

Dennis Lex just stared at him.

"He can't talk," she said.

Myron turned to her. "I don't understand," he said.

"You were right before. It's a hospital. Of sorts. In another era, I suppose one would have called it a private sanitarium."

"How long has your brother been here?"

"Thirty years," she said. She moved toward the bed, and for the first time, she looked down at her brother. "You see, Mr. Bolitar, this is where the wealthy store unpleasantness." She reached down and stroked her brother's cheek. Dennis Lex did not respond. "We're too cultured not to give our loved ones the best. All very humane and practical, don't you know."

Myron waited for her to say more. She kept stroking her brother's cheek. He tried to see her face, but she kept it lowered and away from him.

"Why is he here?" Myron asked.

"I shot him," she said.

Myron opened his mouth, closed it, did the math. "But you were only a child when he disappeared."

"Fourteen years old," she said. "Bronwyn was six." She stopped stroking the cheek. "It's an old story, Mr. Bolitar. You've probably heard it a thousand times. We were playing with a loaded gun. Bronwyn wanted to hold it, I said no, he reached for it, it went off." She said it all in one breath, staring down at her brother, still stroking the cheek. "This is the end result."

Myron looked at the still eyes in the bed. "He's been here since?"

She nodded. "For a while I kept waiting for him to die. So I could officially be a murderer."

"You were a child," Myron said. "It was an accident."

She looked at him and smiled. "My, that means so much coming from you, thank you."

Myron said nothing.

"No matter," she said. "Daddy took care of it. He arranged for my brother to have the best care. He was a very private person, my father. It was his gun. He'd left it where his children could play with it. His business and reputation were both growing. He had political aspirations at the time. He just wanted it all to go away."

"And it did."

She tilted her head back and forth. "Yes."

"What about your mother?"

"What about her?"

"What did she say?"

"My mother hated unpleasantness, Mr. Bolitar. After the incident, she never saw her son again."

Dennis Lex made a sound, a guttural scrape, nothing remotely human. Susan gently shushed him.

"Did you and Bronwyn ever get help?" Myron asked.

She cocked an eyebrow. "Help?"

"Counseling. To help you through it."

She made a face. "Oh please," she said.

Myron stood there, his mind circling nowhere over nothing.

"So now you know the truth, Mr. Bolitar."

"I guess," he said.

"Meaning?"

"I wonder why you told me all this. You could have just shown Dennis to me."

"Because you won't talk."

"How can you be so sure?"

She smiled. "After you shoot your own brother, shooting strangers becomes so easy."

"You don't really believe that."

"No, I suppose not." Susan Lex turned and faced him. "The fact is, you really don't have much to tell. As you said earlier, we both have reasons to keep our mouths shut. You'll be arrested for kidnapping and Lord knows what. The evidence of my crime—if indeed it was a crime—is nonexistent. You'd be worse off than I."

Myron nodded, but his mind still whirred. Her story might be true or just something she told him to gain sympathy, to contain the damage. Still, there was the ring of truth in her words. Maybe her reason for talking was simpler. Maybe, after all this time, she just needed someone who'd listen to her confession. Didn't matter. None of it mattered. There was nothing here. Dennis Lex was truly a dead end.

Myron looked out the window. The sun was starting to dip away. He checked his watch. Jeremy had been missing five hours now—five hours alone with a madman—and Myron's best lead, his *only* lead, was lying brain-damaged in a hospital room.

The sun was still strong, bathing the expansive garden in white. Myron saw what looked like a maze made of shrubbery. He spotted several patients in wheelchairs, legs covered with blankets, sitting by a fountain. Serene. The rays reflected off a pool of water and a statue in the middle of—

He stopped. The statue.

Myron felt the blood in his veins turn to crystal. He shaded his eyes with his hand and squinted again.

"Oh Christ," he said.

Then he sprinted toward the stairs.

34

Susan Lex's helicopter was starting to descend toward the sanitarium's landing pad when Kimberly Green called him on the cell phone.

"We've caught Stan Gibbs," she said. "But the boy wasn't with him."

"That's because he isn't the kidnapper."

"You know something I don't?"

Myron ignored the question. "Has Stan told you anything?"

"Nope. He lawyered up already. Says he won't talk to anyone but you. You, Myron. Why don't I find that particularly surprising?"

Had Myron responded, the helicopter's propeller would have drowned it out. He backed off a few steps. The copter touched down. The pilot stuck his head out and waved to him.

"I'm on my way," Myron shouted into the phone. He switched it off and turned to Susan Lex. "Thank you."

She nodded.

He ducked and ran toward the helicopter. As they rose, Myron looked back down. Susan Lex's chin was tilted up, her eyes still on him. He waved. And she waved back.

Stan was not in a holding cell because they had nothing to hold him on. He sat in a waiting room with his eyes on the table and let his attorney, Clara Steinberg, do the talking. Myron had known Clara—he called her Aunt Clara though there was no familial relationship—since he was too young to remember. Aunt Clara and Uncle Sidney were Mom and Dad's closest friends. Dad had gone to elementary school with Clara. Mom had roomed with her in law school. Aunt Clara, in fact, had set up Mom and Dad on their first date. She liked to remind Myron with a wink that "you wouldn't be here if it weren't for your aunt Clara." Then she'd wink again. Subtle, that Clara. During the holidays, she always pinched Myron's cheeks in admiration of his *punim*.

"Let me set up the ground rules, *bubbe*," she said to him. Clara had gray hair and a pair of oversized glasses that magnified her eyes to Ant-Man size. She looked up at him and the giant eyes seemed to reel in everything all at once. She wore a white blouse with a gray vest, matching skirt, a kerchief around her neck, and teardrop pearl earrings. Think Shtetl Barbara Bush.

"One," she said, "I am Mr. Gibbs's attorney of record. I have requested that this conversation not be overheard. I have changed rooms four times to make sure the authorities don't listen in. But I don't trust them. They think your aunt Clara is an old dodo bird. They think we're going to chat right here."

"We're not?" Myron said.

"We're not," she repeated. There was little hint of the cheek pincher here; if she were an athlete, you'd say that she'd strapped on her game face. "What we're going to do first is stand up. Got me?"

"Stand up," Myron repeated.

"Right. Then I'm going to lead you and Stan outside, across the street. I'm going to remain on the other side of the street with all those friendly agents. We do this right now, quickly, so they won't have a chance to set up surveillance. Understood?"

Myron nodded. Stan kept his eyes on the Formica.

"Good, just so we're all on the same page here." She knocked on the door. Kimberly Green opened it. Clara walked past her without speaking. Myron and Stan followed. Kimberly rushed up behind them.

"Where do you think you're going?"

"Change of plans, doll."

"You can't do that."

"Sure I can. I'm a sweet little old lady."

"I don't care if you're the Queen Mother," Kimberly said. "You're not going anywhere."

"You married, hon?"

"What?"

"Never mind," Clara said. "Try this on for size. See how it fits. My client demands privacy."

"We already promised—"

"Shh, you're talking when you should be listening. My client demands privacy. So he and Mr. Bolitar are going to take a little walk somewhere. You and I will watch from a distance. We will not listen in."

"I already told you—"

"Shh, you're giving me a headache." Aunt Clara rolled her eyes and kept walking. Myron and Stan followed. They reached the doorway. Clara pointed to a bus depot across the street. "Sit over there," she said to them. "On the bench."

Myron said okay. Clara put a hand on his elbow.

"Cross at the corner," she said. "And wait for the light."

The two men walked to the corner and waited for the light before crossing the street. Kimberly Green and her fellow agents fumed. Clara took them by the hand and led them back toward the building's entrance. Stan and Myron sat on the bench. Stan watched a New Jersey Transit bus go by like it carried the secret to life.

"We don't have time to enjoy the scenery, Stan."

Stan leaned forward, put his elbows on his knees. "This is difficult for me."

"If it makes it any easier," Myron said, "I know that the Sow the Seeds kidnapper is your father."

Stan's head fell into his hands.

"Stan?"

"How did you find out?"

"Through Dennis Lex. I found him in a private sanitarium in

Connecticut. He's been there for thirty years. But you already knew that, didn't you?"

Gibbs said nothing.

"At the sanitarium, there's a big garden in the back. With this statue of Diana the Huntress. There's a picture in your condo of you and your father standing in front of that same statue. He was a patient there. You don't have to confirm or deny it. I was just there. Susan Lex has pull. An administrator told us Edwin Gibbs had been in and out of there for fifteen years. The rest is fairly obvious. Your father was there a long time. It'd be easy to learn who else was there, no matter how strict the so-called security. So he knew about Dennis Lex. And he stole his identity. It's a hell of a twist, I'll give him that. Fake IDs used to be somewhat pretty easy to come by. You'd visit a graveyard, find a child who died, request his social security card, bingo. But that doesn't work anymore. Computers closed down that loophole. Nowadays when you die, your social security number dies with you. So your father took the identity of someone still alive, someone who has no use for it, someone committed permanently. In other words, he used the ID of a living person who has no life. And to go deeper undercover, he changed the person's name. Dennis Lex became Davis Taylor. Untraceable."

"Except you traced it."

"I got lucky."

"Go on," Stan said. "Tell me what else you know."

"We don't have time for this, Stan."

"You don't understand," he said.

"What?"

"If you're the one who says it—if you figure it out on your own—it's not as much a betrayal. You see?"

No time to argue. And maybe Myron did see. "Let's start with the question every reporter wanted to know: why you? Why did the Sow the Seeds kidnapper choose you? The answer: because the kidnapper was your father. He knew you wouldn't turn him in. Maybe part of you hoped someone would figure it out. I don't know. I also don't know if you found him or he found you."

"He found me," Stan said. "He came to me as a reporter. Not as a son. He made that clear."

"Sure," Myron said, "double protection. He gets you with the fact that you'd be turning in your own father—plus he gives you an ethical foundation for remaining silent. The beloved First Amendment. You couldn't name a source. It gave you a very neat out—you could be both moralistic and the good son."

Stan looked up. "So you see that I had no choice."

"Oh, I wouldn't be so easy on myself," Myron said. "You weren't being totally altruistic. Everyone says you were ambitious. That played a part here. You got fame out of this. You were handed a monster story—the kind that propels careers into the stratosphere. You were on TV and got your own cable show. You got a big raise and invited to fancy parties. You want to tell me that wasn't a part of it?"

"It was a by-product," Stan said. "It wasn't a factor."

"You say so."

"It's like you said—I couldn't turn him in, even if I wanted to. There was a constitutional principle here. Even if he wasn't my father, I had an obligation—"

"Save it for your minister," Myron said. "Where is he?"

Stan did not reply. Myron looked across the street. Lots of traffic. The cars started blurring and through them, standing on the other side of the street with Kimberly Green, he saw Greg Downing.

"That man over there," Myron said, pointing with his chin. "That's the boy's father."

Stan looked, but his face didn't change.

"There's a kid in danger," Myron said. "That trumps your constitutional cover."

"He's still my father."

"And he's kidnapped a thirteen-year-old boy," Myron said.

Stan looked up. "What would *you* do?"

"What?"

"Would you give up your father? Just like that?"

"If he was kidnapping children? Yeah, I would."

"Do you really think it's that easy?"

"Who said anything about easy?" Myron said.

Stan put his head back in his hands. "He's sick and he needs help."

"And there's also an innocent boy out there."

"So?"

Myron looked at him.

"I don't mean to sound callous, but I don't know this boy. He has no connection to me. My father does. That's what matters here. You hear about a plane crash, right? You hear about how two hundred people die and you sigh and you go on with your life and you thank God it wasn't your loved one in the plane. Don't you do that?"

"What's your point?"

"You do that because the people on the plane are strangers. Like this boy. We don't care about strangers. They don't count."

"Speak for yourself," Myron said.

"Are you close to your father, Myron?"

"Yes."

"And in your heart of hearts, in your deepest, most honest moments, if you could sacrifice his life to save those two hundred people on the airplane, would you do it? Think about it. If God came down to you and said, 'Okay, that plane never crashed. Those people all arrive safely. In exchange, your father will die.' Would you make that trade?"

"I'm not into playing God."

"But you're asking me to," Stan said. "I turn my father in, they'll kill him. He'll get the lethal injection. If that's not playing God, I don't know what is. So I'm asking you. Would you trade those two hundred lives for your father's?"

"We don't have time—"

"Would you?"

"Okay, if it was my father shooting down the plane," Myron said, "yes, Stan, I would make that trade."

"And suppose your father wasn't culpable? If he was sick or deranged?"

"Stan, we don't have time for this."

Something in Stan's face dropped. He closed his eyes.

"There's a boy out there," Myron said. "We can't let him die."

"And if he's already dead?"

"I don't know."

"You'll want my father dead."

"Not by my hand," Myron said.

Stan took a deep breath and looked over at Greg Downing. Greg stared back, stared right through him. "Okay," he said at last. "But we go alone."

"Alone?"

"Just you and me."

Kimberly Green had a major conniption. "Are you insane?"

They were back inside, sitting around the Formica table. Kimberly Green, Rick Peck, and two other faceless feds were hunched together as one. Clara Steinberg sat with her client. Greg sat next to Myron. Jeremy's kidnapping had siphoned all the blood from Greg's face. His hands looked sucked dry, his skin almost crisp, his eyes too solid and unblinking. Myron put a hand on his shoulder. Greg didn't seem to notice.

"You want my client to cooperate or not?" Clara asked.

"I'm supposed to let my number one suspect go?"

"I'm not running away," Stan said.

"How am I supposed to know that?" Kimberly countered.

"It's the only way," Stan said, his voice a plea. "You'll go in with guns blazing. Someone is going to get hurt."

"We're professionals," Green countered. "We don't go in with guns blazing."

"My father is unstable. If he sees a lot of cops, I can guarantee there will be bloodshed."

"Doesn't have to be that way," she said. "It's up to him."

"Exactly," Stan said. "I'm not taking that chance with my father's life. You let us go. You don't follow us. I'll have him surrender to you. Myron will be with me the whole time. He's armed and he has a cell phone."

"Come on," Myron said. "We're wasting time here."

Kimberly Green chewed on her lower lip. "I don't have the authorization—"

"Forget it," Clara Steinberg said.

"Excuse me?"

Clara pointed a meaty finger at Kimberly Green. "Listen up, missy, you haven't arrested Mr. Gibbs, correct?"

Green hesitated. "That's correct."

Clara turned to Stan and Myron and waved the backs of both hands at them. "So shoo, go, good-bye. We're talking nonsense here. Hurry along. Shoo."

Stan and Myron slowly rose.

"Shoo."

Stan looked down at Kimberly. "If I spot a tail, I'm calling this off. You got me?"

She stewed in silence.

"You've been trailing me for three weeks now. I know what one of your tails looks like."

"She won't tail you."

It was Greg Downing. He and Stan locked eyes again. Greg stood. "I want to go with you too," Greg said. "And I probably have the strongest interest in keeping your father alive."

"How do you figure?"

"Your father's bone marrow can save my son's life. If he dies, so does my son. And if Jeremy has been hurt . . . well, I'd like to be there for him."

Stan didn't waste a lot of time thinking about it. "Let's hurry."

35

Stan drove. Greg sat in the front passenger seat, Myron in the back.

"Where are we going?" Myron asked.

"Bernardsville," Stan said. "It's in Morris County."

Myron knew the town.

"My grandmother died three years ago," Stan said. "We haven't sold the house yet. My father sometimes stays there."

"Where else does he stay?"

"Waterbury, Connecticut."

Greg looked back at Myron. The old man, the blond wig. It clicked for both of them at the same time.

"He's Nathan Mostoni?"

Stan nodded. "That's his main alias. The real Nathan Mostoni is another patient at Pine Hills—that's what we call that fancy loony bin, Pine Hills. Mostoni was the one who came up with the idea of using the identification of the committed, mostly for scams. He and my father became close friends. When Nathan slipped into total delirium, my father took his identity."

Greg shook his head, made two fists. "You should have turned the crazy bastard in."

"You love your son, don't you, Mr. Downing?"

Greg gave Stan a look that could have bored holes through titanium. "What the hell does that have to do with anything?"

"Would you want your son to turn you in one day?"

"Don't hand me that. If I'm a raving psychopathic maniac, yeah, my son can turn me in. Or better, he can put a bullet in my head. You knew your old man was sick, right? The least you could have done was get him help."

"We tried," Stan said. "He was in institutions most of his adult life. It didn't do any good. Then he ran off. When he finally called me, I hadn't seen him in eight years. Imagine that. Eight years. He calls me and tells me he needs to talk to me as a reporter. He made that clear. As a reporter. No matter what he told me, I couldn't reveal the source. He made me promise. I was confused as all hell. But I agreed. And then he told me his story. What he'd been doing. I could barely breathe. I wanted to die. I wanted to just dry up and die."

Greg put his fingers to his mouth. Stan concentrated on the road. Myron stared out the window. He thought about the father of three young children, age forty-one; the female college student, age twenty; and the young newlyweds, ages twenty-eight and twenty-seven. He thought about Jeremy's scream over the phone. He thought about Emily waiting at the house, her mind sowing the seeds, sick and blackening.

They got off Route 78 and took 287 north. They exited onto winding streets with no straightaways. Bernardsville was about old money and rustic wealth, a town of converted mills and stone houses and waterwheels. There were fields of long brown grass swaying in death, everything a little too old and too neatly overgrown.

"It's on this road," Stan said.

Myron looked out. His mouth was dry. He felt a tingle deep in his belly. The car traveled down another corkscrew of a street, the loose gravel crunching under the tires. There were deeply wooded lots commingling, with your standard suburban front lawns. Plenty of center-hall colonials and those mid-seventies ranches that aged like milk left out on the counter. A yellow sign warned about children at play, but Myron saw none.

They pulled into a cake-dried driveway with weeds poking up through the cracks. Myron lowered his window. There was plenty of burnt-out grass, but the sweet summer smell of lillies still loomed and even cloyed. Crickets droned. Wildflowers blossomed. Not a hint of menace.

Up ahead Myron spotted what looked like a farmhouse. Black shutters stood out against the white clapboards. There were lights coming from inside, giving the house a glow that was big and soft and oddly welcoming. The front porch was the type that craved a swinging settee and a pitcher of lemonade.

When the car reached the front of the house, Stan shifted into park and turned off the ignition. The crickets eased up. Myron almost waited for someone to note that it was "Quiet" and for someone else to add, "Yeah, too quiet."

Stan turned to them. "I think I should go in first," he said.

Neither man argued. Greg stared out the window at the house, probably conjuring up unspeakable horrors. Myron's left leg started jackhammering. It often did when he was tense. Stan reached for the door handle.

That was when the first bullet smashed through the front passenger-side window.

The glass exploded, and Myron saw Greg's head fly back at a rate it was never supposed to achieve. A thick gob of crimson smacked Myron in the cheek.

"Greg!"

No time. Instincts took over. Myron grabbed Greg, pushed him down, trying to keep his own head down too. Blood. Lots of it. From Greg. He was bleeding, bleeding heavily, but Myron couldn't tell from where. Another bullet rang out. Another window shattered, raining shards of glass down on Myron's head. He kept his hand on top of Greg, tried to cover him, protect him. Greg's own hand fumbled absently on his chest and face, calmly searching for the bullet hole. Blood kept flowing. From the neck. Greg's neck. Or collarbone. Whatever. He couldn't see through the blood. Myron tried to stop the flow with his bare hand, pushing the sticky liquid away, finding the wound with his finger, applying pressure with his palm. But the blood slipped through the cracks between his fingers. Greg looked up at him with big eyes.

Stan Gibbs put his hands over his head and ducked into a quasi-emergency-landing position. "Stop!" he yelled, almost childlike. "Dad!"

Another bullet. More glass shards. Myron reached into his pocket and pulled out his gun. Greg grabbed his hand and pulled it down. Myron looked at him.

"Can't kill him," Greg said to Myron. There was blood in his mouth now. "If he dies . . . Jeremy's only hope."

Myron nodded, but he didn't put the gun away. He looked over at Stan. In the distance, they heard a helicopter. Then sirens. The feds were on their way. No surprise. There was no way they weren't going to follow. By air, at the very least.

Greg's breathing was short spurts. His eyes were going hazy-gray.

"We got to do something here, Stan," Myron said.

"Just stay down," Stan said. Then he opened the car door and shouted, "Dad!"

No reply.

Stan got out of the car. He raised his hands and stood. "Please," he shouted. "They'll be here soon. They'll kill you."

Nothing. The air was so motionless that Myron thought he could still hear the echoes from the gun blasts.

"Dad?"

Myron lifted his head a little and risked a glance. A man stepped out from behind the side of the house. Edwin Gibbs wore full army fatigues with combat boots. He had an ammunition belt hanging off his shoulder. His rifle was pointed toward the ground. Myron could see it was Nathan Mostoni, though he looked twenty years younger. His head was high, chin up. His back was straight.

Greg made a gurgling sound. Myron ripped off his shirt and pushed it against the wound. But Greg's eyes were closing. "Stay with me," Myron urged. "Come on, Greg. Stay here."

Greg did not reply. His eyes fluttered and closed. Myron felt his heart slam into his throat. "Greg?"

He felt for a pulse. It was there. Myron was no doctor, but it didn't feel strong. Oh damn. Oh come on.

Outside the car, Stan moved closer to his father. "Please," Stan said. "Put down the rifle, Dad."

The fed cars poured into the driveway. Brakes squealed. Feds jumped out of their vehicles, took position using the open doors as shields, aimed their weapons. Edwin Gibbs looked confused, panicked, Frankenstein's monster suddenly surrounded by angry villagers. Stan hurried toward him.

The air seemed to thicken, molasses-like. It was hard to move, hard to breathe. Myron could almost feel the officers tense up, fingers itchy, tips touching the cold metal of the trigger. He let go of Greg for a moment and shouted, "You can't shoot him!"

A fed had a megaphone. "Put down the rifle! Now!"

"Don't shoot!" Myron shouted.

For a moment nothing happened. Time did that in-and-out motion where everything rushes and freezes all at one time. Another fed car skidded up the driveway. A news van followed, screeching when it hit the brakes. Stan kept walking toward his father.

"You are surrounded," the megaphone said. "Drop the rifle and put your hands behind your head. Drop to your knees."

Edwin Gibbs looked left, looked right. Then he smiled. Myron felt the dread rise up in his chest. Gibbs lifted his rifle.

Myron rolled out of the car. "No!"

Stan Gibbs broke into a sprint. His father spotted him, his face calm. He aimed the rifle at his approaching son. Stan kept running. Time did stop this time, waiting for the blast of gunfire. But it didn't come. Stan had gained on him too fast. Edwin Gibbs closed his eyes and let his son tackle him. The two men fell to the ground. Stan stayed on top of his father, blanketing him, leaving no space open.

"Don't shoot him," Stan yelled. His voice sounded hurt, again so childlike. "Please don't shoot him."

Edwin Gibbs lay on his back. He let go of the rifle. It dropped into the grass. Stan pushed it away, still on top of his father, still shielding him from harm. They stayed there until the officers took over. They gently removed Stan and then rolled Edwin Gibbs onto his stomach, cuffing his hands behind his back. The news camera caught it all.

Myron turned back to the car. Greg's eyes were still closed. He wasn't moving. Two of the officers ran toward the car, calling into their radios for an ambulance. Nothing Myron could do for Greg now. He looked back at the farmhouse, his heart still lodged in his throat. He ran toward the house and grabbed the knob. The door was locked. He used his shoulder. The door came down. Myron stepped into the foyer.

"Jeremy?" he called out.

But there was no reply.

36

They didn't find Jeremy Downing.

Myron checked every room, every closet, the basement, the garage. Nothing. The feds streamed in with him. They started knocking down walls. They used a heat sensor to check for underground caves or hidden places. Nothing. In the garage, they found a white van. In the back of it, they found one of Jeremy's red sneakers.

But that was it.

News vans, lots of them, gathered at the end of the driveway. What with the kidnapped boy, his famous father shot and in critical condition, a potential serial killer in custody, the connection to Stan Gibbs and the famed plagiarism charges—the story was getting the full, round-the-clock, give-it-a-banner-and-theme-music, death-of-Diana coverage. Stiffly coiffed correspondents flashed their best grim-news teeth and led with phrases like "the vigil continues" or "the search is reaching its *x*th hour" or "behind me lurks the lair" or "we'll be here until."

A recent photograph of Jeremy, the one Emily had on the Web, ran continuously on all the stations. Brokaw, Jennings and Rather interrupted their programming. Viewers called in tips, but so far none amounted to anything.

And the hours passed.

Emily drove to the scene. It played on all the usual outlets, her head lowered, hurrying toward a waiting car like an arrested felon, the flashbulbs creating a grotesque strobe effect. Cameramen elbowed each other out of the way to capture a glimpse of the stricken mother collapsing in the back of the car. They even got a shot of her through the passenger seat crying. Great TV.

Nightfall brought out searchlights. Volunteers and law officials scoured the nearby grounds for signs of recent graves or digging. Nothing. They brought in dogs. Nothing. They spoke to neighbors, some of whom "never trusted that family" but most gave the standard "seemed like nice folk, real quiet neighbors" spiel.

Edwin Gibbs had been taken into custody. They tried to question him at the Bernardsville Police Station, but he wasn't talking. Clara Steinberg became his attorney. She stayed with him. So did Stan. They pleaded with Edwin, Myron guessed, but so far, he hadn't talked.

Back at the farmhouse, the wind picked up. Myron's bad knee ached, each step giving him a fresh jolt of pain. The pain was unpredictable, arriving whenever it damn well pleased, staying on like the most unwelcome houseguest. There was no side benefit to the knee pain, no weather forecasting or anything like that. Some days it just ached. Nothing he could do about it. He approached Emily and put his arm around her.

"He's still out there," Emily said to the dark.

Myron said nothing.

"He's all alone. And it's night. And he's probably scared."

"We'll find him, Em."

"Myron?"

"Hmm."

"Is this more payback for that night?"

Another search party returned, their shoulders slumped in resignation, if not defeat. Odd thing, these search parties. You wanted to find something, yet you didn't want to find something.

"No," Myron said. "I think you were right. I think our mistake was the best thing that could have happened. And maybe there's a price to pay to have something so good."

She closed her eyes, but she did not cry. Myron stayed next to her. The wind howled, scattering the surrounding voices like dead leaves, whipping branches, and whispering in your ear like the most frightening lover.

37

Myron and Win looked through the one-way glass at Clara Steinberg's back and the faces of Stan and Edwin Gibbs. Kimberly Green stood with them. So did Eric Ford. Emily had gone to the hospital to sit vigil while Greg was in surgery. No one seemed to know if he'd make it.

"Why aren't you listening in?" Myron asked.

"Can't," Ford replied. "Attorney-client."

"How long they been at it?"

"On and off since we took him into custody."

Myron checked the clock behind his head. Nearly three in the morning. Evidence collection teams had leveled the house, but still no clue where Jeremy was. Fatigue lined everyone's face, except maybe Win's. Fatigue never registered on his face. Win must internalize it. Or maybe it had something to do with having little to no conscience.

"We don't have time for this," Myron said.

"I know," Eric Ford said. "It's been a long night for all of us."

"Do something."

"Like what?" Ford snapped. "What exactly would you like me to do?"

Win picked up that one. "Perhaps you could speak to Ms. Steinberg in private."

That hooked Ford's attention. "What?"

"Take her into another room," Win said, "and leave me alone with your suspect."

Eric Ford looked at him. "You shouldn't even be here. He"—a gesture toward Myron—"represents the Downing family, as much as I don't like it. But you got no reason to be here."

"Make a reason," Win said.

Eric Ford waved his hand as if this wasn't worth his time.

Win kept the voice at a low, soothing level. "You don't have to be a part of it," he said. "Simply talk to his attorney. Leave Gibbs alone in the room. That's all. Nothing unethical about that."

Ford shook his head. "You're crazy."

"We need answers," Win said.

"And you want to beat them out of him."

"Beating leaves marks," Win said. "I never leave marks."

"That's not how it works, pal. Ever heard of the U.S. Constitution?"

"It's a document," Win said, "not a trump card. You have a choice. The obscure rights of that subhuman"—Win gestured through the glass—"or a young boy's right to live."

Ford leaned his forehead against the glass.

"If the boy dies while we're standing here," Win said, "how will you feel then?"

Ford shut his eyes. In the holding room, Clara Steinberg rose from her chair. She turned, and for the first time, Myron saw her face. He knew that she had represented bad people before—very, very bad people—but whatever horrors she was now hearing had washed away her skin tone and etched in something that would probably never leave. She approached the one-way mirror and knocked. Ford hit the sound switch.

"We need to talk," she said. "Let me out."

Eric Ford met Clara and Stan by the door. "Let's head down this way," he said.

"No," Clara said.

"Pardon me?"

"We'll talk in here," she said, "where I can watch my client. Wouldn't want an accident, now, would we?"

There were no chairs so they all stood by the one-way window—Kimberly Green, Eric Ford, Clara Steinberg, Stan Gibbs, Myron and Win. Stan kept his head down and plucked at his lower lip with his fingers. Myron tried to meet his eyes. Stan never gave him the chance.

"Okay," Clara said. "First off, we need a D.A."

"What for?" Eric Ford asked.

"Because we want a deal."

Ford tried to snicker. "Are you out of your mind?"

"No. My client is the only one who can tell you where Jeremy Downing is. He'll only do so under specific conditions."

"What conditions?"

"That's why we need a D.A."

"A D.A. will back whatever I agree to," Eric Ford said.

"I'll still want it in writing."

"And I want to hear what you're looking for here."

"Okay," Clara said, "here's the deal. We help you find Jeremy Downing. In exchange, you guarantee not to seek the death penalty for Edwin Gibbs. You also agree to psychiatric tests. You then recommend he be placed in a proper mental health facility, not a prison."

"You have to be kidding me."

"There's more," Clara said.

"More?"

"Mr. Edwin Gibbs will also agree to donate bone marrow to Jeremy Downing if the need arises. I understand that Mr. Bolitar is representing the family here. For the record, we should note that he is present as a witness to this agreement."

No one said anything.

"So we clear?" Clara said.

"No," Ford said, "we're not."

Clara adjusted her eyeglasses. "This deal is nonnegotiable." She turned to leave, her gaze snagging on Myron's. Myron just shook his head.

"I'm his attorney," she said to him.

"And you'll let a boy die for him?" Myron said.

"Don't start," Clara said, but her voice was soft.

Myron studied her face again, saw no give. He turned to Ford. "Agree," he said.

"Are you nuts?"

"The family cares about retribution. But they care more about finding their son. Agree to her terms."

"You think I'm taking orders from you?"

Myron's voice was soft. "Come on, Eric."

Ford frowned. He rubbed his face with his hands and then dropped them back to his side. "This agreement assumes, of course, that the boy is still alive."

"No," Clara Steinberg said.

"What?"

"Alive or dead does not change the state of Edwin Gibb's mental health."

"So you don't know if he's alive or—"

"If we did, it would be an attorney-client communication and thus confidential."

Myron looked at her in stark horror. She met his eyes and would not blink. Myron tried Stan, but his head was still lowered. Even Win's face, usually the model of neutrality, was on edge. Win wanted to hurt somebody. He wanted to hurt somebody badly.

"We can't agree to that," Ford said.

"Then there's no deal," Clara said.

"You have to be reasonable—"

"Do we have a deal or not?"

Eric Ford shook his head. "No."

"See you in court, then."

Myron moved into her path.

"Step aside, Myron," Clara said.

He just looked down at her. She raised her eyes.

"You think your mother wouldn't be doing the same thing?" Clara said.

"Leave my mother out of this."

"Step aside," she said again. Aunt Clara was sixty-six. For the first time since he'd known her, she looked older than her age.

Myron turned back to Eric Ford. "Agree," he said.

He shook his head. "The boy is probably dead."

"Probably," Myron repeated. "Not definitely."

Win spoke up this time. "Agree," he said.

Ford looked at him.

"He won't get off easily," Win said.

Stan's head finally rose at that one. "What the hell is that supposed to mean?"

Win gave him flat eyes. "Absolutely nothing."

"I want this man kept away from my father."

Win smiled at him.

"You don't get it, do you?" Stan said. "None of you get it. My father is sick. He's not responsible. We're not making this up. Any competent psychiatrist in the world will agree. He needs help."

"He should die," Win said.

"He's a sick man."

"Sick men die all the time," Win said.

"That's not what I mean. He's like someone who has a heart condition. Or cancer. He needs help."

"He kidnaps and probably kills people," Win said.

"And it doesn't matter why he does it?"

"Of course it doesn't matter," Win said. "He does it. That's enough. He should not be put in a comfortable mental hospital. He should not be allowed to enjoy a wonderful film or read a great book or laugh again. He should not be able to see a beautiful woman or listen to Beethoven or know kindness or love—because his victims never will. What part of that don't you understand, Mr. Gibbs?"

Stan was shaking. "You agree," he said to Ford. "Or we don't help."

"If the boy dies because of this negotiation," Win said to Stan, "you will die."

Clara stepped into Win's face. "You threatening my client?" she shouted.

Win smiled at her. "I never threaten."

"There are witnesses."

"Worried about collecting your fee, Counselor?" Win asked.

"That's enough." It was Eric Ford. He looked at Myron. Myron nodded. "Okay," Ford said slowly. "We agree. Now, where is he?"

"I'll have to take you," Stan said.

"Again?"

"I wouldn't be able to give you directions. I'm not even sure I can find it after all these years."

"But we come along," Kimberly Green said.

"Yes."

There was an empty space, a sudden stillness that Myron didn't like.

"Is Jeremy alive or dead?" Myron asked.

"Truth?" Stan said. "I don't know."

38

Eric Ford drove with Kimberly Green riding shotgun and Myron and Stan in the backseat. Several cars' worth of agents followed them. So too did the press. Nothing they could do about that.

"My mother died in 1977," Stan said. "Cancer. My father was already unwell. The one thing in his life that mattered to him—the one good thing—was my mother. He loved her very much."

The time on the car clock read nearly 4:03 A.M. Stan told them where to turn off Route 15. A sign read DINGSMAN BRIDGE. They were heading into Pennsylvania.

"Whatever sanity was still there, my mother's death stripped away. He watched her suffer. Doctors tried everything—used all their technological advances—but it only made her suffer more. That's when my father started with the strength of the mind. If only my mother hadn't relied on technology, he thought. If only she used her mind instead. If only she'd seen its limitless potential. Technology killed her, he said. It gave her false hope. It stopped her from using the one thing that could save her—the limitless human brain."

No one had a comment.

"We had a summerhouse out here. It was beautiful. Fifteen acres of land, walking distance to a lake. My father used to take me hunting and fishing. But I haven't been out here in years. Haven't even thought about the place. He took my mother out here to die. Then he buried her in the woods. See, it's where her suffering finally ended."

The obvious question hung in the air, unasked: *And who else's?*

Myron would later remember nothing about the drive. No buildings, no landmarks, no trees. Outside his window was total night, the black folding over black, eyes squeezed shut in the darkest of rooms. He sat back and waited.

Stan told them to stop at the foot of a wooded area. More crickets sounded. The other cars pulled up alongside them. Feds got out and started combing the area. Beams from powerful flashlights revealed uneven earth. Myron ignored them. He swallowed and ran. Stan ran with him.

Before morning broke, the federal officers would find graves. They'd find the father of three children, the female college student, and the young newlyweds.

But for now, Myron and Stan kept running. Branches whipped Myron's face. He tripped over a root, curled into a roll, stood back up, kept running. They spotted the small house, barely visible in the faint moonlight. There were no lights on inside, no hint of life. Myron did not bother trying the knob this time. He took it full on, crashing the door down. More darkness. He heard a cry, turned, fumbled for the light switch, flipped it up.

Jeremy was there.

He was chained to a wall—dirty and terrified and still very much alive.

Myron felt his knees buckle, but he fought them and stayed upright. He ran to the boy. The boy stretched out his arms. Myron embraced him and felt his heart fall and shatter. Jeremy was crying. Myron lifted his hand and stroked the boy's hair and shushed him. Like his father. Like his father had done to him countless times. A sudden, beautiful warmth streamed through his veins, tingling his fingers and toes, and for a moment, Myron thought that maybe he understood what his father felt. Myron had always cherished being on the son side of the hug, but now, for just the most fleeting of moments, he experienced something so much stronger—the intensity and overwhelming depth of being on the other side—that it shook every part of him.

"You're okay," Myron said to him, cupping the boy's head. "It's over now."

But it wasn't.

An ambulance came. Jeremy was put inside. Myron called Dr. Karen Singh. She didn't mind being woken at five in the morning. He told her everything.

"Wow," Karen Singh said when he finished.

"Yes."

"We'll get someone to harvest the marrow right away. I'll start prepping Jeremy in the afternoon."

"You mean with chemo."

"Yes," she said. "You done good, Myron. Either way, you should be proud."

"Either way?"

"Come by my office tomorrow afternoon."

Myron felt a thumping in his chest. "What's up?"

"The paternity test," she said. "The results should be in by then."

Jeremy was on his way to the hospital. Myron wandered back outside. The feds were digging. The news vans were there. Stan Gibbs watched the mounds of earth grow, his face now beyond emotion. No sound, not even the crickets now, except for shovel hitting dirt. Myron's knee was acting up. He felt bone-weary. He wanted to find Emily. He wanted to go to the hospital. He wanted to know the results of that test and then he wanted to know what he was going to do with them.

He climbed back up the hill toward the car. More media. Someone called out to him. He ignored them. There were more federal officers working in silence. Myron walked past them. He didn't have the heart to hear what they'd found. Not just yet.

When he reached the top of the landing—when he saw Kimberly Green and the lifeless expression on her face—his heart took one more plummet.

He took another step. "Greg?" he said.

She shook her head, her eyes hazy and unfocused. “They shouldn’t have left him alone,” she said. “They should have watched him. Even after a careful search. You can never search too carefully.”

“Search who?”

“Edwin Gibbs.”

Myron was sure he’d heard wrong. “What about him?”

“They just found him,” she said, having trouble with the words. “He committed suicide in his cell.”

39

Karen Singh summed it up for them: You can't get bone marrow from a dead man.

Emily did not collapse when she heard the news. She took the blow without blinking and immediately segued to the next step. She was on a calmer plane now, somewhere just outside panic.

"We have incredible access to the media right now," Emily said. They were sitting in Karen Singh's hospital office. "We'll make pleas. We'll set up bone marrow drives. The NBA will help. We'll get players to make appearances."

Myron nodded, but the enthusiasm wasn't there. Dr. Singh mimicked his motion.

"When will you have the paternity results?" Emily asked.

"I was just about to call for them," Dr. Singh said.

"I'll leave you two alone, then," Emily said. "I have a press conference downstairs."

Myron looked at her. "You don't want to wait for the results?"

"I already know the results."

Emily left without a backward glance. Karen Singh looked at Myron. Myron folded his hands and put them in his lap.

"You ready?" she asked.

He nodded.

Karen Singh picked up the phone and dialed. Someone on the other end answered. Karen read off a reference number. She waited, tapping a pencil on the desk. Someone on the other end said something. Karen said, "Thank you," hung up, focused her eyes on Myron.

"You're the father."

Myron found Emily in the hospital lobby, giving the press conference. The hospital had set up a podium with their logo perfectly positioned behind it, sure to be picked up by any and all television cameras. Hospital logo. Like they were McDonald's or Toyota, trying to sleaze some free advertising. Emily's statement was direct and heartfelt. Her son was dying. He needed new bone marrow. Everyone who wanted to help should give blood and get registered. She plucked the strings of societal grieving, making sure it rang personal in the same way that Princess Diana's and John Kennedy Jr.'s deaths rang personal, wanting the public to mourn as if they actually knew him. The power of celebrity.

When she finished her statement, Emily hurried off without answering questions. Myron caught up to her in the closed-off area near the elevators. She glanced at him. He nodded, and she smiled.

"So now what are you going to do?" she asked him.

"We have to save him," Myron said.

"Yes."

Behind them the press were still yelling out questions. The sound trickled and then faded into the background. Someone ran by with an empty gurney.

"You said Thursday was the optimum day," Myron said.

Hope lit her eyes. "Yes."

"Okay, then," he said. "We try it on Thursday."

The bullet that had struck Greg had entered in the lower part of his neck and traversed toward his chest. It had stopped short of the heart. But it had done plenty of damage anyway. He survived surgery but remained unconscious in "critical" and "guarded" condition. Myron looked in on him. Greg had tubes in his nose and a frightening assortment of machinery Myron hoped never to understand. He looked like a corpse, waxen and gray-white and sucked dry. Myron sat with him for a few minutes. But not very long.

He returned to the offices of MB SportsReps the next day.

"Lamar Richardson is coming in this afternoon," Esperanza said.

"I know."

"You okay?"

"Dandy."

"Life goes on, huh?"

"Guess so."

Special Agent Kimberly Green came semi-bouncing by a few minutes later. "It's all wrapping up," she told him, and for the first time he saw her smile.

Myron sat back. "I'm listening."

"Edwin Gibbs, under his Dennis Lex/Davis Taylor identity, still had a locker at work. We found the wallets of two of his victims, Robert and Patricia Wilson, in there."

"They were the honeymoon couple?"

"Yes."

They both took a moment, out of respect for the dead, Myron guessed. He pictured a healthy young couple beginning their life, coming to the Big Apple to see some shows and do a little shopping, walking the bustling streets hand in hand, a little scared about the future but ready to give it a go. *El fin.*

Kimberly cleared her throat. "Gibbs also rented a white Ford Windstar using the Davis Taylor credit card. It was one of those automatic reservations. You just make a call, walk straight to the rental, and drive off. No one sees you."

"Where did he pick up the van?"

"Newark Airport."

"I assume that's the van we found in Bernardsville," Myron said.

"The very."

"Tidy," he said, using a Win word. "What else?"

"Preliminary autopsies reveal that all the victims were killed with a thirty-eight. Two shots to the head. No other signs of trauma. We don't think he tortured them or any of that. His modus operandus seemed to involve the early scream and then he just killed them."

"He ends the seed sowing for them," Myron said, "but not the families."

"Right."

"Because for his victims, the terror would be real. He wanted it all in the mind." Myron shook his head. "What did Jeremy tell you about his ordeal?"

"You didn't talk to him about it?"

Myron shifted in his chair. "No."

"Edwin Gibbs wore the same disguise he used at work—the blond wig and beard and glasses. He blindfolded Jeremy as soon as he had him in the van and drove straight to that cabin. Edwin told him to scream into the phone—even made him practice first to make sure he had it right. After the call, Edwin chained him up and left him alone. You know the rest."

Myron nodded. He did.

"What about the plagiarism charge and the novel?"

She shrugged. "It was like you and Stan said. Edwin read it, probably right after his wife was dying of cancer. It influenced him."

Myron stared at her for a moment.

"What?" she said.

"You guys figured that part out when you first got the novel," Myron said. "That Stan hadn't plagiarized. That the book influenced the killer."

She shook her head. "No."

"Come on. You knew that the kidnappings had taken place. You just wanted to put pressure on Stan so he'd talk. And maybe you wanted to embarrass him a little."

"That's not true," Kimberly Green said. "I'm not saying some of our agents didn't take it personally, but we believed that he was the Sow the Seeds kidnapper. I already told you some of the reasons why. Now we know that a lot of the same evidence pointed to his father."

"What same evidence?"

She shook her head. "It's not important anymore. We knew Stan was more here than just a reporter. And we were right. We even thought he was getting stuff wrong on purpose—that he was using the book rather than what he'd really done just to throw us off."

Her words didn't resonate the way the truth does, but Myron didn't argue the point. He scanned his Client Wall and tried to bring his focus around to Lamar Richardson's visit. "So the case is closed."

She smiled. "Like legs in a nunnery."

"You make that one up?"

"Yup."

"Good thing you carry a gun," Myron said. "So are you going to get a big promotion?"

She rose. "I think I get to be a super-secret-special agent now."

Myron smiled. They shook hands. Kimberly left then. Myron sat alone for a while. He rubbed his eyes and thought about what she'd said and what she hadn't said and realized that something was still very wrong.

Lamar Richardson, shortstop extraordinaire, showed up on time and by himself. Positively shocking. The meeting went well. Myron gave his standard spiel, but the standard spiel was pretty good. Damn good, actually. All businesspeople need a spiel. Spiel is good. Esperanza spoke up too. She had started developing her own spiel. Well honed. The perfect complement to Myron's. Quite the partnership, this was becoming.

Win stopped by briefly as planned. If recruitment was a baseball game, Win was the big closer. People knew his name. They checked out his reputation—er, his business reputation, that is. When prospective clients learned that Windsor Horne Lockwood III himself would handle their finances, that Win and Myron further insisted that clients meet with Win at least five times a year, they started smiling. Score one for the small agency.

Lamar Richardson played it close to the vest. He nodded a lot. He asked questions but not too many. Two hours after arriving, he shook their hands and said he'd be in touch. Myron and Esperanza walked him to the elevator and bade him good-bye.

Esperanza turned to Myron. "Well?"

"Got him."

"How can you be so sure?"

"I'm all-seeing," Myron said. "All-knowing."

They moved back into Myron's office and sat down. "If Lamar chooses us over IMG and TruPro"—she stopped, smiled—"we're baaaaack."

"Pretty much."

"And that means Big Cyndi will come back."

"That's supposed to be a good thing, right?"

"You're starting to love her, you know."

"Yeah, don't rub it in."

Esperanza studied his face. She did that a lot. Myron didn't much believe in reading faces. Esperanza did. Especially his. "What happened in that law office?" she asked. "With Chase Layton?"

"I boxed his ears once and punched him seven times."

Her eyes stayed on his face.

"You're supposed to say, 'But you saved Jeremy's life,'" Myron added.

"No, that's Win's line." She adjusted herself and faced him full. She wore an aquamarine business suit, cut low with no blouse, and it was a wonder Lamar had been able to concentrate on anything. Myron was used to her, but the effect was still there, still dazzling. He just saw the dazzle from a different angle.

"Speaking of Jeremy," she said.

"Yes."

"You still blocking?"

Myron thought about it, remembered the embrace in that cabin, stopped. "More than ever," he said.

"So what now?"

"The blood test came back. I'm the father."

Something popped onto her face—regret maybe—but it didn't stay long. "You should tell him the truth."

"Right now I just want to save his life."

She kept studying the face. "Maybe soon," she said.

"Maybe soon what?"

"You'll stop blocking," Esperanza said.

"Yeah, maybe."

"We'll chat then. In the meantime . . ."

"Don't be stupid," he finished for her.

The health club was located in a chi-chi hotel in midtown. The walls were fully mirrored. The ceiling and the trim and the front desk were whole-milk white. Same with the clothes worn by the personal trainers. The weights and exercise machines were sleek and chrome and so beautiful you didn't want to touch them. Everything about the place gleamed; you were almost tempted to work out in sunglasses.

Myron found him on a bench press, struggling without a spotter. Myron waited, watching him wage war on gravity and the barbell. Chase Layton's face was pure red, his teeth gritted, veins in his forehead doing their pop-up video. It took some time, but the attorney achieved victory. He dropped the weight onto the stand. His arms fell to his sides like he'd missed a brain synapse.

"You shouldn't hold your breath," Myron said.

Chase looked over at him. He didn't seem surprised or upset. He sat up, breathing heavily. He wiped his face with a towel.

"I won't take up much of your time," Myron said.

Chase put the towel down and looked at him.

"I just wanted to say that if you want to press charges, Win and I won't get in your way."

Chase did not reply.

"And I'm very sorry for what I did," Myron said.

"I watched the news," Chase said. "You did it to save that boy's life."

"Doesn't excuse it."

"Maybe not." He stood and added a plate to both sides of the bar. "Frankly, Mr. Bolitar, I'm not sure what to think."

"If you want to press charges—"

"I don't."

Myron was not sure what to say, so he settled for "Thank you."

Chase Layton nodded and sat back on the bench. Then he looked at Myron. "Do you want to know what the worst part of it is?"

No, Myron thought. "If you want to tell me."

"The shame," Chase said.

Myron started to open his mouth, but Chase waved him quiet.

"It's not the beating or the pain. It's the feeling of total helplessness. We were primitive. We were man to man. And there was nothing I could do but take it. You made me feel like"—he looked up, found the words, looked straight at Myron—"like I wasn't a real man."

The words made Myron cringe.

"I went to these great schools and joined all the right clubs and made a fortune in my chosen profession. I fathered three kids and raised them and loved them the best I could. Then one day you punch me—and I realize that I'm not a real man."

"You're wrong," Myron said.

"You're going to say that violence is no measure of a man. On some level you're right. But on some level, the base level that makes us men, we both know you're wrong. Don't pretend you don't know what I'm talking about. It'd just be a further insult."

Myron swallowed down the clichés. Chase took deep breaths and reached for the bar.

"Need a spotter?" Myron said.

Chase Layton gripped it and jerked it off the stand. "I don't need anybody," he said.

Thursday came. Karen Singh introduced him to a fer-tility expert named Dr. Barbara Dittrick. Dr. Dittrick handed Myron a small cup and told him to masturbate into it. There were more surreal and embarrassing ex-periences in life, Myron guessed, but being led to a small room to masturbate into a cup while everyone waited for you in the next room had to be right up there with the best of them.

"Step in here, please," Dr. Dittrick said.

Myron frowned at the cup. "I usually insist on flowers and a movie."

"Well, at least you got the movie," she said, pointing at the television. "The TV has X-rated videos." She left the room and closed the door behind her.

Myron checked the titles. *On Golden Blonde. Father Knows Breast* (starring Robert Hung). *Field of Wet Dreams* ("If you watch it, they will come"). He frowned and passed. So to speak. He stared at the swivel leather chair, one of those lean-back kind, where probably hundreds of other men had sat and . . . He covered it with paper towels and did his bit, though it took some time. His imagination was spinning in the wrong direction, generating an aura about as erotic as mole hair on an old man's buttock. When he was, uh, finished, he opened the door and handed the cup to Dr. Dittrick and tried to smile. He felt like the world's biggest doofus. She wore rubber gloves, even though the, uh, specimen was in a cup. Like it might scald her. She brought it to a lab where they "washed" (their expression, not his) the semen. The semen was declared "serviceable but slow." Like it was falling behind in algebra.

"Funny," Emily said. "I usually found Myron to be serviceable but quick."

"Ha-ha," Myron said.

A few hours later Emily was in a hospital bed. Barbara Dittrick smiled while inserting what looked suspiciously like a turkey baster into her and pressed the plunger. Myron took her hand. Emily smiled.

"Romantic," she said.

Myron made a face.

"What?"

"Serviceable?" he said.

She laughed. "But quick."

Dr. Dittrick finished her part. Emily stayed prone for another hour. Myron sat with her. They were doing this to save Jeremy's life. That was all. He didn't let the future enter the equation. He didn't consider the long-term effects or what this might one day mean. Irresponsible, sure. But first things first.

They had to save Jeremy. The hell with the rest.

Terese Collins called him from Atlanta that afternoon. "Can I come up and visit?" she asked.

"The station will give you more time off?"

"Actually, my producer encouraged me."

"Oh?"

"You, my studly friend, are part of a huge story," Terese said.

"You used the words 'studly' and 'huge' in the same sentence."

"That turn you on?"

"Well, it might a lesser man."

"And you are that lesser man."

"I thank you," he said.

"You're also the only one in this story who won't talk to the press."

"So you just want me for my mind," Myron said. "I feel so used."

"Dream on, hot buns. I want your bod. It's my producer who wants your brain."

"Your producer cute?"

"No."

"Terese?"

"Yes."

"I don't want to talk about what happened."

"Good," she said. "Because I don't want to hear it."

There was a brief silence.

"Yeah," Myron said. "I'd like it very much if you came up."

Ten days later, Karen Singh called him at home.

"The pregnancy didn't take."

Myron closed his eyes.

"We can try again next month," she said.

"Thanks for calling, Karen."

"Sure."

There was empty space. "Anything else?" Myron asked.

"There's been a lot of marrow drives," she said.

"I know."

"One donor looks like a match for an AML patient in Maryland. A young mother. She would have probably died if it weren't for these drives."

"Good news," Myron said.

"But no matches for Jeremy."

"Yeah."

"Myron?"

"What?"

"I don't think we have much time here."

*

Terese returned to Atlanta later that day. Win invited Esperanza to his place for a night of mindless television. The three of them sat in their customary spots. Fritos and Indian takeout were on the night's menu. Myron had the remote. He paused when he saw a familiar image on CNN. A basketball superstar simply known as "TC," one of the NBA's most controversial players and a teammate of Greg's, was on *Larry King Live.* His hair was razor-carved to spell out *Jeremy*, and both gold earrings had Jeremy's name on them. He wore a ripped T-shirt that simply read HELP OR JEREMY DIES. Myron smiled. TC was something else, but he'd get the people out in droves.

More flipping. Stan Gibbs was on some talking-head show on MSNBC. Nothing new. The only thing the press loves as much as tearing somebody down is a story of redemption. Bruce Taylor had gotten the exclusive, as promised, and he'd set the tone. The public was mixed on what Stan had done, but for the most part, they sympathized with him. In the end, Stan had risked his own life to catch a killer, saved Jeremy Downing from certain death, and been wrongly accused by a too-eager-to-convict media. The fact that Stan had been confused about turning in his own father played for him, especially since the media was anxious to wipe away the awful mar of plagiarism they'd so quickly tattooed on him. Stan got his column back. Rumor had it his show was coming back too but in a better time slot. Myron wasn't sure what to think. Stan was no hero to him. But so few people were.

Stan, too, was pounding the bone-marrow-drive drum. "This boy needs our help," he said directly into the camera. "Please come down. We'll be here all night."

A blond talking head asked Stan about his own part in this drama, about tackling his father, about racing to the cabin. Stan played the modesty card. Wise. The man knew the media.

"Boring," Esperanza said.

"Agreed," Win said.

"Isn't there a *Partridge Family* marathon on TV Land?"

Myron suddenly stopped.

"Myron?" Win said.

He did not reply.

"Hello, world." Esperanza snapped her fingers in Myron's face. "There's a song that we're singing. Come on, get happy."

Myron switched off the television. He looked at Win, then at Esperanza. "Say one last good-bye to the boy."

Esperanza and Win exchanged a glance.

"You were right, Win."

"About what?"

"Human nature," Myron said.

40

Myron called Kimberly Green at her office. She answered the line and said, "Green."

"I need a favor," Myron said.

"Shit, I thought you were out of my life."

"But never your fantasies. You want to help me or not?"

"Not."

"I need two things."

"Not. I said 'not.' "

"Eric Ford said that the supposedly plagiarized novel was sent directly to you."

"So?"

"Who sent it?"

"You heard him, Myron. It was sent anonymously."

"You have no idea."

"None."

"Where is it now?"

"The book?"

"Yes."

"In an evidence locker."

"Ever do anything with it?"

"Like what?"

Myron waited.

"Myron?"

"I knew you guys were holding something back," he said.

"Listen to me a second—"

"The author of that novel. It was Edwin Gibbs. He wrote it under a pseudonym after his wife died. It makes perfect sense now. You were searching for him right from the get-go. You knew, dammit. You knew the whole time."

"We suspected," she said. "We didn't know."

"All that crap about thinking he was Stan's first victim—"

"It wasn't total crap. We knew it was one of them. We just didn't know which one. We couldn't find Edwin Gibbs until you told us about the Waterbury address. By the time we got there, he was already on his way to kidnap Jeremy Downing. Maybe if you had been more forthcoming—"

"You guys lied to me."

"We didn't lie. We just didn't tell you everything."

"Jesus, you ever listen to yourself?"

"We owed you nothing here, Myron. You weren't a federal agent on this. You were just a pain in the ass."

"A pain in the ass who helped you solve the case."

"And for that I thank you."

Myron's thoughts entered the maze, turned left, turned right, circled back.

"Why doesn't the press know about Gibbs being the author?" Myron asked.

"They will. Ford wants all his ducks in a row first. Then he'll hold yet another big press conference and present it as something new."

"He could do that today," Myron said.

"He could."

"But then the story dies down. Right now the rumors keep it going. Ford gets more time in the limelight."

"He's a politician at heart," she said. "So what?"

Myron took another few turns, hit a few more walls, kept feeling for the way out. "Forget it," he said.

"Good. Can I go now?"

"First I need you to call the national bone marrow registry."

"Why?"

"I need to find out about a donor."

"This case is closed, Myron."

"I know," he said. "But I think a new one might be opening."

Stan Gibbs was at the anchor chair when Myron and Win arrived. His new cable show, *Glib with Gibbs*, was filming in Fort Lee, New Jersey, and the studio, like every television studio Myron had ever seen, looked like a room with the roof ripped off. Wires and lights hung in no discernible pattern. Studios, especially newsrooms, were always much smaller in person than on television. The desks, the chairs, the world map in the background. All smaller. The power of television. A room on a nineteen-inch screen somehow looks smaller in real life.

Stan wore a blue blazer, white shirt, red tie, jeans and sneakers. The jeans would stay under the desk and never get camera time. Classic anchorman-wear. Stan waved to them when they entered. Myron waved back. Win did not.

"We need to talk," Myron said to him.

Stan nodded. He sent away the producers and motioned Myron and Win to the guest chairs. "Sit."

Stan stayed in the anchor chair. Win and Myron sat in guest chairs, which felt pretty strange, as though a home audience were watching. Win checked his reflection in a camera glass and smiled. He liked what he saw.

"Any word on a donor?" Stan asked.

"None."

"Something will come through."

"Yeah," Myron said. "Look, Stan, I need your help."

Stan intertwined his fingers and rested both hands on the anchor desk. "Whatever you need."

"There's a lot of things that don't add up with Jeremy's kidnapping."

"For example?"

"Why do you think your father took a child this time? He never did that before, right? Always adults. Why this time a child?"

Stan mulled it over, chose his words one at a time. "I don't know. I'm not sure taking adults was a pattern or anything. His victims seemed pretty random."

"But this wasn't random," Myron said. "His choosing Jeremy Downing couldn't have been just a coincidence."

Stan thought about that one too. "I agree with you there."

"So he picked him because he was somehow connected with my investigation."

"Seems logical."

"But how would your father have known about Jeremy?"

"I don't know," Stan said. "He might have followed you."

"I don't think so. You see, Greg Downing stayed up in Waterbury after our visit. He kept his eye on Nathan Mostoni. We know he didn't travel out of town until the day before the kidnapping."

Win looked into the camera again. He smiled and waved. Just in case it was on.

"It's strange," Stan said.

"And there's more," Myron said. "Like the call where Jeremy screamed. With the others, your father told the family not to contact the cops. But he didn't this time. Why? And are you aware that he wore a disguise when he kidnapped Jeremy?"

"I heard that, yes."

"Why? If he planned on killing him, why go to the trouble of donning a disguise?"

"He kidnapped Jeremy off the streets," Stan said. "Someone might have been able to identify him."

"Yeah, okay, that makes sense. But then why blindfold Jeremy once he was in the van? He killed all the others. He would have killed Jeremy. So why worry about him seeing his face?"

"I'm not sure," Stan said. "He might have always done it that way, for all we know."

"I guess," Myron said. "But something about it all just rings wrong, don't you think?"

Stan thought about it. "It rings funny," he said slowly. "I'm not sure it rings wrong."

"That's why I came to you. All these questions have been swirling in my head. And then I remembered Win's credo."

Stan Gibbs looked over at Win. Win blinked his eyes and lowered them modestly. "What credo is that?"

"Man is into self-preservation," Myron said. "He is, above all, selfish." He paused a moment. "You agree with that, Stan?"

"To some degree, of course. We're all selfish."

Myron nodded. "You even."

"Yes, of course. And you too, I'm sure."

"The media is making you out to be this noble guy," Myron said. "Torn between family and duty and ultimately doing the right thing. But maybe you're not."

"Not what?"

"Noble."

"I'm not," Stan said. "I did wrong. I never claimed to be a saint."

Myron looked at Win. "He's good."

"Damn good," Win agreed.

Stan Gibbs frowned. "What are you talking about, Myron?"

"Follow me here, Stan. And remember Win's credo. Let's start at the beginning. When your father first contacted you. You talked to him and you decided to write the Sow the Seeds story. What was your motive at first? Were you trying to find an outlet for your fear and guilt? Was it simply to be a good reporter? Or—and here's where we're using the Win credo—did you write it because you knew it would make you a big star?"

Myron looked at him and waited.

"Am I supposed to answer that?"

"Please."

Stan looked in the air and rubbed his fingertips with his thumb. "All of the above, I guess. Yes, I was excited by the story. I thought it could very well be a big deal. If that's selfishness, okay, I'm guilty."

Myron glanced at Win again. "Good."

"Damn good."

"Let's keep following this track, Stan, okay? The story did indeed become a big deal. So did you. You became a celebrity—"

"We covered this already, Myron."

"Right. You're absolutely right. Let's skip to the part where the feds sued you. They demanded to know your source. You refused. Now again there might be several reasons for this. The First Amendment, of course. That could be it. Protecting your father would be another. The combination of the two. But—and again Win's credo—what would be the selfish choice?"

"What do you mean?"

"Think selfishly and you really have only one option."

"That being?"

"If you caved in to the feds—if you said, Okay, now that I'm in legal trouble, my source is my father—well, how would that have looked?"

"Bad," Win said.

"Damn bad. I doubt you'd have been much of a hero if you sold out your father—not to mention the First Amendment—just to save your hide from vague legal threats." Myron smiled. "See what I mean about Win's credo?"

"So you think I acted selfishly by not telling the feds," Stan said.

"It's possible."

"It's also possible that the selfish thing was also the right thing."

"Possible too," Myron agreed.

"I never claimed to be a hero in all this."

"Never denied it either."

Stan smiled this time. "Maybe I didn't deny it because I'm using Win's credo."

"How's that?"

"Denying it would harm me," Stan said. "As would boasting about it."

Myron didn't have a chance to look before he heard Win say, "Damn good."

"I still don't see the relevance of any of this," Stan said.

"Stick with me, I think you will."

Stan shrugged.

"Where were we?" Myron asked.

"The feds take him to court," Win said.

"Right, thanks, the feds take you to court. You battle back. Then something happens you totally didn't foresee. The plagiarism charges. For the sake of discussion, we'll assume the Lex family sent the book to the feds. They wanted to get you off their back—what better way to do that than to ruin your reputation? So what did you do? How did you react to the charges of plagiarism?"

Stan kept quiet. Win said, "He disappeared."

"Correct answer," Myron said.

Win smiled and nodded a thank-you into the camera.

"You took off," Myron said to Stan. "Now the question again is why. Several things come to mind. It could have been because you were trying to protect your father. Or it might have been that you were afraid of the Lex family."

"Which would certainly fit Win's credo," Stan said. "Self-preservation."

"Right. You were afraid they'd harm you."

"Yes."

Myron treaded gently. "But don't you see, Stan? We have to think selfishly too. You're presented with this serious plagiarism charge. What choices did you have? Two really. You could either run off—or you could tell the truth."

Stan said, "I still don't see your point."

"Stay with me. If you told the truth, you would again look like a louse. Here you've been defending the First Amendment and your father and whoops, you get in trouble and you sell them out. No good. You'd still be ruined."

"Damned if you do," Win said. "Damned if you don't."

"Right," Myron said. "So the wise move—the selfish move—was to vanish for a while."

"But I lost everything by vanishing."

"No, Stan, you didn't."

"How can you say that?"

Myron lifted his palms to the skies and grinned. "Look around you."

For the first time, something dark flicked across Stan's face. Myron saw it. So did Win.

"Let's continue, shall we?"

Stan said nothing.

"You go into hiding and start counting your problems. One, your father is a murderer. You're selfish, Stan, but you're not inhumane. You want him off the streets, yet you can't tell on him. Maybe because you love him. Or maybe there's Win's credo."

"Not this time," Stan said.

"Pardon?"

"Win's credo doesn't apply. I kept quiet because I loved my father and because I believe in protecting sources. And I can offer proof."

"I'm listening," Myron said.

"If I wanted to turn my father in—if that would have been in my best interest—I could have done it anonymously." Stan leaned back and folded his arms.

"That's your proof?"

"Sure. I didn't do the selfish thing."

Myron shook his head. "You got to go deeper."

"Deeper how?"

"Turning your father in anonymously wouldn't help you, Stan. Not really. Yes, you needed to put your father behind bars. But more than that, you needed to be redeemed."

Silence.

"So what would answer both those needs? What would put your father away and put you back on top—maybe even more on top than before? First, you had to be patient. That meant staying hidden. Second, you couldn't be the one who turned him in. You had to set him up."

"Set up my father?"

"Yes. You had to leave a trail for the feds to follow. Something subtle, something that would lead to your father, and something you could manipulate at any time. So you took a fake ID, Stan—the same way your father had. You even took a job where people would spot the disguise your father used and hey, maybe you could also tie in your dad's old nemesis the Lex family in the process."

"What the hell are you talking about?"

"You know what bugged me? Your father had been so careful in the past. Now all of a sudden he's leaving incriminating evidence in a locker. He rents the kidnap van on a credit card and leaves a red sneaker in it. It didn't make any sense. Unless someone was setting him up."

Stan's look of disbelief was almost genuine. "You think I killed these people?"

"No," Myron said. "Your father did."

"Then what—?"

"You're the one who used the Dennis Lex identity," Myron said, "not your father."

Stan tried to look stunned, but it wasn't happening.

"You kidnapped Jeremy Downing. And you called me and pretended to be the Sow the Seeds killer."

"And why did I do that?"

"To have this heroic ending. To have your father arrested. To have yourself redeemed."

"How the hell does calling you—"

"To get me interested. You probably learned about my background. You knew I'd investigate. You needed a dupe and a witness. Someone outside the police. I was that dupe."

"The dupe du jour," Win added.

Myron shot him a look. Win shrugged.

"That's ridiculous."

"No, Stan, it adds up. It answers all my earlier questions. How did the kidnapper happen to choose Jeremy? Because you followed me after I left your condo. You saw the feds pick me up. That's how you knew I'd spoken to them. You followed me to Emily's house. From there, any old newsman worth a damn could have figured out her son was the sick kid I told you about. His illness wasn't a secret. So Jeremy's being taken is no longer a coincidence, see?"

Stan folded his arms across his chest. "I see nothing."

"Other questions get answered too now. Like why did the kidnapper wear a disguise and make Jeremy wear a blindfold? Because you couldn't let Jeremy identify you. Why didn't the kidnapper kill Jeremy right away, like he had the others? Same reason you wore the disguise. You had no intention of killing him. Jeremy had to survive the ordeal unharmed. Otherwise you're no hero. Why didn't the kidnapper make his usual demand not to contact the authorities? Because you wanted the feds in. You needed them to witness your heroics. It wouldn't work without their involvement. I wondered how the media was always in the right spot—in Bernardsville, at the cabin. But you set that part up too. Anonymous leaks probably. So the cameras could witness and replay your heroics—your tackling your father, the dramatic rescue of Jeremy Downing. Good television. You knew the power of capturing those moments for all the world to see."

Stan waited. "You finished?"

"Not yet. You see, I think you went too far in spots. Leaving that sneaker in the van, for example. That was overkill. Too obvious. It made me wonder how neatly it all came together in the end. And then I start realizing that I was your main sucker, Stan. You played me like a Stradivarius. But even if I hadn't shown up, you just would have kidnapped someone else. Your main dupes were the feds. For crying out loud, that photograph of your father by the statue was the only picture in the whole condo. It even faced the window. You knew the feds were spying on you. You threw the truth about Dennis Lex right in their faces. Surely they'd go to the sanitarium and put it together. And if not, you could somehow get it out in the end, when they had you in custody. You were all set to cave in and tell on your father when I came through in the clutch. Me, the dupe du jour, saw the truth up at the sanitarium. You must have been so pleased."

"This is crazy."

"It answers all the questions."

"That doesn't mean it's the truth."

"The Davis Taylor address you used at work. It was the same address as your father's in Waterbury. So we would trace it back to him, to Nathan Mostoni. Who else would have done that?"

"My father!"

"Why? Why would your father change identities at all? And if your father needed a new identity, wouldn't he shed the old one? Or hell, at least change addresses? Only you could have pulled it off, Stan. You could have hooked up the extra phone line with no problem. Your father was pretty far gone. He was demented, at the very least. You kidnapped Jeremy. Then you probably told your father to meet you at the house in Bernardsville. He did what you said—for love or because of dementia, I don't know which. Did you know he'd arm himself like that? I doubt it. If Greg had died, you'd probably look worse. But I don't know for sure. Maybe the fact that he fired shots just made you look more heroic in the end. Think selfishly, Stan. That's the key."

Stan shook his head.

" 'Say one last good-bye to the boy,' " Myron said.

"What?"

"That's what the Sow the Seeds killer said to me on the phone. The boy. I made a mistake when he called me. I told him a boy needed help. After that, I only used the word 'child.' When I spoke to Susan Lex. When I spoke to you. I said a thirteen-year-old child needs a transplant."

"So?"

"So when we talked in the car that night, you asked what I was really after, what my real interest in all this was. Remember?"

"Yes."

"And I said I already told you."

"Right."

"And you said, 'That boy who needs a bone marrow transplant?" You said, 'That boy.' How did you know he was a boy, Stan?"

Win turned toward Stan. Stan looked at Win's face.

"Is that your proof?" Stan countered. "I mean, is this supposed to be a Perry Mason moment or something? Maybe you slipped up, Myron. Or maybe I just assumed it was a boy. Or I heard wrong. That's not evidence."

"You're right. It's not. It just got me thinking, that's all."

"Thoughts aren't proof."

"Wow," Win said. "Thoughts aren't proof. I'll have to remember that one."

"But there is proof," Myron said. "Definitive proof."

"Impossible," Stan said, but his voice warbled now. "What?"

"I'll get to that in a moment. First let me back off on my indignation a little."

"I don't understand."

"At the end of the day, what you did was scummy, no question about it. But in its own way, it was almost ethical. Win and I often discuss the ends justifying the means. You could claim that's what happened here. You tried to turn your father in before he struck again. You did all you could to make sure nobody else was harmed. Jeremy was never in any real danger. You couldn't know that Greg would be shot. So in the end, you scared a boy, but so what? Next to the murder and destruction your father would have continued to wreak, it was nothing. So you did some good. The ends perhaps justified the means. Except for one thing."

Stan didn't bite.

"Jeremy's bone marrow transplant. He needs that to live, Stan. You know that. You also know that you're the match, not your father. That was why you slipped him that cyanide pill. Because once we dragged your father to the hospital and realized that he wasn't a match, well, we would have investigated. We would have realized that Edwin Gibbs was not Davis Taylor né Dennis Lex. So you had to have him kill himself and then you pushed for a quick cremation. I don't mean to make it sound as harsh or cold as all that. You didn't murder your father. He took the pill all on his own. He was a sick man. He wanted to die. It's yet another case of the ends justifying the means."

Myron took a moment and just looked into Stan's eyes. Stan did not look away. In a sense, this was more agenting work. Myron was negotiating here—the most important negotiation of his life. He had put his opponent in a corner. Now he needed to reach out. Not help him yet. He had to keep him in the corner. But he had to start reaching out. Just a little.

"You're not a monster," Myron said. "You just didn't count on the complication of being a bone marrow match. You want to do right by Jeremy. It's why you've gone so nuts trying to help the bone marrow drive. If they find another donor, it takes you off the hook. Because you're in this lie too deep now. You couldn't admit the truth—that you are the match. It would ruin you. I understand that."

Stan's eyes were wide and wet, but he was listening.

"Before I told you that I had proof," Myron said. "We checked the bone marrow registry. Know what we found, Stan?"

Stan didn't reply.

"You're not registered," Myron said. "Here you are telling everybody to sign up and you yourself aren't in their computer. The three of us know why. It's because you'd be a match. And if you matched, there would be those questions again."

Stan gave defiance one last shot. "That's not proof."

"Then how will you explain not registering?"

"I don't have to explain anything."

"A blood test will prove it conclusively. The registry still has the blood that Davis Taylor gave during the marrow drive. We can do a DNA test with yours, see if it matches up."

"And if I don't agree to a test?"

Win took that one. "Oh, you'll give blood," he said with just the slightest smile. "One way or another."

Something on Stan's face broke then. He lowered his head. The defiance was over. He was trapped in the corner now. No way to escape. He'd start looking for an ally. It always happened in negotiations. When you're lost, you look for an out. Myron had reached out before. It was time to do it again.

"You don't understand," Stan said.

"Strangely enough, I do." Myron moved a little closer to Stan. He made his voice soft yet unyielding. Total command mode. "Here's what we're going to do, Stan. You and I are going to make a deal."

Stan looked up, confused but also hopeful. "What?"

"You are going to agree to donate bone marrow to save Jeremy's life. You'll do it anonymously. Win and I can set that up. No one will ever know who the donor was. You do that, you save Jeremy, I forget the rest."

"How can I believe you?"

"Two reasons," Myron said. "One, I'm interested in saving Jeremy's life, not ruining yours. Two"—he tilted both palms toward the ceiling—"I'm no better. I bent rules here too. I let the ends justify the means. I assaulted a man. I kidnapped a woman."

Win shook his head. "There's a difference. His reasons were selfish. You, on the other hand, were trying to save a boy's life."

Myron turned to his friend. "Weren't you the one who said that motives are irrelevant? That the act is the act?"

"Sure," Win said. "But I meant that to apply to him, not you."

Myron smiled and faced Stan again. "I'm not your moral superior. We both did wrong. Maybe we can both live with what we've done. But if you let a boy die, Stan, you cross the line. You can't go home again."

Stan closed his eyes. "I would have found a way," he said. "I would have gotten another fake ID, given blood under a pseudonym. I was just hoping—"

"I know," Myron said. "I know all about it."

Myron called Dr. Karen Singh. "I found a matching donor."

"What?"

"I can't explain. But he has to stay anonymous."

"I explained to you that all the bone marrow donors remain anonymous."

"No. The bone marrow registry can't know about this either. We have to find a place that can harvest the marrow without knowing the patient's identity."

"Can't be done."

"Yeah, it can."

"No doctor will agree—"

"We can't play these games, Karen. I have a donor. No one can know who he is. Make it work."

He could hear her breathing.

"He'll have to be retested," she said.

"No problem."

"And pass a physical."

"Done."

"Then okay. Let's get this started."

When Emily heard about the donor, she gave Myron a curious look and waited. He didn't explain. She never asked.

Myron visited the hospital the day before the marrow transplant was to begin. He peeked his head around the doorjamb and saw the boy sleeping. Jeremy was bald from the chemo. His skin had a ghostly glow, like something withering from a lack of sunshine. Myron watched his son sleeping. Then he turned and went home. He didn't come back.

He returned to work at MB SportsReps and lived his life. He visited his father and mother. He hung out with Win and Esperanza. He landed a few new clients and started rebuilding his business. Big Cyndi handed in her wrestling resignation and took over the front desk. His world was wobbly but back on the axis.

Eighty-four days later—Myron kept count—he got a call from Karen Singh. She asked him to visit her office. When he arrived, she wasted no time.

"It worked," she said. "Jeremy went home today."

Myron started to cry. Karen Singh moved around her desk. She sat on the arm of his chair and rubbed his back.

Myron knocked on the half-open door.

"Enter," Greg said.

Myron did so. Greg Downing was sitting up in a chair. He'd grown a beard during his long hospital stretch.

He smiled at Myron. "Nice to see you."

"Same here. I like the beard."

"Gives me that Paul Bunyan touch, don't you think?"

"I was thinking more along the lines of Sebastian Cabot as Mr. French," Myron said.

Greg laughed. "Going home on Friday."

"Great."

Silence.

"You haven't visited much," Greg said.

"Wanted to give you time to heal. And grow that beard in fully."

Greg tried another laugh, but he sort of choked on it. "My basketball career is over, you know."

"You'll get over it."

"That easy?"

Myron smiled. "Who said anything about easy?"

"Yeah."

"But there are more important things in life than basketball," Myron said. "Though sometimes I forget that."

Greg nodded again. Then he looked down and said, "I heard about you finding the donor. I don't know how you did it—"

"It's not important."

He looked up. "Thank you."

Myron was not sure what to say to that. So he kept quiet. And that was when Greg shocked him.

"You know, don't you?"

Myron's heart stopped.

"That was why you helped," Greg said. His voice was pure flat-line. "Emily told you the truth."

The muscles around Myron's throat tightened. There was a whooshing sound in his head.

"Did you take a blood test?" Greg asked.

Myron managed a nod this time. Greg closed his eyes. Myron swallowed and said, "How long . . . ?"

"I'm not sure anymore," Greg said. "I guess right away."

He *knows*. The words fell on Myron, smacking down like raindrops, beading and rolling off, impenetrable. *He's always known. . . .*

"For a while I fooled myself into believing it wasn't so," Greg said. "It's amazing what the mind can do sometimes. But when Jeremy was six, he had his appendix out. I saw his blood type on a chart. It pretty much confirmed what I'd known all along."

Myron didn't know what to say. The realization pushed down on him, swept away the months of blocking like so many children's toys. The mind can indeed do amazing things. He looked at Greg and it was like seeing something in the proper light for the first time and it changed everything. He thought about fathers again. He thought about real sacrifice. He thought about heroes.

"Jeremy's a good boy," Greg said.

"I know," Myron said.

"You remember my father? Screaming on the sidelines like a lunatic?"

"Yes."

"I ended up looking just like him. Spitting image of my old man. He was my blood. And he was the cruelest son of a bitch I ever knew," Greg said. Then he added, "Blood never meant much to me."

A strange echo filled the room. The background noises faded away and there was just the two of them, staring at one another from across the most bizarre chasm.

Greg moved back to the bed. "I'm tired, Myron."

"Don't you think we should talk about this?"

"Yeah," Greg said. He laid back and shut his eyes a little too tightly. "Maybe later. But right now I'm really tired."

At the end of the day, Esperanza stepped into Myron's office, sat down, and said, "I don't know much about family values or what makes a happy family. I don't know the best way to raise a kid or what you have to do to make him happy and well adjusted, whatever the hell 'well adjusted' means. I don't know if it's best to be an only child or have lots of siblings or be raised by two parents or a single parent or a gay couple or a lesbian couple or an overweight albino. But I know one thing."

Myron looked up at her and waited.

"No child could ever be harmed by having you in his life."

Esperanza stood and went home.

Stan Gibbs was playing in the yard with his boys when Myron and Win pulled into the driveway. His wife—at least, Myron guessed it was his wife—sat in a lawn chair and watched. A little boy rode Stan like a horsey. They other boy lay on the ground giggling.

Win frowned. "How very Norman Rockwell."

Myron and Win stepped out of the car. Stan the horsey looked up. The smile stayed on when he saw them, but you could see it starting to lose its grip at the edges. Stan hoisted his son off his back and said something to him Myron couldn't hear. The boy gave an "Aaaw, Dad." Stan jumped to his feet and ruffled the boy's hair. Win frowned again. As Stan jogged toward them, his smile faded away like the end of a song.

"What are you doing here?"

Win said, "Back together with the wife, are we?"

"We're giving it a go."

"Touching," Win said.

Stan turned toward Myron. "What's going on here?"

"Tell the kids to go inside, Stan."

"What?"

Another car pulled in the driveway. Rick Peck was driving. Kimberly Green was in the passenger seat. Stan's face lost color. He snapped a look at Myron.

"We had a deal," he said.

"Remember how I told you that you had two choices when the novel was discovered?"

"I'm not in the mood—"

"I said you could run or you could tell the truth. Remember?"

Stan's façade tottered, and for the first time, Myron saw the rage.

"I left out a third choice. A choice you yourself pointed out to me the first time we met. You could have said that the Sow the Seeds kidnapper was a copycat. That he had read the book. It might have helped you out. Taken some of the heat off."

"I couldn't do that."

"Because it would have led to your father?"

"Yes."

"But you didn't know your father had written the book. Isn't that right, Stan? You said you never knew about the book. I remember that from the first time we talked. I've been watching you say the same thing on TV. You claim you didn't even know your father wrote it."

"All true," Stan said, and the façade slipped back into place. "But—I don't know—maybe subconsciously I suspected something somehow. I can't explain it."

"Good," Myron said.

"Damn good," Win added.

"The problem was," Myron said, "you had to say you hadn't read it. Because if you had, well, Stan, you'd be a plagiarizer. All this work, all your big plans to regain your reputation—it would be for nothing. You'd be ruined."

"We discussed this already."

"No, Stan, we didn't. At least not this part of it." Myron held up the evidence bag with the sheet of paper inside.

Stan set his jaw.

"Know what this is, Stan?"

He said nothing.

"I found it in Melina Garston's apartment. It says 'With love, Dad.' "

Stan swallowed. "So?"

"Something about it bothered me from the beginning. First off, the word 'Dad.' "

"I don't understand—"

"Sure you do, Stan. Melina's sister-in-law called George Garston 'Papa.' When I spoke to him, he referred to himself as 'Papa.' So why would he sign a note like this 'Dad'?"

"That doesn't mean anything."

"Maybe, maybe not. The second thing that bothered me: Who writes a note like this—on the top inside of a folded card? People use the bottom half, right? But see, Stan, this wasn't a card. It was a sheet of a paper folded in half. That's the key. Then there are those tears along the left edge. See them, Stan? Like someone had ripped it out of something."

Win handed Myron the novel that had been sent to Kimberly Green. Myron opened it and laid the piece of paper inside it.

"Something like a book."

It was a perfect match.

"Your father wrote this inscription," Myron said. "To you. Years ago. You'd known about the book all along."

"You can't prove that."

"Come on, Stan. A handwriting analyst will have no trouble with this. The Lexes weren't the ones who found the book. Melina Garston did. You asked her to lie for you in court. She did. But then she started growing suspicious. So she dug around your house and found this book. She's the one who mailed it to Kimberly Green."

"You have no proof—"

"She sent it in anonymously because she still cared about you. She even tore out the inscription so no one, most especially you, would ever know where the book had come from. You had plenty of enemies. Like Susan Lex. And the feds. She probably hoped you'd think they did it. At least for a little while. But you knew right away it was Melina. She didn't count on that. Or your reaction."

Stan's hands tightened into fists. They started shaking.

"The victims' families wouldn't speak to you, Stan. And you needed that for your article. You ended up following the book more than reality. The feds thought it was to fool them. But that wasn't it. Maybe your father told you he was the killer, but nothing else. Maybe the real story wasn't as interesting, so you needed to embellish. Maybe you weren't that good of a writer and you really felt you needed those family quotes. I don't know. But you plagiarized. And the only one who could tie you to that book was Melina Garston. So you killed her."

"You'll never prove it," Stan said.

"The feds will dig hard now. The Lexes will help. Win and I will help. We'll find enough. If nothing else, the jury—and the world—will hear all you did in this. They'll hate you enough to convict."

"You son of a bitch." Stan cocked his fist and aimed it at Myron. With an almost casual movement, Win swept his leg. Stan fell down in a heap. Win pointed and laughed. Stan's sons watched it all.

Kimberly Green and Rick Peck got out of the car. Myron signaled them to wait, but Kimberly Green shook her head. They cuffed Stan hard and dragged him away. His sons still watched. Myron thought about Melina Garston and his silent vow. Then he and Win headed back to the car.

"You always intended to turn him in," Win said.

"Yes. But first I had to make sure he went along with donating the bone marrow."

"And once you knew Jeremy was okay—"

"Then I told Green, yes."

Win started the car. "The evidence is still marginal. A good attorney will be able to poke holes."

"Not my problem," Myron said.

"You'd be willing to let him walk?"

"Yes," Myron said. "But Melina's father has juice. And he won't."

"I thought you advised him against taking the law into his own hands."

Myron shrugged. "No one ever listens to me."

"That's true," Win said.

Win drove.

"I just wonder," Myron said.

"What?"

"Who was the serial killer here? Did his father really do it? Or was it all Stan?"

"Doubt we'll ever know," Win said.

"Probably not."

"It shan't matter," Win said. "They'll get him for Melina Garston."

"I guess," Myron said. Then he frowned and repeated, " 'Shan't'?"

Win shrugged. "So is it finally over, my friend?"

Myron's leg did that nervous jig again. He stopped it and said, "Jeremy."

"Ah," Win said. "Are you going to tell him?"

Myron looked out the window and saw nothing. "Win's credo about selfishness would say yes."

"And Myron's credo?"

"I don't know that it's much different," Myron said.

Jeremy was playing basketball at the Y. Myron stepped into the bleachers, the rickety kind that shake with each step, and sat. Jeremy was still pale. He was thinner than the last time Myron had seen him, but there'd been a growth spurt over the last few months. Myron realized how fast changes take place for the young and felt a deep, hard thud in his chest.

For a while, he just watched the flow of the scrimmage and tried to judge his son's play objectively. Jeremy had the tools, Myron could see that right away, but there was plenty of rust on them. That wouldn't be a problem though. Again with the young. Rust doesn't stay long on the young.

As Myron watched the practice, his eyes widened. He felt his insides shrivel. He thought again about what he was about to do, and a swelling tide rose inside of him, overwhelming him, pulling him under.

Jeremy smiled when he spotted Myron. The smile cleaved Myron's heart in two even pieces. He felt lost, adrift. He thought about what Win had said, about what a real father was, and he thought about what Esperanza had said. He thought about Greg and Emily. He wondered if he should have spoken to his own father about this, if he should have told him that this wasn't a hypothetical, that the bomb had indeed landed, that he needed his help.

Jeremy continued to play, but Myron could see that the boy was distracted by his presence. Jeremy kept sneaking quick glances toward the stands. He played a little harder, picked up the pace a bit. Myron had been there, done that. The desire to impress. It had driven Myron, maybe as much as wanting to win. Shallow, but there you have it.

The coach had his players run a few more drills and then he lined them up on the baseline. They finished up with the aptly named "suicides," which was basically a series of gut-heaving sprints broken up by bending and touching different lines on the floor. Myron might be nostalgic for many things connected to basketball. Suicides were not one of them.

Ten minutes later, with most of the kids still trying to catch their breath, the coach gathered his troops, gave out schedules for the rest of the week, and dispersed the boys with a big handclap. Most of them headed toward the exit, slinging backpacks over their shoulders. Some went into the locker room. Jeremy walked over to Myron slowly.

"Hi," Jeremy said.

"Hi."

Sweat dripped off Jeremy's hair, his face coated and flushed from exertion. "I'm going to shower," he said. "You want to wait?"

"Sure," Myron said.

"Cool, I'll be right back."

The gymnasium emptied out. Myron stood and picked up an errant basketball. His fingers found the grooves right away. He took a few shots, watching the bottom of the net dance as the ball swished through. He smiled and sat back down, still holding the ball. A janitor came in and swept the floor Zamboni-style. His keys jangled. Someone flipped off the overhead lights. Jeremy came back not long after that. His hair was still wet. He, too, had a backpack over his shoulder.

As Win would say, "Showtime."

Myron gripped the ball a little tighter. "Sit down, Jeremy. We need to talk."

The boy's face was serene and almost too beautiful. He slid the backpack off his shoulder and sat down. Myron had rehearsed this part. He had looked at it from all sides, all the pluses and minuses. He had made up his mind and changed it and made it up again. He had, as Win put it, properly tortured himself.

But in the end, he knew there was one universal truth: Lies fester. You try to put them away. You jam them in a box and bury them in the ground. But eventually they eat their way out of coffins. They dig their way out of graves. They may sleep for years. But they always wake up. When they do, they're rested, stronger, more insidious.

Lies kill.

"This is going to be hard to understand—" He stopped. Suddenly his rehearsed speech sounded so damn canned, filled with "It's nobody's fault" and "Adults make mistakes too" and "It doesn't mean your parents love you any less." It was patronizing and stupid and—

"Mr. Bolitar?"

Myron looked up at the boy.

"My mom and dad told me," Jeremy said. "Two days ago."

His chest shuddered. "What?"

"I know you're my biological father."

Myron was surprised and yet he wasn't. Some might say that Emily and Greg had made a preemptive strike, almost like a lawyer who reveals something bad about his own client because he knows the opposition will do it. Lessen the blow. But maybe Emily and Greg had learned the same lesson he had about lies and how they fester. And maybe, once again, they were trying to do what was best for their boy.

"How do you feel about it?" Myron asked.

"Weird, I guess," Jeremy said. "I mean, Mom and Dad keep expecting me to fall apart or something. But I don't see why it has to be such a big deal."

"You don't?"

"Sure, okay, I see it, but"—he stopped, shrugged—"it's not like the whole world's turned inside out or anything. You know what I mean?"

Myron nodded. "Maybe it's because you've already had your world turned inside out."

"You mean being sick and all?"

"Yes."

"Yeah, maybe," he said, thinking about it. "Must be weird for you too."

"Yeah," Myron said.

"I've been thinking about it," Jeremy said. "You want to hear what I've come up with?"

Myron swallowed. He looked into the boy's eyes—serenity, yes, but not through innocence. "Very much," he said.

"You're not my dad," he said simply. "I mean, you might be my father. But you're not my dad. You know what I mean?"

Myron managed a nod

"But"—Jeremy stopped, looked up, shrugged the shrug of a thirteen-year-old—"but maybe you can still be around."

"Around?" Myron repeated.

"Yeah," Jeremy said. He smiled again and *pow*, Myron's chest took another blow. "Around. You know."

"Yeah," Myron said, "I know."

"I think I'd like that."

"Me too," Myron said.

Jeremy nodded. "Cool."

"Yeah."

The gym clock grunted and pushed forward. Jeremy looked at it. "Mom's probably outside waiting for me. We usually stop at the supermarket on the way home. Want to come?"

Myron shook his head. "Not today, thanks."

"Cool." Jeremy stood, watching Myron's face. "You okay?"

"Yeah."

Jeremy smiled. "Don't worry. It's going to work out."

Myron tried to smile back. "How did you get to be so smart?"

"Good parenting," he said. "Combined with good genes."

Myron laughed. "You might want to consider a future in politics."

"Yeah," Jeremy said. "Take it easy, Myron."

"You too, Jeremy."

He watched the boy walk out the door, again with the familiar gait. Jeremy didn't look back. There was the sound of the door closing, the echoes, and then Myron was alone. He turned toward the basket and stared at the hoop until it blurred. He saw the boy's first step, heard his first word, smelled the sweet clean of a young child's pajamas. He felt the smack of a ball against a glove, bent over to help with his homework, stayed up all night when he had a virus, all of it, like his own father had, a whirl of taunting, aching images, as irretrievable as the past. He saw himself hovering in the boy's darkened doorway, the silent sentinel to his adolescence, and he felt what remained of his heart burst into flames.

The images scattered when he blinked. His heart started beating again. He stared again at the basket and waited. This time nothing blurred. Nothing happened.

Tell No One

In loving memory
of my niece Gabi Coben
1997–2000

Our wonderful little Myszka ...

Small said, "But what about when we are dead and gone, will you love me then, does love go on?"

Large held Small snug as they looked out at the night, at the moon in the dark and the stars shining bright. "Small, look at the stars, how they shine and glow, some of the stars died a long time ago. Still they shine in the evening skies, for you see, Small, love like starlight never dies . . ."

– Debi Gliori
No Matter What
(Bloomsbury Publishing)

Acknowledgements

Right then. Before we start, I'd like to introduce the band:

- editor extraordinaire Beth de Guzman, as well as Susan Corcoran, Sharon Lulek, Nita Taublib, Irwyn Applebaum, and the rest of the prime-time players at Bantam Dell
- Lisa Erbach Vance and Aaron Priest, my agents
- Anne Armstrong-Coben, M.D., Gene Riehl, Jeffrey Bedford, Gwendolen Gross, Jon Wood, Linda Fairstein, Maggie Griffin, and Nils Lofgren for their insight and encouragement
- and Joel Gotler, who pushed and prodded and inspired

There should have been a dark whisper in the wind. Or maybe a deep chill in the bone. Something. An ethereal song only Elizabeth or I could hear. A tightness in the air. Some textbook premonition. There are misfortunes we almost expect in life—what happened to my parents, for example—and then there are other dark moments, moments of sudden violence, that alter everything. There was my life before the tragedy. There is my life now. The two have painfully little in common.

Elizabeth was quiet for our anniversary drive, but that was hardly unusual. Even as a young girl, she'd possessed this unpredictable melancholy streak. She'd go quiet and drift into either deep contemplation or a deep funk, I never knew which. Part of the mystery, I guess, but for the first time, I could feel the chasm between us. Our relationship had survived so much. I wondered if it could survive the truth. Or for that matter, the unspoken lies.

The car's air-conditioning whirred at the blue MAX setting. The day was hot and sticky. Classically August. We crossed the Delaware Water Gap at the Milford Bridge and were welcomed to Pennsylvania by a friendly toll collector. Ten miles later, I spotted the stone sign that read Lake Charmaine—private. I turned onto the dirt road.

The tires bore down, kicking up dust like an Arabian stampede. Elizabeth flipped off the car stereo. Out of the corner of my eye, I could tell that she was studying my profile. I wondered what she saw, and my heart started fluttering. Two deer nibbled on some leaves on our right. They stopped, looked at us, saw we meant no harm, went back to nibbling. I kept driving and then the lake rose before us. The sun was now in its death throes, bruising the sky a coiling purple and orange. The tops of the trees seemed to be on fire.

"I can't believe we still do this," I said.

"You're the one who started it."

"Yeah, when I was twelve years old."

Elizabeth let the smile through. She didn't smile often, but when she did, *pow*, right to my heart.

"It's romantic," she insisted.

"It's goofy."

"I love romance."

"You love goofy."

"You get laid whenever we do this."

"Call me Mr. Romance," I said.

She laughed and took my hand. "Come on, Mr. Romance, it's getting dark."

Lake Charmaine. My grandfather had come up with that name, which pissed off my grandmother to no end. She wanted it named for her. Her name was Bertha. Lake Bertha. Grandpa wouldn't hear it. Two points for Grandpa.

Some fifty-odd years ago, Lake Charmaine had been the sight of a rich-kids summer camp. The owner had gone belly-up and Grandpa bought the entire lake and surrounding acreage on the cheap. He'd fixed up the camp director's house and tore down most of the lakefront buildings. But farther in the woods, where no one went anymore, he left the kids' bunks alone to rot. My sister, Linda, and I used to explore them, sifting through their ruins for old treasures, playing hide-and-seek, daring ourselves to seek the Boogeyman we were sure watched and waited. Elizabeth rarely joined us. She liked to know where everything was. Hiding scared her.

When we stepped out of the car, I heard the ghosts. Lots of them here, too many, swirling and battling for my attention. My father's won out. The lake was hold-your-breath still, but I swore I could still hear Dad's howl of delight as he cannonballed off the dock, his knees pressed tightly against his chest, his smile just south of sane, the upcoming splash a virtual tidal wave in the eyes of his only son. Dad liked to land near my sunbathing mother's raft. She'd scold him, but she couldn't hide the laugh.

I blinked and the images were gone. But I remembered how the laugh and the howl and the splash would ripple and echo in the stillness of our lake, and I wondered if ripples and echoes like those ever fully die away, if somewhere in the woods my father's joyful yelps still bounced quietly off the trees. Silly thought, but there you go.

Memories, you see, hurt. The good ones most of all.

"You okay, Beck?" Elizabeth asked me.

I turned to her. "I'm going to get laid, right?"

"Perv."

She started walking up the path, her head high, her back straight. I watched her for a second, remembering the first time I'd seen that walk. I was seven years old, taking my bike—the one with the banana seat and Batman decal—for a plunge down Goodhart Road. Goodhart Road was steep and windy, the perfect thoroughfare for the discriminating Stingray driver. I rode downhill with no hands, feeling pretty much as cool and hip as a seven-year-old possibly could. The wind whipped back my hair and made my eyes water. I spotted the moving van in front of the Ruskins' old house, turned and—first pow—there she was, my Elizabeth, walking with that titanium spine, so poised, even then, even as a seven-year-old girl with Mary Janes and a friendship bracelet and too many freckles.

We met two weeks later in Miss Sobel's second-grade class, and from that moment on—please don't gag when I say this—we were soul mates. Adults found our relationship both cute and unhealthy—our inseparable tomboy-kickball friendship morphing into puppy love and adolescent preoccupation and hormonal high school dating. Everyone kept waiting for us to outgrow each other. Even us. We were both bright kids, especially Elizabeth, top students, rational even in the face of irrational love. We understood the odds.

But here we were, twenty-five-year-olds, married seven months now, back at the spot when at the age of twelve we'd shared our first real kiss.

Nauseating, I know.

We pushed past branches and through humidity thick enough to bind. The gummy smell of pine clawed the air. We trudged through high grass. Mosquitoes and the like buzzed upward in our wake. Trees cast long shadows that you could interpret any way you wanted, like trying to figure out what a cloud looked like or one of Rorschach's inkblots.

We ducked off the path and fought our way through thicker brush. Elizabeth led the way. I followed two paces back, an almost symbolic gesture when I think about it now. I always believed that nothing could drive us apart—certainly our history had proven that, hadn't it?—but now more than ever I could feel the guilt pushing her away.

My guilt.

Up ahead, Elizabeth made a right at the big semi-phallic rock and there, on the right, was our tree. Our initials were, yup, carved into the bark:

E. P.

\+

D. B

And yes, a heart surrounded it. Under the heart were twelve lines, one marking each anniversary of that first kiss. I was about to make a wisecrack about how nauseating we were, but when I saw Elizabeth's face, the freckles now either gone or darkened, the tilt of the chin, the long, graceful neck, the steady green eyes, the dark hair braided like thick rope down her back, I stopped. I almost told her right then and there, but something pulled me back.

"I love you," I said.

"You're already getting laid."

"Oh."

"I love you too."

"Okay, okay," I said, feigning being put out, "you'll get laid too."

She smiled, but I thought I saw hesitancy in it. I took her in my arms. When she was twelve and we finally worked up the courage to make out, she'd smelled wonderfully of clean hair and strawberry Pixie Stix. I'd been overwhelmed by the newness of it, of course, the excitement, the exploration. Today she smelled of lilacs and cinnamon. The kiss moved like a warm light from the center of my heart. When our tongues met, I still felt a jolt. Elizabeth pulled away, breathless.

"Do you want to do the honors?" she asked.

She handed me the knife, and I carved the thirteenth line in the tree. Thirteen. In hindsight, maybe there had been a premonition.

*

It was dark when we got back to the lake. The pale moon broke through the black, a solo beacon. There were no sounds tonight, not even crickets. Elizabeth and I quickly stripped down. I looked at her in the moonlight and felt something catch in my throat. She dove in first, barely making a ripple. I clumsily followed. The lake was surprisingly warm. Elizabeth swam with clean, even strokes, slicing through the water as though it were making a path for her. I splashed after her. Our sounds skittered across the lake's surface like skipping stones. She turned into my arms. Her skin was warm and wet. I loved her skin. We held each other close. She pressed her breasts against my chest. I could feel her heart and I could hear her breathing. Life sounds. We kissed. My hand wandered down the delicious curve of her back.

When we finished—when everything felt so right again—I grabbed a raft and collapsed onto it. I panted, my legs splayed, my feet dangling in the water.

Elizabeth frowned. "What, you going to fall asleep now?"

"Snore."

"Such a man."

I put my hands behind my head and lay back. A cloud passed in front of the moon, turning the blue night into something pallid and gray. The air was still. I could hear Elizabeth getting out of the water and stepping onto the dock. My eyes tried to adjust. I could barely make out her naked silhouette. She was, quite simply, breathtaking. I watched her bend at the waist and wring the water out of her hair. Then she arched her spine and threw her head back.

My raft drifted farther away from shore. I tried to sift through what had happened to me, but even I didn't understand it all. The raft kept moving. I started losing sight of Elizabeth. As she faded into the dark, I made a decision: I would tell her. I would tell her everything.

I nodded to myself and closed my eyes. There was a lightness in my chest now. I listened to the water gently lap against my raft.

Then I heard a car door open.

I sat up.

"Elizabeth?"

Pure silence, except for my own breathing.

I looked for her silhouette again. It was hard to make out, but for a moment I saw it. Or I thought I saw it. I'm not sure anymore or even if it matters. Either way, Elizabeth was standing perfectly still, and maybe she was facing me.

I might have blinked—I'm really not sure about that either—and when I looked again, Elizabeth was gone.

My heart slammed into my throat. "Elizabeth!"

No answer.

The panic rose. I fell off the raft and started swimming toward the dock. But my strokes were loud, maddeningly loud, in my ears. I couldn't hear what, if anything, was happening. I stopped.

"Elizabeth!"

For a long while there was no sound. The cloud still blocked the moon.

Maybe she had gone inside the cabin. Maybe she'd gotten something out of the car. I opened my mouth to call her name again.

That was when I heard her scream.

I lowered my head and swam, swam hard, my arms pumping, my legs kicking wildly. But I was still far from the dock. I tried to look as I swam, but it was too dark now, the moon offering just faint shafts of light, illuminating nothing.

I heard a scraping noise, like something being dragged.

Up ahead, I could see the dock. Twenty feet, no more. I swam harder. My lungs burned. I swallowed some water, my arms stretching forward, my hand fumbling blindly in the dark. Then I found it. The ladder. I grabbed hold, hoisted myself up, climbed out of the water. The dock was wet from Elizabeth. I looked toward the cabin. Too dark. I saw nothing.

"Elizabeth!"

Something like a baseball bat hit me square in the solar plexus. My eyes bulged. I folded at the waist, suffocating from within. No air. Another blow. This time it landed on the top of my skull. I heard a crack in my head, and it felt as though someone had hammered a nail through my temple. My legs buckled and I dropped to my knees. Totally disoriented now, I put my hands against the sides of my head and tried to cover up. The next blow—the final blow—hit me square in the face.

I toppled backward, back into the lake. My eyes closed. I heard Elizabeth scream again—she screamed my name this time—but the sound, all sound, gurgled away as I sank under the water.

1

Eight Years Later

Another girl was about to break my heart. She had brown eyes and kinky hair and a toothy smile. She also had braces and was fourteen years old and—

"Are you pregnant?" I asked.

"Yeah, Dr. Beck."

I managed not to close my eyes. This was not the first time I'd seen a pregnant teen. Not even the first time today. I've been a pediatrician at this Washington Heights clinic since I finished my residency at nearby Columbia-Presbyterian Medical Center five years ago. We serve a Medicaid (read: poor) population with general family health care, including obstetrics, internal medicine, and, of course, pediatrics. Many people believe this makes me a bleeding-heart do-gooder. It doesn't. I like being a pediatrician. I don't particularly like doing it out in the suburbs with soccer moms and manicured dads and, well, people like me.

"What do you plan on doing?" I asked.

"Me and Terrell. We're real happy, Dr. Beck."

"How old is Terrell?"

"Sixteen."

She looked up at me, happy and smiling. Again I managed not to close my eyes.

The thing that always surprises me—always—is that most of these pregnancies are not accidental. These babies want to have babies. No one gets that. They talk about birth control and abstinence and that's all fine and good, but the truth is, their cool friends are having babies and their friends are getting all kinds of attention and so, hey, Terrell, why not us?

"He loves me," this fourteen-year-old told me.

"Have you told your mother?"

"Not yet." She squirmed and looked almost all her fourteen years. "I was hoping you could tell her with me."

I nodded. "Sure."

I've learned not to judge. I listen. I empathize. When I was a resident, I would lecture. I would look down from on high and bestow upon patients the knowledge of how self-destructive their behavior was. But on a cold Manhattan afternoon, a weary seventeen-year-old girl who was having her third kid with a third father looked me straight in the eye and spoke an indisputable truth: "You don't know my life."

It shut me up. So I listen now. I stopped playing Benevolent White Man and became a better doctor. I will give this fourteen-year-old and her baby the absolute best care possible. I won't tell her that Terrell will never stay, that she's just cut her future off at the pass, that if she is like most of the patients here, she'll be in a similar state with at least two more men before she turns twenty.

Think about it too much and you'll go nuts.

We spoke for a while—or, at least, she spoke and I listened. The examining room, which doubled as my office, was about the size of a prison cell (not that I know this from firsthand experience) and painted an institutional green, like the color of a bathroom in an elementary school. An eye chart, the one where you point in the directions the Es are facing, hung on the back of the door. Faded Disney decals spotted one wall while another was covered with a giant food pyramid poster. My fourteen-year-old patient sat on an examining table with a roll of sanitary paper we pulled down fresh for each kid. For some reason, the way the paper rolled out reminded me of wrapping a sandwich at the Carnegie Deli.

The radiator heat was beyond stifling, but you needed that in a place where kids were frequently getting undressed. I wore my customary pediatrician garb: blue jeans, Chuck Taylor Cons, a button-down oxford, and a bright Save the Children tie that screamed 1994. I didn't wear the white coat. I think it scares the kids.

My fourteen-year-old—yes, I couldn't get past her age—was a really good kid. Funny thing is, they all are. I referred her to an obstetrician I liked. Then I spoke to her mother. Nothing new or surprising. As I said, I do this almost every day. We hugged when she left. Over her shoulder, her mother and I exchanged a glance. Approximately twenty-five moms take their children to see me each day; at the end of the week, I can count on one hand how many are married.

Like I said, I don't judge. But I do observe.

After they left, I started jotting notes in the girl's chart. I flipped back a few pages. I'd been following her since I was a resident. That meant she started with me when she was eight years old. I looked at her growth chart. I remembered her as an eight-year-old, and then I thought about what she'd just looked like. She hadn't changed much. I finally closed my eyes and rubbed them.

Homer Simpson interrupted me by shouting, "The mail! The mail is here! Oooo!"

I opened my eyes and turned toward the monitor. This was Homer Simpson as in the TV show *The Simpsons*. Someone had replaced the computer's droning "You've got mail" with this Homer audio wave. I liked it. I liked it a lot.

I was about to check my email when the intercom's squawking stopped my hand. Wanda, a receptionist, said, "You're, uh, hmm, you're, uh . . . Shauna is on the phone."

I understood the confusion. I thanked her and hit the blinking button. "Hello, sweetums."

"Never mind," she said. "I'm here."

Shauna hung up her cellular. I stood and walked down the corridor as Shauna made her entrance from the street. Shauna stalks into a room as though it offends her. She was a plus-size model, one of the few known by one name. Shauna. Like Cher or Fabio. She stood six one and weighed one hundred ninety pounds. She was, as you might expect, a head-turner, and all heads in the waiting room obliged.

Shauna did not bother stopping at Reception and Reception knew better than to try to stop her. She pulled open the door and greeted me with the words "Lunch. Now."

"I told you. I'm going to be busy."

"Put on a coat," she said. "It's cold out."

"Look, I'm fine. The anniversary isn't until tomorrow anyway."

"You're buying."

I hesitated and she knew she had me.

"Come on, Beck, it'll be fun. Like in college. Remember how we used to go out and scope hot babes together?"

"I never scoped hot babes."

"Oh, right, that was me. Go get your coat."

On the way back to my office, one of the mothers gave me a big smile and pulled me aside. "She's even more beautiful in person," she whispered.

"Eh," I said.

"Are you and she . . ." The mother made a together motion with her hands.

"No, she's already involved with someone," I said.

"Really? Who?"

"My sister."

We ate at a crummy Chinese restaurant with a Chinese waiter who spoke only Spanish. Shauna, dressed impeccably in a blue suit with a neckline that plunged like Black Monday, frowned. "Moo shu pork in a tortilla shell?"

"Be adventurous," I said.

We met our first day of college. Someone in the registrar's office had screwed up and thought her name was Shaun, and we thus ended up roommates. We were all set to report the mistake when we started chatting. She bought me a beer. I started to like her. A few hours later, we decided to give it a go because our real roommates might be assholes.

I went to Amherst College, an exclusive small-Ivy institution in western Massachusetts, and if there is a preppier place on the planet, I don't know it. Elizabeth, our high school valedictorian, chose Yale. We could have gone to the same college, but we discussed it and decided that this would be yet another excellent test for our relationship. Again, we were doing the mature thing. The result? We missed each other like mad. The separation deepened our commitment and gave our love a new distance-makes-the-heart-grow-fonder dimension.

Nauseating, I know.

Between bites, Shauna asked, "Can you baby-sit Mark tonight?"

Mark was my five-year-old nephew. Sometime during our senior year, Shauna started dating my older sister, Linda. They had a commitment ceremony seven years ago. Mark was the by-product of, well, their love, with a little help from artificial insemination. Linda carried him to term and Shauna adopted him. Being somewhat old-fashioned, they wanted their son to have a male role model in his life. Enter me.

Next to what I see at work, we're talking *Ozzie and Harriet.*

"No prob," I said. "I want to see the new Disney film anyway."

"The new Disney chick is a babe and a half," Shauna said. "Their hottest since Pocahontas."

"Good to know," I said. "So where are you and Linda going?"

"Beats the hell out of me. Now that lesbians are chic, our social calendar is ridiculous. I almost long for the days when we hid in closets."

I ordered a beer. Probably shouldn't have, but one wouldn't hurt.

Shauna ordered one too. "So you broke up with what's-her-name," she said.

"Brandy."

"Right. Nice name, by the way. She have a sister named Whiskey?"

"We only went out twice."

"Good. She was a skinny witch. Besides, I got someone perfect for you."

"No, thanks," I said.

"She's got a killer bod."

"Don't set me up, Shauna. Please."

"Why not?"

"Remember the last time you set me up?"

"With Cassandra."

"Right."

"So what was wrong with her?"

"For one thing, she was a lesbian."

"Christ, Beck, you're such a bigot."

Her cell phone rang. She leaned back and answered it, but her eyes never left my face. She barked something and flipped the mouthpiece up. "I have to go," she said.

I signaled for the check.

"You're coming over tomorrow night," she pronounced.

I feigned a gasp. "The lesbians have no plans?"

"I don't. Your sister does. She's going stag to the big Brandon Scope formal."

"You're not going with her?"

"Nah."

"Why not?"

"We don't want to leave Mark without us two nights in a row. Linda has to go. She's running the trust now. Me, I'm taking the night off. So come over tomorrow night, okay? I'll order in, we'll watch videos with Mark."

Tomorrow was the anniversary. Had Elizabeth lived, we'd be scratching our twenty-first line in that tree. Strange as this might sound, tomorrow would not be a particularly hard day for me. For anniversaries or holidays or Elizabeth's birthday, I get so geared up that I usually handle them with no problems. It's the "regular" days that are hard. When I flip with the remote and stumble across a classic episode of *The Mary Tyler Moore Show* or *Cheers*. When I walk through a bookstore and see a new title by Alice Hoffman or Anne Tyler. When I listen to the O'Jays or the Four Tops or Nina Simone. Regular stuff.

"I told Elizabeth's mother I'd stop by," I said.

"Ah, Beck . . ." She was about to argue but caught herself. "How about after?"

"Sure," I said.

Shauna grabbed my arm. "You're disappearing again, Beck."

I didn't reply.

"I love you, you know. I mean, if you had any sort of sexual appeal whatsoever, I probably would have gone for you instead of your sister."

"I'm flattered," I said. "Really."

"Don't shut me out. If you shut me out, you shut everyone out. Talk to me, okay?"

"Okay," I said. But I can't.

I almost erased the email.

I get so much junk email, spam, bulk emails, you know the drill, I've become quite handy with the delete button. I read the sender's address first. If it's someone I know or from the hospital, fine. If not, I enthusiastically click the delete button.

I sat at my desk and checked the afternoon schedule. Chock-full, which was no surprise. I spun around in my chair and readied my delete finger. One email only. The one that made Homer shriek before. I did the quick scan, and my eyes got snagged on the first two letters of the subject.

What the—?

The way the window screen was formatted, all I could see were those two letters and the sender's email address. The address was unfamiliar to me. A bunch of numbers @comparama.com.

I narrowed my eyes and hit the right scroll button. The subject appeared a character at a time. With each click, my pulse raced a bit more. My breathing grew funny. I kept my finger on the scroll button and waited.

When I was done, when all the letters showed themselves, I read the subject again and when I did, I felt a deep, hard thud in my heart.

"Dr. Beck?"

My mouth wouldn't work.

"Dr. Beck?"

"Give me a minute, Wanda."

She hesitated. I could still hear her on the intercom. Then I heard it click off.

I kept staring at the screen:

> To: dbeckmd@nyhosp.com
> From: 13943928@comparama.com
> Subject: E.P.+ D.B //////////////////////

Twenty-one lines. I've counted four times already.

It was a cruel, sick joke. I knew that. My hands tightened into fists. I wondered what chicken-shitted son of a bitch had sent it. It was easy to be anonymous in emails—the best refuge of the techno-coward. But the thing was, very few people knew about the tree or our anniversary. The media never learned about it. Shauna knew, of course. And Linda. Elizabeth might have told her parents or uncle. But outside of that . . .

So who sent it?

I wanted to read the message, of course, but something held me back. The truth is, I think about Elizabeth more than I let on—I don't think I'm fooling anyone there—but I never talk about her or what happened. People think I'm being macho or brave, that I'm trying to spare my friends or shunning people's pity or some such nonsense. That's not it. Talking about Elizabeth hurts. A lot. It brings back her last scream. It brings back all the unanswered questions. It brings back the might-have-beens (few things, I assure you, will devastate like the might-have-beens). It brings back the guilt, the feelings, no matter how irrational, that a stronger man—a better man—might have saved her.

They say it takes a long time to comprehend a tragedy. You're numb. You can't adequately accept the grim reality. Again, that's not true. Not for me anyway. I understood the full implications the moment they found Elizabeth's body. I understood that I would never see her again, that I would never hold her again, that we would never have children or grow old together. I understood that this was final, that there was no reprieve, that nothing could be bartered or negotiated.

I started crying immediately. Sobbing uncontrollably. I sobbed like that for almost a week without letup. I sobbed through the funeral. I let no one touch me, not even Shauna or Linda. I slept alone in our bed, burying my head in Elizabeth's pillow, trying to smell her. I went through her closets and pressed her clothes against my face. None of this was comforting. It was weird and it hurt. But it was her smell, a part of her, and I did it anyway.

Well-meaning friends—often the worst kind—handed me the usual clichés, and so I feel in a pretty good position to warn you: Just offer your deepest condolences. Don't tell me I'm young. Don't tell me it'll get better. Don't tell me she's in a better place. Don't tell me it's part of some divine plan. Don't tell me that I was lucky to have known such a love. Every one of those platitudes pissed me off. They made me—and this is going to sound uncharitable—stare at the idiot and wonder why he or she still breathed while my Elizabeth rotted.

I kept hearing that "better to have loved and lost" bullshit. Another falsehood. Trust me, it is not better. Don't show me paradise and then burn it down. That was part of it. The selfish part. What got to me more—what really hurt—was that Elizabeth was denied so much. I can't tell you how many times I see or do something and I think of how much Elizabeth would have loved it and the pang hits me anew.

People wonder if I have any regrets. The answer is, only one. I regret that there were moments I wasted doing something other than making Elizabeth happy.

"Dr. Beck?"

"One more second," I said.

I put my hand on the mouse and moved the cursor over the Read icon. I clicked it and the message came up:

> To: dbeckmd@nyhosp.com
> From: 13943928@comparama.com
> Subject: E.P.+ D.B ////////////////////
> Message: Click on this hyperlink, kiss time, anniversary.

A lead block formed in my chest.

Kiss time?

It was a joke, had to be. I am not big on cryptic. I'm also not big on waiting.

I grabbed the mouse again and moved the arrow over the hyperlink. I clicked and heard the primordial modem screech the mating call of machinery. We have an old system at the clinic. It took a while for the Web browser to appear. I waited, thinking *kiss time, how do they know about kiss time?*

The browser came up. It read error.

I frowned. Who the hell sent this? I tried it a second time, and again the error message came up. It was a broken link.

Who the hell knew about kiss time?

I have never told anyone. Elizabeth and I didn't much discuss it, probably because it was no big deal. We were corny to the point of Pollyanna, so stuff like this we just kept to ourselves. It was embarrassing really, but when we kissed that first time twenty-one years ago, I noted the time. Just for fun. I pulled back and looked at my Casio watch and said, "Six-fifteen."

And Elizabeth said, "*Kiss time.*"

I looked at the message yet again. I started getting pissed now. This was way beyond funny. It's one thing to send a cruel email, but . . .

Kiss time.

Well, kiss time was 6:15 p.m. tomorrow. I didn't have much choice. I'd have to wait until then.

So be it.

I saved the email onto a diskette just in case. I pulled down the print options and hit Print All. I don't know much about computers, but I know that you could sometimes trace the origin of a message from all that gobbledygook at the bottom. I heard the printer purr. I took another look at the subject. I counted the lines again. Still twenty-one.

I thought about that tree and that first kiss, and there in my tight, stifling office I started to smell the strawberry Pixie Stix.

2

At home, I found another shock from the past.

I live across the George Washington Bridge from Manhattan—in the typical American-dream suburb of Green River, New Jersey, a township with, despite the moniker, no river and shrinking amounts of green. Home is Grandpa's house. I moved in with him and a revolving door of foreign nurses when Nana died three years ago.

Grandpa has Alzheimer's. His mind is a bit like an old black-and-white TV with damaged rabbit-ear antennas. He goes in and out and some days are better than others and you have to hold the antennas a certain way and not move at all, and even then the picture does the intermittent vertical spin. At least, that was how it used to be. But lately—to keep within this metaphor—the TV barely flickers on.

I never really liked my grandfather. He was a domineering man, the kind of old-fashioned, lift-by-the-bootstraps type whose affection was meted out in direct proportion to your success. He was a gruff man of tough love and old-world machismo. A grandson who was both sensitive and unathletic, even with good grades, was easily dismissed.

The reason I agreed to move in with him was that I knew if I didn't, my sister would have taken him in. Linda was like that. When we sang at Brooklake summer camp that "He has the whole world in His hands," she took the meaning a little too much to heart. She would have felt obligated. But Linda had a son and a life partner and responsibilities. I did not. So I made a preemptive strike by moving in. I liked living here well enough, I guess. It was quiet.

Chloe, my dog, ran up to me, wagging her tail. I scratched her behind the floppy ears. She took it in for a moment or two and then started eyeing the leash.

"Give me a minute," I told her.

Chloe doesn't like this phrase. She gave me a look—no easy feat when your hair totally covers your eyes. Chloe is a bearded collie, a breed that appears far more like a sheepdog than any sort of collie I've ever seen. Elizabeth and I had bought Chloe right after we got married. Elizabeth had loved dogs. I hadn't. I do now.

Chloe leaned up against the front door. She looked at the door, then at me, then back at the door again. Hint, hint.

Grandpa was slumped in front of a TV game show. He didn't turn toward me, but then again, he didn't seem to be looking at the picture either. His face was stuck in what had become a steady, pallid death-freeze.

The only time I saw the death-freeze melt was when he was having his diaper changed. When that happened, Grandpa's lips thinned and his face went slack. His eyes watered and sometimes a tear escaped. I think he is at his most lucid at the exact moment he craves senility.

God has some sense of humor.

The nurse had left the message on the kitchen table: CALL SHERIFF LOWELL.

There was a phone number scribbled under it.

My head began to pound. Since the attack, I suffer migraines. The blows cracked my skull. I was hospitalized for five days, though one specialist, a classmate of mine at medical school, thinks the migraines are psychological rather than physiological in origin. Maybe he's right. Either way, both the pain and guilt remain. I should have ducked. I should have seen the blows coming. I shouldn't have fallen into the water. And finally, I somehow summoned up the strength to save myself—shouldn't I have been able to do the same to save Elizabeth?

Futile, I know.

I read the message again. Chloe started whining. I put up one finger. She stopped whining but started doing her glance-at-me-and-the-door again.

I hadn't heard from Sheriff Lowell in eight years, but I still remembered him looming over my hospital bed, his face etched with doubt and cynicism.

What could he want after all this time?

I picked up the phone and dialed. A voice answered on the first ring.

"Dr. Beck, thank you for calling me back."

I am not a big fan of caller ID—too Big Brother for my tastes. I cleared my throat and skipped the pleasantries. "What can I do for you, Sheriff?"

"I'm in the area," he said. "I'd very much like to stop by and see you, if that's okay."

"Is this a social call?" I asked.

"No, not really."

He waited for me to say something. I didn't.

"Would now be convenient?" Lowell asked.

"You mind telling me what it's about?"

"I'd rather wait until—"

"And I'd rather you didn't."

I could feel my grip on the receiver tighten.

"Okay, Dr. Beck, I understand." He cleared his throat in a way that indicated he was trying to buy some time. "Maybe you saw on the news that two bodies were found in Riley County."

I hadn't. "What about them?"

"They were found near your property."

"It's not my property. It's my grandfather's."

"But you're his legal custodian, right?"

"No," I said. "My sister is."

"Perhaps you could call her then. I'd like to speak with her too."

"The bodies were not found on Lake Charmaine, right?"

"That's correct. We found them on the western neighboring lot. County property actually."

"Then what do you want from us?"

There was a pause. "Look, I'll be there in an hour. Please see if you can get Linda to come by, will you?"

He hung up.

The eight years had not been kind to Sheriff Lowell, but then again, he hadn't been Mel Gibson to begin with. He was a mangy mutt of a man with features so extra-long hangdog that he made Nixon look as though he'd gotten a nip and tuck. The end of his nose was bulbous to the nth degree. He kept taking out a much-used hanky, carefully unfolding it, rubbing his nose, carefully refolding it, jamming it deep into his back pocket.

Linda had arrived. She leaned forward on the couch, ready to shield me. This was how she often sat. She was one of those people who gave you their full, undivided attention. She fixed you with those big brown eyes and you could look nowhere else. I'm definitely biased, but Linda is the best person I know. Corny, yes, but the fact that she exists gives me hope for this world. The fact that she loves me gives me whatever else I have left.

We sat in my grandparents' formal living room, which I usually do my utmost to avoid. The room was stale, creepy, and still had that old-people's-sofa smell. I found it hard to breathe. Sheriff Lowell took his time getting situated. He gave his nose a few more swipes, took out a pocket pad, licked his finger, found his page. He offered us his friendliest smile and started.

"Do you mind telling me when you were last at the lake?"

"I was there last month," Linda said.

But his eyes were on me. "And you, Dr. Beck?"

"Eight years ago."

He nodded as though he'd expected that response. "As I explained on the phone, we found two bodies near Lake Charmaine."

"Have you identified them yet?" Linda asked.

"No."

"Isn't that odd?"

Lowell thought about that one while leaning forward to pull out the hanky again. "We know that they're both male, both full-grown, both white. We're now searching through missing persons to see what we can come up with. The bodies are rather old."

"How old?" I asked.

Sheriff Lowell again found my eyes. "Hard to say. Forensics is still running tests, but we figure they've been dead at least five years. They were buried pretty good too. We'd never have found them except there was a landslide from that record rainfall, and a bear came up with an arm."

My sister and I looked at each other.

"Excuse me?" Linda said.

Sheriff Lowell nodded. "A hunter shot a bear and found a bone next to the body. It'd been in the bear's mouth. Turned out to be a human arm. We traced it back. Took some time, I can tell you. We're still excavating the area."

"You think there may be more bodies?"

"Can't say for sure."

I sat back. Linda stayed focused. "So are you here to get our permission to dig on Lake Charmaine property?"

"In part."

We waited for him to say more. He cleared his throat and looked at me again. "Dr. Beck, you're blood type B positive, isn't that right?"

I opened my mouth, but Linda put a protective hand on my knee. "What does that have to do with anything?" she asked.

"We found other things," he said. "At the grave site."

"What other things?"

"I'm sorry. That's confidential."

"Then get the hell out," I said.

Lowell did not seem particularly surprised by my outburst. "I'm just trying to conduct—"

"I said, get out."

Sheriff Lowell didn't move. "I know that your wife's murderer has already been brought to justice," he said. "And I know it must hurt like hell to bring this all up again."

"Don't patronize me," I said.

"That's not my intent."

"Eight years ago you thought I killed her."

"That's not true. You were her husband. In such cases, the odds of a family member's involvement—"

"Maybe if you didn't waste time with that crap, you would have found her before—" I jerked back, feeling myself choking up. I turned away. Damn. Damn him. Linda reached for me, but I moved away.

"My job was to explore every possibility," he droned on. "We had the federal authorities helping us. Even your father-in-law and his brother were kept informed of all developments. We did everything we could."

I couldn't bear to hear another word. "What the hell do you want here, Lowell?"

He rose and hoisted his pants onto his gut. I think he wanted the height advantage. To intimidate or something. "A blood sample," he said. "From you."

"Why?"

"When your wife was abducted, you were assaulted."

"So?"

"You were hit with a blunt instrument."

"You know all this."

"Yes," Lowell said. He gave his nose another wipe, tucked the hanky away, and started pacing. "When we found the bodies, we also found a baseball bat."

The pain in my head started throbbing again. "A bat?"

Lowell nodded. "Buried in the ground with the bodies. There was a wooden bat."

Linda said, "I don't understand. What does this have to do with my brother?"

"We found dried blood on it. We've typed it as B positive." He tilted his head toward me. "Your blood type, Dr. Beck."

*

We went over it again. The tree-carving anniversary, the swim in the lake, the sound of the car door, my pitifully frantic swim to shore.

"You remember falling back in the lake?" Lowell asked me.

"Yes."

"And you heard your wife scream?"

"Yes."

"And then you passed out? In the water?"

I nodded.

"How deep would you say the water was? Where you fell in, I mean?"

"Didn't you check this eight years ago?" I asked.

"Bear with me, Dr. Beck."

"I don't know. Deep."

"Over-your-head deep?"

"Yes."

"Right, okay. Then what do you remember?"

"The hospital," I said.

"Nothing between the time you hit the water and the time you woke up at the hospital?"

"That's right."

"You don't remember getting out of the water? You don't remember making your way to the cabin or calling for an ambulance? You did all that, you know. We found you on the floor of the cabin. The phone was still off the hook."

"I know, but I don't remember."

Linda spoke up. "Do you think these two men are more victims of"—she hesitated—"KillRoy?"

She said it in a hush. KillRoy. Just uttering his name chilled the room.

Lowell coughed into his fist. "We're not sure, ma'am. KillRoy's only known victims are women. He never hid a body before—at least, none that we know about. And the two men's skin had rotted so we can't tell if they'd been branded."

Branded. I felt my head spin. I closed my eyes and tried not to hear any more.

3

I rushed to my office early the next morning, arriving two hours before my first scheduled patient. I flipped on the computer, found the strange email, clicked the hyperlink. Again it came up an error. No surprise really. I stared at the message, reading it over and over as though I might find a deeper meaning. I didn't.

Last night, I gave blood. The DNA test would take weeks, but Sheriff Lowell thought they might be able to get a preliminary match earlier. I pushed him for more information, but he remained tight-lipped. He was keeping something from us. What, I had no idea.

As I sat in the examining room and waited for my first patient, I replayed Lowell's visit. I thought about the two bodies. I thought about the bloody wooden bat. And I let myself think about the branding.

Elizabeth's body was found off Route 80 five days after the abduction. The coroner estimated that she'd been dead for two days. That meant she spent three days alive with Elroy Kellerton, aka KillRoy. Three days. Alone with a monster. Three sunrises and sunsets, scared and in the dark and in immense agony. I try very hard not to think about it. There are some places the mind should not go; it gets steered there anyway.

KillRoy was caught three weeks later. He confessed to killing fourteen women on a spree that began with a coed in Ann Arbor and ended with a prostitute in the Bronx. All fourteen women were found dumped on the side of the road like so much refuse. All had also been branded with the letter K. Branded in the same way as cattle. In other words, Elroy Kellerton took a metal poker, stuck it in a blazing fire, put a protective mitt on his hand, waited until the poker turned molten red with heat, and then he seared my Elizabeth's beautiful skin with a sizzling hiss.

My mind took one of those wrong turns, and images started flooding in. I squeezed my eyes shut and wished them away. It didn't work. He was still alive, by the way. KillRoy, I mean. Our appeals process gives this monster the chance to breathe, to read, to talk, to be interviewed on CNN, to get visits from do-gooders, to smile. Meanwhile his victims rot. Like I said, God has some sense of humor.

I splashed cold water on my face and checked the mirror. I looked like hell. Patients started filing in at nine o'clock. I was distracted, of course. I kept one eye on the wall clock, waiting for "kiss time"—6:15 p.m. The clock's hands trudged forward as though bathed in thick syrup.

I immersed myself in patient care. I'd always had that ability. As a kid, I could study for hours. As a doctor, I can disappear into my work. I did that after Elizabeth died. Some people point out that I hide in my work, that I choose to work instead of live. To that cliché I respond with a simple "What's your point?"

At noon, I downed a ham sandwich and Diet Coke and then I saw more patients. One eight-year-old boy had visited a chiropractor for "spinal alignment" eighty times in the past year. He had no back pain. It was a con job perpetrated by several area chiropractors. They offer the parents a free TV or VCR if they bring their kids in. Then they bill Medicaid for the visit. Medicaid is a wonderful, necessary thing, but it gets abused like a Don King undercard. I once had a sixteen-year-old boy rushed to the hospital in an ambulance—for routine sunburn. Why an ambulance instead of a taxi or subway? His mother explained that she'd have to pay for those herself or wait for the government to reimburse. Medicaid pays for the ambulance right away.

At five o'clock, I said good-bye to my last patient. The support staff headed out at five-thirty. I waited until the office was empty before I sat and faced the computer. In the background I could hear the clinic's phones ringing. A machine picks them up after five-thirty and gives the caller several options, but for some reason, the machine doesn't pick up until the tenth ring. The sound was somewhat maddening.

I got online, found the email, and clicked on the hyperlink yet again. Still a no-go. I thought about this strange email and those dead bodies. There had to be a connection. My mind kept going back to that seemingly simple fact. I started sorting through the possibilities.

Possibility one: These two men were the work of KillRoy. True, his other victims were women and easily found, but did that rule out his killing others?

Possibility two: KillRoy had persuaded these men to help him abduct Elizabeth. That might explain a lot. The wooden bat, for one thing, if the blood on it was indeed mine. It also put to rest my one big question mark about the whole abduction. In theory, KillRoy, like all serial killers, worked alone. How, I'd always wondered, had he been able to drag Elizabeth to the car and at the same time lie in wait for me to get out of the water? Before her body surfaced, the authorities had assumed there had been more than one abductor. But once her corpse was found branded with the K, that hypothesis was finessed. KillRoy could have done it, it was theorized, if he'd cuffed or somehow subdued Elizabeth and then gone after me. It wasn't a perfect fit, but if you pushed hard enough, the piece went in.

Now we had another explanation. He had accomplices. And he killed them.

Possibility three was the simplest: The blood on the bat was not mine. B positive is not common, but it's not that rare either. In all likelihood, these bodies had nothing to do with Elizabeth's death.

I couldn't make myself buy it.

I checked the computer's clock. It was hooked into some satellite that gave the exact time.

6:04.42 p.m.

Ten minutes and eighteen seconds to go.

To go to what?

The phones kept ringing. I tuned them out and drummed my fingers. Under ten minutes now. Okay, if there was going to be a change in the hyperlink, it would have probably happened by now. I put my hand on the mouse and took a deep breath.

My beeper went off.

I wasn't on call tonight. That meant it was either a mistake—something made far too often by the clinic night operators—or a personal call. It beeped again. Double beep. That meant an emergency. I looked at the display.

It was a call from Sheriff Lowell. It was marked Urgent.

Eight minutes.

I thought about it but not for very long. Anything was better than stewing with my own thoughts. I decided to call him back.

Lowell again knew who it was before he picked up. "Sorry to bother you, Doc." Doc, he called me now. As though we were chums. "But I just have a quick question."

I put my hand back on the mouse, moved the cursor over the hyperlink, and clicked. The Web browser stirred to life.

"I'm listening," I said.

The Web browser was taking longer this time. No error message appeared.

"Does the name Sarah Goodhart mean anything to you?"

I almost dropped the phone.

"Doc?"

I pulled the receiver away and looked at it as though it had just materialized in my hand. I gathered myself together a piece at a time. When I trusted my voice, I put the phone back to my ear. "Why do you ask?"

Something started coming up on the computer screen. I squinted. One of those sky cams. Or street cam, I guess you'd call this one. They had them all over the Web now. I sometimes used the traffic ones, especially to check out the morning delay on the Washington Bridge.

"It's a long story," Lowell said.

I needed to buy time. "Then I'll call you back."

I hung up. Sarah Goodhart. The name meant something to me. It meant a lot.

What the hell was going on here?

The browser stopped loading. On the monitor, I saw a street scene in black and white. The rest of the page was blank. No banners or titles. I knew you could set it up so that you grabbed only a certain feed. That was what we had here.

I checked the computer clock.

6:12.18 p.m.

The camera was pointing down at a fairly busy street corner, from maybe fifteen feet off the ground. I didn't know what corner it was or what city I was looking at. It was definitely a major city, though. Pedestrians flowed mostly from right to left, heads down, shoulders slumped, briefcases in hand, downtrodden at the end of a workday, probably heading for a train or bus. On the far right, I could see the curb. The foot traffic came in waves, probably coordinated with the changing of a traffic light.

I frowned. Why had someone sent me this feed?

The clock read 6:14.21 p.m. Less than a minute to go.

I kept my eyes glued to the screen and waited for the countdown as though it were New Year's Eve. My pulse started speeding up. Ten, nine, eight . . .

Another tidal wave of humanity passed from right to left. I took my eyes off the clock. Four, three, two. I held my breath and waited. When I glanced at the clock again, it read:

6:15.02 p.m.

Nothing had happened—but then again, what had I expected?

The human tidal wave ebbed and once again, for a second or two, there was nobody in the picture. I settled back, sucking in air. A joke, I figured. A weird joke, sure. Sick even. But nonetheless—

And that was when someone stepped out from directly under the camera. It was as though the person had been hiding there the whole time.

I leaned forward.

It was a woman. That much I could see even though her back was to me. Short hair, but definitely a woman. From my angle, I hadn't been able to make out any faces so far. This was no different. Not at first.

The woman stopped. I stared at the top of her head, almost willing her to look up. She took another step. She was in the middle of the screen now. Someone else walked by. The woman stayed still. Then she turned around and slowly lifted her chin until she looked straight up into the camera.

My heart stopped.

I stuck a fist in my mouth and smothered a scream. I couldn't breathe. I couldn't think. Tears filled my eyes and started spilling down my cheeks. I didn't wipe them away.

I stared at her. She stared at me.

Another mass of pedestrians crossed the screen. Some of them bumped into her, but the woman didn't move. Her gaze stayed locked on the camera. She lifted her hand as though reaching toward me. My head spun. It was as though whatever tethered me to reality had been severed.

I was left floating helplessly.

She kept her hand raised. Slowly I managed to lift my hand. My fingers brushed the warm screen, trying to meet her halfway. More tears came. I gently caressed the woman's face and felt my heart crumble and soar all at once.

"Elizabeth," I whispered.

She stayed there for another second or two. Then she said something into the camera. I couldn't hear her, but I could read her lips.

"I'm sorry," my dead wife mouthed.

And then she walked away.

4

Vic Letty looked both ways before he limped inside the strip mall's Mail Boxes Etc. His gaze slid across the room. Nobody was watching. Perfect. Vic couldn't help but smile. His scam was foolproof. There was no way to trace it back to him, and now it was going to make him big-time rich.

The key, Vic realized, was preparation. That was what separated the good from the great. The greats covered their tracks. The greats prepared for every eventuality.

The first thing Vic did was get a fake ID from that loser cousin of his, Tony. Then, using the fake ID, Vic rented a mailbox under the pseudonym UYS Enterprises. See the brilliance? Use a fake ID *and* a pseudonym. So even if someone bribed the bozo behind the desk, even if someone could find out who rented the UYS Enterprises box, all you'd come up with was the name Roscoe Taylor, the one on Vic's fake ID.

No way to trace it back to Vic himself.

From across the room, Vic tried to see in the little window for Box 417. Hard to make out much, but there was something there for sure. Beautiful. Vic accepted only cash or money orders. No checks, of course. Nothing that could be traced back to him. And whenever he picked up the money, he wore a disguise. Like right now. He had on a baseball cap and a fake mustache. He also pretended to have a limp. He read somewhere that people notice limps, so if a witness was asked to identify the guy using Box 417, what would the witness say? Simple. The man had a mustache and a limp. And if you bribed the dumb-ass clerk, you'd conclude some guy named Roscoe Taylor had a mustache and a limp.

And the real Vic Letty had neither.

But Vic took other precautions too. He never opened the box when other people were around. Never. If someone else was getting his mail or in the general vicinity, he'd act as though he was opening another box or pretend he was filling out a mailing form, something like that. When the coast was clear—and only when the coast was clear—would Vic go over to Box 417.

Vic knew that you could never, ever be too careful.

Even when it came to getting here, Vic took precautions. He'd parked his work truck—Vic handled repairs and installations for CableEye, the East Coast's biggest cable TV operator—four blocks away. He'd ducked through two alleys on his way here. He wore a black windbreaker over his uniform coverall so no one would be able to see the "Vic" sewn over the shirt's right-pocket.

He thought now about the huge payday that was probably in Box 417, not ten feet from where he now stood. His fingers felt antsy. He checked the room again.

There were two women opening their boxes. One turned and smiled absently at him. Vic moved toward the boxes on the other side of the room and grabbed his key chain—he had one of those key chains that jangled off his belt—and pretended to be sorting through them. He kept his face down and away from them.

More caution.

Two minutes later, the two women had their mail and were gone. Vic was alone. He quickly crossed the room and opened his box.

Oh wow.

One package addressed to UYS Enterprises. Wrapped in brown. No return address. And thick enough to hold some serious green.

Vic smiled and wondered: Is that what fifty grand looks like?

He reached out with trembling hands and picked up the package. It felt comfortably heavy in his hand. Vic's heart started jackhammering. Oh, sweet Jesus. He'd been running this scam for four months now. He'd been casting that net and landing some pretty decent fish. But oh lordy, now he'd landed a friggin' whale!

Checking his surroundings again, Vic stuffed the package into the pocket of his windbreaker and hurried outside. He took a different route back to his work truck and started for the plant. His fingers found the package and stroked it. Fifty grand. Fifty thousand dollars. The number totally blew his mind.

By the time Vic drove to the CableEye plant, night had fallen. He parked the truck in the back and walked across the footbridge to his own car, a rusted-out 1991 Honda Civic. He frowned at the car and thought, Not much longer.

The employee lot was quiet. The darkness started weighing against him. He could hear his footsteps, the weary slap of work boots against tar. The cold sliced through his windbreaker. Fifty grand. He had fifty grand in his pocket.

Vic hunched his shoulders and hurried his step.

The truth was, Vic was scared this time. The scam would have to stop. It was a good scam, no doubt about it. A great one even. But he was taking on some big boys now. He had questioned the intelligence of such a move, weighed the pros and cons, and decided that the great ones—the ones who really change their lives—go for it.

And Vic wanted to be a great one.

The scam was simple, which was what made it so extraordinary. Every house that had cable had a switch box on the telephone line. When you ordered some sort of premium channel like HBO or Showtime, your friendly neighborhood cable man came out and flicked a few switches. That switch box holds your cable life. And what holds your cable life holds all about the real you.

Cable companies and hotels with in-room movies always point out that your bill will not list the names of the movies you watch. That might be true, but that doesn't mean they don't know. Try fighting a charge sometime. They'll tell you titles until you're blue in the face.

What Vic had learned right away—and not to get too technical here—was that your cable choices worked by codes, relaying your order information via the cable switch box to the computers at the cable company's main station. Vic would climb the telephone poles, open the boxes, and read off the numbers. When he went back to the office, he'd plug in the codes and learn all.

He'd learn, for example, that at six p.m. on February 2, you and your family rented *The Lion King* on pay-per-view. Or for a much more telling example, that at ten-thirty p.m. on February 7, you ordered a double bill of *The Hunt for Miss October* and *On Golden Blonde* via Sizzle TV.

See the scam?

At first Vic would hit random houses. He'd write a letter to the male owner of the residence. The letter would be short and chilling. It would list what porno movies had been watched, at what time, on what day. It would make it clear that copies of this information would be disseminated to every member of the man's family, his neighbors, his employer. Then Vic would ask for $500 to keep his mouth shut. Not much money maybe, but Vic thought it was the perfect amount—high enough to give Vic some serious green yet low enough so that most marks wouldn't balk at the price.

Still—and this surprised Vic at first—only about ten percent responded. Vic wasn't sure why. Maybe watching porno films wasn't the stigma it used to be. Maybe the guy's wife already knew about it. Hell, maybe the guy's wife watched them with him. But the real problem was Vic's scam was too scattershot.

He had to be more focused. He had to cherry-pick his marks.

That was when he came up with the idea of concentrating on people in certain professions, ones who would have a lot to lose if the information came out. Again the cable computers had all the info he needed. He started hitting up schoolteachers. Day care workers. Gynecologists. Anyone who worked in jobs that would be sensitive to a scandal like this. Teachers panicked the most, but they had the least money. He also made his letters more specific. He would mention the wife by name. He would mention the employer by name. With teachers, he'd promise to flood the Board of Education and the parents of his students with "proof of perversion," a phrase Vic came up with on his own. With doctors, he'd threaten to send his "proof" to the specific licensing board, along with the local papers, neighbors, and patients.

Money started coming in faster.

To date, Vic's scams had netted him close to forty thousand dollars. And now he had landed his biggest fish yet—such a big fish that at first Vic had considered dropping the matter altogether. But he couldn't. He couldn't just walk away from the juiciest score of his life.

Yes, he'd hit someone in the spotlight. A big, big big-time spotlight. Randall Scope. Young, handsome, rich, hottie wife, 2.4 kids, political aspirations, the heir apparent to the Scope fortune. And Scope hadn't ordered just one movie. Or even two.

During a one-month stint, Randall Scope had ordered twenty-three pornographic films.

Ee-yow.

Vic had spent two nights drafting his demands, but in the end he stuck with the basics: short, chilling, and very specific. He asked Scope for fifty grand. He asked that it be in his box by today. And unless Vic was mistaken, that fifty grand was burning a hole in his windbreaker pocket.

Vic wanted to look. He wanted to look right now. But Vic was nothing if not disciplined. He'd wait until he got home. He'd lock his door and sit on the floor and slit open the package and let the green pour out.

Serious big-time.

Vic parked his car on the street and headed up the driveway. The sight of his living quarters—an apartment over a crappy garage—depressed him. But he wouldn't be there much longer. Take the fifty grand, add the almost forty grand he had hidden in the apartment, plus the ten grand in savings ...

The realization made him pause. One hundred thousand dollars. He had one hundred grand in cash. Hot damn.

He'd leave right away. Take this money and head out to Arizona. He had a friend out there, Sammy Viola. He and Sammy were going to start their own business, maybe open a restaurant or nightclub. Vic was tired of New Jersey.

It was time to move on. Start fresh.

Vic headed up the stairs toward his apartment. For the record, Vic had never carried out his threats. He never sent out any letters to anyone. If a mark didn't pay, that was the end of it. Harming them after the fact wouldn't do any good. Vic was a scam artist. He got by on his brains. He used threats, sure, but he'd never carry through with them. It would only make someone mad, and hell, it would probably expose him too.

He'd never really hurt anyone. What would be the point?

He reached the landing and stopped in front of his door. Pitch dark now. The damn lightbulb by his door was out again. He sighed and heaved up his big key chain. He squinted in the dark, trying to find the right key. He did it mostly through feel. He fumbled against the knob until the key found the lock. He pushed open the door and stepped inside and something felt wrong.

Something crinkled under his feet.

Vic frowned. Plastic, he thought to himself. He was stepping on plastic. As though a painter had laid it down to protect the floor or something. He flicked on the light switch, and that was when he saw the man with the gun.

"Hi, Vic."

Vic gasped and took a step back. The man in front of him looked to be in his forties. He was big and fat with a belly that battled against the buttons of his dress shirt and, in at least one place, won. His tie was loosened and he had the worst comb-over imaginable—eight braided strands pulled ear to ear and greased against the dome. The man's features were soft, his chin sinking into folds of flab. He had his feet up on the trunk Vic used as a coffee table. Replace the gun with a TV remote and the man would be a weary dad just home from work.

The other man, the one who blocked the door, was the polar opposite of the big guy—in his twenties, Asian, squat, granite-muscular and cube-shaped with bleached-blond hair, a nose ring or two, and a yellow Walkman in his ears. The only place you might think to see the two of them together would be on a subway, the big man frowning behind his carefully folded newspaper, the Asian kid eyeing you as his head lightly bounced to the too-loud music on his headset.

Vic tried to think. Find out what they want. Reason with them. You're a scam artist, he reminded himself. You're smart. You'll find a way out of this. Vic straightened himself up.

"What do you want?" Vic asked.

The big man with the comb-over pulled the trigger.

Vic heard a pop and then his right knee exploded. His eyes went wide. He screamed and crumbled to the ground, holding his knee. Blood poured between his fingers.

"It's a twenty-two," the big man said, motioning toward the gun. "A small-caliber weapon. What I like about it, as you'll see, is that I can shoot you a lot and not kill you."

With his feet still up, the big man fired again. This time, Vic's shoulder took the hit. Vic could actually feel the bone shatter. His arm flopped away like a barn door with a busted hinge. Vic fell flat on his back and started breathing too fast. A terrible cocktail of fear and pain engulfed him. His eyes stayed wide and unblinking, and through the haze, he realized something.

The plastic on the ground.

He was lying on it. More than that, he was bleeding on it. That was what it was there for. The men had put it down for easy cleanup.

"Do you want to start telling me what I want to hear," the big man said, "or should I shoot again?"

Vic started talking. He told them everything. He told them where the rest of the money was. He told them where the evidence was. The big man asked him if he had any accomplices. He said no. The big man shot Vic's other knee. He asked him again if he had accomplices. Vic still said no. The big man shot him in the right ankle.

An hour later, Vic begged the big man to shoot him in the head.

Two hours after that, the big man obliged.

5

I stared unblinking at the computer screen.

I couldn't move. My senses were past overload. Every part of me was numb.

It couldn't be. I knew that. Elizabeth hadn't fallen off a yacht and assumed drowned, her body never found. She hadn't been burned beyond recognition or any of that. Her corpse had been found in a ditch off Route 80. Battered, perhaps, but she had been positively IDed.

Not by you ...

Maybe not, but by two close family members: her father and her uncle. In fact, Hoyt Parker, my father-in-law, was the one who told me that Elizabeth was dead. He came to my hospital room with his brother Ken not long after I regained consciousness. Hoyt and Ken were large and grizzled and stone-faced, one a New York City cop, the other a federal agent, both war veterans with beefy flesh and large, undefined muscles. They took off their hats and tried to tell me with the semidistant empathy of professionals, but I didn't buy it and they weren't selling too hard.

So what had I just seen?

On the monitor, flows of pedestrians still spurted by. I stared some more, willing her to come back. No dice. Where was this anyway? A bustling city, that was all I could tell. It could be New York for all I knew.

So look for clues, idiot.

I tried to concentrate. Clothes. Okay, let's check out the clothes. Most people were wearing coats or jackets. Conclusion: We were probably somewhere up north or, at least, someplace not particularly warm today. Great. I could rule out Miami.

What else? I stared at the people. The hairstyles? That wouldn't help. I could see the corner of a brick building. I looked for identifiable characteristics, something to separate the building from the norm. Nothing. I searched the screen for something, anything, out of the ordinary.

Shopping bags.

A few people were carrying shopping bags. I tried to read them, but everyone was moving too fast. I willed them to slow down. They didn't. I kept looking, keeping my gaze at knee level. The camera angle wasn't helping here. I put my face so close to the screen, I could feel the heat.

Capital R.

That was the first letter on one bag. The rest was too squiggly to make out. It looked written in some fancy script. Okay, what else? What other clues could I—?

The camera feed went white.

Damn. I hit the reload button. The error screen returned. I went back to the original email and clicked the hyperlink. Another error.

My feed was gone.

I looked at the blank screen, and the truth struck me anew: I'd just seen Elizabeth.

I could try to rationalize it away. But this wasn't a dream. I'd had dreams where Elizabeth was alive. Too many of them. In most, I'd just accept her return from the grave, too thankful to question or doubt. I remember one dream in particular where we were together—I don't remember what we were doing or even where we were—and right then, in mid-laugh, I realized with breath-crushing certainty that I was dreaming, that very soon I'd wake up alone. I remember the dream—me reaching out at that moment and grabbing hold of her, pulling her in close, trying desperately to drag Elizabeth back with me.

I knew dreams. What I had seen on the computer wasn't one.

It wasn't a ghost either. Not that I believe in them, but when in doubt, you might as well keep an open mind. But ghosts don't age. The Elizabeth on the computer had. Not a lot, but it had been eight years. Ghosts don't cut their hair either. I thought of that long braid hanging down her back in the moonlight. I thought about the fashionably short cut I'd just seen. And I thought about those eyes, those eyes that I had looked into since I was seven years old.

It was Elizabeth. She was still alive.

I felt the tears come again, but this time I fought them back. Funny thing. I'd always cried easily, but after mourning for Elizabeth it was as though I couldn't cry anymore. Not that I had cried myself out or used up all my tears or any of that nonsense. Or that I'd grown numb from grief, though that might have been a tiny part of it. What I think happened was that I instinctively snapped into a defensive stance. When Elizabeth died, I threw open the doors and let the pain in. I let myself feel it all. And it hurt. It hurt so damn much that now something primordial wouldn't let it happen again.

I don't know how long I sat there. Half an hour maybe. I tried to slow my breath and calm my mind. I wanted to be rational. I needed to be rational. I was supposed to be at Elizabeth's parents' house already, but I couldn't imagine facing them right now.

Then I remembered something else.

Sarah Goodhart.

Sheriff Lowell had asked if I knew anything about the name. I did.

Elizabeth and I used to play a childhood game. Perhaps you did too. You take your middle name and make it your first, then you take your childhood street name and make it your last. For example, my full name is David Craig Beck and I grew up on Darby Road. I would thus be Craig Darby. And Elizabeth would be ...

Sarah Goodhart.

What the hell was going on here?

I picked up the phone. First I called Elizabeth's parents. They still lived in that house on Goodhart Road. Her mother answered. I told her I was running late. People accept that from doctors. One of the fringe benefits of the job.

When I called Sheriff Lowell, his voice mail picked up. I told him to beep me when he had a chance. I don't have a cell phone. I realize that puts me in the minority, but my beeper leashes me to the outside world too much as it is.

I sat back, but Homer Simpson knocked me out of my trance with another "The mail is here!" I shot forward and gripped the mouse. The sender's address was unfamiliar, but the subject read Street Cam. Another thud in my chest.

I clicked the little icon and the email came up:

> Tomorrow same time plus two hours at Bigfoot.com. A message for you will be left under:
>
> Your user name: Bat Street
>
> Password: Teenage

Beneath this, clinging to the bottom of the screen, just five more words:

> They're watching. Tell no one.

Larry Gandle, the man with the bad comb-over, watched Eric Wu quietly handle the cleanup.

Wu, a twenty-six-year-old Korean with a staggering assortment of body pierces and tattoos, was the deadliest man Gandle had ever known. Wu was built like a small army tank, but that alone didn't mean much. Gandle knew plenty of people who had the physique. Too often, show muscles meant useless muscles.

That was not the case with Eric Wu.

The rock brawn was nice, but the real secret of Wu's deadly strength lay in the man's callused hands—two cement blocks with steel-talon fingers. He spent hours on them, punching cinder blocks, exposing them to extreme heat and cold, performing sets of one-finger push-ups. When Wu put those fingers to use, the devastation to bone and tissue was unimaginable.

Dark rumors swirled around men like Wu, most of which were crap, but Larry Gandle had seen him kill a man by digging his fingers into the soft spots of the face and abdomen. He had seen Wu grab a man by both ears and rip them off in a smooth pluck. He had seen him kill four times in four very different ways, never using a weapon.

None of the deaths had been quick.

Nobody knew exactly where Wu came from, but the most accepted tale had something to do with a brutal childhood in North Korea. Gandle had never asked. There were some night paths the mind was better off not traversing; the dark side of Eric Wu—right, like there might be a light side—was one of them.

When Wu finished wrapping up the protoplasm that had been Vic Letty in the drop cloth, he looked up at Gandle with those eyes of his. Dead eyes, Larry Gandle thought. The eyes of a child in a war newsreel.

Wu had not bothered taking off his headset. His personal stereo did not blare hip hop or rap or even rock 'n' roll. He listened pretty much nonstop to those soothing-sounds CDs you might find at Sharper Image, the ones with names like Ocean Breeze and Running Brook.

"Should I take him to Benny's?" Wu asked. His voice had a slow, odd cadence to it, like a character from a Peanuts cartoon.

Larry Gandle nodded. Benny ran a crematorium. Ashes to ashes. Or, in this case, scum to ashes. "And get rid of this."

Gandle handed Eric Wu the twenty-two. The weapon looked puny and useless in Wu's giant hand. Wu frowned at it, probably disappointed that Gandle had chosen it over Wu's own unique talents, and jammed it in his pocket. With a twenty-two, there were rarely exit wounds. That meant less evidence. The blood had been contained by a vinyl drop cloth. No muss, no fuss.

"Later," Wu said. He picked up the body with one hand as though it were a briefcase and carried it out.

Larry Gandle nodded a good-bye. He took little joy from Vic Letty's pain—but then again, he took little discomfort either. It was a simple matter really. Gandle had to know for absolute certain that Letty was working alone and that he hadn't left evidence around for someone else to find. That meant pushing the man past the breaking point. There was no other way.

In the end, it came down to a clear choice—the Scope family or Vic Letty. The Scopes were good people. They had never done a damn thing to Vic Letty. Vic Letty, on the other hand, had gone out of his way to try to hurt the Scope family. Only one of them could get off unscathed—the innocent, well-meaning victim or the parasite who was trying to feed off another's misery. No choice when you thought about it.

Gandle's cell phone vibrated. He picked it up and said, "Yes."

"They identified the bodies at the lake."

"And?"

"It's them. Jesus Christ, it's Bob and Mel."

Gandle closed his eyes.

"What does it mean, Larry?"

"I don't know."

"So what are we going to do?"

Larry Gandle knew that there was no choice. He'd have to speak with Griffin Scope. It would unearth unpleasant memories. Eight years. After eight years. Gandle shook his head. It would break the old man's heart all over again.

"I'll handle it."

6

Kim Parker, my mother-in-law, is beautiful. She'd always looked so much like Elizabeth that her face had become for me the ultimate what-might-have-been. But Elizabeth's death had slowly sapped her. Her face was drawn now, her features almost brittle. Her eyes had that look of marbles shattered from within.

The Parkers' house had gone through very few changes since the seventies—adhesive wood paneling, wall-to-wall semi-shag carpet of light blue with flecks of white, a faux stone raised fireplace à la the Brady Bunch. Folded TV trays, the kind with white plastic tops and gold metal legs, lined one wall. There were clown paintings and Rockwell collector plates. The only noticeable update was the television. It had swelled over the years from a bouncing twelve-inch black-and-white to the monstrous full-color fifty-incher that now sat hunched in the corner.

My mother-in-law sat on the same couch where Elizabeth and I had so often made out and then some. I smiled for a moment and thought, ah, if that couch could talk. But then again, that hideous chunk of sitting space with the loud floral design held a lot more than lustful memories. Elizabeth and I had sat there to open our college acceptance letters. We cuddled to watch *One Flew Over the Cuckoo's Nest* and *The Deer Hunter* and all the old Hitchcock films. We did homework, me sitting upright and Elizabeth lying with her head on my lap. I told Elizabeth I wanted to be a doctor—a big-time surgeon, or so I thought. She told me she wanted to get a law degree and work with kids. Elizabeth couldn't bear the thought of children in pain.

I remember an internship she did during the summer break after our freshman year of college. She worked for Covenant House, rescuing runaway and homeless children from New York's worst streets. I went with her once in the Covenant House van, cruising up and down Forty-second Street pre-Giuliani, sifting through putrid pools of quasi-humanity for children who needed shelter. Elizabeth spotted a fourteen-year-old hooker who was so strung out that she'd soiled herself. I winced in disgust. I'm not proud of that. These people may have been human, but—I'm being honest here—the filth repulsed me. I helped. But I winced.

Elizabeth never winced. That was her gift. She took the children by the hand. She carried them. She cleaned off that girl and nursed her and talked to her all night. She looked them straight in the eye. Elizabeth truly believed that everyone was good and worthy; she was naïve in a way I wish I could be.

I'd always wondered if she'd died that same way—with that naïveté intact—still clinging through the pain to her faith in humanity and all that wonderful nonsense. I hope so, but I suspect that KillRoy probably broke her.

Kim Parker sat primly with her hands in her lap. She'd always liked me well enough, though during our youth both sets of parents had been concerned with our closeness. They wanted us to play with others. They wanted us to make more friends. Natural, I suppose.

Hoyt Parker, Elizabeth's father, wasn't home yet, so Kim and I chatted about nothing—or, to say the same thing a different way, we chatted about everything except Elizabeth. I kept my eyes focused on Kim because I knew that the mantel was chock-full of photographs of Elizabeth and her heart-splitting smile.

She's alive ...

I couldn't make myself believe it. The mind, I know from my psychiatric rotation in medical school (not to mention my family history), has incredible distortive powers. I didn't believe I was nuts enough to conjure up her image, but then again, crazy people never do. I thought about my mother and wondered what she realized about her mental health, if she was even capable of engaging in serious introspection.

Probably not.

Kim and I talked about the weather. We talked about my patients. We talked about her new part-time job at Macy's. And then Kim surprised the hell out of me.

"Are you seeing anyone?" she asked.

It was the first truly personal question she had ever asked me. It knocked me back a step. I wondered what she wanted to hear. "No," I said.

She nodded and looked as though she wanted to say something else. Her hand fluttered up to her face.

"I date," I said.

"Good," she replied with too hearty a nod. "You should."

I stared at my hands and surprised myself by saying, "I still miss her so much." I didn't plan on that. I planned on keeping quiet and following our usual safe track. I glanced up at her face. She looked pained and grateful.

"I know you do, Beck," Kim said. "But you shouldn't feel guilty about seeing other people."

"I don't," I said. "I mean, it's not that."

She uncrossed her legs and leaned toward me. "Then what is it?"

I couldn't speak. I wanted to. For her sake. She looked at me with those shattered eyes, her need to talk about her daughter so surface, so raw. But I couldn't. I shook my head.

I heard a key in the door. We both turned suddenly, straightening up like caught lovers. Hoyt Parker shouldered open the door and called out his wife's name. He stepped into the den and with a hearty sigh, he put down a gym bag. His tie was loosened, his shirt wrinkled, his sleeves rolled up to the elbows. Hoyt had forearms like Popeye. When he saw us sitting on the couch, he let loose another sigh, this one deeper and with more than a hint of disapproval.

"How are you, David?" he said to me.

We shook hands. His grip, as always, was callous-scratchy and too firm. Kim excused herself and hurried out of the room. Hoyt and I exchanged pleasantries, and silence settled in. Hoyt Parker had never been comfortable with me. There might have been some Electra complex here, but I'd always felt that he saw me as a threat. I understood. His little girl had spent all her time with me. Over the years, we'd managed to fight through his resentment and forged something of a friendship. Until Elizabeth's death.

He blames me for what happened.

He has never said that, of course, but I see it in his eyes. Hoyt Parker is a burly, strong man. Rock-solid, honest Americana. He'd always made Elizabeth feel unconditionally safe. Hoyt had that kind of protective aura. No harm would come to his little girl as long as Big Hoyt was by her side.

I don't think I ever made Elizabeth feel safe like that.

"Work good?" Hoyt asked me.

"Fine," I said. "You?"

"A year away from retirement."

I nodded and we again fell into silence. On the ride over here, I decided not to say anything about what I'd seen on the computer. Forget the fact that it sounded loony. Forget the fact that it would open old wounds and hurt them both like all hell. The truth was, I didn't have a clue what was going on. The more time passed, the more the whole episode felt unreal. I also decided to take that last email to heart. *Tell no one.* I couldn't imagine why or what was going on, but whatever connection I'd made felt frighteningly tenuous.

Nonetheless I still found myself making sure Kim was out of earshot. Then I leaned closer to Hoyt and said softly, "Can I ask you something?"

He didn't reply, offering up instead one of his patented skeptical gazes.

"I want to know—" I stopped. "I want to know how you found her."

"Found her?"

"I mean when you first walked into the morgue. I want to know what you saw."

Something happened to his face, like tiny explosions collapsing the foundation. "For the love of Christ, why would you ask me that?"

"I've just been thinking about it," I said lamely. "With the anniversary and all."

He stood suddenly and wiped his palms on the legs of his pants. "You want a drink?"

"Sure."

"Bourbon okay?"

"That would be great."

He walked over to an old bar cart near the mantel and thus the photographs. I kept my gaze on the floor.

"Hoyt?" I tried.

He twisted open a bottle. "You're a doctor," he said, pointing a glass at me. "You've seen dead bodies."

"Yes."

"Then you know."

I did know.

He brought over my drink. I grabbed it a little too quickly and downed a sip. He watched me and then brought his glass to his lips.

"I know I never asked you about the details," I began. More than that, I had studiously avoided them. Other "families of the victims," as the media referred to us, bathed in them. They showed up every day at KillRoy's trial and listened and cried. I didn't. I think it helped them channel their grief. I chose to channel mine back at myself.

"You don't want to know the details, Beck."

"She was beaten?"

Hoyt studied his drink. "Why are you doing this?"

"I need to know."

He peered at me over the glass. His eyes moved along my face. It felt as though they were prodding my skin. I kept my gaze steady.

"There were bruises, yes."

"Where?"

"David—"

"On her face?"

His eyes narrowed, as though he'd spotted something unexpected. "Yes."

"On her body too?"

"I didn't look at her body," he said. "But I know the answer is yes."

"Why didn't you look at her body?"

"I was there as her father, not an investigator—for the purposes of identification only."

"Was that easy?" I asked.

"Was what easy?"

"Making the identification. I mean, you said her face was bruised."

His body stiffened. He put down his drink, and with mounting dread, I realized I'd gone too far. I should have stuck to my plan. I should have just kept my mouth shut.

"You really want to hear all this?"

No, I thought. But I nodded my head.

Hoyt Parker put down his drink, crossed his arms, and leaned back on his heels. "Elizabeth's left eye was swollen closed. Her nose was broken and flattened like wet clay. There was a slash across her forehead, probably made with a box cutter. Her jaw had been ripped out of its hinges, snapping all the tendons." His voice was a total monotone. "The letter K was burnt into her right cheek. The smell of charred skin was still obvious."

My stomach knotted.

Hoyt's eyes settled onto mine hard. "Do you want to know what was the worst part, Beck?"

I looked at him and waited.

"It still took no time at all," he said. "I knew in an instant that it was Elizabeth."

7

Champagne flutes tinkled in harmony with the Mozart sonata. A harp underscored the subdued pitch of the party chatter. Griffin Scope moved serpentine through the black tuxedos and shimmering gowns. People always used the same word to describe Griffin Scope: billionaire. After that, they might call him businessman or power broker or mention that he was tall or a husband or a grandfather or that he was seventy years old. They might comment on his personality or his family tree or his work ethic. But the first word—in the papers, on television, on people's lists—was always the B word. Billionaire. Billionaire Griffin Scope.

Griffin had been born rich. His grandfather was an early industrialist; his father improved the fortune; Griffin multiplied it several-fold. Most family empires fall apart before the third generation. Not the Scopes'. A lot of that had to do with their upbringing. Griffin, for example, did not attend a prestigious prep school like Exeter or Lawrenceville, as so many of his peers did. His father insisted that Griffin not only attend public school but that he do so in the closest major city, Newark. His father had offices there, thus setting up a fake residence was no problem.

Newark's east side wasn't a bad neighborhood back then—not like now, when a sane person would barely want to drive through it. It was working class, blue collar—tough rather than dangerous.

Griffin loved it.

His best friends from those high school days were still his friends fifty years later. Loyalty was a rare quality; when Griffin found it, he made sure to reward it. Many of tonight's guests were from those Newark days. Some even worked for him, though he tried to make it a point to never be their day-to-day boss.

Tonight's gala celebrated the cause most dear to Griffin Scope's heart: the Brandon Scope Memorial Charity, named for Griffin's murdered son. Griffin had started the fund with a one-hundred-million-dollar contribution. Friends quickly added to the till. Griffin was not stupid. He knew that many donated to curry his favor. But there was more to it than that. During his too-brief life, Brandon Scope touched people. A boy born with so much luck and talent, Brandon had an almost supernatural charisma. People were drawn to him.

His other son, Randall, was a good boy who had grown up to be a good man. But Brandon ... Brandon had been magic.

The pain flooded in again. It was always there, of course. Through the shaking hands and slapping of the backs, the grief stayed by his side, tapping Griffin on the shoulder, whispering in his ear, reminding him that they were partners for life.

"Lovely party, Griff."

Griffin said thank you and moved on. The women were well coiffed and wore gowns that highlighted lovely bare shoulders; they fit in nicely with the many ice sculptures—a favorite of Griffin's wife Allison—that slowly melted atop imported linen tablecloths. The Mozart sonata changed over to one by Chopin. White-gloved servers made the rounds with silver trays of Malaysian shrimp and Omaha tenderloin and a potpourri of bizarre finger-food that always seemed to contain sun-dried tomatoes.

He reached Linda Beck, the young lady who headed up Brandon's charitable fund. Linda's father had been an old Newark classmate too, and she, so like so many others, had become entwined in the massive Scope holdings. She'd started working for various Scope enterprises while still in high school. Both she and her brother had paid for their education with Scope scholarship grants.

"You look smashing," he told her, though in truth he thought she looked tired.

Linda Beck smiled at him. "Thank you, Mr. Scope."

"How many times have I asked you to call me Griff?"

"Several hundred," she said.

"How's Shauna?"

"A little under the weather, I'm afraid."

"Give her my best."

"I will, thank you."

"We should probably meet next week."

"I'll call your secretary."

"Good."

Griffin gave her a peck on the cheek, and that was when he spotted Larry Gandle in the foyer. Larry looked bleary-eyed and disheveled, but then again, he always looked that way. You could slap a custom-cut Joseph Abboud on him, and an hour later he'd still look like someone who'd gotten into a tussle.

Larry Gandle was not supposed to be here.

The two men's eyes met. Larry nodded once and turned away. Griffin waited another moment or two and then followed his young friend down the corridor.

Larry's father, Edward, had also been one of Griffin's classmates from the old Newark days. Edward Gandle died of a sudden heart attack twelve years ago. Damn shame. Edward had been a fine man. Since then, his son had taken over as the Scopes' closest confidant.

The two men entered Griffin's library. At one time, the library had been a wonderful room of oak and mahogany and floor-to-ceiling bookshelves and antique globes. Two years ago, Allison, in a postmodern mood, decided that the room needed a total updating. The old woodwork was torn out and now the room was white and sleek and functional and held all the warmth of a work cubicle. Allison had been so proud of the room that Griffin didn't have the heart to tell her how much he disliked it.

"Was there a problem tonight?" Griffin asked.

"No," Larry said.

Griffin offered Larry a seat. Larry shook him off and started pacing.

"Was it bad?" Griffin asked.

"We had to make certain there were no loose ends."

"Of course."

Someone had attacked Griffin's son Randall—ergo, Griffin attacked back. It was one lesson he never forgot. You don't sit back when you or a loved one is being assaulted. And you don't act like the government with their "proportional responses" and all that nonsense. If someone hurts you, mercy and pity must be put aside. You eliminate the enemy. You scorch the earth. Those who scoffed at this philosophy, who thought it unnecessarily Machiavellian, usually were the ones who caused excess destruction.

In the end, if you eliminate problems swiftly, less blood is shed.

"So what's wrong?" Griffin asked.

Larry kept pacing. He rubbed the front of his bald pate. Griffin didn't like what he was seeing. Larry was not one to get keyed up easily. "I've never lied to you, Griff," he said.

"I know that."

"But there are times for . . . insulation."

"Insulation?"

"Who I hire, for example. I never tell you names. I never tell them names either."

"Those are details."

"Yes."

"What is it, Larry?"

He stopped pacing. "Eight years ago, you'll recall that we hired two men to perform a certain task."

The color drained from Griffin's face. He swallowed. "And they performed admirably."

"Yes. Well, perhaps."

"I don't understand."

"They performed their task. Or, at least, part of it. The threat was apparently eliminated."

Even though the house was swept for listening devices on a weekly basis, the two men never used names. A Scope rule. Larry Gandle often wondered if the rule was for the sake of caution or because it helped depersonalize what they were occasionally forced to do. He suspected the latter.

Griffin finally collapsed into a chair, almost as though someone had pushed him. His voice was soft. "Why are you bringing this up now?"

"I know how painful this must be for you."

Griffin did not reply.

"I paid the two men well," Larry continued.

"As I'd have expected."

"Yes." He cleared his throat. "Well, after the incident, they were supposed to lay low for a while. As a precaution."

"Go on."

"We never heard from them again."

"They'd already collected their money, correct?"

"Yes."

"So what's surprising about that? Perhaps they fled with their newfound wealth. Perhaps they moved across the country or changed identities."

"That," Larry said, "was what we'd always assumed."

"But?"

"Their bodies were found last week. They're dead."

"I still don't see the problem. They were violent men. They probably met a violent end."

"The bodies were old."

"Old?"

"They've been dead at least five years. And they were found buried by the lake where … where the incident took place."

Griffin opened his mouth, closed it, tried again. "I don't understand."

"Frankly, neither do I."

Too much. It was all too much. Griffin had been fighting off the tears all night, what with the gala being in Brandon's honor and all. Now the tragedy of Brandon's murder was suddenly resurfacing. It was all he could do not to break down.

Griffin looked up at his confidant. "This can't come back."

"I know, Griff."

"We have to find out what happened. I mean everything."

"I've kept tabs on the men in her life. Especially her husband. Just in case. Now I've put all our resources on it."

"Good," Griffin said. "Whatever it takes, this gets buried. I don't care who gets buried with it."

"I understand."

"And, Larry?"

Gandle waited.

"I know the name of one man you hire." He meant Eric Wu. Griffin Scope wiped his eyes and started back toward his guests. "Use him."

8

Shauna and Linda rent a three-bedroom apartment on Riverside Drive and 116 Street, not far from Columbia University. I'd managed to find a spot within a block, an act that usually accompanies a parting sea or stone tablet.

Shauna buzzed me up. Linda was still out at her formal. Mark was asleep. I tiptoed into his room and kissed his forehead. Mark was still hanging on to the Pokémon craze and it showed. He had Pikachu sheets, and a stuffed Squirtle doll lay nestled in his arms. People criticize the trend, but it reminded me of my own childhood obsession with Batman and Captain America. I watched him a few more seconds. Cliché to say, yes, but it is indeed the little things.

Shauna stood in the doorway and waited. When we finally moved back into the den, I said, "Mind if I have a drink?"

Shauna shrugged. "Suit yourself."

I poured myself two fingers of bourbon. "You'll join me?"

She shook her head.

We settled onto the couch. "What time is Linda supposed to be home?" I asked.

"Got me," Shauna said slowly. I didn't like the way she did it.

"Damn," I said.

"It's temporary, Beck. I love Linda, you know that."

"Damn," I said again.

Last year, Linda and Shauna had separated for two months. It hadn't been good, especially for Mark.

"I'm not moving out or anything," Shauna said.

"So what's wrong, then?"

"Same ol' same ol'. I have this glamorous high-profile job. I'm surrounded by beautiful, interesting people all the time. Nothing new, right? We all know this. Anyway, Linda thinks I have a wandering eye."

"You do," I said.

"Yeah, sure, but that's nothing new, is it?"

I didn't reply.

"At the end of the day, Linda is the one I go home to."

"And you never take any detours on the way?"

"If I did, they'd be irrelevant. You know that. I don't do well locked in a cage, Beck. I need the stage."

"Nice mix of metaphors," I said.

"At least it rhymed."

I drank in silence for a few moments.

"Beck?"

"What?"

"Your turn now."

"Meaning?"

She shot me a look and waited.

I thought about the "Tell no one" warning at the end of the email. If the message were indeed from Elizabeth—my mind still had trouble even entertaining such a notion—she would know that I'd tell Shauna. Linda—maybe not. But Shauna? I tell her everything. It would be a given.

"There's a chance," I said, "that Elizabeth is still alive."

Shauna didn't break stride. "She ran off with Elvis, right?" When she saw my face, she stopped and said, "Explain."

I did. I told her about the email. I told her about the street cam. And I told her about seeing Elizabeth on the computer monitor. Shauna kept her eyes on me the whole time. She didn't nod or interrupt. When I finished, she carefully extracted a cigarette from its carton and put it in her mouth. Shauna gave up smoking years ago, but she still liked to fiddle with them. She examined the cancer stick, turning it over in her hand as though she'd never seen one before. I could see the gears churning.

"Okay," she said. "So at eight-fifteen tomorrow night, the next message is supposed to come in, right?"

I nodded.

"So we wait until then."

She put the cigarette back in the pack.

"You don't think it's crazy?"

Shauna shrugged. "Irrelevant," she said.

"Meaning?"

"There are several possibilities that'd explain what you just said."

"Including insanity."

"Yeah, sure, that's a strong one. But what's the point of hypothesizing negatively right now? Let's just assume it's true. Let's just assume you saw what you saw and that Elizabeth is still alive. If we're wrong, hey, we'll learn that soon enough. If we're right ..." She knitted her eyebrows, thought about it, shook her head. "Christ, I hope like hell we're right."

I smiled at her. "I love you, you know."

"Yeah," she said. "Everyone does."

When I got home, I poured myself one last quick drink. I took a deep sip and let the warm liquor travel to destinations well known. Yes, I drink. But I'm not a drunk. That's not denial. I know I flirt with being an alcoholic. I also know that flirting with alcoholism is about as safe as flirting with a mobster's underage daughter. But so far, the flirting hasn't led to coupling. I'm smart enough to know that might not last.

Chloe sidled up to me with her customary expression that could be summed up thusly: "Food, walk, food, walk." Dogs are wonderfully consistent. I tossed her a treat and took her for a stroll around the block. The cold air felt good in my lungs, but walking never cleared my head. Walking is, in fact, a tremendous bore. But I liked watching Chloe walk. I know that sounds queer, but a dog derives such pleasure from this simple activity. It made me Zen-happy to watch her.

Back home I moved quietly toward my bedroom. Chloe followed me. Grandpa was asleep. So was his new nurse. She snored with a cartoonlike, high-pitched exhale. I flipped on my computer and wondered why Sheriff Lowell hadn't called me back. I thought about calling him, though the time was nearing midnight. Then I figured: tough.

I picked up the phone and dialed. Lowell had a cell phone. If he was sleeping, he could always turn it off, right?

He answered on the third ring. "Hello, Dr. Beck."

His voice was tight. I also noted that I was no longer Doc.

"Why didn't you call me back?" I asked.

"It was getting late," he said. "I figured I'd catch you in the morning."

"Why did you ask me about Sarah Goodhart?"

"Tomorrow," he said.

"Pardon me?"

"It's late, Dr. Beck. I'm off duty. Besides, I think I'd rather go over this with you in person."

"Can't you at least tell me—?"

"You'll be at your clinic in the morning?"

"Yes."

"I'll call you then."

He bade me a polite but firm good night and then he was gone. I stared at the phone and wondered what the hell that was all about.

Sleep was out of the question. I spent most of the night on the Web, surfing through various city street cams, hoping to stumble across the right one. Talk about the high-tech needle in the worldwide haystack.

At some point, I stopped and slipped under the covers. Part of being a doctor is patience. I constantly give children tests that have life-altering—if not life-ending—implications and tell them and their parents to wait for the results. They have no choice. Perhaps the same could be said for this situation. There were too many variables right now. Tomorrow, when I logged in at Bigfoot under the Bat Street user name and Teenage password, I might learn more.

I stared up at the ceiling for a while. Then I looked to my right—where Elizabeth had slept. I always fell asleep first. I used to lie like this and watch her with a book, her face in profile, totally focused on whatever she was reading. That was the last thing I saw before my eyes closed and I drifted off to sleep.

I rolled over and faced the other way.

At four in the morning, Larry Gandle looked over the bleached-blond locks of Eric Wu. Wu was incredibly disciplined. If he wasn't working on his physical prowess, he was in front of a computer screen. His complexion had turned a sickly blue-white several thousand Web surfs ago, but that physique remained serious cement.

"Well?" Gandle said.

Wu popped the headphones off. Then he folded his marble-column arms across his chest. "I'm confused."

"Tell me."

"Dr. Beck has barely saved any of his emails. Just a few involving patients. Nothing personal. But then he gets two bizarre ones in the last two days." Still not turning from the screen, Eric Wu handed two pieces of paper over his bowling ball of a shoulder. Larry Gandle looked at the emails and frowned.

"What do they mean?"

"I don't know."

Gandle skimmed the message that talked about clicking something at "kiss time." He didn't understand computers—nor did he want to understand them. His eyes traveled back up to the top of the sheet and he read the subject.

E.P.+ D.B. and a bunch of lines.

Gandle thought about it. D.B. David Beck maybe? And E.P. . . .

The meaning landed on him like a dropped piano. He slowly handed the paper back to Wu.

"Who sent this?" Gandle asked.

"I don't know."

"Find out."

"Impossible," Wu said.

"Why?"

"The sender used an anonymous remailer." Wu spoke with a patient, almost unearthly monotone. He used that same tone while discussing a weather report or ripping off a man's cheek. "I won't go into the computer jargon, but there is no way to trace it back."

Gandle turned his attention to the other email, the one with the Bat Street and Teenage. He couldn't make head or tail out of it.

"How about this one? Can you trace it back?"

Wu shook his head. "Also an anonymous remailer."

"Did the same person send both?"

"Your guess would be as good as mine."

"How about the content? Do you understand what either one is talking about?"

Wu hit a few keys and the first email popped up on the monitor. He pointed a thick, veiny finger at the screen. "See that blue lettering there? It's a hyperlink. All Dr. Beck had to do was click it and it would take him someplace, probably a Web site."

"What Web site?"

"It's a broken link. Again, you can't trace it back."

"And Beck was supposed to do this at 'kiss time'?"

"That's what it says."

"Is kiss time some sort of computer term?"

Wu almost grinned. "No."

"So you don't know what time the email refers to?"

"That's correct."

"Or even if we've passed kiss time or not?"

"It's passed," Wu said.

"How do you know?"

"His Web browser is set up to show you the last twenty sites he visited. He clicked the link. Several times, in fact."

"But you can't, uh, follow him there?"

"No. The link is useless."

"What about this other email?"

Wu hit a more few keys. The screen changed and the other email appeared. "This one is easier to figure out. It's very basic, as a matter of fact."

"Okay, I'm listening."

"The anonymous emailer has set up an email account for Dr. Beck," Wu explained. "He's given Dr. Beck a user name and a password and again mentioned kiss time."

"So let me see if I understand," Gandle said. "Beck goes to some Web site. He types in that user name and that password and there'll be a message for him?"

"That's the theory, yes."

"Can we do it too?"

"Sign in using that user name and password?"

"Yes. And read the message."

"I tried it. The account doesn't exist yet."

"Why not?"

Eric Wu shrugged. "The anonymous sender might set up the account later. Closer to kiss time."

"So what can we conclude here?"

"Put simply"—the light from the monitor danced off Wu's blank eyes—"someone is going through a great deal of trouble to stay anonymous."

"So how do we find out who it is?"

Wu held up a small device that looked like something you might find in a transistor radio. "We've installed one of these on his home and work computers."

"What is it?"

"A digital network tracker. The tracker sends digital signals from his computers to mine. If Dr. Beck gets any emails or visits any Web sites or even if he just types up a letter, we'll be able to monitor it all in real time."

"So we wait and watch," Gandle said.

"Yes."

Gandle thought about what Wu had told him—about the lengths someone was going through to remain anonymous—and an awful suspicion started creeping into the pit of his belly.

9

I parked at the lot two blocks from the clinic. I never made it past block one.

Sheriff Lowell materialized with two men sporting buzz cuts and gray suits. The two men in suits leaned against a big brown Buick. Physical opposites. One was tall and thin and white, the other short and round and black; together they looked a little like a bowling ball trying to knock down the last pin. Both men smiled at me. Lowell did not.

"Dr. Beck?" the tall white pin said. He was impeccably groomed—gelled hair, folded hanky in the pocket, tie knotted with supernatural precision, tortoiseshell designer glasses, the kind actors wear when they want to look smart.

I looked at Lowell. He said nothing.

"Yes."

"I'm Special Agent Nick Carlson with the Federal Bureau of Investigation," the impeccably groomed one continued. "This is Special Agent Tom Stone."

They both flashed badges. Stone, the shorter and more rumpled of the two, hitched up his trousers and nodded at me. Then he opened the back door of the Buick.

"Would you mind coming with us?"

"I have patients in fifteen minutes," I said.

"We've already taken care of that." Carlson swept a long arm toward the car door, as though he were displaying a game show prize. "Please."

I got in the back. Carlson drove. Stone squeezed himself into the front passenger seat. Lowell didn't get in. We stayed in Manhattan, but the ride still took close to forty-five minutes. We ended up way downtown on Broadway near Duane Street. Carlson stopped the car in front of an office building marked 26 Federal Plaza.

The interior was basic office building. Men in suits, surprisingly nice ones, moved about with cups of designer coffee. There were women too, but they were heavily in the minority. We moved into a conference room. I was invited to sit, which I did. I tried crossing my legs, but that didn't feel right.

"Can someone tell me what's going on?" I asked.

White-Pin Carlson took the lead. "Can we get you something?" he asked. "We make the world's worst coffee, if you're interested."

That explained all the designer cups. He smiled at me. I smiled back. "Tempting, but no thanks."

"How about a soft drink? We have soft drinks, Tom?"

"Sure, Nick. Coke, Diet Coke, Sprite, whatever the doctor here wants."

They smiled some more. "I'm fine, thanks," I said.

"Snapple?" Stone tried. He once again hitched up his pants. His stomach was the kind of round that made it hard to find a spot where the waistband wouldn't slide. "We got a bunch of different varieties here."

I almost said yes so that they'd get on with it, but I just gently shook him off. The table, some sort of Formica mix, was bare except for a large manila envelope. I wasn't sure what to do with my hands, so I put them on the table. Stone waddled to the side and stood there. Carlson, still taking the lead, sat on the corner of the table and swiveled to look down at me.

"What can you tell us about Sarah Goodhart?" Carlson asked.

I wasn't sure how to answer. I kept trying to figure out the angles, but nothing was coming to me.

"Doc?"

I looked up at him. "Why do you want to know?"

Carlson and Stone exchanged a quick glance. "The name Sarah Goodhart has surfaced in connection with an ongoing investigation," Carlson said.

"What investigation?" I asked.

"We'd rather not say."

"I don't understand. How am I connected into this?"

Carlson let loose a sigh, taking his time on the exhale. He looked over at his rotund partner and suddenly all smiles were gone. "Am I asking a complicated question here, Tom?"

"No, Nick, I don't think so."

"Me neither." Carlson turned his eyes back at me. "Maybe you object to the form of the question, Doc. That it?"

"That's what they always do on *The Practice*, Nick," Stone chimed in. "Object to the form of the question."

"That they do, Tom, that they do. And then they say, 'I'll rephrase,' right? Something like that."

"Something like that, yeah."

Carlson looked me down. "So let me rephrase: Does the name Sarah Goodhart mean anything to you?"

I didn't like this. I didn't like their attitude or the fact that they had taken over for Lowell or the way I was getting grilled in this conference room. They had to know what the name meant. It wasn't that difficult. All you had to do was casually glance at Elizabeth's name and address. I decided to tread gently.

"My wife's middle name is Sarah," I said.

"My wife's middle name is Gertrude," Carlson said.

"Christ, Nick, that's awful."

"What's your wife's middle name, Tom?"

"McDowd. It's a family name."

"I like when they do that. Use a family name as a middle name. Honor the ancestors like that."

"Me too, Nick."

Both men swung their gazes back in my direction.

"What's your middle name, Doc?"

"Craig," I said.

"Craig," Carlson repeated. "Okay, so if I asked you if the name, say"—he waved his arms theatrically—"Craig Dipwad meant anything to you, would you chirp up, 'Hey, my middle name is Craig'?"

Carlson flashed me the hard eyes again.

"I guess not," I said.

"I guess not. So let's try it again: Have you heard the name Sarah Goodhart, yes or no?"

"You mean ever?"

Stone said, "Jesus Christ."

Carlson's face reddened. "You playing semantic games with us now, Doc?"

He was right. I was being stupid. I was flying blind, and that last line of the email—*Tell no one*—kept flashing in my head like something in neon. Confusion took over. They had to know about Sarah Goodhart. This was all a test to see if I was going to cooperate or not. That was it. Maybe. And cooperate about what?

"My wife grew up on Goodhart Road," I said. They both moved back a little, giving me room, folding their arms. They led me to a pool of silence and I foolishly dived in. "See, that's why I said Sarah was my wife's middle name. The Goodhart made me think of her."

"Because she grew up on Goodhart Road?" Carlson said.

"Yes."

"Like the word Goodhart was a catalyst or something?"

"Yes," I said again.

"That makes sense to me." Carlson looked at his partner. "That make sense to you, Tom?"

"Sure," Stone agreed, patting his stomach. "He wasn't being evasive or anything. The word Goodhart was a catalyst."

"Right. That's what got him thinking about his wife."

They both looked at me again. This time I forced myself to keep quiet.

"Did your wife ever use the name Sarah Goodhart?" Carlson asked.

"Use it how?"

"Did she ever say, 'Hi, I'm Sarah Goodhart,' or get an ID with that name or check into some hot-sheets under that name—"

"No," I said.

"You sure?"

"Yes."

"That the truth?"

"Yes."

"Don't need another catalyst?"

I straightened up in the chair and decided to show some resolve. "I don't much like your attitude, Agent Carlson."

His toothy, dentist-proud smile returned, but it was like some cruel hybrid of its earlier form. He held up his hand and said, "Excuse me, yeah, okay, that was rude." He looked around as though thinking about what to say next. I waited.

"You ever beat up your wife, Doc?"

The question hit me like a whiplash. "What?"

"That get you off? Smacking around a woman?"

"What . . . are you insane?"

"How much life insurance did you collect when your wife died?"

I froze. I looked at his face and then at Stone's. Totally opaque. I couldn't believe what I was hearing. "What's going on here?"

"Please just answer the question. Unless, of course, you got something you don't want to tell us."

"It's no secret," I said. "The policy was for two hundred thousand dollars."

Stone whistled. "Two hundred grand for a dead wife. Hey, Nick, where do I get in line?"

"That's a lot of life insurance for a twenty-five-year-old woman."

"Her cousin was starting out with State Farm," I said, my words stumbling over one another. The funny thing is, even though I knew I hadn't done anything wrong—at least not what they thought—I started feeling guilty. It was a weird sensation. Sweat started pouring down my armpits. "She wanted to help him out. So she bought this big policy."

"Nice of her," Carlson said.

"Real nice," Stone added. "Family is so important, don't you think?"

I said nothing. Carlson sat back down on the table's corner. The smile was gone again. "Look at me, Doc."

I did. His eyes bore into mine. I managed to maintain eye contact, but it was a struggle.

"Answer my question this time," he said slowly. "And don't give me shocked or insulted. Did you ever hit your wife?"

"Never," I said.

"Not once?"

"Not once."

"Ever push her?"

"Never."

"Or lash out in anger. Hell, we've all been there, Doc. A quick slap. No real crime in that. Natural when it comes to the affairs of the heart, you know what I mean?"

"I never hit my wife," I said. "I never pushed her or slapped her or lashed out in anger. Never."

Carlson looked over at Stone. "That clear it up for you, Tom?"

"Sure, Nick. He says he never hit her, that's good enough for me."

Carlson scratched his chin. "Unless."

"Unless what, Nick?"

"Well, unless I can provide Dr. Beck here with another one of those catalysts."

All eyes were on me again. My own breaths echoed in my ears, hitched and uneven. I felt light-headed. Carlson waited a beat before he snatched up the large manila envelope. He took his time untying the string flap with long, slender fingers and then he opened the slit. He lifted it high in the air and let the contents fall to the table.

"How's this for a catalyst, huh, Doc?"

They were photographs. Carlson pushed them toward me. I looked down and felt the hole in my heart expand.

"Dr. Beck?"

I stared. My fingers reached out tentatively and touched the surface.

Elizabeth.

They were photographs of Elizabeth. The first one was a close-up of her face. She was in profile, her right hand holding her hair back away from her ear. Her eye was purple and swollen. There was a deep cut and more bruising on her neck, below the ear.

It looked as though she'd been crying.

Another photo was shot from the waist up. Elizabeth stood wearing only a bra, and she was pointing to a large discoloration on her rib cage. Her eyes still had that red-tinged rim. The lighting was strangely harsh, as though the flash itself had sought out the bruise and pulled it closer to the lens.

There were three more photographs—all from various angles and of various body parts. All of them highlighted more cuts and bruises.

"Dr. Beck?"

My eyes jerked up. I was almost startled to see them in the room. Their expressions were neutral, patient. I faced Carlson, then Stone, then I went back to Carlson.

"You think I did this?"

Carlson shrugged. "You tell us."

"Of course not."

"Do you know how your wife got those bruises?"

"In a car accident."

They looked at each other as though I'd told them my dog ate my homework.

"She got into a bad fender-bender," I explained.

"When?"

"I'm not sure exactly. Three, four months before"—the words got stuck for a second—"before she died."

"Did she visit a hospital?"

"No, I don't think so."

"You don't think?"

"I wasn't around."

"Where were you?"

"I was doing a pediatric workshop in Chicago at the time. She told me about the accident when I got home."

"How long after did she tell you?"

"After the accident?"

"Yeah, Doc, after the accident."

"I don't know. Two, three days maybe."

"You two were married by then?"

"For just a few months."

"Why didn't she tell you right away?"

"She did. I mean, as soon as I got home. I guess she didn't want to worry me."

"I see," Carlson said. He looked at Stone. They didn't bother masking their skepticism. "So did you take these pictures, Doc?"

"No," I said. As soon as I did, I wished I hadn't. They exchanged another glance, smelling blood. Carlson tilted his head and moved closer.

"Have you ever seen these pictures before?"

I said nothing. They waited. I thought about the question. The answer was no, but ... where did they get them? Why didn't I know about them? Who took them? I looked at their faces, but they gave away nothing.

It's an amazing thing really, but when you think about it, we learn life's most important lessons from TV. The vast majority of our knowledge about interrogations, Miranda rights, self-incriminations, cross-examinations, witness lists, the jury system, we learn from *NYPD Blue* and *Law & Order* and the like. If I tossed you a gun right now and asked you to fire it, you'd do what you saw on TV. If I told you to look out for a "tail," you'd know what I'm talking about because you'd seen it done on *Mannix* or *Magnum PI*.

I looked up at them and asked the classic question: "Am I a suspect?"

"Suspect for what?"

"For anything," I said. "Do you suspect that I committed any crime?"

"That's a pretty vague question, Doc."

And that was a pretty vague answer. I didn't like the way this was going. I decided to use another line I learned from television.

"I want to call my lawyer," I said.

10

I don't have a criminal lawyer—who does?—so I called Shauna from a pay phone in the corridor and explained the situation. She wasted no time.

"I got just the person," Shauna said. "Sit tight."

I waited in the interrogation room. Carlson and Stone were kind enough to wait with me. They spent the time whispering to each other. Half an hour passed. Again the silence was unnerving. I know that was what they wanted. But I couldn't stop myself. I was innocent, after all. How could I harm myself if I was careful?

"My wife was found branded with the letter K," I said to them.

They both looked up. "Pardon me," Carlson said, craning his long neck back in my direction. "You talking to us?"

"My wife was found branded with the letter K," I repeated. "I was in the hospital after the attack with a concussion. You can't possibly think ..." I let it hang.

"Think what?" Carlson said.

In for a penny, in for a pound. "That I had something to do with my wife's death."

That was when the door burst open, and a woman I recognized from television stamped into the room. Carlson jumped back when he saw her. I heard Stone mumble "Holy shit" under his breath.

Hester Crimstein didn't bother with intros. "Didn't my client ask for counsel?" she asked.

Count on Shauna. I had never met my attorney, but I recognized her from her stints as a "legal expert" on talk shows and from her own *Crimstein on Crime* program on Court TV. On the screen Hester Crimstein was quick and cutting and often left guests in tatters. In person, she had the most bizarre aura of power, the kind of person who looks at everyone as though she were a hungry tiger and they were limping gazelles.

"That's right," Carlson said.

"Yet here you are, all nice and cozy, still questioning him."

"He started talking to us."

"Oh, I see." Hester Crimstein snapped open her briefcase, dug out a pen and paper, and tossed them onto the table. "Write down your names."

"Pardon?"

"Your names, handsome. You know how to spell them, right?"

It was a rhetorical question, but Crimstein still waited for an answer.

"Yeah," Carlson said.

"Sure," Stone added.

"Good. Write them down. When I mention on my show how you two trampled my client's constitutional rights, I want to make sure I get the names right. Print plainly, please."

She finally looked at me. "Let's go."

"Hold up a second," Carlson said. "We'd like to ask your client a few questions."

"No."

"No? Just like that?"

"Exactly like that. You don't talk to him. He doesn't talk to you. Ever. You two understand?"

"Yes," Carlson said.

She turned her glare to Stone.

"Yes," Stone said.

"Swell, fellas. Now are you arresting Dr. Beck?"

"No."

She turned in my direction. "What are you waiting for?" she snapped at me. "We're out of here."

Hester Crimstein didn't say a word until we were safely ensconced in her limousine.

"Where do you want me to drop you off?" she asked.

I gave the driver the clinic's address.

"Tell me about the interrogation," Crimstein said. "Leave out nothing."

I recounted my conversation with Carlson and Stone as best I could. Hester Crimstein didn't so much as glance in my direction. She took out a day planner thicker than my waist and started leafing through it.

"So these pictures of your wife," she said when I finished. "You didn't take them?"

"No."

"And you told Tweedledee and Tweedledum that?"

I nodded.

She shook her head. "Doctors. They're always the worst clients." She pushed back a stand of hair. "Okay, that was dumb of you, but not crippling. You say you've never seen those pictures before?"

"Never."

"But when they asked you that, you finally shut up."

"Yes."

"Better," she said with a nod. "That story about her getting those bruises in a car accident. Is it the truth?"

"Pardon me?"

Crimstein closed her day planner. "Look ... Beck, is it? Shauna says everyone calls you Beck, so you mind if I do the same?"

"No."

"Good. Look, Beck, you're a doctor, right?"

"Right."

"You good at bedside manner?"

"I try to be."

"I don't. Not even a little. You want coddling, go on a diet and hire

Richard Simmons. So let's skip all the pardon-mes and excuse-mes and all that objectionable crap, okay? Just answer my questions. The car accident story you told them. Is it true?"

"Yes."

"Because the feds will check all the facts. You know that, right?"

"I know."

"Okay, fine, just so we're clear here." Crimstein took a breath. "So maybe your wife had a friend take these pictures," she said, trying it on for size. "For insurance reasons or something. In case she ever wanted to sue. That might make sense, if we need to peddle it."

It didn't make sense to me, but I kept that to myself.

"So question uno: Where have these pictures been, Beck?"

"I don't know."

"Dos and tres: How did the feds get them? Why are they surfacing now?"

I shook my head.

"And most important, what are they trying to nail you on? Your wife's been dead for eight years. It's a little late for a spousal battery charge." She sat back and thought about it a minute or two. Then she looked up and shrugged. "No matter. I'll make some calls, find out what's up. In the mean-time, don't be a dimwit. Say nothing to anyone. You understand?"

"Yes."

She sat back and thought about it some more. "I don't like this," she said. "I don't like this even a little bit."

11

On May 12, 1970, Jeremiah Renway and three fellow radicals set off an explosion at Eastern State University's chemistry department. Rumor had it from the Weather Underground that military scientists were using the university labs to make a more powerful form of napalm. The four students, who in a fit of stark originality called themselves Freedom's Cry, decided to make a dramatic albeit showy stand.

At the time, Jeremiah Renway did not know if the rumor was true. Now, more than thirty years later, he doubted it. No matter. The explosion did not damage any of the labs. Two university security guards, however, stumbled across the suspicious package. When one picked it up, the package exploded, killing both men.

Both had children.

One of Jeremiah's fellow "freedom fighters" was captured two days later. He was still in jail. The second died of colon cancer in 1989. The third, Evelyn Cosmeer, was captured in 1996. She was currently serving a seven-year prison sentence.

Jeremiah disappeared into the woods that night and never ventured out. He had rarely seen fellow human beings or listened to the radio or watched television. He had used a telephone only once—and that was in an emergency. His only real connection to the outside world came from newspapers, though they had what happened here eight years ago all wrong.

Born and raised in the foothills of northwest Georgia, Jeremiah's father taught his son all kinds of survival techniques, though his overriding lesson was simply this: You could trust nature but not man. Jeremiah had forgotten that for a little while. Now he lived it.

Fearing they would search near his hometown, Jeremiah took to the woods in Pennsylvania. He hiked around for a while, changing camp every night or two, until he happened upon the relative comfort and security of Lake Charmaine. The lake had old camp bunks that could house a man when the outdoors got a little too nasty. Visitors rarely came to the lake—mostly in the summer, and even then, only on weekends. He could hunt deer here and eat the meat in relative peace. During the few times of the year when the lake was being used, he simply hid or took off for points farther west.

Or he watched.

To the children who used to come here, Jeremiah Renway had been the Boogeyman.

Jeremiah stayed still now and watched the officers move about in their dark windbreakers. FBI windbreakers. The sight of those three letters in big yellow caps still punctured his heart like an icicle.

No one had bothered to yellow-tape the area, probably because it was so remote. Renway had not been surprised when they found the bodies. Yes, the two men had been buried good and deep, but Renway knew better than most that secrets don't like to stay underground. His former partner in crime, Evelyn Cosmeer, who'd transformed herself into the perfect Ohio suburban mom before her capture, knew that. The irony did not escape Jeremiah.

He stayed hidden in the bush. He knew a lot about camouflage. They would not see him.

He remembered the night eight years ago when the two men had died—the sudden gun blasts, the sounds of the shovels ripping into the earth, the grunts from the deep dig. He'd even debated telling the authorities what happened—all of it.

Anonymously, of course.

But in the end he couldn't risk it. No man, Jeremiah knew, was meant for a cage, though some could live through it. Jeremiah could not. He'd had a cousin named Perry who'd been serving eight years in a federal penitentiary. Perry was locked in a tiny cell for twenty-three hours a day. One morning, Perry tried to kill himself by running headfirst into the cement wall.

That would be Jeremiah.

So he kept his mouth shut and did nothing. For eight years anyway.

But he thought about that night a lot. He thought about the young woman in the nude. He thought about the men in wait. He thought about the scuffle near the car. He thought about the sickening, wet sound of wood against exposed flesh. He thought about the man left to die.

And he thought about the lies. The lies, most of all, haunted him.

12

By the time I returned to the clinic, the waiting room was packed with the sniffing and impatient. A television replayed a video of *The Little Mermaid*, automatically rewinding at the end and starting over, the color frayed and faded from overuse. After my hours with the FBI, my mind sympathized with the tape. I kept rehashing Carlson's words—he was definitely the lead guy—trying to figure out what he was really after, but all that did was make the picture murkier and more surreal. It also gave me a whopping headache.

"Yo, Doc."

Tyrese Barton hopped up. He was wearing butt-plunge baggy pants and what looked like an oversized varsity jacket, all done by some designer I never heard of but soon would.

"Hi, Tyrese," I said.

Tyrese gave me a complicated handshake, which was a bit like a dance routine where he leads and I follow. He and Latisha had a six-year-old son they called TJ. TJ was a hemophiliac. He was also blind. I met him after he was rushed in as an infant and Tyrese was seconds away from being arrested. Tyrese claimed I saved his son's life on that day. That was hyperbole.

But maybe I did save Tyrese.

He thought that made us friends—like he was this lion and I was some mouse who pulled a thorn from his paw. He was wrong.

Tyrese and Latisha were never married, but he was one of the few fathers I saw in here. He finished shaking my hands and slipped me two Ben Franklins as though I were a maître d' at Le Cirque.

He gave me the eye. "You take good care of my boy now."

"Right."

"You the best, Doc." He handed me his business card, which had no name, no address, no job title. Just a cell phone number. "You need anything, you call."

"I'll keep that in mind," I said.

Still with the eye. "*Anything*, Doc."

"Right."

I pocketed the bills. We've been going through this same routine for six years now. I knew a lot of drug dealers from working here; I knew none who survived six years.

I didn't keep the money, of course. I gave it to Linda for her charity. Legally debatable, I knew, but the way I figured it, better the money went to charity than to a drug dealer. I had no idea how much money Tyrese had.

He always had a new car, though—he favored BMWs with tinted windows—and his kid's wardrobe was worth more than anything that inhabited my closet. But, alas, the child's mother was on Medicaid, so the visits were free.

Maddening, I know.

Tyrese's cell phone sounded something hip-hop.

"Got to take this, Doc. Bidness."

"Right," I said again.

I do get angry sometimes. Who wouldn't? But through that haze, there are real children here. They hurt. I don't claim that all children are wonderful. They are not. I sometimes treat ones that I know—*know*—will amount to no good. But children are, if nothing else, helpless. They are weak and defenseless. Believe me, I've seen examples that would alter your definition of human beings.

So I concentrate on the children.

I was supposed to work only until noon, but to make up for my FBI detour, I saw patients until three. Naturally, I'd been thinking about the interrogation all day. Those pictures of Elizabeth, battered and defeated, kept popping through my brain like the most grotesque sort of strobe light.

Who would know about those pictures?

The answer, when I took the time to think about it, was somewhat obvious. I leaned forward and picked up the phone. I hadn't dialed this number in years, but I still remembered it.

"Schayes Photography," a woman answered.

"Hi, Rebecca."

"Son of a gun. How are you, Beck?"

"Good. How about yourself?"

"Not bad. Busy as all hell."

"You work too hard."

"Not anymore. I got married last year."

"I know. I'm sorry I couldn't make it."

"Bull."

"Yeah. But congrats anyway."

"So what's up?"

"I need to ask you a question," I said.

"Uh-huh."

"About the car accident."

I hear a tinny echo. Then silence.

"Do you remember the car accident? The one before Elizabeth was killed?"

Rebecca Schayes, my wife's closest friend, did not reply.

I cleared my throat. "Who was driving?"

"What?" She did not say that into the phone. "Okay, hold on." Then back at me: "Look, Beck, something just came up here. Can I call you back in a little while?"

"Rebecca—"

But the line was dead.

*

Here is the truth about tragedy: It's good for the soul.

The fact is, I'm a better person because of the deaths. If every cloud has a silver lining, this one is admittedly pretty flimsy. But there it is. That doesn't mean it's worth it or an even trade or anything like that, but I know I'm a better man than I used to be. I have a finer sense of what's important. I have a keener understanding of people's pain.

There was a time—it's laughable now—when I used to worry about what clubs I belonged to, what car I drove, what college degree I stuck on my wall—all that status crap. I wanted to be a surgeon because that wowed people. I wanted to impress so-called friends. I wanted to be a big man.

Like I said, laughable.

Some might argue that my self-improvement is simply a question of maturity. In part, true. And much of the change is due to the fact I am now on my own. Elizabeth and I were a couple, a single entity. She was so good that I could afford to be not so good, as though her goodness raised us both, was a cosmic equalizer.

Still, death is a great teacher. It's just too harsh.

I wish I could tell you that through the tragedy I mined some undiscovered, life-altering absolute that I could pass on to you. I didn't. The clichés apply—people are what count, life is precious, materialism is over-rated, the little things matter, live in the moment—and I can repeat them to you ad nauseam. You might listen, but you won't internalize. Tragedy hammers it home. Tragedy etches it onto your soul. You might not be happier. But you will be better.

What makes this all the more ironic is that I've often wished that Elizabeth could see me now. Much as I'd like to, I don't believe the dead watch over us or any similar comfort-fantasy we sell ourselves. I believe the dead are gone for good. But I can't help but think: Perhaps now I am worthy of her.

A more religious man might wonder if that is why she's returned.

Rebecca Schayes was a leading freelance photographer. Her work appeared in all the usual glossies, though strangely enough, she specialized in men. Professional athletes who agreed to appear on the cover of, for example, *GQ* often requested her to do the shoot. Rebecca liked to joke that she had a knack for male bodies due to "a lifetime of intense study."

I found her studio on West Thirty-second Street, not far from Penn Station. The building was a butt-ugly semi-warehouse that reeked from the Central Park horse and buggies housed on the ground floor. I skipped the freight elevator and took the stairs.

Rebecca was hurrying down the corridor. Trailing her, a gaunt, black-clad assistant with reedy arms and pencil-sketch facial hair dragged two aluminum suitcases. Rebecca still had the unruly sabra locks, her fiery hair curling angrily and flowing freely. Her eyes were wide apart and green, and if she'd changed in the past eight years, I couldn't see it.

She barely broke stride when she saw me. "It's a bad time, Beck."

"Tough," I said.

"I got a shoot. Can we do this later?"

"No."

She stopped, whispered something to the sulking black-clad assistant, and said, "Okay, follow me."

Her studio had high ceilings and cement walls painted white. There were lots of lighting umbrellas and black screens and extension cords snaking everywhere. Rebecca fiddled with a film cartridge and pretended to be busy.

"Tell me about the car accident," I said.

"I don't get this, Beck." She opened a canister, put it down, put the top back on, then opened it again. "We've barely spoken in, what, eight years? All of a sudden you get all obsessive about an old car accident?"

I crossed my arms and waited.

"Why, Beck? After all this time. Why do you want to know?"

"Tell me."

She kept her eyes averted. The unruly hair fell over half her face, but she didn't bother pushing it back. "I miss her," she said. "And I miss you too."

I didn't reply to that.

"I called," she said.

"I know."

"I tried to stay in touch. I wanted to be there."

"I'm sorry," I said. And I was. Rebecca had been Elizabeth's best friend. They'd shared an apartment near Washington Square Park before we got married. I should have returned her calls or invited her over or made some kind of effort. But I didn't.

Grief can be inordinately selfish.

"Elizabeth told me that you two were in a minor car crash," I went on. "It was her fault, she said. She took her eyes off the road. Is that true?"

"What possible difference does it make now?"

"It makes a difference."

"How?"

"What are you afraid of, Rebecca?"

Now it was her time for silence.

"Was there an accident or not?"

Her shoulders slumped as though something internal had been severed. She took a few deep breaths and kept her face down. "I don't know."

"What do you mean, you don't know?"

"She told me it was a car accident too."

"But you weren't there?"

"No. You were out of town, Beck. I came home one night, and Elizabeth was there. She was bruised up. I asked her what happened. She told me she'd been in a car accident and if anyone asked, we'd been in my car."

"If anyone asked?"

Rebecca finally looked up. "I think she meant you, Beck."

I tried to take this in. "So what really happened?"

"She wouldn't say."

"Did you take her to a doctor?"

"She wouldn't let me." Rebecca gave me a strange look. "I still don't get it. Why are you asking me about this now?"

Tell no one.

"I'm just trying to get a little closure."

She nodded, but she didn't believe me. Neither one of us was a particularly adept liar.

"Did you take any pictures of her?" I asked.

"Pictures?"

"Of her injuries. After the accident."

"God, no. Why would I do that?"

An awfully good question. I sat there and thought about it. I don't know how long.

"Beck?"

"Yeah."

"You look like hell."

"You don't," I said.

"I'm in love."

"It becomes you."

"Thanks."

"Is he a good guy?"

"The best."

"Maybe he deserves you, then."

"Maybe." She leaned forward and kissed my cheek. It felt good, comforting. "Something happened, didn't it?"

This time I opted for the truth. "I don't know."

13

Shauna and Hester Crimstein sat in Hester's swanky midtown law office. Hester finished up her phone call and put the receiver back in the cradle.

"No one's doing much talking," Hester said.

"But they didn't arrest him?"

"No. Not yet."

"So what's going on?" Shauna asked.

"Near as I can tell, they think Beck killed his wife."

"That's nuts," Shauna said. "He was in the hospital, for crying out loud. That KillRoy loony tune is on death row."

"Not for her murder," the attorney replied.

"What?"

"Kellerton's suspected of killing at least eighteen women. He confessed to fourteen, but they only had enough hard evidence to prosecute and convict him on twelve. That was enough. I mean, how many death sentences does one man need?"

"But everyone knows he killed Elizabeth."

"Correction: Everyone *knew*."

"I don't get it. How can they possibly think Beck had anything to do with it?"

"I don't know," Hester said. She threw her feet up on her desk and put her hands behind her head. "At least, not yet. But we'll have to be on our guard."

"How's that?"

"For one thing, we have to assume the feds are watching his every step. Phone taps, surveillance, that kind of thing."

"So?"

"What do you mean, so?"

"He's innocent, Hester. Let them watch."

Hester looked up and shook her head. "Don't be naïve."

"What the hell does that mean?"

"It means that if they tape him having eggs for breakfast, it can be something. He has to be careful. But there's something else."

"What?"

"The feds are going to go after Beck."

"How?"

"Got me, but trust me, they will. They got a hard-on for your friend. And it's been eight years. That means they're desperate. Desperate feds are ugly, constitutional-rights-stamping feds."

Shauna sat back and thought about the strange emails from "Elizabeth."
"What?" Hester said.
"Nothing."
"Don't hold back on me, Shauna."
"I'm not the client here."
"You saying Beck isn't telling me everything?"
An idea struck Shauna with something approaching horror. She thought about it some more, ran the idea over some test tracks, let it bounce around for a few moments.
It made sense, and yet Shauna hoped—nay, prayed—that she was wrong. She stood and hurried toward the door. "I have to go."
"What's going on?"
"Ask your client."

Special agents Nick Carlson and Tom Stone positioned themselves on the same couch over which Beck had recently waxed nostalgic. Kim Parker, Elizabeth's mother, sat across from them with her hands primly in her lap. Her face was a frozen, waxy mask. Hoyt Parker paced.
"So what's so important that you couldn't say anything over the phone?" Hoyt asked.
"We want to ask you some questions," Carlson said.
"What about?"
"Your daughter."
That froze them both.
"More specifically, we'd like to ask you about her relationship with her husband, Dr. David Beck."
Hoyt and Kim exchanged a glance. "Why?" Hoyt asked.
"It involves a matter currently under investigation."
"What matter? She's been dead for eight years. Her killer is on death row."
"Please, Detective Parker. We're all on the same side here."
The room was still and dry. Kim Parker's lips thinned and trembled. Hoyt looked at his wife and then nodded at the two men.
Carlson kept his gaze on Kim. "Mrs. Parker, how would you describe the relationship between your daughter and her husband?"
"They were very close, very much in love."
"No problems?"
"No," she said. "None."
"Would you describe Dr. Beck as a violent man?"
She looked startled. "No, never."
They looked at Hoyt. Hoyt nodded his agreement.
"To your knowledge, did Dr. Beck ever hit your daughter?"
"What?"
Carlson tried a kind smile. "If you could just answer the question."
"Never," Hoyt said. "No one hit my daughter."
"You're certain?"
His voice was firm. "Very."
Carlson looked toward Kim. "Mrs. Parker?"

"He loved her so much."

"I understand that, ma'am. But many wife-beaters profess to loving their wives."

"He never hit her."

Hoyt stopped pacing. "What's going on here?"

Carlson looked at Stone for a moment. "I want to show you some photographs, if I may. They are a bit disturbing, but I think they're important."

Stone handed Carlson the manila envelope. Carlson opened it. One by one, he placed the photographs of the bruised Elizabeth on a coffee table. He watched for a reaction. Kim Parker, as expected, let out a small cry. Hoyt Parker's face seemed at odds with itself, settling into a distant blankness.

"Where did you get these?" Hoyt asked softly.

"Have you seen them before?"

"Never," he said. He looked at his wife. She shook her head.

"But I remember the bruises," Kim Parker offered.

"When?"

"I can't remember exactly. Not long before she died. But when I saw them, they were less"—she searched for the word—"pronounced."

"Did your daughter tell you how she got them?"

"She said she was in a car accident."

"Mrs. Parker, we've checked with your wife's insurance company. She never reported a car accident. We checked police files. No one ever made a claim against her. No policeman ever filled out a report."

"So what are you saying?" Hoyt came in.

"Simply this: If your daughter wasn't in a car accident, how did she get these bruises?"

"You think her husband gave them to her?"

"It's a theory we're working on."

"Based on what?"

The two men hesitated. The hesitation said one of two things: not in front of the lady or not in front of the civilian. Hoyt picked up on it. "Kim, do you mind if I talk to the agents alone for moment?"

"Not at all." She stood on wobbly legs and teetered toward the stairs. "I'll be in the bedroom."

When she was out of sight, Hoyt said, "Okay, I'm listening."

"We don't think Dr. Beck just beat your daughter," Carlson said. "We think he murdered her."

Hoyt looked from Carlson to Stone and back to Carlson, as though waiting for the punch line. When none came, he moved to the chair. "You better start explaining."

14

What else had Elizabeth been keeping from me?

As I headed down Tenth Avenue toward the Quick-n-Park, I again tried to dismiss those photographs as merely a record of her car accident injuries. I remembered how nonchalant Elizabeth had been about the whole thing at the time. Just a fender-bender, she said. No big deal. When I asked for details, she had pretty much brushed me off.

Now I knew that she'd lied to me about it.

I could tell you that Elizabeth never lied to me, but that would be, in light of this recent discovery, a pretty unconvincing argument. This was, however, the first lie I was aware of. I guess we both had our secrets.

When I reached the Quick-n-Park, I spotted something strange—or perhaps, I should say, someone strange. There, on the corner, was a man in a tan overcoat.

He was looking at me.

And he was oddly familiar. No one I knew, but there was still the unease of déjà vu. I'd seen this man before. This morning even. Where? I ran through my morning and spotted him in my mind's eye:

When I pulled over for coffee at eight a.m. The man with the tan overcoat had been there. In the parking lot of Starbucks.

Was I sure?

No, of course not. I diverted my eyes and hurried over to the attendant's booth. The parking attendant—his name tag read Carlo—was watching television and eating a sandwich. He kept his eyes on the screen for half a minute before sliding his gaze toward me. Then he slowly brushed the crumbs off his hands, took my ticket, and stamped it. I quickly paid the man and he handed me my key.

The man in the tan overcoat was still there.

I tried very hard not to look in his direction as I walked to my car. I got in, started it up, and when I hit Tenth Avenue, I checked the rearview mirror.

The man with the tan overcoat didn't so much as glance at me. I kept watching him until I turned toward the West Side Highway. He never looked in my direction. Paranoid. I was going nutsy paranoid.

So why had Elizabeth lied to me?

I thought about it and came up with nothing.

There were still three hours until my Bat Street message came in. Three hours. Man, I needed to distract myself. Thinking too hard about what might be on the other end of that cyber-connection shredded my stomach lining.

I knew what I had to do. I was just trying to delay the inevitable.

*

When I got home, Grandpa was in his customary chair, alone. The television was off. The nurse was yakking on the phone in Russian. She wasn't going to work out. I'd have to call the agency and get her replaced.

Small particles of egg were stuck to the corners of Grandpa's mouth, so I took out a handkerchief and gently scraped them away. Our eyes met, but his gaze was locked on something far beyond me. I saw us all up at the lake. Grandpa would be doing his beloved weight-loss before-and-after pose. He'd turn profile, slump, let his elastic gut hang out, and shout "Before!" and then suck it up and flex and yell "After!" He did it brilliantly. My father would howl. Dad had the greatest, most infectious laugh. It was a total body release. I used to have it too. It died with him. I could never laugh like that again. Somehow it seemed obscene.

Hearing me, the nurse hurried off the phone and hightailed it into the room with a bright smile. I didn't return it.

I eyed the basement door. I was still delaying the inevitable.

No more stalling.

"Stay with him," I said.

The nurse bowed her head and sat down.

The basement had been finished in the days before people finished basements, and it showed. The once-brown shag carpet was pockmarked and water-buckled. Faux white brick made from some sort of bizarre synthetic had been glued to asphalt walls. Some sheets had fallen to the shag; others stopped mid-topple, like columns of the Acropolis.

In the center of the room, the Ping-Pong table's green had been washed to an almost in-vogue spearmint. The torn net looked like the barricades after the French troops stormed. The paddles were stripped down to the splintery wood.

Some cardboard boxes, many sprouting mold, sat on top of the Ping-Pong table. Others were piled in the corner. Old clothes were in wardrobe boxes. Not Elizabeth's. Shauna and Linda had cleared those out for me. Goodwill got them, I think. But some of the other boxes held old items. *Her* items. I couldn't throw them away, and I couldn't let other people have them. I'm not sure why. Some things we pack away, stick in the back of the closet, never expect to see again—but we can't quite make ourselves discard them. Like dreams, I guess.

I wasn't sure where I had put it, but I knew it was there. I started going through old photographs, once again averting my gaze. I was pretty good at that, though as time went on, the photographs hurt less and less. When I saw Elizabeth and me together in some greening Polaroid, it was as though I were looking at strangers.

I hated doing this.

I dug deeper into the box. My fingertips hit something made of felt, and I pulled out her tennis varsity letter from high school. With a sad smirk, I remembered her tan legs and the way her braid bounced as she hopped toward the net. On the court, her face was locked in pure concentration. That was how Elizabeth would beat you. She had decent enough ground strokes and a pretty good serve, but what lifted her above her classmates was that focus.

I put the letter down gingerly and started digging again. I found what I was looking for at the bottom.

Her daily planner.

The police had wanted it after the abduction. Or so I was told. Rebecca came by the apartment and helped them find it. I assume they searched for clues in it—the same thing I was about to do—but when the body popped up with the K branding, they probably stopped.

I thought about that some more—about how everything had been neatly pinned on KillRoy—and another thought scurried through my brain. I ran upstairs to my computer and got online. I found the Web site for the New York City Department of Correction. Tons of stuff on it, including the name and phone number I needed.

I signed off and called Briggs Penitentiary.

That's the prison that holds KillRoy.

When the recording came on, I pressed in the proper extension and was put through. Three rings later, a man said, "Deputy Superintendent Brown speaking."

I told him that I wanted to visit Elroy Kellerton.

"And you are?" he said.

"Dr. David Beck. My wife, Elizabeth Beck, was one of his victims."

"I see." Brown hesitated. "May I ask the purpose of your visit?"

"No."

There was more silence on the line.

"I have the right to visit him if he's willing to see me," I said.

"Yes, of course, but this is a highly unusual request."

"I'm still making it."

"The normal procedure is to have your attorney go through his—"

"But I don't have to," I interrupted. I learned this at a victim's rights Web site—that I could make the request myself. If Kellerton was willing to see me, I was in. "I just want to talk to Kellerton. You have visiting hours tomorrow, don't you?"

"Yes, we do."

"Then if Kellerton agrees, I'll be up tomorrow. Is there a problem with that?"

"No, sir. If he agrees, there's no problem."

I thanked him and hung up the phone. I was taking action. It felt damn good.

The day planner sat on the desk next to me. I was avoiding it again, because as painful as a photograph or recording might be, handwriting was somehow worse, somehow more personal. Elizabeth's soaring capital letters, the firmly crossed ts, the too many loops between letters, the way it all tilted to the right ...

I spent an hour going through it. Elizabeth was detailed. She didn't shorthand much. What surprised me was how well I'd known my wife. Everything was clear, and there were no surprises. In fact, there was only one appointment I couldn't account for.

Three weeks before her death, there was an entry that read simply: *PF.* And a phone number without an area code.

In light of how specific she'd been elsewhere, I found this entry a little unsettling. I didn't have a clue what the area code would be. The call was made eight years ago. Area codes had split and changed several different ways since then.

I tried 201 and got a disconnect. I tried 973. An old lady answered. I told her she'd won a free subscription to the *New York Post.* She gave me her name. Neither initial matched. I tried 212, which was the city. And that was where I hit bingo.

"Peter Flannery, attorney-at-law," a woman said mid-yawn.

"May I speak to Mr. Flannery, please."

"He's in court."

She could have sounded more bored but not without a quality prescription. I heard a lot of noise in the background.

"I'd like to make an appointment to see Mr. Flannery."

"You answering the billboard ad?"

"Billboard ad?"

"You injured?"

"Yes," I said. "But I didn't see an ad. A friend recommended him. It's a medical malpractice case. I came in with a broken arm and now I can't move it. I lost my job. The pain is nonstop."

She set me up for an appointment tomorrow afternoon.

I put the phone back into the cradle and frowned. What would Elizabeth be doing with a probable ambulance-chaser like Flannery?

The sound of the phone made me jump. I snatched it up mid-ring.

"Hello," I said.

It was Shauna. "Where are you?" she asked.

"Home."

"You need to get over here right away," she said.

15

Agent Carlson looked Hoyt Parker straight in the eye. "As you know, we recently found two bodies in the vicinity of Lake Charmaine."

Hoyt nodded.

A cell phone chirped. Stone managed to hoist himself up and said "Excuse me" before lumbering into the kitchen. Hoyt turned back to Carlson and waited.

"We know the official account of your daughter's death," Carlson said. "She and her husband, David Beck, visited the lake for an annual ritual. They went swimming in the dark. KillRoy lay in wait. He assaulted Dr. Beck and kidnapped your daughter. End of story."

"And you don't think that's what happened?"

"No, Hoyt—can I call you Hoyt?"

Hoyt nodded.

"No, Hoyt, we don't."

"So how do you see it?"

"I think David Beck murdered your daughter and pinned it on a serial killer."

Hoyt, a twenty-eight-year veteran of the NYPD, knew how to keep a straight face, but he still leaned back as though the words were jabs at his chin. "Let's hear it."

"Okay, let's start from the beginning. Beck takes your daughter up to a secluded lake, right?"

"Right."

"You've been there?"

"Many times."

"Oh?"

"We were all friends. Kim and I were close to David's parents. We used to visit all the time."

"Then you know how secluded it is."

"Yes."

"Dirt road, a sign that you'd only see if you knew to look for it. It's as hidden as hidden can be. No signs of life."

"What's your point?"

"What are the odds of KillRoy pulling up that road?"

Hoyt raised his palms to the sky. "What are the odds of anyone meeting up with a serial killer?"

"True, okay, but in other cases, there was a logic to it. Kellerton abducted somebody off a city street, he carjacked a victim, even broke into a house.

But think about it. He sees this dirt road and somehow decides to search for a victim up there? I'm not saying it's impossible, but it's highly unlikely."

Hoyt said, "Go on."

"You'll admit that there are plenty of logic holes in the accepted scenario."

"All cases have logic holes."

"Right, okay, but let me try an alternate theory on you. Let's just say that Dr. Beck wanted to kill your daughter."

"Why?"

"For one thing, a two-hundred-thousand-dollar life insurance policy."

"He doesn't need money."

"Everyone needs money, Hoyt. You know that."

"I don't buy it."

"Look, we're still digging here. We don't know all the motivations yet. But let me just go through our scenario, okay?"

Hoyt gave him a suit-yourself shrug.

"We have evidence here that Dr. Beck beat her."

"What evidence? You have some photographs. She told my wife she'd been in a car accident."

"Come on, Hoyt." Carlson swept his hand at the photographs. "Look at the expression on your daughter's face. That look like the face of a woman in a car accident?"

No, Hoyt thought, it didn't. "Where did you find these pictures?"

"I'll get to that in a second, but let's go back to my scenario, okay? Let's assume for the moment that Dr. Beck beat your daughter and that he had a hell of an inheritance coming his way."

"Lot of assuming."

"True, but stay with me. Think of the accepted scenario and all those holes. Now compare it with this one: Dr. Beck brings your daughter up to a secluded spot where he knows there will be no witnesses. He hires two thugs to grab her. He knows about KillRoy. It's in all the papers. Plus your brother worked on the case. Did he ever discuss it with you or Beck?"

Hoyt sat still for a moment. "Go on."

"The two hired thugs abduct and kill your daughter. Naturally, the first suspect will be the husband—always is in a case like this, right? But the two thugs brand her cheek with the letter K. Next thing we know, it's all blamed on KillRoy."

"But Beck was assaulted. His head injury was real."

"Sure, but we both know that's not inconsistent with him being behind it. How would Beck explain coming out of the abduction healthy? 'Hi, guess what, someone kidnapped my wife, but I'm fine'? It'd never play. Getting whacked on the head gave his story credibility."

"He took a hell of a shot."

"He was dealing with thugs, Hoyt. They probably miscalculated. And what about his injury anyway? He tells some bizarre story about miraculously crawling out of the water and dialing 911. I gave several doctors Beck's old medical chart. They claim his account of what he did defies medical logic. It would have been pretty much impossible, given his injuries."

Hoyt considered that. He had often wondered about that himself. How had Beck survived and called for help? "What else?" Hoyt said.

"There's strong evidence that suggests the two thugs, not KillRoy, assaulted Beck."

"What evidence?"

"Buried with the bodies, we found a baseball bat with blood on it. The full DNA match will take a while, but the preliminary results strongly suggest that the blood is Beck's."

Agent Stone plodded back in the room and sat down hard. Hoyt once again said, "Go on."

"The rest is pretty obvious. The two thugs do the job. They kill your daughter and pin it on KillRoy. Then they come back to get the rest of their payment—or maybe they decide to extort more money from Dr. Beck. I don't know. Whatever, Beck has to get rid of them. He sets up a meet in the secluded woods near Lake Charmaine. The two thugs probably thought they were dealing with a wimpy doctor or maybe he caught them unprepared. Either way Beck shoots them and buries the bodies along with the baseball bat and whatever evidence might haunt him later on. The perfect crime now. Nothing to tie him with the murder. Let's face it. If we didn't get enormously lucky, the bodies would have never been found."

Hoyt shook his head. "Hell of a theory."

"There's more."

"Like?"

Carlson looked at Stone. Stone pointed to his cell phone. "I just got a strange phone call from someone at Briggs Penitentiary," Stone said. "It seems your son-in-law called there today and demanded a meeting with KillRoy."

Hoyt now looked openly stunned. "Why the hell would he do that?"

"You tell us," Stone responded. "But keep in mind that Beck knows we're onto him. All of a sudden, he has this overwhelming desire to visit the man he set up as your daughter's killer."

"Hell of a coincidence," Carlson added.

"You think he's trying to cover his tracks?"

"You have a better explanation?"

Hoyt sat back and tried to let all of this settle. "You left something out."

"What?"

He pointed to the photographs on the table. "Who gave you those?"

"In a way," Carlson said, "I think your daughter did."

Hoyt's face looked drained.

"More specifically, her alias did. One Sarah Goodhart. Your daughter's middle name and the name of this street."

"I don't understand."

"At the crime scene," Carlson said. "One of the two thugs—Melvin Bartola—had a small key in his shoe." Carlson held up the key. Hoyt took it from his hand, peering at it as though it held some mystical answer. "See the *UCB* on the flip side?"

Hoyt nodded.

"That stands for United Central Bank. We finally traced this key down to their branch at 1772 Broadway in the city. The key opens Box 174, which is registered to one Sarah Goodhart. We got a search warrant for it."

Hoyt looked up. "The photographs were in there?"

Carlson and Stone glanced at each other. They had already made the decision not to tell Hoyt everything about that box—not until all the tests came back and they knew for sure—but both men nodded now.

"Think about it, Hoyt. Your daughter kept these pictures hidden in a safety-deposit box. The reasons are obvious. Want more? We questioned Dr. Beck. He admitted knowing nothing about the pictures. He'd never seen them before. Why would your daughter hide them from him?"

"You talked to Beck?"

"Yes."

"What else did he say?"

"Not much because he demanded a lawyer." Carlson waited a beat. Then he leaned forward. "He not only lawyered up, he called Hester Crimstein. That sound like the act of an innocent man to you?"

Hoyt actually gripped the sides of the chair, trying to steady himself. "You can't prove any of this."

"Not yet, no. But we know. That's half the battle sometimes."

"So what are you going to do?"

"Only one thing we can do." Carlson smiled at him. "Apply pressure until something breaks."

Larry Gandle looked over the day's developments and mumbled to himself, "Not good."

One, the FBI picks up Beck and questions him.

Two, Beck calls a photographer named Rebecca Schayes. He asks her about an old car accident involving his wife. Then he visits her studio.

A photographer no less.

Three, Beck calls Briggs Penitentiary and says he wants to meet Elroy Kellerton.

Fourth, Beck calls Peter Flannery's office.

All of this was puzzling. None of it was good.

Eric Wu hung up the phone and said, "You're not going to like this."

"What?"

"Our source with the FBI says that they suspect Beck killed his wife."

Gandle nearly fell over. "Explain."

"That's all the source knows. Somehow, they've tied the two dead bodies by the lake to Beck."

Very puzzling.

"Let me see those emails again," Gandle said.

Eric Wu handed them to him. When Gandle thought about who could have sent them, the creeping feeling in the pit of his stomach started to claw and grow. He tried to add the pieces together. He'd always wondered how Beck had survived that night. Now he wondered something else.

Had anyone else survived it?

"What time is it?" Gandle asked.

"Six-thirty."

"Beck still hasn't looked up that Bat-whatever address?"

"Bat Street. And no, he hasn't."

"Anything more on Rebecca Schayes?"

"Just what we already know. Close friend of Elizabeth Parker's. They shared an apartment before Parker married Beck. I checked old phone records. Beck hasn't called her in years."

"So why would he contact her now?"

Wu shrugged. "Ms. Schayes must know something."

Griffin Scope had been very clear. Learn what you can, then bury it.

And use Wu.

"We need to have a chat with her," Gandle said.

16

Shauna met me on the ground floor of a high-rise at 462 Park Avenue in Manhattan.

"Come on," she said without preamble. "I have something to show you upstairs."

I checked my watch. A little under two hours until the Bat Street message came in. We entered an elevator. Shauna hit the button for the twenty-third floor. The lights climbed and the blind-person-counter beeped.

"Hester got me thinking," Shauna said.

"What about?"

"She said the feds would be desperate. That they'd do anything to get you."

"So?"

The elevator sounded its final ding.

"Hang on, you'll see."

The door slid open on a massive cubicle-divided floor. The norm in the city nowadays. Rip off the ceiling and view from above and you'd have a very hard time telling the difference between this floor and a rat maze. From down here too, when you thought about it.

Shauna marched between countless cloth-lined dividers. I trailed in her wake. Halfway down she turned left and then right and then left again.

"Maybe I should drop bread crumbs," I said.

Her voice was flat. "Good one."

"Thank you, I'm here all week."

She wasn't laughing.

"What is this place anyway?" I asked.

"A company called DigiCom. The agency works with them sometimes."

"Doing what?"

"You'll see."

We made a final turn into a cluttered cubbyhole occupied by a young man with a long head and the slender fingers of a concert pianist.

"This is Farrell Lynch. Farrell, this is David Beck."

I shook the slender hand briefly. Farrell said, "Hi."

I nodded.

"Okay," Shauna said. "Key it up."

Farrell Lynch swiveled his chair so that he was facing the computer. Shauna and I watched over his shoulders. He started typing with those slender fingers.

"Keyed up," he said.

"Run it."

He hit the return button. The screen went black and then Humphrey Bogart appeared. He wore a fedora and a trench coat. I recognized the scene right away.The fog, the plane in the background. The finale of *Casablanca.*

I looked at Shauna.

"Wait," she said.

The camera was on Bogie. He was telling Ingrid Bergman that she was getting on that plane with Laszlo and that the problems of three little people didn't amount to a hill of beans in this world. And then, when the camera went back to Ingrid Bergman . . .

. . . it wasn't Ingrid Bergman.

I blinked. There, beneath the famed hat, gazing up at Bogie and bathed in the gray glow, was Shauna.

"I can't go with you, Rick," the computer Shauna said dramatically, "because I'm madly in love with Ava Gardner."

I turned to Shauna. My eyes asked the question. She nodded yes. I said it anyway.

"You think . . ." I stammered. "You think I was fooled by trick photography?"

Farrell took that one. "Digital photography," he corrected me. "Far simpler to manipulate." He spun his chair toward me. "See, computer images aren't film. They're really just pixels in files. Not unlike your word processing document. You know how easy it is to change a word processing document, right? To alter content or fonts or spacing?"

I nodded.

"Well, for someone with even a rudimentary understanding of digital imaging, that's how easy it is to manipulate a computer's streaming images. These aren't pictures, nor are they films or tapes. Computer video streams are simply a bunch of pixels. Anyone can manipulate them. Simply cut and paste and then you run a blend program."

I looked at Shauna. "But she looked older in the video," I insisted. "Different."

Shauna said, "Farrell?"

He hit another button. Bogie returned. When they went to Ingrid Bergman this time, Shauna looked seventy years old.

"Age progression software," Farrell explained. "It's mostly used to age missing children, but nowadays they sell a home version at any software store. I can also change any part of Shauna's image—her hairstyle, her eye color, the size of her nose. I can make her lips thinner or thicker, give her a tattoo, whatever."

"Thank you, Farrell," Shauna said.

She gave him a look of dismissal a blind man could read. "Excuse me," Farrell said before making himself scarce.

I couldn't think.

When Farrell was out of earshot, Shauna said, "I remembered a photo shoot I did last month. One picture came out perfectly—the sponsor loved it—except my earring had slipped down. We brought the image over here. Farrell did a quick cut-and-paste and voilà, my earring was back in the right place."

I shook my head.

"Think about it, Beck. The feds think you killed Elizabeth, but they have no way to prove it. Hester explained how desperate they've become. I started thinking: Maybe they'd play mind games with you. What better mind game than sending you these emails?"

"But kiss time . . . ?"

"What about it?"

"How would they know about kiss time?"

"I know about it. Linda knows about it. I bet Rebecca knows too, maybe Elizabeth's parents. They could have found out."

I felt tears rush up to the surface. I tried to work my voice and managed to croak out, "It's a hoax?"

"I don't know, Beck. I really don't. But let's be rational here. If Elizabeth was alive, where has she been for eight years? Why choose now of all times to come back from the grave—the same time, by coincidence, that the FBI starts suspecting you of killing her? And come on, do you really believe she's still alive? I know you want to. Hell, I want to. But let's try to look at this rationally. When you really think about it, which scenario makes more sense?"

I stumbled back and fell into a chair. My heart started crumbling. I felt the hope start to shrivel up.

A hoax. Has this all been nothing but a hoax?

17

Once he was settled inside Rebecca Schayes's studio, Larry Gandle called his wife on the cell phone. "I'll be home late," he said.

"Don't forget to take your pill," Patty told him.

Gandle had a mild case of diabetes, controlled through diet and a pill. No insulin.

"I will."

Eric Wu, still plugged into his Walkman, carefully laid down a vinyl drop cloth near the door.

Gandle hung up the phone and snapped on a pair of latex gloves. The search was both thorough and time-consuming. Like most photographers, Rebecca Schayes saved tons of negatives. There were four metal file cabinets jammed full of them. They'd checked Rebecca Schayes's schedule. She was finishing up a shoot. She'd be back here to work the darkroom in about an hour. Not enough time.

"You know what would help," Wu said.

"What?"

"Having some idea what the hell we're looking for."

"Beck gets these cryptic emails," Gandle said. "And what does he do? For the first time in eight years, he rushes over to see his wife's oldest friend. We need to know why."

Wu looked through him some more. "Why don't we just wait and ask her?"

"We will, Eric."

Wu nodded slowly and turned away.

Gandle spotted a long metal desk in the darkroom. He tested it. Strong. The size was about right too. You could lay someone on it and tape a limb to each table leg.

"How much duct tape did we bring?"

"Enough," Wu said.

"Do me a favor, then," Gandle said. "Move the drop cloth under the table."

Half an hour until I picked up the Bat Street message.

Shauna's demonstration had hit me like a surprise left hook. I felt groggy, and I took the full count. But a funny thing happened. I got my ass off the canvas. I stood back up and shook off the cobwebs and started circling.

We were in my car. Shauna had insisted on coming back to the house with me. A limousine would take her back in a few hours. I know that she wanted to comfort me, but it was equally clear that she didn't want to go home yet.

"Something I don't get," I said.

Shauna turned to me.

"The feds think I killed Elizabeth, right?"

"Right."

"So why would they send me emails pretending she's alive?"

Shauna had no quick answer.

"Think about it," I said. "You claim that this is some sort of elaborate plot to get me to reveal my guilt. But if I killed Elizabeth, I'd know that it was a trick."

"It's a mind game," Shauna said.

"But that doesn't make sense. If you want to play a mind game with me, send me emails and pretend to be—I don't know—someone who witnessed the murder or something."

Shauna thought about it. "I think they're just trying to keep you off balance, Beck."

"Yeah, but still. It doesn't add up."

"Okay, how long until the next message comes in?"

I checked the clock. "Twenty minutes."

Shauna sat back in her seat. "We'll wait and see what it says."

Eric Wu set up his laptop on the floor in a corner of Rebecca Schayes's studio.

He checked Beck's office computer first. Still idle. The clock read a little past eight o'clock. The clinic was long closed. He switched over to the home computer. For a few seconds there was nothing. And then:

"Beck just signed on," Wu said.

Larry Gandle hurried over. "Can we get on and see the message before him?"

"It wouldn't be a good idea."

"Why not?"

"If we sign in and then he tries to, it will tell him that someone is currently using that screen name."

"He'll know he's being watched?"

"Yes. But it doesn't matter. We're watching him in real time. The moment he reads the message, we'll see it too."

"Okay, let me know when."

Wu squinted at the screen. "He just brought up the Bigfoot site. It should be any second now."

I typed in bigfoot.com and hit the return button.

My right leg started jackhammering. It does that when I'm nervous. Shauna put her hand on my knee. My knee slowed to a stop. She took the hand off. My knee stayed still for a minute, and then it started up again. Shauna put her hand back on my knee. The cycle began again.

Shauna was playing it cool, but I know that she kept sneaking glances at me. She was my best friend. She'd support me to the end. But only an idiot wouldn't be wondering at this juncture if my elevator was stopping at every floor. They say that insanity, like heart disease or intelligence, is hereditary. The thought had been running through my mind since I'd first seen Elizabeth on the street cam. It wasn't a comforting one.

My father died in a car crash when I was twenty. His car toppled over an embankment. According to an eyewitness—a truck driver from Wyoming—my father's Buick drove straight off it. It had been a cold night. The road, while well plowed, was slick.

Many suggested—well, suggested in whispers anyway—that he committed suicide. I don't believe it. Yes, he had been more withdrawn and quiet in his last few months. And yes, I often wonder if all that made him more susceptible to an accident. But suicide? No way.

My mother, always a fragile person of seemingly gentle neuroses, reacted by slowly losing her mind. She literally shrank into herself. Linda tried to nurse her for three years, until even she agreed that Mom needed to be committed. Linda visits her all the time. I don't.

After a few more moments, the Bigfoot home page came up. I found the user name box and typed in Bat Street.

I hit the tab key and in the password text box I typed Teenage. I hit return.

Nothing happened.

"You forgot to click the Sign In icon," Shauna said.

I looked at her. She shrugged. I clicked the icon.

The screen went white. Then an ad for a CD store came up. The bar on the bottom went back and forth in a slow wave. The percentage climbed slowly. When it hit about eighteen percent, it vanished and then several seconds later a message appeared.

> ERROR—Either the user name or password you entered is not in our database.

"Try again," Shauna said.

I did. The same error message came up. The computer was telling me the account didn't even exist.

What did that mean?

I had no idea. I tried to think of a reason that the account wouldn't exist.

I checked the time: 8:13.34 p.m.

Kiss Time

Could that be the answer? Could it be that the account, like the link yesterday, simply didn't exist yet? I mulled that one over. It was possible, of course, but unlikely.

As though reading my mind, Shauna said, "Maybe we should wait until eight-fifteen."

So I tried again at eight-fifteen. At eight-eighteen. At eight-twenty.

Nothing but the same error message.

"The feds must have pulled the plug," Shauna said.

I shook my head, not willing yet to give up.

My leg started shaking again. Shauna used one hand to stop it and one hand to answer her cell phone. She started barking at someone on the other end. I checked the clock. I tried again. Nothing. Twice more. Nothing.

It was after eight-thirty now.

"She, uh, could be late," Shauna said.

I frowned.

"When you saw her yesterday," Shauna tried, "you didn't know where she was, right?"

"Right."

"So maybe she's in a different time zone," Shauna said. "Maybe that's why she's late."

"A different time zone?" I frowned some more. Shauna shrugged.

We waited another hour. Shauna, to her credit, never said I told you so. After a while she put a hand on my back and said, "Hey, I got an idea."

I turned to her.

"I'm going to wait in the other room," Shauna said. "I think that might help."

"How do you figure?"

"See, if this were a movie, this would be the part where I get all fed up by your craziness and storm out and then bingo, the message appears, you know, so only you see it and everyone still thinks you're crazy. Like on Scooby-Doo when only he and Shaggy see the ghost and no one believes them?"

I thought about it. "Worth a try," I said.

"Good. So why don't I go wait in the kitchen for a while? Take your time. When the message comes in, just give a little shout."

She stood.

"You're just humoring me, aren't you?" I said.

Shauna thought about it. "Yeah, probably."

She left then. I turned and faced the screen. And I waited.

18

Nothing's happening," Eric Wu said. "Beck keeps trying to sign on, but all he gets is an error message."

Larry Gandle was about to ask a follow-up question, when he heard the elevator rev up. He checked the clock.

Rebecca Schayes was right on time.

Eric Wu turned away from his computer. He looked at Larry Gandle with the kind of eyes that make a man take a step back. Gandle took out his gun—a nine-millimeter this time. Just in case. Wu frowned. He moved his bulk to the door and flipped off the light.

They waited in the dark.

Twenty seconds later, the elevator stopped on their floor.

Rebecca Schayes rarely thought about Elizabeth and Beck anymore. It had, after all, been eight years. But this morning events had stirred up some long-dormant sensations. Nagging sensations.

About the "car accident."

After all these years, Beck had finally asked her about it.

Eight years ago, Rebecca had been prepared to tell him all about it. But Beck hadn't returned her calls. As time went by—and after an arrest had been made—she saw no point in dredging up the past. It would only hurt Beck. And after KillRoy's arrest, it seemed irrelevant.

But the nagging sensation—the sensation that Elizabeth's bruises from the "car accident" were somehow a precursor to her murder—lingered, even though it made no sense. More than that, the nagging sensation taunted her, making her wonder if she, Rebecca, had insisted, *really* insisted, on finding out the truth about the "car accident," maybe, just maybe, she could have saved her friend.

The lingering, however, faded away over time. At the end of the day, Elizabeth had been her friend, and no matter how close you are, you get over a friend's death. Gary Lamont had come into her life three years ago and changed everything. Yes, Rebecca Schayes, the bohemian photographer from Greenwich Village, had fallen in love with a money-grubbing Wall Street bond trader. They'd gotten married and moved into a trendy high-rise on the Upper West Side.

Funny how life worked.

Rebecca stepped into the freight elevator and slid the gate down. The lights were out, which was hardly unusual in this building. The elevator started heading up to her floor, the churning sound reverberating off the stone. Sometimes at night, she could hear the horses whinny, but they were silent now. The smell of hay and something probably fouler mingled in the air.

She liked being here at night. The way the solitude blended with the city's night noises made her feel her most "artsy."

Her mind started drifting back to the conversation she'd had last night with Gary. He wanted to move out of New York City, preferably to a spacious home on Long Island, at Sands Point, where he'd been raised. The idea of moving to the 'burbs horrified her. More than her love of the city, she knew that it would be the final betrayal of her bohemian roots. She would become what she swore she would never become: her mother and her mother's mother.

The elevator stopped. She lifted the gate and stepped down the corridor. All the lights were off up here. She pulled back her hair and tied it into a thick ponytail. She peered at her watch. Almost nine o'clock. The building would be empty. Of human beings at least.

Her shoes clacked against the cool cement. The truth was—and Rebecca was having a hard time acceptingit, she being a bohemian and all—that the more she thought about it, the more she realized that yes, she wanted children, and that the city was a lousy place to raise them. Children need a backyard and swings and fresh air and . . .

Rebecca Schayes was just reaching a decision—a decision that would have no doubt thrilled her broker husband, Gary—when she stuck her key in the door and opened her studio. She went inside and flipped the light switch.

That was when she saw the weirdly shaped Asian man.

For a moment or two the man simply stared at her. Rebecca stood frozen in his gaze. Then the Asian man stepped to the side, almost behind her, and blasted a fist into the small of her back.

It was like a sledgehammer hit her kidney.

Rebecca crumbled to her knees. The man grabbed her neck with two fingers. He squeezed a pressure point. Rebecca saw bright lights. With his free hand, the man dug with fingers like ice picks under her rib cage. When they reached her liver, her eyes bulged. The pain was beyond anything she'd ever imagined. She tried to scream, but only a choking grunt escaped her mouth.

From across the room, a man's voice sliced through the haze.

"Where is Elizabeth?" the voice asked.

For the first time.

But not the last.

19

I stayed in front of that damn computer and started drinking pretty heavily. I tried logging onto the site a dozen different ways. I used Explorer and then I used Netscape. I cleared my cache and reloaded the pages and signed off my provider and signed back on again.

It didn't matter. I still got the error message.

At ten o'clock, Shauna headed back into the den. Her cheeks were glowing from drink. Mine too, I imagined. "No luck?"

"Go home," I said.

She nodded. "Yeah, I think I'd better."

The limousine was there in five minutes. Shauna wobbled to the curb, fairly wasted on bourbon and Rolling Rock. Me too.

Shauna opened the door and turned back to me. "Were you ever tempted to cheat? I mean, when you two were married."

"No," I said.

Shauna shook her head, disappointed. "You know nothing about how to mess up your life."

I kissed her good-bye and went back inside. I continued to gaze at the screen as though it were something holy. Nothing changed.

Chloe slowly approached a few minutes later. She nudged my hand with her wet nose. Through her forest of hair, our eyes met and I swear that Chloe understood what I was feeling. I'm not one of those who give human characteristics to dogs—for one thing, I think that it might demean them—but I do believe they have a base understanding of what their anthropological counterparts are feeling. They say that dogs can smell fear. Is it such a stretch to believe that they also smell joy or anger or sadness?

I smiled down at Chloe and petted her head. She put a paw on my arm in a comforting gesture. "You want to go for a walk, girl?" I said.

Chloe's reply was to bound about like a circus freak on speed. Like I told you before, it's the little things.

The night air tingled in my lungs. I tried to concentrate on Chloe—her frolicking step, her wagging tail—but I was, well, crestfallen. Crestfallen. That is not a word I use very often. But I thought it fit.

I hadn't fully bought Shauna's too-neat digital-trick hypothesis. Yes, someone could manipulate a photograph and make it part of a video. And yes, someone could have known about kiss time. And yes, someone could have even made the lips whisper "I'm sorry." And yes, my hunger probably helped make the illusion real and made me susceptible to such trickery.

And the biggest yes: Shauna's hypothesis made a hell of a lot more sense than a return from the grave.

But there were two things that overrode a lot of that. First off, I'm not one for flights of fancy. I'm frighteningly boring and more grounded than most. Second, the hunger could have clouded my reasoning, and digital photography could do a lot of things.

But not those eyes . . .

Her eyes. Elizabeth's eyes. There was no way, I thought, that they could be old photographs manipulated into a digital video. Those eyes belonged to my wife. Was my rational mind sure of it? No, of course not. I'm not a fool. But between what I saw and all the questions I'd raised, I had semi-dismissed Shauna's video demonstration. I had come home still believing that I was to receive a message from Elizabeth.

Now I didn't know what to think. The booze was probably helping in that respect.

Chloe stopped to do some prolonged sniffing. I waited under a streetlight and stared at my elongated shadow.

Kiss time.

Chloe barked at a movement in the bush. A squirrel sprinted across the street. Chloe growled and feigned a chase. The squirrel stopped and turned back toward us. Chloe barked a boy-you're-lucky-I'm-on-a-leash sound. She didn't mean it. Chloe was a pure thoroughbred wimp.

Kiss time.

I tilted my head the way Chloe does when she hears a strange sound. I thought again about what I had seen yesterday on my computer—and I thought about the pains someone had gone through to keep this whole thing secret. The unsigned email telling me to click the hyperlink at "kiss time." The second email setting up a new account in my name.

They're watching ...

Someone was working hard to keep these communications under wraps.

Kiss time ...

If someone—okay, if Elizabeth—had simply wanted to give me a message, why hadn't she just called or written it in an email? Why make me jump through all these hoops?

The answer was obvious: secrecy. Someone—I won't say Elizabeth again—wanted to keep it all a secret.

And if you have a secret, it naturally follows that you have someone you want to keep it secret from. And maybe that someone is watching or searching or trying to find you. Either that or you're paranoid. Normally I'd side with paranoid but ...

They're watching ...

What did that mean exactly? Who was watching? The feds? And if the feds were behind the emails in the first place, why would they warn me that way? The feds wanted me to act.

Kiss time ...

I froze. Chloe's head snapped in my direction.

Oh my God, how could I have been so stupid?

*

They hadn't bothered to use the duct tape.

Rebecca Schayes lay upon the table now, whimpering like a dying dog on the side of the road. Sometimes, she uttered words, two or even three at a time, but they never formed a coherent chain. She was too far gone to cry anymore. The begging had stopped. Her eyes were still wide and uncomprehending; they saw nothing now. Her mind had shattered mid-scream fifteen minutes ago.

Amazingly, Wu had left no marks. No marks, but she looked twenty years older.

Rebecca Schayes had known nothing. Dr. Beck had visited her because of an old car accident that wasn't really a car accident. There were pictures too. Beck had assumed she had taken them. She hadn't.

The creeping feeling in his stomach—the one that had started as a mere tickle when Larry Gandle first heard about the bodies being found at the lake—kept growing. Something had gone wrong that night. That much was certain. But now Larry Gandle feared that maybe everything had gone wrong.

It was time to flush out the truth.

He had checked with his surveillance man. Beck was taking his dog for a walk. Alone. In light of the evidence Wu would plant, that would be a terrible alibi. The feds would shred it for laughs.

Larry Gandle approached the table. Rebecca Schayes looked up and made an unearthly noise, a cross between a high-pitched groan and a wounded laugh.

He pressed the gun against her forehead. She made that sound again. He fired twice and all the world fell silent.

I started heading back to the house, but I thought about the warning.

They're watching.

Why take the chance? There was a Kinko's three blocks away. They stay open twenty-four hours a day. When I reached the door, I saw why. It was midnight, and the place was packed. Lots of exhausted businesspeople carrying papers and slides and poster boards.

I stood in a maze line formed by crushed-velvet ropes and waited my turn. It reminded me of visiting a bank in the days before ATMs. The woman in front of me sported a business suit—at midnight—and big enough bags under her eyes to be mistaken for a bellhop. Behind me, a man with curly hair and dark sweats whipped out a cell phone and started pressing buttons.

"Sir?"

Someone with a Kinko's smock pointed at Chloe.

"You can't come in here with a dog."

I was about to tell him I already had but thought better of it. The woman in the business suit didn't react. The curly-haired guy with the dark sweats gave me a what-are-you-gonna-do shrug. I rushed outside, tied Chloe to a parking meter, headed back inside. The curly-haired man let me have my place back in line. Manners.

Ten minutes later, I was at the front of the line. This Kinko's clerk was young and overly exuberant. He showed me to a computer terminal and explained too slowly their per-minute pricing plan.

I nodded through his little speech and signed on to the Web.

Kiss time.

That, I realized, was the key. The first email had said kiss time, not 6:15 p.m. Why? The answer was obvious. That had been code—in case the wrong people got their hands on the email. Whoever had sent it had realized that the possibility of interception existed. Whoever had sent it had known that only I would know what kiss time meant.

That was when it came to me.

First off, the account name Bat Street. When Elizabeth and I were growing up, we used to ride our bikes down Morewood Street on the way to the Little League field. There was this creepy old woman who lived in a faded yellow house. She lived alone and scowled at passing kids. Every town has one of those creepy old ladies. She usually has a nickname. In our case, we'd called her:

Bat Lady.

I brought up Bigfoot again. I typed Morewood into the user name box.

Next to me, the young and exuberant Kinko's clerk was repeating his Web spiel to the curly-haired man with the dark sweat suit. I hit the tab button and moved into the text box for the password.

The clue Teenage was easier. In our junior year of high school, we'd gone to Jordan Goldman's house late one Friday night. There were maybe ten of us. Jordan had found out where his father hid a porn video. None of us had ever seen one before. We all watched, laughing uncomfortably, making the usual snide remarks and feeling deliciously naughty. When we needed a name for our intramural softball team, Jordan suggested we use the movie's stupid title:

Teenage Sex Poodles.

I typed in Sex Poodles under the password. I swallowed hard and clicked the Sign In icon.

I glanced over at the curly-haired man. He was focused on a Yahoo! search. I looked back toward the front desk. The woman in the business suit was frowning at another too-happy-at-midnight Kinko's staff member.

I waited for the error message. But that didn't happen this time. A welcome screen rolled into view. On the top, it read: Hi, Morewood!

Underneath that it said: You have 1 email in your box.

My heart felt like a bird banging against my rib cage.

I clicked on the New Mail icon and did the leg shake again. No Shauna around to stop it. Through the store window I could see my tethered Chloe. She spotted me and started barking. I put a finger to my lips and signaled for her to hush up.

The email message appeared:

Washington Square Park. Meet me at the southeast corner.
Five o'clock tomorrow.
You'll be followed.

And on the bottom:

No matter what, I love you.

Hope, that caged bird that just won't die, broke free. I leaned back. Tears flooded my eyes, but for the first time in a long while, I let loose a real smile.

Elizabeth. She was still the smartest person I knew.

20

At two a.m., I crawled into bed and rolled onto my back. The ceiling started doing the too-many-drinks spins. I grabbed the sides of the bed and hung on.

Shauna had earlier asked if I had ever been tempted to cheat after getting married. She'd added that last part—the "after getting married" part—because she already knew about the other incident.

Technically, I did cheat on Elizabeth once, though cheating doesn't really fit. Cheating denotes doing harm to another. It didn't harm Elizabeth—I'm sure of that—but during my freshman year of college, I partook in a rather pitiful rite of passage known as the collegiate one-night stand. Out of curiosity, I guess. Purely experimental and strictly physical. I didn't like it much. I'll spare you the corny sex-without-love-is-meaningless cliché. It's not. But while I think it's fairly easy to have sex with someone you don't particularly know or like, it's hard to stay the night. The attraction, as it were, was strictly hormonal. Once the, uh, release took place, I wanted out. Sex is for anyone; the aftermath is for lovers.

Pretty nice rationalization, don't you think?

If it matters, I suspect Elizabeth probably did something similar. We both agreed that we would try to "see"—"see" being such a vague, all-encompassing term—other people when we first got to college. Any indiscretion could thus be chalked up to yet another commitment test. Whenever the subject was raised, Elizabeth denied that there had ever been anyone else. But then again, so did I.

The bed continued to spin as I wondered: What do I do now?

For one thing, I wait for five o'clock tomorrow. But I couldn't just sit back until then. I'd done enough of that already, thank you very much. The truth was—a truth I didn't like to admit even to myself—I hesitated at the lake. Because I was scared. I climbed out of the water and paused. That gave whomever a chance to hit me. And I didn't fight back after that first strike. I didn't dive for my assailant. I didn't tackle him or even make a fist. I simply went down. I covered up and surrendered and let the stronger man take away my wife.

Not again.

I considered approaching my father-in-law again—it hadn't escaped my attention that Hoyt might have been less than forthcoming during my previous visit—but what good would that do? Hoyt was either lying or ... or I don't know what. But the message had been clear. *Tell no one.* The only way I could maybe get him to talk would be by telling him what I saw on that street cam. But I wasn't ready to do that yet.

I got out of bed and hopped on the computer. I started surfing again. By morning, I had something of a plan.

Gary Lamont, Rebecca Schayes's husband, didn't panic right away. His wife often worked late, very late, sometimes spending the night on an old cot in the far right corner of her studio. So when four in the morning rolled around and Rebecca still wasn't home, he grew only concerned, not panicked.

At least, that's what he told himself.

Gary called her studio, but the answering machine picked up. Again that wasn't rare. When Rebecca was working, she hated interruptions. She didn't even keep a phone extension in the darkroom. He left a message and settled back into their bed.

Sleep came in fits and spurts. Gary contemplated doing something more, but that would only piss off Rebecca. She was a free spirit, and if there was a tension in their otherwise fulfilling relationship, it had to do with his relatively "traditional" lifestyle "clipping" her creative wings. Her terms.

So he gave her space. To unclip her wings or whatever.

By seven in the morning, concern had segued into something closer to genuine fear. Gary's call woke up Arturo Ramirez, Rebecca's gaunt, black-clad assistant.

"I just got in," Arturo complained groggily.

Gary explained the situation. Arturo, who had fallen asleep in his clothes, did not bother changing. He ran out the door. Gary promised to meet him at the studio. He hopped on the downtown A.

Arturo arrived first and found the studio door ajar. He pushed it open.

"Rebecca?"

No answer. Arturo called her name again. Still no answer. He entered and scanned the studio. She wasn't there. He opened the darkroom door. The usual harsh smell of film-development acids still dominated, but there was something else, something faint and below the surface that still had the ability to make his hair stand on end.

Something distinctly human.

Gary rounded the corner in time to hear the scream.

21

In the morning, I grabbed a bagel and headed west on Route 80 for forty-five minutes. Route 80 in New Jersey is a fairly nondescript strip of pavement. Once you get past Saddle Brook or so, the buildings pretty much vanish and you're faced with identical lines of trees on either side of the road. Only the interstate signs break up the monotony.

As I veered off exit 163 at a town called Gardensville, I slowed the car and looked out at the high grass. My heart started thumping. I had never been here before—I'd purposely avoided this stretch of interstate for the past eight years—but it was here, less than a hundred yards from where I now drove, that they found Elizabeth's body.

I checked the directions I'd printed off last night. The Sussex County coroner's office was on Mapquest.com, so I knew to the tenth of a kilometer how to get there. The building was a blinds-closed storefront with no sign or window lettering, a plain brick rectangle with no frills, but then again, did you want any at a morgue? I arrived a few minutes before eight-thirty and pulled around back. The office was still locked up. Good.

A canary-yellow Cadillac Seville pulled into a spot marked Timothy Harper, County Medical Examiner. The man in the car stubbed out a cigarette—it never ceases to amaze me how many M.E.'s smoke—before he stepped out. Harper was my height, a shade under six feet, with olive skin and wispy gray hair. He saw me standing by the door and set his face. People didn't visit morgues first thing in the morning to hear good news.

He took his time approaching me. "Can I help you?" he said.

"Dr. Harper?"

"Yes, that's right."

"I'm Dr. David Beck." Doctor. So we were colleagues. "I'd like a moment of your time."

He didn't react to the name. He took out a key and unlocked the door. "Why don't we sit in my office?"

"Thank you."

I followed him down a corridor. Harper flicked light switches. The ceiling fluorescents popped on grudgingly and one at a time. The floor was scratched linoleum. The place looked less like a house of death than a faceless DMV office, but maybe that was the point. Our footsteps echoed, mixing with the buzzing from the lights as though keeping the beat. Harper picked up a stack of mail and quick-sorted it as we walked.

Harper's private office, too, was no-frills. There was the same metal desk you might find a teacher using in an elementary school. The chairs were overvarnished wood, strictly functional. Several diplomas spotted one wall. He'd gone to medical school at Columbia, too, I saw, though he'd graduated almost twenty years before me. No family photographs, no golf trophy, no Lucite announcements, nothing personal. Visitors to this office were not in for pleasant chitchat. The last thing they needed to see was someone's smiling grandkids.

Harper folded his hands and put them on the desk. "What can I do for you, Dr. Beck?"

"Eight years ago," I began, "my wife was brought here. She was the victim of a serial killer known as KillRoy."

I'm not particularly good at reading faces. Eye contact has never been my forte. Body language means little to me. But as I watched Harper, I couldn't help but wonder what would make a practiced medical examiner, a man who oft dwelled in the world of the dead, blanch so.

"I remember," he said softly.

"You did the autopsy?"

"Yes. Well, in part."

"In part?"

"Yes. The federal authorities were involved too. We worked on the case in tandem, though the FBI doesn't have coroners, so we took the lead."

"Back up a minute," I said. "Tell me what you saw when they first brought the body in."

Harper shifted in his seat. "May I ask why you want to know this?"

"I'm a grieving husband."

"It was eight years ago."

"We all grieve in our own way, Doctor."

"Yes, I'm sure that's true, but—"

"But what?"

"But I'd like to know what you want here."

I decided to take the direct route. "You take pictures of every corpse brought in here, right?"

He hesitated. I saw it. He saw me seeing it and cleared his throat. "Yes. Currently, we use digital technology. A digital camera, in other words. It allows us to store photographs and various images on a computer. We find it helpful for both diagnosis and cataloguing."

I nodded, not caring. He was chattering. When he didn't continue, I said, "Did you take pictures of my wife's autopsy?"

"Yes, of course. But—how long ago did you say again?"

"Eight years."

"We would have taken Polaroids."

"And where would those Polaroids be right now, Doctor?"

"In the file."

I looked at the tall filing cabinet standing in the corner like a sentinel.

"Not in there," he added quickly. "Your wife's case is closed. Her killer was caught and convicted. Plus it was more than five years ago."

"So where would it be?"

"In a storage facility. In Layton."

"I'd like to see the photographs, if I could."

He jotted something down and nodded at the scrap of paper. "I'll look into it."

"Doctor?"

He looked up.

"You said you remember my wife."

"Well, yes, I mean, somewhat. We don't have many murders here, especially ones so high profile."

"Do you remember the condition of her body?"

"Not really. I mean, not details or anything."

"Do you remember who identified her?"

"You didn't?"

"No."

Harper scratched his temple. "Her father, wasn't it?"

"Do you remember how long it took for him to make an identification?"

"How long?"

"Was it immediate? Did it take a few minutes? Five minutes, ten minutes?"

"I really couldn't say."

"You don't remember if it was immediate or not?"

"I'm sorry, I don't."

"You just said this was a big case."

"Yes."

"Maybe your biggest?"

"We had that pizza delivery thrill kill a few years ago," he said. "But, yes, I'd say it was one of the biggest."

"And yet you don't remember if her father had trouble identifying the body?"

He didn't like that. "Dr. Beck, with all due respect, I don't see what you're getting at."

"I'm a grieving husband. I'm asking some simple questions."

"Your tone," he said. "It seems hostile."

"Should it be?"

"What on earth does that mean?"

"How did you know she was a victim of KillRoy's?"

"I didn't."

"So how did the feds get involved?"

"There were identifying marks—"

"You mean that she was branded with the letter K?"

"Yes."

I was on a roll now, and it felt oddly right. "So the police brought her in. You started examining her. You spotted the letter K—"

"No, they were here right away. The federal authorities, I mean."

"Before the body got here?"

He looked up, either remembering or fabricating. "Or immediately thereafter. I don't remember."

"How did they know about the body so quickly?"

"I don't know."

"You have no idea?"

Harper folded his arms across his chest. "I might surmise that one of the officers on the scene spotted the branding and called the FBI. But that would only be an educated guess."

My beeper vibrated against my hip. I checked it. The clinic with an emergency.

"I'm sorry for your loss," he said in a practiced tone. "I understand the pain you must be going through, but I have a very busy schedule today. Perhaps you can make an appointment at a later date—"

"How long will it take you to get my wife's file?" I asked.

"I'm not even sure I can do that. I mean, I'll have to check—"

"The Freedom of Information Act."

"Pardon me?"

"I looked it up this morning. My wife's case is closed now. I have the right to view her file."

Harper had to know that—I wasn't the first person to ask for an autopsy file—and he started nodding a little too vigorously. "Still, there are proper channels you have to go through, forms to fill out."

"Are you stalling?" I said.

"Excuse me?"

"My wife was the victim of a terrible crime."

"I understand that."

"And I have the right to view my wife's file. If you drag your feet on this, I'm going to wonder why. I've never spoken to the media about my wife or her killer. I'll gladly do so now. And we'll all be wondering why the local M.E. gave me such a hard time over such a simple request."

"That sounds like a threat, Dr. Beck."

I got to my feet. "I'll be back here tomorrow morning," I said. "Please have my wife's file ready."

I was taking action. It felt damn good.

22

Detectives Roland Dimonte and Kevin Krinsky of the NYPD's homicide division arrived first on the scene, even before the uniforms. Dimonte, a greasy-haired man who favored hideous snakeskin boots and an over-chewed toothpick, took the lead. He barked orders. The crime scene was immediately sealed. A few minutes later, lab technicians from the Crime Scene Unit skulked in and spread out.

"Isolate the witnesses," Dimonte said.

There were only two: the husband and the fey weirdo in black. Dimonte noted that the husband appeared distraught, though that could be an act. But first things first.

Dimonte, still chewing on the toothpick, took the fey weirdo—his name, figures, was Arturo—to the side. The kid looked pale. Normally, Dimonte would guess drugs, but the guy had tossed his cookies when he found the body.

"You okay?" Dimonte asked. Like he cared.

Arturo nodded.

Dimonte asked him if anything unusual had happened involving the victim lately. Yes, Arturo replied. What would that be? Rebecca got a phone call yesterday that disturbed her. Who called? Arturo was not sure, but an hour later—maybe less, Arturo couldn't be sure—a man stopped by to see Rebecca. When the man left, Rebecca was a wreck.

Do you remember the man's name?

"Beck," Arturo said. "She called the guy Beck."

Shauna put Mark's sheets in the dryer. Linda came up behind her.

"He's wetting his bed again," Linda said.

"God, you're perceptive."

"Don't be mean." Linda walked away. Shauna opened her mouth to apologize, but nothing came out. When she had moved out the first time—the only time—Mark had reacted badly. It started with bed-wetting. When she and Linda reunited, the bed-wetting stopped. Until now.

"He knows what's going on," Linda said. "He can feel the tension."

"What do you want me to do about that, Linda?"

"Whatever we have to."

"I'm not moving out again. I promised."

"Clearly, that's not enough."

Shauna tossed a sheet of fabric softener into the dryer. Exhaustion lined her face. She didn't need this. She was a big-money model. She couldn't arrive at work with bags under her eyes or a lack of sheen in her hair. She didn't need this shit.

She was tired of it all. Tired of a domesticity that didn't sit well with her. Tired of the pressure from damn do-gooders. Forget the bigotry, that was easy. But the pressure on a lesbian couple with a child—applied by supposedly well-meaning supporters—was beyond suffocating. If the relationship failed, it was a failure for all lesbianism or some such crap, as though hetero couples never break up. Shauna was not a crusader. She knew that. Selfish or not, her happiness would not be sacrificed on the altar of "greater good."

She wondered if Linda felt the same way.

"I love you," Linda said.

"I love you too."

They looked at each other. Mark was wetting his bed again. Shauna wouldn't sacrifice herself for the greater good. But she would for Mark.

"So what do we do?" Linda asked.

"We work it out."

"You think we can?"

"You love me?"

"You know I do," Linda said.

"Do you still think I'm the most exciting, wonderful creature on God's green earth?"

"Oh, yeah," Linda said.

"Me too." Shauna smiled at her. "I'm a narcissistic pain in the ass."

"Oh, yeah."

"But I'm your narcissistic pain in the ass."

"Damn straight."

Shauna moved closer. "I'm not destined for a life of easy relationships. I'm volatile."

"You're sexy as hell when you're volatile," Linda said.

"And even when I'm not."

"Shut up and kiss me."

The downstairs door buzzer sounded. Linda looked at Shauna. Shauna shrugged. Linda pressed the intercom and said, "Yes?"

"Is this Linda Beck?"

"Who is this?"

"I'm Special Agent Kimberly Green with the Federal Bureau of Investigation. I'm with my partner, Special Agent Rick Peck. We'd like to come up and ask you some questions."

Shauna leaned over before Linda could respond. "Our attorney's name is Hester Crimstein," she shouted into the intercom. "You can call her."

"You're not suspects in any crime. We just want to ask you some questions—"

"Hester Crimstein," Shauna interrupted. "I'm sure you have her number. Have a really special day."

Shauna released the button. Linda looked at her. "What the hell was that?"

"Your brother's in trouble."

"What?"

"Sit down," Shauna said. "We need to talk."

Raisa Markov, a nurse who cared for Dr. Beck's grandfather, answered the firm knock. Special agents Carlson and Stone, now working in conjunction with NYPD detectives Dimonte and Krinsky, handed her the document.

"Federal warrant," Carlson announced.

Raisa stepped aside without reacting. She had grown up in the Soviet Union. Police aggression did not faze her.

Eight of Carlson's men flooded into the Beck abode and fanned out.

"I want everything videotaped," Carlson called out. "No mistakes."

They were moving fast in the hope of staying a half-step ahead of Hester Crimstein. Carlson knew that Crimstein, like many a natty defense attorney in this post-OJ era, clung to the claims of police incompetence and/or misconduct like a desperate suitor. Carlson, a rather natty law enforcement officer in his own right, would not let that happen here. Every step / movement / breath would be documented and corroborated.

When Carlson and Stone first burst into Rebecca Schayes's studio, Dimonte had not been happy to see him. There had been the usual local-cops-versus-feds macho-turf posturing. Few things unify the FBI and the local authorities, especially in a big city like New York.

But Hester Crimstein was one of those things.

Both sides knew that Crimstein was a master obscurer and publicity hound. The world would be watching. No one wanted to screw up. That was the driving force here. So they forged an alliance with all the trust of a Palestinian-Israeli handshake, because in the end, both sides knew that they needed to gather and nail down the evidence fast—before Crimstein mucked up the waters.

The feds had gotten the search warrant. For them, it was a simple matter of walking across Federal Plaza to the southern district federal court. If Dimonte and the NYPD had wanted to get one, they'd have had to go to the county courthouse in New Jersey—too much time with Hester Crimstein lurking at their heels.

"Agent Carlson!"

The shout came from the street corner. Carlson sprinted outside, Stone waddling behind him. Dimonte and Krinsky followed. At the curb, a young federal agent stood next to an open trash canister.

"What is it?" Carlson asked.

"Might be nothing, sir, but . . ." The young federal agent pointed down to what looked like a hastily discarded pair of latex gloves.

"Bag them," Carlson said. "I want a gun residue test done right away." Carlson looked over to Dimonte. Time for more cooperation—this time, via competition. "How long will it take to get done at your lab?"

"A day," Dimonte said. He had a fresh toothpick in his mouth now and was working it over pretty well. "Maybe two."

"No good. We'll have to fly the samples down to our lab at Quantico."

"Like hell you will," Dimonte snapped.

"We agreed to go with what's fastest."

"Staying here is fastest," Dimonte said. "I'll see to that."

Carlson nodded. It was as he expected. If you wanted the local cops to make the case a big-time priority, threaten to take it away from them. Competition. It was a good thing.

Half an hour later, they heard another cry, this time coming from the garage. Again they sprinted in that direction.

Stone whistled low. Dimonte stared. Carlson bent down for a better look.

There, under the newspapers in a recycle bin, sat a nine-millimeter handgun. A quick sniff told them the gun had recently been fired.

Stone turned to Carlson. He made sure that his smile was off camera.

"Got him," Stone said softly.

Carlson said nothing. He watched the technician bag the weapon. Then, thinking it all through, he began to frown.

23

The emergency call on my beeper involved TJ. He scraped his arm on a doorjamb. For most kids, that meant a stinging spray of Bactine; for TJ, it meant a night in the hospital. By the time I got there, they had already hooked him up to an IV. You treat hemophilia by administering blood products such as cryoprecipitate or frozen plasma. I had a nurse start him up right away.

As I mentioned earlier, I first met Tyrese six years ago when he was in handcuffs and screaming obscenities. An hour earlier, he had rushed his then nine-month-old son, TJ, into the emergency room. I was there, but I wasn't working the acute side. The attending physician handled TJ.

TJ was unresponsive and lethargic. His breathing was shallow. Tyrese, who behaved, according to the chart, "erratically" (how, I wondered, was a father who rushes an infant to an emergency room supposed to act?), told the attending physician that the boy had been getting worse all day. The attending physician gave his nurse a knowing glance. The nurse nodded and went to make the call. Just in case.

A fundoscopic examination revealed that the infant had multiple retinal hemorrhages bilaterally—that is, the blood vessels in the back of both eyes had exploded. When the physician put the pieces together—retinal bleeding, heavy lethargy, and, well, the father—he made a diagnosis:

Shaken baby syndrome.

Armed security guards arrived in force. They handcuffed Tyrese, and that was when I heard the screamed obscenities. I rounded the corner to see what was up. Two uniformed members of the NYPD arrived. So did a weary woman from ACS—aka the Administration for Children Services. Tyrese tried to plead his case. Everybody shook their heads in that what's-this-world-coming-to way.

I'd witnessed scenes like this a dozen times at the hospital. In fact, I'd seen a lot worse. I'd treated three-year-old girls with venereal diseases. I once ran a rape kit on a four-year-old boy with internal bleeding. In both cases—and in all similar abuse cases I'd been involved with—the perpetrator was either a family member or the mother's most recent boyfriend.

The Bad Man isn't lurking in playgrounds, kiddies. He lives in your house.

I also knew—and this statistic never failed to stagger me—that more than ninety-five percent of serious intracranial injuries in infants were due to child abuse. That made it pretty damn good—or bad, depending on your vantage point—odds that Tyrese had abused his son.

In this emergency room, we've heard all the excuses. The baby fell off the couch. The oven door landed on the baby's head. His older brother dropped a toy on him. You work here long enough, you grow more cynical than the most weathered city cop. The truth is, healthy children tolerate those sorts of accidental blows well. It is very rare that, say, a fall off a couch alone causes retinal hemorrhaging.

I had no problem with the child abuse diagnosis. Not at first blush anyway.

But something about the way Tyrese pleaded his case struck me odd. It was not that I thought he was innocent. I'm not above making quick judgments based on appearance—or, to use a more politically current term, racial profiling. We all do it. If you cross the street to avoid a gang of black teens, you're racial profiling; if you don't cross because you're afraid you'll look like a racist, you're racial profiling; if you see the gang and think nothing whatsoever, you're from some planet I've never visited.

What made me pause here was the pure dichotomy. I had seen a frighteningly similar case during my recent rotation out in the wealthy suburb of Short Hills, New Jersey. A white mother and father, both impeccably dressed and driving a well-equipped Range Rover, rushed their six-month-old daughter into the emergency room. The daughter, their third child, presented the same as TJ.

Nobody shackled the father.

So I moved toward Tyrese. He gave me the ghetto glare. On the street, it fazed me; in here, it was like the big bad wolf blowing at the brick house. "Was your son born at this hospital?" I asked.

Tyrese didn't reply.

"Was your son born here, yes or no?"

He calmed down enough to say "Yeah."

"Is he circumcised?"

Tyrese relit the glare. "You some kind of faggot?"

"You mean there's more than one kind?' I countered. "Was he circumcised here, yes or no?"

Grudgingly, Tyrese said, "Yeah."

I found TJ's social security number and plugged it into the computer. His records came up. I checked under the circumcision. Normal. Damn. But then I saw another entry. This was not TJ's first visit to the hospital. At the age of two weeks, his father brought him in because of a bleeding umbilicus—bleeding from the umbilical cord.

Curious.

We ran some blood tests then, though the police insisted on keeping Tyrese in custody. Tyrese didn't argue. He just wanted the tests done. I tried to have them rushed, but I have no power in this bureaucracy. Few do. Still the lab was able to ascertain through the blood samples that the partial thromboplastin time was prolonged, yet both the prothrombin time and platelet count were normal. Yeah, yeah, but bear with me.

The best—and worst—was confirmed. The boy had not been abused by his ghetto-garbed father. Hemophilia caused the retinal hemorrhages. They had also left the boy blind.

The security guards sighed and uncuffed Tyrese and walked away without a word. Tyrese rubbed his wrists. Nobody apologized or offered a word of sympathy to this man who had been falsely accused of abusing his now-blind son.

Imagine that in the wealthy 'burbs.

TJ has been my patient ever since.

Now, in his hospital room, I stroked TJ's head and looked into his unseeing eyes. Kids usually look at me with undiluted awe, a heady cross between fear and worship. My colleagues believe that children have a deeper understanding than adults of what is happening to them. I think the answer is probably simpler. Children view their parents as both intrepid and omnipotent—yet here their parents are, gazing up at me, the doctor, with a fear-filled longing normally reserved for religious rapture.

What could be more terrifying to a small child?

A few minutes later, TJ's eyes closed. He drifted off to sleep.

"He just bumped into the side of the door," Tyrese said. "That was all. He's blind. Gonna happen, right?"

"We'll need to keep him overnight," I said. "But he'll be fine."

"How?" Tyrese looked at me. "How will he ever be all right when he can't stop bleeding?"

I had no answer.

"I gotta get him out of here."

He didn't mean the hospital.

Tyrese reached into his pocket and started peeling off bills. I wasn't in the mood. I held up a hand and said, "I'll check back later."

"Thanks for coming, Doc. I appreciate it."

I was about to remind him that I had come for his son, not him, but I opted for silence.

Careful, Carlson thought, while his pulse raced. Be oh so careful.

The four of them—Carlson, Stone, Krinsky, and Dimonte—sat at a conference table with Assistant District Attorney Lance Fein. Fein, an ambitious weasel with constantly undulating eyebrows and a face so waxy that it looked ready to melt in extreme heat, strapped on his game face.

Dimonte said, "Let's bust his sorry ass."

"One more time," Lance Fein said. "Put it together for me so that even Alan Dershowitz would want him locked up."

Dimonte nodded at his partner. "Go ahead, Krinsky. Make me wet."

Krinsky took out his pad and started reading:

"Rebecca Schayes was shot twice in the head at very close range with a nine-millimeter automatic pistol. Under a federally issued warrant, a nine-millimeter was located in Dr. David Beck's garage."

"Fingerprints on the gun?" Fein asked.

"None. But a ballistic test confirmed that the nine-millimeter found in Dr. Beck's garage is the murder weapon."

Dimonte smiled and raised his eyebrows. "Anybody else getting hard nipples?"

Fein's eyebrows knitted and dropped. "Please continue," he said.

"Under the same federally issued warrant, a pair of latex gloves was retrieved from a trash canister at Dr. David Beck's residence. Gunpowder residue was found on the right glove. Dr. Beck is right-handed."

Dimonte put up his snakeskin boots and moved the toothpick across his mouth. "Oh, yeah, baby, harder, harder. I like it like that."

Fein frowned. Krinsky, his eyes never leaving the pad, licked a finger and turned the page.

"On the same right-hand latex glove, the lab discovered a hair that has been positively color matched to Rebecca Schayes."

"Oh God! Oh God!" Dimonte started screaming in fake orgasm. Or maybe it was real.

"A conclusive DNA test will take more time," Krinsky went on. "Moreover, fingerprints belonging to Dr. David Beck were found at the murder scene, though not in the darkroom where her body was found."

Krinsky closed up his notebook. All eyes turned to Lance Fein.

Fein stood and rubbed his chin. Dimonte's behavior notwithstanding, they were all suppressing a bit of giddiness. The room crackled with pre-arrest sparks, that heady, addictive high that came with the really infamous cases. There would be press conferences and calls from politicians and pictures in the paper.

Only Nick Carlson remained the tiniest bit apprehensive. He sat twisting and untwisting and retwisting a paper clip. He couldn't stop. Something had crawled into his periphery, hanging on the edges, still out of sight, but there, and irksome as all hell. For one thing, there were the listening devices in Dr. Beck's home. Someone had been bugging him. Tapping his phone too. Nobody seemed to know or care why.

"Lance?" It was Dimonte.

Lance Fein cleared his throat. "Do you know where Dr. Beck is right now?" he asked.

"At his clinic," Dimonte said. "I got two uniforms keeping an eye on him."

Fein nodded.

"Come on, Lance," Dimonte said. "Give it to me, big boy."

"Let's call Ms. Crimstein first," Fein said. "As a courtesy."

Shauna told Linda most of it. She left out the part about Beck's "seeing" Elizabeth on the computer. Not because she gave the story any credence. She'd pretty much proven that it was a digital hoax. But Beck had been adamant. Tell no one. She didn't like having secrets from Linda, but that was preferable to betraying Beck's confidence.

Linda watched Shauna's eyes the whole time. She didn't nod or speak or even move. When Shauna finished, Linda asked, "Did you see the pictures?"

"No."

"Where did the police get them?"

"I don't know."

Linda stood. "David would never hurt Elizabeth."

"I know that."

Linda wrapped her arms around herself. She started sucking in deep breaths. Her face drained of color.

"You okay?" Shauna said.

"What aren't you telling me?"

"What makes you think I'm not telling you something?"

Linda just looked at her.

"Ask your brother," Shauna said.

"Why?"

"It's not my place to tell."

The door buzzed again. Shauna took it this time.

"Yeah?"

Through the speaker: "It's Hester Crimstein."

Shauna hit the release button and left their door open. Two minutes later, Hester hurried into the room.

"Do you two know a photographer named Rebecca Schayes?"

"Sure," Shauna said. "I mean, I haven't seen her in a long time. Linda?"

"It's been years," Linda agreed. "She and Elizabeth shared an apartment downtown. Why?"

"She was murdered last night," Hester said. "They think Beck killed her."

Both women froze as though someone had just slapped them. Shauna recovered first.

"But I was with Beck last night," she said. "At his house."

"Till what time?"

"Till what time do you need?"

Hester frowned. "Don't play games with me, Shauna. What time did you leave the house?"

"Ten, ten-thirty. What time was she killed?"

"I don't know yet. But I have a source inside. He said they have a very solid case against him."

"That's nuts."

A cell phone sounded. Hester Crimstein snatched hers up and pressed it against her ear. "What?"

The person on the other end spoke for what seemed a long time. Hester listened in silence. Her features started softening in something like defeat. A minute or two later, without saying good-bye, she closed the phone with a vicious snap.

"A courtesy call," she mumbled.

"What?"

"They're arresting your brother. We have an hour to surrender him to authorities."

24

All I could think about was Washington Square Park. True, I wasn't supposed to be there for another four hours. But emergencies notwithstanding, today was my day off. Free as a bird, as Lynyrd Skynyrd would sing—and this bird wanted to flock down to Washington Square Park.

I was on my way out of the clinic when my beeper once again sang its miserable song. I sighed and checked the number. It was Hester Crimstein's cell phone. And it was coded for an emergency.

This couldn't be good news.

For a moment or two, I debated not calling back—just continuing to flock—but what would be the point in that? I backpedaled to my examining room. The door was closed, and the red lever was slid into place. That meant another doctor was using the room.

I headed down the corridor, turned left, and found an empty room in the ob-gyn section of the clinic. I felt like a spy in enemy camp. The room gleamed with too much metal. Surrounded by stirrups and other devices that looked frighteningly medieval, I dialed the number.

Hester Crimstein did not bother with hello: "Beck, we got a big problem. Where are you?"

"I'm at the clinic. What's going on?"

"Answer a question for me," Hester Crimstein said. "When was the last time you saw Rebecca Schayes?"

My heart started doing a deep, slow thud. "Yesterday. Why?"

"And before that?"

"Eight years ago."

Crimstein let loose a low curse.

"What's going on?" I asked.

"Rebecca Schayes was murdered last night in her studio. Somebody shot her twice in the head."

A plunging feeling, the one you get moments before you fall asleep. My legs wobbled. I landed with a thump on a stool. "Oh Christ ..."

"Beck, listen to me. Listen closely."

I remembered how Rebecca looked yesterday.

"Where were you last night?"

I pulled the phone away and sucked in some air. Dead. Rebecca was dead. Oddly I kept flashing to the sheen in her beautiful hair. I thought about her husband. I thought about what the nights would bring, lying in that bed, thinking about how that hair used to fan across the pillow.

"Beck?"

"Home," I said. "I was home with Shauna."

"And after that?"

"I took a walk."

"Where?"

"Around."

"Where around?"

I did not reply.

"Listen to me, Beck, okay? They found the murder weapon at your house."

I heard the words, but their meaning was having trouble reaching the cerebrum. The room suddenly felt cramped. There were no windows. It was hard to breathe.

"Do you hear me?"

"Yes," I said. Then, sort of understanding, I said, "That's not possible."

"Look, we don't have time for that now. You're about to be arrested. I spoke to the D.A. in charge. He's a prick and a half, but he agreed to let you surrender."

"Arrested?"

"Stay with me here, Beck."

"I didn't do anything."

"That's irrelevant right now. They're going to arrest you. They're going to arraign you. Then we're going to get you bail. I'm on my way over to the clinic now. To pick you up. Sit tight. Don't say anything to anyone, you hear me? Not to the cops, not to the feds, not to your new buddy in lockup. You understand?"

My gaze got snagged on the clock above the examining table. It was a few minutes after two. Washington Square. I thought about Washington Square. "I can't be arrested, Hester."

"It'll be all right."

"How long?" I said.

"How long what?"

"Until I get bail."

"Can't say for sure. I don't think bail per se will be a problem. You have no record. You're an upstanding member of the community with roots and ties. You'll probably have to surrender your passport—"

"But how long?"

"How long until what, Beck? I don't understand."

"Until I get out."

"Look, I'll try to push them, okay? But even if they rush it—and I'm not saying they will—they still have to send your fingerprints to Albany. That's the rule. If we're lucky—I mean very lucky—we can get you arraigned by midnight."

Midnight?

Fear wrapped itself around my chest like steel bands. Jail meant missing the meet at Washington Square Park. My connection with Elizabeth was so damn fragile, like strands of Venetian glass. If I'm not at Washington Square at five o'clock . . .

"No good," I said.

"What?"

"You have to stall them, Hester. Have them arrest me tomorrow."

"You're kidding, right? Look, they're probably there already, watching you."

I leaned my head out the door and looked down the corridor. I could see only part of the reception desk from my angle, the corner near the right, but it was enough.

There were two cops, maybe more.

"Oh Christ," I said, falling back into the room.

"Beck?"

"I can't go to jail," I said again. "Not today."

"Don't freak out on me here, Beck, okay? Just stay there. Don't move, don't talk, don't do anything. Sit in your office and wait. I'm on my way."

She hung up.

Rebecca was dead. They thought I killed her. Ridiculous, of course, but there had to be a connection. I visited her yesterday for the first time in eight years. That very night she ended up dead.

What the hell was going on here?

I opened the door and peeked my head out. The cops weren't looking my way. I slid out and started down the corridor. There was a back emergency exit. I could sneak out that way. I could make my way down to Washington Square Park.

Was this for real? Was I really going to run away from the police?

I didn't know. But when I reached the door, I risked a look behind me. One of the cops spotted me. He pointed and hurried toward me.

I pushed open the door and ran.

I couldn't believe this. I was running from the police.

The exit door banged into a dark street directly behind the clinic. The street was unfamiliar to me. That might sound strange, but this neighborhood was not mine. I came, I worked, I left. I stayed locked inside a windowless environment, sickened by the lack of sunshine like some dour owl. One parallel block from where I worked and I was in totally alien territory.

I veered right for no particular reason. Behind me I heard the door fling open.

"Stop! Police!"

They actually yelled that. I didn't let up. Would they shoot? I doubted it. Not with all the repercussions in shooting an unarmed man who was in the midst of fleeing. Not impossible—not in this neighborhood anyway—but unlikely.

There weren't many people on this block, but those who were there regarded me with little more than passing, channel-surfing interest. I kept running. The world passed by in a blur. I sprinted past a dangerous-looking man with a dangerous-looking rottweiler. Old men sat at the corner and whined about the day. Women carried too many bags. Kids who probably should have been in school leaned against whatever was available, one cooler than the next.

Me, I was running away from the police.

My mind was having difficulty wrapping itself around that one. My legs were already feeling tingly, but the image of Elizabeth looking into that camera kept shoving me forward, pumping me up.

I was breathing too fast.

You hear about adrenaline, how it spurs you on and gives you uncanny strength, but there's a flip side. The feeling is heady, out of control. It heightens your senses to the point of paralysis. You have to harness the power or it'll choke you down.

I dove down an alleyway—that was what they always do on TV—but it dead-ended into a group of the foulest Dumpsters on the planet. The stench made me draw up like a horse. At one time, maybe when LaGuardia was mayor, the Dumpsters might have been green. All that remained was rust. In many places the rust ate through the metal, facilitating the many rats that poured through like sludge through a pipe.

I looked for some outlet, a door or something, but there was nothing. No back exit at all. I considered smashing a window to gain access, but all the lower ones were barred.

The only way out was the way I'd come in—where the police undoubtedly would see me.

I was trapped.

I looked left, right, and then, oddly enough, I looked up.

Fire escapes.

There were several above my head. Still mining my internal adrenaline drip, I leapt with all my might, stretched high with both hands, and fell flat on my ass. I tried again. Not even close. The ladders were far too high.

Now what?

Maybe I could somehow drag over a Dumpster, stand on it, and leap again. But the tops of the Dumpsters had been totally eaten away. Even if I could get footing on the piles of trash, it would still be too low.

I sucked in air and tried to think. The stench was getting to me; it crawled into my nose and seemed to nest there. I moved back toward the mouth of the alley.

Radio static. Like something you might hear coming from a police radio.

I threw my back against the wall and listened.

Hide. Had to hide.

The static grew louder. I heard voices. The cops were coming closer. I was totally exposed. I flattened myself closer to the wall, like that would help. Like they might turn the corner and mistake me for a mural.

Sirens shattered the still air.

Sirens for me.

Footsteps. They were definitely coming closer. There was only one place to hide.

I quickly discerned which Dumpster might be the least foul, closed my eyes, and dove in.

Sour milk. Very sour milk. That was the first smell that hit me. But it wasn't the only one. Something approaching vomit and worse. I was sitting in it. Something wet and putrid. It was sticking to me. My throat decided to do the gag reflex. My stomach heaved.

I heard someone run by the mouth of the alley. I stayed low.

A rat scrambled over my leg.

I almost screamed, but something in the subconscious kept it in the voice box. God, this was surreal. I held my breath. That lasted only so long. I tried to breathe through my mouth, but I started gagging again. I pressed my shirt against my nose and mouth. That helped, but not much.

The radio static was gone. So, too, were the footsteps. Did I fool them? If so, not for long. More police sirens joined in, harmonizing with the others, a true rhapsody in blue. The cops would have backup now. Someone would return soon. They would check the alley. Then what?

I grabbed hold of the Dumpster's edge to hoist myself out. The rust cut my palm. My hand flew toward my mouth. Bleeding. The pediatrician in me immediately scolded about the dangers of tetanus; the rest of me noted that tetanus would be the least of my worries.

I listened.

No footsteps. No blasts of radio static. Sirens wailed, but what had I expected? More backup. A murderer was on the loose in our fair city. The good guys would come out in force. They'd seal the area and throw a drag-net around it.

How far had I run?

I couldn't say. But I knew one thing. I had to keep moving. I had to put distance between the clinic and my person.

That meant getting out of this alley.

I crept toward the mouth again. Still no footsteps or radio. Good sign. I tried to think for a moment. Fleeing was a great plan, but a destination would make it even better. Keep heading east, I decided, even though it meant less safe neighborhoods. I remember seeing train tracks above-ground.

The subway.

That would get me out of here. All I had to do was get on a train, make a few sudden switches, and I could probably manage to disappear. But where was the closest entrance?

I was trying to conjure up my internal subway map, when a policeman turned into the alley.

He looked so young, so clean-cut and fresh-scrubbed and pink-faced. His blue shirtsleeves were neatly rolled up, two tourniquets on his bloated biceps. He started when he saw me—as surprised to see me as I was to see him.

We both froze. But he froze for a split second longer.

If I had approached him like a boxer or kung-fu expert, I'd probably have ended up picking my teeth out of my skull like so many splinters. But I didn't. I panicked. I worked on pure fear.

I launched myself straight at him.

With my chin tucked tight, I lowered my head and aimed for his center, rocketlike. Elizabeth played tennis. She told me once that when your opponent was at the net, it was often best to slam the ball right at their gut because he or she wouldn't know which way to move. You slow down their reaction time.

That was what happened here.

My body slammed into his. I grabbed hold of his shoulders like a monkey hanging on to a fence. We toppled over. I scrunched up my knees and dug them into his chest. My chin stayed tucked, the top of my head under the young cop's jaw.

We landed with an awful thud.

I heard a cracking noise. A shooting pain ricocheted down from where my skull had connected with his jaw. The young cop made a quiet "pluuu" noise. The air went out of his lungs. His jaw, I think, was broken. The flee panic took total control now. I scrambled off him as though he were a stun gun.

I had assaulted a police officer.

No time to dwell on it. I just wanted to be away from him. I managed to get to my feet and was about to turn and run, when I felt his hand on my ankle. I looked down and our eyes met.

He was in pain. Pain I had caused.

I kept my balance and unleashed a kick. It connected with his ribs. He made a wet "pluuu" sound this time. Blood trickled from his mouth. I couldn't believe what I was doing. I kicked him again. Just hard enough to loosen his grip. I pulled free.

And then I ran.

25

Hester and Shauna took a taxi to the clinic. Linda had taken the number 1 train down to their financial consultant at the World Financial Center to see about liquidating assets for bail.

A dozen police cars were angled in front of Beck's clinic, all pointing in various directions like darts thrown by a drunk. Their lights whirled at full red-blue alert. Sirens whined. More police cars pulled up.

"What the hell is going on?" Shauna asked.

Hester spotted Assistant District Attorney Lance Fein, but not before he spotted her. He stormed toward them. His face was scarlet and the vein in his forehead was pulsing.

"The son of a bitch ran," Fein spat out without preamble.

Hester took the hit and countered: "Your men must have spooked him."

Two more police cars pulled up. So did the Channel 7 news van. Fein cursed under his breath. "The press. Goddammit, Hester. You know how this is going to make me look?"

"Look, Lance—"

"Like a goddamn hack who gives special treatment to the rich, that's how. How could you do this to me, Hester? You know what the mayor is going to do to me? He's going to chew on my ass for jollies. And Tucker"—Tucker was the Manhattan district attorney—"Jesus Christ, can you imagine what he'll do?"

"Mr. Fein!"

One of the police officers was calling him. Fein eyed both of them one more time before turning away with a snap.

Hester quickly spun on Shauna. "Is Beck out of his mind?"

"He's scared," Shauna said.

"He's running away from the police," Hester shouted. "Do you get that? Do you get what that means?" She pointed toward the news van. "The media is here, for Chrissake. They're going to talk about the killer on the run. It's dangerous. It makes him look guilty. Taints the jury pool."

"Calm down," Shauna said.

"Calm down? Do you understand what he's done?"

"He's run away. That's all. Like OJ, right? Didn't seem to hurt him with the jury."

"We're not talking about OJ here, Shauna. We're talking about a rich white doctor."

"Beck's not rich."

"That's not the point, dammit. Everyone is going to want to nail his ass to a wall after this. Forget bail. Forget a fair trial." She took a breath, crossed her arms. "And Fein isn't the only one whose reputation is going to be compromised."

"Meaning?"

"Meaning me!" Hester shrieked. "In one bold stroke, Beck's destroyed my credibility with the D.A.'s office. If I promise to deliver a guy, I have to deliver him."

"Hester?"

"What?"

"I don't give a rat's ass about your reputation right now."

A sudden eruption of noise jolted them both. They turned and saw an ambulance hurry down the block. Somebody cried out. Then another cry. Cops started bouncing around like too many balls released at the same time into a pinball machine.

The ambulance skidded to a stop. The EMTs—one male, one female—jumped out of the cab. Fast. Too fast. They unsnapped the back door and pulled out a stretcher.

"This way!" someone shouted. "He's over here!"

Shauna felt her heart skip a beat. She ran over to Lance Fein. Hester followed. "What's wrong?" Hester asked. "What's happened?"

Fein ignored her.

"Lance?"

He finally faced them. The muscles in his face quaked in rage. "Your client."

"What about him? Is he hurt?"

"He just assaulted a police officer."

This was nuts.

I had crossed a line by running, but attacking that young cop . . . No going back now. So I ran. I sprinted with all I had.

"Officer down!"

Someone actually shouted that. More shouts followed. More radio static. More sirens. They all swirled toward me. My heart leapt into my throat. I kept pumping my legs. They started feeling stiff and heavy, as though the muscles and ligaments were hardening to stone. I was out of shape. Mucus started flowing out of my nose. It mixed with whatever dirt I'd accumulated on my upper lip and snaked into my mouth.

I kept veering from block to block as though that would fool the police. I didn't turn around to see if they were following. I knew they were. The sirens and radio static told me so.

I had no chance.

I dashed through neighborhoods I wouldn't even drive through. I hopped a fence and sprinted through the high grass of what might have once been a playground. People talked about the rising price of Manhattan real estate. But here, not far from the Harlem River Drive, there were vacant lots littered with broken glass and rusted ruins of what might have once been swing sets and jungle gyms and probably cars.

In front of a cluster of low-income high-rises, a group of black teens, all with the gangsta strut and coordinated ensemble, eyed me like a tasty leftover. They were about to do something—I didn't know what—when they realized that the police were chasing me.

They started cheering me on.

"Go, white boy!"

I sort of nodded as I dashed past them, a marathoner grateful for the little boost from the crowd. One of them yelled out, "Diallo!" I kept running, but I knew, of course, who Amadou Diallo was. Everyone in New York did. He'd been shot forty-one times by police officers—and he'd been unarmed. For a moment, I thought it was some kind of warning that the police might fire upon me.

But that wasn't it at all.

The defense in the Amadou Diallo trial claimed that when Diallo reached for his wallet, the officers thought it was a gun. Since then, people had been protesting by quickly reaching into their pockets, withdrawing their wallets, and yelling "Diallo!" Street officers reported that every time someone's hand went into their pockets like that, they still felt the thump of fear.

It happened now. My new allies—allies built on the fact that they probably thought I was a murderer—whipped out their wallets. The two cops on my tail hesitated. It was enough to increase my lead.

But so what?

My throat burned. I was sucking in way too much air. My hightops felt like lead boots. I got lazy. My toe dragged, tripping me up. I lost my balance, skidding across the pavement, scraping my palms and my face and my knees.

I managed to get back up, but my legs were trembling.

Closing in now.

Sweat pasted my shirt to my skin. My ears had that surf rush whooshing through them. I'd always hated running. Born-again joggers described how they got addicted to the rapture of running, how they achieved a nirvana known as runner's high. Right. I'd always firmly believed that—much like the high of auto-asphyxiation—the bliss came more from a lack of oxygen to the brain than any sort of endorphin rush.

Trust me, this was not blissful.

Tired. Too tired. I couldn't keep running forever. I glanced behind me. No cops. The street was abandoned. I tried a door. No go. I tried another. The radio crackle started up again. I ran. Toward the end of the block I spotted a street cellar door slightly ajar. Also rusted. Everything was rusted in this place.

I bent down and pulled at the metal handle. The door gave with an unhappy creak. I peered down into the blackness.

A cop shouted, "Cut him off the other side!"

I didn't bother looking back. I stepped down quickly into the hole. I reached the first step. Shaky. I put my foot out for the second step. But there was none.

I stayed suspended for a second, like Wile E. Coyote after running off a cliff, before I plunged helplessly into the dark pit.

The fall was probably no more than ten feet, but I seemed to take a long time to hit ground. I flailed my arms. It didn't help. My body landed on cement, the impact rattling my teeth.

I was on my back now, looking up. The door slammed closed above me. A good thing, I suppose, but the darkness was now pretty much total. I did a quick survey of my being, the doctor doing an internal exam. Everything hurt.

I heard the cops again. The sirens had not let up, or maybe now the sound was just ringing in my ears. Lots of voices. Lots of radio static.

They were closing in on me.

I rolled onto my side. My right hand pressed down, stinging the cuts in my palms, and my body started to rise. I let the head trail; it screamed in protest when I got to my feet. I almost fell down again.

Now what?

Should I just hide here? No, that wouldn't work. Eventually, they'd start going house to house. I'd be caught. And even if they didn't, I hadn't run with the intention of hiding in a dank basement. I ran so that I could keep my appointment with Elizabeth in Washington Square.

Had to move.

But where?

My eyes started adjusting to the dark, enough to see shadowy shapes anyway. Boxes were stacked haphazardly. There were piles of rags, a few barstools, a broken mirror. I caught my reflection in the glass and almost jumped back at the sight. There was a gash on my forehead. My pants were ripped in both knees. My shirt was tattered like the Incredible Hulk's. I was smeared with enough soot to work as a chimney sweep.

Where to go?

A staircase. There had to be a staircase down here somewhere. I felt my way forward, moving in a sort of spastic dance, leading with my left leg as though it were a white cane. My foot crunched over some broken glass. I kept moving.

I heard what I thought was a mumbling noise, and a giant rag pile rose in my path. What could have been a hand reached out to me like something from a grave. I bit back a scream.

"Himmler likes tuna steaks!" he shouted at me.

The man—yes, I could see now it was clearly a man—started to stand. He was tall and black and he had a beard so white-gray and woolly it looked as though he might be eating a sheep.

"You hear me?" the man shouted. "You hear what I'm telling you?"

He stepped toward me. I shrunk back.

"Himmler! He likes tuna steaks!"

The bearded man was clearly displeased about something. He made a fist and aimed it at me. I stepped to the side without thought. His fist traveled past me with enough momentum—or maybe enough drink—to make him topple over. He fell on his face. I didn't bother to wait. I found the staircase and ran up.

The door was locked.

"Himmler!"

He was loud, too loud. I pressed against the door. No go.

"You hear me? You hear what I'm saying?"

I heard a creak. I glanced behind me and saw something that struck fear straight into my heart.

Sunlight.

Someone had pulled open the same storm door I'd come in from.

"Who's down there?"

A voice of authority. A flashlight started dancing around the floor. It reached the bearded man.

"Himmler likes tuna steaks!"

"That you yelling, old man?"

"You hear me?"

I used my shoulder against the door, putting everything I had behind it. The doorjamb started to crack. Elizabeth's image popped up—the one I'd seen on the computer—her arm raised, her eyes beckoning. I pushed a little harder.

The door gave way.

I fell out onto the ground floor, not far from the building's front door.

Now what?

Other cops were close by—I could still hear the radio static—and one of them was still interviewing Himmler's biographer. I didn't have much time. I needed help.

But from where?

I couldn't call Shauna. The police would be all over her. Same with Linda. Hester would insist I surrender.

Someone was opening the front door.

I ran down the corridor. The floor was linoleum and filthy. The doors were all metal and closed. The motif was chipped paint. I banged open a fire door and headed up the stairwell. At the third floor, I got out.

An old woman stood in the corridor.

She was, I was surprised to see, white. My guess was that she'd probably heard the commotion and stepped out to see what was going on. I stopped short. She stood far enough away from her open door that I could get past her ...

Would I? Would I go that length to get away?

I looked at her. She looked at me. Then she took out a gun.

Oh, Christ ...

"What do you want?" she asked.

And I found myself answering: "May I please use your phone?"

She didn't miss a beat. "Twenty bucks."

I reached into my wallet and plucked out the cash. The old lady nodded and let me in. The apartment was tiny and well kept. There was lace on all the upholstery and on the dark wood tables.

"Over there," she said.

The phone was rotary dial. I jammed my finger into the little holes. Funny thing. I had never called this number before—had never wanted to—but I knew it by heart. Psychiatrists would probably have a field day with that one. I finished dialing and waited.

Two rings later, a voice said, “Yo.”

“Tyrese? It’s Dr. Beck. I need your help.”

26

Shauna shook her head. "Beck hurt someone? That's not possible."

Assistant D.A. Fein's vein started fluttering again. He stepped toward her until his face was right up against hers. "He attacked a police officer in an alley. He probably broke the man's jaw and a couple of ribs." Fein leaned a little closer, his spittle landing on Shauna's cheeks. "You hear what I'm telling you?"

"I hear you," Shauna said. "Now step back, Breath Boy, or I'll knee your balls into your throat."

Fein stayed in place for a screw-you second before turning away. Hester Crimstein did likewise. She started heading back toward Broadway. Shauna chased her.

"Where are you going?"

"I quit," Hester said.

"What?"

"Find him another lawyer, Shauna."

"You can't be serious."

"I am."

"You can't just walk out on him."

"Watch me."

"It's prejudicial."

"I gave them my word he'd surrender," she said.

"Screw your word. Beck's the priority here, not you."

"To you maybe."

"You're putting yourself before a client?"

"I won't work with a man who'd do something like that."

"Who are you kidding? You've defended serial rapists."

She waved a hand. "I'm out of here."

"You're just a goddamn media-hound hypocrite."

"Ouch, Shauna."

"I'll go to them."

"What?"

"I'll go to the media."

Hester stopped. "And say what? That I walked away from a dishonest murderer? Great, go ahead. I'll leak so much shit about Beck, he'll make Jeffrey Dahmer look like a good dating prospect."

"You have nothing to leak," Shauna said.

Hester shrugged. "Never stopped me before."

The two women glared. Neither looked away.

"You may think my reputation is irrelevant," Hester said, her voice suddenly soft. "But it's not. If the D.A.'s office can't rely on my word, I'm useless to my other clients. I'm also useless to Beck. It's that simple. I won't let my practice—and my clients—go down the tubes because your boy acted erratically."

Shauna shook her head. "Just get out my face."

"One more thing."

"What?"

"Innocent men don't run, Shauna. Your boy Beck? Hundred to one he killed Rebecca Schayes."

"You're on," Shauna said. "And one more thing for you too, Hester. You say one word against Beck, and they'll need a soup ladle to bury your remains. We clear?"

Hester didn't reply. She took another step away from Shauna. And that was when the gunfire ripped through the air.

I was in mid-crouch, crawling down a rusted fire escape, when the sound of the gunfire nearly made me topple over. I flattened myself on the grated walk and waited.

More gunfire.

I heard shouts. I should have expected this, but it still packed a wallop. Tyrese told me to climb out here and wait for him. I had wondered how he planned on getting me out. Now I was getting some idea.

A diversion.

In the distance, I heard someone shouting, "White boy shooting up the place!" Then another voice: "White boy with a gun! White boy with a gun!"

More gunfire. But—and I strained my ears—no more police radio static. I stayed low and tried not to think much. My brain, it seemed, had short-circuited. Three days ago, I was a dedicated doctor sleepwalking through my own life. Since then, I had seen a ghost, gotten emails from the dead, had become a suspect in not one but two murders, was on the run from the law, had assaulted a police officer, and had enlisted the aid of a known drug dealer.

Heck of a seventy-two hours.

I almost laughed.

"Yo, Doc."

I looked down. Tyrese was there. So was another black man, early twenties, only slightly smaller than this building. The big man peered up at me with those sleek up-yours sunglasses that fit perfectly with his deadened facial expression.

"Come on, Doc. Let's roll."

I ran down the fire escape stairs. Tyrese kept glancing left and right. The big guy stood perfectly still, his arms folded across his chest in what we used to call the buffalo stance. I hesitated before the last ladder, trying to figure out how to release it so I could reach the ground.

"Yo, Doc, lever on the left."

I found it, pulled, and the ladder slid down. When I reached the bottom, Tyrese made a face and waved his hand in front of his nose. "You ripe, Doc."

"I didn't have a chance to shower, sorry."

"This way."

Tyrese did a quick-walk through the back lot. I followed, having to do a little run to keep up. The big man glided behind us in silence. He never moved his head left or right, but I still got the impression he didn't miss much.

A black BMW with tinted windows, a complicated antenna, and a chain frame on the back license plate was running. The doors were all closed, but I could feel the rap music. The bass vibrated in my chest like a tuning fork.

"The car," I said with a frown. "Isn't it kind of conspicuous?"

"If you five-oh and you looking for a lily-white doctor, where would be the last place you look?"

He had a point.

The big guy opened the back door. The music blared at the volume of a Black Sabbath concert. Tyrese extended his arm doorman-style. I got in. He slid next to me. The big guy bent into the driver's seat.

I couldn't understand much of what the rapper on the CD was saying, but he was clearly pissed off with "da man." I suddenly understood.

"This here is Brutus," Tyrese said.

He meant the big-guy driver. I tried to catch his eye in the rearview mirror, but I couldn't see them through the sunglasses.

"Nice to meet you," I said.

Brutus didn't respond.

I turned my attention back to Tyrese. "How did you pull this off?"

"Coupla my boys are doing some shooting down a Hundred Forty-seventh Street."

"Won't the cops find them?"

Tyrese snorted. "Yeah, right."

"It's that easy?"

"From there, yeah, it's easy. We got this place, see, in Building Five at Hobart Houses. I give the tenants ten bucks a month to stick their garbage in front of the back doors. Blocks it up, see. Cops can't get through. Good place to conduct bidness. So my boys, they pop off some shots from the windows, you know what I'm saying. By the time the cops get through, poof, they gone."

"And who was yelling about a white man with a gun?"

"Couple other of my boys. They just running down the street yelling about a crazy white man."

"Theoretically, me," I said.

"Theoretically," Tyrese repeated with a smile. "That's a nice big word, Doc."

I laid my head back. Fatigue settled down hard on my bones. Brutus drove east. He crossed that blue bridge by Yankee Stadium—I'd never learned the bridge's name—and that meant we were in the Bronx. For a while I slumped down in case someone peered into the car, but then I remembered that the windows were tinted. I looked out.

The area was ugly as all hell, like one of those scenes you see in apocalyptic movies after the bomb detonates. There were patches of what might have once been buildings, all in various states of decay. Structures had crumbled, yes, but as though from within, as though the supporting innards had been eaten away.

We drove a little while. I tried to get a grip on what was going on, but my brain kept throwing up roadblocks. Part of me recognized that I was in something approaching shock; the rest of me wouldn't allow me even to consider it. I concentrated on my surroundings. As we drove a little more—as we dove deeper into the decay—the habitable dwellings dwindled. Though we were probably less than a couple of miles from the clinic, I had no idea where we were. Still the Bronx, I guessed. South Bronx probably.

Worn tires and ripped mattresses lay like war wounded in the middle of the road. Big chunks of cement peeked out from the high grass. There were stripped cars and while there were no fires burning, maybe there should have been.

"You come here much, Doc?" Tyrese said with a small chuckle.

I didn't bother responding.

Brutus pulled the car to a stop in front of yet another condemned building. A chain-link fence encircled the sad edifice. The windows had been boarded over with plywood. I could see a piece of paper glued to the door, probably a demolition warning. The door, too, was plywood. I saw it open. A man stumbled out, raising both hands to shield his eyes from the sun, staggering like Dracula under its onslaught.

My world kept swirling.

"Let's go," Tyrese said.

Brutus was out of the car first. He opened the door for me. I thanked him. Brutus stuck with the stoic. He had the kind of cigar-store-Indian face you couldn't imagine—and probably wouldn't ever want to see—smiling.

On the right, the chain-link had been clipped and pulled back. We crouched through. The stumbling man approached Tyrese. Brutus stiffened, but Tyrese waved him down. The stumbling man and Tyrese greeted each other warmly and performed a complicated handshake. Then they went their separate ways.

"Come in," Tyrese said to me.

I ducked inside, my mind still numb. The stench came first, the acid smells of urine and the never-mistaken stink of fecal matter. Something was burning—I think I knew what—and the damp yellow odor of sweat seemed to be coming from the walls. But there was something else here. The smell, not of death, but of predeath, like gangrene, like something dying and decomposing while still breathing.

The stifling heat was of the blast furnace variety. Human beings—maybe fifty of them, maybe a hundred—littered the floor like losing stubs at an OTB. It was dark inside. There seemed to be no electricity, no running water, no furniture of any sort. Wood planks blocked out most of the sun, the only illumination coming through cracks where the sun sliced through like a reaper's scythe. You could make out shadows and shapes and little more.

I admit to being naïve about the drug scene. In the emergency room, I'd seen the results plenty of times. But drugs never interested me personally.

Booze was my poison of choice, I guess. Still, enough stimuli were getting through that even I could deduce that we were in a crack house.

"This way," Tyrese said.

We started walking through the wounded. Brutus led. The dearly reclined parted for him as though he were Moses. I fell in behind Tyrese. The ends of pipes would light up, popping through the darkness. It reminded me of going to the Barnum and Bailey circus as a kid and twirling those tiny flashlights around in the dark. That was what this looked liked. I saw dark. I saw shadows. I saw the flashes of light.

No music played. No one seemed to talk much either. I heard a hum. I heard the wet sucking sound of the pipes. Shrieks pierced the air every once in a while, the sound not quite human.

I also heard groaning. People were performing the lewdest of sex acts, out in the open, no shame, no attempt at privacy.

One particular sight—I'll spare you the details—made me pull up in horror. Tyrese watched my expression with something close to amusement.

"They run out of money, they trade this"—Tyrese pointed—"for hits."

The bile worked its way into my mouth. I turned to him. He shrugged.

"Commerce, Doc. Makes the world go round."

Tyrese and Brutus kept walking. I staggered alongside. Most of the interior walls had crumbled to the ground. People—old, young, black, white, men, women—hung everywhere, spineless, flopped over like Dali clocks.

"Are you a crackhead, Tyrese?" I said.

"Used to be. Got hooked when I was sixteen."

"How did you stop?"

Tyrese smiled. "You see my man Brutus?"

"Hard to miss him."

"I told him I'd give him a thousand dollars for every week I stayed clean. Brutus moved in with me."

I nodded. That sounded far more effective than a week with Betty Ford.

Brutus opened a door. This room, while not exactly well appointed, at least had tables and chairs, even lights and a refrigerator. I noticed a portable generator in the corner.

Tyrese and I stepped inside. Brutus closed the door and stayed in the corridor. We were left alone.

"Welcome to my office," Tyrese said.

"Does Brutus still help you stay off the junk?"

He shook his head. "Nah, TJ does that now. You know what I'm saying?"

I did. "And you don't have a problem with what you do here?"

"I got lots of problems, Doc." Tyrese sat down and invited me to do the same. His eyes flashed at me, and I didn't like what I saw in them. "I ain't one of the good guys."

I didn't know what to say to that, so I changed subjects. "I have to get down to Washington Square Park by five o'clock."

He leaned back. "Tell me what's up."

"It's a long story."

Tyrese took out a blunt blade and started cleaning his nails. "My kid gets sick, I go to the expert, right?"

I nodded.

"You in trouble with the law, you should do likewise."

"That's some analogy."

"Something bad's happening with you, Doc." He spread his arms. "Bad is my world. I'm the best tour guide there is."

So I told him the story. Almost all of it. He nodded a lot, but I doubted he believed me when I said I had nothing to do with the murders. I doubted he cared either.

"Okay," he said when I finished, "let's get you ready. Then we need to talk about something else."

"What?"

Tyrese did not answer. He moved to what looked like a reinforced metal locker in the corner. He unlocked it with a key, leaned inside, and withdrew a gun.

"Glock, baby, Glock," he said, handing me the gun. I stiffened. An image of black and blood flashed in my mind and quickly fled; I didn't chase it. It had been a long time. I reached out and plucked the gun with two fingers, as though it might be hot. "Gun of champions," he added.

I was going to refuse it, but that would be stupid. They already had me on suspicion of two murders, assaulting a police officer, resisting arrest, and probably a bunch of stuff for fleeing from the law. What's a concealed-weapon charge on top of all that?

"It's loaded," he said.

"Is there a safety or something?"

"Not anymore."

"Oh," I said. I slowly turned it over and over, remembering the last time I held a weapon in my hand. It felt good, holding a gun again. Something about the weight, I guessed. I liked the texture, the cold of the steel, the way it fit perfectly in my palm, the heft. I didn't like that I liked it.

"Take this too." He handed me what looked like a cell phone.

"What's this?" I asked.

Tyrese frowned. "What it look like? A cell phone. But it's got a stolen number. Can't be traced back to you, see?"

I nodded, feeling very much out of my element.

"Got a bathroom behind that door," Tyrese said, gesturing to my right. "No shower but there's a bath. Wash your smelly ass off. I'll get you some fresh clothes. Then Brutus and me, we'll get you down to Washington Square."

"You said you had something you wanted to talk to me about."

"After you get dressed," Tyrese said. "We'll talk then."

27

Eric Wu stared at the sprawling tree. His face was serene, his chin tilted up slightly.

"Eric?" The voice belonged to Larry Gandle.

Wu did not turn around. "Do you know what this tree is called?" he asked.

"No."

"The Hangman's Elm."

"Charming."

Wu smiled. "Some historians believe that during the eighteenth century, this park was used for public executions."

"That's great, Eric."

"Yeah."

Two shirtless men whipped by on Rollerblades. A boom box played Jefferson Airplane. Washington Square Park—named, not surprisingly, for George Washington—was one of those places that tried to cling to the sixties though the grip kept slipping. There were usually protestors of some sort, but they looked more like actors in a nostalgic revival than genuine revolutionaries. Street performers took the stage with a little too much finesse. The homeless were the type of colorful that felt somehow contrived.

"You sure we have this place covered?" Gandle asked.

Wu nodded, still facing the tree. "Six men. Plus the two in the van."

Gandle looked behind him. The van was white with a magnetic sign reading B&T Paint and a phone number and a cute logo of a guy who looked a lot like the Monopoly man holding a ladder and a paintbrush. If asked to describe the van, witnesses would remember, if anything at all, the name of the paint company and maybe the phone number.

Neither existed.

The van was double-parked. In Manhattan, a legally parked work van would be more apt to draw suspicion than one that was double-parked. Still, they kept their eye out. If a police officer approached, they would drive away. They would take the van to a lot on Lafayette Street. They would change license plates and magnetic signs. They would then return.

"You should go back to the van," Wu said.

"Do you think Beck will even make it?"

"Doubt it," Wu said.

"I figured getting him arrested would draw her out," Gandle said. "I didn't figure that he'd have a meet set up."

One of their operatives—the curly-haired man who'd worn sweat pants at Kinko's last night—had seen the message pop up on the Kinko's computer. But by the time he relayed the message, Wu had already planted the evidence at Beck's house.

No matter. It would work out.

"We have to grab them both, but she's the priority," Gandle said. "Worse comes to worst, we kill them. But it would be best to have them alive. So we can find out what they know."

Wu did not respond. He was still staring at the tree.

"Eric?"

"They hung my mother from a tree like this," Wu said.

Gandle wasn't sure how to respond, so he settled for "I'm sorry."

"They thought she was a spy. Six men stripped her naked and took a bullwhip to her. They lashed her for hours. Everywhere. Even the flesh on her face was ripped open. She was conscious the whole time. She kept screaming. It took a long time for her to die."

"Jesus Christ," Gandle said softly.

"When they were done, they hung her on a huge tree." He pointed to the Hangman's Elm. "One just like this. It was supposed to be a lesson, of course. So no one else would spy. But birds and animals got to her. Two days later, there were only bones left on that tree."

Wu put the Walkman back on his ears. He turned away from the tree. "You really should get out of sight," he told Gandle.

Larry had trouble wresting his eyes from the massive elm, but he managed to nod and go on his way.

28

I put on a pair of black jeans with a waist the approximate circumference of a truck tire. I folded over the slack and tightened the belt. The black White Sox's uniform shirt fit like a muumuu. The black baseball cap—it had some logo on it I didn't recognize—already had the bill broken in for me. Tyrese also gave me a pair of the same up-yours sunglasses Brutus favored.

Tyrese almost laughed when I came out of the bathroom. "You look good, Doc."

"I think the word you're looking for is *phat*."

He chuckled and shook his head. "White people." Then his face grew serious. He slid some stapled sheets of paper toward me. I picked it up. On top it read Last Will and Testament. I looked the question at him.

"Been meaning to talk to you about this," Tyrese said.

"About your will?"

"I got two more years on my plan."

"What plan?"

"I do this two more years, I got enough money to get TJ out of here. I figure I got maybe sixty-forty chance of making it."

"What do you mean, making it?"

Tyrese's eyes locked on mine. "You know."

I did know. He meant surviving. "Where will you go?"

He handed me a postcard. The scene was sun, blue water, palm trees. The postcard was crinkled from too much handling. "Down in Florida," he said with a soft lilt in his voice. "I know this place. It's quiet. Gotta pool and good schools. Nobody to start wondering where I got my money, you know what I'm saying?"

I handed him back the picture. "I don't understand what I have to do with this."

"This"—he held up the photograph—"is the plan if the sixty percent happens. That"—he pointed to the will—"that's if the forty plays out."

I told him that I still didn't understand.

"I went downtown six months ago, you know what I'm saying. Got a fancy lawyer. Cost me two grand for a coupla hours with him. His name is Joel Marcus. If I die, you have to go see him. You the executor of my will. I got some papers locked up. They'll tell you where the money is."

"Why me?"

"You care about my boy."

"What about Latisha?"

He scoffed. "She a woman, Doc. Soon as I hit the pavement, she be looking for another cock, you know what I'm saying? Probably get knocked up again. Maybe get back on the stuff." He sat back and folded his arms. "Can't trust women, Doc. You should know that."

"She's TJ's mother."

"Right."

"She loves him."

"Yeah, I know that. But she just a woman, you know what I'm saying? You give her this kind of cash, she'll blow it in a day. That's why I set up some trust funds and shit. You the executor. She want money for TJ, you have to approve it. You and this Joel Marcus."

I would have argued that it was sexist and that he was a Neanderthal, but this hardly seemed the time. I shifted in the chair and looked at him. Tyrese was maybe twenty-five years old. I had seen so many like him. I had always lumped them into a single entity, blurring their faces into a dark mass of bad. "Tyrese?"

He looked at me.

"Leave now."

He frowned.

"Use the money you have. Get a job down in Florida. I'll lend you more if you need it. But take your family and go now."

He shook his head.

"Tyrese?"

He stood up. "Come on, Doc. We best get going."

"We're still looking for him."

Lance Fein fumed, his waxy face almost dripping. Dimonte chewed. Krinsky took notes. Stone hitched up his pants.

Carlson was distracted, bent over a fax that had just come through in the car.

"What about the gunshots?" Lance Fein snapped.

The uniformed officer—Agent Carlson hadn't bothered learning his name—shrugged. "Nobody knows anything. I think they were probably unrelated."

"Unrelated?" Fein shrieked. "What kind of incompetent idiot are you, Benny? They were running down the street yelling about a white guy."

"Well, no one knows nothing now."

"Lean on them," Fein said. "Lean on them hard. I mean, for crying out loud, how the hell does a guy like this escape, huh?"

"We'll get him."

Stone tapped Carlson on the shoulder. "What's up, Nick?"

Carlson frowned at the printout. He didn't speak. He was a neat man, orderly to the point of obsessive-compulsive. He washed his hands too much. He often locked and unlocked his door a dozen times before leaving the house. He stared some more because something here just did not mesh.

"Nick?"

Carlson turned toward him. "The thirty-eight we found in Sarah Goodhart's safety-deposit box."

"The one the key on the body led us to?"

"Right."

"What about it?" Stone asked.

Carlson kept frowning. "There's lots of holes here."

"Holes?"

"First off," Carlson continued, "we assume the Sarah Goodhart safety-deposit box was Elizabeth Beck's, right?"

"Right."

"But someone's paid the bill for the box every year for the past eight years," Carlson said. "Elizabeth Beck is dead. Dead women pay no tabs."

"Her father maybe. I think he knows more than he's letting on."

Carlson didn't like it. "How about those listening devices we found at Beck's house? What's the deal there?"

"I don't know," Stone replied with a shrug. "Maybe someone else in the department suspected him too."

"We'd have heard by now. And this report on that thirty-eight we found in the box." He motioned toward it. "You see what the ATF came back with?"

"No."

"Bulletproof had no hits, but that's not surprising since the data doesn't go back eight years anyway." Bulletproof, a bullet-analyzing module used by the Bureau of Alcohol, Tobacco and Firearms, was used to link data from past crimes with more recently discovered firearms. "But the NTC got a hit." NTC stood for the National Tracing Center. "Guess who the last registered owner was."

He handed Stone the printout. Stone scanned down and found it. "Stephen Beck?"

"David Beck's father."

"He died, right?"

"Right."

Stone handed it back to him. "So his son probably inherited the weapon," he said. "It was Beck's gun."

"So why would his wife keep it locked in a safety-deposit box with those photographs?"

Stone considered that one a minute. "Maybe she feared he'd use it on her."

Carlson frowned some more. "We're missing something."

"Look, Nick, let's not make this more complicated than we have to. We got Beck nailed good on the Schayes murder. It'll be a righteous collar. Let's just forget about Elizabeth Beck, okay?"

Carlson looked at him. "Forget about her?"

Stone cleared his throat and spread his hands. "Let's face it. Nailing Beck on Schayes, that'll be a piece of pie. But his wife—Christ, that case is eight years old. We got some scraps, okay, but we're not going to get him for it. It's too late. Maybe"—he gave too dramatic a shrug—"maybe it's best to let sleeping dogs lie."

"What the hell are you talking about?"

Stone moved closer and beckoned Carlson to bend down. "Some people at the Bureau would rather we didn't dig this all up."

"Who doesn't want us digging what up?"

"It's not important, Nick. We're all on the same side, right? If we find out KillRoy didn't kill Elizabeth Beck, it just opens a can of worms, right? His lawyer will probably ask for a new trial—"

"They never tried him for Elizabeth Beck."

"But we wrote her off as KillRoy's handiwork. It would add doubt, that's all. It's neater this way."

"I don't want neat," Carlson said. "I want the truth."

"We all want that, Nick. But we want justice even more, right? Beck will get a life sentence for Rebecca Schayes. KillRoy will stay in jail. That's how it should be."

"There are holes, Tom."

"You keep saying that, but I don't see any. You were the one who first came up with Beck being good for his wife's murder."

"Exactly," Carlson said. "For his wife's murder. Not Rebecca Schayes's."

"I don't get what you mean."

"The Schayes murder doesn't fit."

"You kidding me? It makes it more solid. Schayes knew something. We started closing in. Beck had to shut her up."

Carlson frowned again.

"What?" Stone continued. "You think Beck's visit to her studio yesterday—right after we pressured him—was just a coincidence?"

"No," Carlson said.

"Then what, Nick? Don't you see? Schayes's murder fits in beautifully."

"A little too beautifully," Carlson said.

"Ah, don't start with that crap."

"Let me ask you something, Tom. How well did Beck plan and execute his wife's murder?"

"Pretty damn well."

"Exactly. He killed every witness. He got rid of the bodies. If it wasn't for the rainfall and that bear, we'd have nothing. And let's face it. Even with that, we still don't have enough to indict, much less convict."

"So?"

"So why is Beck suddenly so stupid? He knows we're after him. He knows that Schayes's assistant will be able to testify that he saw Rebecca Schayes the day of the murder. So why would he be stupid enough to keep the gun in his garage? Why would he be stupid enough to leave those gloves in his own trash can?"

"Easy," Stone said. "He rushed this time. With his wife, he had plenty of time to plan."

"Did you see this?"

He handed Stone the surveillance report.

"Beck visited the medical examiner this morning," Carlson said. "Why?"

"I don't know. Maybe he wanted to know if there was anything incriminating in the autopsy file."

Carlson frowned yet again. His hands were itching for another wash. "We're missing something, Tom."

"I don't see what, but hey, either way, we got to get him into custody.

Then we can sort it out, okay?"

Stone headed over to Fein. Carlson let the doubts sink in. He thought again about Beck's visit to the medical examiner's office. He took out his phone, wiped it down with a handkerchief, and pressed the digits. When someone answered, he said, "Get me the Sussex County medical examiner."

29

In the old days—ten years ago anyway—she had friends living at the Chelsea Hotel on West Twenty-third Street. The hotel was half tourist, half residential, all-around kooky. Artists, writers, students, methadone addicts of every stripe and persuasion. Black fingernails, goth-white face paint, bloodred lipstick, hair without a trace of curl—all in the days before it was mainstream.

Little had changed. It was a good place to remain anonymous.

After grabbing a slice of pizza across the street, she'd checked in and had not ventured out of her room. New York. She'd once called this city home, but this was only her second visit in the past eight years.

She missed it.

With too practiced a hand, she tucked her hair under the wig. Today's color would be blond with dark roots. She put on a pair of wire-rim glasses and jammed the implants into her mouth. They changed the shape of her face.

Her hands were shaking.

Two airplane tickets sat on the kitchen table. Tonight, they would take British Airways Flight 174 from JFK to London's Heathrow Airport, where her contact would meet them with new identities. Then they would take the train to Gatwick and take the afternoon flight to Nairobi, Kenya. A jeep would take them near the foothills of Mount Meru in Tanzania, and a three-day hike would follow.

Once they were there—in one of the few spots on this planet with no radio, no television, no electricity—they would be free.

The names on the tickets were Lisa Sherman. And David Beck.

She gave her wig one more tug and stared at her reflection. Her eyes blurred, and for a moment, she was back at the lake. Hope ignited in her chest, and for once she did nothing to extinguish it. She managed a smile and turned away.

She took the elevator to the lobby and made a right on Twenty-third Street.

Washington Square Park was a nice walk from here.

Tyrese and Brutus dropped me on the corner of West Fourth and Lafayette streets, about four blocks east of the park. I knew the area well enough. Elizabeth and Rebecca had shared an apartment on Washington Square, feeling deliciously avant garde in their West Village digs—the photographer and the social-working attorney, striving for Bohemia as they mingled with their fellow suburban-raised wannabes and trust-fund revolutionaries. Frankly I never quite bought it, but that was okay.

I was attending Columbia Medical School at the time, and technically, I lived uptown on Haven Avenue near the hospital now known as New York-Presbyterian. But naturally I spent a lot of time down here.

Those were good years.

Half an hour until the meet time.

I headed down West Fourth Street past the Tower Records and into a region of the city heavily occupied by New York University. NYU wanted you to know this. They staked claim to this land with garish purple NYU-logo flags everywhere. Ugly as hell, this garish purple set against Greenwich Village's subdued brick. Very possessive and territorial too, thought I, for such a liberal enclave. But there you go.

My heart pounded on my chest wall as though it wanted to break free.

Would she be there already?

I didn't run. I kept cool and tried to distract myself from what the next hour or so could bring. The wounds from my recent ordeal were in that state between burn and itch. I caught my reflection in a building window and couldn't help but notice that I looked utterly ridiculous in my borrowed garb. Gangsta Prep. Yo, word.

My pants kept sliding down. I hitched them up with one hand and tried to keep pace.

Elizabeth might be at the park.

I could see the square now. The southeast corner was only a block away. There seemed to be a rustle in the air, the onset of a storm maybe, but that was probably my imagination shifting into high gear. I kept my head lowered. Had my picture reached the television yet? Had the anchors broken in with a be-on-the-lookout announcement? I doubted it. But my eyes still stayed on the pavement.

I hurried my step. Washington Square had always been too intense for me during the summer months. It was trying too hard—too much happening with just a little too much desperation. Manufactured edge, I called it. My favorite spot was the large clutter of humanity near the cement game tables. I played chess there sometimes. I was pretty good, but in this park, chess was the great equalizer. Rich, poor, white, black, homeless, high-rised, rental, co-oped—all harmonized over the age-old black and white figurines. The best player I'd ever seen down here was a black man who spent most of his pre-Giuliani afternoons harassing motorists for change with his squeegee.

Elizabeth wasn't there yet.

I took a seat on a bench.

Fifteen more minutes.

The tightness in my chest increased fourfold. I had never been so scared in my entire life. I thought about Shauna's technological demonstration. A hoax? I wondered again. What if this was all a hoax? What if Elizabeth was indeed dead? What would I do then?

Useless speculation, I told myself. A waste of energy.

She had to be alive. There was no other choice.

I sat back and waited.

*

"He's here," Eric Wu said into his cell phone.

Larry Gandle looked out the van's tinted window. David Beck was indeed where he was supposed to be, dressed like a street punk. His face was covered with scrapes and flowering bruises.

Gandle shook his head. "How the hell did he pull it off?"

"Well," Eric Wu said in that singsong voice, "we can always ask him."

"We need this to go smoothly, Eric."

"Yes indeed."

"Is everybody in place?"

"Of course."

Gandle checked his watch. "She should be here any minute now."

Located between Sullivan and Thompson streets, Washington Square's most striking edifice was a high tower of washed-brown brick on the south side of the park. Most believed that the tower was still part of the Judson Memorial Church. It wasn't. For the past two decades, the tower held NYU student dorm rooms and offices. The top of the tower was easily accessible to anyone who looked as though she knew where she was going.

From up here, she could look down at the whole park. And when she did, she started to cry.

Beck had come. He wore the most bizarre disguise, but then again, the email had warned him that he might be followed. She could see him sitting on that bench, all alone, waiting, his right leg shaking up and down. His leg always did that when he was nervous.

"Ah, Beck …"

She could hear the pain, the bitter agony, in her own voice. She kept staring at him.

What had she done?

So stupid.

She forced herself to turn away. Her legs folded and she slid with her back against the wall until she reached the floor. Beck had come for her.

But so had they.

She was sure of it. She had spotted three of them, at the very least. Probably more. She had also spotted the B&T Paint van. She'd dialed the number on the van's sign, but it was out of service. She checked with directory assistance. There was no B&T Paint.

They'd found them. Despite all her precautions, they were here.

She closed her eyes. Stupid. So stupid. To think that she could pull this off. How could she have allowed it to happen? Yearning had clouded her judgment. She knew that now. Somehow, she had fooled herself into believing that she could turn a devastating catastrophe—the two bodies being discovered near the lake—into some sort of divine windfall.

Stupid.

She sat up and risked another look at Beck. Her heart plummeted like a stone down a well. He looked so alone down there, so small and fragile and helpless. Had Beck adjusted to her death? Probably. Had he fought through what happened and made a life for himself? Again probably. Had he recovered from the blow only to have her stupidity whack him over the head again?

Definitely.

The tears returned.

She took out the two airplane tickets. Preparation. That had always been the key to her survival. Prepare for every eventuality. That was why she had planned the meet here, at a public park she knew so well, where she would have this advantage. She hadn't admitted it to herself, but she'd known that this possibility—no, this likelihood—existed.

It was over.

The small opening, if there had ever been one, had been slammed shut.

Time to go. By herself. And this time for good.

She wondered how he'd react to her not showing up. Would he keep scouring his computer for emails that would never come? Would he search the faces of strangers and imagine he saw hers? Would he just forget and go on—and, when she really mined her true feelings, did she want him to?

No matter. Survival first. His anyway. She had no choice. She had to go.

With great effort, she tore her gaze away and hurried down the stairs. There was a back exit that led out to West Third Street, so she'd never even had to enter the park. She pushed the heavy metal door and stepped outside. Down Sullivan Street, she found a taxi on the corner of Bleecker.

She leaned back and closed her eyes.

"Where to?" the driver asked.

"JFK Airport," she said.

30

Too much time passed.

I stayed on the bench and waited. In the distance I could see the park's famed marble arch. Stanford White, the famous turn-of-the-century architect who murdered a man in a jealous fit over a fifteen-year-old girl, had purportedly "designed" it. I didn't get that. How do you design something that is a replica of someone else's work? The fact that the Washington Arch was a direct rip-off of the Arc de Triomphe in Paris was no secret. New Yorkers got excited over what was in effect a facsimile. I had no idea why.

You couldn't touch the arch anymore. A chain-link fence, not unlike the ones I'd just seen in the South Bronx, encircled it so as to discourage "graffiti artists." The park was big on fences. Almost all grassy areas were lined with loose fencing—double fencing in most places.

Where was she?

Pigeons waddled with the type of possessiveness usually associated with politicians. Many flocked in my direction. They pecked my sneakers and then looked up as though disappointed they weren't edible.

"Ty usually sits there."

The voice came from a homeless guy wearing a pinwheel hat and Spock ears. He sat across from me.

"Oh," I said.

"Ty feeds them. They like Ty."

"Oh," I said again.

"That's why they're all over you like that. They don't like you or nothing. They think maybe you're Ty. Or a friend of Ty's."

"Uh-huh."

I checked my watch. I had been sitting here the better part of two hours. She wasn't coming. Something had gone wrong. Again I wondered if it had all been a hoax, but I quickly pushed it away. Better to continue assuming that the messages were from Elizabeth. If it's all a hoax, well, I'd learn that eventually.

No matter what, I love you ...

That was what the message said. No matter what. As though something might go wrong. As though something could happen. As though I should just forget about it and go on.

To hell with that.

It felt strange. Yes, I was crushed. The police were after me. I was exhausted and beaten up and near the edge sanity-wise. And yet I felt stronger than I had in years. I didn't know why. But I knew I was not going to let it go. Only Elizabeth knew all those things—kiss time, the Bat Lady, the Teenage Sex Poodles. Ergo, it was Elizabeth who had sent the emails. Or someone who was making Elizabeth send them. Either way, she was alive. I had to pursue this. There was no other way.

So, what next?

I took out my new cell phone. I rubbed my chin for a minute and then came up with an idea. I pressed in the digits. A man sitting across the way—he'd been reading a newspaper for a very long time there—sneaked a glance at me. I didn't like that. Better safe than sorry. I stood and moved out of hearing distance.

Shauna answered the phone. "Hello?"

"Old man Teddy's phone," I said.

"Beck? What the hell—?"

"Three minutes."

I hung up. I figured that Shauna and Linda's phone would be tapped. The police would be able to hear every word we said. But one floor below them lived an old widower named Theodore Malone. Shauna and Linda looked in on him from time to time. They had a key to his apartment. I'd call there. The feds or cops or whoever wouldn't have a tap on that phone. Not in time anyway.

I pressed the number.

Shauna sounded out of breath. "Hello?"

"I need your help."

"Do you have any idea what's going on?"

"I assume there's a massive manhunt for me." I still felt oddly calm—in the eye, I guess.

"Beck, you have to turn yourself in."

"I didn't kill anyone."

"I know that, but if you stay out there—"

"Do you want to help me or not?" I interrupted.

"Tell me," she said.

"Have they established a time for the murder yet?"

"Around midnight. Their timetable is a little tight, but they figure you took off right after I left."

"Okay," I said. "I need you to do something for me."

"Name it."

"First off, you have to pick up Chloe."

"Your dog?"

"Yes."

"Why?"

"For one thing," I said, "she needs a walk."

Eric Wu spoke on his cell phone. "He's on the phone, but my man can't get close enough."

"Did he make your guy?"

"Possibly."

"Maybe he's calling off the meet then."

Wu did not reply. He watched as Dr. Beck pocketed his cell phone and started crossing through the park.

"We have a problem," Wu said.

"What?"

"It appears as though he's leaving the park."

There was silence on the other end of the line. Wu waited.

"We lost him before," Gandle said.

Wu did not reply.

"We can't risk it, Eric. Grab him. Grab him now, find out what he knows, and end it."

Eric nodded a signal in the direction of the van. He started walking toward Beck. "Done."

I headed past the park's statue of Garibaldi unsheathing his sword. Strangely enough, I had a destination in mind. Forget visiting KillRoy, that was out for now. But the PF from Elizabeth's diary, aka Peter Flannery, ambulance-chaser-at-law, was another matter. I could still get to his office and have a chat with him. I had no idea what I would learn. But I'd be doing something. That would be a start.

A playground was nestled up on my right, but there were fewer than a dozen children in there. On my left, "George's Dog Park," a glorified doggy run, was chock-full of bandanna-clad canines and their parental alternatives. On the park's stage, two men juggled. I walked past a group of poncho-sheathed students sitting in a semi-circle. A dyed-blond Asian man built like the Thing from the Fantastic Four glided to my right. I glanced behind me. The man who'd been reading the newspaper was gone.

I wondered about that.

He had been there almost the whole time I was. Now, after several hours, he decided to leave at the exact time I did. Coincidence? Probably.

You'll be followed ...

That was what the email had said. It didn't say maybe. It seemed, in hindsight, pretty sure of itself. I kept walking and thought about it a little more. No way. The best tail in the world wouldn't have stuck with me after what I'd just been through today.

The guy with the newspaper couldn't have been following me. At least, I couldn't imagine it.

Could they have intercepted the email?

I couldn't see how. I'd erased it. It had never even been on my own computer.

I crossed Washington Square West. When I reached the curb, I felt a hand on my shoulder. Gentle at first. Like an old friend sneaking up behind me. I turned and had enough time to see it was the Asian guy with the dyed hair.

Then he squeezed my shoulder.

31

His fingers bore into the joint's crevice like spearheads.

Pain—crippling pain—slashed down my left side. My legs gave out. I tried to scream or fight, but I couldn't move. A white van swung up next to us. The side door slid open. The Asian guy moved his hand onto my neck. He squeezed the pressure points on either side, and my eyes started rolling back. With his other hand, he toyed with my spine and I bent forward. I felt myself folding up.

He shoved me toward the van. Hands reached from inside the back and dragged me in. I landed on the cool metal floor. No seats in here. The door closed. The van pulled back into the traffic.

The whole episode—from the hand touching my shoulder to the van starting up—took maybe five seconds.

The Glock, I thought.

I tried to reach for it, but someone leapt on my back. My hands were pinned down. I heard a snap, and my right arm was cuffed at the wrist to the floorboard. They flipped me over, nearly ripping my shoulder out of the socket. Two of them. I could see them now. Two men, both white, maybe thirty years old. I could see them clearly. Too clearly. I could identify them. They would have to know that.

This wasn't good.

They cuffed my other hand so I was spread-eagle on the floorboard. Then they sat on my legs. I was chained down now and totally exposed.

"What do you want?" I asked.

No one answered. The van pulled to a quick stop around the corner. The big Asian guy slid in, and the van started up again. He bent down, gazing at me with what looked like mild curiosity.

"Why were you at the park?" he asked me.

His voice threw me. I had expected something growling or menacing, but his tone was gentle, high-pitched, and creepily childlike.

"Who are you?" I asked.

He slammed his fist in my gut. He punched me so hard, I was sure his knuckles scraped the van floor. I tried to bend or crumple into a ball, but the restraints and the men sitting on my legs made that impossible. Air. All I wanted was air. I thought that I might throw up.

You'll be followed . . .

All the precautions—the unsigned emails, the code words, the warnings—they all made sense now. Elizabeth was afraid. I didn't have all the answers yet—hell, I barely had any of them—but I finally understood that her cryptic communications were a result of fear. Fear of being found.

Found by these guys.

I was suffocating. Every cell in my body craved oxygen. Finally, the Asian nodded at the other two men. They got off my legs. I snapped my knees toward my chest. I tried to gather some air, thrashing around like an epileptic. After a while, my breath came back. The Asian man slowly kneeled closer to me. I kept my eyes steady on his. Or, at least, I tried to. It wasn't like staring into the eyes of a fellow human being or even an animal. These were the eyes of something inanimate. If you could look into the eyes of a file cabinet, this would be what it felt like.

But I did not blink.

He was young too, my captor—no more than twenty, twenty-five tops. He put his hand on the inside of my arm, right above the elbow. "Why were you in the park?" he asked again in his singsong way.

"I like the park," I said.

He pressed down hard. With just two fingers. I gasped. The fingers knifed through my flesh and into a bundle of nerves. My eyes started to bulge. I had never known pain like this. It shut down everything. I flailed like a dying fish on the end of a hook. I tried to kick, but my legs landed like rubber bands. I couldn't breathe.

He wouldn't let go.

I kept expecting him to release the grip or let up a bit. He didn't. I started making small whimpering sounds. But he held on, his expression one of boredom.

The van kept going. I tried to ride out the pain, to break it down into intervals or something. But that didn't work. I needed relief. Just for a second. I needed him to let go. But he remained stonelike. He kept looking at me with those empty eyes. The pressure built in my head. I couldn't speak—even if I wanted to tell him what he wanted to know, my throat had shut down. And he knew that.

Escape the pain. That was all I could think about. How could I escape the pain? My entire being seemed to focus and converge on that nerve bundle in my arm. My body felt on fire, the pressure in my skull building.

With my head seconds from exploding, he suddenly released his grip. I gasped again, this time in relief. But it was short-lived. His hand began to snake down to my lower abdomen and stopped.

"Why were you in the park?"

I tried to think, to conjure up a decent lie. But he didn't give me time. He pinched deeply, and the pain was back, somehow worse than before. His finger pierced my liver like a bayonet. I started bucking against the restraints. My mouth opened in a silent scream.

I whipped my head back and forth. And there, in mid-whip, I saw the back of the driver's head. The van had stopped, probably for a traffic light. The driver was looking straight ahead—at the road, I guess. Then everything happened very fast.

I saw the driver's head swivel toward his door window as though he'd heard a noise. But he was too late. Something hit him in the side of the skull. He went down like a shooting gallery mallard. The van's front doors opened.

"Hands up now!"

Guns appeared. Two of them. Aimed in the back. The Asian guy let go. I flopped back, unable to move.

Behind the guns I saw two familiar faces, and I almost cried out in joy.

Tyrese and Brutus.

One of the white guys made a move. Tyrese casually fired his weapon. The man's chest exploded. He fell back with his eyes open. Dead. No doubt about that. In the front, the driver groaned, starting to come to. Brutus elbowed him hard in the face. The driver went quiet again.

The other white guy had his hands up. My Asian tormenter never changed his expression. He looked on as though from a distance, and he didn't raise or lower his hands. Brutus took the driver's seat and shifted into gear. Tyrese kept his weapon pointed straight at the Asian guy.

"Uncuff him," Tyrese said.

The white guy looked at the Asian. The Asian nodded his consent. The white guy uncuffed me. I tried to sit up. It felt as if something inside me had shattered and the shards were digging into tissue.

"You okay?" Tyrese asked.

I managed a nod.

"You want me to waste them?"

I turned to the still-breathing white guy. "Who hired you?"

The white guy slid his eyes toward the young Asian. I did the same.

"Who hired you?" I asked him.

The Asian finally smiled, but it didn't change his eyes. And then, once again, everything happened too fast.

I never saw his hand shoot out, but next thing I knew the Asian guy had me by the scruff of my neck. He hurled me effortlessly at Tyrese. I was actually airborne, my legs kicking out as though that might slow me down. Tyrese saw me coming, but he couldn't duck out of the way. I landed on him. I tried to roll off quickly, but by the time we righted ourselves, the Asian had gotten out via the van's side door.

He was gone.

"Fucking Bruce Lee on steroids," Tyrese said.

I nodded.

The driver was stirring again. Brutus prepared a fist, but Tyrese shook him off. "These two won't know dick," he said to me.

"I know."

"We can kill them or let them go." Like it was no big deal either way, a coin toss.

"Let them go," I said.

Brutus found a quiet block, probably someplace in the Bronx, I can't be sure. The still-breathing white guy got out on his own. Brutus heaved the driver and the dead guy out like yesterday's refuse. We started driving again. For a few minutes, nobody spoke.

Tyrese laced his hands behind his neck and settled back. "Good thing we hung around, huh, Doc?"

I nodded at what I thought might be the understatement of the millennium.

32

The old autopsy files were kept in a U-Store-'Em in Layton, New Jersey, not far from the Pennsylvania border. Special Agent Nick Carlson arrived on his own. He didn't like storage facilities much. They gave him the black-cat creeps. Open twenty-four hours a day, no guard, a token security camera at the entrance ... God only knows what lay padlocked in these houses of cement. Carlson knew that many were loaded with drugs, money, and contraband of all sorts. That didn't bother him much. But he remembered a few years back when an oil executive had been kidnapped and crate-stored in one. The executive had suffocated to death. Carlson had been there when they found him. Ever since, he imagined *living* people in here too, right now, the inexplicably missing, just yards from where he stood, chained in the dark, straining against mouth gags.

People often note that it's a sick world. They had no idea.

Timothy Harper, the county medical examiner, came out of a garagelike facility, holding a large manila envelope closed with a wrap-around string. He handed Carlson an autopsy file with Elizabeth Beck's name on it.

"You have to sign for it," Harper said.

Carlson signed the form.

"Beck never told you why he wanted to see it?" Carlson asked.

"He talked about being a grieving husband and something about closure, but outside of that ..." Harper shrugged.

"Did he ask you anything else about the case?"

"Nothing that sticks out."

"How about something that doesn't stick out?"

Harper thought about it a moment. "He asked if I remembered who identified the body."

"Did you?"

"Not at first, no."

"Who did identify her?"

"Her father. Then he asked me how long it took."

"How long what took?"

"The identification."

"I don't understand."

"Neither did I, quite frankly. He wanted to know if her father had made the ID immediately or if it took a few minutes."

"Why would he want to know that?"

"I have no idea."

Carlson tried to find an angle on that one, but nothing came to him.

"How did you answer him?"

"With the truth actually. I don't remember. I assume he did it in a timely fashion or I'd remember it better."

"Anything else?"

"Not really, no," he said. "Look, if we're done here, I got two kids who smashed a Civic into a telephone pole waiting for me."

Carlson gripped the file in his hand. "Yeah," he said. "We're done. But if I need to reach you?"

"I'll be at the office."

Peter Flannery, Attorney-at-Law was stenciled in faded gold into the door's pebbled glass. There was a hole in the glass the size of a fist. Someone had patched it up with gray duct tape. The tape looked old.

I kept the brim of my cap low. My insides ached from my ordeal with the big Asian guy. We had heard my name on the radio station that promises the world in exchange for twenty-two minutes. I was officially a wanted man.

Hard to wrap ye olde brain around that one. I was in huge trouble and yet that all seemed strangely remote, as though that were happening to someone with whom I was vaguely acquainted. I, me, the guy right here, didn't care much. I had a single focus: finding Elizabeth. The rest felt like scenery.

Tyrese was with me. Half a dozen people were scattered about the waiting room. Two wore elaborate neck braces. One had a bird in a cage. I had no idea why. No one bothered to glance up at us, as though they'd weighed the effort of sliding their eyes in our direction against the possible benefits and decided, hey, it isn't worth it.

The receptionist wore a hideous wig and looked at us as though we'd just plopped out of a dog's behind.

I asked to see Peter Flannery.

"He's with a client." She wasn't clacking gum, but it was close.

Tyrese took over then. Like a magician with a great sleight of hand, he flourished a roll of cash thicker than my wrist. "Tell him we be offering a retainer." Then, grinning, he added, "One for you too, we get in to see him right away."

Two minutes later, we were ushered into Mr. Flannery's inner sanctum. The office smelled of cigar smoke and Lemon Pledge. Snap-together furniture, the kind you might find at K-mart or Bradlees, had been stained dark, feigning rich oak and mahogany and working about as well as a Las Vegas toupee. There were no school diplomas on the wall, just that phony nonsense people put up to impress the easily impressed. One commemorated Flannery's membership in the "International Wine-tasting Association." Another ornately noted that he attended a "Long Island Legal Conference" in 1996. Big wow. There were sun-faded photos of a younger Flannery with what I guessed were either celebrities or local politicians, but nobody I recognized. The office staple of a golf foursome photo mounted wood-plaque-like adorned a prize spot behind the desk.

"Please," Flannery said with a big wave of his hand. "Have a seat, gentlemen."

I sat. Tyrese stayed standing, crossed his arms, and leaned against the back wall.

"So," Flannery said, stretching the word out like a wad of chaw, "what can I do for you?"

Peter Flannery had that athlete-gone-to-seed look. His once-golden locks had thinned and fled. His features were malleable. He wore a rayon three-piece suit—I hadn't seen one in a while—and the vest even had the pocket watch attached to a faux gold chain.

"I need to ask you about an old case," I said.

His eyes still had the ice blue of youth, and he aimed them my way. On the desk, I spotted a photograph of Flannery with a plump woman and a girl of maybe fourteen who was definitely in the throes of awkward adolescence. They were all smiling, but I saw a wince there too, as though they were bracing for a blow.

"An old case?" he repeated.

"My wife visited you eight years ago. I need to know what it was about."

Flannery's eyes flicked toward Tyrese. Tyrese still had the folded arms and showed him nothing more than the sunglasses. "I don't understand. Was this a divorce case?"

"No," I said.

"Then . . . ?" He put his hands up and gave me the I'd-like-to-help shrug. "Attorney-client confidentiality. I don't see how I can help you."

"I don't think she was a client."

"You're confusing me, Mr.—" He waited for me to fill in the blank.

"Beck," I said. "And it's doctor, not mister."

His double chin went slack at my name. I wondered if maybe he had heard the news reports. But I didn't think that was it.

"My wife's name is Elizabeth."

Flannery said nothing.

"You remember her, don't you?"

Again he flipped a glance at Tyrese.

"Was she a client, Mr. Flannery?"

He cleared his throat. "No," he said. "No, she wasn't a client."

"But you remember meeting her?"

Flannery shifted in his chair. "Yes."

"What did you discuss?"

"It's been a long time, Dr. Beck."

"Are you saying you don't remember?"

He didn't answer that one directly. "Your wife," he said. "She was murdered, wasn't she? I remember seeing something about it on the news."

I tried to keep us on track. "Why did she come here, Mr. Flannery?"

"I'm an attorney," he said, and he almost puffed out his chest.

"But not hers."

"Still," he said, trying to gain some sort of leverage, "I need to be compensated for my time." He coughed into his fist. "You mentioned something about a retainer."

I looked over my shoulder, but Tyrese was already on the move. The cash roll was out and he was peeling bills. He tossed three Ben Franklins on the desk, gave Flannery a hard sunglass glare, and then stepped back to his spot.

Flannery looked at the money but didn't touch it. He bounced his fingertips together and then flattened his palms against each other. "Suppose I refuse to tell you."

"I can't see why you would," I said. "Your communications with her don't fall under privilege, do they?"

"I'm not talking about that," Flannery said. His eyes pierced mine and he hesitated. "Did you love your wife, Dr. Beck?"

"Very much."

"Have you remarried?"

"No," I said. Then: "What does that have to do with anything?"

He settled back. "Go," he said. "Take your money and just go."

"This is important, Mr. Flannery."

"I can't imagine how. She's been dead for eight years. Her killer is on death row."

"What are you afraid to tell me?"

Flannery didn't answer right away. Tyrese again peeled himself off the wall. He moved closer to the desk. Flannery watched him and surprised me with a tired sigh. "Do me a favor," he said to Tyrese. "Stop with the posturing, okay? I've repped psychos who make you look like Mary Poppins."

Tyrese looked as though he might react, but that wouldn't help. I said his name. He looked at me. I shook my head. Tyrese backed off. Flannery was plucking at his lower lip. I let him. I could wait.

"You don't want to know," he said to me after a while.

"Yeah, I do."

"It can't bring your wife back."

"Maybe it can," I said.

That got his attention. He frowned at me, but something there softened.

"Please," I said.

He swiveled his seat to the side and tilted way back, staring up at window blinds that had turned yellow and crusty sometime during the Watergate hearings. He folded his hands and rested them on his paunch. I watched the hands rise and fall as he breathed.

"I was a public defender back then," he began. "You know what that is?"

"You defended the indigent," I said.

"Something like that. The Miranda rights—they talk about having the right to counsel if you can afford one. I'm the guy you get when you can't."

I nodded, but he was still looking at the blinds.

"Anyway, I was assigned one of the most prominent murder trials in the state."

Something cold wormed into my stomach. "Whose?" I asked.

"Brandon Scope's. The billionaire's son. Do you remember the case?"

I froze, terrified. I could barely breathe. Little wonder Flannery's name had seemed familiar. Brandon Scope. I almost shook my head, not because I didn't remember the case, but because I wanted him to say anything but that name.

For the sake of clarity, let me give you the newspaper account: Brandon Scope, age thirty-three, was robbed and murdered eight years ago. Yes, eight years ago. Maybe two months before Elizabeth's murder. He was shot twice and dumped near a housing project in Harlem. His money was gone. The media played all the violins on this one. They made much of Brandon Scope's charitable work. They talked about how he helped street kids, how he preferred working with the poor to running Daddy's multinational conglomerate, that kind of spin. It was one of those murders that "shock a nation" and lead to plenty of finger-pointing and hand-wringing. A charitable foundation had been set up in young Scope's name. My sister, Linda, runs it. You wouldn't believe the good she does there.

"I remember it," I said softly.

"Do you remember that an arrest was made?"

"A street kid," I said. "One of the kids he helped, right?"

"Yes. They arrested Helio Gonzalez, then age twenty-two. A resident of Barker House in Harlem. Had a felony sheet that read like a Hall of Famer's career stats. Armed robbery, arson, assault, a real sunshine, our Mr. Gonzalez."

My mouth was dry. "Weren't the charges eventually dropped?" I asked.

"Yes. They didn't have much really. His fingerprints were found at the scene, but so were plenty of others. There were strands of Scope's hair and even a speck of matching blood found where Gonzalez lived. But Scope had been to the building before. We could have easily claimed that was how that material got there. Nonetheless, they had enough for an arrest, and the cops were sure something more would break."

"So what happened?" I asked.

Flannery still wouldn't look at me. I didn't like that. Flannery was the kind of guy who lived for the Willy Loman world of shined shoes and eye contact. I knew the type. I didn't want anything to do with them, but I knew them.

"The police had a solid time of death," he continued. "The M.E. got a good liver temperature reading. Scope was killed at eleven. You might be able to stretch it a half hour in either direction, but that was about it."

"I don't understand," I said. "What does this have to do with my wife?"

He bounced the fingertips again. "I understand that your wife worked with the poor as well," he said. "In the same office with the victim, as a matter of fact."

I didn't know where this was going, but I knew I wasn't going to like it. For the most fleeting of seconds, I wondered if Flannery was right, if I really didn't want to hear what he had to say, if I should just pick myself out of the chair and forget all about this. But I said, "So?"

"That's noble," he said with a small nod. "Working with the downtrodden."

"Glad you think so."

"It's why I originally went into law. To help the poor."

I swallowed down the bile and sat a little straighter. "Do you mind telling me what my wife has to do with any of this?"

"She freed him."

"Who?"

"My client. Helio Gonzalez. Your wife freed him."

I frowned. "How?"

"She gave him an alibi."

My heart stopped. So did my lungs. I almost pounded on my chest to get the inner workings started up again.

"How?" I asked.

"How did she give him an alibi?"

I nodded numbly, but he still wasn't looking. I croaked out a yes.

"Simple," he said. "She and Helio had been together during the time in question."

My mind started to flail, adrift in the ocean, no life preserver in reach. "I never saw anything about this in the papers," I said.

"It was kept quiet."

"Why?"

"Your wife's request, for one. And the D.A.'s office didn't want their wrongful arrest made more public. So it was all done as quietly as possible. Plus there were, uh, problems with your wife's testimony."

"What problems?"

"She sort of lied at first."

More flailing. Sinking under. Coming to the surface. Flailing. "What are you talking about?"

"Your wife claimed that she was doing some career counseling with Gonzalez at the charity office at the time of the murder. Nobody really bought that."

"Why not?"

He cocked a skeptical eyebrow. "Career counseling at eleven at night?"

I nodded numbly.

"So as Mr. Gonzalez's attorney, I reminded your wife that the police would investigate her alibi. That, for example, the counseling offices had security cameras and there would be tapes of the comings and goings. That was when she came clean."

He stopped.

"Go on," I said.

"It's obvious, isn't it?"

"Tell me anyway."

Flannery shrugged. "She wanted to spare herself—and you, I guess—the embarrassment. That was why she insisted on secrecy. She was at Gonzalez's place, Dr. Beck. They'd been sleeping together for two months."

I didn't react. No one spoke. In the distance, I heard a bird squawk. Probably the one in the waiting room. I got to my feet. Tyrese took a step back.

"Thank you for your time," I said in the calmest voice you ever heard.

Flannery nodded at the window blinds.

"It's not true," I said to him.

He didn't respond. But then again, I hadn't expected him to.

33

Carlson sat in the car. His tie was still knotted meticulously. His suit jacket was off, hung on a wooden hanger on the backseat hook. The air-conditioning blew loud and hard. Carlson read the autopsy envelope: Elizabeth Beck, Case File 94-87002. His fingers started unwinding the string. The envelope opened. Carlson extracted the contents and spread them out on the passenger seat.

What had Dr. Beck wanted to see?

Stone had already given him the obvious answer: Beck wanted to know if there was anything that might incriminate him. That fit into their early theories, and it had, after all, been Carlson who'd first started questioning the accepted scenario on Elizabeth Beck's murder. He had been the first to believe that the killing was not what it appeared to be—that indeed it was Dr. David Beck, the husband, who had planned the murder of his wife.

So why had he stopped buying it?

He had carefully reviewed the holes now poking through that theory, but Stone had been equally convincing in patching them back up. Every case has holes. Carlson knew that. Every case has inconsistencies. If it doesn't, ten to one you've missed something.

So why did he now have doubts about Beck's guilt?

Perhaps it had something to do with the case becoming too neat, all the evidence suddenly lining up and cooperating with their theory. Or maybe his doubts were based on something as unreliable as "intuition," though Carlson had never been a big fan of that particular aspect of investigative work. Intuition was often a way of cutting corners, a nifty technique of replacing hard evidence and facts with something far more elusive and capricious. The worst investigators Carlson knew relied on so-called intuition.

He picked up the top sheet. General information. Elizabeth Parker Beck. Her address, her birth date (she'd been twenty-five when she died), Caucasian female, height five seven, weight 98 pounds. Thin. The external examination revealed that rigor mortis had resolved. There were blisters on the skin and fluid leaks from the orifices. That placed the time of death at more than three days. The cause of death was a knife wound to the chest. The mechanism of death was loss of blood and dramatic hemorrhaging of the right aorta. There were also cut wounds on her hands and fingers, theoretically because she tried to defend herself against a knife attack.

Carlson took out his notebook and Mont Blanc pen. He wrote Defensive knife wounds?!?! and then he underlined it several times. Defensive wounds. That wasn't KillRoy's style. KillRoy tortured his victims. He bound them with rope, did whatever, and once they were too far gone to care, he killed them.

Why would there be defensive knife wounds on her hands?

Carlson kept reading. He scanned through hair and eye color, and then, halfway down the second page, he found another shocker.

Elizabeth Beck had been branded postmortem.

Carlson reread that. He took out his notebook and scratched down the word postmortem. That didn't add up. KillRoy had always branded his victims while they were alive. Much was made at trial about how he liked the smell of sizzling flesh, how he enjoyed the screams of his victims while he seared them.

First, the defensive wounds. Now this. Something wasn't meshing.

Carlson took off his glasses and closed his eyes. Mess, he thought to himself. Mess upset him. Logic holes were expected, yes, but these were turning into gaping wounds. On the one hand, the autopsy supported his original hypothesis that Elizabeth Beck's murder had been staged to look like the work of KillRoy. But now, if that were true, the theory was coming unglued from the other side.

He tried to take it step by step. First, why would Beck be so eager to see this file? On the surface, the answer was now obvious. Anybody who scrutinized these results would realize that there was an excellent chance that KillRoy had not murdered Elizabeth Beck. It was not a given, however. Serial killers, despite what you might read, are not creatures of habit. KillRoy could have changed his M.O. or sought some diversity. Still, with what Carlson was reading here, there was enough to make one ponder.

But all of this just begged what had become the big question: Why hadn't anybody noticed these evidentiary inconsistencies back then?

Carlson sorted through possibilities. KillRoy had never been prosecuted for Elizabeth Beck's murder. The reasons were now pretty clear. Perhaps the investigators suspected the truth. Perhaps they realized that Elizabeth Beck didn't fit, but publicizing that fact would only aid KillRoy's defense. The problem with prosecuting a serial killer is that you cast a net so wide, something is bound to slither out. All the defense has to do is pick apart one case, find discrepancies with one murder, and bang, the other cases are tainted by association. So without a confession, you rarely try him for all the murders at once. You do it step by step. The investigators, realizing this, probably just wanted the murder of Elizabeth Beck to go away.

But there were big problems with that scenario too.

Elizabeth Beck's father and uncle—two men in law enforcement—had seen the body. They had in all likelihood seen this autopsy report. Wouldn't they have wondered about the inconsistencies? Would they have let her murderer go free just to secure a conviction on KillRoy? Carlson doubted it.

So where did that leave him?

He continued through the file and stumbled across yet another stunner. The car's air-conditioning was seriously chilling him now, reaching bone. Carlson slid down a window and pulled the key out of the ignition. The top of the sheet read: Toxicology Report. According to the tests, cocaine and heroin had been found in Elizabeth Beck's bloodstream; moreover, traces were found in the hair and tissues, indicating that her use was more than casual.

Did that fit?

He was thinking about it, when his cell phone rang. He picked it up. "Carlson."

"We got something," Stone said.

Carlson put down the file. "What?"

"Beck. He's booked on a flight to London out of JFK. It leaves in two hours."

"I'm on my way."

Tyrese put a hand on my shoulder as we walked. "Bitches," he said for the umpteenth time. "You can't trust them."

I didn't bother replying.

It surprised me at first that Tyrese would be able to track down Helio Gonzalez so quickly, but the street network was as developed as any other. Ask a trader at Morgan Stanley to locate a counterpart at Goldman Sachs and it would be done in minutes. Ask me to refer a patient to pretty much any other doctor in the state, and it takes one phone call. Why should street felons be different?

Helio was fresh off a four-year stint upstate for armed robbery. He looked it too. Sunglasses, a doo-rag on his head, white T-shirt under a flannel shirt that had only the top button buttoned so that it looked like a cape or bat wings. The sleeves were rolled up, revealing crude prison tattoos etched onto his forearm and the prison muscles coiling thereunder. There is an unmistakable look to prison muscles, a smooth, marblelike quality as opposed to their puffier health club counterparts.

We sat on a stoop somewhere in Queens. I couldn't tell you where exactly. A Latin rhythm tah-tah-tahhed, the beat driving into my chest. Dark-haired women sauntered by in too-clingy spaghetti-strap tops. Tyrese nodded at me. I turned to Helio. He had a smirk on his face. I took in the whole package and one word kept popping into my brain: scum. Unreachable, unfeeling scum. You looked at him, and you knew that he would continue to leave serious destruction in his wake. The question was how much. I realized that this view was not charitable. I realized, too, that based on surfaces, the very same could be said for Tyrese. That didn't matter. Elizabeth may have believed in the redemption for the street-hardened or morally anesthetized. I was still working on it.

"Several years ago, you were arrested for the murder of Brandon Scope," I began. "I know you were released, and I don't want to cause you any trouble. But I need to know the truth."

Helio took off his sunglasses. He flicked a glance at Tyrese. "You bring me a cop?"

"I'm not a cop," I said. "I'm Elizabeth Beck's husband."

I wanted a reaction. I didn't get one.

"She's the woman who gave you the alibi."

"I know who she is."

"Was she with you that night?"

Helio took his time. "Yeah," he said slowly, smiling at me with yellow teeth. "She was with me all night."

"You're lying," I said.

Helio looked back over at Tyrese. "What is this, man?"

"I need to know the truth," I said.

"You think I killed that Scope guy?"

"I know you didn't."

That surprised him.

"What the hell is going on here?" he said.

"I need you to confirm something for me."

Helio waited.

"Were you with my wife that night, yes or no?"

"What you want me to say, man?"

"The truth."

"And if the truth is she was with me all night?"

"It's not the truth," I said.

"What makes you so sure?"

Tyrese joined in. "Tell the man what he wants to know."

Helio took his time again. "It's like she said. I did her, all right? Sorry, man, but that's what happened. We were doing it all night."

I looked at Tyrese. "Leave us alone a second, okay?"

Tyrese nodded. He got up and walked to his car. He leaned against the side door, arms folded, Brutus by his side. I turned my gaze back to Helio.

"Where did you first meet my wife?"

"At the center."

"She tried to help you?"

He shrugged, but he wouldn't look at me.

"Did you know Brandon Scope?"

A flicker of what might have been fear crossed his face. "I'm going, man."

"It's just you and me, Helio. You can frisk me for a wire."

"You want me to give up my alibi?"

"Yeah."

"Why would I do that?"

"Because someone is killing everyone connected with what happened to Brandon Scope. Last night, my wife's friend was murdered in her studio. They grabbed me today, but Tyrese intervened. They also want to kill my wife."

"I thought she was dead already."

"It's a long story, Helio. But it's all coming back. If I don't find out what really happened, we're all going to end up dead."

I didn't know if this was true or hyperbole. I didn't much care either.

"Where were you that night?" I pressed.

"With her."

"I can prove you weren't," I said.

"What?"

"My wife was in Atlantic City. I have her old charge records. I can prove it. I can blow your alibi right out of the water, Helio. And I'll do it. I know you didn't kill Brandon Scope. But so help me, I'll let them execute you for it if you don't tell me the truth."

A bluff. A great big bluff. But I could see that I'd drawn blood.

"Tell me the truth, and you stay free," I said.

"I didn't kill that dude, I swear it, man."

"I know that," I said again.

He thought about it. "I don't know why she did it, all right?"

I nodded, trying to keep him talking.

"I robbed a house out in Fort Lee that night. So I had no alibi. I thought I was going down for it. She saved my ass."

"Did you ask her why?"

He shook his head. "I just went along. My lawyer told me what she said. I backed her up. Next thing I knew, I was out."

"Did you ever see my wife again?"

"No." He looked up at me. "How come you so sure your wife wasn't doing me?"

"I know my wife."

He smiled. "You think she'd never cheat?"

I didn't reply.

Helio stood up. "Tell Tyrese he owes me one."

He chuckled, turned, walked away.

34

No luggage. An e-ticket so she could check in by machine rather than with a person. She waited in a neighboring terminal, keeping her eye on the departure screen, waiting for the On Time next to her flight to evolve into Boarding.

She sat in a chair of molded plastic and looked out onto the tarmac. A TV blared CNN. "Next up *Headline Sports.*" She made her mind blank. Five years ago, she had spent time in a small village outside Goa, India. Though a true hellhole, the village had something of a buzz about it because of the one-hundred-year-old yogi who lived there. She had spent time with the yogi. He had tried to teach her meditation techniques, pranayama breathing, mind cleansing. But none of it ever really stuck. There were moments when she could sink away into blackness. More often, though, wherever she sank, Beck was there.

She wondered about her next move. There was no choice really. This was about preservation. Preservation meant fleeing. She had made a mess and now she was running away again, leaving others to clean it up. But what other option was there? They were onto her. She had been careful as hell, but they had still been watching. Eight years later.

A toddler scrambled toward the plate-glass window, his palms hitting it with a happy splat. His harried father chased him down and scooped him up with a giggle. She watched and her mind scrambled to the obvious what-could-have-beens. An old couple sat to her right, chatting amiably about nothing. As teenagers, she and Beck would watch Mr. and Mrs. Steinberg stroll up Downing Place arm in arm, every night without fail, long after their children had grown and fled the nest. That would be their lives, Beck had promised. Mrs. Steinberg died when she was eighty-two. Mr. Steinberg, who had been in amazingly robust health, followed four months later. They say that happens a lot with the elderly, that—to paraphrase Springsteen—two hearts become one. When one dies, the other follows. Was that how it was with her and David? They had not been together sixty-one years like the Steinbergs, but when you think about it in relative terms, when you consider that you barely have any memories of your life before age five, when you figure that she and Beck had been inseparable since they were seven, that they could barely unearth any memory that didn't include the other, when you think of the time spent together not just in terms of years but in life percentages, they had more vested in each other than even the Steinbergs.

She turned and checked the screen. Next to British Airways Flight 174, the word Boarding started to flash.

Her flight was being called.

*

Carlson and Stone, along with their local buddies Dimonte and Krinsky, stood with the British Airways reservation manager.

"He's a no-show," the reservation manager, a blue-and-white-uniformed woman with a kerchief, a beautiful accent, and a name tag reading Emily told them.

Dimonte cursed. Krinsky shrugged. This was not unexpected. Beck had been successfully eluding a manhunt all day. It was a long shot that he would be dumb enough to try to board a flight using his real name.

"Dead end," Dimonte said.

Carlson, who still had the autopsy file clutched against his hip, asked Emily, "Who is your most computer-literate employee?"

"That would be me," she said with a competent smile.

"Please bring up the reservation," Carlson said.

Emily did as he requested.

"Can you tell me when he booked the flight?"

"Three days ago."

Dimonte leapt on that one. "Beck planned to run. Son of a bitch."

Carlson shook his head. "No."

"How do you figure?"

"We've been assuming that he killed Rebecca Schayes to shut her up," Carlson explained. "But if you're going to leave the country, why bother? Why take the risk of waiting three days and trying to get away with another murder?"

Stone shook his head. "You're overthinking this one, Nick."

"We're missing something," Carlson insisted. "Why did he all of a sudden decide to run in the first place?"

"Because we were onto him."

"We weren't onto him three days ago."

"Maybe he knew it was a matter of time."

Carlson frowned some more.

Dimonte turned to Krinsky. "This is a waste of time. Let's get the hell out of here." He looked at Carlson. "We'll leave a couple of uniforms around just in case."

Carlson nodded, only half listening. When they left, he asked Emily, "Was he traveling with anyone?"

Emily hit some keys. "It was a solo booking."

"How did he book it? In person? On the phone? Did he go through a travel agency?"

She clicked the keys again. "It wasn't through a travel agency. That much I can tell you because we'd have a marking to pay a commission. The reservation was made directly with British Airways."

No help there. "How did he pay?"

"Credit card."

"May I have the number, please?"

She gave it to him. He passed it over to Stone. Stone shook his head. "Not one of his cards. At least, not one we know about."

"Check it out," Carlson said.

Stone's cell phone was already in his hand. He nodded and pressed the keypad.

Carlson rubbed his chin. "You said he booked his flight three days ago."

"That's correct."

"Do you know what time he booked it?"

"Actually yes. The computer stamps it in. Six-fourteen in the p.m."

Carlson nodded. "Okay, great. Can you tell me if anyone else booked at around the same time?"

Emily thought about it. "I've never tried that," she said. "Hold on a moment, let me see something." She typed. She waited. She typed some more. She waited. "The computer won't sort by booking date."

"But the information is in there?"

"Yes. Wait, hold up." Her fingers started clacking again. "I can paste the information onto a spreadsheet. We can put fifty bookings per screen. It will make it faster."

The first group of fifty had a married couple who booked the same day but hours earlier. Useless. The second group had none. In the third group, however, they hit bingo.

"Lisa Sherman," Emily pronounced. "Her flight was booked the same day, eight minutes later."

It didn't mean anything on its own, of course, but Carlson felt the hair on the back of his neck stand up.

"Oh, this is interesting," Emily added.

"What?"

"Her seat assignment."

"What about it?"

"She was scheduled to sit next to David Beck. Row sixteen, seats E and F."

He felt the jolt. "Has she checked in?"

More typing. The screen cleared. Another came up. "As a matter of fact, she has. She's probably boarding as we speak."

She adjusted her purse strap and stood. Her step was brisk, her head high. She still had the glasses and the wig and implants. So did the photograph of Lisa Sherman in her passport.

She was four gates away when she heard a snippet of the CNN report. She stopped short. A man wheeling an industrial-size piece of carry-on ran into her. He made a rude hand gesture as though she'd cut him off on a freeway. She ignored him and kept her eyes on the screen.

The anchorwoman was doing the report. In the right-hand corner of the screen was a photograph of her old friend Rebecca Schayes side by side with an image of ... of Beck.

She hurried closer to the screen. Under the images in a bloodred font were the words *Death in the Darkroom.*

"... David Beck, suspected in the slaying. But is that the only crime they believe he's committed? CNN's Jack Turner has more."

The anchorwoman disappeared. In her place, two men with NYPD windbreakers rolled out a black body bag on a stretcher. She recognized the building at once and almost gasped. Eight years. Eight years had passed, but

Rebecca still had her studio in the same location.

A man's voice, presumably Jack Turner's, began his report: "It's a twisted tale, this murder of one of New York's hottest fashion photographers. Rebecca Schayes was found dead in her darkroom, shot twice in the head at close range." They flashed a photograph of Rebecca smiling brightly. "The suspect is her longtime friend, Dr. David Beck, an uptown pediatrician." Now Beck's image, no smile, lit up the screen. She almost fell over.

"Dr. Beck narrowly escaped arrest earlier today after assaulting a police officer. He is still at large and assumed armed and dangerous. If you have any information on his whereabouts ..." A phone number appeared in yellow. Jack Turner read out the number before continuing.

"But what has given this story an added twist are the leaks coming out of Manhattan's Federal Building. Presumably, Dr. Beck has been linked to the murder of two men whose bodies were recently unearthed in Pennsylvania, not far from where Dr. Beck's family has a summer residence. And the biggest shocker of all: Dr. David Beck is also a suspect in the eight-year-old slaying of his wife, Elizabeth."

A photograph of a woman she barely recognized popped up. She suddenly felt naked, cornered. Her image vanished as they went back to the anchorwoman, who said, "Jack, wasn't it believed that Elizabeth Beck was the victim of serial killer Elroy 'KillRoy' Kellerton?"

"That's correct, Terese. Authorities aren't doing much talking right now, and officials deny the reports. But the leaks are coming to us from very reliable sources."

"Do the police have a motive, Jack?"

"We haven't heard one yet. There has been some speculation that there may have been a love triangle here. Ms. Schayes was married to a Gary Lamont, who remains in seclusion. But that's little more than conjecture at this point."

Still staring at the TV screen, she felt the tears start welling up.

"And Dr. Beck is still at large tonight?"

"Yes, Terese. The police are asking for the public's cooperation, but they stress that no one should approach him on their own."

Chatter followed. Meaningless chatter.

She turned away. Rebecca. Oh God, not Rebecca. And she'd gotten married. Had probably picked out dresses and china patterns and done all those things they used to mock. How? How had Rebecca gotten tangled up in all this? Rebecca hadn't known anything.

Why had they killed her?

Then the thought hit her anew: What have I done?

She had come back. They had started looking for her. How would they have gone about that? Simple. Watch the people she was closest to. Stupid. Her coming back had put everyone she cared about in danger. She had messed up. And now her friend was dead.

"British Airways Flight 174, departing for London. All rows may now board."

There was no time to beat herself up. Think. What should she do? Her loved ones were in danger. Beck—she suddenly remembered his silly disguise—was on the run. He was up against powerful people. If they were trying to frame him for murder—and that seemed pretty obvious right now—he'd have no chance.

She couldn't just leave. Not yet. Not until she knew that Beck was safe.

She turned and headed for an exit.

When Peter Flannery finally saw the news reports on the David Beck manhunt, he picked up the phone and dialed a friend at the D.A.'s office.

"Who's running the Beck case?" Flannery asked.

"Fein."

A true ass, Flannery thought. "I saw your boy today."

"David Beck?"

"Yeah," Flannery said. "He paid me a visit."

"Why?"

Flannery kicked back his BarcaLounger. "Maybe you should put me through to Fein."

35

When night fell, Tyrese found me a room at the apartment of Latisha's cousin. We couldn't imagine that the police would unearth my connection with Tyrese, but why take the chance?

Tyrese had a laptop. We hooked it up. I checked my email, hoping for a message from my mysterious mailer. Nothing under my work account. Nothing under my home account. I tried the new one at bigfoot.com. Nothing there either.

Tyrese had been looking at me funny since we'd left Flannery's office. "I ask you something, Doc?"

"Go ahead," I said.

"When that mouthpiece said about that guy being murdered—"

"Brandon Scope," I added.

"Yeah, him. You look like someone hit you with a stun gun."

It had felt it. "You're wondering why?"

Tyrese shrugged.

"I knew Brandon Scope. He and my wife shared an office at a charitable foundation in the city. And my father grew up with and worked for his father. In fact, my father was in charge of teaching Brandon about the family holdings."

"Uh-huh," Tyrese said. "What else?"

"That's not enough?"

Tyrese waited. I turned to face him. He kept his eyes steady and for a moment I thought he could see all the way to the blackest corners of my soul. Thankfully, the moment passed. Tyrese said, "So what do you want to do next?"

"Make a few phone calls," I said. "You sure they can't be traced back here?"

"Can't see how. Tell you what, though. We'll do it with a conference call to another cell phone. Make it that much harder."

I nodded. Tyrese set it up. I had to dial another number and tell somebody I didn't know what numbers to dial. Tyrese headed for the door. "I'm gonna check on TJ. I'll be back in an hour."

"Tyrese?"

He looked back. I wanted to say thanks, but somehow it didn't feel right. Tyrese understood. "Need you to stay alive, Doc. For my kid, see?"

I nodded. He left. I checked my watch before dialing Shauna's cell phone. She answered on the first ring. "Hello?"

"How's Chloe?" I asked.

"Great," she said.

"How many miles did you walk?"

"At least three. More like four or five." Relief coursed through me. "So what's our next—"

I smiled and disconnected the phone. I dialed up my forwarding buddy and gave him another number. He mumbled something about not being a goddamn operator, but he did as I asked.

Hester Crimstein answered as though she were taking a bite out of the receiver. "What?"

"It's Beck," I said quickly. "Can they listen in, or do we have some kind of attorney-client protection here?"

There was a strange hesitation. "It's safe," she said.

"I had a reason for running," I began.

"Like guilt?"

"What?"

Another hesitation. "I'm sorry, Beck. I screwed up. When you ran like that, I freaked out. I said some stupid things to Shauna, and I quit as your attorney."

"Never told me," I said. "I need you, Hester."

"I won't help you run."

"I don't want to run anymore. I want to surrender. But on our terms."

"You're not in any position to dictate terms, Beck. They're going to lock you up tight. You can forget bail."

"Suppose I offer proof I didn't kill Rebecca Schayes."

Another hesitation. "You can do that?"

"Yes."

"What sort of proof?"

"A solid alibi."

"Provided by?"

"Well," I said, "that's where it gets interesting."

Special Agent Carlson picked up his cell phone. "Yeah."

"Got something else," his partner Stone said.

"What?"

"Beck visited a cheap mouthpiece named Flannery a few hours ago. A black street kid was with him."

Carlson frowned. "I thought Hester Crimstein was his attorney."

"He wasn't looking for legal representation. He wanted to know about a past case."

"What case?"

"Some all-purpose perp named Gonzalez was arrested for killing Brandon Scope eight years ago. Elizabeth Beck gave the guy a hell of an alibi. Beck wanted to know all about it."

Carlson felt his head doing a double spin. How the hell . . . ?

"Anything else?"

"That's it," Stone said. "Say, where are you?"

"I'll talk to you later, Tom." Carlson hung up the phone and pressed in another number.

A voice answered, "National Tracing Center."

"Working late, Donna?"

"And I'm trying to get out of here, Nick. What do you want?"

"A really big favor."

"No," she said. Then with a big sigh, "What?"

"You still have that thirty-eight we found in the Sarah Goodhart safety-deposit box?"

"What about it?"

He told her what he wanted. When he finished, she said, "You're kidding, right?"

"You know me, Donna. No sense of humor."

"Ain't that truth." She sighed. "I'll put in a request, but there's no way it'll get done tonight."

"Thanks, Donna. You're the best."

When Shauna entered the building's foyer, a voice called out to her.

"Excuse me. Miss Shauna?"

She looked at the man with the gelled hair and expensive suit. "And you are?"

"Special Agent Nick Carlson."

"Nighty-night, Mr. Agent."

"We know he called you."

Shauna patted her mouth in a fake yawn. "You must be proud."

"Ever hear the terms aiding and abetting and accessory after the fact?"

"Stop scaring me," she said in an exaggerated monotone, "or I might just make wee-wee right here on the cheap carpeting."

"You think I'm bluffing?"

She put out her hands, wrists together. "Arrest me, handsome." She glanced behind him. "Don't you guys usually travel in pairs?"

"I'm here alone."

"So I gather. Can I go up now?"

Carlson carefully adjusted his glasses. "I don't think Dr. Beck killed anyone."

That stopped her.

"Don't get me wrong. There's plenty of evidence he did it. My colleagues are all convinced he's guilty. There is still a massive manhunt going on."

"Uh-huh," Shauna said with more than a hint of suspicion in her voice. "But somehow you see through all that?"

"I just think something else is going on here."

"Like what?"

"I was hoping you could tell me."

"And if I suspect that this is a trick?"

Carlson shrugged. "Not much I can do about that."

She mulled it over. "It doesn't matter," she said. "I don't know anything."

"You know where he's hiding."

"I don't."

"And if you did?"

"I wouldn't tell you. But you already know that."

"I do," Carlson said. "So I guess you won't tell me what all that talk about walking his dog was about."

She shook her head. "But you'll find out soon enough."

"He'll get hurt out there, you know. Your friend assaulted a cop. That makes it open season on him."

Shauna kept her gaze steady. "Not much I can do about that."

"No, I guess not."

"Can I ask you something?"

"Shoot," Carlson said.

"Why don't you think he's guilty?"

"I'm not sure. Lots of little things, I guess." Carlson tilted his head. "Did you know that Beck was booked on a flight to London?"

Shauna let her eyes take in the lobby, trying to buy a second or two. A man entered and smiled appreciatively at Shauna. She ignored him. "Bull," she said at last.

"I just came from the airport," Carlson continued. "The flight was booked three days ago. He was a no-show, of course. But what was really odd was that the credit card used to purchase the ticket was in the name of Laura Mills. That name mean anything to you?"

"Should it?"

"Probably not. We're still working on it, but apparently it's a pseudonym."

"For whom?"

Carlson shrugged. "Do you know a Lisa Sherman?"

"No. How does she fit in?"

"She was booked on the same flight to London. In fact, she was supposed to sit next to our boy."

"Another no-show?"

"Not exactly. She checked in. But when they called the flight, she never boarded. Weird, don't you think?"

"I don't know what to think," Shauna said.

"Unfortunately, nobody could give us an ID on Lisa Sherman. She didn't check any luggage and she used an e-ticket machine. So we started running a background check. Any guess what we found?"

Shauna shook her head.

"Nothing," Carlson replied. "It looks like another pseudonym. Do you know the name Brandon Scope?"

Shauna stiffened. "What the hell is this?"

"Dr. Beck, accompanied by a black man, visited an attorney named Peter Flannery today. Flannery defended a suspect in the murder of Brandon Scope. Dr. Beck asked him about that and about Elizabeth's role in his release. Any clue why?"

Shauna started fumbling in her purse.

"Looking for something?"

"A cigarette," she said. "You have one?"

"Sorry, no."

"Damn." She stopped, met his eye. "Why are you telling me all this?"

"I have four dead bodies. I want to know what's going on."

"Four?"

"Rebecca Schayes, Melvin Bartola, Robert Wolf—those are the two men we found at the lake. And Elizabeth Beck."

"KillRoy killed Elizabeth."

Carlson shook his head.

"What makes you so sure?"

He held up the manila folder. "This, for one."

"What is it?"

"Her autopsy file."

Shauna swallowed. Fear coursed through her, tingling her fingers. The final proof, one way or the other. She tried very hard to keep her voice steady. "Can I take a look?"

"Why?"

She didn't reply.

"And more important, why was Beck so eager to see it?"

"I don't know what you mean," she said, but the words rang hollow in her own ears and, she was sure, his.

"Was Elizabeth Beck a drug user?" Carlson asked.

The question was a total surprise. "Elizabeth? Never."

"You're sure?"

"Of course. She worked with drug addicts. That was part of her training."

"I know a lot of vice cops who enjoy a few hours with a prostitute."

"She wasn't like that. Elizabeth was no Goody Two-shoes, but drugs? Not a chance."

He held up the manila envelope again. "The tox report showed both cocaine and heroin in her system."

"Then Kellerton forced them into her."

"No," Carlson said.

"What makes you so sure?"

"There are other tests, Shauna. Tissue and hair tests. They show a pattern of use going back several months at the least."

Shauna felt her legs weaken. She slumped against a wall. "Look, Carlson, stop playing games with me. Let me see the report, okay?"

Carlson seemed to consider it. "How about this?" he said. "I'll let you see any one sheet in here. Any one piece of information. How about that?"

"What the hell is this, Carlson?"

"Good night, Shauna."

"Whoa, whoa, hold up a sec." She licked her lips. She thought about the strange emails. She thought about Beck's running from the cops. She thought about the murder of Rebecca Schayes and the toxicology report that couldn't be. All of a sudden, her convincing demonstration on digital imaging manipulation didn't seem so convincing.

"A photograph," she said. "Let me see a photograph of the victim."

Carlson smiled. "Now, that's very interesting."

"Why's that?"

"There are none in here."

"But I thought—"

"I don't understand it either," Carlson interrupted. "I've called Dr.

Harper. He was the M.E. on this one. I'm seeing if he can find out who else has signed out for this file. He's checking as we speak."

"Are you saying someone stole the photographs?"

Carlson shrugged. "Come on, Shauna. Tell me what's going on."

She almost did. She almost told him about the emails and the street cam link. But Beck had been firm. This man, for all his fancy talk, could still be the enemy. "Can I see the rest of the file?"

He moved it toward her slowly. The hell with blasé, she thought. She stepped forward and grabbed it from his hand. She tore it open and found the first sheet. As her eyes traveled down the page, a block of ice hardened in her stomach. She saw the body's height and the weight and stifled a scream.

"What?" Carlson asked.

She didn't reply.

A cell phone rang. Carlson scooped it out of his pants pocket. "Carlson."

"It's Tim Harper."

"Did you find the old logs?"

"Yes."

"Did someone else sign out Elizabeth Beck's autopsy?"

"Three years ago," Harper said. "Right after it was placed into cold storage. One person signed it out."

"Who?"

"The deceased's father. He's also a police officer. His name is Hoyt Parker."

36

Larry Gandle sat across from Griffin Scope. They were outside in the garden portico behind Scope's mansion. Night had taken serious hold, blanketing the manicured grounds. The crickets hummed an almost pretty melody, as though the super-rich could even manipulate that. Tinkling piano music spilled from the sliding glass doors. Lights from inside the house provided a modicum of illumination, casting shadows of burnt red and yellow.

Both men wore khakis. Larry wore a blue Polo shirt. Griffin had on a silk button-down from his tailor in Hong Kong. Larry waited, a beer cooling his hand. He watched the older man sitting in perfect copper-penny silhouette, facing his vast backyard, his nose tilted up slightly, his legs crossed. His right hand dangled over the arm of the chair, amber liquor swirling in his snifter.

"You have no idea where he is?" Griffin asked.

"None."

"And these two black men who rescued him?"

"I have no idea how they're involved. But Wu is working on it."

Griffin took a sip of his drink. Time trudged by, hot and sticky. "Do you really believe she's still alive?"

Larry was about to launch into a long narrative, offering evidence for and against, showing all the options and possibilities. But when he opened his mouth, he simply said, "I do."

Griffin closed his eyes. "Do you remember the day your first child was born?"

"Yes."

"Did you attend the birth?"

"I did."

"We didn't do that in our day," Griffin said. "We fathers paced in a waiting room with old magazines. I remember the nurse coming out to get me. She brought me down the hall and I still remember turning the corner and seeing Allison holding Brandon. It was the strangest feeling, Larry. Something welled up inside me so that I thought I might burst. The feeling was almost too intense, too overwhelming. You couldn't sort through or comprehend it. I assume that all fathers experience something similar."

He stopped. Larry looked over. Tears ran down the old man's cheeks, sparkling off the low light. Larry remained still.

"Perhaps the most obvious feelings on that day are joy and apprehension—apprehension in the sense that you are now responsible for this little person. But there was something else there too. I couldn't put my finger on it exactly. Not then anyway. Not until Brandon's first day of school."

Something caught in the old man's throat. He coughed a bit and now Larry could see more tears. The piano music seemed softer now. The crickets hushed as though they were listening too.

"We waited together for the school bus. I held his hand. Brandon was five years old. He looked up at me in that way children do at that age. He wore brown pants that already had a grass stain on the knee. I remember the yellow bus pulling up and the sound the door made when it opened. Then Brandon let go of my hand and started climbing up the steps. I wanted to reach out and snatch him back and take him home, but I stood there, frozen. He moved inside the bus and I heard that noise again and the door slid closed. Brandon sat by a window. I could see his face. He waved to me. I waved back and as the bus pulled away, I said to myself, 'There goes my whole world.' That yellow bus with its flimsy metal sides and its driver I didn't know from Adam chariotted away what was in effect everything to me. And at that moment, I realized what I had felt the day of his birth. Terror. Not just apprehension. Cold, stark terror. You can fear illness or old age or death. But there's nothing like that small stone of terror that sat in my belly as I watched that bus pull away. Do you understand what I'm saying?"

Larry nodded. "I think I do."

"I knew then, at that moment, that despite my best efforts, something bad could happen to him. I wouldn't always be there to take the blow. I thought about it constantly. We all do, I guess. But when it happened, when—" He stopped and finally faced Larry Gandle. "I still try to bring him back," he said. "I try to bargain with God, offering him anything and everything if he'll somehow make Brandon alive. That won't happen, of course. I understand that. But now you come here and tell me that while my son, my whole world, rots in the ground … she lives." He started shaking his head. "I can't have that, Larry. Do you understand?"

"I do," he said.

"I failed to protect him once. I won't fail again."

Griffin Scope turned back to his garden. He took another sip of his drink. Larry Gandle understood. He rose and walked back into the night.

At ten o'clock, Carlson approached the front door of 28 Goodhart Road. He didn't worry much about the late hour. He had seen downstairs lights on and the flicker of a television, but even without that, Carlson had more important worries than someone's beauty sleep.

He was about to reach for the bell when the door opened. Hoyt Parker was there. For a moment they both stood, two boxers meeting at center ring, staring each other down as the referee reiterated meaningless instructions about low blows and not punching on the break.

Carlson didn't wait for the bell. "Did your daughter take drugs?"

Hoyt Parker took it with little more than a twitch. "Why do you want to know?"

"May I come in?"

"My wife is sleeping," Hoyt said, slipping outside and closing the door behind him. "You mind if we talk out here?"

"Suit yourself."

Hoyt crossed his arms and bounced on his toes a bit. He was a burly guy in blue jeans and a T-shirt that fit less snugly ten pounds ago. Carlson knew that Hoyt Parker was a veteran cop. Cute traps and subtlety would not work here.

"Are you going to answer my question?" Carlson asked.

"Are you going to tell me why you want to know?" Hoyt replied.

Carlson decided to change tactics. "Why did you take the autopsy pictures from your daughter's file?"

"What makes you think I took them?" There was no outrage, no loud, phony denials.

"I looked at the autopsy report today," Carlson said.

"Why?"

"Pardon me?"

"My daughter has been dead for eight years. Her killer is in jail. Yet you decide to look at her autopsy report today. I'd like to know why."

This was going nowhere and going there fast. Carlson decided to give a little, put down his guard, let him wade in, see what happened. "Your son-in-law visited the county M.E. yesterday. He demanded to see his wife's file. I was hoping to find out why."

"Did he see the autopsy report?"

"No," Carlson said. "Do you know why he'd be so eager to see it?"

"No idea."

"But you seemed concerned."

"Like you, I find the behavior suspicious."

"More than that," Carlson said. "You wanted to know if he'd actually gotten his hands on it. Why?"

Hoyt shrugged.

"Are you going to tell me what you did with the autopsy pictures?"

"I don't know what you're talking about," he replied in a flat voice.

"You were the only person to sign out this report."

"And that proves what?"

"Were the photographs there when you viewed the file?"

Hoyt's eyes flickered, but there was little delay. "Yes," he said. "Yes, they were."

Carlson couldn't help but smile. "Good answer." It had been a trap, and Hoyt had avoided it. "Because if you answered no, I'd have to wonder why you didn't report it then and there, wouldn't I?"

"You have a suspicious mind, Agent Carlson."

"Uh-huh. Any thoughts on where those photos might be?"

"Probably misfiled."

"Right, sure. You don't seem very upset over it."

"My daughter's dead. Her case is closed. What's to get upset about?"

This was a waste of time. Or maybe it wasn't. Carlson wasn't getting much information, but Hoyt's demeanor spoke volumes.

"So you still think KillRoy murdered your daughter?"

"Without question."

Carlson held up the autopsy report. "Even after reading this?"

"Yes."

"The fact that so many of the wounds were postmortem doesn't trouble you?"

"It gives me comfort," he said. "It means my daughter suffered less."

"That's not what I mean. I'm talking in terms of the evidence against Kellerton."

"I don't see anything in that file that contradicts that conclusion."

"It's not consistent with the other murders."

"I disagree," Hoyt said. "What was not consistent was the strength of my daughter."

"I'm not sure I follow."

"I know that Kellerton enjoyed torturing his victims," Hoyt said. "And I know that he usually branded them while they were still alive. But we theorized that Elizabeth had tried to escape or, at the very least, fought back. The way we saw it, she forced his hand. He had to subdue her and in doing so, he ended up killing her. That explains the knife wounds on her hands. That explains why the branding was postmortem."

"I see." A surprise left hook. Carlson tried to keep on his feet. It was a good answer—a hell of a good answer. It made sense. Even the smallest victims can make plenty of trouble. His explanation made all the apparent inconsistencies wonderfully consistent. But there were still problems. "So how do you explain the tox report?"

"Irrelevant," Hoyt said. "It's like asking a rape victim about her sexual history. It doesn't matter if my daughter was a teetotaler or a crack fiend."

"Which was she?"

"Irrelevant," he repeated.

"Nothing's irrelevant in a murder investigation. You know that."

Hoyt took a step closer. "Be careful," he said.

"You threatening me?"

"Not at all. I'm just warning you that you shouldn't be so quick to victimize my daughter a second time."

They stood there. The final bell had sounded. They were now waiting for a decision that would be unsatisfactory no matter how the judges leaned.

"If that's all," Hoyt said.

Carlson nodded and took a step back. Parker reached for the doorknob.

"Hoyt?"

Hoyt turned back around.

"So there's no misunderstanding," Carlson said. "I don't believe a word you just said. We clear?"

"Crystal," Hoyt said.

37

When Shauna arrived at the apartment, she collapsed onto her favorite spot on the couch. Linda sat next to her and patted her lap. Shauna laid her head down. She closed her eyes as Linda caressed her hair.

"Is Mark okay?" Shauna asked.

"Yes," Linda said. "Do you mind telling me where you were?"

"Long story."

"I'm only sitting here waiting to hear about my brother."

"He called me," Shauna said.

"What?"

"He's safe."

"Thank God."

"And he didn't kill Rebecca."

"I know that."

Shauna turned her head to look up. Linda was blinking her eyes. "He's going to be okay," Shauna said.

Linda nodded, turned away.

"What is it?"

"I took those pictures," Linda said.

Shauna sat up.

"Elizabeth came to my office. She was hurt pretty badly. I wanted her to go to a hospital. She said no. She just wanted to make a record of it."

"It wasn't a car accident?"

Linda shook her head.

"Who hurt her?"

"She made me promise not to tell."

"Eight years ago," Shauna said. "Tell me."

"It's not that simple."

"Like hell it's not." Shauna hesitated. "Why would she go to you anyway? And how can you think of protecting ..." Her voice faded away. She looked at Linda hard. Linda didn't flinch, but Shauna thought about what Carlson had told her downstairs.

"Brandon Scope," Shauna said softly.

Linda didn't reply.

"He's the one who beat her up. Oh Christ, no wonder she came to you. She wanted to keep it a secret. Me or Rebecca, we would have made her go to the police. But not you."

"She made me promise," Linda said.

"And you just accepted that?"

"What was I supposed to do?"

"Drag her ass down to the police station."

"Well, we can't all be as brave and strong as you, Shauna."

"Don't give me that crap."

"She didn't want to go," Linda insisted. "She said that she needed more time. That she didn't have enough proof yet."

"Proof of what?"

"That he assaulted her, I guess. I don't know. She wouldn't listen to me. I couldn't just force her."

"Oh right—and that was likely."

"What the hell does that mean?"

"You were involved in a charity financed by his family with his face at the helm," Shauna said. "What would happen if it got out that he beat up a woman?"

"Elizabeth made me promise."

"And you were only too happy to keep your mouth shut, right? You wanted to protect your damn charity."

"That's not fair—"

"You put it over her well-being."

"Do you know how much good we do?" Linda shouted. "Do you know how many people we help?"

"On the blood of Elizabeth Beck," Shauna said.

Linda slapped her across the face. The slap stung. They stared at each other, breathing hard. "I wanted to tell," Linda said. "She wouldn't let me. Maybe I was weak, I don't know. But don't you dare say something like that."

"And when Elizabeth was kidnapped at the lake—what did you think, for crying out loud?"

"I thought it might be connected. I went to Elizabeth's father. I told him what I knew."

"What did he say?"

"He thanked me and said he knew about it. He also told me not to say anything because the situation was delicate. And then when it became clear that KillRoy was the murderer—"

"You decided to keep silent."

"Brandon Scope was dead. What good would dragging his name through the mud do?"

The phone rang. Linda reached for it. She said hello, paused, and then she handed the phone to Shauna. "For you."

Shauna didn't look at her as she took the receiver. "Hello?"

"Meet me down at my office," Hester Crimstein told her.

"Why the hell should I?"

"I'm not big on apologies, Shauna. So let's just agree that I'm a big fat idiot and move on. Grab a taxi and come down here. We've got an innocent man to rescue."

Assistant District Attorney Lance Fein stormed into Crimstein's conference room looking like a sleep-deprived weasel on too many amphetamines. The two homicide detectives Dimonte and Krinsky followed in his wake. All three had faces taut as piano wire.

Hester and Shauna stood on the other side of the table. "Gentlemen," Hester said with a sweep of her hand, "please have a seat."

Fein eyed her, then shot a look of pure disgust at Shauna. "I'm not here for you to jerk me around."

"No, I'm sure you do enough of that in the privacy of your own home," Hester said. "Sit."

"If you know where he is—"

"Sit, Lance. You're giving me a headache."

Everyone sat. Dimonte put his snakeskin boots up on the table. Hester took both hands and knocked them off, never letting her smile falter. "We are here, gentlemen, with one aim: saving your careers. So let's get to it, shall we?"

"I want to know—"

"Shh, Lance. I'm talking here. Your job is to listen and maybe nod and say things like 'Yes, ma'am' and 'Thank you, ma'am.' Otherwise, well, you're toast."

Lance Fein gave her the eye. "You're the one helping a fugitive escape justice, Hester."

"You're sexy when you talk tough, Lance. Actually, you're not. Listen up, okay, because I don't want to have to repeat myself. I'm going to do you a favor, Lance. I'm not going to let you look like a total idiot on this. An idiot, okay, nothing to be done about that, but maybe, if you listen carefully, not a total idiot. You with me? Good. First off, I understand you have a definitive time of death on Rebecca Schayes now. Midnight, give or take a half hour. We pretty clear on that?"

"So?"

Hester looked at Shauna. "You want to tell him?"

"No, that's okay."

"But you're the one who did all the hard work."

Fein said, "Cut the crap, Crimstein."

The door behind them opened. Hester's secretary brought the sheets of paper over to her boss along with a small cassette tape. "Thank you, Cheryl."

"No problem."

"You can go home now. Come in late tomorrow."

"Thanks."

Cheryl left. Hester took out her half-moon reading glasses. She slipped them on and started reading the pages.

"I'm getting tired of this, Hester."

"You like dogs, Lance?"

"What?"

"Dogs. I'm not a big fan of them myself. But this one ... Shauna, you have that photograph?"

"Right here." Shauna held up a large photograph of Chloe for all to see. "She's a bearded collie."

"Isn't she cute, Lance?"

Lance Fein stood. Krinsky stood too. Dimonte didn't budge. "I've had enough."

"You leave now," Hester said, "and this dog will piss all over your career like it's a fire hydrant."

"What the hell are you talking about?"

She handed two of the sheets to Fein. "That dog proves Beck didn't do it. He was at Kinko's last night. He entered with the dog. Caused quite a ruckus, I understand. Here are four statements from independent witnesses positively IDing Beck. He rented some computer time while there—more precisely, from four past midnight to twelve twenty-three a.m., according to their billing records." She grinned. "Here, fellas. Copies for all of you."

"You expect me to take these at face value?"

"Not all. Please, by all means, follow up."

Hester tossed a copy at Krinsky and another at Dimonte. Krinsky gathered it up and asked if he could use a phone.

"Sure," Crimstein said. "But if you're going to make any toll calls, kindly charge it to the department." She gave him a sickly sweet smile. "Thanks so much."

Fein read the sheet, his complexion turning to something in the ash-gray family.

"Thinking about expanding the time of death a bit?" Hester asked. "Feel free, but guess what? There was bridge construction that night. He's covered."

Fein was actually quaking. He muttered something under his breath that might have rhymed with "witch."

"Now, now, Lance." Hester Crimstein made a tsk-tsk noise. "You should be thanking me."

"What?"

"Just think of how I could have sandbagged you. There you are, all those cameras, all that delightful media coverage, ready to announce the big arrest of this vicious murderer. You put on your best power tie, make that big speech about keeping the streets safe, about what a team effort the capture of this animal was, though really you should be getting all the credit. The flashbulbs start going off. You smile and call the reporters by their first names, all the while imagining your big oak desk in the governor's mansion—and then bam, I lower the boom. I give the media this airtight alibi. Imagine, Lance. Man, oh, man, do you owe me, or what?"

Fein shot daggers with his eyes. "He still assaulted a police officer."

"No, Lance, he didn't. Think spin, my friend. Fact: You, Assistant District Attorney Lance Fein, jumped to the wrong conclusion. You hunted down an innocent man with your storm troopers—and not just an innocent man, but a doctor who chooses to work for lower pay with the poor instead of in the lucrative private sector." She sat back, smiling. "Oh, this is good, let me see. So while using dozens of city cops at Lord-knows-what expense, all with guns drawn and chasing down this innocent man, one officer, young and beefy and gung-ho, traps him in an alleyway and starts pounding on him. Nobody else is in sight, so this young cop takes it upon himself to make this scared man pay. Poor, persecuted Dr. David Beck, a widower I might add, did nothing but lash out in self-defense."

"That'll never sell."

"Sure it will, Lance. I don't want to sound immodest, but who's better at spin than yours truly? And wait, you haven't heard me wax philosophical on the comparisons between this case and Richard Jewell, or on the overzealousness of the D.A.'s office, or how they were so eager to pin this on Dr. David Beck, hero to the downtrodden, that they obviously planted evidence at his residence."

"Planted?" Fein was apoplectic. "Are you out of your mind?"

"Come on, Lance, we know Dr. David Beck couldn't have done it. We have a proof-positive alibi in the testimony of four—ah, hell, we'll dig up more than four before this is through—independent, unbiased witnesses that he didn't do it. So how did all that evidence get there? You, Mr. Fein, and your storm troopers. Mark Fuhrman will look like Mahatma Gandhi by the time I'm through with you."

Fein's hands tightened into fists. He gulped down a few breaths and made himself lean back. "Okay," he began slowly. "Assuming this alibi checks out—"

"Oh it will."

"*Assuming* it does, what do you want?"

"Well now, that's an awfully good question. You're in a bind, Lance. You arrest him, you look like an idiot. You call off the arrest, you look like an idiot. I'm not sure I see any way around it." Hester Crimstein stood, started pacing as though working a closing. "I've looked into this and I've thought about it and I think I've found a way to minimize the damage. Care to hear it?"

Fein glared some more. "I'm listening."

"You've done one thing smart in all this. Just one, but maybe it's enough. You've kept your mug away from the media. That's because, I imagine, it would be a tad embarrassing trying to explain how this doctor escaped your dragnet. But that's good. Everything that has been reported can be blamed on anonymous leaks. So here's what you do, Lance. You call a press conference. You tell them that the leaks are false, that Dr. Beck is being sought as a material witness, nothing more than that. You do not suspect him in this crime—in fact, you're certain he didn't commit it—but you learned that he was one of the last people to see the victim alive and wanted to speak with him."

"That'll never fly."

"Oh it'll fly. Maybe not straight and true, but it'll stay aloft. The key will be me, Lance. I owe you one because my boy ran. So I, the enemy of the D.A.'s office, will back you up. I'll tell the media how you cooperated with us, how you made sure that my client's rights were not abused, that Dr. Beck and I wholeheartedly support your investigation and look forward to working with you."

Fein kept still.

"It's like I said before, Lance. I can spin for you or I can spin against you."

"And in return?"

"You drop all these silly assault and resisting charges."

"No way."

Hester motioned him toward the door. "See you in the funny pages."

Fein's shoulders slumped ever so slightly. His voice, when he spoke, was soft. "If we agree," he said, "your boy will cooperate? He'll answer all my questions?"

"Please, Lance, don't try to pretend you're in any condition to negotiate. I've laid out the deal. Take it—or take your chances with the press. Your choice. The clock is ticking." She bounced her index finger back and forth and made a tick-tock sound.

Fein looked at Dimonte. Dimonte chewed his toothpick some more. Krinsky got off the phone and nodded at Fein. Fein in turn nodded at Hester. "So how do we handle this?"

38

I woke up and lifted my head and almost screamed. My muscles were two steps beyond stiff and sore; I ached in parts of my body I didn't know I had. I tried to swing my legs out of bed. Swing was a bad idea. A very bad idea. Slow. That was the ticket this morning.

My legs hurt most, reminding me that despite my quasi-marathon of yesterday, I was pathetically out of shape. I tried to roll over. The tender spots where the Asian guy had attacked felt as though I'd ripped sutures. My body longed for a couple of Percodans, but I knew that they would put me on Queer Street, and that's not where I wanted to be right now.

I checked my watch. Six a.m. It was time for me to call Hester back. She picked up on the first ring.

"It worked," she said. "You're free."

I felt only mild relief.

"What are you going to do?" she asked.

A hell of a question. "I'm not sure."

"Hold on a sec." I heard another voice in the background. "Shauna wants to talk to you."

There was a fumbling sound as the phone changed hands, and then Shauna said, "We need to talk."

Shauna, never one for idle pleasantries or subtleties, still sounded uncharacteristically strained and maybe even—hard to imagine—scared. My heart started doing a little giddyap.

"What is it?"

"This isn't for the phone," she said.

"I can be at your place in an hour."

"I haven't told Linda about, uh, you know."

"Maybe it's time to," I said.

"Yeah, okay." Then she added with surprising tenderness, "Love you, Beck."

"Love you too."

I half crouched, half crawled toward the shower. Furniture helped support my stiff-legged stumble and keep me upright. I stayed under the spray until the hot water ran out. It helped ease the soreness, but not a lot.

Tyrese found me a purple velour sweat suit from the Eighties Al Sharpton collection. I almost asked for a big gold medallion.

"Where you gonna go?" he asked me.

"To my sister's for now."

"And then?"

"To work, I guess."

Tyrese shook his head.

"What?" I asked.

"You up against some bad dudes, Doc."

"Yeah, I kinda put that together."

"Bruce Lee ain't gonna let this slide."

I thought about that. He was right. Even if I wanted to, I couldn't just go home and wait for Elizabeth to make contact again. In the first place, I'd had enough with the passive; gentle repose simply was not on the Beck agenda anymore. But equally important, the men in that van were not about to forget the matter and let me go merrily on my way.

"I watch your back, Doc. Brutus too. Till this is over."

I was about to say something brave like "I can't ask you to do that" or "You have your own life to lead," but when you thought about it, they could either do this or deal drugs. Tyrese wanted to help—perhaps even needed to help—and let's face it, I needed him. I could warn him off, remind him of the danger, but he understood these particular perils far better than I did. So in the end, I just accepted with a nod.

Carlson got the call from the National Tracing Center earlier than he expected.

"We were able to run it already," Donna said.

"How?"

"Heard of IBIS?"

"Yeah, a little." He knew that IBIS stood for Integrated Ballistic Identification System, a new computer program that the Bureau of Alcohol, Tobacco and Firearms used to store bullet and shell casings. Part of the ATF's new Ceasefire program.

"We don't even need the original bullet anymore," she went on. "They just had to send us the scanned images. We can digitize and match them right on the screen."

"And?"

"You were right, Nick," she said. "It's a match."

Carlson disconnected and placed another call. When the man on the other end picked up, he asked, "Where's Dr. Beck?"

39

Brutus hooked up with us on the sidewalk. I said, "Good morning." He said nothing. I still hadn't heard the man speak. I slid into the backseat. Tyrese sat next to me and grinned. Last night he had killed a man. True, he had done so in defense of my life, but from his casual demeanor, I wasn't even sure he remembered pulling the trigger. I more than anyone should understand what he was going through, but I didn't. I'm not big on moral absolutes. I see the grays. I make the calls. Elizabeth had a clearer view of her moral compass. She would be horrified that a life had been lost. It wouldn't have mattered to her that the man was trying to kidnap, torture, and probably kill me. Or maybe it would. I don't really know anymore. The hard truth is, I didn't know everything about her. And she certainly didn't know everything about me.

My medical training insists that I never make that sort of moral call. It's a simple rule of triage: The most seriously injured gets treated first. It doesn't matter who they are or what they've done. You treat the most grievously wounded. That's a nice theory, and I understand the need for such thinking. But if, say, my nephew Mark were rushed in with a stab wound and some serial pedophile who stabbed him came in at the same time with a life-threatening bullet in the brain, well, come on. You make the call, and in your heart of hearts, you know that the call is an easy one.

You might argue that I'm nesting myself on an awfully slippery slope. I would agree with you, though I might counter that most of life is lived out there. The problem was, there were repercussions when you lived in the grays—not just theoretical ones that taint your soul, but the brick-and-mortar ones, the unforeseeable destruction that such choices leave behind. I wondered what would have happened if I had told the truth right from the get-go. And it scared the hell out of me.

"Kinda quiet, Doc."

"Yeah," I said.

Brutus dropped me off in front of Linda and Shauna's apartment on Riverside Drive.

"We'll be around the corner," Tyrese said. "You need anything, you know my number."

"Right."

"You got the Glock?"

"Yes."

Tyrese put a hand on my shoulder. "Them or you, Doc," he said. "Just keep pulling the trigger."

No grays there.

I stepped out of the car. Mothers and nannies ambled by, pushing complicated baby strollers that fold and shift and rock and play songs and lean back and lean forward and hold more than one kid, plus an assortment of diapers, wipes, Gerber snacks, juice boxes (for the older sibling), change of clothing, bottles, even car first-aid kits. I knew all this from my own practice (being on Medicaid did not preclude one from affording the high-end Peg Perego strollers), and I found this spectacle of bland normalcy cohabiting in the same realm as my recent ordeal to be something of an elixir.

I turned back toward the building. Linda and Shauna were already running toward me. Linda got there first. She wrapped her arms around me. I hugged her back. It felt nice.

"You're okay?" Linda said.

"I'm fine," I said.

My assurances did not stop Linda from repeating the question several more times in several different ways. Shauna stopped a few feet away. I caught her eye over my sister's shoulder. Shauna wiped tears from her eyes. I smiled at her.

We continued the hugs and kisses through the elevator ride. Shauna was less effusive than usual, staying a bit out of the mix. An outsider might claim that this made sense, that Shauna was giving the sister and brother some space during this tender reunion. That outsider wouldn't know Shauna from Cher. Shauna was wonderfully consistent. She was prickly, demanding, funny, bighearted, and loyal beyond all reason. She never put on masks or pretenses. If your thesaurus had an antonym section and you looked up the phrase "shrinking violet," her lush image would stare back at you. Shauna lived life in your face. She wouldn't take a step back if smacked across the mouth with a lead pipe.

Something inside me started to tingle.

When we reached the apartment, Linda and Shauna exchanged a glance. Linda's arm slipped off me. "Shauna wants to talk to you alone first," she said. "I'll be in the kitchen. You want a sandwich?"

"Thanks," I said.

Linda kissed me and gave me one more squeeze, as though making sure I was still there and of substance. She hurried out of the room. I looked over at Shauna. She kept her distance. I put out my hands in a "Well?" gesture.

"Why did you run?" Shauna asked.

"I got another email," I said.

"At that Bigfoot account?"

"Yes."

"Why did it come in so late?"

"She was using code," I said. "It just took me time to figure it out."

"What kind of code?"

I explained about the Bat Lady and the Teenage Sex Poodles.

When I finished, she said, "That's why you were using the computer at Kinko's? You figured it out during your walk with Chloe?"

"Yes."

"What did the email say exactly?"

I couldn't figure out why Shauna was asking all these questions. On top of what I've already said, Shauna was strictly a big-picture person. Details were not her forte; they just muddied and confused. "She wanted me to meet her at Washington Square Park at five yesterday," I said. "She warned me that I'd be followed. And then she told me that no matter what, she loved me."

"And that's why you ran?" she asked. "So you wouldn't miss the meeting?"

I nodded. "Hester said I wouldn't get bail until midnight at the earliest."

"Did you get to the park in time?"

"Yes."

Shauna took a step closer to me. "And?"

"She never showed."

"And yet you're still convinced that Elizabeth sent you that email?"

"There's no other explanation," I said.

She smiled when I said that.

"What?" I asked.

"You remember my friend Wendy Petino?"

"Fellow model," I said. "Flaky as a Greek pastry."

Shauna smiled at the description. "She took me to dinner once with her"—she made quote marks with her fingers—"spiritual guru. She claimed that he could read minds and tell the future and all that. He was helping her communicate with her dead mother. Wendy's mother had committed suicide when she was six."

I let her go on, not interrupting with the obvious "what's the point?" Shauna was taking her time here, but I knew that she'd get to it eventually.

"So we finish dinner. The waiter serves us coffee. Wendy's guru—he had some name like Omay—he's staring at me with these bright, inquisitive eyes, you know the type, and he hands me the bit about how he senses—that's how he says it, senses—that maybe I'm a skeptic and that I should speak my mind. You know me. I tell him he's full of shit and I'm tired of him stealing my friend's money. Omay doesn't get angry, of course, which really pisses me off. Anyway, he hands me a little card and tells me to write anything I want on it—something significant about my life, a date, a lover's initials, whatever I wanted. I check the card. It looks like a normal white card, but I still ask if I can use one of my own. He tells me to suit myself. I take out a business card and flip it over. He hands me a pen, but again I decide to use my own—in case it's a trick pen or something, what do I know, right? He has no problem with that either. So I write down your name. Just Beck. He takes the card. I'm watching his hand for a switch or whatever, but he just passes the card to Wendy. He tells her to hold it. He grabs my hand. He closes his eyes and starts shaking like he's having a seizure and I swear I feel something course through me. Then Omay opens his eyes and says, 'Who's Beck?' "

She sat down on the couch. I did likewise.

"Now, I know people have good sleight of hand and all that, but I was there. I watched him up close. And I almost bought it. Omay had special abilities. Like you said, there was no other explanation. Wendy sat there with this satisfied smile plastered on her face. I couldn't figure it out."

"He did research on you," I said. "He knew about our friendship."

"No offense, but wouldn't he guess I'd put my own son's name or maybe Linda's? How would he know I'd pick you?"

She had a point. "So you're a believer now?"

"Almost, Beck. I said I almost bought it. Ol' Omay was right. I'm a skeptic. Maybe it all pointed to him being psychic, except I knew he wasn't. Because there are no such things as psychics—just like there are no such things as ghosts." She stopped. Not exactly subtle, my dear Shauna.

"So I did some research," she went on. "The good thing about being a famous model is that you can call anyone and they'll talk to you. So I called this illusionist I'd seen on Broadway a couple of years ago. He heard the story and then he laughed. I said what's so funny. He asked me a question: Did this guru do this after dinner? I was surprised. What the hell could that have to do with it? But I said yes, how did you know? He asked if we had coffee. Again I said yes. Did he take his black? One more time I said yes." Shauna was smiling now. "Do you know how he did it, Beck?"

I shook my head. "No clue."

"When he passed the card to Wendy, it went over his coffee cup. Black coffee, Beck. It reflects like a mirror. That's how he saw what I'd written. It was just a dumb parlor trick. Simple, right? Pass the card over your cup of black coffee and it's like passing it over a mirror. And I almost believed him. You understand what I'm saying here?"

"Sure," I said. "You think I'm as gullible as Flaky Wendy."

"Yes and no. See, part of Omay's con is the want, Beck. Wendy falls for it because she wants to believe in all that mumbo-jumbo."

"And I want to believe Elizabeth is alive?"

"More than any dying man in a desert wants to find an oasis," she said. "But that's not really my point either."

"Then what is?"

"I learned that just because you can't see any other explanation doesn't mean that one doesn't exist. It just means you can't see it."

I leaned back and crossed my legs. I watched her. She turned away from my gaze, something she never does. "What's going on here, Shauna?"

She wouldn't face me.

"You're not making any sense," I said.

"I think I was pretty damn clear—"

"You know what I mean. This isn't like you. On the phone you said you needed to talk to me. Alone. And for what? To tell me that my dead wife is, after all, still dead?" I shook my head. "I don't buy it."

Shauna didn't react.

"Tell me," I said.

She turned back. "I'm scared," she said in a tone that made the hair on the back of my neck stand up.

"Of what?"

The answer didn't come right away. I could hear Linda rustling around in the kitchen, the tinkling of plates and glasses, the sucking pop when she opened the refrigerator. "That long warning I just gave you," Shauna finally continued. "That was as much for me as for you."

"I don't understand."

"I've seen something." Her voice died out. She took a deep breath and tried again. "I've seen something that my rational mind can't explain away. Just like in my story about Omay. I know there has to be another explanation, but I can't find it." Her hands started moving, her fingers fidgeting with buttons, pulling imaginary threads off her suit. Then she said it: "I'm starting to believe you, Beck. I think maybe Elizabeth is still alive."

My heart leapt into my throat.

She rose quickly. "I'm going to mix a mimosa. Join me?"

I shook my head.

She looked surprised. "You sure you don't want—"

"Tell me what you saw, Shauna."

"Her autopsy file."

I almost fell over. It took me a little time to find my voice. "How?"

"Do you know Nick Carlson from the FBI?"

"He questioned me," I said.

"He thinks you're innocent."

"Didn't sound that way to me."

"He does now. When all that evidence started pointing at you, he thought it was all too neat."

"He told you that?"

"Yes."

"And you believed him?"

"I know it sounds naïve, but yeah, I believed him."

I trusted Shauna's judgment. If she said that Carlson was on the level, he was either a wonderful liar or he'd seen through the frame-up. "I still don't understand," I said. "What does that have to do with the autopsy?"

"Carlson came to me. He wanted to know what you were up to. I wouldn't tell him. But he was tracking your movements. He knew that you asked to see Elizabeth's autopsy file. He wondered why. So he called the coroner's office and got the file. He brought it with him. To see if I could help him out on that."

"He showed it to you?"

She nodded.

My throat was dry. "Did you see the autopsy photos?"

"There weren't any, Beck."

"What?"

"Carlson thinks someone stole them."

"Who?"

She shrugged. "The only other person to sign out the file was Elizabeth's father."

Hoyt. It all circled back to him. I looked at her. "Did you see any of the report?"

Her nod was more tentative this time.

"And?"

"It said Elizabeth had a drug problem, Beck. Not just that there were drugs in her system. He said that the reports showed the abuse was long-term."

"Impossible," I said.

"Maybe, maybe not. That alone wouldn't be enough to convince me. People can hide drug abuse. It's not likely, but neither is her being alive. Maybe the tests were wrong or inconclusive. Something. There are explanations, right? It can somehow be explained away."

I licked my lips. "So what couldn't be?" I asked.

"Her height and weight," Shauna said. "Elizabeth was listed as five seven and under a hundred pounds."

Another sock in the gut. My wife was five four and closer to a hundred fifteen pounds. "Not even close," I said.

"Not even."

"She's alive, Shauna."

"Maybe," she allowed, and her gaze flicked toward the kitchen. "But there's something more."

Shauna turned and called out Linda's name. Linda stepped into the doorway and stayed there. She looked suddenly small in her apron. She wrung her hands and wiped them on the apron front. I watched my sister, puzzled.

"What's going on?" I said.

Linda started speaking. She told me about the photographs, how Elizabeth had come to her to take them, how she'd been only too happy to keep her secret about Brandon Scope. She didn't sugarcoat or offer explanations, but then again, maybe she didn't have to. She stood there and poured it all out and waited for the inevitable blow. I listened with my head down. I couldn't face her, but I easily forgave. We all have our blind spots. All of us.

I wanted to hug her and tell her that I understood, but I couldn't quite pull it off. When she'd finished, I merely nodded and said, "Thanks for telling me."

My words were meant to be a dismissal. Linda understood. Shauna and I sat there in silence for almost a full minute.

"Beck?"

"Elizabeth's father has been lying to me," I said.

She nodded.

"I've got to talk to him."

"He didn't tell you anything before."

True enough, I thought.

"Do you think it'll be different this time?"

I absentmindedly patted the Glock in my waistband. "Maybe," I said.

Carlson greeted me in the corridor. "Dr. Beck?" he said.

Across town at the same time, the district attorney's office held a press conference. The reporters were naturally skeptical of Fein's convoluted explanation (vis-à-vis me), and there was a lot of backpedaling and finger-pointing and that sort of thing. But all that seemed to do was confuse the issue. Confusion helps. Confusion leads to lengthy reconstruction and clarification and exposition and several other "tions." The press and their public prefer a simpler narrative.

It probably would have been a rougher ride for Mr. Fein, but by coincidence, the D.A.'s office used this very same press conference to release indictments against several high-ranking members of the mayor's administration along with a hint that the "tentacles of corruption"—their phrase—may even reach the big man's office. The media, an entity with the collective attention span of a Twinkie-filled two-year-old, immediately focused on this shiny new toy, kicking the old one under the bed.

Carlson stepped toward me. "I'd like to ask you a few questions."

"Not now," I said.

"Your father owned a gun," he said.

His words rooted me to the floor. "What?"

"Stephen Beck, your father, purchased a Smith and Wesson thirty-eight. The registration showed that he bought it several months before he died."

"What does that have to do with anything?"

"I assume you inherited the weapon. Am I correct?"

"I'm not talking to you." I pressed the elevator button.

"We have it," he said. I turned, stunned. "It was in Sarah Goodhart's safety-deposit box. With the pictures."

I couldn't believe what I was hearing. "Why didn't you tell me this before?"

Carlson gave me a crooked smile.

"Oh right, I was the bad guy back then," I said. Then, making a point of turning away, I added, "I don't see the relevance."

"Sure you do."

I pressed the elevator button again.

"You went to see Peter Flannery," Carlson continued. "You asked him about the murder of Brandon Scope. I'd like to know why."

I pressed the call button and held it down. "Did you do something to the elevators?"

"Yes. Why did you see Peter Flannery?"

My mind made a few quick deductions. An idea—a dangerous thing under the best of circumstances—came to me. Shauna trusted this man. Maybe I could too. A little anyway. Enough. "Because you and I have the same suspicions," I said.

"What's that?"

"We're both wondering if KillRoy murdered my wife."

Carlson folded his arms. "And what does Peter Flannery have to do with that?"

"You were tracking down my movements, right?"

"Yes."

"I decided to do the same with Elizabeth's. From eight years ago. Flannery's initials and phone number were in her day planner."

"I see," Carlson said. "And what did you learn from Mr. Flannery?"

"Nothing," I lied. "It was a dead end."

"Oh, I don't think so," Carlson said.

"What makes you say that?"

"Are you familiar with how ballistic tests work?"

"I've seen them on TV."

"Put simply, every gun makes a unique imprint on the bullet it fires. Scratches, grooves—unique to that weapon. Like fingerprints."

"That much I know."

"After your visit to Flannery's office, I had our people run a specific ballistic match on the thirty-eight we found in Sarah Goodhart's safety-deposit box. Know what I found?"

I shook my head, but I knew.

Carlson took his time before he said, "Your father's gun, the one you inherited, killed Brandon Scope."

A door opened and a mother and her teen son stepped into the hall. The teen was in mid-whine, his shoulder slumped in adolescent defiance. His mother's lips were pursed, her head held high in the don't-wanna-hear-it position. They came toward the elevator. Carlson said something into a walkie-talkie. We both stepped away from the elevator bank, our eyes locked in a silent challenge.

"Agent Carlson, do you think I'm a killer?"

"Truth?" he said. "I'm not sure anymore."

I found his response curious. "You're aware, of course, that I'm not obligated to speak to you. In fact, I can call Hester Crimstein right now and nix everything you're trying to do here."

He bristled, but he didn't bother denying it. "What's your point?"

"Give me two hours."

"To what?"

"Two hours," I repeated.

He thought about it. "Under one condition."

"What?"

"Tell me who Lisa Sherman is."

That genuinely puzzled me. "I don't know the name."

"You and she were supposed to fly out of the country last night."

Elizabeth.

"I don't know what you're talking about," I said. The elevator dinged. The door slid open. The pursed-lips mom and her slumped adolescent stepped inside. She looked back at us. I signaled for her to hold the door.

"Two hours," I said.

Carlson nodded grudgingly. I hopped into the elevator.

40

"You're late!" the photographer, a tiny man with a fake French accent, shouted at Shauna. "And you look like—*comment dit-on*?—like something flushed through the *toilette*."

"Up yours, Frédéric," Shauna snapped back, not knowing or caring if that was his name. "Where you from anyway, Brooklyn?"

He threw his hands up. "I cannot work like this!"

Aretha Feldman, Shauna's agent, hurried over. "Don't worry, François. Our makeup man will work magic on her. She always looks like hell when she arrives. We'll be right back." Aretha grabbed Shauna's elbow hard but never let up the smile. To Shauna, sotto voce, she said, "What the hell is wrong with you?"

"I don't need this crap."

"Don't play prima donna with me."

"I had a rough night, okay?"

"Not okay. Get in that makeup chair."

The makeup artist gasped in horror when he saw Shauna. "What are those bags under your eyes?" he cried. "Are we doing a shoot for Samsonite luggage now?"

"Ha-ha." Shauna moved toward the chair.

"Oh," Aretha said. "This came for you." She held an envelope in her hand.

Shauna squinted. "What is it?"

"Beats me. A messenger service dropped it off ten minutes ago. Said it was urgent."

She handed the envelope to Shauna. Shauna took it in one hand and flipped it over. She looked at the familiar scrawl on the front of the envelope—just the word "Shauna"—and felt her stomach clench.

Still staring at the handwriting, Shauna said, "Give me a second."

"Now's not the time—"

"A second."

The makeup artist and agent stepped away. Shauna slit open the seal. A blank white card with the same familiar handwriting fell out. Shauna picked it up. The note was brief: "Go to the ladies' room."

Shauna tried to keep her breath even. She stood.

"What's wrong?" Aretha said.

"I have to pee," she said, the calmness in her voice surprising even her. "Where's the head?"

"Down the hall on the left."

"I'll be right back."

Two minutes later, Shauna pushed the bathroom door. It didn't budge. She knocked. "It's me," she said. And waited.

A few seconds later, she heard the bolt slide back. More silence. Shauna took a deep breath and pushed again. The door swung open. She stepped onto the tile and stopped cold. There, across the room, standing in front of the near stall, was a ghost.

Shauna choked back a cry.

The brunette wig, the weight loss, the wire-framed spectacles—none of it altered the obvious.

"Elizabeth ..."

"Lock the door, Shauna."

Shauna obeyed without thought. When she turned around, she took a step toward her old friend. Elizabeth shrunk back.

"Please, we don't have much time."

For perhaps the first time in her life, Shauna was at a loss for words.

"You have to convince Beck I'm dead," Elizabeth said.

"A little late for that."

Her gaze swept the room as though looking for an escape route. "I made a mistake coming back. A stupid, stupid mistake. I can't stay. You have to tell him—"

"We saw the autopsy, Elizabeth," Shauna said. "There's no putting this genie back in the bottle."

Elizabeth's eyes closed.

Shauna said, "What the hell happened?"

"It was a mistake to come here."

"Yeah, you said that already."

Elizabeth started chewing on her lower lip. Then: "I have to go."

"You can't," Shauna said.

"What?"

"You can't run away again."

"If I stay, he'll die."

"He's already dead," Shauna said.

"You don't understand."

"Don't have to. If you leave him again, he won't survive. I've been waiting eight years for him to get over you. That's what's supposed to happen, you know. Wounds heal. Life goes on. But not for Beck." She took a step toward Elizabeth. "I can't let you run away again."

There were tears in all four eyes.

"I don't care why you left," Shauna said, inching closer. "I just care that you're back."

"I can't stay," she said weakly.

"You have to."

"Even if it means his death?"

"Yeah," Shauna said without hesitation. "Even if. And you know what I'm saying is true. That's why you're here. You know you can't leave again. And you know I won't let you."

Shauna took another step.

"I'm so tired of running," Elizabeth said softly.

"I know."

"I don't know what to do anymore."

"Me neither. But running isn't an option this time. Explain it to him, Elizabeth. Make him understand."

Elizabeth lifted her head. "You know how much I love him?"

"Yeah," Shauna said, "I do."

"I can't let him get hurt."

Shauna said, "Too late."

They stood now, a foot apart. Shauna wanted to reach out and hold her, but she stayed still.

"Do you have a number to reach him?" Elizabeth said.

"Yeah, he gave me a cell—"

"Tell him Dolphin. I'll meet him there tonight."

"I don't know what the hell that means."

Elizabeth quickly slid past her, peeked out the bathroom door, slithered through it. "He'll understand," she said. And then she was gone.

41

As usual, Tyrese and I sat in the backseat. The morning sky was a charcoal ash, the color of tombstone. I directed Brutus where to turn off after we crossed the George Washington Bridge. Behind his sunglasses, Tyrese studied my face. Finally he asked, "Where we going?"

"My in-laws."

Tyrese waited for me to say more.

"He's a city cop," I added.

"What's his name?"

"Hoyt Parker."

Brutus smiled. Tyrese did likewise.

"You know him?"

"Never worked with the man myself, but, yeah, I heard the name."

"What do you mean, worked with the man?"

Tyrese waved me off. We hit the town border. I had gone through several surreal experiences over the past three days—chalk "driving through my old neighborhood with two drug dealers in a car with tinted windows" as another. I gave Brutus a few more directions before we pulled up to the memory-laden split-level on Goodhart.

I stepped out. Brutus and Tyrese sped off. I made it to the door and listened to the long chime. The clouds grew darker. A lightning bolt ripped the sky at the seam. I pressed the chime again. Pain traveled down my arm. I still ached all over hell from yesterday's combination of torture and overexertion. For a moment, I let myself wonder what would have happened if Tyrese and Brutus hadn't shown up. Then I shoved that thought away hard.

Finally I heard Hoyt say, "Who is it?"

"Beck," I said.

"It's open."

I reached for the knob. My hand stopped an inch before touching the brass. Weird. I had visited here countless times in my life, but I never remembered Hoyt asking who it was at the door. He was one of the guys who preferred direct confrontation. No hiding in the bushes for Hoyt Parker. He feared nothing, and dammit, he would prove it every step of the way. You ring his bell, he opens the door and faces you full.

I looked behind me. Tyrese and Brutus were gone—no smarts in loitering in front of a cop's house in a white suburb.

"Beck?"

No choice. I thought about the Glock. As I put my left hand on the knob, I put my right closer to my hip. Just in case. I turned the knob and pushed the door. My head leaned through the crack.

"I'm in the kitchen," Hoyt called out.

I stepped all the way inside and closed the door behind me. The room smelled of a lemon disinfectant, one of those plug-in-a-socket cover-up brands. I found the odor cloying.

"You want something to eat?" Hoyt asked.

I still couldn't see him. "No, thanks."

I waded across the semi-shag toward the kitchen. I spotted the old photographs on the mantel, but this time I didn't wince. When my feet reached linoleum, I let my eyes take in the room. Empty. I was about to turn back when I felt the cold metal against my temple. A hand suddenly snaked around my neck and jerked back hard.

"You armed, Beck?"

I didn't move or speak.

With the gun still in place, Hoyt dropped the arm from my neck and patted me down. He found the Glock, pulled it out, skidded it across the linoleum.

"Who dropped you off?"

"A couple of friends," I managed to say.

"What sort of friends?"

"What the hell is this, Hoyt?"

He backed off. I turned around. The gun was pointed at my chest. The muzzle looked enormous to me, widening like a giant mouth readying to swallow me whole. It was hard to wrest my gaze from that cold, dark tunnel.

"You come here to kill me?" Hoyt asked.

"What? No." I forced myself to look up. Hoyt was unshaven. His eyes were red-tinged, his body was swaying. Drinking. Drinking a lot.

"Where's Mrs. Parker?" I asked.

"She's safe." An odd reply. "I sent her away."

"Why?"

"I think you know."

Maybe I did. Or was starting to.

"Why would I want to hurt you, Hoyt?"

He kept the gun pointed at my chest. "Do you always carry a concealed weapon, Beck? I could have you thrown in jail for that."

"You've done worse to me," I replied.

His face fell. A low groan escaped his lips.

"Whose body did we cremate, Hoyt?"

"You don't know shit."

"I know that Elizabeth is still alive," I said.

His shoulders slumped, but the weapon stayed right in place. I saw his gun hand tense, and for a moment, I was sure he was going to shoot. I debated jumping away, but it wasn't as though he couldn't nail me with the second round.

"Sit down," he said softly.

"Shauna saw the autopsy report. We know it wasn't Elizabeth in that morgue."

"Sit down," he repeated, raising the gun a bit, and I believe that he might have shot me if I didn't obey. He led me back to the living room. I sat on the hideous couch that had witnessed so many memorable moments, but I had the feeling that they would be pretty much Bic flicks next to the bonfire about to engulf this room.

Hoyt sat across from me. The weapon was still up and centered at my middle. He never let his hand rest. Part of his training, I supposed. Exhaustion bled from him. He looked like a balloon with a slow leak, deflating almost imperceptibly.

"What happened?" I asked.

He didn't answer my question. "What makes you think she's alive?"

I stopped. Could I have been wrong here? Was there any way he didn't know? No, I decided quickly. He had seen the body at the morgue. He had been the one who identified her. He had to be involved. But then I remembered the email.

Tell no one ...

Had it been a mistake to come here?

Again no. That message had been sent before all this—in practically another era. I had to make a decision here. I had to push, take some action.

"Have you seen her?" he asked me.

"No."

"Where is she?"

"I don't know," I said.

Hoyt suddenly cocked his head. He signaled me to silence with a finger to his lips. He stood and crept toward the window. The shades were all drawn. He peeked through the side.

I stood.

"Sit down."

"Shoot me, Hoyt."

He looked at me.

"She's in trouble," I said.

"And you think you can help her?" He made a sneering noise. "I saved both your lives that night. What did you do?"

I felt something in my chest contract. "I got knocked unconscious," I said.

"Right."

"You . . ." I was having trouble articulating. "You saved us?"

"Sit down."

"If you know where she is—"

"We wouldn't be having this conversation," he finished.

I took another step toward him. Then another. He aimed the gun at me. I did not stop. I walked until the muzzle pressed against my sternum. "You're going to tell me," I said. "Or you're going to kill me."

"You're willing to take that gamble?"

I looked him straight in the eye and really held the stare for perhaps the first time in our long relationship. Something passed between us, though I'm not sure what. Resignation on his part maybe, I don't know. But I stayed put. "Do you have any idea how much I miss your daughter?"

"Sit down, David."

"Not until—"

"I'll tell you," he said softly. "Sit down."

I kept my eyes on his as I backed up to the couch. I lowered myself onto the cushion. He put the gun down on the side table. "You want a drink?"

"No."

"You better have one."

"Not now."

He shrugged and walked over to one of those chintzy pull-down bars. It was old and loose. The glasses were in disarray, tinkling against one another, and I was more certain than ever that this had not been his first foray into the liquor cabinet today. He took his time pouring the drink. I wanted to hurry him, but I had done enough pushing for the time being. He needed this, I figured. He was gathering his thoughts, sorting through them, checking the angles. I expected as much.

He cupped the glass in both hands and sank into the chair. "I never much liked you," he said. "It was nothing personal. You come from a good family. Your father was a fine man, and your mother, well, she tried, didn't she." One hand held the drink while the other ran through his hair. "But I thought your relationship with my daughter was"—he looked up, searching the ceiling for the words—"a hindrance to her growth. Now ... well, now I realize how incredibly lucky you both were."

The room chilled a few degrees. I tried not to move, to quiet my breath, anything so as not to disturb him.

"I'll start with the night at the lake," he said. "When they grabbed her."

"Who grabbed her?"

He stared down into his glass. "Don't interrupt," he said. "Just listen."

I nodded, but he didn't see. He was still staring down at his drink, literally looking for answers in the bottom of a glass.

"You know who grabbed her," he said, "or you should by now. The two men they found buried up there." His gaze suddenly swept the room. He snatched up his weapon and stood, checking the window again. I wanted to ask what he expected to see out there, but I didn't want to throw off his rhythm.

"My brother and I got to the lake late. Almost too late. We set up to stop them midway down the dirt road. You know where those two boulders are?"

He glanced toward the window, then back at me. I knew the two boulders. They sat about half a mile down the dirt road from Lake Charmaine. Both huge, both round, both almost the exact same size, both perfectly placed on either side of the road. There were all kinds of legends about how they got there.

"We hid behind them, Ken and me. When they came close, I shot out a tire. They stopped to check it. When they got out of the car, I shot them both in the head."

With one more look out the window, Hoyt moved back to his chair. He put down the weapon and stared at his drink some more. I held my tongue and waited.

"Griffin Scope hired those two men," he said. "They were supposed to interrogate Elizabeth and then kill her. Ken and I got wind of the plan and headed up to the lake to stop them." He put up his hand as if to silence a question, though I hadn't dared open my mouth. "The hows and whys aren't important. Griffin Scope wanted Elizabeth dead. That's all you need to know. And he wouldn't stop because a couple of his boys got killed. Plenty more where they came from. He's like one of those mythical beasts where you cut off the head and it grows two more." He looked at me. "You can't fight that kind of power, Beck."

He took a deep sip. I kept still.

"I want you to go back to that night and put yourself in our position," he continued, moving closer, trying to engage me. "Two men are lying dead on that dirt road. One of the most powerful men in the world sent them to kill you. He has no qualms about taking out the innocent to get to you. What can you do? Suppose we decided to go to the police. What would we tell them? A man like Scope doesn't leave any evidence behind—and even if he did, he has more cops and judges in his pocket than I have hairs on my head. We'd be dead. So I ask you, Beck. You're there. You have two men dead on the ground. You know it won't end there. What do you do?"

I took the question as rhetorical.

"So I presented these facts to Elizabeth, just like I'm presenting them to you now. I told her that Scope would wipe us out to get to her. If she ran away—if she went into hiding, for example—he'd just torture us until we gave her up. Or he'd go after my wife. Or your sister. He'd do whatever it took to make sure Elizabeth was found and killed." He leaned closer to me. "Do you see now? Do you see the only answer?"

I nodded because it was all suddenly transparent. "You had to make them think she was dead."

He smiled, and new goose bumps surfaced all over me. "I had some money saved up. My brother Ken had more. We also had the contacts. Elizabeth went underground. We got her out of the country. She cut her hair, learned to wear disguises, but that was probably overkill. No one was really looking for her. For the past eight years she's been bouncing around third world countries, working for the Red Cross or UNICEF or whatever organization she could hook up with."

I waited. There was so much he hadn't yet told me, but I sat still. I let the implications seep in and shake me at the core. Elizabeth. She was alive. She had been alive for the past eight years. She had been breathing and living and working. . . . It was too much to compute, one of those incomprehensible math problems that make the computer shut down.

"You're probably wondering about the body in the morgue."

I allowed myself a nod.

"It was pretty simple really. We get Jane Does in all the time. They get stored in pathology until somebody gets bored with them. Then we stick them in a potter's field out on Roosevelt Island. I just waited for the next Caucasian Jane Doe who'd be a near enough match to pop up. It took longer than I expected. The girl was probably a runaway stabbed by her pimp, but, of course, we'll never know for sure. We also couldn't leave Elizabeth's murder open. You need a fall guy, Beck. For closure. We chose

KillRoy. It was common knowledge that KillRoy branded the faces with the letter K. So we did that to the corpse. That only left the problem of identification. We toyed around with the idea of burning her beyond recognition, but that would have meant dental records and all that. So we took a chance. The hair matched. The skin tone and age were about right. We dumped her body in a town with a small coroner's office. We made the anonymous call to the police ourselves. We made sure we arrived at the medical examiner's office at the same time as the body. Then all I had to do was make a tearful ID. That's how the large majority of murder victims are identified. A family member IDs them. So I did, and Ken backed me up. Who would question that? Why on earth would a father and uncle lie?"

"You took a hell of a risk," I said.

"But what choice did we have?"

"There had to be other ways."

He leaned closer. I smelled his breath. The loose folds of skin by his eyes drooped low. "Again, Beck, you're on that dirt road with those two bodies—hell, you're sitting here right now with the benefit of hindsight. So tell me: What should we have done?"

I didn't have an answer.

"There were other problems too," Hoyt added, sitting back a bit. "We were never totally sure that Scope's people would buy the whole setup. Luckily for us, the two lowlifes were supposed to leave the country after the murder. We found plane tickets to Buenos Aires on them. They were both drifters, unreliable types. That all helped. Scope's people bought it, but they kept tabs on us—not so much because they thought she was still alive, but they worried that maybe she had given one of us some incriminating material."

"What incriminating material?"

He ignored the question. "Your house, your phone, probably your office. They've been bugged for the past eight years. Mine too."

That explained the careful emails. I let my eyes wander around the room.

"I swept for them yesterday," he said. "The house is clean."

When he was silent for a few moments, I risked a question. "Why did Elizabeth choose to come back now?"

"Because she's foolish," he said, and for the first time, I heard anger in his voice. I gave him some time. He calmed, the red swells in his face ebbing away. "The two bodies we buried," he said quietly.

"What about them?"

"Elizabeth followed the news on the Internet. When she read that they'd been discovered, she figured, same as me, that the Scopes might realize the truth."

"That she was still alive?"

"Yes."

"But if she were overseas, it would still take a hell of a lot to find her."

"That's what I told her. But she said that wouldn't stop them. They'd come after me. Or her mother. Or you. But"—again he stopped, dropped his head—"I don't know how important all that was."

"What do you mean?"

"Sometimes I think she wanted it to happen." He fiddled with the drink, jiggled the ice. "She wanted to come back to you, David. I think the bodies were just an excuse."

I waited again. He drank some more. He took another peek out the window.

"It's your turn," he said to me.

"What?"

"I want some answers now," he said. "Like how did she contact you. How did you get away from the police. Where you think she is."

I hesitated, but not very long. What choice did I really have here? "Elizabeth contacted me by anonymous emails. She spoke in code only I'd understand."

"What kind of code?"

"She made references to things in our past."

Hoyt nodded. "She knew they might be watching."

"Yes." I shifted in my seat. "How much do you know about Griffin Scope's personnel?" I asked.

He looked confused. "Personnel?"

"Does he have a muscular Asian guy working for him?"

Whatever color was left on Hoyt's face flowed out as though through an open wound. He looked at me in awe, almost as though he wanted to cross himself. "Eric Wu," he said in a hushed tone.

"I ran into Mr. Wu yesterday."

"Impossible," he said.

"Why?"

"You wouldn't be alive."

"I got lucky." I told him the story. He looked near tears.

"If Wu found her, if he got to her before he got to you ..." He closed his eyes, wishing the image away.

"He didn't," I said.

"How can you be so sure?"

"Wu wanted to know why I was in the park. If he had her already, why bother with that?"

He nodded slowly. He finished his drink and poured himself another. "But they know she's alive now," he said. "That means they're going to come after us."

"Then we'll fight back," I said, with far more bravery than I felt.

"You didn't hear me before. The mystical beast keeps growing more heads."

"But in the end, the hero always defeats the beast."

He scoffed at that one. Deservedly, I might add. I kept my eyes on him. The grandfather clock ding-donged. I thought about it some more.

"You have to tell me the rest," I said.

"Unimportant."

"It's connected with Brandon Scope's murder, isn't it?"

He shook his head without conviction.

"I know that Elizabeth gave an alibi to Helio Gonzalez," I said.

"It's not important, Beck. Trust me."

"Been there, done that, got screwed," I said.

He took another swig.

"Elizabeth kept a safety-deposit box under the name Sarah Goodhart," I said. "That's where they found those pictures."

"I know," Hoyt said. "We were in a rush that night. I didn't know she'd already given the key to them. We emptied their pockets, but I never checked their shoes. Shouldn't have mattered, though. I had no intention of them ever being found."

"She left more in that box than just the photographs," I continued.

Hoyt carefully set down his drink.

"My father's old gun was in there too. A thirty-eight. You remember it?"

Hoyt looked away and his voice was suddenly soft. "Smith and Wesson. I helped him pick it out."

I felt myself start shaking again. "Did you know that Brandon Scope was killed with that gun?"

His eyes shut tight, like a child wishing away a bad dream.

"Tell me what happened, Hoyt."

"You know what happened."

I couldn't stop quaking. "Tell me anyway."

Each word came out like body blows. "Elizabeth shot Brandon Scope."

I shook my head. I knew it wasn't true.

"She was working side by side with him, doing that charity work. It was just a question of time before she stumbled across the truth. That Brandon was running all this penny-ante crap, playing at being a tough street guy. Drugs, prostitution, I don't even know what."

"She never told me."

"She didn't tell anyone, Beck. But Brandon found out. He beat the hell out of her to warn her off. I didn't know it then, of course. She gave me the same story about a bad fender-bender."

"She didn't kill him," I insisted.

"It was self-defense. When she didn't stop investigating, Brandon broke into your home, and this time he had a knife. He came at her . . . and she shot him. Total self-defense."

I couldn't stop shaking my head.

"She called me, crying. I drove over to your place. When I got there"—he paused, his breath caught—"he was already dead. Elizabeth had that gun. She wanted me to call the police. I talked her out of it. Self-defense or not, Griffin Scope would kill her and worse. I told her to give me a few hours. She was shaky, but she finally agreed."

"You moved the body," I said.

He nodded. "I knew about Gonzalez. The punk was on his way to a fulfilling life of crime. I've seen the type enough to know. He'd already gotten off on a technicality for one murder. Who better to frame?"

It was becoming so clear. "But Elizabeth wouldn't let that happen."

"I didn't count on that," he said. "She heard on the news about the arrest, and that was when she decided to make up that alibi. To save Gonzalez from"—sarcastic finger-quote marks—"a grave injustice." He shook his head. "Worthless. If she'd just let that scumbag take the fall, it would have been all over."

I said, "Scope's people found out about her making up that alibi."

"Someone inside leaked it to them, yeah. Then they started sending their own people around, and they found out about her investigation. The rest became obvious."

"So that night at the lake," I said. "It was about revenge."

He mulled that over. "In part, yes. And in part it was about covering up the truth about Brandon Scope. He was a dead hero. Maintaining that legacy meant a lot to his father."

And, I thought, to my sister.

"I still don't get why she kept that stuff in a safety-deposit box," I said.

"Evidence," he said.

"Of what?"

"That she killed Brandon Scope. And that she did it in self-defense. No matter what else happened, Elizabeth didn't want someone else to take the blame for what she did. Naïve, wouldn't you say?"

No, I wouldn't. I sat there and let the truth try to settle in. Not happening. Not yet anyway. Because this wasn't the full truth. I knew that better than anyone. I looked at my father-in-law, the sagging skin, the thinning hair, the softening gut, the still-impressive but eroding frame. Hoyt thought that he knew what had really happened with his daughter. But he had no idea how wrong he was.

I heard a thunderclap. Rain pounded the windows like tiny fists.

"You could have told me," I said.

He shook his head, this time putting more into it. "And what would you have done, Beck? Follow her? Run away together? They would have learned the truth and killed us all. They were watching you. They still are. We told no one. Not even Elizabeth's mother. And if you need proof we did the right thing, look around you. It's eight years later. All she did was send you a few anonymous emails. And look what happened."

A car door slammed. Hoyt pounced toward the window like a big cat. He peered out again. "Same car you arrived in. Two black men inside."

"They're here for me."

"You sure they don't work for Scope?"

"Positive." On cue, my new cell phone rang. I picked it up.

"Everything okay?" Tyrese asked.

"Yes."

"Step outside."

"Why?"

"You trust that cop?"

"I'm not sure."

"Step outside."

I told Hoyt that I had to go. He seemed too drained to care. I retrieved the Glock and hurried for the door. Tyrese and Brutus were waiting for me. The rain had let up a bit, but none of us seemed to care.

"Got a call for you. Stand over there."

"Why?"

"Personal," Tyrese said. "I don't want to hear it."

"I trust you."

"Just do what I say, man."

I moved out of hearing distance. Behind me I saw the shade open up. Hoyt peered out. I looked back at Tyrese. He gestured for me to put the phone to my ear. I did. There was silence and then Tyrese said, "Line clear, go ahead."

The next voice I heard was Shauna's. "I saw her."

I remained perfectly still.

"She said for you to meet her tonight at the Dolphin."

I understood. The line went dead. I walked back to Tyrese and Brutus. "I need to go somewhere on my own," I said. "Where I can't be followed."

Tyrese glanced at Brutus. "Get in," Tyrese said.

42

Brutus drove like a madman. He took one-way streets in the wrong direction. He made sudden U-turns. From the right lane, he'd cut across traffic and make a left through a red light. We were making excellent time.

The MetroPark in Iselin had a train heading toward Port Jervis that left in twenty minutes. I could rent a car from there. When they dropped me off, Brutus stayed in the car. Tyrese walked me to the ticket counter.

"You told me to run away and not come back," Tyrese said.

"That's right."

"Maybe," he said, "you should do the same."

I put my hand out for him to shake. Tyrese ignored it and hugged me fiercely. "Thank you," I said softly.

He released his grip, adjusted his shoulders so that his jacket relaxed down, fixed his sunglasses. "Yeah, whatever." He didn't wait for me to say anything more before heading back to the car.

The train arrived and departed on schedule. I found a seat and collapsed into it. I tried to make my mind go blank. It wouldn't happen. I glanced around. The car was fairly empty. Two college girls with bulky backpacks jabbered in the language of "like" and "you know." My eyes drifted off. I spotted a newspaper—more specifically, a city tabloid—that someone had left on a seat.

I moved over and picked it up. The coveted cover featured a young starlet who'd been arrested for shoplifting. I flipped pages, hoping to read the comics or catch up on sports—anything mindless would do. But my eyes got snagged on a picture of, well, me. The wanted man. Amazing how sinister I looked in the darkened photo, like a Mideast terrorist.

That was when I saw it. And my world, already off kilter, lurched again.

I wasn't actually reading the article. My eyes were just wandering down the page. But I saw the names. For the first time. The names of the men who'd been found dead at the lake. One was familiar.

Melvin Bartola.

It couldn't be.

I dropped the paper and ran, opening those sliding doors until I found a conductor two cars away. "Where's the next stop?" I asked him.

"Ridgemont, New Jersey."

"Is there a library near the station?"

"I wouldn't know."

I got off there anyway.

*

Eric Wu flexed his fingers. With a small, tight push, he forced the door.

It hadn't taken him long to track down the two black men who'd helped Dr. Beck escape. Larry Gandle had friends in the police department. Wu had described the men to them, and then he went through the proper mug books. Several hours later, Wu spotted the image of a thug named Brutus Cornwall. They made a few calls and learned that Brutus worked for a drug dealer named Tyrese Barton.

Simple.

The chain lock snapped. The door flew open, the knob banging against the wall. Latisha looked up, startled. She was about to scream, but Wu moved fast. He clamped his hand over her mouth and lowered his lips to her ear. Another man, someone Gandle had hired, came in behind him.

"Shh," Wu said almost gently.

On the floor, TJ played with his Hot Wheels. He tilted his head at the noise and said, "Mama?"

Eric Wu smiled down at him. He let Latisha go and knelt to the floor. Latisha tried to stop him, but the other man held her back. Wu rested his enormous hand on the boy's head. He stroked TJ's hair as he turned to Latisha.

"Do you know how I can find Tyrese?" he asked her.

Once off the train, I took a taxi to the rent-a-car place. The green-jacketed agent behind the counter gave me directions to the library. It took maybe three minutes to get there. The Ridgemont library was a modern facility, nouveau colonial brick, picture windows, beech-wood shelves, balconies, turrets, coffee bar. At the reference desk on the second floor, I found a librarian and asked if I could use the Internet.

"Do you have ID?" she asked.

I did. She looked at it. "You have to be a county resident."

"Please," I said. "It's very important."

I expected to see a no-yield, but she softened. "How long do you think you'll be?"

"No more than a few minutes."

"That computer over there"—she pointed to a terminal behind me—"it's our express terminal. Anyone can use it for ten minutes."

I thanked her and hurried over. Yahoo! found me the site for the *New Jersey Journal*, the major newspaper of Bergen and Passaic counties. I knew the exact date I needed. Twelve years ago on January twelfth. I found the search archive and typed in the information.

The Web site went back only six years.

Damn.

I hurried back over to the librarian. "I need to find a twelve-year-old article from the *New Jersey Journal*," I said.

"It wasn't in their Web archive?"

I shook my head.

"Microfiche," she said, slapping the sides of her chair to rise. "What month?"

"January."

She was a large woman and her walk was labored. She found the roll in a file drawer and then helped me thread the tape through the machine. I sat down. "Good luck," she said.

I fiddled with the knob, as if it were a throttle on a new motorcycle. The microfiche shrieked through the mechanism. I stopped every few seconds to see where I was. It took me less than two minutes to find the right date. The article was on page three.

As soon as I saw the headline, I felt the lump in my throat.

Sometimes I swear that I actually heard the screech of tires, though I was asleep in my bed many miles away from where it happened. It still hurt—maybe not as much as the night I lost Elizabeth, but this was my first experience with mortality and tragedy and you never really get over that. Twelve years later, I still remember every detail of that night, though it comes back to me in a tornado blur—the predawn doorbell, the solemn-faced police officers at the door, Hoyt standing with them, their soft, careful words, our denials, the slow realization, Linda's drawn face, my own steady tears, my mother still not accepting, hushing me, telling me to stop crying, her already frayed sanity giving way, her telling me to stop acting like a baby, insisting that everything was fine, then suddenly, coming close to me, marveling at how big my tears were, too big, she said, tears that big belonged on the face of a child, not a grown-up, touching one, rubbing it between her forefinger and her thumb, stop crying David!, growing angrier because I couldn't stop, her screams then, screaming at me to stop crying, until Linda and Hoyt stepped in and shushed her and someone gave her a sedative, not for the first or last time. It all came back to me in an awful gush. And then I read the article and felt the impact jar me in a whole new direction:

CAR DRIVES OVER RAVINE

One Dead, Cause Unknown

Last night at approximately 3:00 AM, a Ford Taurus driven by Stephen Beck of Green River, New Jersey, ran off a bridge in Mahwah, not far from the New York state border. Road conditions were slick due to the snowstorm, but officials have not yet made a ruling on what caused the accident. The sole witness to the accident, Melvin Bartola, a truck driver from Cheyenne, Wyoming—

I stopped reading. Suicide or accident. People had wondered which. Now I knew it was neither.

Brutus said, "What's wrong?"

"I don't know, man." Then, thinking about it, Tyrese added, "I don't want to go back."

Brutus didn't reply. Tyrese sneaked a glance at his old friend. They had started hanging out together in third grade. Brutus hadn't been much of a talker back then either. Probably too busy getting his ass whipped twice a day—home and school—until Brutus figured out the only way he was going to survive was to become the meanest son of a bitch on the block. He started taking a gun to school when he was eleven. He killed for the first time when he was fourteen.

"Ain't you tired of it, Brutus?"

Brutus shrugged. "All we know."

The truth sat there, heavy, unmoving, unblinking.

Tyrese's cell phone trilled. He picked it up and said, "Yo."

"Hello, Tyrese."

Tyrese didn't recognize the strange voice. "Who is this?"

"We met yesterday. In a white van."

His blood turned to ice. Bruce Lee, Tyrese thought. Oh, damn ... "What do you want?"

"I have somebody here who wants to say hi."

There was a brief silence and then TJ said, "Daddy?"

Tyrese whipped off his sunglasses. His body went rigid. "TJ? You okay?"

But Eric Wu was back on the line. "I'm looking for Dr. Beck, Tyrese. TJ and I were hoping you could help me find him."

"I don't know where he is."

"Oh, that's a shame."

"Swear to God, I don't know."

"I see," Wu said. Then: "Hold on a moment, Tyrese, would you? I'd like you to hear something."

43

The wind blew, the trees danced, the purple-orange of sunset was starting to give way to a polished pewter. It frightened me how much the night air felt exactly the same as it had eight years ago, the last time I'd ventured near these hallowed grounds.

I wondered if Griffin Scope's people would think to keep an eye on Lake Charmaine. It didn't matter really. Elizabeth was too clever for that. I mentioned earlier that there used to be a summer camp here before Grandpa purchased the property. Elizabeth's clue—Dolphin—was the name of a cabin, the one where the oldest kids had slept, the one deepest in the woods, the one we rarely dared to visit.

The rental car climbed what had once been the camp's service entrance, though it barely existed anymore. From the main road you couldn't make it out, the high grass hiding it like the entrance to the Batcave. We still kept a chain across it, just in case, with a sign that read No Trespassing. The chain and sign were both still there, but the years of neglect showed. I stopped the car, unhooked the chain, wrapped it around the tree.

I slid back into the driver's seat and headed up to the old camp mess hall. Little of it remained. You could still see the rusted, overturned remnants of what had once been ovens and stoves. Some pots and pans littered the ground, but most had been buried over the years. I got out and smelled the sweet of the green. I tried not to think about my father, but in the clearing, when I was able to look down at the lake, at the way the moon's silver sparkled on the crisp surface, I heard the old ghost again and wondered, this time, if it wasn't crying out for revenge.

I hiked up the path, though that, too, was pretty much nonexistent. Odd that Elizabeth would pick here to meet. I mentioned before that she never liked to play in the ruins of the old summer camp. Linda and I, on the other hand, would marvel when we stumbled over sleeping bags or freshly emptied tin cans, wondering what sort of drifter had left them behind and if, maybe, the drifter was still nearby. Elizabeth, far smarter than either of us, didn't care for that game. Strange places and uncertainty scared her.

It took ten minutes to get there. The cabin was in remarkably good shape. The ceiling and walls were all still standing, though the wooden steps leading to the door were little more than splinters. The Dolphin sign was still there, hanging vertically on one nail. Vines and moss and a mélange of vegetation I couldn't name had not been dissuaded by the structure; they burrowed in, surrounded it, slithered through holes and windows, consumed the cabin so that it now looked like a natural part of the landscape.

"You're back," a voice said, startling me.

A male voice.

I reacted without thought. I jumped to the side, fell on the ground, rolled, pulled out the Glock, and took aim. The man merely put his hands up in the air. I looked at him, keeping the Glock on him. He was not what I expected. His thick beard looked like a robin's nest after a crow attack. His hair was long and matted. His clothes were tattered camouflage. For a moment, I thought I was back in the city, faced with another homeless panhandler. But the bearings weren't right. The man stood straight and steady. He looked me dead in the eye.

"Who the hell are you?" I said.

"It's been a long time, David."

"I don't know you."

"Not really, no. But I know you." He gestured with his head toward the bunk behind me. "You and your sister. I used to watch you play up here."

"I don't understand."

He smiled. His teeth, all there, were blindingly white against the beard. "I'm the Boogeyman."

In the distance, I heard a family of geese squawk as they glided to a landing on the lake's surface. "What do you want?" I asked.

"Not a damn thing," he said, still smiling. "Can I put my hands down?"

I nodded. He dropped his hands. I lowered my weapon but kept it at the ready. I thought about what he'd said and asked, "How long have you been hiding up here?"

"On and off for"—he seemed to be doing some kind of calculation with his fingers—"thirty years." He grinned at the dumbstruck expression on my face. "Yeah, I've watched you since you were this high." He put his hand at knee level. "Saw you grow up and—" He paused. "Been a long time since you been up here, David."

"Who are you?"

"My name is Jeremiah Renway," he said.

I couldn't place the name.

"I've been hiding from the law."

"So why are you showing yourself now?"

He shrugged. "Guess I'm glad to see you."

"How do you know I won't tell the authorities on you?"

"I figure you owe me one."

"How's that?"

"I saved your life."

I felt the ground beneath me shift. "What?"

"Who do you think pulled you out of the water?" he asked.

I was dumbstruck.

"Who do you think dragged you into the house? Who do you think called the ambulance?"

My mouth opened, but no words came out.

"And"—his smile spread—"who do you think dug up those bodies so someone would find them?"

It took me a while to find my voice. "Why?" I managed to ask.

"Can't say for sure," he said. "See, I did something bad a long time ago. Guess I thought this was a chance at redemption or something."

"You mean you saw . . . ?"

"Everything," Renway finished for me. "I saw them grab your missus. I saw them hit you with the bat. I saw them promise to pull you out if she told them where something was. I saw your missus hand them a key. I saw them laugh and force her into the car while you stayed underwater."

I swallowed. "Did you see them get shot?"

Renway smiled again. "We've chatted long enough, son. She's waiting for you now."

"I don't understand."

"She's waiting for you," he repeated, turning away from me. "By the tree." Without warning, he sprinted into the woods, darting through the brush like a deer. I stood there and watched him vanish in the thicket.

The tree.

I ran then. Branches whipped my face. I didn't care. My legs begged me to let up. I paid them no heed. My lungs protested. I told them to toughen up. When I finally made the right at the semi-phallic rock and rounded the path's corner, the tree was still there. I moved closer and felt my eyes start to well up.

Our carved initials—E.P. + D.B.—had darkened with age. So, too, had the thirteen lines we had carved out. I stared for a moment, and then I reached out and tentatively touched the grooves. Not of the initials. Not of the thirteen lines. My fingers traced down the eight fresh lines, still white and still sticky from sap.

Then I heard her say, "I know you think it's goofy."

My heart exploded. I turned behind me. And there she was.

I couldn't move. I couldn't speak. I just stared at her face. That beautiful face. And those eyes. I felt as though I were falling, plummeting down a dark shaft. Her face was thinner, her Yankee cheekbones more pronounced, and I don't think I had ever seen anything so perfect in all my life.

I reminded myself of the teasing dreams then—the nocturnal moments of escape when I would hold her in my arms and stroke her face and all the while feel myself being pulled away, knowing even as I had been bathing in the bliss that it was not real, that soon I'd be flung back into the waking world. The fear that this might be more of the same engulfed me, crushing the wind out of my lungs.

Elizabeth seemed to read what I was thinking and nodded as if to say "Yeah, this is real." She took a tentative step toward me. I could barely breathe, but I managed to shake my head and point at the carved lines and say, "I think it's romantic."

She muffled a sob with her hand and sprinted toward me. I opened my arms and she jumped in. I held her. I held her as tight as I could. My eyes squeezed shut. I smelled the lilac and cinnamon in her hair. She buried her face into my chest and sobbed. We gripped and regripped. She still ... fit. The contours, the grooves of our bodies needed no adjusting. I cupped the back of her head. Her hair was shorter, but the texture hadn't changed. I could feel her shaking and I'm sure she could feel the same emanating from me.

Our first kiss was exquisite and familiar and frighteningly desperate, two people who'd finally reached the surface after misjudging the depth of the water. The years began to melt away, winter giving way to spring. So many emotions ricocheted through me. I didn't sort through them or try to figure them out. I just let it all happen.

She lifted her head and looked into my eyes and I couldn't move. "I'm sorry," she said, and I thought my heart would shatter all over again.

I held her. I held her, and I wondered if I would ever risk letting her go. "Just don't leave me again," I said.

"Never."

"Promise?"

"Promise," she said.

We kept the embrace. I pressed against the wonder of her skin. I touched the muscles in her back. I kissed the swan neck. I even looked up to the heavens as I just held on. How? I wondered. How could this not be another cruel joke? How could she still be alive and back with me?

I didn't care. I just wanted it to be real. I wanted it to last.

But even as I held her against me, the sound of the cell phone, like something from my teasing dreams, started pulling me away. For a moment, I debated not answering it, but with all that had happened, that wasn't really an option. Loved ones had been left lying in our wake. We couldn't just abandon them. We both knew that. Still keeping one arm around Elizabeth—I'd be damned if I was ever going to let her go—I put the phone to my ear and said hello.

It was Tyrese. And as he spoke, I could feel it all start to slip away.

44

We parked in the abandoned lot at Riker Hill Elementary School and cut across the grounds, holding hands. Even in the dark, I could see that very little had changed from the days when Elizabeth and I had frolicked here. The pediatrician in me couldn't help but notice the new safety features. The swing set had stronger chains and harnessed seats now. Soft mulch was spread thickly under the jungle gyms in case a kid fell. But the kickball field, the soccer field, the blacktop with its painted-on hopscotch and four-square courts—they were all the same as when we were kids.

We walked past the window of Miss Sobel's second-grade class, but it was so long ago now that I think neither of us felt more than a ripple of nostalgia. We ducked into the woods, still hand in hand. Neither one of us had taken the path in twenty years, but we still knew the way. Ten minutes later, we were in Elizabeth's backyard on Goodhart Road. I turned to her. She stared at her childhood house with moist eyes.

"Your mother never knew?" I asked her.

She shook her head. She turned to me. I nodded and slowly let go of her hand.

"Are you sure about this?" she asked.

"No choice," I said.

I didn't give her a chance to argue. I stepped away and headed for the house. When I reached the sliding glass door, I cupped my hands around my eyes and peered in. No sign of Hoyt. I tried the back door. It was unlocked. I turned the knob and went inside. No one was there. I was about to head out when I saw a light snap on in the garage. I went through the kitchen and into the laundry room. I opened the door to the garage slowly.

Hoyt Parker sat in the front seat of his Buick Skylark. The engine was off. He had a drink in his hand. When I opened the door, he lifted his gun. Then, seeing me, he lowered it back to his side. I took the two steps down to the cement and reached for the passenger door handle. The car was unlocked. I opened the door and slid in next to him.

"What do you want, Beck?" There was the slur of drink in his speech.

I made a production of settling back in the seat. "Tell Griffin Scope to release the boy," I said.

"I don't know what you're talking about," he replied without an iota of conviction.

"Graft, payola, on the take. Choose your own term, Hoyt. I know the truth now."

"You don't know shit."

"That night at the lake," I said. "When you helped convince Elizabeth not to go to the police."

"We talked about that already."

"But now I'm curious, Hoyt. What were you really afraid of—that they'd kill her or that you'd be arrested too?"

His eyes lazily drifted toward me. "She'd be dead if I hadn't convinced her to run."

"I don't doubt that," I said. "But still it was lucky for you, Hoyt—shooting down two birds with one stone like that. You were able to save her life—and you were able to stay out of jail."

"And why exactly would I go to jail?"

"Are you denying you were on Scope's payroll?"

He shrugged. "You think I'm the only one who took their money?"

"No," I said.

"So why would I be more worried than the next cop?"

"Because of what you'd done."

He finished his drink, looked around for the bottle, poured himself some more. "I don't know what the hell you're talking about."

"Do you know what Elizabeth was investigating?"

"Brandon Scope's illegal activities," he said. "Prostitution. Underage girls. Drugs. The guy was playing at being Mr. Bad."

"What else?" I said, trying to stop quivering.

"What are you talking about?"

"If she kept digging, she might have stumbled across a bigger crime." I took a deep breath. "Am I right, Hoyt?"

His face sagged when I said that. He turned and stared straight out the front windshield.

"A murder," I said.

I tried to follow his gaze, but all I saw were Sears Craftsman tools hanging neatly on a pegboard. The screwdrivers with their yellow-and-black handles were lined up in perfect size order, flat-tops on the left, Phillips head on the right. Three wrenches and a hammer separated them.

I said, "Elizabeth wasn't the first one who wanted to bring Brandon Scope down." Then I stopped and waited, waited until he looked at me. It took some time, but eventually he did. And I saw it in his eyes. He didn't blink or try to hide it. I saw it. And he knew that I saw it.

"Did you kill my father, Hoyt?"

He took a deep swig from the glass, swished it around his mouth, and swallowed hard. Some of the whiskey spilled onto his face. He didn't bother to wipe it away. "Worse," he said, closing his eyes. "I betrayed him."

The rage boiled up in my chest, but my voice stayed surprisingly even. "Why?"

"Come on, David. You must have figured that out by now."

Another flash of fury shot across me. "My father worked with Brandon Scope," I began.

"More than that," he interjected. "Griffin Scope had your dad mentor him. They worked very closely together."

"Like with Elizabeth."

"Yes."

"And while working with him, my father discovered what a monster Brandon really was. Am I right?"

Hoyt just drank.

"He didn't know what to do," I continued. "He was afraid to tell, but he couldn't just let it go. The guilt ate at him. That was why he was so quiet the months before his death." I stopped and thought about my father, scared, alone, nowhere to turn. Why hadn't I seen it? Why hadn't I looked past my own world and seen his pain? Why hadn't I reached out to him? Why hadn't I done something to help him?

I looked at Hoyt. I had a gun in my pocket. How simple it would be. Just take out the gun and pull the trigger. Bam. Gone. Except I knew from personal experience that it wouldn't solve a damn thing. Just the opposite, in fact.

"Go on," Hoyt said.

"Somewhere along the line, Dad decided to tell a friend. But not just any friend. A cop, a cop who worked in the city where the crimes were being committed." My blood started boiling, threatening again to erupt. "You, Hoyt."

Something in his face shifted.

"I got it right so far?"

"Pretty much," he replied.

"You told the Scopes, didn't you?"

He nodded. "I thought they'd transfer him or something. Keep him away from Brandon. I never thought ..." He made a face, clearly hating the self-justification in his own voice. "How did you know?"

"The name Melvin Bartola, for starters. He was the witness to the supposed accident that killed my father, but, of course, he worked for Scope too." My father's smile flashed in front of me. I tightened my hands into fists. "And then there was the lie you told about saving my life," I continued. "You did go back to the lake after you shot Bartola and Wolf. But not to save me. You looked, you saw no movement, and you figured I was dead."

"Figured you were dead," he repeated. "Not wanted you dead."

"Semantics," I said.

"I never wanted you to get hurt."

"But you weren't very broken up about it either," I said. "You went back to the car and told Elizabeth that I had drowned."

"I was just trying to convince her to disappear," he said. "It helped too."

"You must have been surprised when you heard I was still alive."

"More like shocked. How did you survive anyway?"

"It's not important."

Hoyt settled back as though from exhaustion. "Guess not," he said. His expression veered again and I was surprised when he said, "So what else do you want to know?"

"You're not denying any of this?"

"Nope."

"And you knew Melvin Bartola, right?"

"That's right."

"Bartola tipped you off about the hit on Elizabeth," I said. "I can't figure out what happened exactly. Maybe he had a conscience. Maybe he didn't want her to die."

"Bartola a conscience?" He chuckled. "Please. He was a low-life murdering scum. He came to me because he thought he could double-dip. Collect from the Scopes and from me. I told him I'd double his money and help him out of the country if he helped me fake her death."

I nodded, seeing it now. "So Bartola and Wolf told Scope's people that they were going to lie low after the killing. I wondered why their disappearance didn't raise more eyebrows, but thanks to you, Bartola and Wolf were supposed to go away."

"Yes."

"So what happened? Did you double-cross them?"

"Men like Bartola and Wolf—their word means nothing. No matter how much I paid them, I knew that they'd come back for more. They'd get bored living out of the country or maybe they'd get drunk and boast about it in a bar. I've dealt with this type of garbage my whole life. I couldn't risk that."

"So you killed them."

"Yep," he said without an ounce of regret.

I knew it all now. I just didn't know how it was all going to play out. "They're holding a little boy," I said to him. "I promised I'd turn myself in if they let him go. You call them. You help make the trade."

"They don't trust me anymore."

"You've worked for Scope for a long time," I said. "Come up with something."

Hoyt sat there and thought about it. He looked at his tool wall again, and I wondered what he was seeing. Then slowly, he lifted the gun and pointed it at my face. "I think I got an idea," he said.

I didn't blink. "Open the garage door, Hoyt."

He didn't move.

I reached across him to the visor and pressed the garage's remote. The door came to life with a whir. Hoyt watched it rise. Elizabeth stood there, not moving. When it was open all the way, her gaze settled hard on her father's.

He flinched.

"Hoyt?" I said.

His head snapped toward me. With one hand he grabbed my hair. He pressed the gun against my eye. "Tell her to move out of the way."

I stayed still.

"Do it or you die."

"You wouldn't. Not in front of her."

He leaned closer to me. "Just do it, dammit." His voice was more like an urgent plea than a hostile command. I looked at him and felt something strange course through me. Hoyt turned on the ignition. I faced the front and gestured for her to move out of the way. She hesitated, but eventually she stepped to the side. Hoyt waited until she was clear of his path. Then he hit the gas. We flew past her with a jerk. As we hurtled away, I turned and watched out the back window as Elizabeth grew dimmer, fainter, until finally she was gone.

Again.

I sat back and wondered if I would ever see her again. I had feigned confidence before, but I knew the odds. She fought me on it. I explained that I had to do this. I needed to be the one doing the protecting this time. Elizabeth hadn't liked it, but she understood.

In the past few days I'd learned that she was alive. Would I trade my life for that? Gladly. I understood that going in. A strange, peaceful feeling came over me as I drove with the man who betrayed my father. The guilt that had weighed me down for so long finally lifted its hold. I knew now what I had to do—what I had to sacrifice—and I wondered if there was ever any choice, if it had been preordained to end like this.

I turned to Hoyt and said, "Elizabeth didn't kill Brandon Scope."

"I know," he interrupted, and then he said something that shook me to the core: "I did."

I froze.

"Brandon beat up Elizabeth," he went on quickly. "He was going to kill her. So I shot him when he got to the house. Then I framed Gonzalez, just like I said before. Elizabeth knew what I had done. She wouldn't let an innocent man take the fall. So she made up that alibi. Scope's people heard about it and it made them wonder. When they then began to suspect that maybe Elizabeth was the killer"—he stopped, kept his eyes on the road, summoned something from deep inside—"God help me, I let them."

I handed him the cell phone. "Call," I said.

He did. He called a man named Larry Gandle. I had met Gandle several times over the years. His father had gone to high school with mine. "I have Beck," Hoyt told him. "We'll meet you at the stables, but you have to release the kid."

Larry Gandle said something I couldn't make out.

"As soon as we know the kid is safe, we'll be there," I heard Hoyt say. "And tell Griffin I have what he wants. We can end this without hurting me or my family."

Gandle spoke again and then I heard him click off the line. Hoyt handed me back the phone.

"Am I part of your family, Hoyt?"

He aimed the gun at my head again. "Slowly take out your Glock, Beck. Two fingers."

I did as he asked. He hit the electric window slide.

"Toss it out the window."

I hesitated. He pushed the muzzle into my eye. I flipped the gun out of the car. I never heard it land.

We drove in silence now, waiting for the phone to ring again. When it did, I was the one who answered it. Tyrese said in a soft voice, "He's okay."

I hung up, relieved.

"Where are you taking me, Hoyt?"

"You know where."

"Griffin Scope will kill us both."

"No," he said, still pointing the gun at me. "Not both."

45

We turned off the highway and headed into the rural. The number of streetlights dwindled until the only illumination came from the car's headlights. Hoyt reached into the backseat and pulled out a manila envelope.

"I have it here, Beck. All of it."

"All of what?"

"What your father had on Brandon. What Elizabeth had on Brandon."

I was puzzled for a second. He'd had it with him the whole time. And then I wondered. The car. Why had Hoyt gone to the car?

"Where are the copies?" I asked.

He grinned as though happy I had asked. "There aren't any. It's all here."

"I still don't understand."

"You will, David. I'm sorry, but you're my fall guy now. It's the only way."

"Scope won't buy it," I said.

"Yeah, he will. Like you said, I've worked for him a long time. I know what he wants to hear. Tonight it ends."

"With my death?" I asked.

He didn't reply.

"How are you going to explain it to Elizabeth?"

"She might end up hating me," he said. "But at least she'll be alive."

Up ahead, I could see the estate's gated back entrance. Endgame, I thought. The uniformed security guard waved us through. Hoyt kept the gun on me. We started up the drive and then, without warning, Hoyt slammed on the brake.

He spun toward me. "You wearing a wire, Beck?"

"What? No."

"Bullshit, let me see." He reached for my chest. I leaned away. He lifted the gun higher, closed the gap between us, and then started patting me down. Satisfied, he sat back.

"You're lucky," he said with a sneer.

He shifted back into drive. Even in the dark, you could get a feel for the lushness of the grounds. Trees stood silhouetted against the moon, swaying even though there seemed to be no wind. In the distance, I saw a burst of lights. Hoyt followed the road toward them. A faded gray sign told us we'd arrived at the Freedom Trails Stables. We parked in the first spot on the left. I looked out the window. I don't know much about the housing of horses, but this sprawl was impressive. There was one hangar-shaped building large enough to house a dozen tennis courts. The stables themselves were V-shaped and stretched as far as I could see. There was a sprouting fountain in the middle of the grounds. There were tracks and jumps and obstacle courses.

They were also men waiting for us.

With the weapon still on me, Hoyt said, "Get out."

I did. When I closed the door, the slam echoed in the stillness. Hoyt came around to my side of the car and jammed the gun into the small of my back. The smells brought on a quick spell of 4-H-fair déjà vu. But when I saw the four men in front of me, two of whom I recognized, the image fled.

The other two—the two I had never seen before—were both armed with some sort of semiautomatic rifle. They pointed them at us. I barely shuddered. I guess that I was getting used to weapons aimed in my direction. One of the men stood on the far right near the stable entrance. The other was leaning against a car on the left.

The two men I had recognized were huddled together under a light. One was Larry Gandle. The other was Griffin Scope. Hoyt nudged me forward with the gun. As we moved toward them, I saw the door to the big building open.

Eric Wu stepped out.

My heart thumped against my rib cage. I could hear my breath in my ears. My legs tingled. I might be immune to weapon intimidation, but my body remembered Wu's fingers. I involuntarily slowed a step. Wu hardly glanced at me. He walked straight to Griffin Scope and handed him something.

Hoyt made me stop when we were still a dozen yards away. "Good news," he called out.

All eyes turned to Griffin Scope. I knew the man, of course. I was, after all, the son of an old friend and the brother of a trusted employee. Like most everyone else, I'd been in awe of the burly man with the twinkle in his eye. He was the guy you wanted to notice you—a back-slap buy-you-a-drink compadre who had the rare ability to walk the tightrope between friend and employer. It was a mix that rarely worked. The boss either lost respect when he became a friend, or the friend was resented when he suddenly had to be the boss. That wasn't a problem for a dynamo like Griffin Scope. He'd always known how to lead.

Griffin Scope looked puzzled. "Good news, Hoyt?"

Hoyt tried a smile. "Very good news, I think."

"Wonderful," Scope said. He glanced at Wu. Wu nodded but stayed where he was. Scope said, "So tell me this good news, Hoyt. I'm all a-twitter."

Hoyt cleared his throat. "First of all, you have to understand. I never meant to harm you. In fact, I went to great lengths to make sure nothing incriminating ever got out. But I also needed to save my daughter. You can understand that, can't you?"

A shadow flickered across Scope's face. "Do I understand the desire to protect a child?" he asked, his voice a quiet rumble. "Yes, Hoyt, I think I do."

A horse neighed in the distance. All else was silence. Hoyt licked his lips and held up the manila envelope.

"What's that, Hoyt?"

"Everything," he replied. "Photographs, statements, tapes. Everything that my daughter and Stephen Beck had on your son."

"Are there copies?"

"Only one," Hoyt said.

"Where?"

"In a safe place. An attorney has it. If I don't call him in an hour and give him the code, he releases them. I don't mean this as a threat, Mr. Scope. I would never reveal what I know. I have as much to lose as anyone."

"Yes," Scope said. "You do at that."

"But now you can leave us alone. You have it all. I'll send the rest. There is no need to hurt me or my family."

Griffin Scope looked at Larry Gandle, then at Eric Wu. The two perimeter men with the weapons seemed to tense. "What about my son, Hoyt? Someone shot him down like a dog. Do you expect me to just let that go?"

"That's just it," Hoyt said. "Elizabeth didn't do it."

Scope narrowed his eyes in what was supposed to be profound interest, but I thought I saw something else there, something akin to bemusement. "Pray tell," he said. "Then who did?"

I heard Hoyt swallow hard. He turned and looked at me. "David Beck."

I wasn't surprised. I wasn't angry either.

"He killed your son," he continued quickly. "He found out what was going on and he took vengeance."

Scope made a production of gasping and putting his hand on his chest. Then he finally looked at me. Wu and Gandle turned my way too. Scope met my eyes and said, "What do you have to say in your defense, Dr. Beck?"

I thought about it. "Would it do any good to tell you he's lying?"

Scope didn't reply to me directly. He turned to Wu and said, "Please bring me that envelope."

Wu had the walk of a panther. He headed toward us, smiling at me, and I felt a few of my muscles contract instinctively. He stopped in front of Hoyt and put out his hand. Hoyt handed him the envelope. Wu took the envelope with one hand. With the other—I've never seen anyone move so fast—he snatched away Hoyt's gun as though from a child, and tossed it behind him.

Hoyt said, "What the—?"

Wu punched him deep in the solar plexus. Hoyt fell to his knees. We all stood and watched as he dropped to all fours, retching. Wu circled, took his time, and placed his kick squarely on Hoyt's rib cage. I heard something snap. Hoyt rolled onto his back, blinking, his arms and legs splayed.

Griffin Scope approached, smiling down at my father-in-law. Then he held up something in the air. I squinted. It was small and black.

Hoyt looked up, spitting out blood. "I don't understand," he managed.

I could see what was in Scope's hand now. It was a microcassette player. Scope pressed the play button. I heard first my own voice, then Hoyt's:

"Elizabeth didn't kill Brandon Scope."

"I know. I did."

Scope snapped off the tape recorder. Nobody spoke. Scope glared down at my father-in-law. As he did, I realized a number of things. I realized that if Hoyt Parker knew that his house was bugged, he'd also know that it was more than likely that the same would be true of his car. That was why he left the house when he spotted us in the backyard. That was why he waited for me in the car. That was why he interrupted me when I said that Elizabeth didn't kill Brandon Scope. That was why he confessed to the murder in a place where he knew they'd be listening. I realized that when he patted me down, he did indeed feel the wire that Carlson had put on my chest, that he wanted to make sure that the feds, too, would hear everything and that Scope wouldn't bother frisking me. I realized that Hoyt Parker was taking the fall, that while he had done many terrible things, including betraying my father, this had all been a ruse, a last chance at redemption, that in the end, he, not I, would sacrifice himself to save us all. I also realized that for his plan to work, he had to do one more thing. So I stepped away. And even as I heard the FBI helicopters start to descend, even as I heard Carlson's voice through a megaphone shout for everyone to freeze, I watched Hoyt Parker reach into his ankle holster, pull out a gun, and fire it three times at Griffin Scope. Then I watched him turn the gun around.

I shouted "No!" but the final blast smothered it out.

46

We buried Hoyt four days later. Thousands of uniformed cops showed up to pay their respects. The details of what had happened at the Scope estate weren't out yet, and I wasn't sure they ever would be. Even Elizabeth's mother hadn't pushed for answers, but perhaps that had more to do with the fact that she was delirious with joy over her daughter's return from the dead. It made her not want to ask too many questions or look at the cracks too closely. I could relate.

For now, Hoyt Parker had died a hero. And maybe that was true. I'm not the best judge.

Hoyt had written a long confession, basically restating what he had told me in the car. Carlson showed it to me.

"Does this end it?" I asked.

"We still have to make a case against Gandle and Wu and some of the others," he said. "But with Griffin Scope dead, everyone's cutting deals now."

The mythical beast, I thought. You don't chop off its head. You stab it in the heart.

"You were smart to come to me when they kidnapped that little boy," Carlson said to me.

"What was my alternative?"

"Good point." Carlson shook my hand. "Take care of yourself, Dr. Beck."

"You too," I said.

You may want to know if Tyrese ever goes down to Florida and what happens to TJ and Latisha. You may be wondering if Shauna and Linda stay together and what that means to Mark. But I can't tell any of that because I don't know.

This story ends now, four days after the death of Hoyt Parker and Griffin Scope. It is late. Very late. I am lying in bed with Elizabeth, watching her body rise and fall in sleep. I watch her all the time. I don't close my eyes much. My dreams have perversely reversed themselves. It is in my dreams now that I lose her—where she is dead again and I am alone. So I hold her a lot. I am clingy and needy. So is she. But we'll work that out.

As though she feels my eyes on her, Elizabeth rolls over. I smile at her. She smiles back and I feel my heart soar. I remember the day at the lake. I remember drifting on that raft. And I remember my decision to tell her the truth.

"We need to talk," I say.

"I don't think so."

"We're not good at keeping secrets from each other, Elizabeth. It's what caused this mess in the first place. If we had just told each other everything ..." I didn't finish.

She nods. And I realize that she knows. That she's always known.

"Your father," I say. "He always thought you killed Brandon Scope."

"That's what I told him."

"But in the end—" I stop, start again. "When I said in the car that you didn't kill him, do you think he realized the truth?"

"I don't know," Elizabeth says. "I like to think that maybe he did."

"So he sacrificed himself for us."

"Or he tried to stop you from doing it," she says. "Or maybe he died still thinking I killed Brandon Scope. We'll never really know. And it doesn't matter."

We look at each other.

"You knew," I say, my chest hitching. "From the beginning. You—"

She hushes me with a finger on my lips. "It's okay."

"You put all that stuff in the safety-deposit box," I say, "for me."

"I wanted to protect you," she says.

"It was in self-defense," I say, again remembering the feel of the gun in my hand, the sickening backfire when I pulled the trigger.

"I know," she says, wrapping her arms around my neck and pulling me close. "I know."

You see, I was the one who was home when Brandon Scope broke into our house eight years ago. I was the one lying alone in the bed when he sneaked up with the knife. We struggled. I fumbled for my father's gun. He lunged again. I shot and killed him. And then, in a panic, I ran. I tried to gather my thoughts, figure out what to do. When I came to my senses, when I returned to the house, the body was gone. So was the gun. I wanted to tell her. I was going to at the lake. But in the end, I never said anything about it. Until now.

Like I told you earlier, if I had just told the truth from the get-go ...

She pulls me closer.

"I'm here," Elizabeth whispers.

Here. With me. It would take a while to accept that. But I would. We hold each other and drift off to sleep. Tomorrow morning we would wake up together. And the morning after that too. Her face would be the first I'd see every day. Her voice would be the first I'd hear.

And that, I knew, would always be enough.

Gone For Good

For Anne
A ma vie coeur entier

Acknowledgments

The author wishes to thank the following for their technical expertise: Jim White, Executive Director, Covenant House Newark; Anne Armstrong-Coben, M.D., Medical Director, Covenant House Newark; Frank Gilliam, Outreach Manager, Covenant House Atlantic City; Mary Ann Daly, Director of Community Programs, Covenant House Atlantic City; Kim Sutton, Resident Manager, Covenant House Atlantic City; Steven Miller, M.D., Director of Pediatric Emergency Medicine, Children's Hospital of New York-Presbyterian, Columbia University; Douglas P. Lyle, M.D.; Richard Donner (for the final push); Linda Fairstein, Manhattan Assistant District Attorney; Gene Riehl, FBI (retired); Jeffrey Bedford, FBI, Special Agent—all of whom provided the author with wonderful insights and now get to see him distort and dismiss them to suit his own purposes.

Covenant House is a real organization, though I took great liberties here. I made up a lot of stuff—that's why it's called fiction—but I tried to get the caring heart and soul of this important charity right. Those interested in helping or learning more should check out www.covenanthouse.org.

The author also wishes to thank his great team: Irwyn Applebaum, Nita Taublib, Danielle Perez, Barb Burg, Susan Corcoran, Cynthia Lasky, Betsy Hulsebosch, Jon Wood, Joel Gotler, Maggie Griffin, Lisa Erbach Vance, and Aaron Priest. You all mean a great deal to me.

To repeat: this is a work of fiction. That means I make stuff up.

1

Three days before her death, my mother told me—these weren't her last words, but they were pretty close—that my brother was still alive.

That was all she said. She didn't elaborate. She said it only once. And she wasn't doing very well. Morphine had already applied its endgame heart squeeze. Her skin was in that cusp between jaundice and fading summer tan. Her eyes had sunken deep into her skull. She slept most of the time. She would, in fact, have only one more lucid moment—if indeed this had been a lucid moment, which I very much doubted—and that would be a chance for me to tell her that she had been a wonderful mother, that I loved her very much, and good-bye. We never said anything about my brother. That didn't mean we weren't thinking about him as though he were sitting bedside too.

"He's alive."

Those were her exact words. And if they were true, I didn't know if it would be a good thing or bad.

We buried my mother four days later.

When we returned to the house to sit shivah, my father stormed through the semi-shag in the living room. His face was red with rage. I was there, of course. My sister, Melissa, had flown in from Seattle with her husband, Ralph. Aunt Selma and Uncle Murray paced. Sheila, my soul mate, sat next to me and held my hand.

That was pretty much the sum total.

There was only one flower arrangement, a wonderful monster of a thing. Sheila smiled and squeezed my hand when she saw the card. No words, no message, just the drawing

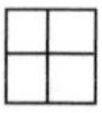

Dad kept glancing out the bay windows—the same windows that had been shot out with a BB gun twice in the past eleven years—and muttered under his breath, "Sons of bitches." He'd turn around and think of someone else who hadn't shown. "For God's sake, you'd think the Bergmans would have at least made a goddamn appearance." Then he'd close his eyes and look away. The anger would consume him anew, blending with the grief into something I didn't have the strength to face.

One more betrayal in a decade filled with them.

I needed air.

I got to my feet. Sheila looked up at me with concern. "I'm going to take a walk," I said softly.

"You want company?"

"I don't think so."

Sheila nodded. We had been together nearly a year. I've never had a partner so in sync with my rather odd vibes. She gave my hand another I-love-you squeeze, and the warmth spread through me.

Our front-door welcome mat was harsh faux grass, like something stolen from a driving range, with a plastic daisy in the upper left-hand corner. I stepped over it and strolled up Downing Place. The street was lined with numbingly ordinary aluminum-sided split-levels, circa 1962. I still wore my dark gray suit. It itched in the heat. The savage sun beat down like a drum, and a perverse part of me thought that it was a wonderful day to decay. An image of my mother's light-the-world smile—the one before it all happened—flashed in front of my eyes. I shoved it away.

I knew where I was headed, though I doubt if I would have admitted it to myself. I was drawn there, pulled by some unseen force. Some would call it masochistic. Others would note that maybe it had something to do with closure. I thought it was probably neither.

I just wanted to look at the spot where it all ended.

The sights and sounds of summer suburbia assaulted me. Kids squealed by on their bicycles. Mr. Cirino, who owned the Ford/Mercury dealership on Route 10, mowed his lawn. The Steins—they'd built up a chain of appliance stores that were swallowed up by a bigger chain—were taking a stroll hand in hand. There was a touch football game going on at the Levines' house, though I didn't know any of the participants. Barbecue smoke took flight from the Kaufmans' backyard.

I passed by the Glassmans' old place. Mark "the Doof" Glassman had jumped through the sliding glass doors when he was six. He was playing Superman. I remembered the scream and the blood. He needed over forty stitches. The Doof grew up and became some kind of IPO-start-up zillionaire. I don't think they call him the Doof anymore, but you never know.

The Marianos' house, still that horrid shade of phlegm yellow with a plastic deer guarding the front walk, was on the bend. Angela Mariano, our local bad girl, was two years older than us and like some superior, awe-inducing species. Watching Angela sunning in her backyard in a gravity-defying ribbed halter top, I had felt the first painful thrusts of deep hormonal longing. My mouth would actually water. Angela used to fight with her parents and sneak smokes in the toolshed behind her house. Her boyfriend drove a motorcycle. I ran into her last year on Madison Avenue in midtown. I expected her to look awful—that was what you always hear happens to that first lust-crush—but Angela looked great and seemed happy.

A lawn sprinkler did the slow wave in front of Eric Frankel's house at 23 Downing Place. Eric had a space-travel-themed bar mitzvah at the Chanticleer in Short Hills when we were both in seventh grade. The ceiling was done up planetarium style—a black sky with star constellations. My seating card told me that I was sitting at "Table Apollo 14." The centerpiece was an ornate model rocket on a green fauna launching pad. The waiters, adorned in realistic space suits, were each supposed to be one of the Mercury 7. "John Glenn" served us. Cindi Shapiro and I had sneaked into the chapel room and made out for over an hour. It was my first time. I didn't know what I was doing. Cindi did. I remember it was glorious, the way her tongue caressed and jolted me in unexpected ways. But I also remember my initial wonderment evolving after twenty minutes or so into, well, boredom—a confused "what next?" along with a naïve "is that all there is?"

When Cindi and I stealthily returned to Cape Kennedy's Table Apollo 14, ruffled and in fine post-smooch form (the Herbie Zane Band serenading the crowd with "Fly Me to the Moon"), my brother, Ken, pulled me to the side and demanded details. I, of course, too gladly gave them. He awarded me with that smile and slapped me five. That night, as we lay on the bunk beds, Ken on the top, me on the bottom, the stereo playing Blue Oyster Cult's "Don't Fear the Reaper" (Ken's favorite), my older brother explained to me the facts of life as seen by a ninth-grader. I'd later learn he was mostly wrong (a little too much emphasis on the breast), but when I think back to that night, I always smile.

"He's alive. . . ."

I shook my head and turned right at Coddington Terrace by the Holders' old house. This was the same route Ken and I had taken to get to Burnet Hill Elementary School. There used to be a paved path between two houses to make the trip shorter. I wondered if it was still there. My mother—everyone, even kids, had called her Sunny—used to follow us to school quasi-surreptitiously. Ken and I would roll our eyes as she ducked behind trees. I smiled, thinking about her overprotectiveness now. It used to embarrass me, but Ken would simply shrug. My brother was securely cool enough to let it slide. I wasn't.

I felt a pang and moved on.

Maybe it was just my imagination, but people began to stare. The bicycles, the dribbling basketballs, the sprinklers and lawn mowers, the cries of touch footballers—they all seemed to hush as I passed. Some stared out of curiosity because a strange man strolling in a dark gray suit on a summer evening was something of an oddity. But most, or again so it seemed, looked on in horror because they recognized me and couldn't believe that I would dare tread upon this sacred soil.

I approached the house at 147 Coddington Terrace without hesitation. My tie was loosened. I jammed my hands in my pockets. I toed the spot where curb met pavement. Why was I here? I saw a curtain move in the den. Mrs. Miller's face appeared at the window, gaunt and ghostlike. She glared at me. I didn't move or look away. She glared some more—and then to my surprise, her face softened. It was as though our mutual agony had made some sort of connection. Mrs. Miller nodded at me. I nodded back and felt the tears begin to well up.

You may have seen the story on *20/20* or *PrimeTime Live* or some other television equivalent of fish wrap. For those who haven't, here's the official account: On October 17 eleven years ago, in the township of Livingston, New Jersey, my brother, Ken Klein, then twenty-four, brutally raped and strangled our neighbor Julie Miller.

In her basement. At 147 Coddington Terrace.

That was where her body was found. The evidence wasn't conclusive as to if she'd actually been murdered in that poorly finished subdwelling or if she'd been dumped postmortem behind the water-stained zebra-striped couch. Most assume the former. My brother escaped capture and ran off to parts unknown—at least, again, according to the official account.

Over the past eleven years, Ken has eluded an international dragnet. There have however been "sightings."

The first came about a year after the murder from a small fishing village in northern Sweden. Interpol swooped in, but somehow my brother evaded their grasp. Supposedly he was tipped off. I can't imagine how or by whom.

The next sighting occurred four years later in Barcelona. Ken had rented—to quote the newspaper accounts—"an oceanview hacienda" (Barcelona is not on an ocean) with—again I will quote—"a lithe, dark-haired woman, perhaps a flamenco dancer." A vacationing Livingston resident, no less, reported seeing Ken and his Castilian paramour dining beachside. My brother was described as tan and fit and wore a white shirt opened at the collar and loafers without socks. The Livingstonite, one Rick Horowitz, had been a classmate of mine in Mr. Hunt's fourth-grade class. During a three-month period, Rick entertained us by eating caterpillars during recess.

Barcelona Ken yet again slipped through the law's fingers.

The last time my brother was purportedly spotted he was skiing down the expert hills in the French Alps (interestingly enough, Ken never skied before the murder). Nothing came of it, except a story on *48 Hours.* Over the years, my brother's fugitive status had become the criminal version of a VH1 *Where Are They Now?*, popping up whenever any sort of rumor skimmed the surface or, more likely, when one of the network's fish wraps was low on material.

I naturally hated television's "team coverage" of "suburbia gone wrong" or whatever similar cute moniker they came up with. Their "special reports" (just once, I'd like to see them call it a "normal report, everyone has done this story") always featured the same photographs of Ken in his tennis whites—he was a nationally ranked player at one time—looking his most pompous. I can't imagine where they got them. In them Ken looked handsome in that way people hate right away. Haughty, Kennedy hair, suntan bold against the whites, toothy grin, Photograph Ken looked like one of those people of privilege (he was not) who coasted through life on his charm (a little) and trust account (he had none).

I had appeared on one of those magazine shows. A producer reached me—this was pretty early on in the coverage—and claimed that he wanted to present "both sides fairly." They had plenty of people ready to lynch my brother, he noted. What they truly needed for the sake of "balance" was someone who could describe the "real Ken" to the folks back home.

I fell for it.

A frosted-blond anchorwoman with a sympathetic manner interviewed me for over an hour. I enjoyed the process actually. It was therapeutic. She thanked me and ushered me out and when the episode aired, they used only one snippet, removing her question ("But surely, you're not going to tell us that your brother was perfect, are you? You're not trying to tell us he was a saint, right?") and editing my line so that I appeared in nose-pore-enhancing extreme close-up with dramatic music as my cue, saying, "Ken was no saint, Diane."

Anyway, that was the official account of what happened.

I've never believed it. I'm not saying it's not possible. But I believe a much more likely scenario is that my brother is dead—that he has been dead for the past eleven years.

More to the point, my mother always believed that Ken was dead. She believed it firmly. Without reservation. Her son was not a murderer. Her son was a victim.

"He's alive. . . .He didn't do it."

The front door of the Miller house opened. Mr. Miller stepped through it. He pushed his glasses up his nose. His fists rested on his hips in a pitiful Superman stance.

"Get the hell out of here, Will," Mr. Miller said to me.

And I did.

The next big shock occurred an hour later.

Sheila and I were up in my parents' bedroom. The same furniture, a sturdy, faded swirling gray with blue trim, had adorned this room for as long as I could remember. We sat on the king-size bed with the weak-springed mattress. My mother's most personal items—the stuff she kept in her bloated nightstand drawers—were scattered over the duvet. My father was still downstairs by the bay windows, staring out defiantly.

I don't know why I wanted to sift through the things my mother found valuable enough to preserve and keep near her. It would hurt. I knew that. There is an interesting correlation between intentional pain infliction and comfort, a sort of playing-with-fire approach to grieving. I needed to do that, I guess.

I looked at Sheila's lovely face—tilted to the left, eyes down and focused—and I felt my heart soar. This is going to sound a little weird, but I could stare at Sheila for hours. It was not just her beauty—hers was not what one would call classical anyway, her features a bit off center from either genetics or, more likely, her murky past—but there was an animation there, an inquisitiveness, a delicacy too, as if one more blow would shatter her irreparably. Sheila made me want to—bear with me here—be brave for her.

Without looking up, Sheila gave a half-smile and said, "Cut it out."

"I'm not doing anything."

She finally looked up and saw the expression on my face. "What?" she asked.

I shrugged. "You're my world," I said simply.

"You're pretty hot stuff yourself."

"Yeah," I said. "Yeah, that's true."

She feigned a slap in my direction. "I love you, you know."

"What's not to love?"

She rolled her eyes. Then her gaze fell back onto the side of my mother's bed. Her face quieted.

"What are you thinking about?" I asked.

"Your mother." Sheila smiled. "I really liked her."

"I wish you had known her before."

"Me too."

We started going through the laminated yellow clippings. Birth announcements—Melissa's, Ken's, mine. There were articles on Ken's tennis exploits. His trophies, all those bronze men in miniature in mid-serve, still swarmed his old bedroom. There were photographs, mostly old ones from before the murder. Sunny. It had been my mother's nickname since childhood. It suited her. I found a photo of her as PTA president. I don't know what she was doing, but she was onstage and wearing a goofy hat and all the other mothers were cracking up. There was another one of her running the school fair. She was dressed in a clown suit. Sunny was the favorite grown-up among my friends. They liked when she drove the carpool. They wanted the class picnic at our house. Sunny was parental cool without being cloying, just "off" enough, a little crazy perhaps, so that you never knew exactly what she would do next. There had always been an excitement—a crackle if you will—around my mother.

We kept it up for more than two hours. Sheila took her time, looking thoughtfully at every picture. When she stopped at one in particular, her eyes narrowed. "Who's that?"

She handed me the photograph. On the left was my mother in a semi-obscene yellow bikini, I'd say, 1972ish, looking very curvy. She had her arm around a short man with a dark mustache and happy smile.

"King Hussein," I said.

"Pardon me?"

I nodded.

"As in the kingdom of Jordan?"

"Yep. Mom and Dad saw him at the Fontainebleau in Miami."

"And?"

"Mom asked him if he'd pose for a picture."

"You're kidding."

"There's the proof."

"Didn't he have guards or something?"

"I guess she didn't look armed."

Sheila laughed. I remember Mom telling me about the incident. Her posing with King Hussein, Dad's camera not working, his muttering under his breath, his trying to fix it, her glaring at him to hurry, the king standing patiently, his chief of security checking the camera, finding the problem, fixing it, handing it back to Dad.

My mom, Sunny.

"She was so lovely," Sheila said.

It's an awful cliché to say that a part of her died when they found Julie

Miller's body, but the thing about clichés is that they're often dead-on. My mother's crackle quieted, smothered. After hearing about the murder, she never threw a tantrum or cried hysterically. I often wish she had. My volatile mother became frighteningly even. Her whole manner became flat, monotone—*passionless* would be the best way to describe it—which in someone like her was more agonizing to witness than the most bizarre histrionics.

The front doorbell rang. I looked out the bedroom window and saw the Eppes-Essen deli delivery van. Sloppy joes for the, uh, mourners. Dad had optimistically ordered too many platters. Delusional to the end. He stayed in this house like the captain of the *Titanic.* I remember the first time the windows had been shot out with the BB gun not long after the murder—the way he shook his fist with defiance. Mom, I think, wanted to move. Dad would not. Moving would be a surrender in his eyes. Moving would be admitting their son's guilt. Moving would be a betrayal.

Dumb.

Sheila had her eyes on me. Her warmth was almost palpable, more sunbeam on my face, and for a moment I just let myself bathe in it. We'd met at work about a year before. I'm the senior director of Covenant House on 41st Street in New York City. We're a charitable foundation that helps young runaways survive the streets. Sheila had come in as a volunteer. She was from a small town in Idaho, though she seemed to have very little small-town girl left in her. She told me that many years ago, she too had been a runaway. That was all she would tell me about her past.

"I love you," I said.

"What's not to love?" she countered.

I did not roll my eyes. Sheila had been good to my mother toward the end. She'd take the Community Bus Line from Port Authority to Northfield Avenue and walk over to the St. Barnabas Medical Center. Before her illness, the last time my mom had stayed at St. Barnabas was when she delivered me. There was probably something poignantly life-cycling about that, but I couldn't see it just then.

I had however seen Sheila with my mother. And it made me wonder. I took a risk.

"You should call your parents," I said softly.

Sheila looked at me as though I'd just slapped her across the face. She slid off the bed.

"Sheila?"

"This isn't the time, Will."

I picked up a picture frame that held a photo of my tanned parents on vacation. "Seems as good as any."

"You don't know anything about my parents."

"I'd like to," I said.

She turned her back to me. "You've worked with runaways," she said.

"So?"

"You know how bad it can be."

I did. I thought again about her slightly off-center features—the nose, for example, with the telltale bump—and wondered. "I also know it's worse if you don't talk about it."

"I've talked about it, Will."

"Not with me."

"You're not my therapist."

"I'm the man you love."

"Yes." She turned to me. "But not now, okay? Please."

I had no response to that one, but perhaps she was right. My fingers were absently toying with the picture frame. And that was when it happened.

The photograph in the frame slid a little.

I looked down. Another photograph started peeking out from underneath. I moved the top one a little farther. A hand appeared in the bottom photograph. I tried pushing it some more, but it wouldn't go. My finger found the clips on back. I slid them to the side and let the back of the frame drop to the bed. Two photographs floated down behind it.

One—the top one—was of my parents on a cruise, looking happy and healthy and relaxed in a way I barely remember them ever being. But it was the second photograph, the hidden one, that caught my eye.

The red-stamped date on the bottom was from less than two years ago. The picture was taken atop a field or hill or something. I saw no houses in the background, just snowcapped mountains like something from the opening scene of *The Sound of Music.* The man in the picture wore shorts and a backpack and sunglasses and scuffed hiking boots. His smile was familiar. So was his face, though it was more lined now. His hair was longer. His beard had gray in it. But there was no mistake.

The man in the picture was my brother, Ken.

2

My father was alone on the back patio. Night had fallen. He sat very still and stared out at the black. As I came up behind him, a jarring memory rocked me.

About four months after Julie's murder, I found my father in the basement with his back to me just like this. He thought that the house was empty. Resting in his right palm was his Ruger, a .22 caliber gun. He cradled the weapon tenderly, as though it were a small animal, and I never felt so frightened in my entire life. I stood there, frozen. He kept his eyes on the gun. After a few long minutes, I quickly tiptoed to the top of the stairs and faked like I'd just come in. By the time I trudged down the steps, the weapon was gone.

I didn't leave his side for a week.

I slipped now through the sliding glass door. "Hey," I said to him.

He spun around, his face already breaking into a wide smile. He always had one for me. "Hey, Will," he said, the gravel voice turning tender. Dad was always happy to see his children. Before all this happened, my father was a fairly popular man. People liked him. He was friendly and dependable, if not a little gruff, which just made him seem all the more dependable. But while my father might smile at you, he didn't care a lick. His world was his family. No one else mattered to him. The suffering of strangers and even friends never really reached him—a sort of family-centeredness.

I sat in the lounge chair next to him, not sure how to raise the subject. I took a few deep breaths and listened to him do the same. I felt wonderfully safe with him. He might be older and more withered, and by now I was the taller, stronger man—but I knew that if trouble surfaced, he'd still step up and take the hit for me.

And that I'd still slip back and let him.

"Have to cut that branch back," he said, pointing into the dark.

I couldn't see it. "Yeah," I said.

The light from the sliding glass doors hit his profile. The anger had dissolved now, and the shattered look had returned. Sometimes I think that he had indeed tried to step up and take the hit when Julie died, but it had knocked him on his ass. His eyes still had that burst-from-within look, that look of someone who had unexpectedly been punched in the gut and didn't know why.

"You okay?" he asked me. His standard opening refrain.

"I'm fine. I mean, not fine but . . ."

Dad waved his hand. "Yeah, dumb question," he said.

We fell back into silence. He lit a cigarette. Dad never smoked at home. His children's health and all that. He took a drag and then, as if suddenly remembering, he looked at me and stamped it out.

"It's all right," I said.

"Your mother and I agreed that I would never smoke at home."

I didn't argue with him. I folded my hands and put them on my lap. Then I dived in. "Mom told me something before she died."

His eyes slid toward me.

"She said that Ken was still alive."

Dad stiffened, but only for a second. A sad smile came to his face. "It was the drugs, Will."

"That's what I thought," I said. "At first."

"And now?"

I looked at his face, searching for some sign of deception. There had been rumors, of course. Ken wasn't wealthy. Many wondered how my brother could have afforded to live in hiding for so long. My answer, of course, was that he hadn't—that he died that night too. Others, maybe most people, believed that my parents somehow sneaked him money.

I shrugged. "I wonder why after all these years she would say that."

"The drugs," he repeated. "And she was dying, Will."

The second part of that answer seemed to encompass so much. I let it hang a moment. Then I asked, "Do you think Ken's alive?"

"No," he said. And then he looked away.

"Did Mom say anything to you?"

"About your brother?"

"Yes."

"Pretty much what she told you," he said.

"That Ken was alive?"

"Yes."

"Anything else?"

Dad shrugged. "She said he didn't kill Julie. She said he'd be back by now except he had to do something first."

"Do what?"

"She wasn't making sense, Will."

"Did you ask her?"

"Of course. But she was just ranting. She couldn't hear me anymore. I shushed her. I told her it'd be okay."

He looked away again. I thought about showing him the photograph of Ken but decided against it. I wanted to think it through before I started us down that path.

"I told her it'd be okay," he repeated.

Through the sliding glass door, I could see one of those photo cubes, the old color images sun-faded into a blur of yellow-green. There were no recent pictures in the room. Our house was trapped in a time warp, frozen solid eleven years ago, like in that old song where the grandfather clock stops when the old man dies.

"I'll be right back," Dad said.

I watched him stand and walk until he thought he was out of sight. But

I could see his outline in the dark. I saw him lower his head. His shoulders started to shake. I don't think that I had ever seen my father cry. I didn't want to start now.

I turned away and remembered the other photograph, the one still upstairs of my parents on the cruise looking tan and happy, and I wondered if maybe he was thinking about that too.

When I woke late that night, Sheila wasn't in bed.

I sat up and listened. Nothing. At least, not in the apartment. I could hear the normal late-night street hum drifting up from three floors below. I looked over toward the bathroom. The light was out. All lights, in fact, were out.

I thought about calling out to her, but there was something fragile about the quiet, something bubblelike. I slipped out of bed. My feet touched down on the wall-to-wall carpet, the kind apartment buildings make you use so as to stifle noise from below or above.

The apartment wasn't big, just one bedroom. I padded toward the living room and peeked in. Sheila was there. She sat on the windowsill and looked down toward the street. I stared at her back, the swan neck, the wonderful shoulders, the way her hair flowed down the white skin, and again I felt the stir. Our relationship was still on the border of the early throes, the gee-it's-great-to-be-alive love where you can't get enough of each other, that wonderful run-across-the-park-to-see-her stomach-flutter that you know, *know*, would soon darken into something richer and deeper.

I'd been in love only once before. And that was a very long time ago.

"Hey," I said.

She turned just a little, but it was enough. There were tears on her cheeks. I could see them sliding down in the moonlight. She didn't make a sound—no cries or sobs or hitching chest. Just the tears. I stayed in the doorway and wondered what I should do.

"Sheila?"

On our second date, Sheila performed a card trick. It involved my picking two cards, putting them in the middle of the deck while she turned her head, and her throwing the entire deck save my two cards onto the floor. She smiled widely after performing this feat, holding up the two cards for my inspection. I smiled back. It was—how to put this?—goofy. Sheila was indeed goofy. She liked card tricks and cherry Kool-Aid and boy bands. She sang opera and read voraciously and cried at Hallmark commercials. She could do a mean imitation of Homer Simpson and Mr. Burns, though her Smithers and Apu were on the weak side. And most of all, Sheila loved to dance. She loved to close her eyes and put her head on my shoulder and fade away.

"I'm sorry, Will," Sheila said without turning around.

"For what?" I said.

She kept her eyes on the view. "Go back to bed. I'll be there in a few minutes."

I wanted to stay or offer up words of comfort. I didn't. She wasn't reachable right now. Something had pulled her away. Words or action would be either superfluous or harmful. At least, that was what I told myself. So I made a huge mistake. I went back to bed and waited.

But Sheila never came back.

3

Las Vegas, Nevada

Morty Meyer was in bed, dead asleep on his back, when he felt the gun muzzle against his forehead.

"Wake up," a voice said.

Morty's eyes went wide. The bedroom was dark. He tried to raise his head, but the gun held him down. His gaze slid toward the illuminated clock-radio on the night table. But there was no clock there. He hadn't owned one in years, now that he thought about it. Not since Leah died. Not since he'd sold the four-bedroom colonial.

"Hey, I'm good for it," Morty said. "You guys know that."

"Get up."

The man moved the gun away. Morty lifted his head. With his eyes adjusting, he could make out a scarf over the man's face. Morty remembered the radio program *The Shadow* from his childhood. "What do you want?"

"I need your help, Morty."

"We know each other?"

"Get up."

Morty obeyed. He swung his legs out of bed. When he stood, his head reeled in protest. He staggered, caught in that place where the drunk-buzz is winding down and the hangover is gathering strength like an oncoming storm.

"Where's your medical bag?" the man asked.

Relief flooded Morty's veins. So that was what this was about. Morty looked for a wound, but it was too dark. "You?" he asked.

"No. She's in the basement."

She?

Morty reached under the bed and pulled out his leather medical bag. It was old and worn. His initials, once shiny in gold leaf, were gone now. The zipper didn't close all the way. Leah had bought it when he'd graduated from Columbia University's medical school more than forty years before. He'd been an internist in Great Neck for the three decades following that. He and Leah had raised three boys. Now here he was, approaching seventy, living in a one-bedroom dump and owing money and favors to pretty much everyone.

Gambling. That'd been Morty's addiction of choice. For years, he'd been something of a functioning gambleholic, fraternizing with those particular inner demons yet keeping them on the fringe. Eventually, however, the demons caught up to him. They always do. Some had claimed that Leah had been a facilitator. Maybe that was true. But once she died, there was no reason to fight anymore. He let the demons claw in and do their worst.

Morty had lost everything, including his medical license. He moved out west to this shithole. He gambled pretty much every night. His boys—all grown and with families—didn't call him anymore. They blamed him for their mother's death. They said that he'd aged Leah before her time. They were probably right.

"Hurry," the man said.

"Right."

They started down the basement stairs. Morty could see the light was on. This building, his crappy new abode, used to be a funeral home. Morty rented a bedroom on the ground floor. That gave him use of the basement—where the bodies used to be stored and embalmed.

In the basement's back corner, a rusted playground slide ran down from the back parking lot. That was how they used to bring the bodies down—park-'n-slide. The walls were blanketed with tiles, though many were crumbling from years of neglect. You had to use a pair of pliers to get the water running. Most of the cabinet doors were gone. The death stench still hovered, an old ghost refusing to leave.

The injured woman was lying on a steel table. Morty could see right away that this didn't look good. He turned back to the Shadow.

"Help her," he said.

Morty didn't like the timbre of the man's voice. There was anger there, yes, but the overriding emotion was naked desperation, his voice more a plea than anything else. "She doesn't look good," Morty said.

The man pressed the gun against Morty's chest. "If she dies, you die."

Morty swallowed. Clear enough. He moved toward her. Over the years, he'd treated plenty of men down here—but this would be the first woman. That was how Morty made his quasi-living. Stitch and run. If you go to an emergency room with a bullet or stab wound, the doctor on duty had a legal obligation to report it. So they came instead to Morty's makeshift hospital.

He flashed back to the triage lessons of medical school. The ABCs, if you will. Airway, Breathing, Circulation. Her breaths were raspy and filled with spittle.

"You did this to her?"

The man did not reply.

Morty worked on her the best he could. Patchwork really. Get her stabilized, he thought. Stabilized and out of here.

When he was done, the man lifted her gently. "If you say anything—"

"I've been threatened by worse."

The man hurried out with the woman. Morty stayed in the basement. His nerves felt frayed from the surprise wake-up. He sighed and decided to head back to bed. But before he went up the stairs, Morty Meyer made a crucial error.

He looked out the back window.

The man carried the woman to the car. He carefully, almost tenderly, laid her down in the back. Morty watched the scene. And then he saw movement.

He squinted. And that was when he felt the shudder rip through him.

Another passenger.

There was a passenger in the back of the car. A passenger who very much did not belong. Morty automatically reached for the phone, but before he even picked up the receiver, he stopped. Who would he call? What would he say?

Morty closed his eyes, fought it off. He trudged back up the steps. He crawled back into bed and pulled the covers up over him. He stared at the ceiling and tried to forget.

4

The note Sheila left me was short and sweet:

Love you always.
S

She hadn't come back to bed. I assume that she'd spent the entire evening staring out the window. There'd been silence until I heard her slip out at around five in the morning. The time wasn't that odd. Sheila was an early riser, the sort who reminded me of that old army commercial about doing more before nine than most people did all day. You know the type: She makes you feel like a slacker, and you love her for it.

Sheila had told me once—and only once—that she was used to getting up early because of her years working on the farm. When I pressed her for details, she quickly clammed up. The past was the line in the sand. Cross it at your own peril.

I was more confused by her behavior than worried.

I showered and dressed. The photograph of my brother was in my desk drawer. I took it out and studied it for a long time. There was a hollow sensation in my chest. My mind whirled and danced, but coming through all that was one pretty basic thought:

Ken had pulled it off.

You may have been wondering what'd convinced me that he'd been dead all these years. Part of it, I confess, was old-fashioned intuition mixed with blind hope. I loved my brother. And I knew him. Ken was not perfect. Ken was quick to anger and thrived on confrontation. Ken was mixed up in something bad. But Ken was not a murderer. I was sure of that.

But there was more to the Klein family theory than this bizarre faith. First off, how could Ken have survived on the run like this? He'd only had eight hundred dollars in the bank. Where did he get the resources to elude this international manhunt? And what possible motive could there have been for killing Julie? How come he never contacted us during the past eleven years? Why was he so on edge when he came home for that final visit? Why did he tell me that he was in danger? And why, looking back on it, didn't I push him to tell me more?

But most damaging—or encouraging, depending on your viewpoint—was the blood found at the scene. Some of it belonged to Ken. A large splotch of his blood was in the basement, and small drips made a trail up the stairs and out the door. And then another splotch was found on a shrub in the Millers' backyard. The Klein family theory was that the real murderer had killed Julie and seriously wounded (and eventually killed) my brother. The police's theory was simpler: Julie had fought back.

There was one more thing that backed the family theory—something directly attributable to me, which was why, I guess, no one took it seriously.

That is, I saw a man lurking near the Miller house that night.

Like I said, the authorities and press have pretty much dismissed this—I am, after all, interested in clearing my brother—but it is important in understanding why we believe what we believe. In the end, my family had a choice. We could accept that my brother murdered a lovely young woman for no reason, that he then lived without any visible income in hiding for eleven years (this—don't forget—despite extensive media coverage and a major police search)—or we could believe that he had consensual sex with Julie Miller (ergo much of the physical evidence), and that whatever mess he had gotten himself into, whoever had terrified Ken so, maybe whoever I saw outside the house on Coddington Terrace that night had somehow set him up for a murder and made sure his body would never be found.

I'm not saying it was a perfect fit. But we knew Ken. He didn't do what they said. So what was the alternative?

Some people did give credence to our family's theory, but most were conspiracy nuts, the kind who think Elvis and Jimi Hendrix are jamming on some island off Fiji. The TV stories gave it lip service that was so tongue-in-cheek you'd expect your television to smirk at you. As time went by, I grew quieter in my defense of Ken. Selfish as this might sound, I wanted a life. I wanted a career. I didn't want to be the brother of a famous murderer on the run.

Covenant House, I'm sure, had reservations about hiring me. Who would blame them? Even though I'm a senior director, my name is kept off the letterhead. I never appear at fund-raising functions. My job is strictly behind-the-scenes. And most of the time, that's okay with me.

I looked again at the picture of a man so familiar yet totally unknown to me.

Had my mother been lying from the beginning?

Had she been helping Ken while telling my father and me she thought he was dead? When I think back on it now, it was my mother who had been the strongest proponent of the Ken-dead theory. Had she been sneaking him money the whole time? Had Sunny known where he was from the start?

Questions to ponder.

I wrested my eyes away and opened a kitchen cabinet. I'd already decided that I wouldn't go out to Livingston this morning—the thought of sitting in that coffin of a house for another day made me want to scream—and I really needed to go to work. My mother, I was sure, would not only understand but encourage. So I poured myself a bowl of Golden Grahams cereal and dialed Sheila's work voice mail. I told her I loved her and I asked her to call me.

My apartment—well, it's *our* apartment now—is on 24th Street and Ninth Avenue, not far from the Chelsea Hotel. I usually walk the seventeen blocks north to Covenant House, which was on 41st Street, not far from the West Side Highway. This used to be a great location for a runaway shelter in the days before the cleanup of 42nd Street, when this stretch of stench was a bastion of in-your-face degradation. Forty-second Street had been a sort of Hell's Gate, a place for the grotesquely amative intermingling of species. Commuters and tourists would walk past prostitutes and dealers and pimps and head shops and porno palaces and movie theaters, and when they'd reach the end, they'd either be titillated or they'd want to take a shower and get a shot of penicillin. In my view, the perversion was so dirty, so depressing, it had to weigh you down. I am a man. I have lusts and urges like most guys I know. But I never understood how anyone could confuse the filth of toothless crackheads for eroticism.

The city's cleanup, in a sense, made our jobs harder. The Covenant House rescue van had known where to cruise. The runaways were out in the open, more obvious. Now our task wasn't as clear-cut. And worse, the city itself wasn't really cleaner—just cleaner to look at. The so-called decent folk, those commuters and tourists I mentioned before, were no longer subjected to blacked-out windows reading ADULTS ONLY or crumbling marquees announcing pun-porn titles like SHAVING RYAN'S PRIVATES or BONFIRE OF THE PANTIES. But sleaze like this never really dies. Sleaze is a cockroach. It survives. It burrows and it hides. I don't think you can kill it.

And there are negatives to hiding the sleaze. When sleaze is obvious, you can scoff and feel superior. People need that. It's an outlet for some. Another advantage to in-the-open sleaze: Which would you rather face—an obvious frontal assault or a snakelike danger gliding through the high grass? Finally—and maybe I'm looking at this too closely—you can't have a front without a back, you can't have an up without a down, and I'm not sure you can have light without dark, purity without sleaze, good without evil.

The first honk didn't make me turn around. I live in New York City. Avoiding honks while strolling the avenues was tantamount to avoiding water while swimming. So it was not until I heard the familiar voice yell "Hey, asshole" that I turned around. The Covenant House van screeched alongside me. Squares was the driver and sole occupant. He lowered the window and whipped off his sunglasses.

"Get in," he said.

I opened the door and hopped up. The outreach van smelled of cigarettes and sweat and faintly of bologna from the sandwiches we hand out every night. There were stains of every size and stripe on the carpeting. The glove compartment was just an empty cavern. The springs in the seats were shot.

Squares kept his eyes on the road. "What the hell are you doing?"

"Going to work."

"Why?"

"Therapy," I said.

Squares nodded. He'd been up all night driving the van—an avenging angel searching for kids to rescue. He didn't look worse for wear, but then again, he hadn't started out too sparkly anyway. His hair was eighties Aerosmith-long, parted in the middle and on the greasy side. I don't think

I'd ever seen him clean-shaven, but I'd never seen him with a full beard or even a nifty-neat *Miami Vice* growth either. The patches of skin that were visible were pockmarked. His work boots were scuffed to a near whiteness. His jeans looked like they'd been trampled in a prairie by buffalo, and the waist was too big, giving him that ever-desirable repairman-butt-plunge look. A pack of Camels was rolled up in his sleeve. His teeth were tobacco-stained the yellow of a Ticonderoga pencil.

"You look like shit," he said.

"That means something," I said, "coming from you."

He liked that one. We called him Squares, short for Four Squares, because of the tattoo on his forehead. It was, well, four squares, two by two, so that it looked exactly like a four squares court you still see on playgrounds. Now that Squares was a big-time yoga instructor with videos and a chain of schools, most people assumed that the tattoo was some sort of significant Hindu symbol. Not so.

At one time, it had been a tattoo of a swastika. He'd just added four lines. Closed it up.

It was hard for me to imagine this. Squares is probably the least judgmental person I've ever known. He's probably also my closest friend. When he first told me the origins of the squares, I was appalled and shocked. He never explained or apologized, and like Sheila, he never talked about his past. Others have filled in pieces. I understand better now.

"Thanks for sending the flowers," I said.

Squares didn't reply.

"And for showing up," I added. He had brought a group of Covenant House friends in the van. They'd pretty much made up the entire nonfamily funeral brigade.

"Sunny was great people," he said.

"Yeah."

A moment of silence. Then Squares said, "But what a shitty turnout."

"Thanks for pointing that out."

"I mean, Jesus, how many people were there?"

"You're quite the comfort, Squares. Thanks, man."

"You want comfort? Know this: People are assholes."

"Let me get out a pen and write that down."

Silence. Squares stopped for a red light and sneaked a glance at me. His eyes were red. He unrolled the cigarette pack from his sleeve. "You want to tell me what's wrong?"

"Uh, well, see, the other day? My mother died."

"Fine," he said, "don't tell me."

The light turned green. The van started up again. The image of my brother in that photograph flashed across my eyes. "Squares?"

"I'm listening."

"I think," I said, "that my brother is still alive."

Squares didn't say anything right away. He withdrew a cigarette from the pack and put it in his mouth.

"Quite the epiphany," he said.

"Epiphany," I repeated with a nod.

"Been taking night courses," he said. "So why the sudden change of heart?"

He pulled into the small Covenant House lot. We used to park out on the street, but people would break in and sleep there. We did not call the cops, of course, but the expense of the broken windows and stripped locks became cumbersome. After a while, we kept the van doors unlocked so the inhabitants could just go inside. In the morning, whoever was first to arrive at the center would knock against the van. The night's tenants would get the message and scurry away.

We had to stop that too, though. The van became—not to get too graphic here—too disgusting for use. The homeless are not always pretty. They vomit. They soil themselves. They often cannot find rest-room facilities. Enough said.

Still sitting in the van, I wondered how to approach this. "Let me ask you a question."

He waited.

"You've never given me your take on what happened to my brother," I said.

"That a question?"

"More an observation. Here's the question: How come?"

"How come I never gave you my take on your brother?"

"Yes."

Squares shrugged. "You never asked."

"We talked about it a lot."

Squares shrugged again.

"Okay, I'm asking now," I said. "Did you think he's alive?"

"Always."

Just like that. "So all those talks we had, all those times I made convincing arguments to the contrary . . ."

"I wondered who you were trying to convince, me or you."

"You never bought my arguments?"

"Nope," Squares said. "Never."

"But you never argued with me either."

Squares took a deep drag on the cigarette. "Your delusion seemed harmless."

"Ignorance is bliss, eh?"

"Most of the time, yeah."

"But I made some valid points," I said.

"You say so."

"You don't think so?"

"I don't think so," Squares said. "You thought your bro didn't have the resources to hide, but you don't need resources. Look at the runaways we meet every day. If one of them really wanted to disappear, presto, they'd be gone."

"There isn't an international manhunt for any of them."

"International manhunt," Squares said with something close to disgust. "You think every cop in the world wakes up wondering about your brother?"

He had a point—especially now that I realized he may have gotten financial help from my mother. "He wouldn't kill anyone."

"Bullshit," Squares said.

"You don't know him."

"We're friends, right?"

"Right."

"You believe that one day I used to burn crosses and shout 'Heil Hitler'?"

"That's different."

"No, it's not." We stepped out of the van. "You asked me once why I didn't get rid of the tattoo altogether, remember?"

I nodded. "And you told me to fuck off."

"Right. But the fact is, I could have removed it by laser or done a more elaborate cover-up. But I keep it because it reminds me."

"Of what? The past?"

Squares flashed the yellows. "Of potential," he said.

"I don't know what that means."

"Because you're hopeless."

"My brother would never rape and murder an innocent woman."

"Some yoga schools teach mantras," Squares said. "But repeating something over and over does not make it true."

"You're pretty deep today," I said.

"And you're acting like an asshole." He stubbed out the cigarette. "You going to tell me why you've had this change of heart?"

We were near the entrance.

"In my office," I said.

We hushed as we entered the shelter. People expect a dump, but our shelter is anything but. Our philosophy is that this should be a place you'd want your own kids to stay if they were in trouble. That comment stuns donors at first—like most charities, this one seems very removed from them—but it also strikes them where they live.

Squares and I were silent now, because when we are in our house, all our focus, all our concentration, is aimed at the kids. They deserve nothing less. For once in their often sad lives, they are what matters most. Always. We greet each kid like—and pardon the way I phrase this—a long-lost brother. We listen. We never hurry. We shake hands and hug. We look them in the eye. We never look over their shoulder. We stop and face them full. If you try to fake it, these kids will pick it up in a second. They have excellent bullshit-o-meters. We love them hard in here, totally and without conditions. Every day we do that. Or we just go home. It doesn't mean that we are always successful. Or even successful most of the time. We lose a lot more than we save. They get sucked back down into the streets. But while here, in our house, they will stay in comfort. While here, they will be loved.

When we entered my office, two people—one woman, one man—were waiting for us. Squares stopped short. He lifted his nostrils and sniffed the air, hound-dog style.

"Cops," he said to me.

The woman smiled and stepped forward. The man stayed behind her, casually leaning again the wall. "Will Klein?"

"Yes?" I said.

She unfurled her ID with a flourish. The man did the same thing. "My name is Claudia Fisher. This is Darryl Wilcox. We're both special agents for the Federal Bureau of Investigation."

"The feds," Squares said to me, thumbs up, like he was impressed I ranked such attention. He squinted at the ID, then at Claudia Fisher. "Hey, how come you cut your hair?"

Claudia Fisher snapped the ID closed. She arched an eyebrow at Squares. "And you are?"

"Easily aroused," he said.

She frowned and slid her eyes back to me. "We'd like a few words with you." Then she added, "Alone."

Claudia Fisher was short and semi-perky, the dedicated student/athlete from high school who was a little too tightly wound—the type who had fun but never spontaneously. Her hair was indeed short and feathered back, a bit too late-seventies but it fit. She had small hoop earrings and a strong bird nose.

We are naturally suspicious of law enforcement here. I have no desire to protect criminals, but I do not want to be a tool in their apprehension either. This place has to be a safe haven. Cooperating with law enforcement would cripple our street cred—and really, our street cred is everything. I like to think of us as neutral. Switzerland for the runaways. And of course, my personal history—the way the feds have handled my brother's situation—does little to endear me to them either.

"I'd rather he stayed," I said.

"This has nothing to do with him."

"Think of him as my attorney."

Claudia Fisher took Squares in—the jeans, the hair, the tattoo. He pulled on imaginary lapels and wriggled his eyebrows.

I moved to my desk. Squares flopped into the chair in front of it and threw his work boots onto the desktop. They landed with a dusty thud. Fisher and Wilcox remained standing.

I spread my hands. "What can I do for you, Agent Fisher?"

"We're looking for one Sheila Rogers."

That had not been what I expected.

"Can you tell us where we might find her?"

"Why are you looking for her?" I asked.

Claudia Fisher gave me a patronizing smile. "Would you mind just telling us where she is?"

"Is she in trouble?"

"Right now"—she paused a beat and changed the smile—"we'd just like to ask her some questions."

"What about?"

"Are you refusing to cooperate with us?"

"I'm not refusing anything."

"Then please tell us where we might locate Sheila Rogers."

"I'd like to know why."

She looked at Wilcox. Wilcox gave her a very small nod. She turned back to me. "Earlier today, Special Agent Wilcox and I visited Sheila Rogers's place of employment on 18th Street. She was not present. We inquired as to where we might locate her. Her employer informed us that she had called in sick. We checked her last known place of residence. The landlord informed us that she moved out several months ago. Her current residence was listed as yours, Mr. Klein, on 378 West 24th Street. We visited there. Sheila Rogers was not present."

Squares pointed at her. "You talk real purdy."

She ignored him. "We don't want trouble, Mr. Klein."

"Trouble?" I said.

"We need to question Sheila Rogers. We need to question her right away. We can do it the easy way. Or, if you choose not to cooperate, we can travel an alternate, though less pleasant, avenue."

Squares rubbed his hands together. "Ooo, a threat."

"What's it going to be, Mr. Klein?"

"I'd like you to leave," I said.

"How much do you know about Sheila Rogers?"

This was turning weird. My head started aching. Wilcox reached into his jacket pocket and took out a sheet of paper. He handed it to Claudia Fisher. "Are you aware," Fisher said, "of Ms. Rogers's criminal record?"

I tried to keep a straight face, but even Squares reacted to that one.

Fisher started reading from the sheet of paper. "Shoplifting. Prostitution. Possession with intent to sell."

Squares made a scoffing noise. "Amateur hour."

"Armed robbery."

"Better," Squares said with a nod. He looked up at Fisher. "No conviction on that one, right?"

"That's correct."

"So maybe she didn't do it."

Fisher frowned again.

I plucked at my lower lip.

"Mr. Klein?"

"Can't help you," I said.

"Can't or won't."

I still plucked. "Semantics."

"This must all seem a little déjà-vu, Mr. Klein."

"What the hell is that supposed to mean?"

"Covering up. First for your brother. Now your lover."

"Go to hell," I said.

Squares made a face at me, clearly disappointed with my admittedly lame retort.

Fisher didn't back off. "You're not thinking this through," she said.

"How's that?"

"The repercussions," she went on. "For example: How do you think the Covenant House donors would take it if you were arrested for, say, aiding and abetting?"

Squares took that one. "You know who you should ask?"

Claudia Fisher crinkled her nose at him, as if he were something she'd just scraped off her shoe.

"Joey Pistillo," Squares said. "I bet Joey would know."

Now it was Fisher and Wilcox's turn to rock back on their heels.

"You got a cell phone?" Squares asked. "We can ask him right now."

Fisher looked at Wilcox, then at Squares. "Are you telling us that you know Assistant Director in Charge Joseph Pistillo?" she asked.

"Call him," Squares said. Then: "Oh, wait, you probably don't know his private line." Squares stretched out his hand and wiggled his finger in a give-me gesture. "You mind?"

She handed him the phone. Squares pressed the number pad and put the phone to his ear. He leaned all the way back, his feet still on the desk; if he'd been wearing a cowboy hat, it'd be pulled down over his eyes for a little siesta.

"Joey? Hey, man, how are you?" Squares listened for a minute and then he burst out laughing. He schmoozed a bit and I watched Fisher and Wilcox turn white. Normally I'd enjoy this power play—between his checkered past and current celebrity status, Squares was one degree of separation from almost everyone—but my mind was reeling.

After a few minutes, Squares handed Agent Fisher the cell phone. "Joey wants to talk to you."

Fisher and Wilcox stepped out in the corridor and closed the door.

"Dude, the feds," Squares said, thumbs up again, still impressed.

"Yeah, I'm pretty thrilled," I said.

"That's something, huh. I mean, about Sheila having a record. Who'd have guessed?"

Not me.

When Fisher and Wilcox returned, the color had returned to their faces. Fisher handed the phone to Squares with too courteous a smile.

Squares put it to his ear and said, "What's up, Joey?" He listened for a while. Then he said, "Okay," and hung up.

"What?" I said.

"That was Joey Pistillo. Top gun for the FBI on the East Coast."

"And?"

"He wants to see you in person," Squares said. He looked off.

"What?"

"I don't think we're going to like what he has to say."

5

Assistant Director in Charge Joseph Pistillo not only wanted to see me in person, but alone.

"I understand your mother passed away," he said.

"How do you understand?"

"Pardon?"

"Did you read the obituary in the paper?" I asked. "Did a friend tell you? How did you come to understand that she passed away?"

We looked at each other. Pistillo was a burly man, bald except for a close-cropped fringe of gray, shoulders like bowling balls, gnarled hands folded on his desk.

"Or," I went on, feeling the old anger creep in, "did you have an agent watching us. Watching her. At the hospital. On her deathbed. At her funeral. Was one of your agents the new orderly the nurses whispered about? Was one of your agents the limousine driver who forgot the funeral director's name?"

Neither one of us broke eye contact.

"I'm sorry for your loss," Pistillo said.

"Thank you."

He leaned back. "Why won't you tell us where Sheila Rogers is?"

"Why won't you tell me why you're looking for her?"

"When did you see her last?"

"Are you married, Agent Pistillo?"

He didn't break stride. "Twenty-six years. We have three kids."

"You love your wife?"

"Yes."

"So if I came to you and made demands and threats involving her, what would you do?"

Pistillo nodded slowly. "If you worked for the Federal Bureau of Investigation, I'd tell her to cooperate."

"Just like that?"

"Well"—he raised his index finger—"with one caveat."

"What's that?"

"That she was innocent. If she's innocent, I'd have no fears."

"So you wouldn't wonder what it was all about?"

"Wonder? Sure. Demand to know . . ." He let his voice trail off. "Let me ask you a hypothetical now."

He paused. I sat up.

"I know that you think your brother is dead."

Another pause. I stayed quiet.

"But suppose you found out that he's alive and hiding—and suppose on top of that, you found out he killed Julie Miller." He sat back. "Hypothetically, of course. This is all just a hypothetical."

"Go on," I said.

"Well, what would you do? Would you turn him in? Would you tell him he's on his own? Or would you help him?"

More silence.

I said, "You didn't bring me here to play hypotheticals."

"No," he said, "I didn't."

There was a computer monitor on the right side of his desk. He turned the screen so that I could see it. Then he pressed some buttons. A color image came up, and something inside me clenched.

An ordinary-looking room. Tall lamp in the corner overturned. Beige carpet. Coffee table on its side. A mess. Like a tornado aftermath or something. But in the center of the room, a man lay in a puddle of what I assumed was blood. The blood was dark, beyond crimson, beyond rust, almost black. The man lay faceup, his arms and legs splayed in such way that he looked like he'd been dropped from a great height.

As I looked at the image on the monitor, I could feel Pistillo's eyes on me, gauging my reaction. My eyes flicked to his and then back at the screen.

He pressed the keyboard. Another image replaced the blood-soaked one. The same room. The lamp was out of sight now. Blood still stained the carpet—but there was another body now, this one curled up in the fetal position. The first man wore a black T-shirt and black pants. This one wore a flannel shirt and blue jeans.

Pistillo hit another key. Now the photograph was wide framed. Both bodies now. The first in the center of the room. The second, closer to the door. I could see only one face—from this angle it was not a familiar one—but the other was blocked from view.

Panic rose up in me. Ken, I thought. Could one of them be . . . ?

But then I remembered their questions. This wasn't about Ken.

"These pictures were taken in Albuquerque, New Mexico, over the weekend," Pistillo said.

I frowned. "I don't understand."

"The crime scene was something of a mess, but we still found some hairs and fibers." He smiled at me. "I'm not great on the technical aspects of our work. They have tests nowadays that you simply can't believe. But sometimes it's still the classics that get you through the day."

"Am I supposed to know what you're talking about?"

"Someone had wiped the place pretty good, but the crime-scene people still lifted a set of fingerprints—one clean set that didn't belong to either of the victims. We ran them through the computer and got a hit early this morning." He leaned forward and the smile was gone now. "You want to make a guess?"

I saw Sheila, my beautiful Sheila, staring out the window.

"I'm sorry, Will."

"They belong to your girlfriend, Mr. Klein. The same one with a criminal record. The same one we're suddenly having a lot of trouble finding."

6

Elizabeth, New Jersey

They were near the cemetery now.

Philip McGuane sat in the back of his handcrafted Mercedes limousine—a stretch model equipped with armor-reinforced sides and bulletproof one-way windows at a cost of four hundred thou—and stared out at the blur of fast-food restaurants, tacky stores, and aged strip malls. A scotch and soda, freshly mixed in the limo's wet bar, was cupped in his right hand. He looked down at the amber liquor. Steady. That surprised him.

"You okay, Mr. McGuane?"

McGuane turned to his companion. Fred Tanner was huge, the approximate size and consistency of a city brownstone. His hands were manhole covers with sausagelike fingers. His gaze was one of supreme confidence. Old school, Tanner was—still with his shellac-shiny suit and the ostentatious pinky ring. Tanner always wore the ring, a garish, oversize gold thing, twisting and toying with it whenever he spoke.

"I'm fine," McGuane lied.

The limousine exited Route 22 at Parker Avenue. Tanner kept fiddling with the pinky ring. He was fifty, a decade and a half older than his boss. His face was a weathered monument of harsh planes and right angles. His hair was meticulously mowed into a severe crew cut. McGuane knew that Tanner was very good—a cold, disciplined and lethal son of a bitch for whom mercy was about as relevant a concept as feng shui. Tanner was adept at using those huge hands or a potpourri of firearms. He had gone up against some of the cruelest and had always come out on top.

But this, McGuane knew, was taking it to a whole new level.

"Who is this guy anyway?" Tanner asked.

McGuane shook his head. His own suit was a hand-tailored Joseph Abboud. He rented three floors on Manhattan's lower west side. In another era, McGuane might have been called a consigliore or capo or some such nonsense. But that was then, this is now. Gone (long gone, despite what Hollywood might want you to believe) were the days of backroom hangouts and velour sweats—days Tanner undoubtedly still longed for. Now you had offices and a secretary and a computer-generated payroll. You paid taxes. You owned legit businesses.

But you were no better.

"And why we driving way out here anyway?" Tanner went on. "He should come to you, no?"

McGuane didn't reply. Tanner wouldn't understand.

If the Ghost wants to meet, you meet.

Didn't matter who you were. To refuse would mean that the Ghost would come to you. McGuane had excellent security. He had good people. But the Ghost was better. He had patience. He would study you. He would wait for an opening. And then he would find you. Alone. You knew that.

No, better to get it over with. Better to go to him.

A block away from the cemetery, the limousine pulled to a stop.

"You understand what I want," McGuane said.

"I got a man in place already. It's taken care of."

"Don't take him out unless you see my signal."

"Right, yeah. We've gone over this."

"Don't underestimate him."

Tanner gripped the door handle. Sunlight glistened off the pinky ring. "No offense, Mr. McGuane, but he's just some guy, right? Bleeds red like the rest of us?"

McGuane was not so sure.

Tanner stepped out, moving gracefully for a man carrying such bulk. McGuane sat back and downed a long swig of scotch. He was one of the most powerful men in New York. You don't get there—you don't reach that pinnacle—without being a cunning and ruthless bastard. You show weakness, you're dead. You limp, you die. Simple as that.

And most of all, you never back down.

McGuane knew all that—knew it as well as anyone—but right now, more than anything, he wanted to run away. Just pack what he could and simply disappear.

Like his old friend Ken.

McGuane met the driver's eyes in the rearview mirror. He took a deep breath and nodded. The car started moving again. They turned left and slid past the gates of Wellington Cemetery. Tires crunched loose gravel. McGuane told the driver to stop. The driver obeyed. McGuane stepped out and moved to the front of the car.

"I'll call you when I need you."

The driver nodded and pulled out.

McGuane was alone.

He pulled up his collar. His gaze swept over the graveyard. No movement. He wondered where Tanner and his man had hidden themselves. Probably closer to the meet site. In a tree or behind a shrub. If they were doing it right, McGuane would never see them.

The sky was clear. The wind whipped him like a reaper's scythe. He hunched his shoulders. The traffic sounds from Route 22 spilled up over sound barriers and serenaded the dead. The smell of something freshly baked wafted in the still air and for a moment McGuane thought of cremation.

No sign of anyone.

McGuane found the path and headed east. As he passed the stones and markers, his eyes unconsciously checked birth and death dates. He calculated ages and wondered about what fate had befallen the young ones. He hesitated when he saw a familiar name. Daniel Skinner. Dead at age thirteen. A smiling angel had been sculpted into the tombstone. McGuane chuckled softly at the image. Skinner, a vicious bully, had been repeatedly tormenting a fourth-grader. But on that day—May 11, according to the tombstone—that rather unique fourth-grader had brought a kitchen knife for protection. His first and only thrust punctured Skinner's heart.

Bye, bye, Angel.

McGuane tried to shrug it off.

Had it all started here?

He moved on. Up ahead, he made a left and slowed his pace. Not far now. His eyes scanned the surroundings. Still no movement. It was quieter back here—peaceful and green. Not that the inhabitants seemed to care. He hesitated, veered left again, and moved down the row until he arrived at the right grave.

McGuane stopped. He read the name and the date. His mind traveled back. He wondered what he felt and realized that the answer was, not much. He didn't bother looking around anymore. The Ghost was here somewhere. He could feel him.

"You should have brought flowers, Philip."

The voice, soft and silky with a hint of a lisp, chilled his blood. McGuane slowly turned to look behind him. John Asselta approached, flowers in his hand. McGuane stepped away. Asselta's eyes met his, and McGuane could feel a steel claw reach into his chest.

"It's been a long time," the Ghost said.

Asselta, the man McGuane knew as the Ghost, moved toward the tombstone. McGuane stayed perfectly still. The temperature seemed to drop thirty degrees when the Ghost walked past.

McGuane held his breath.

The Ghost knelt and gently placed the flowers on the ground. He stayed down there for a moment, his eyes closed. Then he stood, reached out with the tapered fingers of a pianist, and caressed the tombstone with too much intimacy.

McGuane tried not to watch.

The Ghost had skin like cataracts, milky and marshlike. Blue veins ran down his almost-pretty face like dyed tear tracks. His eyes were shale, almost colorless. His head, too big for his narrow shoulders, was shaped like a lightbulb. The sides of his skull were freshly shaved, a sprout of mud-brown hairs sticking up from the middle and cascading out like a fountain. There was something delicate, even feminine, in his features—a nightmare version of a Dresden doll.

McGuane took another step back.

Sometimes you meet a person whose innate goodness bursts at you with an almost blinding light. And then sometimes, you meet the direct opposite—someone whose very presence smothers you in a heavy cloak of decay and blood.

"What do you want?" McGuane asked.

The Ghost lowered his head. "Have you heard the expression that there are no atheists in foxholes?"

"Yes."

"It's a lie, you know," the Ghost said. "In fact, just the opposite is true. When you are in a foxhole, when you are face-to-face with death—that is when you know for sure that there is no God. It's why you fight to survive, to draw one more breath. It's why you call out to any and every entity—because you don't want to die. Because in your heart of hearts, you know that death is the endgame. No hereafter. No paradise. No God. Just nothingness."

The Ghost looked up at him. McGuane stayed still.

"I've missed you, Philip."

"What do you want, John?"

"I think you know."

McGuane did, but he said nothing.

"I understand," the Ghost continued, "that you are in something of a bind."

"What have you heard?"

"Just rumors." The Ghost smiled. His mouth was a thin razor slice, and the sight of it nearly made McGuane scream. "It's why I'm back."

"It's my problem."

"If only that were true, Philip."

"What do you want, John?"

"The two men you sent to New Mexico. They failed, correct?"

"Yes."

The Ghost whispered, "I won't."

"I still don't understand what you want."

"You would agree, would you not, that I have something of a stake in this too?"

The Ghost waited. McGuane finally nodded. "I guess you do."

"You have sources, Philip. Access to information I don't." The Ghost looked at the tombstone, and for a moment McGuane thought he saw something almost human there. "Are you sure he's back?"

"Fairly sure," McGuane said.

"How do you know?"

"Someone with the FBI. The men we sent to Albuquerque were supposed to confirm it."

"They underestimated their foe."

"Apparently."

"Do you know where he ran to?"

"We're working on it."

"But not very hard."

McGuane said nothing.

"You'd prefer that he vanish again. Am I right?"

"It'd make things easier."

The Ghost shook his head. "Not this time."

There was silence.

"So who would know where he is?" the Ghost asked.

"His brother perhaps. The FBI picked Will up an hour ago. For questioning."

That got the Ghost's attention. His head popped up. "Questioning about what?"

"We don't know yet."

"Then," the Ghost said softly, "that might be a good place for me to start."

McGuane managed a nod. And that was when the Ghost stepped toward him. He put out his hand. McGuane shuddered, couldn't move.

"Afraid to shake an old friend's hand, Philip?"

He was. The Ghost took another step closer. McGuane's breathing was shallow. He thought about signaling Tanner.

One bullet. One bullet could end this.

"Shake my hand, Philip."

It was a command, and McGuane obeyed it. Almost against his will, his hand rose from his side and slowly reached out. The Ghost, he knew, killed people. Lots of them. With ease. He was Death. Not just a killer. But Death itself—as though the Ghost's very touch could prick your skin, enter your bloodstream, send out a poison that would puncture your heart like the kitchen knife the Ghost had used so long ago.

McGuane averted his eyes.

The Ghost quickly closed the gap between them and clasped McGuane's hand in his own. McGuane bit back a scream. He tried to pull away from the clammy trap. The Ghost held on.

Then McGuane felt something—something cold and sharp digging into his palm.

The grip tightened. McGuane gasped in pain. Whatever the Ghost had in his hand speared into a nerve bundle like a bayonet. The grip tightened a little more. McGuane dropped to one knee.

The Ghost waited until McGuane looked up. The two men's eyes met, and McGuane was sure that his lungs would stop, that his organs would simply shut down one by one. The Ghost loosened his grip. He slipped the sharp something into McGuane's hand and folded his fingers over it. Then, finally, the Ghost let go and stepped back.

"It could be a lonely ride back, Philip."

McGuane found his voice. "What the hell is that supposed to mean?"

But the Ghost turned and walked away. McGuane looked down and opened his fist.

There in his hand, twinkling in the sunlight, was Tanner's gold pinky ring.

7

After my meeting with Assistant Director Pistillo, Squares and I hopped in the van. "Your apartment?" he asked me.

I nodded.

"I'm listening," he said.

I recounted my conversation with Pistillo.

Squares shook his head. "Albuquerque. Hate that place, man. You ever been?"

"No."

"You're in the Southwest yet everything feels pseudo-Southwest. Like the whole place is a Disney facsimile."

"I'll keep that in mind, Squares, thanks."

"So when did Sheila go?"

"I don't know," I said.

"Think. Where were you last weekend?"

"I was at my folks'."

"And Sheila?"

"She was supposed to be in the city."

"You called her?"

I thought about it. "No, she called me."

"Caller ID?"

"The number was blocked."

"Anybody who can confirm she was in the city?"

"I don't think so."

"So she could have been in Albuquerque," Squares said.

I considered that. "There are other explanations," I said.

"Like?"

"The fingerprints could be old."

Squares frowned, kept his eyes on the road.

"Maybe," I went on, "she went out to Albuquerque last month or hell, last year. How long do fingerprints last anyway?"

"Awhile, I think."

"So maybe that's what happened," I said. "Or maybe her prints were on, say, a piece of furniture—a chair maybe—and maybe the chair was in New York and then it was shipped out to New Mexico."

Squares adjusted his sunglasses. "Reaching."

"But possible."

"Yeah, sure. And hey, maybe someone borrowed her fingers. You know. Took them to Albuquerque for the weekend."

A taxi cut us off. We made a right turn, nearly clipping a group of people standing three feet off the curb. Manhattanites always do that. No one ever waits for the light on the actual sidewalk. They step into the fold, risk their lives to gain yet another imaginary edge.

"You know Sheila," I said.

"I do."

It was hard to utter the words, but there it was: "Do you really think she could be a killer?"

Squares was quiet a moment. A light turned red. He pulled the van to a stop and looked at me. "Starting to sound like your brother all over again."

"All I'm saying, Squares, is that there are other possibilities."

"And all I'm saying, Will, is that your head is up your sphincter."

"Meaning?"

"A chair, for chrissake? Are you for real? Last night Sheila cried and told you she was sorry—and in the morning, poof, she's gone. Now the feds tell us her fingerprints were found at a murder scene. And what do you come up with? Friggin' shipped chairs and old visits."

"It doesn't mean she killed anyone."

"It means," Squares said, "that she's involved."

I let that one sink in. I sat back and looked out the window and saw nothing.

"You have a thought, Squares?"

"Not a one."

We drove some more.

"I love her, you know."

"I know," Squares said.

"Best-case scenario, she lied to me."

He shrugged. "Worse things."

I wondered. I remembered our first full night together, lying in bed, Sheila's head on my chest, her arm draped over me. There was such contentment there, such a feeling of peace, of the world being so right. We just stayed there. I don't know how long anymore. "No past," she said softly, almost to herself. I asked her what she meant. She kept her head on my chest, her eyes away from me. And she said nothing more.

"I have to find her," I said.

"Yeah, I know."

"You want to help?"

Squares shrugged. "You won't be able to do it without me."

"There's that," I said. "So what should we do first?"

"To quote an old proverb," Squares said, "before we go forward, we have to look back."

"You just make that up?"

"Yeah."

"Guess it makes sense, though."

"Will?"

"Yeah?"

"Not to state the obvious or anything, but if we look back, you may not like what we see."

"Almost assuredly," I agreed.

Squares dropped me by the door and drove back to Covenant House. I entered the apartment and tossed my keys on the table. I would have called out Sheila's name—just to make sure she hadn't come home—but the apartment felt so empty, so drained of energy, I didn't bother. The place I'd called home for the past four years seemed somehow different to me, foreign. There was a stale feel to it, as though it'd been empty for a long time.

So now what?

Search the place, I guess. Look for clues, whatever that meant. But what struck me immediately was how spartan Sheila had been. She took pleasure in the simple, even seemingly mundane, and taught me how to do the same. She had very few possessions. When she'd moved in, she'd only brought one suitcase. She wasn't poor—I'd seen her bank statements and she'd paid for more than her share here—but she'd always been one of those people who lived by that "possessions own you, not the other way around" philosophy. Now I wondered about that, about the fact that possessions don't so much own you as bind you down, give you roots.

My XXL Amherst College sweatshirt lay over a chair in the bedroom. I picked it up, feeling a pang in my chest. We spent homecoming weekend at my alma mater last fall. There's a hill on Amherst's campus, a steep slope that starts a-high on a classic New England quad and slides toward a vast expanse of athletic fields. Most students, in a fit of originality, call this hill "the Hill."

Late one night Sheila and I walked the campus, hand in hand. We lay on the Hill's soft grass, stared at the pure fall sky, and talked for hours. I remember thinking that I had never known such a sense of peace, of calm and comfort and, yes, joy. Still on our backs, Sheila put her palm on my stomach and then, eyes on the stars, she slipped her hand under the waistband of my pants. I turned just a little and watched her face. When her fingers hit, uh, pay dirt, I saw her wicked grin.

"That's giving it the old college try," she'd said.

And okay, maybe I was turned on as all get-out, but it was at that very moment, on that hill, her hand in my pants, when I first realized, really realized with an almost supernatural certainty, that she was the one, that we would always be together, that the shadow of my first love, my only love before Sheila, the one that haunted me and drove away the others, had finally been banished.

I looked at the sweatshirt and for a moment, I could smell the honeysuckle and foliage all over again. I pressed it against me and wondered for the umpteenth time since I'd spoken to Pistillo: Was it all a lie?

No.

You don't fake that. Squares might be right about people's capacity to do violence. But you can't fake a connection like ours.

The note was still on the counter.

Love you always.
S

I had to believe that. I owed Sheila that much. Her past was her past. I had no claim to it. Whatever had happened, Sheila must have had her reasons. She loved me. I knew that. My task now was to find her, to help her, to figure a way back to . . . I don't know . . . us.

I would not doubt her.

I checked the drawers. Sheila had one bank account and one credit card—at least, that I knew of. But there were no papers anywhere—no old statements, no receipts, no bankbooks, nothing. They'd all been thrown away, I guess.

The computer screen saver, the ever-popular bouncing lines, disappeared when I moved the mouse. I signed on, switched over to Sheila's screen name, clicked Old Mail. Nothing. Not one. Odd. Sheila didn't use the Net often—very rarely in fact—but to not have one old email?

I clicked Filing Cabinet. Empty too. I checked under Bookmarked Web sites. More nothing. I checked the history. *Nada.*

I sat back and stared at the screen. A thought floated to the surface. I considered it for a moment, wondering if such an act would be a betrayal. No matter. Squares had been right about looking back in order to figure out where to go next. And he was right that I might not like what I find.

I logged on to switchboard.com, a massive online telephone directory. Under Name I typed Rogers. The state was Idaho. The city was Mason. I knew that from the form she'd filled out when she volunteered at Covenant House.

There was only one listing. On a slip of scrap paper, I jotted down the phone number. Yes, I was going to call Sheila's parents. If we were going to go back, we might as well go all the way.

Before I could reach for the receiver, the phone rang. I picked it up, and my sister, Melissa, said, "What are you doing?"

I thought about how to put it and settled for: "I have something of a situation here."

"Will," she said, and I could hear the older-sister tone, "we're mourning our mother here."

I closed my eyes.

"Dad's been asking about you. You have to come."

I looked around the stale, foreign apartment. No reason to hang here. And I thought about the picture still in my pocket—the image of my brother on the mountain.

"I'm on my way," I said.

Melissa greeted me at the door and asked, "Where's Sheila?"

I mumbled something about a previous commitment and ducked inside.

We actually had a real-life nonfamily visitor today—an old friend of my father's named Lou Farley. I don't think they'd seen each other in ten years. Lou Farley and my father traded stories with too much gusto and from too long ago. Something about an old softball team, and I had a vague recollection of my father suiting up in a maroon uniform of heavy polyester knit, a Friendly's Ice Cream logo emblazoned across the chest. I could still hear the scrape of his cleats on the driveway, feel the weight of his hand on my shoulder. So long ago. He and Lou Farley laughed. I hadn't heard my father laugh like that in years. His eyes were wet and far away. My mother would sometimes go to the games too. I can see her sitting in the bleachers with her sleeveless shirt and tanned, toned arms.

I glanced out the window, still hoping Sheila might show up, that this could still all somehow be one big misunderstanding. Part of me—a big part of me—blocked. While my mother's death had long been expected—Sunny's cancer, as was often the case, had been a slow, steady death march with a sudden downhill plunge at the end—I was still too raw to accept all that was happening.

Sheila.

I had loved and lost once before. When it comes to affairs of the heart, I confess to a streak of dated thinking. I believe in a soul mate. We all have that first love. When mine left me, she blew a hole straight through my heart. For a long time, I thought I'd never recover. There were reasons for that. Our ending felt incomplete, for one. But no matter. After she dumped me—at the end of the day, that's what she did—I was convinced that I was doomed to either settle for someone . . . lesser . . . or be forever alone.

And then I met Sheila.

I thought about the way Sheila's green eyes bore into me. I thought about the silky feel of her red hair. I thought about how the initial physical attraction—and it was immense, overwhelming—had segued and spread to all corners of my being. I thought about her all the time. I had flutters in my stomach. I could feel my heart do a little two-step whenever I first laid eyes on that face. I'd be in the van with Squares and all of a sudden he'd punch my shoulder because my mind had floated away, floated to a place Squares jokingly called Sheila Land, leaving a dorky smile behind. I felt heady. We cuddled and watched old movies on video, stroking each other, teasing, seeing how long we could hold out, warm comfort and hot arousal doing battle until, well, that was why VCRs have a pause button.

We held hands. We took long walks. We sat in the park and whispered snide comments about strangers to each other. At parties, I'd love to stand on the other side of the room and look at her from afar, watch her walk and move and talk to others and then, when our eyes would meet, there'd be a jolt, a knowing glance, a lascivious smile.

Sheila once asked me to fill out some stupid survey she found in a magazine. One of the questions was: What is your lover's biggest weakness? I thought about it and wrote, "Often forgets her umbrella in restaurants." She loved that, though she pressed for more. I reminded her that she listened to boy bands and old ABBA records. She nodded solemnly and promised that she would try to change.

We talked about everything but the past. I see that a lot in my line of work. It didn't trouble me much. Now, in hindsight, I wondered, but back then it had added, I don't know, an air of mystery maybe. And more than that—bear with me again—it was as though there were no life before us. No love, no partners, no past, born the day we met.

Yeah, I know.

Melissa sat next to my father. I saw them both in profile. The resemblance was strong. I favored my mother. Melissa's husband, Ralph, circled the buffet table. He was middle-manager America, a man of shortsleeve dress shirts over wife-beater T's, a good ol' boy with a firm handshake, shined shoes, slicked hair, limited intelligence. He never loosened his tie, not exactly uptight but comfortable only when things are in their proper place.

I have nothing in common with Ralph, but to be fair, I really don't know him very well. They live in Seattle and almost never come back. Still, I can't help but remember when Melissa was going through her wild stage, sneaking around with local bad boy Jimmy McCarthy. What a gleam in her eye there had been back then. How spontaneous and outrageously, even inappropriately, funny she could be. I don't know what happened, what changed her, what had scared her so. People claim that it was just maturity. I don't think that's the full story. I think there was something more.

Melissa—we'd always called her Mel—signaled me with her eyes. We slid into the den. I reached into my pocket and touched the photograph of Ken.

"Ralph and I are leaving in the morning," she told me.

"Fast," I said.

"What's that supposed to mean?"

I shook my head.

"We have children. Ralph has work."

"Right," I said. "Nice of you to show up at all."

Her eyes went wide. "That's a horrible thing to say."

It was. I looked behind me. Ralph sat with Dad and Lou Farley, downing a particularly messy sloppy joe, the coleslaw nestling in the corner of his lips. I wanted to tell her that I was sorry. But I couldn't. Mel was the oldest of us, three years older than Ken, five years my senior. When Julie was found dead, she ran away. That was the only way to put it. She upped with her new husband and baby and moved across the country. Most of the time I understood, but I still felt the anger of what I perceived as abandonment.

I thought again about the picture of Ken in my pocket and made a sudden decision. "I want to show you something."

I thought I saw Melissa wince, as if bracing for a blow, but that might have been projection. Her hair was pure Suzy Homemaker, what with the suburban-blond frost and bouncy shoulder-length—probably just the way Ralph liked it. It looked wrong to me, out of place on her.

We moved a little farther away until we were near the door leading to the garage. I looked back. I could still see my father and Ralph and Lou Farley.

I opened the door. Mel looked at me curiously but she followed. We stepped onto the cement of the chilly garage. The place was done up in Early American Fire Hazard. Rusted paint cans, moldy cardboard boxes, baseball bats, old wicker, treadless tires—all strewn about as though there'd been an explosion. There were oil stains on the floor, and the dust made it all drab and faded gray and hard to breathe. A rope still hung from the ceiling. I remembered when my father had cleared out some space, attached a tennis ball to that rope so I could practice my baseball swing. I couldn't believe it was still there.

Melissa kept her eyes on me.

I wasn't sure how to do this.

"Sheila and I were going through Mom's things yesterday," I began.

Her eyes narrowed a little. I was about to start explaining, how we had sifted through her drawers and looked at the laminated birth announcements and that old program from when Mom played Mame in the Little Livingston production and how Sheila and I bathed ourselves in the old pictures—remember the one with King Hussein, Mel?—but none of that passed my lips.

Without saying another word, I reached into my pocket, plucked out the photograph, and held it up in front of her face.

It didn't take long. Melissa turned away as if the photo could scald her. She gulped a few deep breaths and stepped back. I moved toward her, but she held up a hand, halting me. When she looked up again, her face was a total blank. No surprise anymore. No anguish or joy either. Nothing.

I held it up again. This time she didn't blink.

"It's Ken," I said stupidly.

"I can see that, Will."

"That's the sum total of your reaction?"

"How would you like me to react?"

"He's alive. Mom knew it. She had this picture."

Silence.

"Mel?"

"He's alive," she said. "I heard you."

Her response—or lack thereof—left me speechless.

"Is there anything else?" Melissa asked.

"What . . . that's all you have to say?"

"What else is there to say, Will?"

"Oh, right, I forgot. You have to get back to Seattle."

"Yes."

She stepped away from me.

The anger resurfaced. "Tell me something, Mel. Did running away help?"

"I didn't run away."

"Bullshit," I said.

"Ralph got a job out there."

"Right."

"How dare you judge me?"

I flashed back to when the three of us played Marco Polo for hours in the motel pool near Cape Cod. I flashed back to the time Tony Bonoza spread rumors about Mel, how Ken's face had turned red when he'd heard, how he'd taken Bonoza on, even though he'd given up two years and twenty pounds.

"Ken is alive," I said again.

Her voice was a plea. "And what do you want me to do about it?"

"You act like it doesn't matter."

"I'm not sure it does."

"What the hell is that supposed to mean?"

"Ken's not a part of our lives anymore."

"Speak for yourself."

"Fine, Will. He's not a part of my life anymore."

"He's your brother."

"Ken made his choices."

"And now—what?—he's dead to you?"

"Wouldn't it be better if he were?" She shook her head and closed her eyes. I waited. "Maybe I did run away, Will. But so did you. We had a choice. Our brother was either dead or a brutal killer. Either way, yes, he's dead to me."

I held up the picture again. "He doesn't have to be guilty, you know."

Melissa looked at me, and suddenly she was the older sister again. "Come on, Will. You know better."

"He defended us. When we were kids. He looked out for us. He loved us."

"And I loved him. But I also saw him for what he was. He was drawn to violence, Will. You know that. Yes, he stuck up for us. But don't you think part of that was because he enjoyed it? You know he was mixed up in something bad when he died."

"That doesn't make him a killer."

Melissa closed her eyes again. I could see her mining for some inner strength. "For crying out loud, Will, what was he doing that night?"

Our eyes met and held. I said nothing. A sudden chill blew across my heart.

"Forget the murder, okay? What was Ken doing having sex with Julie Miller?"

Her words penetrated me, blossomed in my chest, big and cold. I couldn't breathe. My voice, when I finally found it, was tinny, faraway. "We'd been broken up for over a year."

"You telling me you were over her?"

"I . . . she was free. He was free. There was no reason—"

"He betrayed you, Will. Face it already. At the very least, he slept with the woman you loved. What kind of brother does that?"

"We broke up," I said, floundering. "I held no claim to her."

"You loved her."

"That has nothing to do with it."

She wouldn't take her eyes off mine. "Now who's running away?"

I stumbled back and half collapsed onto the cement stairs. My face dropped into my hands. I put myself together a piece at a time. It took a while. "He's still our brother."

"So what do you want to do? Find him? Hand him over to the police? Help him keep hiding? What?"

I had no answer.

Melissa stepped over me and opened the door to head back into the den. "Will?"

I looked up at her.

"This isn't my life anymore. I'm sorry."

I saw her then as a teenager, lying on her bed, jabbering away, her hair overteased, the smell of bubble gum in the air. Ken and I would sit on the floor of her room and roll our eyes. I remembered her body language. If Mel was lying on her belly, her feet kicking in the air, she was talking about boys and parties and that nonsense. But when she lay on her back and stared at the ceiling, well, that was for dreams. I thought about her dreams. I thought about how none of them had come true.

"I love you," I said.

And, as though she could see into my thoughts, Melissa started to cry.

We never forget our first love. Mine ended up being murdered.

Julie Miller and I met when her family moved onto Coddington Terrace during my freshman year at Livingston High. We started dating two years later. We went to the junior and senior proms. We were voted class couple. We were pretty much inseparable.

Our breakup was surprising only in its outright predictability. We went off to separate colleges, sure our commitment could stand the time and distance. It couldn't, though it hung on for longer than most. During our junior year, Julie called me on the phone and said that she wanted to see other people, that she'd already started dating a senior named—I'm not kidding here—Buck.

I should have gotten over it. I was young and this was hardly an unusual rite of passage. And I probably would have. Eventually. I mean, I dated. It was taking time, but I was starting to accept reality. Time and distance helped with that.

But then Julie died, and it seemed as though a part of my heart would never break free of her grip from the grave.

Until Sheila.

I didn't show the picture to my father.

I got back to my apartment at ten o'clock at night. Still empty, still stale, still foreign. No messages on the machine. If this was life without Sheila, I wanted no part of it.

The scrap of paper with her parents' Idaho phone number was still on the desk. What was the time difference in Idaho? One hour? Maybe two? I didn't remember. But that made it either eight or nine o'clock at night.

Not too late to call.

I collapsed into the chair and stared at the phone as if it'd tell me what to do. It didn't. I picked up the scrap of paper. When I'd told Sheila to call her parents, her face had lost all color. That had been yesterday. Just yesterday. I wondered what I should do and my first thought, my very first, was that I should ask my mother, that she would know the right answer.

A fresh wave of sadness pulled me under.

In the end, I knew that I had to act. I had to do something. And this, calling Sheila's parents, was all I could come up with.

A woman answered on the third ring. "Hello?"

I cleared my throat. "Mrs. Rogers?"

There was a pause. "Yes?"

"My name is Will Klein."

I waited, seeing if the name meant anything to her. If it did, she wasn't letting me know.

"I'm a friend of your daughter's."

"Which daughter?"

"Sheila," I said.

"I see," the woman said. "I understand she's been in New York."

"Yes," I said.

"Is that where you're calling from?"

"Yes."

"What can I do for you, Mr. Klein?"

That was a good question. I didn't really know myself, so I started with the obvious. "Do you have any idea where she is?"

"No."

"You haven't seen or spoken to her?"

In a tired voice, she said, "I haven't seen or spoken to Sheila in years."

I opened my mouth, closed it, tried to see a route to take, kept running into roadblocks. "Are you aware that she's missing?"

"The authorities have been in touch with us, yes."

I switched hands and brought the receiver up to my other ear. "Could you tell them anything useful?"

"Useful?"

"Do you have any idea where she might have gone? Where she'd run away to? A friend or a relative who might help?"

"Mr. Klein?"

"Yes."

"Sheila has not been a part of our life for a long time."

"Why not?"

I just blurted that out. I imagined a rebuke, of course, a big, fat none-of-your-business. But again she fell into silence. I tried to wait her out, but she was better at that than I.

"It's just that"—I could hear myself begin to stammer—"she's a wonderful person."

"You're more than a friend, aren't you, Mr. Klein?"

"Yes."

"The authorities. They mentioned that Sheila was living with a man. I assume they were talking about you?"

"We've been together about a year," I said.

"You sound as though you're worried about her."

"I am."

"You love her, then?"

"Very much."

"But she's never told you about her past."

I wasn't sure how to respond to that one, though the answer was obvious. "I'm trying to understand," I said.

"It's not like that," she said. "I don't even understand."

My neighbor picked now to blast his new stereo with quadraphonic speakers. The bass shook the wall. I was on the portable phone, so I moved toward the far end of the apartment.

"I want to help her," I said.

"Let me ask you something, Mr. Klein."

Her tone made my grip on the receiver tighten.

"The federal agent who came by," she went on. "He said they don't know anything about it."

"About what?" I asked.

"About Carly," Mrs. Rogers said. "About where she is."

I was confused. "Who's Carly?"

There was another long pause. "May I give you a word of advice, Mr. Klein?"

"Who's Carly?" I asked again.

"Get on with your life. Forget you ever knew my daughter."

And then she hung up.

8

I grabbed a Brooklyn Lager from the fridge and slid open the glass door. I stepped out onto what my Realtor had optimistically dubbed a "veranda." It was the approximate size of a baby crib. One person, perhaps two, if they stood very still, could stand on it at one time. There were, of course, no chairs, and being on the third floor, not much of a view. But it was air and night and I still liked it.

At night, New York is well lit and unreal, filled with a blue-black glow. This may be the city that never sleeps, but if my street was an indication, it could sneak in a serious nap. Parked cars sat crammed along the curb, bumper grinding bumper, seemingly jockeying for position long after their owners had abandoned them. Night sounds throbbed and hummed. I heard music. I heard clatter from the pizza place across the street. I heard the steady whooshing from the West Side Highway, gentle now, Manhattan's lullaby.

My brain slipped into numb. I didn't know what was happening. I didn't know what to do next. My call to Sheila's mother raised more questions than it answered. Melissa's words still stung, but she'd raised an interesting point: Now that I knew Ken was alive, what was I prepared to do about it?

I wanted to find him, of course.

I wanted to find him very badly. But so what? Forget the fact that I wasn't a detective or up to the task. If Ken wanted to be found, he'd come to me. Searching him out could only lead to disaster.

And maybe I had another priority.

First my brother had run off. Now my lover vanishes into thin air. I frowned. It was a good thing I didn't have a dog.

I was raising the bottle to my lip when I noticed him.

He stood on the corner, maybe fifty yards from my building. He wore a trench coat and what might have been a fedora, his hands in his pockets. His face from this distance looked like a white orb shining against a dark backdrop, featureless and too round. I couldn't see his eyes, but I knew he was looking at me. I could feel it, the weight of his stare. It was palpable.

The man didn't move.

There weren't many pedestrians on the street, but the ones who were there, they, well, they *moved.* That was what New Yorkers did. They moved. They walked. They walked with purpose. Even when they stood for a light or passing car, they bounced, always at the ready. New Yorkers moved. There was no still in them.

But this man stood like stone. Staring at me. I blinked hard. He was still there. I turned away and then looked back. He was still there, unmoving. And one more thing.

Something about him was familiar.

I didn't want to take that too far. We were at a pretty good distance and it was nighttime and my vision is not the best, especially in streetlight. But the hair on the back of my neck rose like on an animal sensing terrible danger.

I decided to stare back, see how he reacted. He didn't move. I don't know how long we stood there like that. I could feel the blood leaving my fingertips. Cold settled in near the edges, but something at my center gathered strength. I didn't look away. And neither did the featureless face.

The phone rang.

I wrested my vision away. My watch said it was nearly eleven P.M. Late for a call. Without a backward glance, I stepped back inside and picked up the receiver.

Squares said, "Sleepy?"

"No."

"Want to take a ride?"

He was taking out the van tonight. "You learn something?"

"Meet me at the studio. Half an hour."

He hung up. I walked back to the terrace and looked down. The man was gone.

The yoga school was simply called Squares. I made fun of it, of course. Squares had become one word, like Cher or Fabio. The school, studio, whatever you want to call it, was located in a six-story walk-up on University Place off Union Square. The beginnings had been humble. The school had toiled in happy obscurity. Then a certain celebrity, a major pop star you know too well, "discovered" Squares. She told her friends. A few months later, *Cosmo* picked it up. Then *Elle*. Somewhere along the line, a big infomercial company asked Squares to do a video. Squares, a firm believer in selling out, delivered the goods. The Yoga Squared Workout—the name is copyrighted—took off. Hey, Squares even shaved on the day they taped.

The rest was history.

Suddenly, no Manhattan or Hamptons social event could deem itself "a happening" without everyone's favorite fitness guru. Squares turned down most invitations, but he quickly learned how to network. He rarely had time to teach anymore. If you want to take any of the classes, even ones taught by his most junior students, the waitlist is at least two months. He charges twenty-five dollars per class. He has four studios. The smallest holds fifty students. The largest close to two hundred. He has twenty-four teachers who rotate in and out. As I approached the school now, it was eleven-thirty at night and three classes were still in session.

Do the math.

In the elevator I started hearing the painful strains of sitar music blending with the lapping of cascading waterfalls, a mingling of sounds I find about as soothing as a cat hit with a stun gun. The gift shop greets you first, filled with incense and books and lotions and tapes and videos and CD-

ROMs and DVDs and crystals and beads and ponchos and tie-dye. Behind the counter were two anorexic twentysomething-year-olds dressed in black, their entire personas reeking of granola. Forever young. Just wait. One male, one female, though it wasn't easy to tell which was which. Their voices were even and just this side of patronizing—maître d's at a trendy new restaurant. Their body piercings—and there were lots of them—were filled with silver and turquoise.

"Hi," I said.

"Please remove your shoes," Probably Male said.

"Right."

I slipped them off.

"And you are?" Probably Female asked.

"Here to see Squares. I'm Will Klein."

The name meant nothing to them. Must be new. "Do you have an appointment with Yogi Squares?"

"Yogi Squares?" I repeated.

They stared at me.

"Tell me," I said. "Is Yogi Squares smarter than the average Squares?"

No laughter from the kiddies. Big surprise. She typed something into the computer terminal. They both frowned at the monitor. He picked up the phone and dialed. The sitar music blared. I felt a whopper headache brewing.

"Will?"

A wonderfully leotard-clad Wanda swept into the room, head high, clavicle prominent, eyes taking in everything. She was Squares's lead teacher and lover. They'd been together for three years now. Said leotard was lavender and oh-so-right. Wanda was a bold vision—tall, long-limbed, and lithe, achingly beautiful, and black. Yes, black. The irony did not escape those of us who knew Squares's—pardon the pun—checkered past.

She wrapped her arms around me, her embrace as warm as wood smoke. I wished it would last forever.

"How are you, Will?" she said softly.

"Better."

She pulled back, those eyes searching for the lie. She'd been to my mother's funeral. She and Squares had no secrets. Squares and I had no secrets. Like an algebra proof using the communicative property, you could thus deduce that she and I had no secrets.

"He's finishing up a class," she said. "Pranayama breathing."

I nodded.

She tilted her head as though she'd just thought of something. "Do you have a second before you go?" Her voice aimed for casual but couldn't quite get there.

"Sure," I said.

She padded—Wanda was too graceful to merely walk—down the corridor. I followed, my eyes level with her swanlike neck. We passed a fountain so large and ornate I wanted to toss a penny in it. I peeked in one of the studios. Total silence, save heavy breathing. It looked like a movie set. Gorgeous people—I don't know how Squares found so many gorgeous people—packed side by side in warrior pose, faces serenely blank, legs spread, hands out, front knees at a ninety-degree angle.

The office Wanda shared with Squares was on the right. She lowered herself onto a chair as though it were made of Styrofoam and crossed her legs into a lotus. I sat across from her in a more conventional style. She didn't speak for a few moments. Her eyes closed and I could see her willing herself to relax. I waited.

"I didn't tell you this," she said.

"Okay."

"I'm pregnant."

"Hey, that's great." I started to rise to offer up a congratulatory hug.

"Squares isn't handling it well."

I stopped. "What do you mean?"

"He's freaking out."

"How?"

"You didn't know, right?"

"Right."

"He tells you everything, Will. He's known for a week." I saw her point.

"He probably didn't want to say anything," I said, "what with my mother and all."

She looked at me hard and said, "Don't do that."

"Yeah, sorry."

Her eyes skittered away from mine. The cool façade. There were cracks there now. "I expected him to be happy."

"He wasn't?"

"I think he wants me to"—she seemed out of words—"end it."

That knocked me back a step. "He said that?"

"He hasn't said anything. He's working the van extra nights. He's taking on more classes."

"He's avoiding you."

"Yes."

The office door opened without knocking. Squares leaned his unshaven mug into the doorway. He gave Wanda a cursory smile. She turned away. Squares gave me the thumb. "Let's rock and roll."

We didn't speak until we were safely ensconced in the van.

Squares said, "She told you."

It was a statement, not a question, so I didn't bother confirming or denying.

He put the key in the ignition. "We're not talking about it," he said.

Another statement that required no response.

The Covenant House van heads straight into the bowels. Many of our kids come to our doors. Many others are rescued in this van. The job of outreach is to connect with the community's seedy underbelly—meet the runaway kids, the street urchins, the ones too often referred to as the "throwaways." A kid living on the street is a bit like—and please pardon the analogy here—a weed. The longer he's on the street, the harder it is to pull him out by the root.

We lose a lot of these kids. More than we save. And forget the weed analogy. It's stupid because it implies that we're getting rid of something bad and preserving something good. In fact, it's just the opposite. Try this instead: The street is more like a cancer. Early screening and preventive treatment is the key to long-term survival.

Not much better, but you get the gist.

"The feds exaggerated," Squares said.

"How so?"

"Sheila's record."

"Go on."

"The arrests. They were all a long time ago. You want to hear this?"

"Yes."

We started driving deep into the gloom. The city's hooker hangouts are fluid. Often you'll find them near the Lincoln Tunnel or Javits Center, but lately the cops have been cracking down. More cleanup. So the hookers flowed south to the meat-packing district on 18th Street and the far west side. Tonight the hookers were out in force.

Squares gestured with his head. "Sheila could have been any one of them."

"She worked the street?"

"A runaway from the Midwest. Got off the bus and straight into the life."

I'd seen it too many times to shock me. But this wasn't a stranger or street kid at the end of her rope. This was the most amazing woman I had ever known.

"A long time ago," Squares said as though reading my thoughts. "Her first arrest was age sixteen."

"Prostitution?"

He nodded. "Three more like that in the next eighteen months, working, according to her file, for a pimp named Louis Castman. Last time she was carrying two ounces and a knife. They tried to bust her for both dealing and armed robbery, but it got kicked."

I looked out the window. The night had turned gray, washed out. You see so much bad on these streets. We work hard to stop some of it. I know we succeed. I know we turn lives around. But I know that what happens here, in the vibrant cesspool of night, never leaves them. The damage is done. You may work around it. You may go on. But the damage is permanent.

"What are you afraid of?" I asked him.

"We're not talking about it."

"You love her. She loves you."

"And she's black."

I turned to him and waited. I know that he didn't mean the obvious by this. He was not being racist. But it's like I told you. The damage is permanent. I had seen the tension between them. It wasn't nearly as powerful as the love, but it was there.

"You love her," I repeated.

He kept driving.

"Maybe that was part of the initial attraction," I said. "But she's not your redemption anymore. You're in love with her."

"Will?"

"Yeah?"

"Enough."

Squares suddenly veered the van to the right. Headlights splashed over the children of the night. They didn't scatter like rats under the onslaught. They, in fact, stared mutely, barely blinking. Squares narrowed his eyes, spotted his prey, and pulled to a stop.

We got out in silence. The children looked at us with dead eyes. I remembered a line of Fantine's in *Les Misérables*—the musical version, I don't know if it's in the book: "Don't they know they're making love to what's already dead?"

There were girls and boys and cross-dressers and transsexuals. I have seen every known perversion out here, though—and I'm sure I'll get accused of sexism here—I don't think I've ever seen a female customer. I'm not saying that women never buy sex. I'm sure they do. But they don't seem to cruise the streets to do it. The street customers, the johns, are always men. They may want a buxom woman or a skinny one, young, old, straight, kinky to unfathomable levels, big men, little boys, animals, whatever. Some may even have a woman with them, dragging a girlfriend or wife into the fray. But the customers trolling these byways are men.

Despite all the talk about unfathomable kink, these men for the most part come here to purchase a certain . . . act, if you will. Something performed on them, one that can easily take place in a parked car. It makes sense for both, when you think about it. Convenience, for one thing. You don't need the expense and time of finding a room. Your concern about sexually transmitted diseases, while still there, is lessened. Pregnancy is not an issue. You don't need to fully undress. . . .

I'll spare you further details.

The street veterans—by veterans, I mean anyone over the age of eighteen—greeted Squares warmly. They knew him. They liked him. They were a bit wary of my presence. It had been a while since I'd been in the trenches. Still, some of the old-timers recognized me and in a bizarre way, I was glad to see them.

Squares approached a hooker named Candi, though I deduced that Candi was probably not her real name. No flies on me. She pointed with her chin at two shivering girls huddled in a doorway. I looked at them, no more than sixteen years old, their faces painted like two little girls who'd found Mommy's makeup case, and my heart sank. They were dressed in shorter-than-short shorts, high boots with stiletto heels, fake fur. I often wondered where they find these outfits, if the pimps had special hooker stores or what.

"Fresh meat," Candi said.

Squares frowned, nodded. Many of our best leads come from the veterans. There are two reasons for this. One—the cynical reasoning—is that taking the newbies out of circulation eliminates competition. If you live out in the streets, you get ugly in a hurry. Candi was, quite frankly, hideous. This life ages you faster than any black hole. The new girls, though forced to stay huddled in doorways until they earn turf, are going to get noticed.

But that view is, I think, uncharitable. Reason two, the bigger reason, was that—and please don't think me naïve here—they want to help. They see themselves. They see the fork in the road and while they might not readily admit they took the wrong prong, they know that it's too late for them. They can't go back. I used to argue with the Candis of the world. I used to insist that it was never too late, that there was still time. I was wrong. Here again is why we need to reach them quickly. There is a certain point that once passed, you cannot save them. The destruction is irreversible. The street consumes them. They fade away. They become part of the night, one single dark entity. They are lost to us. They will probably die here or end up in jail or insane.

"Where's Raquel?" Squares said.

"Working a car job," Candi said.

"She coming back here?"

"Yeah."

Squares nodded and turned to the two new girls. One was already leaning into a Buick Regal. You cannot imagine the frustration. You want to step in and stop it. You want to pull the girl away and reach your hand down the john's throat and rip out his lungs. You want to at least chase him away or take a photograph or . . . or something. But you do none of that. If you do any of that, you lose the trust. You lose the trust, you're useless.

It was hard to do nothing. Fortunately I'm not particularly brave or confrontational. Maybe that makes it easier.

I watched the passenger door open. The Buick Regal seemed to devour the child. She disappeared slowly, sinking into the dark. I watched and I don't think I ever felt so helpless. I looked at Squares. His eyes were focused on the car. The Buick pulled away. The girl was gone as though she'd never existed. If the car chooses not to return, it would forever be that way.

Squares approached the remaining new girl. I followed, staying a few steps behind him. The girl's lower lip quivered as though holding back tears, but her eyes blazed with defiance. I wanted to pull her into the van, by force if necessary. So much of this task is restraint. It was why Squares was the master. He stopped about a yard away, careful not to invade her space.

"Hi," he said.

She looked him over and muttered, "Hey."

"I was hoping you could help me out." Squares took another step and pulled a photograph out of his pocket. "I'm wondering if you've seen her."

The girl did not look at the picture. "I haven't seen anyone."

"Please," Squares said with a smile damn near celestial. "I'm not a cop."

She tried to look tough. "Figured that," she said. "You talking to Candi and all."

Squares moved a little closer. "We, that is, my friend here and I"—I waved on cue, smiled—"we're trying to save this girl."

Curious now, she narrowed her eyes. "Save her how?"

"Some bad people are after her."

"Who?"

"Her pimp. See, we work for Covenant House. You heard of that?"

She shrugged.

"It's a place to hang out," Squares said, trying to downplay it. "No big deal. You can stop in and have a hot meal, a warm bed to sleep in, use the phone, get some clothes, whatever. Anyway, this girl"—he held up the photograph, a school portrait of a white girl in braces—"her name is Angie." Always give a name. It personalizes it. "She's been staying with us. Taking a couple of courses. She's a really funny kid. And she got a job too. Turning her life around, you know?"

The girl said nothing.

Squares held out his hand. "Everyone calls me Squares," he said.

The girl sighed, took the hand. "I'm Jeri."

"Nice to meet you."

"Yeah. But I haven't seen this Angie. And I'm kinda busy here."

Here was where you had to read. If you push too hard, you lose them forever. They burrow back into their hole and never come out. All you want to do now—all you can do now—is plant the seed. You let her know that there is a haven for her, a safe place, where she can get a meal and find shelter. You give her a way off the street for just one night. Once she gets there, you show the unconditional love. But not now. Now it scares them. Now it chases them away.

As much as it ripped you apart inside, you could not do any more.

Very few people could do Squares's job for very long. And the ones who lasted, the ones who were particularly good at it, they were just . . . slightly off center. You had to be.

Squares hesitated. He has used this "missing girl" gig as an icebreaker for as long as I've known him. The girl in the picture, the real Angie, died fifteen years ago, out on the street, from exposure. Squares found her behind a Dumpster. At the funeral, Angie's mother gave him that photograph. I don't think I've ever seen him without it.

"Okay, thanks." Squares took out a card and handed it to her. "If you do see her, will you let me know? You can call anytime. Any reason."

She took the card, fingered it. "Yeah, maybe."

Another hesitation. Then Squares said, "See you around."

"Yeah."

We then did the most unnatural thing in the world. We walked away.

Raquel's real name was Roscoe. At least that was what he or she told us. I never know if I should address Raquel as a he or a she. I should probably ask him/her.

Squares and I found the car parked in front of a sealed-off delivery entrance. A common place for street work. The car windows were fogged up, but we kept our distance anyway. Whatever was going on in there—and we had a pretty good idea what—was not something we cared to witness.

The door opened a minute later. Raquel came out. As you may have guessed by now, Raquel was a cross-dresser, hence the gender confusion. With transsexuals, okay, you refer to them as "she." Cross-dressing is a bit trickier. Sometimes the "she" applies. Sometimes it's just a tad too politically correct.

That was probably the case with Raquel.

Raquel rolled out of the car, reached into his purse, and took out the Binaca spray. Three blasts, a pause, a thought, then three more blasts. The car pulled away. Raquel turned toward us.

Many transvestites are beautiful. Raquel was not. He was black, six-six, and comfortably on the north side of three hundred pounds. He had biceps like giant hogs wrestling in sausage casing, and his six-o'clock shadow reminded me of Homer Simpson's. He had a voice so high pitched it made Michael Jackson sound like a teamster boss—Betty Boop sucking helium.

Raquel claimed to be twenty-nine years old, but he'd been saying that for the six years I'd known him. He worked five nights a week, rain or shine, and had a rather devoted following. He could get off the streets if he wanted. He could find a place to work out of, set up appointments, that kind of thing. But Raquel liked it out here. That was one of the things people did not get. The street may be dark and dangerous, but it was also intoxicating. The night had an energy, an electricity. You felt wired out on the street. For some of our kids, the choice may be a menial job at Mickey D's versus the thrill of the night—and that, when you have no future, was no choice at all.

Raquel spotted us and started tottering in our direction on stiletto heels. Men's shoes size fourteen. No easy task, I assure you. Raquel stopped under a streetlamp. His face was worn like a rock battered by centuries of storms. I didn't know his back story. He lies a lot. One legend had him as an all-American football player who blew out a knee. Another time I'd heard him say that he'd gotten a college scholarship based on high SAT scores. Still another pegged him as a Gulf War veteran. Choose one of those or create your own.

Raquel greeted Squares with a hug and peck on the cheek. He then turned his attention to me.

"You looking so good, Sweet Willy," Raquel said.

"Gee thanks, Raquel," I said.

"Tasty enough to eat."

"I've been working out," I said. "Makes me extra yummy."

Raquel threw an arm around my shoulder. "I could fall in love with a man like you."

"I'm flattered, Raquel."

"Man like you, he could take me away from all this."

"Ah, but think of all the broken hearts you'd leave in these sewers."

Raquel giggled. "Got that right."

I showed Raquel a photograph of Sheila, the only one I had. Weird when I think back on it now. Neither one of us were picture-takers, but to have only one photograph?

"You recognize her?" I asked him.

Raquel studied the picture. "This your woman," he said. "I seen her at the shelter once."

"Right. You know her from anyplace else?"

"Nope. Why?"

There was no reason to lie. "She's run off. I'm looking for her."

Raquel studied the picture some more. "Can I keep this?"

I'd made some color copies at the office, so I handed it to him.

"I'll ask around," Raquel said.

"Thanks."

He nodded.

"Raquel?" It was Squares. Raquel turned to him. "You remember a pimp named Louis Castman?"

Raquel's face went slack. He started looking around.

"Raquel?"

"I gotta get back to work, Squares. Bidness, you know."

I stepped in his way. He looked down at me as if I were dandruff flakes he might flick off his shoulder.

"She used to work the streets," I said to him.

"Your girl?"

"Yes."

"And she worked for Castman?"

"Yes."

Raquel crossed himself. "A bad man, Sweet Willy. Castman was the worst."

"How so?"

He licked his lips. "Girls out here. They just a commodity, you know what I'm saying. Merchandise. It bidness with most folk out here. They make money, they stay. They don't make money, well, you know."

I did.

"But Castman"—Raquel whispered his name the way some people whispered the word *cancer*—"he was different."

"How?"

"He'd damage his own merchandise. Sometimes just for fun."

Squares said, "You keep referring to him in the past tense."

"That's 'cause he ain't been around in, oh, three years."

"He alive?"

Raquel became very quiet. He looked off. Squares and I exchanged a glance, waited.

"He still alive," Raquel said. "I guess."

"What does that mean?"

Raquel just shook his head.

"We need to speak with him," I said. "Do you know where we can find him?"

"I just heard rumors."

"What kind of rumors?"

Raquel shook his head again. "Check out a place on the corner of Wright Street and Avenue D in the South Bronx. Heard he might be there."

Raquel walked away then, steadier on the stiletto heels. A car drove up, stopped, and again I watched a human being disappear into the night.

9

Most neighborhoods, you'd hesitate about waking someone at one in the morning. This wasn't one of them. The windows were all boarded up. The door was a hunk of plywood. I'd tell you the paint was peeling, but it would probably be more apt to say it was shedding.

Squares knocked on the plywood door and immediately a woman shouted, "What do you want?"

Squares did the talking. "We're looking for Louis Castman."

"Go away."

"We need to speak with him."

"You got a warrant?"

"We're not with the police."

"Who are you?" the woman asked.

"We work for Covenant House."

"No runaways here," she shouted, nearly hysterical. "Go away."

"You have a choice," Squares said. "We talk to Castman ourselves right now, or we come back with a bunch of nosy cops."

"I didn't do nothing."

"I can always make something up," Squares said. "Open the door."

The woman made a fast decision. We heard a bolt slide, then another, then a chain. The door opened a crack. I started toward it, but Squares blocked me with his arm. Wait until the door opened all the way.

"Hurry," the woman said with a witchlike cackle. "Get inside. Don't want nobody seeing."

Squares gave the door a shove. It opened all the way. We stepped through the frame, and the woman closed the door. Two things hit me at the same time. First, the dark. The only light was a low-watt lamp in the far right-hand corner. I saw a threadbare reading chair, a coffee table, and that was about it. Second, the smell. Take your most vivid remembrance of fresh air and the great outdoors and then imagine the polar opposite. The stuffiness made me afraid to inhale. Part hospital, part something I couldn't quite place. I wondered when the last time a window had been opened, and the room seemed to whisper, *Never.*

Squares turned to the woman. She'd shrunk back into a corner. We could see only a silhouette in the darkness. "They call me Squares," he said.

"I know who you are."

"Have we met?"

"That's not important."

"Where is he?" Squares asked.

"There's only one other room in here," she said, raising her hand in a slow point. "He might be asleep."

Our eyes started to adjust. I stepped toward her. She didn't back away. I got closer. When she lifted her head, I almost gasped. I mumbled an apology and started backing away.

"No," she said. "I want you to see."

She crossed the room, stopped in front of the lamp, and faced us full. To our credit, neither Squares nor I flinched. But it wasn't easy. Whoever had disfigured her had done it with great care. She'd probably been a looker at one time, but it was as though she'd gone through some anti-plastic-surgery regimen. A perhaps once-well-shaped nose had been squelched like a beetle under a heavy boot. Once-smooth skin had been split and ripped. The corners of her mouth had been torn to the point where it was hard to tell where it ended. Dozens of raised angry purple scars crisscrossed her face, like the work of a three-year-old given free rein with a Crayola. Her left eye wandered off to the side, dead in its socket. The other stared at us unblinking.

Squares said, "You used to be on the street."

She nodded.

"What's your name?"

Moving her mouth seemed to take great effort. "Tanya."

"Who did that to you?"

"Who do you think?"

We did not bother replying.

"He's through that door," she said. "I take care of him. I never hurt him. You understand? I never raise a hand to him."

We both nodded. I didn't know what to make of that. I don't think Squares did either. We moved to the door. Not a sound. Perhaps he was asleep. I didn't really care. He'd wake up. Squares put his hand on the knob and looked back at me. I let him know that I'd be fine. He opened the door.

Lights were on in there. Full blast, in fact. I had to shade my eyes. I heard a beeping noise and saw some sort of medical machine near the bed. But that wasn't what first drew my eye.

The walls.

That was what you noticed first. The walls were corked—I could see a little of the brown—but more than that, they were blanketed with photographs. Hundreds of photographs. Some blown up to poster size, some your classic three-by-fives, most somewhere in between—all hung on the cork by clear pushpins.

And they were all pictures of Tanya.

At least, that was what I guessed. The pictures were all pre-disfiguration. And I had been right. Tanya had been beautiful once. The photos, mostly glamour shots from what appeared to be a model's portfolio, were inescapable. I looked up. More photographs, a ceiling fresco from hell.

"Help me. Please."

The small voice came from the bed. Squares and I moved toward it. Tanya came in behind us and cleared her voice. We turned. In the harsh light, her scars seemed almost alive, squirming across her face like dozens of worms. The nose was not just flattened, but misshapen, claylike. The old photographs seemed to glow, swarming her in a perverse before-and-after aura.

The man in the bed groaned.

We waited. Tanya turned the good eye first toward me, then toward Squares. The eye seemed to dare us to forget, to etch this image into our brains, to remember what she'd once been and what he'd done to her.

"A straight razor," she said. "A rusted one. It took him over an hour to do this. And he didn't just slice up my face."

Without another word, Tanya moved out of the room. She closed the door behind her.

We stood in silence for a moment. Then Squares said, "Are you Louis Castman?"

"You cops?"

"Are you Castman?"

"Yes. And I did it. Christ, whatever you want me to confess to, I did it. Just get me out of here. For the love of God."

"We're not cops," Squares said.

Castman lay flat on his back. There was some kind of tube connected to his chest. The machine kept beeping and something kept rising and falling accordionlike. He was a white guy, newly shaven, fresh-scrubbed. His hair was clean. His bed had rails and controls. I saw a bedpan in the corner and a sink. Other than that, the room was empty. No drawers, no dressers, no TV, no radio, no clock, no books, no newspapers, no magazines. The window shades were pulled down.

I had a sick feeling in the pit of my stomach.

"What's wrong with you?" I asked.

Castman's eyes—and only his eyes—turned toward me. "I'm paralyzed," he said. "A fucking quadriplegic. Below the neck"—he stopped, closed his eyes—"nothing."

I was not sure how to begin. Neither, it seemed, was Squares.

"Please," Castman said. "You gotta get me out of here. Before . . ."

"Before what?"

He closed his eyes, opened them again. "I got shot, what, three, four years ago maybe? I don't know anymore. I don't know what day or month or even year it is. The light's always on, so I don't know if it's day or night. I don't know who's president." He swallowed, not without some effort. "She's crazy, man. I try screaming for help, it don't do no good. She got the place lined with cork. I just lay here, all day, looking at these walls."

I found it hard to find my voice. Squares, however, was unfazed. "We're not here for your life story," he said. "We want to ask you about one of your girls."

"You got the wrong guy," he said. "I haven't worked the streets in a long time."

"That's okay. She hasn't worked in a long time either."

"Who?"

"Sheila Rogers."

"Ah." Castman smiled at the name. "What do you want to know?"

"Everything."

"And if I refuse to tell you?"

Squares touched my shoulder. "We're leaving," he said to me.

Castman's voice was pure panic. "What?"

Squares looked down at him. "You don't want to cooperate, Mr. Castman, that's fine. We won't bother you further."

"Wait!" he shouted. "Okay, look, you know how many visitors I've had since I been here?"

"Don't care," Squares said.

"Six. A grand total of six. And none in, I don't know, has to be a year at least. And all six were my old girls. They came here to laugh at me. Watch me shit myself. And you want to hear something sick? I looked forward to it. Anything to break up the monotony, you know what I mean?"

Squares looked impatient. "Sheila Rogers."

The tube made a wet, sucking noise. Castman opened his mouth. A bubble formed. He closed his mouth and tried again. "I met her—God, I'm trying to think—ten, fifteen years ago. I was working the Port Authority. She came off a bus from Iowa or Idaho, some shithole like that."

Working the Port Authority. I knew the routine well. Pimps wait at the terminal. They look for kids fresh off the bus—the desperate, the runaways, the raw meat, coming to the Big Apple to be models or actresses or start anew or flee from boredom or escape abuse. The pimps watch like the predators that they are. And then they swoop in, take them down, gnaw on the carcass.

"I had a good rap," Castman said. "First off, I'm a white guy. The Midwest meat. It's almost all white breast. They're afraid of the strutting brothers. But me, I was different. I'd wear a nice business suit. I'd carry a briefcase. I'd be a little more patient. So anyway, that day I was waiting by Gate 127. It was a favorite of mine. Got a good view of maybe six different arrivals. Sheila came off the bus and man, she was smoking hot. Maybe sixteen years old and prime-time. A virgin too, though I couldn't tell that right off. I'd learn all about that later."

I felt my muscles tighten. Squares slowly slid his body between the bed and me.

"So I started sweet-talking her. Sling her my best bits, you know?"

We knew.

"So I give her the line about making her a big-time model. But smooth. Not like the other assholes. I'm like silk. But Sheila, she was smarter than most. Cautious. I could tell she wasn't buying it all the way, but that was okay. See, I don't press. I act legit. End of the day, they want to believe, right? They all hear stories about some supermodel being discovered at the Dairy Queen or some such shit, and hey, that's why they come in the first place."

The machine stopped beeping. I heard it gurgle. Then it started beeping again.

"So Sheila sort of crosses her arms, right. She tells me straight up that she never parties or any of that. I tell her hey, no problem, I'm not into that either. I'm a businessman, I say. A professional photographer and talent scout. We'll take some pictures. That's all. Get a portfolio going. Straight up—no partying, no drugs, no nudity, nothing she isn't totally comfortable with. And I'm a pretty good photographer, you know. I got an eye for it. See these walls? These shots of Tanya—I took them."

I looked at the photographs of the once-beautiful Tanya, and the chill struck me deep in my heart. When I looked back at the bed, Castman was staring at me.

"You," he said.

"What about me?"

"Sheila." He smiled. "She means something to you, am I right?"

I didn't reply.

"You *love* her."

He stretched out the word *love*. Mocking me. I kept still.

"Hey, I don't blame you, man. That was some quality tang. And, man, she could suck the—"

I started toward him. Castman laughed. Squares stepped in the way. He looked me straight in the eye and shook his head. I backed off. He was right.

Castman stopped laughing, but his eyes stayed on me. "You want to know how I turned your girl out, lover boy?"

I said nothing.

"Same way as I did Tanya out there. See, I went for the prime cuts, the ones the brothers couldn't get their hooks into. A high-end operation. So I gave Sheila the rap, and eventually I got her into my studio for a shoot. That was it. All I need to do. Put a fork in her, she's done."

"How?" I asked.

"You really want to hear this?"

"How?"

Castman closed his eyes, the smile still there, savoring the memory. "I took a bunch of photos of her. All nice and legit. And when we were done, I put a knife to her throat. Then I cuffed her to a bed in a room that was"—he chuckled, let his eyes open and roll—"corked. I drugged her up. I filmed her when she was half out of it, made it all look very consensual. That, by the way, was how your Sheila lost her virginity. On video. With yours truly. Magical, am I right?"

The rage flared again, started boiling over, consuming me. I didn't know how much longer I could keep from wringing his neck. But that, I reminded myself, was what he wanted.

"Where was I? Oh, right, I cuffed her and shot her up for maybe a week. Prime stuff too. Expensive. But hey, it's a business expense. All businesses got their training regimens, right? Eventually Sheila got hooked, and let me tell you, you can't put that genie back in the bottle. By the time I uncuffed her, that girl would lick out my toe jam for a hit, you know what I mean?"

He stopped as though waiting for applause. It felt as if something were shredding my insides.

Squares kept his voice flat. "So after this, you put her on the street?"

"Yup. Taught her some tricks too. How to get a guy off fast. How to take on more than one guy at a time. All that, I was her teacher."

I thought that I might throw up.

"Go on," Squares said.

"No," he said. "Not until—"

"Then we'll bid you good-bye."

"Tanya," he said.

"What about her?"

Castman licked his lips. "Can you give me some water?"

"No. What about Tanya?"

"The bitch keeps me here, man. It ain't right. Yeah, I hurt her. But I had my reason. She wanted to leave, marry this john from Garden City. She thought they were in love. I mean, come on, this look like *Pretty Woman* to you? She was going to take some of my best girls with her. They could live out in Garden City with her and this john, get cleaned up, some such shit. I couldn't stand for that."

"So," Squares said, "you taught her a lesson."

"Yeah, sure. It's how it is."

"You messed up her face with a razor."

"Not just her face—guy might be into putting a bag over the head, you know what I mean? But yeah, you get the gist. It was a lesson to the other girls too. But see—and here's the funny part—her boyfriend, the john, he didn't know what I'd done. So he comes down from his big house in Garden City, all set up to rescue Tanya, right? The dumbass has a twenty-two. I laugh at him. And he shoots me. This dipwad accountant from Garden City. He shoots me under the armpit with a twenty-two and bam, the bullet goes into my spine. I'm left like this. You believe that? And then, oh, this is precious, after he shoots me, Mr. Garden City sees what I did to Tanya and you know what he does, this great love of hers?"

He waited. We figured it was rhetorical and kept still.

"He freaks out and dumps her. Get it? He sees my handiwork on Tanya, and he just runs out on her. Her great love. Wants nothing to do with her. They never see each other again."

Castman started laughing again. I tried to stay still and breathe.

"So I'm in the hospital," he continued, "totally out of it. Tanya's got nothing. So she signs me out. She brings me here. And now she takes care of me. You understand what I'm saying? She's prolonging my life. I refuse to eat, she sticks a tube down my throat. Look, I'll tell you what you want to know. But you got to do something for me."

"What?" Squares said.

"Kill me."

"No can do."

"Tell the police, then. Let them arrest me. I'll confess to everything."

Squares said, "What happened to Sheila Rogers?"

"Promise me."

Squares looked at me. "We got enough here. Let's go."

"Okay, okay, I'll tell you. Just . . . just think about it, okay?"

He shifted his eyes from Squares to me then back to Squares again. Squares showed him nothing. I have no idea what was on my face. "I don't know where Sheila is now. Hell, I don't really understand what happened."

"How long did she work for you?"

"Two years. Maybe three."

"And how did she get free?"

"Huh?"

"You don't seem like the sort of guy who lets employees branch out," Squares said. "So I'm asking what happened to her."

"She worked the streets, right. Started getting some regulars. She was good at what she did. And somewhere along the way, she hooked up with some bigger players. It happens. Not often. But it happens."

"What do you mean, bigger players?"

"Dealers. Big-time dealers, I think. She started muling and delivering, I think. And worse, she started getting clean. I was going to lean on her, like you said, but she had some heavy-duty friends."

"Like who?"

"You know Lenny Misler?"

Squares leaned back. "The attorney?"

"The mob attorney," Castman corrected him. "She got picked up carrying. He repped her."

Squares frowned. "Lenny Misler took on the case of a streetwalker caught carrying?"

"You see my point? She comes out, I start sniffing around, you know. Find out what's she up to. A couple of major-league goons pay me a visit. They tell me to stay away. I'm not stupid. Plenty more tang where that came from."

"What happened next?"

"Never saw her again. Last I heard she was going to college. You believe that?"

"Do you know what college?"

"No. I'm not even sure it's true. Could have been just a rumor."

"Anything else?"

"Nope."

"No other rumors?"

Castman's eyes started moving, and I could see the desperation. He wanted to keep us there. But he had nothing else to tell us. I looked at Squares. He nodded and turned to leave. I followed.

"Wait!"

We ignored him.

"Please, man, I'm begging you. I told you everything, right? I cooperated. You can't just leave me here."

I saw his endless days and nights in the room, and I didn't care.

"Fucking assholes!" he shouted. "Hey, man, you. Lover boy. You enjoy my leftovers, you hear. And remember this: Everything she does to you, every time she gets you off—I taught her that. You hear me? You hear what I'm saying?"

My cheeks flushed, but I didn't turn around. Squares opened the door.

"Shit." Castman's voice was softer now. "It doesn't leave, you know."

I hesitated.

"She may look all nice and clean. But where she's been, you don't ever come back. You know what I'm saying?"

I tried to shut out his words. But they hammered their way in and bounced around my skull. I walked out and closed the door. Back in the dark. Tanya met us on the way out.

"Are you going to tell?" she asked, her words slurred.

I never hurt him. That was what she said. She never raised a hand to him. Too true.

Without another word, we hurried back outside, almost diving into the night air. We sucked down deep breaths, divers breaking the surface short on air, got back to the van, and drove away.

10

Grand Island, Nebraska

Sheila wanted to die alone.

Strangely enough, the pain was diminishing now. She wondered why. There was no light, though, no moment of stark clarity. There was no comfort in death. No angels surrounded her. No long-gone relatives—she thought of her grandmother, the woman who'd made her feel special, who'd called her "Treasure"—came and held her hand.

Alone. In the dark.

She opened her eyes. Was she dreaming right now? Hard to say. She'd been hallucinating earlier. She'd been slipping in and out of consciousness. She remembered seeing Carly's face and begging her to go away. Had that been real? Probably not. Probably an illusion.

When the pain got bad, really bad, the line between awake and sleep, between reality and dreams, blurred. She did not fight it anymore. It was the only way you could survive the agony. You try to block the pain. That doesn't work. You try to break the pain down into manageable time intervals. That doesn't work either. Finally, you find the only outlet available: your sanity.

You let go of your sanity.

But if you can recognize what's happening, are you really letting go?

Deep philosophical questions. They were for the living. In the end, after all the hopes and dreams, after all the damage and rebuilding, Sheila Rogers would end up dying young and in pain and at the hands of another.

Poetic justice, she supposed.

Because now, as she felt something inside her cleave and tear and pull away, there was indeed a clarity. A horrible, inescapable one. The blinders were being lifted, and for once she could see the truth.

Sheila Rogers wanted to die alone.

But he was in the room with her. She was sure of it. She could feel his hand resting gently on her forehead now. It made her cold. As she felt the life force slipping away, she made one last plea.

"Please," she said. "Go away."

11

Squares and I did not discuss what we'd seen. We also did not call the police. I pictured Louis Castman trapped in that room, unable to move, nothing to read, no TV or radio, nothing to look at except those old photographs. If I were a better person, I might have even cared.

I also thought about the Garden City man who'd shot Louis Castman and then turned his back, his rejection probably scarring Tanya worse than Castman ever could. I wondered if Mr. Garden City still thought about Tanya or if he'd just gone on as if she'd never existed. I wondered if her face haunted his dreams.

I doubted it.

I thought about all this because I was curious and horrified. But I also did it because it stopped me from thinking about Sheila, about what she'd been, about what Castman had done to her. I reminded myself that she was the victim here, kidnapped and raped and worse, and that nothing she had done had been her fault. I should not view her any differently. But this clearheaded and obvious rationale would not stick.

And I hated myself for that.

It was nearly four in the morning when the van pulled up to my building.

"What do you make of it so far?" I asked.

Squares stroked his stubble. "What Castman said at the end there. About it never leaving her. He's right, you know."

"You speaking from experience?"

"As a matter of fact, I am."

"So?"

"So my guess is that something from her past came back and got her."

"We're on the right track then."

"Probably," Squares said.

I grabbed the door handle and said, "Whatever she's done—whatever you've done—it may never leave you. But it doesn't condemn you either."

Squares stared out the window. I waited. He kept staring. I stepped out and he drove away.

A message on the phone knocked me back a step. I checked the time on the LCD. The message had been left at 11:47 P.M. Awfully late. I figured it had to be family. I was wrong.

I hit the play button and a young woman said, "Hi, Will."

I didn't recognize the voice.

"It's Katy. Katy Miller."

I stiffened.

"Long time, right? Look, I, uh, sorry I'm calling so late. You're probably asleep, I don't know. Listen, Will, could you give me a call as soon as you get this? I don't care what time it is. I just, well, I need to talk to you about something."

She left her number. I stood there, dumbstruck. Katy Miller. Julie's little sister. The last time I'd seen her . . . she'd been six years old or so. I smiled, remembering a time—sheesh, Katy couldn't have been more than four—when she had hidden behind her father's army trunk and jumped out at an inopportune time. I remember Julie and I covering ourselves with a blanket, no time to pull up our pants, trying not to laugh our asses off.

Little Katy Miller.

She'd be, what, seventeen or eighteen by now. Odd to think about. I knew the effect Julie's death had on my family, and I could pretty much surmise what it had done to Mr. and Mrs. Miller. But I'd never really considered the impact on little Katy. I thought again about that time Julie and I had pulled up the blanket giggling, and now I remembered that we'd been in the basement. We'd been messing around on the very couch where Julie would be found murdered.

Why, after all these years, was Katy calling me?

It could be just a condolence call, I reminded myself, though that seemed odd on several levels, not the least of which would be the hour of her call. I replayed the message, searching for a hidden meaning. I didn't find one. She had said to call anytime. But it was four in the A.M., and I was exhausted. Whatever it was, it could wait until morning.

I climbed into bed and remembered the last time I'd seen Katy Miller. My family had been asked to stay away from the funeral. We complied. But two days later, I went by myself to the graveyard off Route 22. I sat by Julie's tombstone. I said nothing. I did not cry. I did not feel comfort or closure or anything else. The Miller family pulled up in their white Oldsmobile Cierra, and I made myself scarce. But I'd met little Katy's eyes. There was a strange resignation in her face, a knowing that went beyond her years. I saw sadness and horror and maybe I saw pity too.

I left the graveyard then. I had not seen or spoken to her since.

12

Belmont, Nebraska

Sheriff Bertha Farrow had seen worse.

Murder scenes were bad, but for overall vomit-inducing, bone-crunching, head-splitting, blood-splattering grossness, it was hard to beat the metal-against-flesh effect of an old-fashioned automobile accident. A head-on collision. A truck crossing the divider. A tree that splits the car from the bumper to the backseat. A high-speed tumble over a guardrail.

Now, that did serious damage.

And yet this sight, this dead woman at this fairly bloodless scene, was somehow much worse. Bertha Farrow could see the woman's face—her features twisted in fear, uncomprehending, maybe desperate—and she could see that the woman had died in great pain. She could see the mangled fingers, the misshapen rib cage, the bruises, and she knew that the damage here had been done by a fellow human being, flesh against flesh. This was not the result of a patch of ice or someone changing radio stations at eighty miles an hour or a rush truck delivery or the ill effects of alcohol or speed.

This had been intentional.

"Who found her?" she asked her deputy George Volker.

"The Randolph boys."

"Which ones?"

"Jerry and Ron."

Bertha calculated. Jerry would be about sixteen. Ron fourteen.

"They were walking with Gypsy," the deputy added. Gypsy was the Randolphs' German shepherd. "He sniffed her out."

"Where are the boys now?"

"Dave took them home. They were kinda shook up. I got statements. They don't know nothing."

Bertha nodded. A station wagon came tearing up the highway. Clyde Smart, the county medical examiner, stopped his wagon with a screech. The door flew open, and Clyde sprinted toward them. Bertha cupped a hand over her eyes.

"No rush, Clyde. She ain't going anywhere."

George snickered.

Clyde Smart was used to this. He was closing in on fifty, about Bertha's age. The two had been in office for nearly two decades. Clyde ignored her joke and ran past them. He looked down at the body, and his face dropped.

"Sweet Jesus," the M.E. said.

Clyde squatted beside her. He gently pushed the hair back from the corpse's face. "Oh God," he said. "I mean—" He stopped, shook his head.

Bertha was used to him too. Clyde's reaction did not surprise her. Most M.E.s, she knew, stayed clinical and detached. Not Clyde. People were not tissue and messy chemicals to him. She'd seen Clyde cry over bodies plenty of times. He handled each DOA with incredible, almost ridiculous, respect. He performed autopsies as though he could make the person recover. He'd deliver bad news to families, and he'd genuinely share their grief.

"Can you give me an approximate time of death?" she asked.

"Not long," Clyde said softly. "The skin is still in early rigor mortis. I'd say no more than six hours. I'll get a liver temperature reading and—" He spotted the hand with the fingers that jutted out in unnatural directions. "Oh my God," he said again.

Bertha looked back at her deputy. "Any ID?"

"None."

"Possible robbery?"

"Too brutal," Clyde said. He looked up. "Someone wanted her to suffer."

There was a moment of silence. Bertha could see tears forming in Clyde's eyes.

"What else?" she asked.

Clyde quickly looked back down. "She's no vagrant," he said. "Well dressed and nourished." He checked her mouth. "Decent enough dental work."

"Any signs of rape?"

"She's dressed," Clyde said. "But my God, what wasn't done to her? Very little blood here, certainly not enough for this to be the murder scene. My guess is that someone drove by and dumped her here. I'll know more when I get her on the table."

"Okay then," Bertha said. "Let's check Missing Persons and run her prints."

Clyde nodded as Sheriff Bertha Farrow started walking away.

13

I didn't have to call Katy back.

The ring hit me like a cattle prod. My sleep had been so deep, so total and dreamless, there could be no slow swim to the surface. One moment I was drowning in the black. The next I jolted upright, heart racing. I checked the digital clock: 6:58 A.M.

I groaned and leaned over. The caller ID was blocked. A useless contraption. Everyone you'd want to avoid or who'd wanted to hide simply paid for the block.

My voice sounded too awake in my own ears as I chirped a merry "Hello?"

"Uh, Will Klein?"

"Yes?"

"It's Katy Miller." Then, as if an afterthought, "Julie's sister."

"Hi, Katy," I said.

"I left a message for you last night."

"I didn't get in until four in the morning."

"Oh. I guess I woke you up then."

"Don't worry about it," I said.

Her voice sounded sad and young and forced. I remembered when she was born. I did a little math. "You're, what, a senior now?"

"I start college in the fall."

"Where?"

"Bowdoin. It's a small college."

"In Maine," I said. "I know it. It's an excellent school. Congratulations."

"Thanks."

I sat up a little more, trying to think of a way to bridge the silence. I fell back on the classics: "It's been a long time."

"Will?"

"Yes?"

"I'd like to see you."

"Sure, that would be great."

"How about today?"

"Where are you?" I asked.

"I'm in Livingston," she said. Then added, "I saw you come by our house."

"I'm sorry about that."

"I can come to the city if you want."

"No need," I said. "I'll be out visiting my father today. How about we hook up before that?"

"Yeah, okay," she said. "But not here. You remember the basketball courts by the high school?"

"Sure," I said. "I'll meet you there at ten."

"Okay."

"Katy," I said, switching ears. "I don't mind telling you that this call is a little weird."

"I know."

"What do you want to see me about?"

"What do you think?" she replied.

I did not answer right away, but that did not matter. She was already off the line.

14

Will left his apartment. The Ghost watched.

The Ghost did not follow him. He knew where Will was going. But as he watched, his fingers flexed and tightened, flexed and tightened. His forearms bunched. His body quaked.

The Ghost remembered Julie Miller. He remembered her naked body in that basement. He remembered the feel of her skin, warm at first, for just a little while, and then slowly stiffening into something akin to wet marble. He remembered the purple-yellow of her face, the pinpoints of red in the bulging eyes, her features contorted in horror and surprise, shattered capillaries, the saliva frozen down the side of her face like a knife scar. He remembered the neck, the unnatural bend in death, the way the wire had actually slashed deep into her skin, slicing through the esophagus, nearly decapitating her.

All that blood.

Strangulation was his favorite method of execution. He had visited India to study the Thuggee, the so-called cult of silent assassins, who'd perfected the secret art of strangulation. Over the years, the Ghost had mastered guns and knives and the like, but when possible, he still preferred the cold efficiency, the final silence, the bold power, the personal touch of strangulation.

A careful breath.

Will disappeared from view.

The brother.

The Ghost thought about all those kung fu movies, the ones where one brother is murdered and the other lives to avenge the death. He thought about what would happen if he simply killed Will Klein.

No, this was not about that. This went way beyond revenge.

Still he wondered about Will. He was the key, after all. Had the years changed him? The Ghost hoped so. But he would find out soon enough.

Yes, it was almost time to meet with Will and catch up on old times.

The Ghost crossed the street toward Will's building.

Five minutes later, he was in the apartment.

I took the Community Bus Line out to the intersection of Livingston Avenue and Northfield. The hotbed of the great suburb of Livingston. An old elementary school had been converted into a poor man's strip mall with specialty stores that never seemed to do any business. I hopped off the bus along with several domestic workers heading out from the city. The bizarre symmetry of reverse commute. Those who lived in towns like Livingston head into the city in the morning; those who clean their houses and watch their children do the opposite. Balance.

I headed down Livingston Avenue toward Livingston High School, which was clustered together with the Livingston Public Library, the Livingston Municipal Court Building, and the Livingston police station. See a pattern here? All four edifices were made of brick and looked as though they were built at the same time, from the same architect, from the same supply of brick—as though one building had begot another.

I grew up here. As a child, I borrowed the classics by C. S. Lewis and Madeleine L'Engle from that library. I fought (and lost) a speeding ticket in that municipal building when I was eighteen. I spent my high school years, one of six hundred kids in my graduating class, in the cluster's biggest building.

I took the circle halfway around and veered to the right. I found the basketball courts and stood under a rusted rim. The town tennis courts were on my left. I played tennis in high school. I was actually pretty good too, though I never had the heart for sports. I lacked the competitive spirit to be great. I didn't want to lose, but I didn't fight hard enough to win.

"Will?"

I turned and when I saw her, I felt my blood turn to ice. The clothes were different—hip-hugging jeans, circa-seventies clogs, a too-tight too-short shirt that revealed a flat, albeit pierced, belly—but the face and the hair . . . It felt like I was falling. I looked away for a moment, in the direction of the soccer field, and I could have sworn I saw Julie out there.

"I know," Katy Miller said. "Like seeing a ghost, right?"

I turned back to her.

"My dad," she said, jamming her tiny hands into the tight jean pockets. "He still can't look at me straight on without crying."

I did not know what to say to that. She came closer to me. We both faced the high school. "You went here, right?" I asked.

"Graduated last month."

"Like it?"

She shrugged. "Glad to get out."

The sun shone, making the building a cold silhouette, and for a moment, it looked a bit like a prison. High school is like that. I was fairly popular in high school. I was vice president of the student council. I was co-captain of the tennis team. I had friends. But as I tried to dig up a pleasant memory, none came. They were all tainted with the insecurity that marks those years. In hindsight, high school—adolescence, if you will—feels a little like protracted combat. You just need to survive, get through it, come out of it okay. I wasn't happy in high school. I'm not sure you're supposed to be.

"I'm sorry about your mother," Katy said.

"Thank you."

She took a pack of cigarettes out of her back pocket and offered me one. I shook her off. I watched her light up and resisted the urge to lecture. Katy's eyes took in everything but me. "I was an accident, you know. I came late. Julie was already in high school. My parents were told they couldn't have more children. Then . . ." She shrugged again. "So they weren't expecting me."

"It's not like the rest of us are well planned," I said.

She laughed a little at that, and the sound echoed deep inside me. It was Julie's laugh, even the way it faded away.

"Sorry about my dad," Katy said. "He just freaked when he saw you."

"I shouldn't have done that."

She took too long a drag and tilted her head. "Why did you?"

I thought about the answer. "I don't know," I said.

"I saw you. From the moment you turned the corner. It was weird, you know. I remember as a little kid watching you walk from your house. My bedroom. I mean, I'm still in the same bedroom, so it's like I was watching the past or something. It felt weird."

I looked to my right. The drive was empty now, but during the school year, that was where the parents sat in cars and waited for their kids. Maybe my high school memories are not all good, but I remember my mom picking me up there in her old red Volkswagen. She'd be reading a magazine and the bell would ring and I'd walk toward her and when she'd spot me, when she first raised her head and sensed that I was coming near, her smile, that Sunny smile, would burst forth from deep in her heart, that blinding smile of unconditional love, and I realized now with a hard thud that nobody would ever smile at me that way again.

Too much, I thought. Being here. The visual echo of Julie on Katy's face. The memories. It was all too much.

"You hungry?" I asked her.

"Sure, I guess."

She had a car, an old Honda Civic. Trinkets, lots of them, hung from the rearview mirror. The car smelled of bubble gum and fruity shampoo. I didn't recognize the music blaring from the speakers, but I didn't mind it either.

We drove to a classic New Jersey diner on Route 10 without speaking. There were autographed photographs of local anchormen behind the counter. Each booth had a mini-jukebox. The menu was slightly longer than a Tom Clancy novel.

A man with a heavy beard and heavier deodorant asked us how many. We told him that we were two. Katy added that we wanted a smoking table. I didn't know smoking sections still existed, but apparently big diners are throwbacks. As soon as we sat, she pulled the ashtray toward her, almost as if for protection.

"After you came by the house," she said, "I went to the graveyard."

The water boy filled our glasses. She inhaled on the cigarette and did that lean-back-and-up blowout. "I haven't gone in years. But after I saw you, I don't know, I felt like I should."

She still would not look at me. I find this a lot with the kids at the shelter. They avoid your eyes. I let them. It does not mean anything. I try to hold their gaze, but I've learned that eye contact is overrated.

"I barely remember Julie anymore. I see the pictures and I don't know if my memories are real or something I made up myself. I think, oh I remember when we went on the teacups at Great Adventure and then I'll see the picture and I won't know if I really remember it or if I just remember the picture. You know what I mean?"

"I think so, yes."

"And after you came by, I mean, I had to get out of the house. My dad was raging. My mom was crying. I just had to get out."

"I didn't mean to upset anyone," I said.

She waved my words away. "It's okay. It's good for them in a weird way. Most of the time we tiptoe around it, you know. It's creepy. Sometimes I wish . . . I wish I could just scream, 'She's dead.' " Katy leaned forward. "You want to hear something totally freaky?"

I gestured for her to go ahead.

"We haven't changed the basement. That old couch and TV. That ratty carpet. That old trunk I used to hide behind. They're all still there. Nobody uses them. But they're there. And our laundry room is still down there. We have to walk through that room to get to it. You understand what I'm saying? That's how we live. We tiptoe around upstairs, you know, like we're living on ice and we're afraid the floor is going to crack and we're all going to fall down into that basement."

She stopped and sucked on the cigarette as if it were an air hose. I sat back. Like I said before: I'd never really thought about Katy Miller, about what the murder of her sister had done to her. I thought about her parents, of course. I thought about the devastation. I often wondered why they'd stayed in the house, but then again, I never really understood why my parents had not moved either. I mentioned before the link between comfort and self-inflicted pain, the desire to hold on because suffering was preferable to forgetting. Staying in that house had to be the ultimate example.

But I'd never really considered the case of Katy Miller, about what it must have been like growing up among those ruins, with your sister's look-alike specter forever at your side. I looked at Katy again, as if for the first time. Her eyes continued to dart about like scared birds. I could see tears there now. I reached out and took her hand, again so like her sister's. The past came at me so hard I nearly fell back.

"This is so weird," she said.

Truer words, I thought. "For me too."

"It needs to end, Will. My whole life . . . whatever really happened that night, it needs to end. Sometimes I hear on TV when they catch the bad guy someone says, 'It won't bring her back,' and I think, 'Duh.' But that's not the point. It ends. You catch the guy, it gives it some kind of finality. People need that."

I had no idea where she was going with this. I tried to pretend that she was one of the center's kids, that she'd come in needing my help and love. I sat and looked at her and tried to let her know that I was here to listen.

"You don't know how much I hated your brother—not just for what he did to Julie, but for what he did to the rest of us by running away. I prayed they'd find him. I had this dream where he'd be surrounded and he put up a fight and then the cops would smoke him. I know you don't want to hear this. But I need you to understand."

"You wanted closure," I said.

"Yeah," she said. "Except . . ."

"Except what?"

She looked up and for the first time our eyes locked. I grew cold again. I wanted to withdraw my hand, but I could not move. "I saw him," she said.

I thought that I heard wrong.

"Your brother. I saw him. At least I think it was him."

I found my voice enough to ask, "When?"

"Yesterday. At the graveyard."

The waitress came over then. She withdrew the pencil from her ear and asked what we wanted. For a moment neither of us spoke. The waitress cleared her throat. Katy ordered some sort of salad. The waitress looked at me. I asked for a cheese omelette. She asked what kind of cheese—American, Swiss, cheddar. I said cheddar would be fine. Did I want home fries or french fries with that? Home fries. White toast, rye toast, wheat toast. Rye. And nothing to drink, thank you.

The waitress finally left.

"Tell me," I said.

Katy stubbed out the cigarette. "It's like I said before. I went to the graveyard. Just to get out of the house. Anyway, you know where Julie's buried, right?"

I nodded.

"That's right. I saw you there. Couple of days after her funeral."

"Yes," I said.

She leaned forward. "Did you love her?"

"I don't know."

"But she broke your heart."

"Maybe," I said. "A long time ago."

Katy stared down at her hands.

"Tell me what happened," I said.

"He looked pretty different. Your brother, I mean. I don't remember him much. Just a little. And I've seen pictures." She stopped.

"Are you saying he was standing by Julie's grave?"

"By a willow tree."

"What?"

"There's a tree there. Maybe a hundred feet away. I didn't come in the front gate. I hopped a fence. So he wasn't expecting me. See, I came up from the back and I saw this guy standing under the willow tree and he's just staring in the direction of Julie's stone. He never heard me. He was just lost, you know. I tapped him on the shoulder. He jumped like a mile in the air and when he turned around and saw me . . . well, you see what I look like. He nearly screamed. He thought I was a ghost or something."

"And you were sure it was Ken?"

"Not sure, no. I mean, how could I be?" She took out another cigarette and then said, "Yeah. Yeah, I know it was him."

"But how could you be sure?"

"He told me he didn't do it."

My head spun. My hands fell to my sides and gripped the cushion. When I finally spoke, my words came out slowly. "What exactly did he say?"

"At first, just that. 'I didn't kill your sister.' "

"What did you do?"

"I told him he was a liar. I told him I was going to scream."

"Did you?"

"No."

"Why not?"

Katy still had not lit the new cigarette. She withdrew it from her lips and put it on the tabletop. "Because I believed him," she said. "Something in his voice, I don't know. I'd hated him for so long. You have no idea how much. But now . . ."

"So what did you do?"

"I stepped back. I was still going to scream. But he came toward me. He took my face in his hands and looked me in the eye and said, 'I'm going to find the killer, I promise.' That was it. He looked at me a little more. Then he let go and ran off."

"Have you told—"

She shook her head. "No one. Sometimes I'm not even sure it happened. Like I imagined the whole thing. Dreamt it or made it up. Like my memories of Julie." She looked up at me. "Do you think he killed Julie?"

"No," I said.

"I've seen you on the news," she said. "You've always thought he was dead. Because they found some of his blood at the scene."

I nodded.

"Do you still believe that?"

"No," I said. "I don't believe that anymore."

"What made you change your mind?"

I didn't know how to reply to that. "I guess," I said, "I'm looking for him too."

"I want to help."

She'd said want. But I know she meant need.

"Please, Will. Let me help."

And I said okay.

15

Belmont, Nebraska

Sheriff Bertha Farrow frowned over Deputy George Volker's shoulder. "Hate these things," she said.

"You shouldn't," Volker replied, fingers dancing on the keyboard. "Computers are our friends."

She frowned some more. "So what is our friend doing now?"

"Scanning Jane Doe's fingerprints."

"Scanning?"

"How to explain this to a total technophobe . . . ?" Volker looked up and rubbed his chin. "It's like a Xerox machine and fax machine in one. It makes a copy of the fingerprint and then it emails it over to the CJIS in West Virginia."

CJIS stood for Criminal Justice Information Services. Now that every police force was online—even those in the most hillbilly of Hicksville boonies like them—fingerprints could be sent over the Internet for identification. If the fingerprints were listed in the National Crime Information Center's enormous database, they'd have a match and a positive ID in no time.

"I thought the CJIS was in Washington," Bertha said.

"Not anymore. Senator Byrd got it moved."

"Good man to have as senator."

"Oh yeah."

Bertha hoisted her holster and headed down the corridor. Her police station shared space with Clyde's morgue, which was convenient if sporadically pungent. The morgue had terrible ventilation, and every once in a while a heavy cloud of formaldehyde and decay floated out and hovered.

With only a moment's hesitation, Bertha Farrow opened the door to the morgue. There were no gleaming drawers or shiny instruments or any of the stuff that you see on TV. Clyde's morgue was pretty close to makeshift. The job was only part-time because, let's face it, there was not that much to do. Car accident victims were pretty much the extent out here. Last year, Don Taylor had gotten drunk and shot himself in the head by accident. His long-suffering wife liked to joke that ol' Don fired because he looked in the mirror and mistook himself for a moose. Marriage. But really, that was about it. The morgue—hell, the term was a generous description of this converted janitorial room—could only hold maybe two corpses at a time. If Clyde needed more storage, he used Wally's funeral home facilities.

Jane Doe's body was on the table. Clyde stood over her. He wore blue scrubs and pale surgical gloves. He was crying. Opera blared from the boom box, the wail of something appropriately tragic.

"Open her up yet?" Bertha asked, though the answer was obvious.

Clyde wiped his eyes with two fingers. "No."

"You waiting for her permission?"

He shot Bertha a red-eyed glare. "I'm still doing the external."

"How about a cause of death, Clyde?"

"Won't know for sure until I complete the autopsy."

Bertha moved closer to him. She put her hand on his shoulder, faking comfort and pretending to bond. "How about a preliminary guess, Clyde?"

"She was beaten pretty badly. See here?"

He pointed to where you might normally find a rib cage. There was little definition. The bones had caved in, crushed down like a boot on Styrofoam.

"Lots of bruising," Bertha said.

"Discoloration, yeah, but see here?" He put his finger on something poking up the skin near the stomach.

"Broken ribs?"

"Smashed ribs," he corrected her.

"How?"

Clyde shrugged. "Probably used a heavy ball peen hammer, something like that. My guess—and it's only a guess—is that one of the ribs splintered off and pierced a major organ. It might have punctured a lung or sliced through her belly. Or maybe she got lucky and it went straight through her heart."

Bertha shook her head. "She don't seem the lucky type to me."

Clyde turned away. He lowered his head and started crying again. His body heaved from the stifled sobs.

"These marks on her breasts," Bertha said.

Without looking he said, "Cigarette burns."

What she'd figured. Mangled fingers, cigarette burns. You did not have to be Sherlock Holmes to deduce that she was tortured.

"Do it all, Clyde. Blood samples, tox screen, everything."

He sniffled and finally turned back around. "Yeah, Bertha, sure, okay."

The door behind them opened. They both turned. It was Volker. "Got a hit," he said.

"Already?"

George nodded. "Top of the NCIC list."

"What do you mean, top of the list?"

Volker gestured toward the body on the table. "Our Jane Doe," he said. "She was wanted by none other than the FBI."

16

Katy dropped me off on Hickory Place, maybe three blocks from my parents' house. We did not want anybody to see us together. That was probably paranoia on our part, but I figured, what the hell.

"So what now?" Katy asked.

I had been wondering that myself. "I'm not sure. But if Ken didn't kill Julie—"

"Then someone else did."

"Man," I said, "we're good at this."

She smiled. "So I guess we look for suspects?"

It sounded ridiculous—who were we, the Mod Squad?—but I nodded.

"I'll start checking," she said.

"Checking what?"

She gave me a teenager shrug, using her whole body. "I don't know. Julie's past, I guess. Figure out who'd have wanted to kill her."

"The police did that."

"They only looked at your brother, Will."

She had a point. "Okay," I said, again feeling ridiculous.

"Let's hook up later tonight."

I nodded and slid out. Nancy Drew sped off without a good-bye. I stood there and soaked in the solitude. I was not all that eager to move.

The streets of suburbia were empty, but the well-paved driveways were full. The paneled station wagons of my youth had been replaced by a vast variety of quasi-off-road vehicles—minivans, family trucks (whatever that meant), SUVs. Most of the houses were in the classic split-level mode of the circa-1962 housing boom. Many were bloated with additions. Others had undergone extensive exterior renovations circa 1974 involving too-white, too-smooth stone; the look had aged about as well as the powder-blue tux I'd worn to the prom.

When I arrived at our house, there were no cars out front and no mourners inside. No surprise there. I called out to my father. No answer. I found him alone in the basement with a cutting razor in his hand. He was in the middle of the room, surrounded by old wardrobe boxes. The sealing tape had been sliced open. Dad stood perfectly still among the boxes. He did not turn around when he heard my footsteps.

"So much already packed away," he said softly.

The boxes had belonged to my mother. My father reached into one and plucked out a thin silver headband. He turned to me and held it up. "You remember this?"

We both smiled. Everyone, I guess, goes through fashion stages, but not like my mother. She set them, defined them, became them. There was her Headband Era, for example. She'd grown her hair out and worn a potpourri of the multihued bands like an Indian princess. For several months—I'd say the Headband Era lasted maybe six—you would never see her without one. When the headbands were retired, the Suede-Fringe Period began in earnest. That was followed by the Purple Renaissance—not my favorite, I assure you, like living with a giant eggplant or Jimi Hendrix groupie—and then the Riding-Crop Age—this from a woman whose closest connection to a horse was seeing Elizabeth Taylor in *National Velvet.*

The fashion stages, like so many other things, ended with Julie Miller's murder. My mom—Sunny—packed the clothes away and stored them in the dingiest corner of the basement.

Dad flipped the headband back into the box. "We were going to move, you know."

I hadn't.

"Three years ago. We were going to get a condo in West Orange and maybe a winter place in Scottsdale, near Cousin Esther and Harold. But when we found out your mother was sick, we put it all on hold." He looked at me. "You thirsty?"

"Not really."

"How about a Diet Coke? I know I could use one."

Dad hurried past me and toward the stairs. I looked at the old boxes, my mother's handwriting on the sides in thick marker. On the shelf in the back I could still see two of Ken's old tennis rackets. One was the first he'd ever used, when he was only three. Mom had saved it for him. I turned away and followed him. When we reached the kitchen, he opened the refrigerator door.

"You want to tell me what happened yesterday?" he began.

"I don't know what you mean."

"You and your sister." Dad pulled out a two-liter bottle of Diet Coke. "What was that all about?"

"Nothing," I said.

He nodded as he opened a cabinet. He took out two glasses, opened the freezer, filled them with ice. "Your mother used to eavesdrop on you and Melissa," he said.

"I know."

He smiled. "She wasn't very discreet. I'd tell her to cut it out, but she'd just tell me to hush, it was a mother's job."

"You said, me and Melissa."

"Yes."

"Why not Ken?"

"Maybe she didn't want to know." He poured the sodas. "Very curious about your brother lately."

"It's a natural enough question."

"Sure, natural. And after the funeral, you were asking me if I think he's still alive. And then the next day, you and Melissa have an argument about him. So I'll ask you one more time: What's going on?"

The photograph was still in my pocket. Don't ask me why. I'd made color copies with my scanner that morning. But I couldn't let go of it.

When the doorbell rang, we both jumped, startled. We looked at each other. Dad shrugged. I told him I'd get it. I took a quick sip of the Diet Coke and put it back on the counter. I trotted to the front door. When I opened it, when I saw who it was, I nearly toppled back.

Mrs. Miller. Julie's mom.

She held out a platter wrapped with aluminum foil. Her eyes were lowered as though she were making an offering on an altar. For a moment, I froze, unsure what to say. She glanced up. Our eyes met just as they had when I stood on her curb two days earlier. The pain I saw in them felt alive, electric. I wondered if she felt the same coming from mine.

"I just thought . . ." she began. "I mean, I just . . ."

"Please," I said. "Come in."

She tried to smile. "Thank you."

My father moved from the kitchen and said, "Who's there?"

I backed up. Mrs. Miller stepped into view, still holding up the platter as if for protection. My father's eyes widened, and I saw something behind them burst.

His voice was a rage-filled whisper. "What the hell are you doing here?"

"Dad," I said.

He ignored me. "I asked you a question, Lucille. What the hell do you want?"

Mrs. Miller lowered her head.

"Dad," I said more urgently.

But it was no use. His eyes had gone small and black. "I don't want you here," he said.

"Dad, she came to offer—"

"Get out."

"Dad!"

Mrs. Miller shrunk back. She pushed the platter into my hands. "I better go, Will."

"No," I said. "Don't."

"I shouldn't have come."

Dad shouted, "Damn right you shouldn't have come."

I shot him a glare, but his eyes stayed on her.

With her eyes still lowered, Mrs. Miller said, "I'm sorry for your loss."

But my father was not through. "She's dead, Lucille. It doesn't do any good now."

Mrs. Miller fled then. I stood holding the platter. I looked at my father in disbelief. He looked back and said, "Throw that crap away."

I was not sure what to do here. I wanted to follow her, to apologize, but she was halfway up the block and moving fast. My father had moved back into the kitchen. I followed, slamming the platter down on the counter.

"What the hell was that about?" I asked.

He picked up his drink. "I don't want her here."

"She came to pay her respects."

"She came to ease her guilt."

"What are you talking about?"

"Your mother is dead. There's nothing she can do for her now."

"That doesn't make any sense."

"Your mother called Lucille. Did you know that? Not long after the murder. She wanted to offer her condolences. Lucille told her to go to hell. She blamed us for raising a murderer. That's what she said. It was our fault. We raised a murderer."

"That was eleven years ago, Dad."

"Do you have any idea what that did to your mother?"

"Her daughter had just been murdered. She was in a lot of pain."

"So she waits until now to make it right? When it won't do any good?" He shook his head sternly. "I don't want to hear it. And your mother, well, she can't."

The front door opened then. Aunt Selma and Uncle Murray entered with their grieving smiles in place. Selma took over the kitchen. Murray busied himself with a loose wall plate he'd spotted yesterday.

And my father and I stopped talking.

17

Special Agent Claudia Fisher stiffened her spine and knocked on the door.

"Come in."

She turned the knob and entered the office of Assistant Director in Charge Joseph Pistillo. The ADIC—immaturely nicknamed, naturally enough, a-dick—ran the New York office. Outside of the director in Washington, an ADIC was the most senior and powerful agent in the FBI.

Pistillo looked up. He did not like what he saw. "What?"

"Sheila Rogers was found dead," Fisher reported.

Pistillo cursed. "How?"

"She was found on a roadside in Nebraska. No ID. They ran her prints through NCIC and got a hit."

"Damn."

Pistillo chewed on a cuticle. Claudia Fisher waited.

"I want a visual confirmation," he said.

"Done."

"What?"

"I took the liberty of emailing Sheriff Farrow the mug shots of Sheila Rogers. She and the M.E. confirmed it was the same woman. The height and weight match too."

Pistillo leaned back. He grabbed a pen, raised it to eye level, and studied it. Fisher stood at attention. He signaled for her to sit. She obeyed. "Sheila Rogers's parents live in Utah, right?"

"Idaho."

"Whatever. We need to contact them."

"I have the local police on standby. The chief knows the family personally."

Pistillo nodded. "Okay, good." He took the pen out of his mouth. "How was she killed?"

"Probably internal bleeding from a beating. The autopsy is still under way."

"Jesus."

"She was tortured. Her fingers had been snapped back and twisted, probably by a pair of pliers. There were cigarette burns on her torso."

"How long has she been dead?"

"She probably died sometime last night or early in the morning."

Pistillo looked at Fisher. He remembered how Will Klein, the lover, had sat in that very chair yesterday. "Fast," he said.

"Excuse me?"

"If, as we were led to believe, she ran away, they found her fast."

"Unless," Fisher said, "she ran to them."

Pistillo leaned back. "Or she never ran at all."

"I'm not following."

He studied the pen some more. "Our assumption has always been that Sheila Rogers fled because of her connection to the Albuquerque murders, right?"

Fisher tilted her head back and forth. "Yes and no. I mean, why come back to New York just to run away again?"

"Maybe she wanted to go to the mother's funeral, I don't know," he said. "Either way, I don't think that's the case anymore. Maybe she never knew we were on to her. Maybe—stay with me here, Claudia—maybe someone kidnapped her."

"How would that have worked?" Fisher asked.

Pistillo put down the pen. "According to Will Klein, she left the apartment at, what, six in the morning?"

"Five."

"Fine, five. So let's put this together using the accepted scenario. Sheila Rogers walks out at five. She goes into hiding. Someone finds her and tortures her and dumps her in the boonies of Nebraska. That sound about right?"

Fisher nodded slowly. "Like you said, fast."

"Too fast?"

"Maybe."

"Time-phase-wise," Pistillo said, "it's far more likely that someone grabbed her right away. As soon as she left the apartment."

"And flew her to Nebraska?"

"Or drove like a demon."

"Or . . . ?" Fisher began.

"Or?"

She looked at her boss. "I think," she said, "that we're both coming to the same conclusion. The time line is too close. She probably disappeared the night before."

"Which means?"

"Which means that Will Klein lied to us."

Pistillo grinned. "Exactly."

Fisher's words started coming fast now. "Okay, here's a more likely scenario: Will Klein and Sheila Rogers go to the funeral of Klein's mother. They return to his parents' house afterward. According to Klein, they drive back to their apartment that night. But we have no independent confirmation of that. So maybe"—she tried to slow down but that wasn't happening—"maybe they don't head home. Maybe he hands her over to an accomplice, who tortures and kills her and dumps the body. Will meanwhile drives back to his apartment. He goes to work in the morning. When Wilcox and I brace him at his office, he makes up this story about her leaving in the morning."

Pistillo nodded. "Interesting theory."

She stood at attention.

"Do you have a motive?" he asked.

"He needed to silence her."

"For?"

"Whatever happened in Albuquerque."

They both mulled it over in silence.

"I'm not convinced," Pistillo said.

"Neither am I."

"But we agree that Will Klein knows more than he's saying."

"For certain."

Pistillo let loose a long breath. "Either way, we need to give him the bad news about Ms. Rogers's demise."

"Yes."

"Call that local chief out in Utah."

"Idaho."

"Whatever. Have him inform the family. Then get them on a plane for official identification."

"What about Will Klein?"

Pistillo thought about that. "I'll reach out to Squares. Maybe he can help us deliver the blow."

18

My apartment door was ajar.

After Aunt Selma and Uncle Murray's arrival, my father and I carefully avoided each other. I love my father. I think I have made that pretty clear. But a small part of me irrationally blames him for my mother's death. I don't know why I feel that way, and it is very hard to admit this even to myself, but from the moment she first became ill, I looked at him differently. As though he hadn't done enough. Or perhaps I blamed him for not saving her after Julie Miller's murder. He hadn't been strong enough. He hadn't been a good enough husband. Couldn't true love have helped Mom recover, salved her spirit?

Like I said, irrational.

My door was only open a crack, but it made me pause. I always lock it—hey, I live in a doorman-free building in Manhattan—but then again I had not been thinking straight of late. Perhaps in my haste to meet Katy Miller I'd just forgotten. That would be natural enough. And the dead bolt gets stuck sometimes. Maybe I'd never fully closed the door in the first place.

I frowned. Not likely.

I put my hand on a door panel and pushed ever so slightly. I waited to hear the door creak. It did not. I heard something. Faint at first. I leaned my head through the opening and immediately felt my insides turn to ice.

Nothing I saw was out of the ordinary. The lights were out, as a matter of fact. The blinds were drawn, so there was not much illumination. No, nothing out of the ordinary—or again, nothing that I could see. I stayed in the corridor and leaned in a little more.

But I could hear music.

Again, that alone would not cause too much alarm. I do not make it a practice to leave music playing like some security-conscious New Yorkers, but I confess to a major streak of absentmindedness. I could have left my CD player on. That alone would not chill me like this.

What did chill me, however, was the song selection.

That was what was getting to me. The song playing—I tried to remember when I last heard it—was "Don't Fear the Reaper." I shuddered.

Ken's favorite song.

By Blue Oyster Cult, a heavy metal band, though this song, their most famous, was more subdued, almost ethereal. Ken used to grab his tennis racket and fake-guitar the solos. And I know that I do not have a copy of that particular song on any of my CDs. No way, unh-unh. Too many memories.

What the hell was going on here?

I stepped into the room. As I said before, the lights were out. It was dark. I stopped and felt awfully stupid. Hmm. Why not just flick on the lights, numbnuts? Wouldn't that be a good idea?

As I reached for the switch, another inner voice said, Better yet, why not just run? That was what we always yell at the movie screens, right? The killer is hiding inside the house. The stupid teenager, after finding her best friend's decapitated corpse, decides that this would be the perfect time to stroll through the darkened house instead of, say, fleeing and screaming like a mad animal.

Gee, all I had to do was strip down to a bra and I could be playing the part.

The song faded down in a guitar solo. I waited for the silence. It was brief. The song started up again. The same song.

What the hell was going on?

Flee and scream. That was the ticket. I would do just that. Except for one thing. I had not stumbled across any headless corpse. So how would this play out here? What exactly would I do? Call the police? I could just see that. What seems to be the problem, sir? Well, my stereo is playing my brother's favorite song so I decided to start running down the hall screaming. Can you rush over here with guns drawn? Uh-huh, sure, we're on our way.

How dorky would that sound?

And even if I assumed that someone had broken in, that there was indeed a prowler still in my apartment, someone who had brought his own CD with him . . .

. . . well, who was that most likely to be?

My heart picked up a beat as my eyes began to adjust to the dark. I decided to leave the lights off. If there was an intruder, there was no reason to let him know I was standing there, an easy target. Or would turning on the light scare him into view?

Christ, I'm not good at this.

I decided to leave the lights off.

Okay, fine, let's play it that way. Lights stay off. Now what?

The music. Follow the music. It was coming from my bedroom. I turned in that direction. The door was closed. I stepped toward it. Carefully. I was not going to be a total idiot. I opened the front door all the way and left it like that—in case I had to scream or make a run for it.

I moved forward in a sort of spastic slide, leading with the left foot but keeping the right toes firmly pointed toward the exit. It reminded me of one of Squares's yoga stances. You spread your legs and you bend one way but both your weight and your "awareness" go in the opposite direction. The body moves one way, the mind another. This was what some yogis, not Squares thankfully, referred to as "spreading your consciousness."

I slid a yard. Then another. Blue Oyster Cult's Buck Dharma—the fact that I remembered not only that name, but that his real name was Donald Roeser said a lot about my childhood—sang how we can be like they are, like Romeo and Juliet.

In a word: dead.

I reached the bedroom door. I swallowed and pushed against the frame. No go. I'd have to turn the knob. My hand gripped the metal. I looked over my shoulder. The door was still wide open. My right foot stayed pointed in that direction, though I could no longer be sure of my "awareness." I turned the knob as silently as possible, but it still sounded like a gunshot in my ear.

I pushed just a little, just to clear the frame. I let go of the knob. The music was louder now. Crisp and clear. Probably playing on the Bose CD player Squares had gotten me for my birthday two years ago.

I stuck my head in, just for a quick look. And that was when someone grabbed me by the hair.

I barely had time to gasp. My head was tugged forward so hard, my feet left the ground. I flew across the room, my hands stretched out Superman style, and landed in a thudding belly flop.

The air left my lungs with a whoosh. I tried to roll over, but he—I assumed it was a he—was already on top of me. His legs straddled my back. An arm snaked around my throat. I tried to struggle, but his grip was impossibly strong. He pulled back and I gagged.

I couldn't move. Totally at his mercy, he lowered his head toward mine. I could feel his breath in my ear. He did something with his other arm, got a better angle or counterweight, and squeezed. My windpipe was being crushed.

My eyes bulged. I pawed at my throat. Useless. My fingernails tried to dig into his forearm, but it was like trying to penetrate mahogany. The pressure in my head was building, growing unbearable. I flailed. My attacker did not budge. My skull felt like it was about to explode. And then I heard the voice:

"Hey, Willie boy."

That voice.

I placed it instantly. I had not heard it in—Christ, I tried to remember—ten, fifteen years maybe? Since Julie's death anyway. But there are certain sounds, voices mostly, that get stored in a special section of the cortex, on the survival shelf if you will, and as soon as you hear them, your every fiber tenses, sensing danger.

He let go of my neck—suddenly and completely. I collapsed to the floor, thrashing, gagging, trying to dislodge something imaginary from my throat. He rolled off me and laughed. "You've gone soft on me, Willie boy."

I flipped over and scooted away in a back crawl. My eyes confirmed what my ears had already told me. I could not believe it. He had changed, but there was no mistake.

"John?" I said. "John Asselta?"

He smiled that smile that touched nothing. I felt myself drop back in time. The fear—the fear I hadn't experienced since adolescence—surfaced. The Ghost—that was what everyone called him, though no one had the courage to say it to his face—had always had that effect on me. I don't think I was alone in that. He terrified pretty much everyone, though I had always been protected. I was Ken Klein's little brother. For the Ghost, that was enough.

I have always been a wimp. I have shied away from physical confrontations all my life. Some claim that makes me prudent and mature. But that was not it. The truth is, I am a coward. I am deathly afraid of violence. That might be normal—survival instinct and all—but it still shames me. My brother, who was, strangely enough, the Ghost's closest friend, had the enviable aggression that separated the wanna-bes from the greats. His tennis, for example, reminded some of a young John McEnroe in that take-on-the-world, pit-bull, won't-lose, borderline going-too-far competitiveness. Even as a child, he'd battle you to the death—and then stomp on the remains after you fell. I was never like that.

I scrambled to my feet. Asselta rose straight up, like a spirit from the grave. He spread his arms. "No hug for an old friend, Willie boy?"

He approached, and before I could react, he embraced me. He was pretty short, what with that strange long-torso, short-arms build. His cheek pressed my chest. "Been a long time," he said.

I was not sure what to say, where to start. "How did you get in?"

"What?" He released me. "Oh, the door was open. I'm sorry about sneaking up on you like that but . . ." He smiled, shrugged it away. "You haven't changed a bit, Willie boy. You look good."

"You shouldn't have just . . ."

He tilted his head, and I remembered the way he would simply lash out. John Asselta had been a classmate of Ken's, two years ahead of me at Livingston High School. He captained the wrestling team and was the Essex County lightweight champ two years running. He probably would have won the states, but he got disqualified for purposely dislocating a rival's shoulder. His third violation. I still remember the way his opponent screamed in pain. I remembered how some of the spectators got violently ill at the sight of the dangling appendage. I remembered Asselta's small smile as they carted his opponent away.

My father claimed that the Ghost had a Napoleon complex. That explanation seemed too simplistic to me. I don't know what it was, if the Ghost needed to prove himself or if he had an extra Y chromosome or if he was just the meanest son of a bitch in existence.

Whatever, he was definitely a psycho.

No way around it. He enjoyed hurting people. An aura of destruction surrounded his every step. Even the big jocks steered clear of him. You never met his eye, never got in his path, because you never knew what could provoke him. He would strike with no hesitation. He'd break your nose. He'd knee you in the balls. He'd gouge your eyes. He would hit you when your back was turned.

He gave Milt Saperstein a concussion during my sophomore year. Saperstein, a nerdy freshman complete with pocket protector against polyester print, had made the mistake of leaning up against the Ghost's locker. The Ghost smiled and let him go with a pat on the back. Later that day, Saperstein was walking between classes when, bam, the Ghost ran up behind him and smashed his forearm into Milt's head. Saperstein never saw him coming. He crumbled to the ground, and with a laugh, the Ghost stomped on his skull. Milt had to be taken to the emergency room at St. Barnabas.

No one saw a thing.

When he was fourteen—if legend was true—the Ghost killed a neighbor's dog by sticking firecrackers up his rectum. But worse than that, worse than pretty much anything, were the rumors that the Ghost, at the tender age of ten, stabbed a kid named Daniel Skinner with a kitchen knife. Supposedly Skinner, who was a couple of years older, picked on the Ghost, and the Ghost had responded with a knife strike straight to the heart. Rumor also had it that he spent some time in both juvie and therapy and that neither one had stuck. Ken claimed ignorance on the subject. I asked my father about it once, but he would neither confirm nor deny.

I tried to push the past away. "What do you want, John?"

I never understood my brother's friendship with him. My parents had not been happy about it either, though the Ghost could be charming with adults. His almost albino complexion—ergo the nickname—belied gentle features. He was almost pretty, with long lashes and a Dudley Do-Right cleft in the chin. I had heard that after graduation he had gone into the military. Supposedly he'd been enlisted in something clandestine involving Special Ops or Green Berets, something like that, but nobody could confirm that with any certainty.

The Ghost did the head-tilt again. "Where's Ken?" he asked in that silky, pre-strike voice.

I did not respond.

"I've been gone a long time, Willie boy. Overseas."

"Doing what?" I asked.

He flashed me the teeth again. "Now that I'm back, I thought I'd look up my old best bud."

I did not know what to say to that. But I suddenly flashed to when I stood on the veranda last night. The man staring at me from the end of the street. It had been the Ghost.

"So, Willie boy, where can I find him?"

"I don't know."

He put his hand up to his ear. "Excuse me?"

"I don't know where he is."

"But how can that be? You're his brother. He loved you so."

"What do you want here, John?"

"Say," he said, and he showed the teeth yet again, "whatever happened to your high school hottie Julie Miller? You two get hitched?"

I stared at him. He held the smile. He was putting me on, I knew that. He and Julie had, strangely enough, been close. I never understood that. Julie had claimed to see something there, something under the lashing-out psychosis. I once joked that she must have pulled a thorn from his paw. I wondered now how to play it. I actually considered running, but I knew that I would never make it. I also knew that I was no match for him.

This was creeping me out big-time.

"You've been gone a long time?" I asked.

"Years, Willie boy."

"So when was the last time you saw Ken?"

He feigned deep thought. "Oh, must have been, what, twelve years ago? I've been overseas since. Haven't kept up."

"Uh-huh."

He narrowed his eyes. "You sound like you're doubting me, Willie boy." He moved closer to me. I tried not to flinch. "You afraid of me?"

"No."

"Big bro's not here to protect you anymore, Willie boy."

"And we're not in high school either, John."

He looked up into my eyes. "You think the world's so different now?"

I tried to hold my ground.

"You look scared, Willie boy."

"Get out," I said.

His reply was sudden. He dropped to the floor and whipped out my legs from under me. I fell hard on my back. Before I could move, he had me wrapped up in an elbow lock. There was already tremendous pressure on the joint, but then he lifted up against my triceps. The elbow started bending the wrong way. A deep pain knifed down my arm.

I tried to move with it. Give way. Anything to relieve the pressure.

The Ghost spoke in the calmest voice I've ever heard. "You tell him no more hiding, Willie boy. You tell him other people could get hurt. Like you. Or your dad. Or your sister. Or maybe even that little Miller vixen you met with today. You tell him that."

His hand speed was unearthly. In one move, he released my arm and shot his fist straight into my face. My nose exploded. I fell back against the floor, my head swimming, only half conscious. Or maybe I passed out. I don't know anymore.

When I looked up again, the Ghost had vanished.

19

Squares handed me a freezer bag of ice. "Yeah, but I oughta see the other guy, right?"

"Right," I said, putting the bag on my rather tender nose. "He looks like a matinee idol."

Squares sat on the couch and threw his boots up on the coffee table. "Explain."

I did.

"Guy sounds like a prince," Squares said.

"Did I mention that he tortured animals?"

"Yep."

"Or that he had a skull collection in his bedroom?"

"Say, that must have impressed the ladies."

"I don't get it." I lowered the bag. My nose felt like it was jammed with crushed-up pennies. "Why would the Ghost be looking for my brother?"

"Hell of a question."

"You think I should call the cops?"

Squares shrugged. "Give me his full name again."

"John Asselta."

"I assume you don't have a current residence."

"No."

"But he grew up in Livingston?"

"Yes," I said. "On Woodland Terrace. Fifty-seven Woodland Terrace."

"You remember his address?"

Now it was my turn to shrug. That was the way Livingston was. You remembered stuff like that. "His mother, I don't know what her deal was. She ran away or something when he was very young. His dad lived in a bottle. Two brothers, both older. One—I think his name was Sean—was a Vietnam vet. He had this long hair and matted beard and all he'd do was walk around town talking to himself. Everyone figured he was crazy. Their yard was like a junkyard, always overgrown. People in Livingston didn't like that. The cops used to ticket them for it."

Squares wrote down the info. "Let me look into it."

My head ached. I tried to focus. "Did you have someone like that in your school?" I asked. "A psycho who'd just hurt people for the fun of it?"

"Yeah," Squares said. "Me."

I found it hard to believe. I knew abstractly Squares had been a punk of biblical proportions, but the idea that he'd been like the Ghost, that I'd have shuddered as he passed me in the halls, that he would crack a skull and laugh at the sound . . . it just would not compute.

I put the ice back on my nose, wincing when it touched down.

Squares shook his head. "Baby."

"Pity you didn't consider a career in medicine."

"Your nose is probably broken," he said.

"I figured."

"You want to go to the hospital?"

"Nah, I'm a tough guy."

That made him snicker. "Nothing they could do anyway." Then he stopped, gnawed on the inside of his cheek, said, "Something's come up."

I did not like the tone of his voice.

"I got a call from our favorite fed, Joe Pistillo."

Again I lowered down the ice. "Did they find Sheila?"

"Don't know."

"What did he want?"

"Wouldn't say. He just asked me to bring you in."

"When?"

"Now. He said he was calling me as a courtesy."

"Courtesy for what?"

"Damned if I know."

"My name is Clyde Smart," the man said in the gentlest voice Edna Rogers had ever heard. "I'm the county medical examiner."

Edna Rogers watched her husband, Neil, shake the man's hand. She settled for just a nod in his direction. The woman sheriff was there. So was one of her deputies. They all, Edna Rogers thought, had properly solemn faces. The man named Clyde was trying to dispense some comforting words. Edna Rogers shut him out.

Clyde Smart finally moved to the table. Neil and Edna Rogers, married forty-two years, stood next to each other and waited. They did not touch. They did not gather strength from one another. Many years had passed since they had last leaned on each other.

Finally, the medical examiner stopped talking and pulled back the sheet.

When Neil Rogers saw Sheila's face, he reeled back like a wounded animal. He kept his eyes up now and let out a cry that reminded Edna of a coyote when a storm is brewing. She knew from her husband's anguish, even before looking herself, that there would be no reprieve, no last-minute miracle. She summoned the courage and gazed at her daughter. She reached out a hand—the maternal desire to comfort, even in death, never let up—but she made herself stop.

Edna continued to stare down until her vision blurred, until Edna could almost see Sheila's face transforming, the years running backward, peeling down, until her firstborn was her baby again, her whole life ahead of her, a second chance for her mother to do it right.

And then Edna Rogers started to cry.

20

"What happened to your nose?" Pistillo asked me.

We were back in his office. Squares stayed in the waiting room. I sat in the armchair in front of Pistillo's desk. His chair, I noticed this time, was set a little higher than mine, probably for reasons of intimidation. Claudia Fisher, the agent who'd visited me at Covenant House, stood behind me with her arms crossed.

"You should see the other guy," I said.

"You got into a fight?"

"I fell," I said.

Pistillo didn't believe me, but that was okay. He put both hands on his desk. "We'd like you to run through it again for us," he said.

"Through what?"

"How Sheila Rogers disappeared."

"Have you found her?"

"Just bear with us please." He coughed into his fist. "What time did Sheila Rogers leave your apartment?"

"Why?"

"Please, Mr. Klein, if you could just help us out here."

"I think she left around five in the morning."

"You're sure about that?"

"Think," I said. "I used the word *think*."

"Why aren't you sure?"

"I was asleep. I thought I heard her leave."

"At five?"

"Yes."

"You looked at the clock?"

"Are you for real? I don't know."

"How else would you know it was five?"

"I have a great internal clock, I don't know. Can we move on?"

He nodded and shifted in his seat. "Ms. Rogers left you a note, correct?"

"Yes."

"Where was the note?"

"You mean, where in the apartment?"

"Yes."

"What's the difference?"

He offered up his most patronizing smile. "Please."

"On the kitchen counter," I said. "It's made of Formica, if that helps."

"What did the note say exactly?"

"That's personal."

"Mr. Klein—"

I sighed. No reason to fight him. "She told me that she'd love me always."

"What else?"

"That was it."

"Just that she'd love you always?"

"Yep."

"Do you still have the note?"

"I do."

"May we see it?"

"May you tell me why I'm here?"

Pistillo sat back. "After leaving your father's house, did you and Ms. Rogers head straight back to your apartment?"

The change of subject threw me. "What are you talking about?"

"You attended your mother's funeral, correct?"

"Yes."

"Then you and Sheila Rogers returned to your apartment. That was what you told us, no?"

"That's what I told you."

"And is it the truth?"

"Yes."

"Did you stop on the way home?"

"No."

"Can anyone verify that?"

"Verify that I didn't stop?"

"Verify that you two went back to your apartment and stayed there for the remainder of the evening."

"Why would anyone have to verify that?"

"Please, Mr. Klein."

"I don't know if anyone can verify it or not."

"Did you talk with anyone?"

"No."

"Did a neighbor see you?"

"I don't know." I looked over my shoulder at Claudia Fisher. "Why don't you canvass the neighborhood? Isn't that what you guys are famous for?"

"Why was Sheila Rogers in New Mexico?"

I turned back around. "I don't know that she was."

"She never told you that she was going?"

"I know nothing about it."

"How about you, Mr. Klein?"

"How about me what?"

"Do you know anyone in New Mexico?"

"I don't even know the way to Santa Fe."

"San Jose," Pistillo corrected him, smiling at the lame joke. "We have a list of your recent incoming calls."

"How nice for you."

He sort of shrugged. "Modern technology."

"And that's legal? You having my phone records?"

"We got a warrant."

"I bet you did. So what do you want to know?"

Claudia Fisher moved for the first time. She handed me a sheet of paper. I glanced down at what appeared to be a photocopy of a phone bill. One number—an unfamiliar one—was highlighted in yellow.

"Your residence received a phone call from a pay phone in Paradise Hills, New Mexico, the night before your mother's funeral." He leaned in a little closer. "Who was that call from?"

I studied the number, totally confused yet again. The call had come in at six-fifteen in the evening. It'd lasted eight minutes. I did not know what it meant, but I didn't like the whole tone of this conversation. I looked up.

"Should I have a lawyer?"

That slowed Pistillo down. He and Claudia Fisher exchanged another glance. "You can always have a lawyer," he said a little too carefully.

"I want Squares in here."

"He's not a lawyer."

"Still. I don't know what the hell is going on, but I don't like these questions. I came down because I thought you had information for me. Instead, I'm being interrogated."

"Interrogated?" Pistillo spread his hands. "We're just chatting."

A phone trilled behind me. Claudia Fisher snapped up her cell phone à la Wyatt Earp. She put it to her ear and said, "Fisher." After listening for about a minute, she hung up without saying good-bye. Then she nodded some kind of confirmation at Pistillo.

I stood up. "I've had enough of this."

"Sit down, Mr. Klein."

"I'm tired of your bullshit, Pistillo. I'm tired of—"

"That call," he interjected.

"What about it?"

"Sit down, Will."

He'd used my first name. I did not like the sound of it. I stood where I was and waited.

"We were just waiting for visual confirmation," he said.

"Of what?"

He did not reply to my query. "So we flew Sheila Rogers's parents in from Idaho. They made it official, though the fingerprints had already told us what we needed to know."

His face grew soft. My knees buckled, but I managed to stay upright. He looked at me now with heavy eyes. I started to shake my head, but I knew there was no way to duck the blow.

"I'm sorry, Will," Pistillo said. "Sheila Rogers is dead."

21

Denial is an amazing thing.

Even as I felt my stomach twist and drop, even as I felt the ice spread out and chill me from the center, even as I felt the tears push hard against my eyes, I somehow managed to detach. I nodded while concentrating on the few details that Pistillo was willing to give me. She'd been dumped on the side of a road in Nebraska, he said. I nodded. She'd been murdered in—to use Pistillo's words—"a rather brutal fashion." I nodded some more. She had been found with no ID on her, but the fingerprints had matched and then Sheila's parents had flown in and identified the body for official purposes. I nodded again.

I did not sit. I did not cry. I stood perfectly still. I felt something inside me harden and grow. It pressed against my rib cage, made it almost impossible to breathe. I heard his words as though from afar, as though through a filter or from underwater. I flashed to a simple moment: Sheila reading on our couch, her legs tucked under her, the sleeves of her sweater stretched too long. I saw the focus on her face, the way she prepared her finger for the next page turn, the way her eyes narrowed during certain passages, the way she looked up and smiled when she realized that I was staring.

Sheila was dead.

I was still back there, with Sheila, back in our apartment, grasping smoke, trying to hold on to what was already gone, when Pistillo's words cut through the haze.

"You should have cooperated with us, Will."

I surfaced as if from a sleep. "What?"

"If you'd told us the truth, maybe we could have saved her."

Next thing I remember, I was out in the van.

Squares alternated between pounding on the steering wheel and swearing vengeance. I had never seen him so agitated. My reaction had been just the opposite. It was like someone had pulled out my plug. I stared out the window. Denial was still holding, but I could feel reality start hammering against the walls. I wondered how long before the walls collapsed under the onslaught.

"We'll get him," Squares said yet again.

For the moment, I did not much care.

We double-parked in front of the apartment building. Squares jumped out.

"I'll be fine," I said.

"I'll walk you up anyway," he said. "I want to show you something."

I nodded numbly.

When we entered, Squares reached into his pocket and pulled out a gun. He swept through the apartment, gun drawn. No one. He handed me the weapon.

"Lock the door. If that creepy asshole comes back, blow him away."

"I don't need this," I said.

"Blow him away," he repeated.

I kept my eyes on the gun.

"You want me to stay?" he asked.

"I think I'm better off alone."

"Yeah, okay, but you need me, I got the cell. Twenty-four, seven."

"Right. Thanks."

He left without another word. I put the gun on the table. Then I stood and looked at our apartment. Nothing of Sheila was here anymore. Her smell had faded. The air felt thinner, less substantial. I wanted to close all the windows and doors, batten them down, try to preserve something of her.

Someone had murdered the woman I love.

For the second time?

No. Julie's murder had not felt like this. Not even close. Denial was, yep, still there, but a voice was whispering through the cracks: Nothing would be the same ever again. I knew that. And I knew that I would not recover this time. There are blows you can take and get back up from—like what happened with Ken and Julie. This was not like that. Lots of feelings ricocheted through me. But the most dominant was despair.

I would never be with Sheila again. Someone had murdered the woman I love.

I concentrated on the second part. Murdered. I thought about her past, about the hell she had gone through. I thought about how valiantly she'd struggled, and I thought about how someone—probably someone from her past—had sneaked up behind her and snatched it all away.

Anger began to seep in too.

I moved over to the desk, bent down, and reached into the back of the bottom drawer. I pulled out the velour box, took a deep breath, and opened it.

The ring's diamond was one-point-three carats, with G color, VI rating, round cut. The platinum band was simple with two rectangle baguettes. I'd bought it from a booth in the diamond district on 47th Street two weeks ago. I'd only shown it to my mother, and I had planned on proposing, so she could see. But Mom had no good days after that. I waited. Still, it gave me comfort that she'd known that I had found someone and that she more than approved. I had just been waiting for the right time, what with my mother dying and all, to give it to Sheila.

Sheila and I had loved each other. I would have proposed in some corny, awkward, quasi-original way and her eyes would have misted over and then she would have said yes and thrown her arms around me. We would have gotten married and been life partners. It would have been great.

Someone had taken all that away.

The wall of denial began to buckle and crack. Grief spread over me, ripping the breath from my lungs. I collapsed into a chair and hugged my knees against my chest. I rocked back and forth and started to cry, really cry, gut-wrenching, soul-tearing cries.

I don't know how long I sobbed. But after a while, I forced myself to stop. That was when I decided to fight back against the grief. Grief paralyzes. But not anger. And the anger was there too, lingering, looking for an opening.

So I let it in.

22

When Katy Miller heard her father raise his voice, she stopped in the doorway.

"Why would you go over there?" he shouted.

Her mother and father stood in the den. The room, like so much of the house, had a hotel-chain feel to it. The furniture was functional, shiny, sturdy, and totally lacking in warmth. The oils on the wall were inconsequential images of sailing ships and still lifes. There were no figurines, no vacation souvenirs, no collections, no family photographs.

"I went to pay my respects," her mother said.

"Why the hell would you do that?"

"I thought it was the right thing to do."

"The right thing? Her son murdered our daughter."

"Her son," Lucille Miller repeated. "Not her."

"Don't give me that crap. She raised him."

"That doesn't make her responsible."

"You never believed that before."

Her mother kept her spine stiff. "I've believed it for a long time," she said. "I just haven't said anything."

Warren Miller turned away and began to pace. "And that jackass threw you out?"

"He's in pain. He just lashed out."

"I don't want you to go back," he said, waving an impotent finger. "You hear me? For all you know, she helped that murdering son of a bitch hide."

"So?"

Katy stifled a gasp. Mr. Miller's head snapped around. "What?"

"She was his mother. Would we have done differently?"

"What are you talking about?"

"If it was the other way around. If Julie had killed Ken and needed to hide. What would you have done?"

"You're talking nonsense."

"No, Warren, I'm not. I want to know. I want to know if the roles were reversed, what would we have done? Would we have turned Julie in? Or would we have tried to save her?"

As her father turned away, he spotted Katy in the doorway. Their eyes met and for the umpteenth time in her life, he could not hold his daughter's gaze. Without another word Warren Miller stormed upstairs. He made his way into the new "computer room" and closed the door. The "computer room" was Julie's old bedroom. For nine years it had remained exactly the same as the day Julie died. Then one day, without warning, her father had gone into the room and packed up everything and stored it away. He painted the walls white and bought a new computer desk at Ikea. Now it was the computer room. Some took this as a sign of closure or, at least, moving on. The truth was just the opposite. The whole act was forced, a dying man showing he can get out of bed when all it really did was make him sicker. Katy never went in there. Now that the room had no tangible signs of Julie, her spirit seemed somehow more aggressive. You relied on your mind now instead of your eyes. You conjured up what you were never meant to see.

Lucille Miller headed into the kitchen. Katy followed in silence. Her mother began to wash dishes. Katy watched, wishing—also for the umpteenth time—that she could say something that would not wound her mother deeper. Her parents never talked to her about Julie. Never. Over the years, she had caught them discussing the murder maybe half a dozen times. It always ended like this. In silence and tears.

"Mom?"

"It's okay, honey."

Katy stepped closer. Her mother scrubbed harder. Katy noticed that her mother's hair had more streaks of white. Her back was a little more bent, her complexion grayer.

"Would you have?" Katy asked.

Her mother said nothing.

"Would you have helped Julie run?"

Lucille Miller kept scrubbing. She loaded the dishwasher. She poured in the detergent and turned it on. Katy waited a few more moments. But her mother would not speak.

Katy tiptoed upstairs. She heard her father's anguished sobs emanating from the computer room. The sound was muffled by the door but not nearly enough. Katy stopped and rested her palm on the wood. She thought that maybe she could feel the vibrations. Her father's sobs were always so total, so full-body. His choked voice begged, "Please, no more" over and over, as if imploring some unseen tormenter to put a bullet in his brain. Katy stood there and listened, but the sound did not let up.

After a while she had to turn away. She continued to her own room. Then she packed her clothes in a knapsack and prepared herself to end this once and for all.

I was still sitting in the dark with my knees up against my chest.

It was near midnight. I screened calls. Normally I would have turned off the phone, but the denial was still potent enough to make me hope that maybe Pistillo would call and tell me it was all a big mistake. The mind does that. It tries to find a way out. It makes deals with God. It makes promises. It tries to convince itself that maybe there is a reprieve, that this could all be a dream, the most vicious of nightmares, and that somehow you can find your way back.

I had picked up the phone only once and that was for Squares. He told me that the kids at Covenant House wanted to have a memorial service for

Sheila tomorrow. Would that be all right? I told him that I thought Sheila would have really liked that.

I looked out the window. The van circled the block again. Yep, Squares. Protecting me. He had been circling all night. I knew that he would not stray far. He probably hoped that trouble arose just so he could unload on someone. I thought about Squares's comment that he had not been all that different from the Ghost. I thought about the power of the past and what Squares had gone through and what Sheila had gone through and marveled at how they'd found the strength to swim against the riptide.

The phone rang again.

I looked down into my beer. I was not one for drinking away my problems. I sort of wished that I were. I wanted to be numb right now, but the opposite was happening. My skin was being ripped off so that I could feel everything. My arms and legs grew impossibly heavy. It felt as though I were sinking under, drowning, that I would always be just inches from the surface, my legs held by invisible hands, unable to break free.

I waited for the answering machine to pick up. After the third ring, I heard a click and then my voice said to leave a message at the beep. When the beep sounded I heard a semi-familiar voice.

"Mr. Klein?"

I sat up. The woman on the answering machine tried to stifle a sob.

"This is Edna Rogers. Sheila's mother."

My hand shot out and snatched the receiver. "I'm here," I said.

Her answer was to cry. I started crying too.

"I didn't think it would hurt so much," she said after some time had passed.

Alone in what had been our apartment, I started rocking back and forth.

"I cut her out of my life so long ago," Mrs. Rogers continued. "She wasn't my daughter anymore. I had other children. She was gone. For good. That's not what I wanted. It was just the way it was. Even when the chief came to my house, even when he told me she was dead, I didn't react. I just nodded and stiffened my back, you know?"

I didn't know. I said nothing. I just listened.

"And then they flew me out here. To Nebraska. They said they had her fingerprints already, but they needed a family member to identify her. So Neil and me, we drove to the airport in Boise and flew here. They took us to this little station. On TV they always do it behind glass. You know what I mean? They stand outside and they wheel in the body and it's behind glass. But not here. They brought me into this office and there was this . . . this lump covered with a sheet. She wasn't even on a stretcher. She was on a table. And then this man pulled back the sheet and I saw her face. For the first time in fourteen years, I saw Sheila's face. . . ."

She lost it then. She started crying and for a long time there was no letup. I held the receiver to my ear and waited.

"Mr. Klein," she began.

"Please call me Will."

"You loved her, Will, didn't you?"

"Very much."

"And you made her happy?"

I thought about the diamond ring. "I hope so."

"I'm staying overnight in Lincoln. I want to fly to New York tomorrow morning."

"That would be nice," I said. I told her about the memorial service.

"Will there be time for us to talk afterward?" she asked.

"Of course."

"There are some things I need to know," she said. "And there are some things—some hard things—I have to tell you."

"I'm not sure I understand."

"I'll see you tomorrow, Will. We'll talk then."

I had one visitor that night.

At one in the morning, the doorbell rang. I figured it was Squares. I managed to get to my feet and shuffle across the floor. Then I remembered the Ghost. I glanced back. The gun was still on the table. I stopped.

The bell sounded again.

I shook my head. No. I was not that far gone. Not yet anyhow. I moved toward the door and looked through the peephole. But it wasn't Squares or the Ghost.

It was my father.

I opened the door. We stood and looked at each other as if from a great distance. He was out of breath. His eyes were swollen and tinged with red. I stood there, unmoving, feeling everything inside me collapse away. He nodded and held out his arms and beckoned me forward. I stepped into his embrace. I pressed my cheek against the scratchy wool of his sweater. It smelled wet and old. I started to sob. He shushed me and stroked my hair and pulled me closer. I felt my legs give way. But I did not slide down. My father held me up. He held me up for a very long time.

23

Las Vegas

Morty Meyer split the tens. He signaled the dealer to hit both. The first came up a nine, the second an ace. Nineteen on the first hand. And blackjack.

He was on a roll. Eight straight hands had gone his way, twelve of the last thirteen—up a solid eleven grand. Morty was in the zone. The ever-elusive winner's high tingled down his arms and legs. It felt delicious. Nothing like it. Gambling, Morty had learned, was the ultimate temptress. You come after her, she scorns you, rejects you, makes you miserable, and then, when you're ready to give her up, she smiles at you, puts her warm hand on your face, gently caresses you, and it feels so good, so damn good. . . .

The dealer busted. Oh yes, another winner. The dealer, a hausfrau with overtreated haylike hair, swept up the cards and gave him his chips. Morty was winning. And yes, despite what those bozos at Gamblers Anonymous tried to peddle, you could indeed win at a casino. Someone had to win, didn't they? Look at the odds, for chrissake. The house can't beat everyone. Hell, with dice you can actually play on the house's side. So, of course, some people won. Some people went home with money. Had to be. Impossible any other way. To say no one won was just part of the overreaching GA crap that left the organization with no credibility. If they start off lying to you, how can you trust them to help?

Morty played in Las Vegas, Las Vegas— the real Las Vegas, the city itself, no strip-strolling tourist trade in pseudo-suede and sneakers, no whistling and hollering or squeals of joy, no faux Statue of Liberty or Eiffel Tower, no Cirque du Soleil, no roller coasters, no 3-D movie rides or gladiator costumes or dancing water fountains or bogus volcanoes or kid-appeal arcades. This was downtown Las Vegas. This was where grimy men with barely a mouth of teeth per table, the dust from their pickups still coming off them with each shoulder slump, lost their meager paychecks. The players here were bleary-eyed, exhausted, their faces lined, their hard times baked on by the sun. A man came here after slaving at a job that he hated because he did not want to go home to his trailer or equivalent, his abode with the broken TV, the screaming babies, the let-herself-go wife who used to stroke him in the back of that pickup and now eyed him with naked repulsion. He came here with the closest thing that he would ever know to hope, with that wispy belief that he was one score away from changing his life. But the hope never lasted. Morty was not even sure it was ever really there. Deep down, the players knew it was never meant to be. They would always be on the toe end of the kick. They were destined for a lifetime of disappointment, for slouching with their faces forever pressed against the glass.

The table changed dealers. Morty leaned back. He stared at his winnings and the old shadow crossed over him again: He missed Leah. Some days he still woke up and turned to her, and when he remembered, the sorrow consumed him. He would not be able to get out of bed. He looked now at the grimy men in this casino. When he was younger, Morty would have called them losers. But they had an excuse for being here. They may as well have been born with the loser L branded into their behinds. Morty's parents, immigrants from a shtetl in Poland, had sacrificed for him. They had sneaked into this country, faced terrible poverty an ocean away from everything familiar, fought and clawed—all so their son would have a better life. They had worked themselves to an early-ish grave, hanging on just long enough to see Morty graduate medical school, to see that their struggle had meant something, had steered the genealogical trajectory for the better now and forever. They died in peace.

Morty was dealt a six up, seven down. He hit and got a ten. Busted. He lost the next hand too. Damn. He needed this money. Locani, a classic leg-breaking bookie, wanted his cash. Morty, a loser's loser when you really think about it, had stalled him by offering up information. He had told Locani about the masked man and injured woman. At first, Locani did not seem to care, but the word spread and all of a sudden someone wanted details.

Morty told them *almost* everything.

He did not, would not, tell them about the passenger in the backseat. He did not have a clue what was going on, but there were some things even he would not do. Low as he had sunk, Morty would not tell them about that.

He was dealt two aces. He split them. A man sat next to him. Morty felt rather than saw him. He felt him in his old bones, as though the man were an incoming weather front. He did not turn his head, afraid, as irrational as this sounded, even to look.

The dealer hit both hands. A king and a jack. Morty had just gotten two blackjacks.

The man leaned close and whispered, "Quit while you're ahead, Morty."

Morty slowly turned and saw a man with eyes of washed-out gray and skin that went beyond white, too translucent really, so that you felt as though you could see his every vein. The man smiled.

"It might be time," the silvery whisper continued, "to cash in your chips."

Morty tried not to shudder. "Who are you? What do you want?"

"We need to chat," the man said.

"About what?"

"About a certain patient who recently visited your esteemed practice."

Morty swallowed. Why had he opened his mouth to Locani? He should have stalled with something else, anything else. "I already told them everything I know."

The pale man cocked his head. "Did you, Morty?"

"Yes."

Those washed-out eyes fell on him hard. Neither man spoke or moved. Morty felt his face redden. He tried to stiffen his back, but he could feel himself wither under the gaze.

"I don't think you have, Morty. I think you're holding back."

Morty said nothing.

"Who else was in the car that night?"

He stared at his chips and tried not to shudder. "What are you talking about?"

"There was someone else, wasn't there, Morty?"

"Hey, leave me alone, will you? I'm on a roll here."

Rising from his seat, the Ghost shook his head. "No, Morty," he said, touching him gently on the arm. "I would say that your luck is about to take a turn for the worse."

24

The memorial service was held in the Covenant House auditorium.

Squares and Wanda sat on my right, my father on my left. Dad kept his arm behind me, sometimes rubbing my back. It felt nice. The room was packed, mostly with the kids. They hugged me and cried and told me how much they'd miss Sheila. The service lasted almost two hours. Terrell, a fourteen-year-old who'd been selling himself for ten dollars a pop, played a song on the trumpet that he'd composed in her memory. It was the saddest, sweetest sound I'd ever heard. Lisa, who was seventeen years old and diagnosed bipolar, spoke of how Sheila had been the only one she could talk to when she learned that she was pregnant. Sammy told a funny story about how Sheila tried to teach him how to dance to that "crappy white-girl" music. Sixteen-year-old Jim told the mourners that he had given up on himself, that he'd been ready to commit suicide, and when Sheila smiled at him, he realized that there was indeed good in this world. Sheila convinced him to stay another day. And then another.

I pushed away the pain and listened closely because these kids deserved that. This place meant so much to me. To us. And when we had doubts about our success, about how much we were helping, we always remembered that it was all about the kids. They were not cuddly. Most were unattractive and hard to love. Most would live terrible lives and end up in jail or on the streets or dead. But that did not mean you gave up. It meant just the opposite, in fact. It meant we had to love them all the more. Unconditionally. Without a flinch. Sheila had known that. It had mattered to her.

Sheila's mother—at least, I assumed it was Mrs. Rogers—came in about twenty minutes into the ceremony. She was a tall woman. Her face had the dry, brittle look of something left too long in the sun. Our eyes met. She looked a question at me, and I nodded a yes. As the service continued, I turned and glanced at her every once in a while. She sat perfectly still, listening to the words about her daughter with something approaching awe.

At one point, when we rose as a congregation, I saw something that surprised me. I'd been gazing over the sea of familiar faces, when I spotted a familiar figure with a scarf covering most of her face.

Tanya.

The scarred woman who took "care" of that scum Louis Castman. Again I assumed that it was Tanya. I was fairly certain. Same hair, same height and build, and even though most of her face was covered, I could still see something familiar in the eyes. I had not really thought about it before, but of course there was a chance that she and Sheila had known each other from their days on the street.

We sat back down.

Squares spoke last. He was eloquent and funny and brought Sheila to life in a way I knew I never could. He told the kids how Sheila had been "one of you," a struggling runaway who'd fought her own demons. He remembered her first day here. He remembered watching Sheila bloom. And mostly, he said, he remembered watching her fall in love with me.

I felt hollow. My insides had been scooped out, and again I was struck with the realization that this pain would be permanent, that I could stall, that I could run around and investigate and dig for some inner truth, but in the end, it would change nothing. My grief would forever be by my side, my constant companion in lieu of Sheila.

When the ceremony ended, no one knew exactly what to do. We all sat for an awkward moment, no one moving, until Terrell started playing his trumpet again. People rose. They cried and hugged me all over again. I don't know how long I stood there and took it all in. I was thankful for the outpouring, but it made me miss Sheila all the more. The numb slid back up because this was all too raw. Without the numb, I wouldn't get through it.

I looked for Tanya, but she was gone.

Someone announced that there was food in the cafeteria. The mourners slowly milled toward it. I spotted Sheila's mother standing in a corner, both hands clutching a small purse. She looked drained, as if the vitality had leaked out from a still-open wound. I made my way toward her.

"You're Will?" she said.

"Yes."

"I'm Edna Rogers."

We did not hug or kiss cheeks or even shake hands.

"Where can we talk?" she asked.

I led her down the corridor toward the stairs. Squares picked up that we wanted to be alone and diverted foot traffic. We passed the new medical facility, the psychiatric offices, the drug treatment areas. Many of our runaways are new or expectant mothers. We try to treat them. Many others have serious mental problems. We try to help them too. And of course, a whole slew of them have a potpourri of drug problems. We do our best there too.

We found an empty dorm room and stepped inside. I closed the door. Mrs. Rogers showed me her back. "It was a beautiful service," she said.

I nodded.

"What Sheila became—" She stopped, shook her head. "I had no idea. I wish I could have seen that. I wish that she'd called and told me."

I did not know what to say to that.

"Sheila never gave me a moment of pride when she was alive." Edna Rogers tugged a handkerchief out of her bag as though someone inside were putting up a fight. She gave her nose a quick, decisive swipe, and then tucked it away again. "I know that sounds unkind. She was a beautiful baby. And she was fine in elementary school. But somewhere along the way"—

she looked away, shrugged—"she changed. She became surly. Always complaining. Always unhappy. She stole money from my purse. She ran away time after time. She had no friends. The boys bored her. She hated school. She hated living in Mason. Then one day she dropped out of school and ran away. Except this time she never came back."

She looked at me as if expecting a response.

"You never saw her again?" I asked.

"Never."

"I don't understand," I said. "What happened?"

"You mean what made her finally run away?"

"Yes."

"You think there was some big event, right?" Her voice was louder now, challenging. "Her father must have abused her. Or maybe I beat her. Something that explains it all. That's the way it works. Nice and tidy. Cause and effect. But there was nothing like that. Her father and I, we weren't perfect. Far from it. But it wasn't our fault either."

"I didn't mean to imply—"

"I know what you were implying."

Her eyes ignited. She pursed her lips and looked a dare at me. I wanted off this subject.

"Did Sheila ever call you?" I said.

"Yes."

"How often?"

"The last time was three years ago."

She stopped, waiting for me to continue.

I asked, "Where was she when she called?"

"She wouldn't tell me."

"What did she say?"

This time it took her a long while to respond. Edna Rogers began to circle the room and look at the beds and the dressers. She fluffed a pillow and tucked in a sheet corner. "Once every six months or so, Sheila would call home. She was usually stoned or drunk or high, whatever. She'd get all emotional. She'd cry and I'd cry and she'd say horrible things to me."

"Like what?"

She shook her head. "Downstairs. What that man with the tattoo on his forehead said. About you two meeting here and falling in love. That true?"

"Yes."

She stood upright and looked at me. Her lips curled into what might pass for a smile. "So," she said, and I heard something creep into her voice, "Sheila was sleeping with her boss."

Edna Rogers curled the smile some more, and it was like looking at a different person.

"She was a volunteer," I said.

"Uh-huh. And what exactly was she volunteering to do for you, Will?"

I felt a shiver skitter down my back.

"Still want to judge me?" she asked.

"I think you should leave."

"Can't take the truth, is that it? You think I'm some kind of monster. That

I gave up on my kid for no good reason."

"It's not my place to say."

"Sheila was a miserable kid. She lied. She stole—"

"Maybe I'm beginning to understand," I said.

"Understand what?"

"Why she ran away."

She blinked and then glared at me. "You didn't know her. You still don't."

"Didn't you hear a thing that was said down there?"

"I heard." Her voice grew softer. "But I never knew that Sheila. She'd never let me. The Sheila I knew—"

"In all due deference, I'm really not in the mood to hear you trash her any further."

Edna Rogers stopped. She closed her eyes and sat on the edge of a bed. The room grew very still. "That's not why I came here."

"Why did you come?"

"I wanted to hear something good, for one thing."

"You got that," I said.

She nodded. "That I did."

"What else do you want?"

Edna Rogers stood. She stepped toward me, and I fought off the desire to move away. She looked me straight in the eye. "I'm here about Carly."

I waited. When she did not elaborate, I said, "You mentioned that name on the phone."

"Yes."

"I didn't know any Carly then, and I don't know any now."

She showed me the cruel, curled smile again. "You wouldn't be lying to me, would you, Will?"

I felt a fresh shiver. "No."

"Sheila never mentioned the name Carly?"

"No."

"You're sure about that?"

"Yes. Who is she?"

"Carly is Sheila's daughter."

I was struck dumb. Edna Rogers saw my reaction. She seemed to enjoy it.

"Your lovely volunteer never mentioned that she had a daughter, did she?"

I said nothing.

"Carly is twelve years old now. And no, I don't know who the father is. I don't think Sheila did either."

"I don't understand," I said.

She reached into her purse and took out a picture. She handed it to me. It was one of those newborn hospital shots. A baby wrapped in a blanket, new eyes blinking out, unseeing. I flipped it over. The handwriting said "Carly." The date of birth was written under it.

My head began to spin.

"The last time Sheila called me was on Carly's ninth birthday," she said. "And I spoke to her myself. Carly, that is."

"So where is she now?"

"I don't know," Edna Rogers said. "That's why I'm here, Will. I want to find my granddaughter."

25

When I stumbled back home, Katy Miller was sitting by my apartment door, her knapsack between her splayed legs.

She scrambled to her feet. "I called but . . ."

I nodded.

"My parents," Katy told me. "I just can't stay in that house another day. I thought maybe I could crash on your couch."

"It's not a good time," I said.

"Oh."

I put the key in the door.

"It's just that I've been trying to put it together, you know. Like we said. Who could have killed Julie. And I started wondering. How much do you know about Julie's life after you two broke up?"

We both stepped inside the apartment. "I don't know if now is a good time."

She finally saw my face. "Why? What happened?"

"Someone very close to me died."

"You mean your mother?"

I shook my head. "Someone else close to me. She was murdered."

Katy gasped and dropped the knapsack. "How close?"

"Very."

"A girlfriend?"

"Yes."

"Someone you loved?"

"Very much."

She looked at me.

"What?" I said.

"I don't know, Will. It's like someone murders the women you love."

The same thought I'd earlier pushed away. Vocalized, it sounded even more ridiculous. "Julie and I broke up more than a year before her murder."

"So you were over her?"

I did not want to travel that route again. I said, "What about Julie's life after we broke up?"

Katy fell onto the couch the way teenagers do, as if she had no bones. Her right leg was draped over the arm, her head back with the chin tilted up. She wore ripped jeans again and another top that was so tight it looked like the bra was on the outside. Her hair was tied back in a ponytail. A few of the strands fell loose and onto her face.

"I started thinking," she said, "if Ken didn't kill her, someone else did, right?"

"Right."

"So I started looking into her life at the time. You know, calling old friends, trying to remember what was going on with her, that kind of thing."

"And what did you find?"

"That she was pretty messed up."

I tried to focus on what she was saying. "How so?"

She dropped both legs to the floor and sat up. "What do you remember?"

"She was a senior at Haverton."

"No."

"No?"

"Julie dropped out."

That surprised me. "You're sure?"

"Senior year," she said. Then she asked, "When did you last see her, Will?"

I thought about it. It had indeed been a while. I told her so.

"So when you broke up?"

I shook my head. "She ended it on the phone."

"For real?"

"Yes."

"Cold," Katy said. "And you just accepted that?"

"I tried to see her. But she wouldn't let me."

Katy looked at me as though I'd just spouted the lamest excuse in the history of mankind. Looking back on it, I guess maybe she was right. Why hadn't I gone to Haverton? Why hadn't I demanded to meet face-to-face?

"I think," Katy said, "Julie ended up doing something bad."

"What do you mean?"

"I don't know. Maybe that's going too far. I don't remember much, but I remember she seemed happy before she died. I hadn't seen her that happy in a long time. I think maybe she was getting better, I don't know."

The doorbell rang. My shoulders slumped at the sound. I was not much in the mood for more company. Katy, reading me, jumped up and said, "I'll get it."

It was a deliveryman with a fruit basket. Katy took the basket and brought it back into the room. She dropped it on the table. "There's a card," she said.

"Open it."

She plucked it out of the tiny envelope. "It's a condolence basket from some of the kids at Covenant House." She pulled something from an envelope. "A mass card too."

Katy kept staring at the card.

"What's the matter?"

Katy read it again. Then she looked up at me. "Sheila Rogers?"

"Yes."

"Your girlfriend's name was Sheila Rogers?"

"Yeah, why?"

Katy shook her head and put down the card.

"What is it?"

"Nothing," she said.

"Don't give me that. Did you know her?"

"No."

"Then what is it?"

"Nothing." Katy's voice was firmer this time. "Just drop it, okay?"

The phone rang. I waited for the machine. Through the speaker I heard Squares say, "Pick it up."

I did.

Without preamble, Squares said, "You believe the mother? About Sheila having a daughter?"

"Yes."

"So what are we going to do about it?"

I had been thinking about it since I first heard the news. "I have a theory," I said.

"I'm a-listening."

"Maybe Sheila's running away had something to do with her daughter."

"How?"

"Maybe she was trying to find Carly or bring her back. Maybe she learned that Carly was in trouble. I don't know. But something."

"Sounds semi-logical."

"And if we can trace Sheila's steps," I said, "maybe we can find Carly."

"And maybe we'll end up like Sheila."

"A risk," I agreed.

There was a hesitation. I looked over at Katy. She was staring off, plucking her lower lip.

"So you want to continue," Squares said.

"Yes, but I don't want to put you in danger."

"So this is the part where you tell me I can step away at any time?"

"Right, and then this is the part where you say you'll stick with me to the end."

"Cue the violins," Squares said. "Now that we're past all that, Roscoe via Raquel just called me. He may have come up with a serious lead on how Sheila ran. You game for a night ride?"

"Pick me up," I said.

26

Philip McGuane saw his old nemesis on the security camera. His receptionist buzzed him.

"Mr. McGuane?"

"Send him in," he said.

"Yes, Mr. McGuane. He's with—"

"Her too."

McGuane stood. He had a corner office overlooking the Hudson River near the isle of Manhattan's southwestern tip. In the warmer months, the new mega-cruise ships with their neon decor and atrium lobbies glided by, some climbing as high as his window. Today nary a stir. McGuane kept flicking the remote on the security camera, keeping up with his federal antagonist Joe Pistillo and the female underling he had in tow.

McGuane spent a lot on security. It was worth it. His system employed eighty-three cameras. Every person who entered his private elevator was digitally recorded from several angles, but what really made the system stand out was that the camera angles were designed to shoot in such a way that anyone entering could be made to look as though they were also leaving. Both the corridor and elevator were painted spearmint green. That might not seem like much—it was, in effect, rather hideous—but to those who understood special effects and digital manipulation, it was key. An image on the green background could be plucked out and placed on another background.

His enemies felt comfortable coming here. This was, after all, his office. No one, they surmised, would be brazen enough to kill someone on his own turf. That was where they were wrong. The brazen nature, the very fact that the authorities would think the same thing—and the fact that he could offer up evidence that the victim had left the facility unharmed—made it the ideal spot to strike.

McGuane pulled out an old photograph from his top drawer. He had learned early that you never underestimate a person or a situation. He also realized that by making opponents underestimate him, he could finagle the advantage. He looked now at the picture of the three seventeen-year-old boys—Ken Klein, John "the Ghost" Asselta, and McGuane. They'd grown up in the suburb of Livingston, New Jersey, though McGuane had lived on the opposite side of town from Ken and the Ghost. They hooked up in high school, drawn to each other, noticing—or perhaps this was giving them all too much credit—a kinship in the eyes.

Ken Klein had been the fiery tennis player, John Asselta the psycho wrestler, McGuane the wow-'em charmer and student council president. He looked at the faces in the photograph. You would never see it. All you saw were three popular high school kids. Nothing beyond that façade. When those kids shot up Columbine a few years back, McGuane had watched the media reaction with fascination. The world looked for comfortable excuses. The boys were outsiders. The boys were teased and bullied. The boys had absent parents and played video games. But McGuane knew that none of that mattered. It may have been a slightly different era, but that could have been them—Ken, John, and McGuane—because the truth is, it does not matter if you are financially comfortable or loved by your parents or if you keep to yourself or fight to stay afloat in the mainstream.

Some people have that rage.

The office door opened. Joseph Pistillo and his young protégée entered. McGuane smiled and put away the photograph.

"Ah, Javert," he said to Pistillo. "Do you still hunt me when all I did was steal some bread?"

"Yeah," Pistillo said. "Yeah, that's you, McGuane. The innocent man hounded."

McGuane turned his attention to the female agent. "Tell me, Joe, why do you always have such a lovely colleague with you?"

"This is Special Agent Claudia Fisher."

"Charmed," McGuane said. "Please have a seat."

"We'd rather stand."

McGuane shrugged a suit-yourself and dropped into his chair. "So what can I do for you today?"

"You're having a tough time, McGuane."

"Am I?"

"Indeed."

"And you're here to help? How special."

Pistillo snorted. "Been after you a long time."

"Yes, I know, but I'm fickle. Suggestion: Send a bouquet of roses next time. Hold the door for me. Use candlelight. A man wants to be romanced."

Pistillo put two fists on the desk. "Part of me wants to sit back and watch you get eaten alive." He swallowed, tried to hold something deep inside him in check. "But a bigger part of me wants to see you rot in jail for what you've done."

McGuane turned to Claudia Fisher. "He's very sexy when he talks tough, don't you think?"

"Guess who we just found, McGuane?"

"Hoffa? About time too."

"Fred Tanner."

"Who?"

Pistillo smirked. "Don't play that with me. Big thug. Works for you."

"I believe he's in my security department."

"We found him."

"I didn't know he was lost."

"Funny."

"I thought he was on vacation, Agent Pistillo."

"Permanently. We found him in the Passaic River."

McGuane frowned. "How unsanitary."

"Especially with two bullet holes in the head. We also found a guy named Peter Appel. Strangled. He was an ex-army sharpshooter."

"Be all that you can be."

Only one strangled, McGuane thought. The Ghost must have been disappointed that he'd had to shoot the other.

"Yeah, well, let's see," Pistillo went on. "We have these two men dead. Plus we have the two guys in New Mexico. That's four."

"And you didn't use your fingers. They're not paying you enough, Agent Pistillo."

"You want to tell me about it?"

"Very much," McGuane said. "I admit it. I killed them all. Happy?"

Pistillo leaned over the desk so that their faces were inches apart. "You're about to go down, McGuane."

"And you had onion soup for lunch."

"Are you aware," Pistillo said, not backing off, "that Sheila Rogers is dead too?"

"Who?"

Pistillo stood back up. "Right. You don't know her either. She doesn't work for you."

"Many people work for me. I'm a businessman."

Pistillo looked over at Fisher. "Let's go," he said.

"Leaving so soon?"

"I've waited a long time for this," Pistillo said. "What do they say? Revenge is a dish best served cold."

"Like vichyssoise."

Another smirk from Pistillo. "Have a nice day, McGuane."

They left. McGuane sat there and did not move for ten minutes. What had been the purpose of that visit? Simple. To shake him up. More underestimation. He hit line three, the safe phone, the one checked daily for listening devices. He hesitated. Dialing the number. Would that show panic?

He weighed the pros and cons and decided to risk it.

The Ghost answered on the first ring with a drawn-out "Hello?"

"Where are you?"

"Just off the plane from Vegas."

"Learn anything?"

"Oh yes."

"I'm listening."

"There was a third person in the car with them," the Ghost said.

McGuane shifted in his seat. "Who?"

"A little girl," the Ghost said. "No more than eleven or twelve years old."

27

Katy and I were on the street when Squares pulled up. She leaned over and kissed me on the cheek. Squares arched an eyebrow in my direction. I frowned at him.

"I thought you were staying on my couch," I said to her.

Katy had been distracted since the fruit basket's arrival. "I'll be back tomorrow."

"And you don't want to tell me what's going on?"

She stuck her hands deep in her pockets and shrugged. "I just need to do a little research."

"On?"

She shook her head. I did not press it. She gave me a quick grin before taking off. I got in the van.

Squares said, "And she is?"

I explained as we headed uptown. There were dozens of sandwiches and blankets packed in the bag. Squares handed them out to the kids. The sandwiches and blankets, in the same vein as his rap about the missing Angie, made excellent icebreakers, and even if they didn't, at least the kids would have something to eat and something to keep them warm. I had seen Squares work wonders with those items. The first night, a kid would most likely refuse any help at all. He or she might even curse or become hostile. Squares would take no offense. He'd just keep coming at him. Squares believed that consistency was the key. Show the kid you're there all the time. Show the kid you're not leaving. Show the kid it's unconditional.

A few nights later, that kid will take the sandwich. Another, he'll want a blanket. After a while, he'll start looking for you and the van.

I reached back and lifted a sandwich into view. "You're working again tonight?"

He lowered his head and looked at me above his sunglasses. "No," he said dryly, "I'm just really hungry."

He drove some more.

"How long are you going to avoid her, Squares?"

Squares flipped on the radio. Carly Simon's "You're So Vain." Squares sang along. Then he said, "Remember this song?"

I nodded.

"That rumor that it was about Warren Beatty. Was that true?"

"Don't know," I said.

We drove some more.

"Let me ask you something, Will."

He kept his eyes on the road. I waited.

"How surprised were you to learn that Sheila had a kid?"

"Very."

"And," he went on, "how surprised would you be to learn I had one too?"

I looked at him.

"You don't understand the situation, Will."

"I'd like to."

"Let's concentrate on one thing at a time."

The traffic was miraculously light this evening. Carly Simon faded away and then the Chairman of the Board begged his woman to give him just a little more time and their love would surely grow. Such desperation in that simple plea. I love this song.

We cut across town and took the Harlem River Drive north. When we passed a group of kids huddled under an overpass, Squares pulled over and shifted into park.

"Quick work stop," he said.

"You want help?"

Squares shook his head. "It won't take long."

"You going to use the sandwiches?"

Squares examined his potential help-ees and considered. "Nah. Got something better."

"What?"

"Phone cards." He handed me one. "I got TeleReach to donate over a thousand of them. The kids go nuts for them."

They did too. As soon as they saw them, the kids flocked to him. Count on Squares. I watched the faces, tried to separate the smeared mass into individuals with wants and dreams and hopes. Kids do not survive long out here. Forget the incredible physical dangers. They can often get past that. It is the soul, the sense of self, that erodes out here. Once the erosion reaches a certain level, well, that's the ball game.

Sheila had been saved before reaching that level.

Then someone had killed her.

I shook it off. No time for that now. Focus on the task at hand. Keep moving. Action kept the grief at bay. Let it fuel you, not slow you down.

Do it—corny as it might sound—for her.

Squares returned a few minutes later. "Let's rock and roll."

"You haven't told me where we're going."

"Corner of 128th Street and Second Avenue. Raquel will meet us there."

"And what's there?"

He grinned. "A possible clue."

We exited the highway and passed a sprawl of housing projects. From two blocks away, I spotted Raquel. This was not difficult. Raquel was the size of a small principality and dressed like an explosion at the Liberace museum. Squares slowed the van next to him and frowned.

"What?" Raquel said.

"Pink pumps with a green dress?"

"It's coral and turquoise," Raquel said. "Plus the magenta purse pulls it all together."

Squares shrugged and parked in front of a storefront with a faded sign that read GOLDBERG PHARMACY. When I stepped out, Raquel wrapped me in an embrace that felt like wet foam rubber. He reeked of Aqua Velva, and my mind couldn't help but think that in this case, indeed, there was something about an Aqua Velva man.

"I'm so sorry," he whispered.

"Thank you."

He released me, and I was able to breathe again. He was crying. His tears grabbed hold of his mascara and ran it down his face. The colors mixed and got diverted in the rough of his beard, so that his face started looking like a candle in the back of Spencer's Gifts.

"Abe and Sadie are inside," Raquel said. "They're expecting you."

Squares nodded and headed into the pharmacy. I followed. A ding-dong sounded when we entered. The smell reminded me of a cherry tree–shaped freshener dangling from a rearview window. The store shelves were high and packed and tight. I saw bandages and deodorants and shampoos and cough medicines, all laid out with seemingly little organization.

An old man with half-moon reading glasses on a chain appeared. He wore a sweater-vest over a white shirt. His hair was high and thick and white and looked like a powdered wig from Bailey's. His eyebrows were extra bushy, giving him the look of an owl.

"Look! It's Mr. Squares!"

The two men hugged, the old man giving Squares's back a few hard pats. "You look good," the old man said.

"You too, Abe."

"Sadie," he shouted. "Sadie, Mr. Squares is here."

"Who?"

"The yoga guy. With that tattoo."

"The one on his forehead?"

"That's him."

I shook my head and leaned toward Squares. "Is there anyone you don't know?"

He shrugged. "I've lived a charmed life."

Sadie, an older woman who would never see five feet even in Raquel's highest pumps, stepped down from behind the pharmacy stand. She frowned at Squares and said, "You look skinny."

"Leave him alone," Abe said.

"Shush you. You eating enough?"

"Sure," Squares said.

"You're bones. Pure bones."

"Sadie, can you leave the man alone?"

"Shush you." She smiled conspiratorially. "I got kugel. You want some?"

"Maybe later, thanks."

"I'll put some in the Tupperware."

"That would be nice, thank you." Squares turned to me. "This is my friend, Will Klein."

The two old people showed me sad eyes. "He's the boyfriend?"

"Yes."

They inspected me. Then they looked at each other.

"I don't know," Abe said.

"You can trust him," Squares said.

"Maybe we can, maybe we can't. But we're like priests here. We don't talk. You know that. And she was particularly adamant. We were to say nothing, no matter what."

"I know that."

"We talk, what good are we?"

"I understand."

"We talk, we could be killed."

"No one will know. I give you my word."

The old couple looked at each other some more. "Raquel," Abe said. "He's a good boy. Or girl. I don't know, I get so confused sometimes."

Squares stepped toward them. "We need your help."

Sadie took her husband's hand in a gesture so intimate I almost turned away. "She was such a beautiful girl, Abe."

"And so nice," he added. Abe sighed and looked at me. The door opened and the ding-dong chimed again. A disheveled black man walked in and said, "Tyrone sent me."

Sadie moved toward him. "I'll take care of you over here," she said.

Abe kept staring at me. I looked at Squares. I didn't understand any of this.

Squares took off his sunglasses. "Please, Abe," he said. "It's important."

Abe held up a hand. "Okay, okay, just stop with the face, please." He waved us forward. "Come this way."

We walked to the back of the store. He lifted the counter flap, and we walked under. We passed the pills, the bottles, the bags of filled prescriptions, the mortars and pestles. Abe opened a door. We headed down into the basement. Abe flicked on the light.

"This," he announced, "is where it all happens."

I saw very little. There was a computer, a printer, and a digital camera. That was about it. I looked at Abe and then at Squares.

"Does someone want to clue me in?"

"Our business is simple," Abe said. "We keep no records. If the police want to take this computer, fine, go ahead. They'll learn nothing. All the records are located up here." He tapped his forehead with his finger. "And hey, lots of those records are getting lost every day, am I right, Squares?"

Squares smiled at him.

Abe spotted my confusion. "You still don't get it?"

"I still don't get it."

"Fake IDs," Abe said.

"Oh."

"I'm not talking about the ones underage kids use to drink."

"Right, okay."

He lowered his voice. "You know anything about them?"

"Not much."

"I'm talking here about the ones people need to disappear. To run away. To start again. You're in trouble? Poof, I'll make you disappear. Like a magician, no? You need to go away, really go away, you don't go to a travel agent. You come to me."

"I see," I said. "And there's a big need for your"—I wasn't sure of the term—"services?"

"You'd be surprised. Oh, it's not usually very glamorous. Lots of times it's just parole jumpers. Or bail jumpers. Or someone the authorities are looking to arrest. We service a lot of illegal immigrants too. They want to stay in the country, so we make them citizens." He smiled at me. "And every once in a while we get someone nicer."

"Like Sheila," I said.

"Exactly. You want to know how it works?"

Before I could answer, Abe had started up again. "It's not like on the TV," he said. "On the TV they always make it so complicated, am I right? They look for a kid who died and then they send away for his birth certificate or something like that. They make up all these complicated forgeries."

"That's not how it's done?"

"That's not how it's done." He sat at the computer terminal and started typing. "First of all, that would take too long. Second, with the Net and the Web and all that nonsense, dead people quickly become dead. They don't stay alive anymore. You die, so does your social security number. Otherwise I could just use the social security numbers of old people who die, right? Or people who die in middle age? You understand?"

"I think so," I said. "So how do you create a fake identity?"

"Ah, I don't create them," Abe said with a big smile. "I use real ones."

"I don't follow."

Abe frowned at Squares. "I thought you said he worked the street."

"A long time ago," Squares said.

"Yeah, okay, let's see." Abe Goldberg turned back to me. "You saw that man upstairs. The one who came in after you."

"Yes."

"He looks unemployed, no? Probably homeless."

"I wouldn't know."

"Don't play politically correct with me. He looked like a vagrant, am I right?"

"I guess."

"But he's a person, see. He has a name. He had a mother. He was born in this country. And"—he smiled and waved his hands theatrically—"he has a social security number. He might even have a driver's license, maybe an expired one. No matter. As long as he has a social security number, he exists. He has an identity. You follow?"

"I follow."

"So let's say he needs a little money. For what, I don't want to know. But he needs money. What he doesn't need is an identity. He's out on the street, so what good is it doing him? It's not like he has a credit rating or owns land. So we run his name through this little computer here." He patted the top of the monitor. "We see if he has any outstanding warrants against him. If he doesn't—and most don't—then we buy his ID. Let's say his name is John Smith. And let's say you, Will, need to be able to check into hotels or whatever under a name other than your own."

I saw where he was heading. "You sell me his social security number and I become John Smith."

Abe snapped his fingers. "Bingo."

"But suppose we don't look alike."

"There's no physical descriptions associated with your social security number. Once you have it, you call up any bureau and you can get whatever paperwork you need. If you're in a rush, I have the equipment here to give you an Ohio driver's license. But it won't hold up under tough scrutiny. But the thing is, the identity will."

"Suppose our John Smith gets rousted and needs an ID."

"He can use it too. Heck, five people can use it at the same time. Who's going to know? Simple, am I right?"

"Simple," I agreed. "So Sheila came to you?"

"Yes."

"When?"

"What, two, three days ago. Like I said before, she wasn't our usual customer. Such a nice girl. So beautiful too."

"Did she tell you where she was going?"

Abe smiled and touched my arm. "Does this look like an ask-a-lot-of-questions business? They don't want to say—and I don't want to know. You see, we never talk. Not a word. Sadie and I have our reputation, and like I said upstairs, loose lips can get you killed. You understand?"

"Yes."

"In fact, when Raquel first put out feelers, we didn't say boo. Discretion. That's what this business is about. We love Raquel. But we still said nothing. Zip, not a word."

"So what made you change your mind?"

Abe looked hurt. He turned to Squares, then back to me. "What, you think we're animals? You think we don't feel anything?"

"I didn't mean—"

"The murder," he interrupted. "We heard what happened to that poor, lovely girl. It isn't right." He threw up his hands. "But what can I do? I can't go to the police, am I right? Thing is, I trust Raquel and Mr. Squares here. They're good men. They dwell in the dark but they shine a light. Like my Sadie and me, see?"

The door above us opened, and Sadie came down. "I've closed up," she said.

"Good."

"So where were you?" she asked him.

"I was telling him why we may be willing to talk."

"Okay."

Sadie Goldberg slowly felt her way down the stairs. Abe turned his owl eyes on me again and said, "Mr. Squares tells us that there is a little girl involved here."

"Her daughter," I said. "She's probably about twelve years old."

Sadie clucked a tsk-tsk. "You don't know where she is."

"That's right."

Abe shook his head. Sadie moved next to him, their bodies touching, somehow fitting together. I wondered how long they'd been married, if they had children, where they'd come from, how they came to these shores, how they ended up in this business.

"You want to know something?" Sadie said to me.

I nodded.

"Your Sheila. She had"—she raised two fists in the air—"a special something. A spirit about her. She was beautiful, of course, but there was something more. The fact that she's gone . . . we feel lessened. She came in and she looked so scared. And maybe the identity we gave her didn't hold up. Maybe that's why she's dead."

"So," Abe said, "we want to help." He wrote something down on a piece of paper and handed it to me. "The name we gave her was Donna White. That's the social security number. I don't know if it'll help you or not."

"And the real Donna White?"

"A homeless crack addict."

I stared down at the scrap of paper.

Sadie moved toward me and put a hand on my cheek. "You look like a nice man."

I looked up at her.

"Find that little girl," she said.

I nodded once and then again. Then I promised that I would.

28

Katy Miller was still shaking when she arrived at her house.

This can't be, she thought. It's a mistake. I got the name wrong.

"Katy?" her mother called out.

"Yeah."

"I'm in the kitchen."

"I'll be there in a little while, Mom."

Katy headed for the basement door. When her hand reached the knob, she stopped.

The basement. She hated to go down there.

You would think that after so many years, she'd be desensitized to the threadbare couch and water-stained carpet and so-old-it's-not-even-cable-ready television. She wasn't. For all her senses knew, her sister's body was still down there, bloated and decayed, the stench of death so thick it made it hard to swallow.

Her parents understood. Katy never had to do laundry. Her father never asked her to fetch his toolbox or get a fresh bulb from the storage room. If a task required a trip into these bowels, her mother and father tried to take it on for her.

But not this time. This time, she was on her own.

At the top of the stairs she flicked the light switch. One naked bulb—the glass fixture had broken during the murder—came to life. She crept down the stairs. She kept her line of vision up and over the couch and carpet and TV.

Why did they still live here?

It made little sense to her. When JonBenét was murdered, the Ramseys had moved across the country. But then again, everyone thought that they killed her. The Ramseys were probably running away from the stares of neighbors as much as the memory of their daughter's demise. That, of course, was not the case here.

But still, there was something about this town. Her parents had stayed. And so had the Kleins. Neither had been willing to surrender.

What did that mean?

She found Julie's trunk in the corner. Her father had put some kind of wooden crate under it in case of a flood. Katy flashed back and saw her sister packing for college. She remembered crawling into the trunk as Julie packed, pretending at first that the trunk was a protective fort and then, after that, pretending that Julie might pack her up too, so that they could go to college together.

There were boxes piled on the top. Katy removed them and put them in a corner. She examined the trunk's lock. There was no key, but all she needed was a flat edge. She found an old butter knife with the stored silver. She stuck it into the opening and turned. The lock fell open. She unsnapped the two clasps and slowly, like Van Helsing opening Dracula's coffin, she lifted the lid.

"What are you doing?"

Her mother's voice startled her. She leapt back.

Lucille Miller moved closer. "Isn't that Julie's trunk?"

"Jesus, Mom, you scared the hell out of me."

Her mother came closer. "What are you doing with Julie's trunk?"

"I'm . . . I'm just looking."

"At what?"

Katy straightened up. "She was my sister."

"I know that, honey."

"Don't I have a right to miss her too?"

Her mother looked at her for a long time. "And that's why you're down here?"

Katy nodded.

"Is everything else okay?" her mother asked.

"Fine."

"You've never been one for reminiscing, Katy."

"You've never let me," she said.

Her mother considered that. "I guess that's true."

"Mom?"

"Yes?"

"Why did you stay?"

For a moment, her mother seemed ready to give Katy the usual rebuff about not wanting to talk about it. But—what with Will's surprise visit to the curb and her working up the courage to pay her respects to the Klein family—this was turning into a rather bizarre week. Her mother sat on one of the boxes. She smoothed out her skirt.

"When a tragedy hits you," her mother began. "I mean, when it first hits you, it's the end of the world. It's like being dumped in the ocean during a storm. The water tosses you and thrashes you and there is nothing you can do but try to stay afloat. Part of you—maybe even most of you—doesn't even want to keep your head above water. You want to stop fighting and just sink away. But you can't. The survival instinct won't let you—or maybe, in my case, it was because I had another child to raise. I don't know. But either way, like it or not, you stay afloat."

Her mother wiped the corner of her eye with one finger. She sat up a little and forced a smile. "My analogy isn't holding," she said.

Katy took her mother's hand. "It sounds pretty good to me."

"Maybe," Mrs. Miller allowed, "but you see, after a while, the storm part is over. And that's when it gets even worse. I guess you can say you're washed up onshore. But all that thrashing and tossing has caused irreparable harm. You are in tremendous pain. And that's still not the end of it. Because now you're left with an awful alternative."

Katy waited, still holding her mother's hand.

"You can try to move past the pain. You can try to forget and get on with your life. But for your father and me"—Lucille Miller closed her eyes and shook her head firmly—"forgetting would be too obscene. We couldn't betray your sister like that. The pain may be enormous, but how could we go on if we abandoned Julie? She existed. She was real. I know that doesn't make sense."

But, Katy thought, maybe it did.

They sat in silence. Eventually Lucille Miller let go of Katy's hand. She slapped her thighs and stood. "I'll leave you alone now."

Katy listened to her footsteps. Then she turned back to the trunk. She dug through the contents. It took her nearly half an hour, but she found it.

And it changed everything.

29

When we were back in the van, I asked Squares what we should do next.

"I have a source," he said, a true understatement if ever I've heard one. "We'll run the name Donna White through the airline computers, see if we can figure out when she flew out or where she stayed, something."

We lapsed into silence.

"Someone has to say it," Squares began.

I stared down at my hands. "Go ahead, then."

"What are you trying to do here, Will?"

"Find Carly," I said too quickly.

"And then what? Raise her as your own?"

"I don't know."

"You realize, of course, that you're using this to block."

"So are you."

I looked out the car window. The neighborhood was full of rubble. We drove past housing projects that housed mostly misery. I looked for something good. I didn't see any.

"I was going to propose," I said.

Squares kept driving, but I saw something in his posture give way.

"I bought a ring. I showed it to my mother. I was just waiting for some time to pass. You know, after my mom's death and all."

We stopped at a red light. Squares would not turn and look at me.

"I have to keep searching," I said, "because I'm not sure what I'll do if I don't. I'm not suicidal or anything, but if I stop running"—I stopped, tried to think how to say this, settled for the simple—"it'll catch up to me."

"It's going to catch you eventually, no matter what," Squares said.

"I know. But by then, maybe I'll have done something good. Maybe I'll have saved her daughter. Maybe, even though she's dead, I'll have helped her."

"Or," Squares countered, "you might find out that she was not the woman you believed her to be. That she fooled us all and worse."

"Then so be it," I said. "You still with me?"

"To the end, Kemosabi."

"Good, because I think I have an idea."

His leather face cracked into that smile. "Rock and roll, dude. Lay it on me."

"We've been forgetting something."

"What?"

"New Mexico. Sheila's fingerprints were found at a murder scene in New Mexico."

He nodded. "You think that murder has something to do with Carly?"

"Could be."

He nodded. "But we don't even know who was killed in New Mexico. Hell, we don't even know where the murder scene is exactly."

"That's where my plan comes into action," I said. "Drop me off at home. I think I need to do a little Web surfing."

Yes, I had a plan.

It stood to reason that the FBI were not the ones to discover the bodies. Probably a local cop did. Or maybe a neighbor. Or a relative. And since this murder had taken place in a town not already anesthetized to such sudden violence, the crime had probably been reported in the local paper.

I surfed to refdesk.com and clicked on national newspapers. They had thirty-three listings for New Mexico. I tried the ones in the Albuquerque area. I sat back and let the page load. Found one. Okay, good. I clicked on to the archives and started searching. I typed "murder" in. Too many hits. I tried "double murder." That didn't work either. I tried another paper. Then another.

It took almost an hour, but I finally nailed it:

TWO MEN FOUND MURDERED

Small community shocked

by Yvonne Sterno

Late last night, the gated Albuquerque suburb of Stonepointe was reeling from news that two men were both shot in the head, probably in broad daylight, and found in one of the community's homes. "I didn't hear a thing," said Fred Davison, a neighbor. "I just can't believe something like this could happen in our community." The two men remain unidentified. Police had no comment other than to say that they were investigating. "This is an ongoing investigation. We're following several leads." The homeowner is listed as Owen Enfield. An autopsy is scheduled for this morning.

That was about it. I searched the next day. Nothing. I searched the day after. Still nothing. I searched for all the stories written by Yvonne Sterno. There were pieces on local weddings and charity events. Nothing, not another word, about the murders.

I sat back.

Why weren't there more stories?

One way to find out. I picked up the phone and began to dial the number for the *New Mexico Star-Beacon*. Maybe I'd get lucky and reach Yvonne Sterno. And maybe she'd tell me something.

The switchboard was one of those machines that ask you to spell your party's last name. I had dialed the S-T-E-R when the machine cut in and told me to hit the pound key if I was trying to reach Yvonne Sterno. I followed orders. Two rings later a machine picked up.

"This is Yvonne Sterno at the *Star-Beacon*. I'm either on the phone or away from my desk."

I hung up. I was still online so I brought up switchboard.com. I typed in Sterno's name and tried the Albuquerque area. Bingo. A "Y and M Sterno" was listed as living at 25 Canterbury Drive in Albuquerque. I dialed the number. A woman answered.

"Hello?" Then she shouted, "Quiet back there, Mommy's on the phone."

The squeal of young children did not let up.

"Yvonne Sterno?"

"You selling something?"

"No."

"Then yes, speaking."

"My name is Will Klein—"

"Sure sounds like you're selling something."

"I'm not," I said. "Are you the same Yvonne Sterno that writes for the *Star-Beacon*?"

"What did you say your name was?" Before I could reply, she shouted, "Hey, I told you two to knock if off. Tommy, give him the Game Boy. No, now!" Back to me. "Hello?"

"My name is Will Klein. I wanted to talk to you about that double murder you wrote about recently."

"Uh-huh. And what's your interest in the case?"

"I just have a few questions."

"I'm not a library, Mr. Klein."

"Please, call me Will. And bear with me for just a moment. How often do murders occur in places like Stonepointe?"

"Rarely."

"And double murders where the victims are found like this?"

"This would be the first that I'm aware of."

"So," I said, "why didn't it get more coverage?"

The kids erupted again. So did Yvonne Sterno. "That's it! Tommy, get up to your room. Right, right, save it for the judge, bud, let's move. And you, give me that Game Boy. Hand it over before I stick it down the disposal." I heard the phone being picked up again. "And again I will ask you: What's your interest in the case?"

I knew enough reporters to know that the way to their hearts is through their byline. "I may have pertinent information on the case."

"Pertinent," she repeated. "That's a good word there, Will."

"I think you'll find what I say interesting."

"Where you calling from anyway?"

"New York City," I said.

There was a pause. "A long way from the murder scene."

"Yes."

"So I'm listening. What, pray tell, will I find both pertinent and interesting?"

"First I need to know a few basics."

"That's not how I work, Will."

"I looked up your other pieces, Mrs. Sterno."

"It's miz. And since we're all buddy-buddy, just call me Yvonne."

"Fine," I said. "You mostly do features, Yvonne. You cover weddings. You cover society dinners."

"They have great eats, Will, and I look fabulous in a black dress. What's your point?"

"A story like this doesn't fall in your lap every day."

"Okay, you're getting me all hot and bothered here. Your point?"

"My point is, take a chance. Just answer a few questions. What's the harm? And who knows, maybe I'm legit."

When she did not respond, I pushed ahead.

"You land a big murder story like this. But the article doesn't list victims or suspects or any real details."

"I didn't know any," she said. "The report came in over the scanner late at night. We barely made it in time for the morning edition."

"So why no follow-up? This had to be a huge event. Why was there only that one piece?"

Silence.

"Hello?"

"Give me a second. The kids are acting up again."

Only I wasn't hearing any noise this time.

"I was closed down," she said softly.

"Meaning?"

"Meaning we were lucky to get even that much into the paper. By the next morning there were feds all over the place. The local SAC—"

"SAC?"

"Special Agent in Charge. The head fed in the area. He got my boss to shut the story down. I tried a little on my own, but all I got was a bunch of no-comments."

"Is that odd?"

"I don't know, Will. I haven't covered a murder before. But yeah, I'd say it sounds pretty odd."

"What do you take it to mean?"

"From the way my boss has been acting?" Yvonne took a deep breath. "It's big. Very big. Bigger than a double murder. Your turn, Will."

I wondered how far I should go. "Are you aware of any fingerprints found at the scene?"

"No."

"There was one set belonging to a woman."

"Go on."

"That woman was found dead yesterday."

"Whoa, Nelly. Murdered?"

"Yes."

"Where?"

"A small town in Nebraska."

"Her name?"

I leaned back. "Tell me about the homeowner, Owen Enfield."

"Oh I see. Back and forth. I give, you give."

"Something like that. Was Enfield one of the victims?"

"I don't know."

"What do you know about him?"

"He's lived there three months."

"Alone?"

"According to neighbors, he moved in alone. A woman and child have been hanging around a lot the last few weeks."

Child.

A tremor started in my heart. I sat up. "How old was the child?"

"I don't know. School age."

"Like maybe twelve."

"Yeah maybe."

"Boy or girl."

"Girl."

I froze.

"Yo, Will, you there?"

"Got a name on the girl?"

"No. No one really knew anything about them."

"Where are they now?"

"I don't know."

"How can that be?"

"One of the great mysteries of life, I guess. I haven't been able to track them down. But like I said, I'm off the case. I haven't been trying all that hard."

"Can you find out where they are?"

"I can try."

"Is there anything else? Have you heard the name of a suspect or one of the victims, anything?"

"Like I said, it's been quiet. I only work at the paper part-time. As you might have been able to discern, I'm a full-time mother. I just caught the story because I was the only one in when it came over the band. But I have a few good sources."

"We need to find Enfield," I said. "Or at least the woman and girl."

"Seems like a good place to start," she agreed. "You want to tell me your interest in all this?"

I thought about that. "You up for rattling cages, Yvonne?"

"Yeah, Will. Yeah, I am."

"Are you any good?"

"Want a demonstration?"

"Sure."

"You may be calling me from New York City, but you're actually from New Jersey. In fact—though there must certainly be more than one Will Klein out there—my bet is you're the brother of an infamous murderer."

"An alleged infamous murderer," I corrected her. "How did you know?"

"I have Lexis-Nexis on my home computer. I plugged in your name and that's what came up. One of the articles mentioned that you now live in Manhattan."

"My brother had nothing to do with any of this."

"Sure, and he was innocent of killing your neighbor too, right?"

"That's not what I mean. Your double murder has nothing to do with him."

"Then what's your connection?"

I let loose a breath. "Someone else who was very close to me."

"Who?"

"My girlfriend. Her fingerprints were the ones found at the scene."

I heard the kids act up again. It sounded like they were running through the room making siren noises. Yvonne Sterno did not yell at them this time. "So it was your girlfriend who was found dead in Nebraska?"

"Yes."

"And that's your interest in this?"

"Part of it."

"What's the other part?"

I was not prepared yet to tell her about Carly. "Find Enfield," I said.

"What was her name, Will? Your girlfriend."

"Just find him."

"Hey, you want us to work together? You don't hold out on me. I can find out in five seconds by looking it up anyway. Just tell me."

"Rogers," I said. "Her name was Sheila Rogers."

I heard her typing some more. "I'll do my best, Will," she said. "Hang tight, I'll call you soon."

30

I had a strange quasi-dream.

I say "quasi" because I was not fully asleep. I floated in that groove between slumber and consciousness, that state where you sometimes stumble and plummet and need to grab the sides of the bed. I lay in the dark, my hands behind my head, my eyes closed.

I mentioned earlier how Sheila had loved to dance. She even made me join a dance club at the Jewish Community Center in West Orange, New Jersey. The JCC was close to both my mother's hospital and the house in Livingston. We'd go out every Wednesday to visit my mother and then at six-thirty head for our meeting with our fellow dancers.

We were the youngest couple in the club by—and this is just a rough estimate—seventy-five years, but man, the older folks knew how to move. I'd try to keep up, but there was simply no way. I felt self-conscious in their company. Sheila did not. Sometimes, in the middle of a dance, she would let go of my hands and sway away from me. Her eyes would close. There would be a sheen on her face as she totally disappeared in the bliss.

There was one older couple in particular, the Segals, who'd been dancing together since a USO gathering in the forties. They were a handsome, graceful couple. Mr. Segal always wore a white ascot. Mrs. Segal wore something blue and a pearl choker. On the floor, they were pure magic. They moved like lovers. They moved like one. During the breaks, they were outgoing and friendly to the rest of us. But when the music played, they saw only each other.

On a snowy night last February—we thought that the club would probably be canceled, but it wasn't—Mr. Segal showed up by himself. He still wore the white ascot. His suit was impeccable. But one look at the tightness in his face and we knew. Sheila gripped my hand. I could see a tear escape from her eye. When the music started, Mr. Segal stood, stepped without hesitation onto the dance floor, and danced by himself. He put out his arms and moved as though his wife were still there. He guided her across the floor, cradling her ghost so gently that none of us dared disturb him.

The next week Mr. Segal did not show at all. We heard from some of the others that Mrs. Segal had lost a longtime battle with cancer. But she danced until the end. The music started up then. We all found our partners and took to the floor. And as I held Sheila close, impossibly close, I realized that, sad as the Segal story was, they'd had it better than anyone I had ever known.

Here was where I entered the quasi-dream, though from the beginning I recognized that it was just that. I was back at the JCC Dance Club. Mr. Segal was there. So were a bunch of people I had never seen before, all without partners. When the music started, we all danced by ourselves. I looked around. My father was there, doing a clumsy solo fox-trot. He nodded at me.

I watched the others dance. They all clearly felt the presence of their dearly departed. They looked into their partners' ghostly eyes. I tried to follow suit, but something was wrong. I saw nothing. I was dancing alone. Sheila would not come to me.

Far away, I heard the phone ring. A deep voice on the answering machine penetrated my dream. "This is Lieutenant Daniels of the Livingston Police Department. I am trying to reach Will Klein."

In the background, behind Lieutenant Daniels, I heard the muffled laugh of a young woman. My eyes flew open, and the JCC Dance Club disappeared. As I reached for the phone, I heard the young woman whoop another laugh.

It sounded like Katy Miller.

"Perhaps I should call your parents," Lieutenant Daniels was saying to whoever was laughing.

"No." It was Katy. "I'm eighteen. You can't make me—"

I picked up the phone. "This is Will Klein."

Lieutenant Daniels said, "Hi, Will. This is Tim Daniels. We went to school together, remember?"

Tim Daniels. He'd worked at the local Hess station. He used to wear his oil-smeared uniform to school, complete with his name embroidered on the pocket. I guessed that he still liked uniforms.

"Sure," I said, totally confused now. "How's it going?"

"Good, thanks."

"You're on the force now?" Nothing gets by me.

"Yep. And I still live in town. Married Betty Jo Stetson. We have two daughters."

I tried to conjure up Betty Jo, but nothing came. "Wow, congrats."

"Thanks, Will." His voice grew grave. "I, uh, read about your mother in the *Tribune*. I'm sorry."

"I appreciate that, thanks," I said.

Katy Miller started laughing again.

"Look, the reason I'm calling is, well, I guess you know Katy Miller?"

"Yes."

There was a moment of silence. He probably remembered that I'd dated her older sister and what fate had befallen her. "She asked me to call you."

"What's the problem?"

"I found Katy on the Mount Pleasant playground with a half-empty bottle of Absolut. She's totally blitzed. I was going to call her parents—"

"Forget that!" Katy shouted again. "I'm eighteen!"

"Right, whatever. Anyway, she asked me to call you instead. Hey, I remember when we were kids. We weren't perfect either, you know what I mean?"

"I do," I said.

And that was when Katy yelled something, and my body went rigid. I hoped that I'd heard wrong. But her words, and the almost mocking way she shouted them, worked like a cold hand pressed against the back of my neck.

"Idaho!" she yelled. "Am I right, Will? Idaho!"

I gripped the receiver, sure I heard wrong. "What is she saying?"

"I don't know. She keeps yelling out something about Idaho, but she's still pretty wasted."

Katy again: "Friggin' Idaho! Potato! Idaho! I'm right, aren't I?"

My breath had gone shallow.

"Look, Will, I know it's late, but can you come down and get her?"

I found my voice enough to say, "I'm on my way."

31

Squares crept up the stairs rather than risk the noise from the elevator waking Wanda.

The Yoga Squared Corporation owned the building. He and Wanda lived on the two floors above the yoga studio. It was three in the morning. Squares slid open the door. The lights were out. He stepped into the room. The streetlights provided harsh slivers of illumination.

Wanda sat on the couch in the dark. Her arms and legs were crossed.

"Hey," he said very softly, as if afraid of waking someone up, though there was no one else in the building.

"Do you want me to get rid of it?" she said.

Squares wished that he had kept his sunglasses on. "I'm really tired, Wanda. Just let me grab a few hours of sleep."

"No."

"What do you want me to say here?"

"I'm still in the first trimester. All I'd have to do is swallow a pill. So I want to know. Do you want to get rid of it?"

"So all of a sudden it's up to me?"

"I'm waiting."

"I thought you were the great feminist, Wanda. What about a woman's right to choose?"

"Don't hand me that crap."

Squares jammed his hands in his pockets. "What do you want to do?"

Wanda turned her head to the side. He could see the profile, the long neck, the proud bearing. He loved her. He had never loved anyone before, and no one had ever loved him either. When he was very small, his mother liked to burn him with her curling iron. She finally stopped when he was two years old—on the very day, coincidentally, that his father beat her to death and hung himself in a closet.

"You wear your past on your forehead," Wanda said. "We don't all have that luxury."

"I don't know what you mean."

Neither of them had turned on the light. Their eyes were adjusting, but everything was a murky haze and maybe that made it easier.

Wanda said, "I was valedictorian of my high school class."

"I know."

She closed her eyes. "Let me just say this, okay?"

Squares nodded for her to proceed.

"I grew up in a wealthy suburb. There were very few black families. I was the only black girl in my class of three hundred. And I was ranked first. I had my pick of colleges. I chose Princeton."

He knew all this already, but he said nothing.

"When I got there, I started to feel like I didn't measure up. I won't go into the whole diagnosis, about my lack of self-worth and all that. But I stopped eating. I lost weight. I became anorexic. I wouldn't eat anything I couldn't get rid of. I would do sit-ups all day. I dropped under ninety pounds and I would still look at myself in the mirror and hate the fatty who stared back at me."

Squares moved closer to her. He wanted to take her hand. But idiot that he was, he did not.

"I starved myself to the point where I had to be hospitalized. I damaged my organs. My liver, my heart, the doctors still are not sure how much. I never went into cardiac arrest, but for a while, I think I was pretty close. I eventually recovered—I won't go into that either—but the doctors told me that I'd probably never get pregnant. And if I did, I'd most likely not be able to carry to term."

Squares stood over her. "And what does your doctor say now?" he asked.

"She makes no promises." Wanda looked at him. "I've never been so scared in my life."

He felt his heart crumble in his chest. He wanted to sit next to her and put his arms around her. But again something held him back and he hated himself for it. "If going through with this is a risk to your health—" he began.

"Then it's my risk," she said.

He tried to smile. "The great feminist returns."

"When I said I was scared, I wasn't just talking about my health."

He knew that.

"Squares?"

"Yeah."

Her voice was nearly a plea. "Don't shut me out, okay?"

He did not know what to say, so he settled for the obvious. "It's a big step."

"I know."

"I don't think," he said slowly, "that I'm equipped to handle it."

"I love you."

"I love you too."

"You're the strongest man I've ever known."

Squares shook his head. Some drunk on the street started scream-singing that love grows where his Rosemary goes and nobody knows but him. Wanda uncrossed her arms and waited.

"Maybe," Squares began, "we shouldn't go through with this. For the sake of your health, if nothing else."

Wanda watched him step back and away. Before she could reply, he was gone.

I rented a car at a twenty-four-hour place on 37th Street and drove out to the Livingston police station. I had not been in these hallowed halls since the

Burnet Hill Elementary School class trip when I was in first grade. On that sunny morning, we were not allowed to see the station's holding cell where I now found Katy because, like tonight, someone had been in it. The idea of that—that maybe a big-time criminal was locked up just yards from where we stood—was about as cool an idea as a first-grader can wrap his brain around.

Detective Tim Daniels greeted me with too firm a handshake. I noticed that he hoisted his belt a lot. He jangled—or his keys or cuffs or whatever did—whenever he walked. His build was beefier than in his youth, but his face remained smooth and unblemished.

I filled out some paperwork and Katy was released into my custody. She had sobered up in the hour it took me to get out there. There was no laugh in her now. Her head hung low. Her face had taken on a classic teenage-sullen posture.

I thanked Tim again. Katy did not even attempt a smile or wave. We started for the car, but when we were out in the night air, she grabbed my arm.

"Let's take a walk," Katy said.

"It's four in the morning. I'm tired."

"I'll throw up if I sit in a car."

I stopped. "Why were you yelling about Idaho on the phone?"

But Katy was already crossing Livingston Avenue. I started after her. She picked up speed as she reached the town circle. I caught up.

"Your parents are going to be worried," I said.

"I told them I was staying with a friend. It's okay."

"You want to tell me why you were drinking alone."

Katy kept walking. Her breathing grew deeper. "I was thirsty."

"Uh-huh. And why were you yelling about Idaho?"

She looked at me but didn't break stride. "I think you know."

I grabbed her arm. "What kind of game are you playing here?"

"I'm not the one playing games here, Will."

"What are you talking about?"

"Idaho, Will. Your Sheila Rogers was from Idaho, right?"

Again her words hit me like a body blow. "How did you know that?"

"I read it."

"In the paper?"

She chuckled. "You really don't know?"

I took hold of her shoulders. "What are you talking about?"

"Where did your Sheila go to college?" she asked.

"I don't know."

"I thought you two were madly in love."

"It's complicated."

"I bet it is."

"I still don't understand, Katy."

"Sheila Rogers went to Haverton, Will. With Julie. They were in the same sorority."

I stood, stunned. "That's not possible."

"I can't believe you don't know. Sheila never told you?"

I shook my head. "Are you sure?"

"Sheila Rogers of Mason, Idaho. Majored in communications. It's all in the sorority booklet. I found it in an old trunk in the basement."

"I don't get it. You remembered her name after all these years?"

"Yeah."

"How come? I mean, do you remember the name of everyone in Julie's sorority?"

"No."

"So why would you remember Sheila Rogers?"

"Because," Katy said, "Sheila and Julie were roommates."

32

Squares arrived at my apartment with bagels and spreads from a place cleverly christened La Bagel on 15th and First. It was ten a.m., and Katy was sleeping on the couch. Squares lit up a cigarette. I noticed that he was still wearing the same clothes from last night. This was not easy to discern—it was not as though Squares was a leading figure in the haut monde community—but this morning he looked extra disheveled. We sat at the stools by the kitchen counter.

"Hey," I said, "I know you want to blend in with the street people but . . ."

He took a plate out of a cabinet. "You going to keep wowing me with the funny lines, or are you going to tell me what happened?"

"Is there a reason I can't do both?"

He lowered his head and again looked at me over the sunglasses. "That bad?"

"Worse," I said.

Katy stirred on the couch. I heard her say "Ouch." I had the extra-strength Tylenol at the ready. I handed her two with a glass of water. She downed them and stumbled toward the shower. I returned to the stool.

"How does your nose feel?" Squares asked.

"Like my heart moved up there and is trying to thump its way out."

He nodded and took a bite out of a bagel with lox spread. He chewed slowly. His shoulders drooped. I knew that he had not stayed home that night. I knew that something had happened between him and Wanda. And mostly, I knew that he did not want me to ask about it.

"You were saying about worse?" he prompted.

"Sheila lied to me," I said.

"We knew that already."

"Not like this."

He kept chewing.

"She knew Julie Miller. They were sorority sisters in college. Roommates even."

He stopped chewing. "Come again?"

I told him what I'd learned. The shower stayed on the whole time. I imagined that Katy would ache from the alcohol aftereffects for some time yet. Then again, the young recuperate faster than the rest of us.

When I finished filling him in, Squares leaned back, crossed his arms, and grinned. "Styling," he said.

"Yeah. Yeah, that's the word that came to my mind too."

"I don't get it, man." He started spreading another bagel. "Your old girlfriend, who was murdered eleven years ago, was college roommates with your most recent girlfriend, who was also murdered."

"Yes."

"And your brother was blamed for the first murder."

"Yes again."

"Okay, yeah." Squares nodded confidently. Then: "I still don't get it."

"It had to be a setup somehow," I said.

"What was a setup?"

"Sheila and me." I tried to shrug. "It must have all been a setup. A lie."

He made a yes-and-no gesture with his head. His long hair fell onto his face. He pushed it back. "To what end?"

"I don't know."

"Think about it."

"I have," I said. "All night."

"Okay, suppose you're right. Suppose Sheila did lie to you or, I don't know, set you up somehow. You with me?"

"With you."

He raised both palms. "To what end?"

"Again I don't know."

"Then let's go through the possibilities," Squares said. He raised his finger. "One, it could be a giant coincidence."

I just looked at him.

"Hold up, you dated Julie Miller, what, more than twelve years ago?"

"Yes."

"So maybe Sheila didn't remember. I mean, do you remember the name of every friend's ex? Maybe Julie never talked about you. Or maybe Sheila just forgot your name. And then years later you two meet . . ."

I just looked at him some more.

"Yeah, okay, that's pretty begging," he agreed. "Let's forget that. Possibility two"—Squares raised another finger, paused, looked up in the air—"hell, I'm lost here."

"Right."

We ate. He mulled it over some more. "Okay, let's assume that Sheila knew exactly who you were from the beginning."

"Let's."

"I still don't get it, man. What are we left with here?"

"Styling," I replied.

The shower stopped. I picked up a poppy-seed bagel. The seeds stuck to my hand.

"I've been thinking about it all night," I said.

"And?"

"And I keep coming back to New Mexico."

"How so?"

"The FBI wanted to question Sheila about an unsolved double murder in Albuquerque."

"So?"

"Years earlier, Julie Miller was also murdered."

"Also unsolved," Squares said, "though they suspect your brother."

"Yes."

"You see a connection between the two," Squares said.

"There has to be."

Squares nodded. "Okay, I see point A and I see point B. But I don't see how you get from one to the other."

"Neither," I said, "do I."

We grew silent. Katy peeked her head through the doorway. Her face had that morning-after pallor. She groaned and said, "I just upchucked again."

"Appreciate the update," I said.

"Where's my clothes?"

"The bedroom closet," I said.

She gestured an in-pain thank-you and closed the door. I looked at the right side of the couch, the spot where Sheila liked to read. How could this be happening? The old adage "Better to have loved and lost than to never have loved at all" came to me. I wondered about that. But more than that, I wondered what was worse—to lose the love of a lifetime or to realize that maybe she never loved you at all.

Some choice.

The phone rang. This time I did not wait for the machine. I lifted the receiver and said hello.

"Will?"

"Yes?"

"It's Yvonne Sterno," she said. "Albuquerque's answer to Jimmy Olsen."

"What have you got?"

"I've been up all night working on this."

"And?"

"And it keeps getting weirder."

"I'm listening."

"Okay, I got my contact to go through the deeds and tax records. Now understand that my contact is a government employee, and I got her to go in during her off hours. You usually have a better chance of turning water into wine or having my uncle pick up a check than getting a government employee to show up—"

"Yvonne?" I interrupted.

"Yeah?"

"Assume that I'm already impressed by your resourcefulness. Tell me what you got."

"Yeah, okay, you're right," she said. I heard papers being shuffled. "The murder-scene house was leased by a corporation called Cripco."

"And they are?"

"Untraceable. It's a shell. They don't seem to do anything."

I thought about that.

"Owen Enfield also had a car. A gray Honda Accord. Also leased by the fine folks at Cripco."

"Maybe he worked for them."

"Maybe. I'm trying to check that now."

"Where's the car now?"

"That's another interesting thing," Yvonne said. "The police found it abandoned in a mall in Lacida. That's about two hundred miles east of here."

"So where is Owen Enfield?"

"My guess? He's dead. For all we know, he was one of the victims."

"And the woman and little girl? Where are they?"

"No clue. Hell, I don't even know who they are."

"Did you talk to the neighbors?"

"Yes. It's like I said before: No one knew much about them."

"How about a physical description?"

"Ah."

"Ah what?"

"That's what I wanted to talk to you about."

Squares kept eating, but I could tell he was listening. Katy was still in my room, either dressing or making another offering to the porcelain gods.

"The descriptions were pretty vague," Yvonne continued. "The woman was in her mid-thirties, attractive, and a brunette. That's about as much as any of the neighbors could tell me. No one knew the little girl's name. She was around eleven or twelve with sandy-brown hair. One neighbor described her as cute as a button, but what kid that age isn't? Mr. Enfield was described as six feet with a gray crew cut and goatee. Forty years old, more or less."

"Then he wasn't one of the victims," I said.

"How do you know?"

"I saw a photo of the crime scene."

"When?"

"When I was questioned by the FBI about my girlfriend's whereabouts."

"You could see the victims?"

"Not clearly, but enough to know that neither had a crew cut."

"Hmm. Then the whole family has up and vanished."

"Yes."

"There's one other thing, Will."

"What's that?"

"Stonepointe is a new community. Everything is fairly self-contained."

"Meaning?"

"Are you familiar with QuickGo, the convenience store chain?"

"Sure," I said. "We have QuickGos out here too."

Squares took off his sunglasses and looked a question at me. I shrugged and he moved toward me.

"Well, there's a big QuickGo at the edge of the complex," Yvonne said. "Almost all the residents use it."

"So?"

"One of the neighbors swore she saw Owen Enfield there at three o'clock on the day of the murders."

"I'm not following you, Yvonne."

"Well," she said, "the thing is, all the QuickGos have security cameras." She paused. "You following me now?"

"Yeah, I think so."

"I already checked," she went on. "They keep them for a month before they tape over them."

"So if we can get that tape," I began, "we might be able to get a good view of Mr. Enfield."

"Big if, though. The store manager was firm. There was no way he was going to turn anything over to me."

"There has to be a way," I said.

"I'm open to ideas, Will."

Squares put his hand on my shoulder. "What?"

I covered the mouthpiece and filled him in. "You know anybody connected to QuickGo?" I said.

"Incredible as this might sound, the answer is nope."

Damn. We mulled it over for a bit. Yvonne started humming the QuickGo jingle, one of those torturous tunes that enters through the ear canal and proceeds to ricochet around the skull in search of an escape route it will never find. I remembered the new commercial campaign, the one where they updated the old jingle by adding an electric guitar and a synthesizer and bass, and fronting the band with a big-time pop star simply known as Sonay.

Hold the phone. Sonay.

Squares looked at me. "What?"

"I think you may be able to help after all," I said.

33

Sheila and Julie had been members of Chi Gamma sorority. I still had the rent-a-car from my late-night sojourn to Livingston, so Katy and I decided to take the two-hour drive up to Haverton College in Connecticut and see what we could learn.

Earlier in the day, I called the Haverton registrar's office to do a little fact-checking. I'd learned that the sorority's housemother back then had been one Rose Baker. Ms. Baker had retired three years ago and moved into a campus house directly across the street. She was to be the main target of our pseudo-investigation.

We pulled in front of the Chi Gamma house. I remembered it from my too-infrequent visits during my Amherst College days. You could tell right off that it was a sorority house. It had that antebellum, faux Greco-Roman-columns-thing going on, all in white, and with soft ruffled edges that gave the whole edifice a feminine feel. Something about it reminded me of a wedding cake.

Rose Baker's residence was, to speak kindly, more modest. The house had started life as a small Cape Cod, but somewhere along the way the lines had been ironed flat. The one-time red color was now a dull clay. The window lace looked cat-shredded. Shingles had flaked off as if the house had an acute case of seborrhea.

Under normal circumstances, I would have made an appointment of some kind. On TV, they never do that. The detective shows up and the person is always home. I always found that both unrealistic and unwieldy, yet perhaps now I understood a little better. First off, the chatty lady in the registrar's office informed me that Rose Baker rarely left home, and when she did, she rarely strayed far. Second—and I think, more important—if I called Rose Baker and she asked me why I wanted to see her, what would I say? Hi, let's talk murder? No, better just to show up with Katy and see where that got us. If she was not in, we could always explore the archives in the library or visit the sorority house. I had no idea what good any of this would do, but hey, we were just flying blind here.

As we approached Rose Baker's door, I could not help but feel a pang of envy for the knapsack-laden students I saw walking to and fro. I'd loved college. I loved everything about it. I loved hanging out with sloppy slacker friends. I loved living on my own, doing laundry too rarely, eating pepperoni pizza at midnight. I loved chatting with the accessible, hippielike professors. I loved debating lofty issues and harsh realities that never, ever, penetrated the green of our campus.

When we reached the overly cheerful welcome mat, I heard a familiar song wafting through the wooden portal. I made a face and listened closer. The sound was muffled, but it sounded like Elton John—more specifically, his song "Candle in the Wind" from the classic *Goodbye Yellow Brick Road* double album. I knocked on the door.

A woman's voice chimed, "Just a minute."

A few seconds later, the door opened. Rose Baker was probably in her seventies and dressed, I was surprised to see, for a funeral. Her wardrobe, from the big-brimmed hat with matching veil to the sensible shoes, was black. Her rouge looked as if it'd been liberally applied via an aerosol can. Her mouth formed a nearly perfect "O" and her eyes were big red saucers, as if her face had frozen immediately after being startled.

"Mrs. Baker?" I said.

She lifted the veil. "Yes?"

"My name is Will Klein. This is Katy Miller."

The saucer eyes swiveled toward Katy and locked into position.

"Is this a bad time?" I asked.

She seemed surprised by the question. "Not at all."

I said, "We'd like to speak with you, if that's okay."

"Katy Miller," she repeated, her eyes still on her.

"Yes, ma'am," I said.

"Julie's sister."

It was not a question, but Katy nodded anyway. Rose Baker pushed open the screen door. "Please come in."

We followed her into the living room. Katy and I stopped short, taken aback by what we saw.

It was Princess Di.

She was everywhere. The entire room was sheathed, blanketed, overrun with Princess Di paraphernalia. There were photographs, of course, but also tea sets, commemorative plates, embroidered pillows, lamps, figurines, books, thimbles, shot glasses (how respectful), a toothbrush (eeuw!), a night-light, sunglasses, salt-'n-pepper shakers, you name it. I realized that the song I was hearing was not the original Elton John–Bernie Taupin classic, but the more recent Princess Di tribute version, the lyrics now offering a good-bye to our "English rose." I had read somewhere that the Di-tribute version was the biggest-selling single in world history. That said something, though I was not sure I wanted to know what.

Rose Baker said, "Do you remember when Princess Diana died?"

I looked at Katy. She looked at me. We both nodded yes.

"Do you remember the way the world mourned?"

She looked at us some more. And we nodded again.

"For most people, the grief, the mourning, it was just a fad. They did it for a few days, maybe a week or two. And then"—she snapped her fingers, magician style, her saucer eyes bigger than ever—"it was over for them. Like she never existed at all."

She looked at us and waited for clucks of agreement. I tried not to make a face.

"But for some of us, Diana, Princess of Wales, well, she really was an angel. Too good for this world maybe. We won't ever forget her. We keep the light burning."

She dabbed her eye. A sarcastic rejoinder came to my lips, but I bit it back.

"Please," she said. "Have a seat. Would you care for some tea?"

Katy and I both politely declined.

"A biscuit, then?"

She produced a plate with cookies in the shape of, yup, Princess Diana's profile. Sprinkles formed the crown. We begged off, neither of us much in the mood to nibble on dead Di. I decided to start right in.

"Mrs. Baker," I said, "you remember Katy's sister, Julie?"

"Yes, of course." She put down the plate of cookies. "I remember all of the girls. My husband, Frank—he taught English here—died in 1969. We had no children. My family had all passed away. That sorority house, those girls, for twenty-six years they were my life."

"I see," I said.

"And Julie, well, late at night, when I lay in bed in the dark, her face comes to me more than most. Not just because she was a special child—oh, and she was—but of course, because of what happened to her."

"You mean her murder?" It was a dumb thing to say, but I was new at this. I just wanted to keep her talking.

"Yes." Rose Baker reached out and took Katy's hand. "Such a tragedy. I'm so sorry for your loss."

Katy said, "Thank you."

Uncharitable as this might sound, my mind could not help but think: Tragedy, yes, but where was Julie's image—or the image of Rose Baker's husband or family, for that matter—in this swirling potpourri of royal grief?

"Mrs. Baker, do you remember another sorority sister named Sheila Rogers?" I asked.

Her face pinched up and her voice was short. "Yes." She shifted primly. "Yes, I do."

From her reaction, it was pretty obvious that she had not heard about the murder. I decided not to tell her yet. She clearly had a problem with Sheila, and I wanted to know what it was. We needed honesty here. If I were to tell her that Sheila was dead now, she might sugarcoat her answers. Before I could follow up, Mrs. Baker held up her hand. "May I ask you a question?"

"Of course."

"Why are you asking me all this now?" She looked at Katy. "It all happened so long ago."

Katy took that one. "I'm trying to find the truth."

"The truth about what?"

"My sister changed while she was here."

Rose Baker closed her eyes. "You don't need to hear this, child."

"Yes," Katy said, and the desperation in her voice was palpable enough to knock out a window. "Please. We need to know."

Rose Baker kept her eyes closed for another moment or two. Then she nodded to herself and opened them. She folded her hands and put them in her lap. "How old are you?"

"Eighteen."

"About the age Julie was when she first came here." Rose Baker smiled. "You look like her."

"So I've been told."

"It's a compliment. Julie lit up a room. In many ways she reminds me of Diana herself. Both of them were beautiful. Both of them were special—almost divine." She smiled and wagged a finger. "Ah, and both had a wild streak. Both were inordinately stubborn. Julie was a good person. Kind, smart as a whip. She was an excellent student."

"Yet," I said, "she dropped out."

"Yes."

"Why?"

She turned her eyes on me. "Princess Di tried to be firm. But no one can control the winds of fate. They blow as they may."

Katy said, "I'm not following you."

A Princess Di clock chimed the hour, the sound a hollow imitation of Big Ben. Rose Baker waited for it to grow silent again. Then she said, "College changes people. Your first time away, your first time on your own . . ." She drifted off, and for a moment I thought I'd have to nudge her into continuing. "I'm not saying this right. Julie was fine at first, but then she, well, she started to withdraw. From all of us. She cut classes. She broke up with her hometown boyfriend. Not that that was unusual. Almost all the girls do first year. But in her case, it came so late. Junior year, I think. I thought she really loved him."

I swallowed, kept still.

"Earlier," Rose Baker said, "you asked me about Sheila Rogers."

Katy said, "Yes."

"She was a bad influence."

"How so?"

"When Sheila joined us that same year"—Rose put a finger to her chin and tilted her head as if a new idea had just forced its way in—"well, maybe she was the winds of fate. Like the paparazzi that made Diana's limousine speed up. Or that awful driver, Henri Paul. Did you know that his blood alcohol level was three times the legal limit?"

"Sheila and Julie became friends?" I tried.

"Yes."

"Roommates, right?"

"For a time, yes." Her eyes were moist now. "I don't want to sound melodramatic, but Sheila Rogers brought something bad to Chi Gamma. I should have thrown her out. I know that now. But I had no proof of wrongdoing."

"What did she do?"

She shook her head again.

I thought about it for a moment. Junior year, Julie had visited me at Amherst. I, on the other hand, had been discouraged from coming down to Haverton, which was a little strange. I flashed back to the last time Julie and I had been together. She had set up a quiet getaway at a bed and breakfast in Mystic instead of having us stay on campus. At the time, I'd thought it romantic. Now, of course, I knew better.

Three weeks later, Julie called and broke it off with me. But looking back on it now, I remembered that she had been acting both lethargic and strange during that visit. We were in Mystic only one night and even as we made love, I could feel her fading away from me. She blamed it on her studies, said that she'd been cramming big-time. I bought it because, in hindsight, I wanted to.

When I now added it all together, the solution was fairly obvious. Sheila had come here straight from the abuse of Louis Castman and drugs and the streets. That life is not so easy to leave behind. My guess was, she dragged some of that decay with her. It does not take much to poison the well. Sheila arrives at the start of Julie's junior year, Julie begins to act erratically.

It made sense.

I tried another tack. "Did Sheila Rogers graduate?"

"No, she dropped out too."

"The same time as Julie?"

"I'm not even sure either of them officially dropped out. Julie just stopped going to class toward the end of the year. She stayed in her room a lot. She slept past noon. When I confronted her"—her voice caught—"she moved out."

"Where did she move to?"

"An apartment off campus. Sheila stayed there too."

"So when exactly did Sheila Rogers drop out?"

Rose Baker pretended to think about it. I say pretend, because I could see that she knew the answer right away and that this act was somehow for our benefit. "I think Sheila left after Julie died."

"How long after?" I asked.

She kept her eyes down. "I don't remember ever seeing her after the murder."

I looked at Katy. Her eyes, too, were on the floor. Rose Baker put a trembling hand to her mouth.

"Do you know where Sheila went?" I asked.

"No. She was gone. That was all that mattered."

She would not look at us anymore. I found that troubling.

"Mrs. Baker?"

She still would not face me.

"Mrs. Baker, what else happened?"

"Why are you here?" she asked.

"We told you. We wanted to know—"

"Yes, but why now?"

Katy and I looked at each other. She nodded. I turned to Rose Baker and said, "Yesterday, Sheila Rogers was found dead. She was murdered."

I thought that maybe she had not heard me. Rose Baker kept her gaze locked on a black-velvet Diana, a grotesque and frightening reproduction. Diana's teeth were blue, and her skin looked like a bad bottle-tan. Rose stared at the image and I started thinking again about the fact that there were no pictures of her husband or her family or her sorority girls—only this dead stranger from overseas. And I wondered about how I was dealing with all this death, how I kept chasing shadows to divert the pain, and I wondered if maybe there was something like that going on here too.

"Mrs. Baker?"

"Was she strangled like the others?"

"No," I said. And then I stopped. I turned to Katy. She had heard it too. "Did you say others?"

"Yes."

"What others?"

"Julie was strangled," she said.

"Right."

Her shoulders slumped. The wrinkles on her face seemed more pronounced now, the crevices sinking deeper into the flesh. Our visit had unleashed demons she had stuffed in boxes or maybe buried beneath the Di accoutrements. "You don't know about Laura Emerson, do you?"

Katy and I exchanged another glance. "No," I said.

Rose Baker's eyes started darting across the walls again. "Are you sure you won't have some tea?"

"Please, Mrs. Baker. Who is Laura Emerson?"

She stood and hobbled over to the fireplace mantel. Her fingers reached out and gently touched down on a ceramic bust of Di. "Another sorority sister," she said. "Laura was a year behind Julie."

"What happened to her?" I asked.

She found a piece of dirt stuck on the ceramic bust. She used her nail to scratch it off. "Laura was found dead near her home in North Dakota eight months before Julie. She'd been strangled too."

Icy hands were grabbing at my legs, pulling me back under. Katy's face was white. She shrugged at me, letting me know that this was new to her too.

"Did they ever find her killer?" I asked.

"No," Rose Baker said. "Never."

I tried to sift through it, process this new data, get a grip on what this all meant. "Mrs. Baker, did the police question you after Julie's murder?"

"Not the police," she said.

"But someone did?"

She nodded. "Two men from the FBI."

"Do you remember their names?"

"No."

"Did they ask you about Laura Emerson?"

"No. But I told them anyway."

"What did you say?"

"I reminded them that another girl had been strangled."

"How did they react to that?"

"They told me that I should keep that to myself. That saying something could compromise the investigation."

Too fast, I thought. This was all coming at me too fast. It would not compute. Three young women were dead. Three women from the same sorority house. That was a pattern if ever I saw one. A pattern meant that Julie's murder was not the random, solo act of violence that the FBI had led us—and the world—to believe.

And worst of all, the FBI knew it. They had lied to us all these years.

The question now was, why.

34

Man, I had a good head of steam going. I wanted to explode into Pistillo's office. I wanted to burst in and grab him by the lapels and demand answers. But real life does not work that way. Route 95 was littered with construction delays. We hit terrible traffic on the Cross Bronx Expressway. The Harlem River Drive crawled like a wounded soldier. I leaned on the horn and swerved in and out of lanes, but in New York, that just raises you to average.

Katy used her cell phone to call her friend Ronnie, who she said was good with computers. Ronnie checked out Laura Emerson on the Internet, pretty much confirming what we already knew. She'd been strangled eight months before Julie. Her body had been found at the Court Manor Motor Lodge in Fessenden, North Dakota. The murder received extensive though vague local coverage for two weeks before fading off the front page and into stardust. There was no mention of sexual assault.

I veered hard off the exit, drove through a red light, found the Kinney parking lot near Federal Plaza, pulled in. We hurried toward the building. I kept my head high and my feet in motion, but alas, there was a security checkpoint. We had to walk through a metal detector. My keys set it off. I emptied my pockets. Now it was my belt. The guard ran a wand that looked like a vibrator over my persons. Okay, we were cleared.

When we reached Pistillo's office, I demanded to see him in my firmest voice. His secretary appeared unintimidated. She smiled with the genuineness of a politician's wife and sweetly asked us to have a seat. Katy looked at me and shrugged. I would not sit. I paced like a caged lion, but I could feel my fury ebbing.

Fifteen minutes later, the secretary told us that Assistant Director in Charge Joseph Pistillo—that was exactly how she said it, with the full title—would see us now. She opened the door. I blasted into the office.

Pistillo was already standing and at the ready. He gestured at Katy. "Who is this?"

"Katy Miller," I said.

He looked stunned. He said to her, "What are you doing with him?"

But I was not about to be sidetracked. "Why didn't you ever say anything about Laura Emerson?"

He turned back to me. "Who?"

"Don't insult me, Pistillo."

Pistillo waited a beat. Then he said, "Why don't we all sit?"

"Answer my question."

He lowered himself into his seat, his eyes never leaving me. His desk looked shiny and sticky. The smell of lemon Pledge clawed at the air.

"You're in no position to make demands," he said.

"Laura Emerson was strangled eight months before Julie."

"So?"

"Both of them were from the same sorority house."

Pistillo steepled his fingers. He played the wait game and won.

I said, "Are you going to tell me you didn't know about it?"

"Oh, I knew."

"And you don't see a connection?"

"That's correct."

His eyes were steady, but he was practiced at this.

"You can't be serious," I said.

He let his gaze wander the walls now. There was not much to look at it. There was a photograph of President Bush and an American flag and a few diplomas. That was pretty much it. "We looked into it at the time, of course. I think the local media picked up on it too. They might have even run something—I don't remember anymore. But in the end none of them saw a true connection."

"You have to be kidding."

"Laura Emerson was strangled in another state at another time. There were no signs of rape or sexual assault. She was found in a motel. Julie"—he turned to Katy—"your sister was found in her home."

"And the fact that they both belonged to the same sorority?"

"A coincidence."

"You're lying," I said.

He did not like that, and his face reddened a shade. "Watch it," he said, pointing a beefy finger in my direction. "You have no standing here."

"Are you telling us that you saw no link between the murders?"

"That's right."

"And what about now, Pistillo?"

"What about now?"

The rage was building back up again. "Sheila Rogers was a member of that sorority too. Is that another coincidence?"

That caught him off guard. He leaned back, trying to get some distance. Was it because he didn't know or because he didn't think I'd find out about it? "I'm not going to talk to you about an ongoing investigation."

"You knew," I said slowly. "And you knew that my brother was innocent."

He shook his head, but there was nothing behind it. "I knew—correction: know—nothing of the sort."

But I did not believe him. He had been lying from the start. Of that I was now certain. He stiffened as though bracing for my next outburst. But, to my surprise, my voice grew suddenly soft.

"Do you realize what you've done?" I said, barely a whisper. "The damage to my family. My father, my mother . . . ?"

"This doesn't involve you, Will."

"Like hell it doesn't."

"Please," he said. "Both of you. Stay out of this."

I stared at him. "No."

"For your own sakes. You're not going to believe this, but I'm trying to protect you."

"From?"

He did not reply.

"From?" I repeated.

He slapped the arms of his chair and stood. "This conversation is over."

"What do you really want with my brother, Pistillo?"

"I'm not going to comment any further on an ongoing investigation." He moved toward the door. I tried to block his path. He gave me his hardest look and walked around me. "You stay away from my investigation, or I'll arrest you for hindering."

"Why are you trying to frame him?"

Pistillo stopped and turned around. I saw something change his demeanor. A straightening of the spine maybe. A quick flicker in the eyes. "You want to get into truths, Will?"

I did not like his change of tone. I suddenly wasn't sure of the answer. "Yes."

"Then," he said slowly, "let's start with you."

"What about me?"

"You've always been so convinced your brother was innocent," he continued, his posture more aggressive now. "How come?"

"Because I know him."

"Really? So how close were you and Ken near the end?"

"We were always close."

"Saw him often, did you?"

I shuffled my feet. "You don't have to see someone a lot to be close."

"Is that a fact? So tell us, Will: Who do you think killed Julie Miller?"

"I don't know."

"Well then, let's examine what you think happened, shall we?" Pistillo strode toward me. Somewhere along the way, I had lost the upper hand. There was fire in his belly now, and I had no idea why. He stopped just close enough to start invading my space. "Your dear brother, the one you were so close to, had sexual relations with your old girlfriend the night of the murder. Isn't that your theory, Will?"

I might have squirmed. "Yes."

"Your ex-girlfriend and your brother doing the nasty." He made a tsk-tsk noise. "That must have infuriated you."

"What are you babbling about?"

"The truth, Will. We want to deal in truths, right? So come on, let's all put our cards on the table." His eyes stayed on me, level and cool. "Your brother comes home for the first time in, what, two years. And what does he do? He strolls down the block and has intercourse with the girl you loved."

"We'd broken up," I said, though even I could hear the whiny weakness in my own voice.

He gave a small smirk. "Sure, that always ends it, doesn't it? Open season on her after that—especially for a beloved brother." Pistillo stayed in my face. "You claim that you saw someone that night. Someone mysteriously lurking around the Miller house."

"That's right."

"How exactly did you see him?"

"What do you mean?" I asked. But I knew.

"You said you saw someone by the Miller house, correct?"

"Yes."

Pistillo smiled and spread his hands. "But you see, you never told us what *you* were doing there that night, Will." He said it in a casual, almost singsong voice. "You, Will. Outside the Miller house. Alone. Late at night. With your brother and your ex alone inside . . ."

Katy turned and looked at me.

"I was taking a walk," I said quickly.

Pistillo paced, pressing his advantage. "Uh-huh, sure, okay, so let's see if we got this straight. Your brother is having sex with the girl you still loved. You happen to be taking a walk by her house that night. She ends up dead. We find your brother's blood at the scene. And you, Will, *know* that your brother didn't do it."

He stopped and gave me the grin again. "So if you were the investigating officer, who would you suspect?"

A large stone was crushing my chest. I could not speak.

"If you're suggesting . . ."

"I'm suggesting you go home," Pistillo said. "That's all. Go home, both of you, and stay the hell out of this."

35

Pistillo offered to find Katy a ride home. She declined and said that she would stay with me. He didn't like that, but what could he do?

We drove back to the apartment in silence. Once inside, I showed her my impressive collection of takeout menus. She ordered Chinese. I ran downstairs and picked it up. We spread the white boxes out on the table. I sat in my usual seat. Katy sat in Sheila's. I flashed back to Chinese with Sheila—her hair tied back, fresh out of the shower and smelling sweet, in that terry-cloth robe, the freckles on her chest . . .

It was odd what you would always remember.

The grief roared back at me in high, crippling waves. Whenever I stopped moving, it hit me hard and deep. Grief wears you down. If you don't guard against it, it will exhaust you past the point of caring.

I dumped some fried rice on my plate and followed it up with a dash of lobster sauce. "Are you sure you still want to stay tonight?"

Katy nodded.

"I'll give you the bedroom," I said.

"I'd rather sleep on the couch."

"You sure?"

"Positive."

We pretended to eat.

"I didn't kill Julie," I said.

"I know."

We pretended to eat some more.

She finally asked, "Why were you there that night?"

I tried to smile. "You don't buy that I was taking a walk?"

"No."

I put down the chopsticks as if they could shatter. I wondered how to explain this, here in my apartment, talking to the sister of the woman I once loved, sitting in the chair of the woman I'd wanted to marry. Both murdered. Both connected to me. I looked up and said, "I guess that maybe I wasn't really over Julie."

"You wanted to see her?"

"Yes."

"And?"

"I rang the bell," I said. "But nobody answered."

Katy thought about it. She looked down at her plate and tried to sound casual. "Your timing was strange."

I picked up the chopsticks.

"Will?"

I kept my head down.

"Did you know your brother was there?"

I moved the food around the plate. She lifted her head and watched me. I heard my neighbor open and close his door. A horn honked. Someone on the street was shouting in what might have been Russian.

"You knew," Katy said. "You knew Ken was at our house. With Julie."

"I didn't kill your sister."

"What happened, Will?"

I folded my arms across my chest. I leaned back, closed my eyes, tilted my head all the way back. I did not want to go back there, but what choice did I have? Katy wanted to know. She deserved to know.

"It was such a strange weekend," I began. "Julie and I had been broken up over a year. I hadn't seen her in all that time. I'd tried to bump into her on school breaks, but she never seemed to be around."

"She hadn't been home in a long while," Katy said.

I nodded. "The same with Ken. That was what made it all so bizarre. All of a sudden, all three of us are back in Livingston at the same time. I can't remember the last time that happened. Ken was acting strangely too. He was looking out the window all the time. He wouldn't leave the house. He was up to something. I don't know what. Anyway, he asked me if I was still hung up on Julie. I told him no. That we were history."

"You lied to him."

"It was like . . ." I tried to figure out how to explain this. "My brother was like a god to me. He was strong and brave and . . ." I shook my head. I was not saying this right. I started again. "When I was sixteen, my parents took the family on a trip to Spain. The Costa del Sol. The whole place was one big party scene. It was sort of like Florida spring break for the Europeans. Ken and I hung out at this one disco near our hotel. On our fourth night there, a guy bumped me on the dance floor. I looked over at him. He laughed at me. I went back to dancing. Then another guy bumped me. I tried to ignore him too. Then the first guy, he ran up to me and just pushed me down." I stopped, tried to blink away the memory as if it were sand in my eye. I looked at her. "Do you know what I did?"

She shook her head.

"I yelled for Ken. I didn't jump up. I didn't push the guy back. I yelled for my big brother and scrambled away."

"You were scared."

"Always," I said.

"That's natural."

I didn't think so.

"So did he come?" she asked.

"Of course."

"And?"

"A fight broke out. There was a big group of them from some Scandinavian country. Ken got the hell beat out of him."

"And you?"

"I never so much as threw a punch. I hung back and tried to reason with them, convince them to stop." The shame flushed my cheeks yet again. My brother, who had been in more than his share of fights, was right. A beating hurts for a little while. The shame of cowardice never leaves. "Ken broke his arm during the scuffle. His right arm. He was an incredible tennis player. Nationally ranked. Stanford was interested in him. His serve was never the same after that. He ended up not going to college."

"That's not your fault."

How wrong she was. "The point is, Ken always defended me. Sure, we fought the way brothers do. He'd tease me mercilessly. But he'd step in the way of a freight train to protect me. And me, I never had the courage to reciprocate."

Katy put her hand to her chin.

"What?" I said.

"It's odd, that's all."

"What is?"

"That your brother would be insensitive enough to sleep with Julie."

"It wasn't his fault. He asked me if I was over her. I told him I was."

"You gave him the green light," she said.

"Yes."

"But then you ended up following him."

"You don't understand," I said.

"No, I do," Katy said. "We all do stuff like that."

36

I fell into such a deep sleep that I never heard him sneak up on me.

I had found fresh sheets and blankets for Katy, made sure she was comfortable on the couch, taken a shower, tried to read. The words swam by in a murky haze. I'd go back and reread and re-forget the same paragraph over and over again. I signed on to the Internet and surfed. I did a few push-ups, sit-ups, yoga stretches Squares had taught me. I did not want to lie down. I did not want to stop, to let the grief catch me again unawares.

I was a worthy adversary, but eventually sleep managed to corner and take me down. I was out, falling in a totally dreamless pit, when I felt a jerk on my hand and heard the click. Still asleep, I tried to pull my hand back to my side, but it would not move.

Something metallic dug into my wrist.

My eyelids were fluttering open when he leapt on top of me. He landed hard, knocking the wind out of my lungs. I gulped as whoever he was straddled my chest. His knees pinned down my shoulders. Before I could mount any sort of serious struggle, my attacker yanked my free hand to the side above my head. I didn't hear the click this time, but I felt the cold metal close around my skin.

Both of my hands were cuffed to the bed.

My veins flooded with ice. For a moment I simply shut down, just as I always had during physical altercations. I opened my mouth, about to scream or at least say something. My attacker grabbed the back of my head and pulled me forward. Without hesitation, he ripped off a piece of duct tape and covered my mouth. Then, for good measure, he started winding a fresh band of tape around the back of my skull and over my mouth, ten maybe fifteen times, as if he were shrink-wrapping my head.

I could no longer speak or cry out. Breathing was a chore—I had to suck the air through my broken nose. It hurt like hell. My shoulders ached from the cuffs and his body weight. I struggled, which was totally futile. I tried to buck him off me. More futile. I wanted to ask him what he wanted, what he planned to do now that I was helpless.

And that was when I thought about Katy alone in the other room.

The bedroom was dark. My assailant was no more than a shadow to me. He wore a mask of some kind, something dark, but I could not see what, if anything, was on it. Breathing was becoming nearly impossible. I snorted through the pain.

Whoever he was, he finished taping my mouth. He hesitated for only a second before bouncing off me. And then, as I watched in helpless horror, he headed for the bedroom door, opened it, stepped into the room where Katy was sleeping, and closed the door behind him.

My eyes bulged. I tried to scream, but the tape muffled any sound. I bucked like a bronco. I kicked and flailed. No progress.

Then I stopped and listened. For a moment there was nothing. Pure silence.

And then Katy screamed.

Oh Christ. I bucked some more. Her scream had been brief, cut off midway, as though someone had turned off a switch. Panic took full flight now. Full, red-alert panic. I jerked hard on both cuffs. I twisted my head back and forth. Nothing.

Katy screamed again.

The sound was fainter this time—the gasp of a wounded animal. No way anyone would hear it, and even if they did, nobody would react. Not in New York. Not at this time of night. And even if they did—even if someone called the police or rushed to her rescue—it would be too late.

I freaked out then.

My sanity felt as though it were being torn in two. I went nuts. I thrashed around, seizure style. My nose hurt like hell. I swallowed some of the fibers from the duct tape. I struggled some more.

But I made no progress.

Oh God. Okay, calm down. Be cool. Think a second.

I turned my head toward my right cuff. It did not feel that tight. There was give there. Okay, maybe, if I went a little slower, I could pull my hand out. That was it. Calm down. Try to narrow your hand, squeeze it through.

So I tried. I tried to will my hand into something thinner. I rounded my palm by forcing the bottom of my thumb toward the bottom of my pinky. Then I pulled down, slowly at first, then with more force. No go. The skin bunched around the metal ring and then started ripping. I did not care. I kept pulling.

It wasn't working.

The other room had gone quiet.

I strained my ears for a sound. Any sound at all. Nothing. I tried to curl up my body, tried to lift myself off the bed so hard that, I don't know, maybe the bed would lift up too. Just an inch or two and then maybe it'd break on the way down. I bucked some more. The bed did indeed slide a few inches out. But it was not doing any good.

I was still trapped.

I heard Katy scream again. And in a scared, panic-filled voice, she shouted, "John—"

And then she was cut off again.

John, I thought. She'd said John.

Asselta?

The Ghost . . .

Oh no, please, oh God, no. I heard something muffled. Voices. A groan maybe. Like something being smothered by a pillow. My heart beat wildly against my rib cage. The fear struck at me from every angle. I flung my head from side to side, looked for something, anything.

The phone.

Could I . . . ? My legs were still free. Maybe I could swing them up, grab the phone with my feet, drop the receiver into my hand. From there I could, I don't know, maybe dial 911 or 0. My feet were already on the rise. I contracted the muscles in my abdomen, lifted my legs, swung them to the right. But I was still in hysteria mode. My weight teetered to the side. I lost control of my legs. I pulled back up, trying to regain balance, and when I did, my foot hit the phone.

The receiver clattered to the floor.

Damn.

Now what? My mind snapped—I mean, I totally lost it. I thought of animals caught in those claw traps, the ones who gnaw off a limb to escape. I thrashed to exhaustion, at my wit's end and about to give up, when I remembered something Squares had taught me.

Plow pose.

That's what it was called. In Hindu: Halāsana. You usually do it from a shoulder stand. You lie on your back and flip your legs all the way over your head as you lift your hips. Your toes would touch the floor behind your head. I did not know if I could go that far, but it didn't matter. I crunched my stomach and swung my legs up as hard as I could. I threw them back behind me. The balls of my feet thudded against the wall. My chest was up against my chin, making it harder than ever to breathe.

I pushed against the wall with my legs. The adrenaline kicked in. The bed slid away from the wall. I pushed some more, got enough room. Okay, good. Now for the hard part. If the cuffs were too tight, if they did not allow my wrists to turn within them, I would either not be able to make it or dislocate both shoulders. No matter.

Silence, dead silence, from the other room.

I let my legs fall toward the floor. I was doing, in effect, a back somersault off the bed. The weight of my legs gave me the momentum and—in a stroke of luck—my wrists turned in the cuffs. My feet landed hard. I went with it, scraping the front of my thighs and abdomen on the low headboard.

When I finished, I was standing up behind the bed.

My hands were still cuffed. My mouth was still taped. But I was standing. I felt another surge of adrenaline.

Okay, now what?

No time. I bent my knees. I lowered my shoulder to the back of the headboard and I drove the bed toward the door as if I were an offensive lineman and the bed was a tackle sled. My legs moved like pistons. I did not hesitate. I did not let up.

The bed crashed into the door.

The collision was jarring. Pain knifed down my shoulder, my arms, my spine. Something popped and hot pain flooded my joints. Ignoring it, I pulled back and rammed the door again. Then again. The tape made my scream audible only in my own ears. The third time, I pulled extra hard on both cuffs at the precise moment the bed made contact with the wall.

The bed rails gave way.

I was free.

I pushed the bed away from the door. I tried unwrapping the tape from my mouth, but it was taking too long. I grabbed the knob and turned it. I flung open the door and leapt into the darkness.

Katy was on the floor.

Her eyes were closed. Her body was limp. The man was straddling her chest. He had his hands on her throat.

He was choking her.

Without hesitation, I launched myself at him, rocketlike. It seemed to take me a long time to reach him, as if I were leaping through syrup. He saw me coming—had plenty of time to prepare—but it still meant that he would have to release her throat. He turned and faced me. I still couldn't see anything but a black outline. He grabbed hold of my shoulders, put his foot into my stomach, and using my own momentum, he simply rolled back.

I flew across the room. My arms windmilled in the air. But I lucked out again. Or so I thought. I landed on the soft reading chair. It wobbled for a second. Then it toppled over from my weight. My head bounced hard against the side table before banging to the floor.

I fought off the dizziness and tried to get to my knees. When I started rising for a second offensive, I saw something that terrified me like nothing before ever had.

The black-clad assailant was up too. He had a knife now. And he was heading toward Katy with it.

Everything slowed down. What happened next took no more than a second or two. But in my mind's eye, it happened in some alternate time warp. Time does that. It is indeed relative. Moments fly by. And moments freeze-frame.

I was too far away to reach him. I knew that. Even through the dizziness, through the blow from hitting my head on the table . . .

The table.

Where I'd placed Squares's gun.

Was there time to reach it and turn and fire? My eyes were still on Katy and her assailant. No. Not enough time. I knew that immediately.

The man bent over and grabbed Katy by the hair.

As I went for the gun, I pawed at the tape on my mouth. The tape shifted enough for me to shout, "Freeze or I'll shoot!"

His head turned in the dark. I was already scrambling on the floor. I moved flat on my stomach, crawling commando style. He saw that I was unarmed and turned back to finish what he had started. My hand found the gun. No time to aim. I pulled the trigger.

The man startled back from the sound.

That bought me time. I swung around with the gun, already pulling the trigger again. The man rolled back like a gymnast. I could still barely make him out, just a shadow. I started moving the gun toward the black mass, still firing. How many bullets did this thing hold? How many had I fired?

He jerked back, but kept on moving. Had I hit him?

The man jumped toward the door. I yelled for him to stop. He didn't. I considered firing into his back, but something, perhaps a fly-through of humanity, made me stop. He was already out the door. And I had bigger worries.

I looked down at Katy. She was not moving.

37

Another officer—the fifth, by my count—came to hear my story.

"I want to know how she is first," I said.

The doctor had stopped working on me. In the movies, the doctor always defends his patients. He tells the cop that they cannot question him right now, that he needs his rest. My doctor, an emergency room intern from, I think, Pakistan, had no such hang-up. He popped back my shoulder while they began their grilling. He poured iodine on my wrist wounds. He toyed with my nose. He took out a hacksaw—what a hospital was doing with a hacksaw I don't want to know—and cut off my handcuffs, all while I got grilled. I was still wearing my sleeping boxers and pajama top. The hospital had covered my bare feet with paper sandals.

"Just answer my question," the cop said.

This had been going on for two hours now. The adrenaline had died down, and the ache was starting to gnaw on my bones. I'd had enough.

"Yeah, okay, you got me," I said. "First, I put cuffs on both my hands. Then I broke up some furniture, fired several bullets into the walls, choked her nearly to death in my own apartment, and then called the police on myself. You got me."

"Could have worked that way," the officer said. He was a big man with a waxy mustache that made me think of a barbershop quartet. He had given me his name, but I stopped caring three cops ago.

"Excuse me?"

"A ruse maybe."

"I dislocated my shoulder and cut up my hands and broke my bed to divert suspicion?"

He gave a classic cop-shrug. "Hey, I had a guy one time, he cut off his dick so we wouldn't think he killed his girl. Said a bunch of black guys attacked them. Thing is, he only meant to cut it a little but he ended up slicing all the way through."

"That's a great story," I said.

"Could be the same thing here."

"My penis is fine, thanks for caring."

"You tell us about some guy breaking in. Neighbors heard the shots."

"Yes."

He gave me the skeptical eyes. "So how come none of your neighbors saw him running out?"

"Because—and this is just a wild stab in the dark—it was two in the morning?"

I was still sitting up on the examining table. My legs hung off. They were starting to go to sleep from the angle. I hopped down.

"Where do you think you're going?" the cop asked.

"I want to see Katy."

"I don't think so." The cop twitched the mustache. "Her parents are with her right now."

He studied my face for a reaction. I tried not to give him one.

The mustache twitched. "Her father has some pretty strong opinions about you," he said.

"I bet he does."

"He thinks you did this."

"For what purpose?"

"You mean what motive?"

"No, I mean purpose, intent. Do you think I was trying to kill her?"

He crossed his arms and shrugged. "Sounds reasonable to me."

"Then why did I call you while she was still alive?" I asked. "I went through this big ruse, right? So why didn't I finish her off?"

"Strangling someone isn't that easy," he said. "Maybe you thought she was dead."

"You realize, of course, how idiotic that sounds."

The door behind him opened, and Pistillo entered. He gave me a look as heavy as the ages. I closed my eyes and massaged the bridge of my nose with my forefinger and thumb. Pistillo was with one of the cops who had questioned me earlier. The cop signaled to his mustached compadre. The mustached cop looked annoyed by the interruption, but he followed the other one out the door. I was alone now with Pistillo.

He did not say anything at first. Pistillo circled the room, studying the glass jar of cotton balls, the tongue depressors, the hazardous-waste disposal can. Hospital rooms normally smell of antiseptic, but this one reeked of male-flight-attendant cologne. I did not know if it was from a doctor or cop, but I could see Pistillo's nose twitch in disgust. I was already used to it.

"Tell me what happened," he said.

"Didn't your friends with the NYPD fill you in?"

"I told them I wanted to hear it from you," Pistillo said. "Before they throw your ass in jail."

"I want to know how Katy is."

He weighed my request for a second or two. "Her neck and vocal cords will be sore, but she'll be fine."

I closed my eyes and let the relief flow over me.

"Start talking," Pistillo said.

I told him what happened. He stayed quiet until I got to the part about her shouting out the name "John."

"Any idea who John is?" he asked.

"Maybe."

"I'm listening."

"A guy I knew when I was growing up. His name is John Asselta."

Pistillo's face dropped.

"You know him?" I asked.

He ignored my question. "What makes you think she was talking about Asselta?"

"He's the one who broke my nose."

I filled him in on the Ghost's break-in and assault. Pistillo did not look happy.

"Asselta was looking for your brother?"

"That's what he said."

His face reddened. "Why the hell didn't you tell me this before?"

"Yeah, it's weird," I said. "You've always been the guy I could turn to, the friend I could trust with anything."

He stayed angry. "Do you know anything about John Asselta?"

"We grew up in the same town. We used to call him the Ghost."

"He's one of the most dangerous wackos out there," Pistillo said. He stopped, shook his head. "It couldn't have been him."

"What makes you say that?"

"Because you're both alive."

Silence.

"He's a stone-cold killer."

"So why isn't he in jail?" I asked.

"Don't be naïve. He's good at what he does."

"Killing people?"

"Yes. He lives overseas, no one knows where exactly. He's worked for government death squads in Central America. He helped despots in Africa." Pistillo shook his head. "No, if Asselta wanted her dead, we'd be tying a toe tag on her right about now."

"Maybe she meant another John," I said. "Or maybe I just heard wrong."

"Maybe." He thought about that. "One other thing I don't get. If the Ghost or anyone else wanted to kill Katy Miller, why not just do it? Why go to the trouble of cuffing you down?"

That had troubled me too, but I had come up with one possibility. "Maybe it was a setup."

He frowned. "How do you figure?"

"The killer cuffs me to the bed. He chokes Katy to death. Then"—I could feel a tingle on my scalp—"maybe he'd set it up to make it look like I did it." I looked up at him.

Pistillo frowned. "You're not going to say 'Like my brother,' are you?"

"Yeah," I said. "Yeah, I think I am."

"That's horseshit."

"Think about it, Pistillo. One thing you guys could never explain: Why was my brother's blood at the scene?"

"Julie Miller fought him off."

"You know better. There was too much blood for that." I moved closer to him. "Ken was framed eleven years ago, and maybe tonight someone wanted history to repeat itself."

He scoffed. "Don't be melodramatic. And let me tell you something. The cops aren't buying your Houdini-cuff-escape story. They think you tried to kill her."

"What do you think?" I asked him.

"Katy's father is here. He's riled up as all hell."

"That's hardly surprising."

"It makes you wonder, though."

"You know I didn't do it, Pistillo. And despite your theatrics yesterday, you know I didn't kill Julie."

"I warned you to stay away."

"And I chose not to heed your warning."

Pistillo let loose a long breath and nodded. "Exactly, tough guy, so here's how we're going to play it." He stepped closer and tried to stare me down. I did not blink. "You're going to jail."

I sighed. "I think I've already surpassed my minimum daily requirement of threats today."

"No threat, Will. You're going to be shipped off to jail this very night."

"Fine, I want a lawyer."

He looked at his watch. "Too late for that. You'll spend the night in lockup. Tomorrow you'll get arraigned. The charges will be attempted murder and assault two. The D.A.'s office will claim that you're a flight risk—case in point: your brother—and they'll ask for the judge to deny bail. My guess is, the judge will grant it."

I started to speak but he held up a hand. "Save your breath because—and you're not going to like this—I don't care if you did it or not. I'm going to find enough evidence to convict you. And if I can't find it, I'll create it. Go ahead, tell your lawyer about this chat. I'll just deny it. You're a murder suspect who's helped hide his killer-brother for eleven years. I'm one of the country's most respected law enforcement agents. Who do you think they'll believe?"

I looked at him. "Why are you doing this?"

"I told you to stay away."

"What would you have done if you were in my place? If it was your brother?"

"That's not the point. You didn't listen. And now your girlfriend is dead and Katy Miller just barely escaped with her life."

"I never hurt either one of them."

"Yeah, you did. You caused it. If you'd listened to me, you think they'd be where they are now?"

His words hit home, but I pushed on. "And what about you, Pistillo? What about your burying Laura Emerson's connection—"

"Hey, I'm not here to play point-counterpoint with you. You're going to jail tonight. And make no mistake, I'll get you convicted."

He headed for the door.

"Pistillo?" When he turned around, I said, "What are you really after here?"

He stopped and leaned so that his lips were only inches from my ear. He whispered, "Ask your brother," and then he was gone.

38

I spent the night in the precinct holding pen at Midtown South on West 35th Street. The cell reeked of urine and vomit and that sour-vodka smell when a drunk sweats. It was still a step up from the aroma of flight-attendant cologne. I had two cellmates. One was a cross-dressing hooker who cried a lot and seemed confused about sitting or standing when using the metal toilet. My other cellmate was a black man who slept the whole time. I have no jail stories about being beaten or robbed or raped. The night was totally uneventful.

Whoever was working the night shift spun a CD of Bruce Springsteen's "Born to Run." Talk about comfort food. Like every good Jersey boy, I had the lyrics memorized. This may sound strange, but I always thought of Ken when I listened to the Boss's power ballads. We were not blue collar or suffering hard times, and neither of us had been into fast cars or hanging out on the shore (in Jersey, it's always "the shore," never "the beach")—then again, judging by what I've seen at recent E Street Band concerts, that was probably true of most of his listeners—but there was something in the stories of struggle, the spirit of a man in chains trying to break free, of wanting something more and finding the courage to run away, that not only resonated with me but made me think of my brother, even before the murder.

But tonight, when Bruce sang that she was so pretty he got lost in the stars, I thought about Sheila. And I ached all over again.

My one call had been to Squares. I woke him up. When I told him what happened, he said, "Bummer." Then he promised to find me a good lawyer and see what he could learn about Katy's condition.

"Oh, the security tapes from that QuickGo," Squares said.

"What about them?"

"Your idea worked. We'll be able to see them tomorrow."

"If they let me out of here."

"Yeah, I guess," Squares said. Then he added, "If they don't give you bail, man, that would suck."

In the morning, the cops escorted me down to central booking at 100 Centre Street. The corrections department took over from there. I was held in a pen located in the basement. If you no longer believe that America is a melting pot, you should spend some time with the potpourri of (in)humanity that inhabits this mini–United Nations. I heard at least ten different languages. There were shades of skin color that could inspire the people at Crayola. There were baseball caps and turbans and toupees and even a fez. Everyone talked at the same time. And when I could understand them—hey, even when I couldn't—they were all claiming innocence.

Squares was there when I stood before the judge. So was my new attorney, a woman named Hester Crimstein. I recognized her from some famous case, but I could not put my finger on which one. She introduced herself to me and never looked my way again. She turned and stared at the young D.A. as though he were a bleeding boar and she was a panther with an industrial-sized case of piles.

"We request that Mr. Klein be held over without bail," the young D.A. said. "We believe that he is a very serious flight risk."

"Why's that?" the judge, who seemed to be perspiring boredom from every pore, asked.

"His brother, a murder suspect, has been on the run for the past eleven years. Not only that, your honor, but his brother's victim was this victim's sister."

That got the judge's attention. "Come again?"

"The defendant, Mr. Klein, is accused of trying to murder one Katherine Miller. Mr. Klein's brother, Kenneth, is a suspect in the eleven-year-old murder of Julie Miller, the victim's older sister."

The judge, who'd been rubbing his face, stopped abruptly. "Oh, wait, I remember the case."

The young D.A. smiled as if he'd been given a gold star.

The judge turned to Hester Crimstein. "Ms. Crimstein?"

"Your honor, we believe that all charges against Mr. Klein should be dropped immediately," she said.

The judge started rubbing his face again. "Label me shocked, Ms. Crimstein."

"Short of that, we believe that Mr. Klein should be released on his own recognizance. Mr. Klein has no criminal record at all. He has a job working with the poor in this city. He has roots in the community. As for that ridiculous comparison to his brother, that's guilt by association at its worst."

"You don't think the people have a valid concern, Ms. Crimstein?"

"Not at all, your honor. I understand that Mr. Klein's sister recently got her hair permed. Does that make it more likely that he will do the same?"

There was laughter.

The young D.A. was feeling his oats. "Your honor, with all due deference to my colleague's silly analogy—"

"What's silly about it?" Crimstein snapped.

"Our point is that Mr. Klein certainly has the resources to flee."

"That's ludicrous. He has no more means than anyone else. The reason they're making this claim is because they believe his brother fled—and no one is even sure about that. He may be dead. But either way, your honor, the assistant district attorney is leaving out one crucial element in all this."

Hester Crimstein turned to the young D.A. and smiled.

"Mr. Thomson?" the judge said.

Thomson, the young D.A., kept his head down.

Hester Crimstein waited another beat and then dove in. "The victim of this heinous crime, one Katherine Miller, claimed this morning that Mr. Klein was innocent."

The judge did not like that. "Mr. Thomson?"

"That's not exactly true, your honor."

"Not exactly?"

"Ms. Miller claimed that she did not see her assailant. It was dark. He wore a mask."

"And," Hester Crimstein finished for him, "she said that it wasn't my client."

"She said she did not *believe* it was Mr. Klein," Thomson countered. "But, your honor, she's injured and confused. She didn't see the attacker, so she really couldn't rule him out—"

"We're not trying the case here, counselor," the judge interrupted. "But your request for no bail is denied. Bail is set at thirty thousand dollars."

The judge banged the gavel. And I was free.

39

I wanted to head up to the hospital and see Katy. Squares shook his head and told me that would be a bad idea. Her father was there. He refused to leave her side. He had hired an armed guard to stand outside her door. I understood. Mr. Miller had failed to protect one daughter. He would never let himself do that again.

I called the hospital on Squares's cell phone, but the switchboard operator said that no calls were allowed. I dialed a local florist and sent her a get-well bouquet. It seemed pretty simplistic and dumb—Katy gets nearly strangled to death in my apartment and I send a basket with flowers, a teddy bear, and a mini-Mylar balloon on a stick—but it was the only way I could come up with to let her know that I was thinking of her.

Squares drove his own car, a 1968 venetian-blue Coupe de Ville that was about as inconspicuous as our cross-dressing friend Raquel/Roscoe at a Daughters of the American Revolution gathering, through the Lincoln Tunnel. Tough going, the tunnel, as always. People claimed that the traffic was getting worse. I'm not so sure. As a kid, our family car—in those days, one of those paneled station wagons—used to creep through that tunnel every other Sunday. I remember how sluggish that trek would be, in the dark, those stupid yellow warning lights hanging batlike from the tunnel's ceiling as if we really needed to be told to go slow, that little glass booth with the worker in it, the soot painting the tunnel tiles a urine-hued ivory, all of us peering anxiously ahead for the breaking light of day, and then, finally, with those metal-looking rubber dividers rising in greeting, we would ascend into the world of high-rises, an alternate reality, as if we'd traveled through a transporter. We'd go to the Ringling Bros. and Barnum & Bailey circus and twirl those little lights on a string, or maybe Radio City Music Hall for some show that dazzled for about ten minutes and then bored, or stand in line for half-priced tickets at the TKTS booth, or browse the books at the big Barnes & Noble (I think there was only one back then), or hit the Museum of Natural History, or a street fair—my mom's favorite was September's New York Is Book Country on Fifth Avenue.

My father would grumble about the traffic and the parking and the all-purpose "filth," but my mother loved New York. She longed for the theater, the arts, the razz and jangle of the city. Sunny had managed to shrink herself enough to fit into the suburban world of carpools and tennis sneakers, but her dreams, those long-ago suppressed longings, were right there, right beneath the surface. She loved us, I know that, but sometimes, when I sat behind her in that station wagon and watched her looking out the car window, I wondered if she would have been happier without us.

"Smart thinking," Squares said.

"What?"

"Remembering that Sonay was a devout practitioner of Yoga Squared."

"So how did it work?"

"I called Sonay and told her our problem. She told me that QuickGo was run by two brothers, Ian and Noah Muller. She called them, told them what she wanted, and . . ." Squares shrugged.

I shook my head. "You are amazing."

"Yes. Yes, I am."

QuickGo's offices were housed in a warehouse off Route 3 in the heart of northern New Jersey's swamps. New Jersey gets goofed on a lot, mostly because our most-traveled byroads cut through the butt-ugliest sections of the so-called Garden State. I am one of those who staunchly defend my home state. Most of New Jersey is surprisingly gorgeous, but our critics do score points on two fronts. One, our cities are beyond decay. Trenton, Newark, Atlantic City, take your pick. They get and deserve little respect. Take Newark as a case in point. I have friends who grew up in Quincy, Massachusetts. They always say they are from Boston. I have friends who grew up in Bryn Mawr. They always say they are from Philadelphia. I grew up less than nine miles from the heart of Newark. I have never once said or heard anyone I know say that they were from Newark.

Two—and I don't care what others say—there is an odor in the North Jersey marshlands. It is often faint but nonetheless unmistakable. It is not pleasant. It does not smell like nature. It smells like smoke and chemicals and a leaking septic tank. That was the odor that greeted us as we stepped out of the car at the QuickGo warehouse.

Squares said, "Did you fart?"

I looked at him.

"Hey, just trying to break the tension."

We headed into the warehouse. The Muller brothers were worth close to a hundred million dollars each, yet they shared a small office that sat in the middle of a hangarlike room. Their desks, which looked like something bought at an elementary school closeout, were pushed together facing each other. Their chairs were pre-ergonomics shellacked-wood. There were no computers or fax machines or photocopiers, just the desks, tall metal filing cabinets, and two phones. All four walls were glassed. The brothers liked to look out at the cargo boxes and forklifts. They did not much care who looked in.

The brothers looked alike and were dressed the same. They wore what my father called "charcoal slacks" with white button-downs over V-neck Ts. The shirts were buttoned low enough that their gray chest hair jutted out like steel wool. The brothers rose and aimed their widest smiles at Squares.

"You must be Ms. Sonay's guru," one said. "Yogi Squares."

Squares replied with a serene, wise-man head nod.

They both rushed over and shook his hand. I half expected them to take a knee.

"We had them overnight the tapes," the taller of the brothers said, clearly looking for approval. Squares deigned another nod at him. They led us across the cement floor. I heard the beep-beep of vehicles in reverse. Garagelike doors were opened and trucks were loaded. The brothers greeted every worker, and the workers responded.

We entered a windowless room with a Mr. Coffee on the counter. A TV with a coat-hanger antenna and VCR sat on one of those metal carts I had not seen since the days when the A-V kid would wheel them into my elementary school class.

The taller brother turned on the TV. Pure static blew forth. He stuck a tape in the VCR. "This tape covers twelve hours," he said. "You told me the guy was in the store around three o'clock, right?"

"That's what we were told," Squares said.

"I have it set at two forty-five. The tape moves pretty quickly since it only captures an image every three seconds. Oh, and the fast forward doesn't work, sorry. We don't have a remote control either, so just press the Play button right here whenever you're ready. We figured you'd want privacy so we'll leave. Take your time."

"We may need to keep the tape," Squares said.

"Not a problem. We can make copies."

"Thank you."

One brother shook Squares's hand again. The other—I'm not making this up—bowed. Then we were left alone. I approached the VCR and pressed Play. The static disappeared. So did the sound. I played with the volume button on the TV, but, of course, there was no sound.

The images were in black and white. There was a clock on the bottom of the screen. The camera pointed at the cash register from above. A young woman with long blond hair worked it. Her moving in jerky, every-three-second clips made me dizzy.

"How are we going to know this Owen Enfield?" Squares asked.

"We look for a forty-year-old guy with a crew cut, I guess."

Watching now, I realized that this task might be easier than I'd first thought. The customers were all elderly and in golf-club garb. I wondered if Stonepointe catered mostly to retirees. I made a mental note to ask Yvonne Sterno.

At 3:08.15, we spotted him. His back anyway. He wore shorts and a collared shortsleeve shirt. We could not see his face, but he had a crew cut. He headed past the register and down the last aisle. We waited. At 3:09.24, our potential Owen Enfield turned the corner, heading back toward the long-haired blonde at the cash register. He carried a half-gallon of what looked like milk and a loaf of bread. I put my hand near the pause button so I could stop it and get a better look.

But there was no need.

The Vandyke beard might throw you off. So, too, the close-cropped gray hair. If I had casually stumbled across this tape, or if I had walked past him on a busy street, I might not have noticed. But I was anything but casual right now. I was concentrating. And I knew. I hit the pause button anyway: 3:09.51.

Any doubts were erased. I stood there, unmoving. I did not know if I should celebrate or cry. I turned toward Squares. His eyes were on me instead of the screen. I nodded at him, confirming what he already suspected.

Owen Enfield was my brother, Ken.

40

The intercom buzzed.

"Mr. McGuane?" the receptionist, part of his security force, asked.

"Yes."

"Joshua Ford and Raymond Cromwell are here."

Joshua Ford was the senior partner at Stanford, Cummings, and Ford, a firm that employed more than three hundred attorneys. Raymond Cromwell would thus be the note-taking, extra-hour-billing underling. Philip watched them both on the monitor. Ford was a big guy, six-four, two-twenty. He had a reputation for being tough, aggressive, nasty, and fitting that profile, he worked his face and mouth as though he were chomping on either a cigar or human leg. Cromwell, in contrast, was young, soft, manicured, and waxy-smooth.

McGuane looked over at the Ghost. The Ghost smiled, and McGuane felt another cold gust. Again he wondered about the intelligence of bringing Asselta in on this. In the end, he had decided that it would be okay. The Ghost had a stake in this too.

Besides, the Ghost was good at this.

Still keeping his eyes on that skin-crawling smile, McGuane said, "Please send in Mr. Ford alone. Make sure that Mr. Cromwell is comfortable in the waiting room."

"Yes, Mr. McGuane."

McGuane had debated how to play this. He did not care for violence for violence's sake, but he never shrank from it either. It was a means to an end. The Ghost was right about that atheist-in-foxhole crap. The truth is, we are mere animals, organisms even, slightly more complex than your basic paramecium. You die, you're gone. It was pure megalomania to think we humans are somehow above death, that we, unlike any other creature, have the ability to transcend it. In life, sure, we are special, dominant, because we are the strongest and most ruthless. We rule. But in death, to believe that we are somehow special in God's eyes, that we can worm our way into his good graces by kissing his ass, well, and not to sound like a Communist here, but that's the sort of thinking that the rich have used to keep the poor in place since the beginning of man's rule.

The Ghost moved toward the door.

You take the edge any way you can get it. McGuane often trod along byways others considered taboo. You were never supposed to kill, for example, a fed or a D.A. or a cop. McGuane had killed all three. You were never supposed to attack, to use another example, powerful people who could make trouble and draw attention.

McGuane did not buy that one either.

When Joshua Ford opened the door, the Ghost had the iron baton ready. It was the approximate length of a baseball bat, with a powerful spring that helped it snap with the force of a blackjack. If you were to hit someone on the head with any kind of force, it would crush the skull like an eggshell.

Joshua Ford entered with a rich-man's swagger. He smiled at McGuane. "Mr. McGuane."

McGuane smiled back. "Mr. Ford."

Sensing someone to his right, Ford turned toward the Ghost, his hand outstretched for a customary shake. The Ghost had his eyes elsewhere. He aimed the metal bar for the shin and hit it flush. Ford cried out and dropped to the floor like a marionette with its strings cut. The Ghost hit him again, this time in the right shoulder. Ford felt his arm go dead. The Ghost smashed the baton against the rib cage. There was a cracking sound. Ford tried to roll into a ball.

From across the room, McGuane asked, "Where is he?"

Joshua Ford swallowed and croaked, "Who?"

Big mistake. The Ghost snapped the weapon down on the man's ankle. Ford howled. McGuane looked behind him at the security monitor. Cromwell was comfortably ensconced in the waiting room. He would hear nothing. Neither would anybody else.

The Ghost hit the lawyer again, finding the same spot on the ankle. There was a crunching sound like a truck tire over a beer bottle. Ford put up a hand, pleading for mercy.

Over the years, McGuane had learned that it was best to strike before you interrogate. Most people, when presented with the threat of pain, will try to talk their way out of it. That goes double for men who are accustomed to using their mouths. They'll search for angles, for half-truths, for credible lies. They are rational, the assumption goes, and thus their opponents must be the same. Words can be used to defuse.

You need to strip them of that delusion.

The pain and fear that accompany a sudden physical assault are devastating to the psyche. Your cognitive reasoning—your intelligentsia, if you will, your evolved man—fades away, caves in. You are left with the Neanderthal, the primitive true-you who knows only to escape pain.

The Ghost looked over at McGuane. McGuane nodded. The Ghost stepped back and let McGuane move closer.

"He stopped in Vegas," McGuane explained. "That was his big mistake. He visited a doctor there. We checked the nearby pay phones for out-of-state calls made an hour before and an hour after his visit. There was only one call of interest. To you, Mr. Ford. He called you. And just to make sure, I had a man watch your office. The feds paid you a visit yesterday. So you see, it all adds up. Ken had to have a lawyer. He'd want someone tough and independent and not connected in any way to me. That would be you."

Joshua Ford said, "But—"

McGuane held up his hand to stop him. Ford obeyed and closed his mouth. McGuane stepped back, looked at the Ghost, and said, "John."

The Ghost advanced and without hesitating, he whacked Ford on the side of the arm above the elbow. The elbow bent back the wrong way. Ford's face lost whatever color was left.

"If you deny or pretend you don't know what I'm talking about," McGuane said, "my friend here will stop the love taps and start to hurt you. Do you understand?"

Ford took a few seconds. When he finally looked up, McGuane was surprised by the steadiness of the man's gaze. Ford looked at the Ghost, then at McGuane. "Go to hell," Ford spat out.

The Ghost looked at McGuane. He arched an eyebrow, smiled, and said, "Brave."

"John . . ."

But the Ghost ignored him. He whipped the iron bar across Ford's face. There was a wet ripping sound as his head snapped to the side. Blood squirted across the room. Ford fell back and did not move. The Ghost lined up for another blow to the knee.

McGuane said, "Is he still conscious?"

That made the Ghost pause. He bent down. "Conscious," the Ghost reported, "but his breathing is sporadic." He stood back up. "Another blow and Mr. Ford might go nighty-night."

McGuane thought about that. "Mr. Ford?"

Ford looked up.

"Where is he?" McGuane asked again.

This time Ford shook his head.

McGuane walked over to the monitor. He swiveled it so that Joshua Ford could see the screen. Cromwell was sitting cross-legged, sipping coffee.

The Ghost pointed at the monitor. "He wears nice shoes. Are they Allen-Edmonds?"

Ford tried to sit up. He got his hands underneath him, tried to push, fell back.

"How old is he?" McGuane asked.

Ford did not reply.

The Ghost lifted the bar. "He asked you—"

"Twenty-nine."

"Married?"

Ford nodded.

"Kiddies?"

"Two boys."

McGuane studied the monitor some more. "You're right, John. Those are nice shoes." He turned to Ford. "Tell me where Ken is, or he dies."

The Ghost carefully put down the metal bar. He reached into his pocket and pulled out a Thuggee strangulation stick. The handle portion was made of mahogany. It was eight inches long and two inches in diameter. The surface was octagonal. Deep grooves were cut into it, making it easier to grip. There was a braided rope attached to either end. The rope was made of horsehair.

"He's got nothing to do with this," Ford said.

"Listen to me closely," McGuane said. "I'm only going to say this once."

Ford waited.

"We never bluff," McGuane said.

The Ghost smiled. McGuane waited a beat, his eyes on Ford. Then he hit the intercom button. The security receptionist responded.

"Yes, Mr. McGuane."

"Bring Mr. Cromwell here."

"Yes, sir."

They both watched the monitor as a beefy security guard came to the door and waved toward Cromwell. Cromwell uncrossed his legs, put down his coffee, rose, straightened out his jacket. He followed the security guard out the door. Ford turned to McGuane. Their eyes met and locked.

"You're a stupid man," McGuane said.

The Ghost regripped the wooden handle and waited.

The security guard opened the door. Raymond Cromwell entered with his smile at the ready. When he saw the blood and his boss crumbled on the floor, his face dropped like someone had short-circuited the muscles. "What the—?"

The Ghost stepped behind Cromwell and kicked the back of both legs. Cromwell let out a cry and dropped to his knees. The Ghost's moves were practiced, effortlessly graceful, like a grotesque ballet.

The rope dropped over the younger man's head. When it fully circled his neck, the Ghost jerked back violently while simultaneously putting his knee against Cromwell's spine. The rope tightened hard against Cromwell's waxy-smooth skin. The Ghost twisted the handle, effectively cutting off blood flow to the brain. Cromwell's eyes bulged. His hands pawed at the rope. The Ghost held on.

"Stop!" Ford shouted. "I'll talk!"

But there was no reply.

The Ghost kept his gaze on his victim. Cromwell's face was a horrid shade of purple.

"I said—" Ford quickly turned to McGuane. McGuane stood at ease with his arms folded. The two men locked eyes. The quiet sounds, the awful gurgling struggle coming from Cromwell, echoed in the stillness.

Ford whispered, "Please."

But McGuane shook his head and repeated his earlier statement: "We never bluff."

The Ghost turned the handle one more time and held on.

41

I had to tell my father about the security tape.

Squares dropped me off at a bus stop near the Meadowlands. I had no idea what to do about what I'd just seen. Somewhere along the New Jersey Turnpike, while staring out at the decaying industrial plants, my brain slipped on the autopilot. It was the only way to keep moving.

Ken was indeed alive.

I had seen the proof. He had been living in New Mexico and using the name Owen Enfield. Part of me was ecstatic. There was a chance at redemption, a chance to be with my brother again, a chance—dare I even think of it?—to make this all right.

But then I thought about Sheila.

Her fingerprints had been found in my brother's house, along with two dead bodies. How did Sheila fit into all this? I had no idea—or maybe I just didn't want to face the obvious. She had betrayed me—when my mind would function, the only scenarios I could come up with involved betrayal of one form or another—and if I dwelled on that for too long, if I really allowed myself to sink into the simple memories—the way she tucked her feet under her when we talked on the couch, the way she pulled her hair back as though she were standing under a waterfall, the way she smelled in that terry-cloth robe when she came out of the shower, the way she wore my oversize sweatshirts on fall nights, the way she hummed in my ear when we danced, the way she could stop my breath with a look from across the room—that it had all been some sort of elaborate lie . . .

Autopilot.

So I plodded on with one thought in mind: closure. My brother and my lover had both left me without warning, gone before good-bye. I knew that I could never put any of this behind me until I knew the truth. Squares had warned me about this in the beginning, about maybe not liking what I found, but maybe in the end, this was all necessary. Maybe now, finally, it was my turn to be brave. Maybe now I would save Ken instead of the other way around.

So that was what I'd focus on: Ken was alive. He was innocent—if I had been subconsciously harboring any doubts before, Pistillo had erased them. I could see and be with him again. I could—I don't know—avenge the past, let my mother rest in peace, something.

On this, the last day of our official mourning, my father was not at the house. Aunt Selma was in the kitchen. She told me that he'd taken a walk. Aunt Selma wore an apron. I wondered where she had gotten it. We did not have one, I was certain of that. Had Selma brought it with her? She seemed always to be wearing an apron, even when she wasn't, if you know what I mean. I watched her cleaning out the sink. Selma, Sunny's quiet sister, labored quietly. I had always taken her for granted. I think most people did. Selma was just . . . there. She was one of those people who lived life below the radar, as though she were afraid of drawing the attention of the fates. She and Uncle Murray had no children. I did not know why, though I'd once overheard my parents talking about a stillborn. I stood and looked at her, as if for the first time, just looking at yet another human being struggling every day to do right.

"Thank you," I said to her.

Selma nodded.

I wanted to tell her that I loved her and appreciated her and wanted us, especially now that Mom was gone, to be closer, that I know Mom would have wanted that. But I couldn't. I hugged her instead. Selma stiffened at first, startled by my aberrant display of affection, but then she relaxed.

"It'll be okay," she told me.

I knew my father's favorite walking route. I crossed Coddington Terrace, carefully avoiding the Miller house. My father, I knew, did that too. He had changed the route years ago. I cut through both the Jarats' and Arnays' yards, and then took the path that crossed the Meadowbrook to the town's Little League fields. The fields were empty, the season over, and my father sat alone on the top row of the metal bleachers. I remembered how much he loved coaching, that white T-shirt with the three-quarter-length green sleeves, the word *Senators* across the front, the green cap with the *S* sitting too high on his head. He loved the dugout, hanging his arms casually off the dusty rafters, the sweat forming in the pits. He'd put his right foot on the first cinder step, the left on the concrete, and in one fluid smooth motion he'd take the cap off, do the forearm swipe of the brow, put the cap neatly back in place. His face glowed on those late-spring nights, especially when Ken played. He coached with Mr. Bertillo and Mr. Horowitz, his two best friends, beer buddies, both dead of heart attacks before sixty, and I know that as I sat next to him now, he could still hear those clapping hands and that repetitive banter and smell that sweet Little League clay-dirt.

He looked at me and smiled. "Remember the year your mom umped?"

"A little, I guess. What was I, four?"

"Yeah, something like that." He shook his head, still smiling, lost in the memory. "This was during the height of your mother's women's lib stage. She wore these slogan T-shirts that said A WOMAN'S PLACE IS IN THE HOUSE AND SENATE, stuff like that. Keep in mind that this was a few years before girls were allowed to play Little League, okay? So somewhere along the way, your mom learned that there were no female umpires. She checked the rule book and saw that there was nothing forbidding that."

"So she signed up?"

"Yep."

"And?"

"Well, the elder statesmen threw a fit, but the rules were the rules. So they let her ump. But there were a couple of problems."

"Like?"

"Like she was the worst umpire in the world." Dad smiled again, a smile I rarely saw anymore, a smile so firmly rooted in the past that it made me ache. "She barely knew the rules. Her eyesight, as you know, was terrible. I remember in her first game she stuck up her thumb and yelled 'Safe.' Whenever she made a call, she'd go through all these gyrations. Like something Bob Fosse choreographed."

We both chuckled and I could almost see him watching her, waving off her theatrics, half embarrassed, half thrilled.

"Didn't the coaches go nuts?"

"Sure, but you know what the league did?"

I shook my head.

"They teamed her up with Harvey Newhouse. You remember him?"

"His son was in my class. He played pro football, right?"

"For the Rams, yeah. Offensive tackle. Harvey must have been three hundred pounds. So he took behind the plate and your mom took the field and whenever a coach would get out of hand, Harvey would just glare at him and the coach sat back down."

We chuckled again and then fell gently into silence, both of us wondering how a spirit like that could be smothered away, even before the onset of the disease. He finally turned and looked at me. His eyes widened when he noticed the bruises.

"What the hell happened to you?"

"It's okay," I said.

"Did you get in a fight?"

"I'm fine, really. I need to talk to you about something."

He was quiet. I wondered how to approach this, but Dad took care of that.

"Show me," he said.

I looked at him.

"Your sister called this morning. She told me about the picture."

I still had it with me. I pulled it out. He took it in his palm, as though afraid that he might crush it. He looked down and said, "My God." His eyes began to glisten.

"You didn't know?" I said.

"No." He looked at the photograph again. "Your mother never said anything until, you know." I saw something cross his face. His wife, his life partner, had kept this from him, and it hurt.

"There's something else," I said.

He turned to me.

"Ken's been living in New Mexico." I gave him a thumbnail sketch of what I'd learned. Dad took it in quietly and steadily, as if he'd found his sea legs.

When I'd finished, Dad said, "How long had he been living out there?"

"Just a few months. Why?"

"Your mother said he was coming back. She said he'd be back when he proved his innocence."

We sat in silence. I let my mind wander. Suppose, I thought, it went something like this: Eleven years ago, Ken was framed. He ran off and lived overseas—in hiding or something, just like the news report. Years pass. He comes back home.

Why?

Was it, like my mother had said, to prove his innocence? That made sense, I guess, but why now? I didn't know, but whatever the reason, Ken did indeed return—and it backfired on him. Someone found out.

Who?

The answer seemed obvious: whoever murdered Julie. That person, be it a he or she, would need to silence Ken. And then what? No idea. There were still pieces missing.

"Dad?"

"Yes."

"Did you ever suspect Ken was alive?"

He took his time. "It was easier to think he was dead."

"That's not an answer."

He let his gaze roam again. "Ken loved you so much, Will."

I let that hang in the air.

"But he wasn't all good."

"I know that," I said.

He let that settle in. "When Julie was murdered," my father said, "Ken was already in trouble."

"What do you mean?"

"He came home to hide."

"From what?"

"I don't know."

I thought about it. I again remembered that he had not been home in at least two years and that he'd seemed on edge, even as he asked me about Julie. I just didn't know what that all meant.

Dad said, "Do you remember Phil McGuane?"

I nodded. Ken's old friend from high school, the "class leader" who was now reputed to be "connected." "I heard he moved into the Bonannos' old place."

"Yes."

During my childhood, the Bonannos, famed old-time mafiosi, had lived in Livingston's biggest estate, the one with the big iron gate and the driveway guarded by two stone lions. Rumor had it—as you may have surmised, suburbia is rife with rumors—that there were bodies buried on the property and that the fence could electrocute and if a kid tried to sneak through the woods out back, he'd get shot in the head. I doubt any of those stories were true, but the police finally arrested Old Man Bonanno when he was ninety-one.

"What about him?" I asked.

"Ken was mixed up with McGuane."

"How?"

"That's all I know."

I thought about the Ghost. "Was John Asselta involved too?"

My father went rigid. I saw fear in his eyes. "Why would you ask me that?"

"The three of them were all friends in high school," I began—and then I decided to go the rest of the way. "I saw him recently."

"Asselta?"

"Yes."

His voice was soft. "He's back?"

I nodded.

Dad closed his eyes.

"What is it?"

"He's dangerous," my father said.

"I know that."

He pointed at my face. "Did he do that?"

Good question, I thought. "In part, at least."

"In part?"

"It's a long story, Dad."

He closed his eyes again. When he opened them, he put his hands on his thighs and stood. "Let's go home," he said.

I wanted to ask him more, but I knew that now was not the time. I followed him. Dad had a hard time getting down the rickety bleacher steps. I offered him a hand. He refused it. When we both reached the gravel, we turned toward the path. And there, smiling patiently with his hands in his pockets, stood the Ghost.

For a moment I thought it was my imagination, as if our thinking about him had conjured up this horrific mirage. But I heard the sharp intake of air coming from my father. And then I heard that voice.

"Ah, isn't this touching?" the Ghost said.

My father stepped in front of me as though trying to shield me. "What do you want?" he shouted.

But the Ghost laughed. " 'Gee, son, when I struck out in the big game,' " he said, mocking, " 'it took a whole roll of Life Savers to make me feel better.' "

We stayed rooted to the spot. The Ghost looked up at the sky, closed his eyes, took a great big sniff of air. "Ah, Little League." He lowered his gaze to my father. "Do you remember that time my old man showed up at a game, Mr. Klein?"

My father set his jaw.

"It was a great moment, Will. Really. A classic. My dear ol' dad was so wasted, he took a leak right on the side of the snack bar. Can you imagine? I thought Mrs. Tansmore was going to have a stroke." He laughed heartily, the sound clawing at me as it echoed. When it died down, he added, "Good times, eh?"

"What do you want?" my father said again.

But the Ghost was on his own track now. He would not be derailed. "Say, Mr. Klein, do you remember coaching that all-star team in the state finals?"

My father said, "I do."

"Ken and I were in, what, fourth grade, was it?"

Nothing from my father this time.

The Ghost snapped, "Oh wait." The smile slid off his face. "I almost forgot. I missed that year, didn't I? And the next year too. Jail time, don't you know."

"You never went to jail," my father said.

"True, true, you're absolutely right, Mr. Klein. I was"—the Ghost made quote marks with his skinny fingers—"hospitalized. You know what that means, Willie boy? They lock up a child with the most depraved whack-jobs that ever cursed this wretched planet, so as to make him all better. My first roommate, his name was Timmy, was a pyromaniac. At the tender age of thirteen, Timmy killed his parents by setting them on fire. One night he stole a book of matches from a drunk orderly and lit up my bed. I got to go to the medical wing for three weeks. I almost set myself on fire so I wouldn't have to go back."

A car drove down Meadowbrook Road. I could see a little boy in the back, perched high by a safety seat of some kind. There was no wind. The trees stood too still.

"That was a long time ago," my father said softly.

The Ghost's eyes narrowed as if he were giving my father's words very special attention. Finally he nodded and said, "Yes, yes, it was. You're right about that too, Mr. Klein. And it wasn't like I had a great home life to begin with. I mean, what were my prospects anyway? You could almost look at what happened to me as a blessing: I could get therapy instead of living with a father who beat me."

I realized then that he was talking about the killing of Daniel Skinner, the bully who'd been stabbed with the kitchen knife. But what struck me then, what gave me pause, was how his story sounded like the kids we help at Covenant House—abusive home life, early crime, some form of psychosis. I tried to look at the Ghost like that, as if he were just one of my kids. But the picture would not hold. He was not a kid anymore. I don't know when they cross over, at what age they go from being a kid who needs help to a degenerate who should be locked up, or even if that was fair.

"Hey, Willie boy?"

The Ghost tried to meet my eye then, but my father leaned in the way of even his gaze. I put a hand on his shoulder as if to tell him I could handle it.

"What?" I said.

"You do know I was"—again with the finger quotes—"hospitalized again, don't you?"

"Yes," I said.

"I was a senior. You were a sophomore."

"I remember."

"I had only one visitor the whole time I was there. Do you know who it was?"

I nodded. The answer was Julie.

"Ironic, don't you think?"

"Did you kill her?" I asked.

"Only one of us here is to blame."

My father stepped back in the way. "That's enough," he said.

I slid to the side. "What do you mean?"

"You, Willie boy. I mean you."

I was confused. "What?"

"That's enough," my father said again.

"You were supposed to fight for her," the Ghost went on. "You were supposed to protect her."

The words, even coming from this lunatic, pierced my chest like an ice pick.

"Why are you here?" my father demanded.

"The truth, Mr. Klein? I'm not exactly sure."

"Leave my family alone. You want someone, you take me."

"No, sir, I don't want you." He considered my father, and I felt something cold coil in the pit of my belly. "I think I prefer you this way."

The Ghost gave a little wave good-bye then and stepped into the wooded area. We watched him move deeper into the brush, fading away until, like his nickname, he vanished. We stood there for another minute or two. I could hear my father's breathing, hollow and tinny, as if coming up from a deep cavern.

"Dad?"

But he had already started toward the path. "Let's go home, Will."

42

My father would not talk.

When we got back to the house, he headed up to his bedroom, the one he had shared with my mother for nearly forty years, and closed the door. There was so much coming at me now. I tried to sort through it, but it was too much. My brain threatened to shut down. And still I didn't know enough. Not yet anyway. I needed to learn more.

Sheila.

There was one more person who might be able to shed some light on the enigma that had been the love of my life. So I made my excuses, said my good-byes, and headed back into the city. I hopped on a subway and headed up to the Bronx. The skies had started to darken and the neighborhood was bad, but for once in my life, I was beyond being scared.

Before I even knocked, the door opened a crack, the chain in place. Tanya said, "He's asleep."

"I want to talk to you," I said.

"I have nothing to say."

"I saw you at the memorial service."

"Go away."

"Please," I said. "It's important."

Tanya sighed and took off the chain. I slipped inside. The dim lamp was on in the far corner, casting the faintest of glows. As I let my eyes wander over this most depressing place, I wondered if Tanya was not as much a prisoner here as Louis Castman. I faced her. She shrunk back as if my gaze had the ability to scald.

"How long do you plan on keeping him here?" I asked.

"I don't make plans," she replied.

Tanya did not offer me a seat. We both just stood there, facing each other. She crossed her arms and waited.

"Why did you come to the service?" I asked.

"I wanted to pay my respects."

"You knew Sheila?"

"Yes."

"You were friends?"

Tanya may have smiled. Her face was so mangled, the scars running jagged lines with her mouth, I couldn't be sure. "Not even close."

"Why did you come then?"

She cocked her head to the side. "You want to hear something weird?"

I was not sure how to respond, so I settled for a nod.

"That was the first time I've been out of this apartment in sixteen months."

I was not sure how to respond to that either, so I tried, "I'm glad you came."

Tanya looked at me skeptically. The room was silent save for her breathing. I don't know what was physically wrong with her, if it was connected to the brutal slashing or not, but every breath sounded as though her throat were a narrow straw with a few drops of liquid stuck inside.

I said, "Please tell me why you came."

"It's like I told you. I wanted to pay my respects." She paused. "And I thought I could help."

"Help?"

She looked at the door to Louis Castman's bedroom. I followed her gaze. "He told me why you came here. I thought maybe I could fill in some more of the pieces."

"What did he say?"

"That you were in love with Sheila." Tanya moved closer to the lamp. It was hard not to look away. She finally sat and gestured for me to do likewise. "Is that true?"

"Yes."

"Did you murder her?" Tanya asked.

The question startled me. "No."

She did not seem convinced.

"I don't understand," I said. "You came to help?"

"Yes."

"Then why did you run off?"

"You haven't figured that out?"

I shook my head.

She sat—more like collapsed—onto a chair. Her hands fell into her lap, and her body started rocking back and forth.

"Tanya?"

"I heard your name," she said.

"Pardon?"

"You asked why I ran off." She stopped rocking. "It was because I heard your name."

"I don't understand."

She looked at the door again. "Louis didn't know who you were. Neither did I—not until I heard your name at the service, when Squares eulogized her. You're Will Klein."

"Yes."

"And"—her voice grew soft now, so soft I had to lean forward to hear it—"you're Ken's brother."

Silence.

"You knew my brother?"

"We met. A long time ago."

"How?"

"Through Sheila." She straightened her back and looked at me. It was odd. They say that the eyes are the windows to the soul. That's nonsense.

Tanya's eyes were normal. I saw no scars there, no hint of defect, no shade of her history or her torments. "Louis told you about a big-time gangster who got involved with Sheila."

"Yes."

"That was your brother."

I shook my head. I was about to protest further, but I held it back when I saw that she had more to say.

"Sheila never fit into this lifestyle. She was too ambitious. She and Ken found each other. He helped set her up at a fancy college in Connecticut, but that was more to sell drugs than anything else. Out here, you see guys slicing up each other's intestines for a spot on a street corner. But a fancy rich-kid school, if you could move in and control that, you could score an easy mint."

"And you're saying that my brother set this up?"

She started rocking again. "Are you seriously telling me you didn't know?"

"Yes."

"I thought—" She stopped.

"What?"

She shook her head. "I don't know what I thought."

"Please," I said.

"It's just weird. First Sheila's with your brother. Now she pops up again with you. And you act like you don't know anything about it."

Again, I did not know how to respond. "So what happened to Sheila?"

"You'd know better than me."

"No, I mean back then. When she was up at this college."

"I never saw her after she left the life. I got a couple of calls, that's all. But those stopped too. But Ken was bad news. You and Squares, you seemed nice. Like maybe she found some good. But then when I heard your name . . ." She shrugged the thought away.

"Does the name Carly mean anything to you?" I asked.

"No. Should it?"

"Did you know that Sheila had a daughter?"

That got Tanya rocking again. Her voice was pained. "Oh God."

"You knew?"

She shook her head hard. "No."

I followed right up. "Do you know a Philip McGuane?"

Still shaking her head. "No."

"How about John Asselta? Or Julie Miller?"

"No," she said quickly. "I don't know any of these people." She stood now and spun away from me. "I had hoped she escaped," she said.

"She did," I said. "For a time."

I saw her shoulders slump. Her breathing seemed even more labored. "It should have ended better for her."

Tanya started toward the door then. I did not follow. I looked back to Louis Castman's room. Again I thought that there were two prisoners here. Tanya stopped. I could feel her eyes on me. I turned to her.

"There are surgeries," I said to her. "Squares knows people. We can help."

"No, thank you."

"You can't live on vengeance forever."

She tried a smile. "You think that's what this is about?" She pointed to her mutilated face. "You think I keep him here because of this?"

I was confused again.

Tanya shook her head. "He told you how he recruited Sheila?"

I nodded.

"He gives himself all the credit. He talks about his natty clothes and smooth lines. But most of the girls, even the ones fresh off the bus, they're afraid to go with a guy alone. So you see, what really made the difference was that Louis had a partner. A woman. To help close the sale. To lull the girls into feeling safe."

She waited. Her eyes were dry. A tremor began deep inside me and spread out. Tanya moved to the door. She opened it for me. I left and never went back.

43

There were two phone messages on my voice mail. The first was from Sheila's mother, Edna Rogers. Her tone was stiff and impersonal. The funeral would be in two days, she stated, at a chapel in Mason, Idaho. Mrs. Rogers gave me times and addresses and directions from Boise. I saved the message.

The second was from Yvonne Sterno. She said it was urgent that I call her right away. Her tone was one of barely restrained excitement. That made me uneasy. I wondered if she'd learned the true identity of Owen Enfield—and if she had, would that be a positive or negative thing?

Yvonne answered on the first ring.

"What's up?" I asked.

"Got something big here, Will."

"I'm listening."

"We should have realized it earlier."

"What's that?"

"Put the pieces together. A guy with a pseudonym. The FBI's strong interest. All the secrecy. A small community in a quiet area. You with me?"

"Not really, no."

"Cripco was the key," she went on. "As I said, it's a dummy corporation. So I checked with a few sources. Truth is, they don't try to hide them that hard. The cover isn't that deep. The way they figure it, if someone spots the guy, they know or they don't know. They aren't going to do a big background check."

"Yvonne?" I said.

"What?"

"I don't have a clue what you're talking about."

"Cripco, the company who leased the house and the car, traces back to the United States marshal's office."

Once again I felt my head teeter and spin. I let it go and a bright hope surfaced in the dark, murky blur. "Wait a second," I said. "Are you saying that Owen Enfield is an undercover agent?"

"No, I don't think so. I mean, what would he be investigating at Stonepointe—someone cheating at gin rummy?"

"What then?"

"The U.S. marshal—not the FBI—runs the witness protection program."

More confusion. "So you're saying that Owen Enfield . . . ?"

"That the government was hiding him here, yeah. They gave him a new identity. The key, like I said before, is that they don't take the background that deep. A lot of people don't know that. Hell, sometimes they're even dumb about it. My source at the paper was telling me about this black drug dealer from Baltimore who they stuck in a lily-white suburb outside Chicago. A total screwup. That wasn't the case here, but if, say, Gotti were searching for Sammy the Bull, they'd either recognize him or not. They wouldn't bother checking his background to make sure. You know what I mean?"

"I think so."

"So the way I figure it, this Owen Enfield was bad news. Most of the guys in witness protection are. So he's in the program and for some reason he murders these two guys and runs off. The FBI doesn't want that out. Think how embarrassing it would be—the government cuts a deal with a guy and then he goes on a murder spree? Bad press all the way around, you know what I mean?"

I didn't say anything.

"Will?"

"Yeah."

There was a pause. "You're holding out on me, aren't you?"

I thought about what to do.

"Come on," she said. "Back and forth, remember? I give, you give."

I don't know what I would have said—if I would have told her that my brother and Owen Enfield were one and the same, if I would have concluded that publicizing this was better than keeping it in the dark—but the decision was taken from me. I heard a click and then the phone went dead.

There was a sharp knock on the door.

"Federal officers. Open up now."

I recognized the voice. It belonged to Claudia Fisher. I reached for the knob, twisted it, and was nearly knocked over. Fisher burst in with a gun drawn. She told me to put my hands up. Her partner, Darryl Wilcox, was with her. They both looked pale, weary, and maybe even frightened.

"What the hell is this?" I said.

"Hands up now!"

I did as she asked. She took out her cuffs, and then, as though thinking better of it, she stopped. Her voice was suddenly soft. "You'll come without a hassle?" she asked.

I nodded.

"Then come on, let's go."

44

I did not argue. I did not call their bluff or demand a phone call or any of that. I did not even ask them where we were going. Such protestations at this delicate juncture would, I knew, be either superfluous or harmful.

Pistillo had warned me to stay away. He had gone so far as to have me arrested for a crime I did not commit. He'd promised to frame me if need be. And still I had not backed down. I wondered where I'd unearthed this newfound bravery and I realized that it was simply a matter of having nothing more to lose. Maybe that was what bravery always is—being past the point of giving a rat's ass. Sheila and my mother were dead. My brother had been lost to me. You corner a man, even one as weak as this one, and you see the animal emerge.

We pulled up to a row of houses in Fair Lawn, New Jersey. Everywhere I looked I saw the same thing: tidy lawns, overdone flower beds, rusted once-white furniture, hoses snaking through the grass attached to sprinklers that vacillated in a lazy haze. We approached a house no different from any other. Fisher tried the knob. It was unlocked. They led me through a room with a pink sofa and console TV. Photographs of two boys ran along the top of the console. The photos were in age order, starting with two infants. In the last one, the boys, both teenagers now, were formally dressed, each bussing a cheek of a woman I assumed was their mother.

The kitchen had a swing door. Pistillo sat at the Formica table with an iced tea. The woman in the photograph, the probable mother, stood by the sink. Fisher and Wilcox made themselves scarce. I stayed standing.

"You have my phone tapped," I said.

Pistillo shook his head. "A tap just tells you where a call originated. What we're using here are listening devices. And just so we're clear, they were court ordered."

"What do you want from me?" I asked him.

"The same thing I've wanted for eleven years," he said. "Your brother."

The woman at the sink turned on the faucet. She rinsed out a glass. More photos, some with the woman, some with Pistillo and other youngsters but again mostly the same two boys, had been hung on the refrigerator by magnets. These were more recent and casual shots—at the shore, in the yard, that kind of thing.

Pistillo said, "Maria?"

The woman shut off the water and turned toward him.

"Maria, this is Will Klein. Will, Maria."

The woman—I assumed that this was Pistillo's wife—dried her hands on a dish towel. Her grip was firm.

"Nice to meet you," she said a little too formally.

I mumbled and nodded, and when Pistillo signaled, I sat on a metal chair with vinyl padding.

"Would you like something to drink, Mr. Klein?" Maria asked me.

"No, thank you."

Pistillo raised his glass of iced tea. "Dynamite stuff. You should have a glass."

Maria kept hovering. I finally accepted the iced tea just so we could move on. She took her time pouring and putting the glass in front of me. I thanked her and tried a smile. She tried one back, but it flickered even weaker than mine.

She said, "I'll wait in the other room, Joe."

"Thanks, Maria."

She pushed through the swinging door.

"That's my sister," he said, still looking at the door she'd just gone through. He pointed to the snapshots on the refrigerator. "Those are her two boys. Vic Junior is eighteen now. Jack is sixteen."

"Uh-huh." I folded my hands and rested them on the table. "You've been listening in on my calls."

"Yes."

"Then you already know that I don't have a clue where my brother is."

He took a sip of the iced tea. "That I do." He was still staring at the refrigerator; he head-gestured for me to do likewise. "You notice anything missing from those pictures?"

"I'm really not in the mood for games, Pistillo."

"No, me neither. But take a longer look. What's missing?"

I did not bother to look because I already knew. "The father."

He snapped his fingers and pointed at me like a game show host. "Got it on the first try," he said. "Impressive."

"What the hell is this?"

"My sister lost her husband twelve years ago. The boys, well, you can do the math on your own. They were six and four. Maria raised them on her own. I pitched in where I could, but an uncle isn't a father, you know what I mean?"

I said nothing.

"His name was Victor Dober. That name mean anything to you?"

"No."

"Vic was murdered. Shot twice in the head execution-style." He drained his iced tea and then added, "Your brother was there."

My heart lurched inside my chest. Pistillo stood, not waiting for a reaction. "I know my bladder is going to regret this, Will, but I'm going to have another glass. You want anything while I'm up?"

I tried to work through the shock. "What do you mean, my brother was there?"

But Pistillo was taking his time now. He opened the freezer, took out an ice tray, broke it open in the sink. The cubes clattered against the ceramic. He fished some out with his hand and filled his glass. "Before we begin, I want you to make a promise."

"What?"

"It involves Katy Miller."

"What about her?"

"She's just a kid."

"I know that."

"This is a dangerous situation. You don't have to be a genius to figure that out. I don't want her getting hurt again."

"Neither do I."

"So we agree then," he said. "Promise me, Will. Promise me you won't involve her anymore."

I looked at him and I knew that point was not negotiable. "Okay," I said. "She's out."

He checked my face, looking for the lie, but on this point he was right. Katy had already paid a huge price. I'm not sure I could stand it if she was forced to pay a higher one.

"Tell me about my brother," I said.

He finished pouring the iced tea and settled back into his chair. He looked at the table and then raised his eyes. "You read in the paper about the big busts," Pistillo began. "You read about how the Fulton Fish Market's been cleaned up. You see the parade of old men doing the perp walk on the news, and you think, those days are over. The mob is gone. The cops have won."

He finished pouring the iced tea and sat back down. My own throat suddenly felt parched, sandy, as if it might close up altogether. I took a deep sip from my glass. The tea was too sweet.

"Do you know anything about Darwin?" he asked.

I thought the question was rhetorical, but he waited for an answer. I said, "Survival of the strongest, all that."

"Not the strongest," he said. "That's the modern interpretation, and it's wrong. The key for Darwin was not that the strongest survive—the most adaptable do. See the difference?"

I nodded.

"So the smarter bad guys, they adapted. They moved their business out of Manhattan. They sold drugs, for example, in the less competitive burbs. For your basic corruption, they started feeding on the Jersey cities. Camden, for example. Three of the last five mayors have been convicted of crimes. Atlantic City, I mean, c'mon, you don't cross the street without graft. Newark and all that revitalization bullshit. Revitalization means money. Money means kickbacks and graft."

I shifted in my chair. "Is there a point to this, Pistillo?"

"Yeah, asshole, there's a big point." His face reddened. His features remained steady, though not without great effort. "My brother-in-law—the father of those boys—tried to clean the streets of these scumbags. He worked undercover. Someone found out. And he and his partner ended up dead."

"And you think my brother was involved in that?"

"Yeah. Yeah, I do."

"You have proof?"

"Better than that." Pistillo smiled. "Your brother confessed."

I leaned back as if he'd taken a swing at me. I shook my head. Calm down. He would say and do anything, I reminded myself. Hadn't he been willing to frame me just last night?

"But we're getting ahead of ourselves, Will. And I don't want you to get the wrong idea. We don't think your brother killed anyone."

Another whiplash. "But you just said—"

He held up a hand. "Hear me out, okay?"

Pistillo rose again. He needed time. I could see that. His face was surprisingly matter-of-fact, composed even, but that was because he was jamming the rage back in the closet. I wondered if that closet door would hold. I wondered how often, when he looked at his sister, that door gave way and the rage was let loose.

"Your brother worked for Philip McGuane. I assume you know who he is."

I was giving him nothing. "Go on."

"McGuane is more dangerous than your pal Asselta, mostly because he's smarter. The OCID considers him one of the top guns on the East Coast."

"OCID?"

"Organized Crime Investigation Division," he said. "At a young age, McGuane saw the writing on the wall. Talk about adapting, this guy is the ultimate survivor. I won't go into detail about the current state of organized crime—the new Russians, the Triad, the Chinese, the old-world Italians. McGuane stayed two steps ahead of the competition. He was a boss by the time he was twenty-three. He works all the classics—drugs, prostitution, loan-sharking—but he specializes in graft and kickbacks and setting up his drug trade in less competitive spots away from the city."

I thought about what Tanya had said, about Sheila selling up at Haverton College.

"McGuane killed my brother-in-law and his partner, a guy named Curtis Angler. Your brother was involved. We arrested him but on lesser charges."

"When?"

"Six months before Julie Miller was murdered."

"How come I never heard anything about it?"

"Because Ken didn't tell you. And because we didn't want your brother. We wanted McGuane. So we flipped him."

"Flipped him?"

"We gave Ken immunity in exchange for his cooperation."

"You wanted him to testify against McGuane?"

"More than that. McGuane was careful. We didn't have enough to nail him on the murder indictment. We needed an informant. So we wired him up and sent him back in."

"You're saying that Ken worked undercover for you?"

Something flashed hard in Pistillo's eyes. "Don't glamorize it," he snapped. "Your low-life brother wasn't a law enforcement officer. He was just a scumbag trying to save his own skin."

I nodded, reminding myself yet again that this could all be a lie. "Go on," I said again.

He reached back and grabbed a cookie from the counter. He chewed slowly and washed it down with the iced tea. "We don't know what happened exactly. I can only give you our working theory."

"Okay."

"McGuane found out. You have to understand. McGuane is a brutal son of a bitch. Killing someone is always an option for him, you know, like deciding to take the Lincoln or Holland Tunnel. A matter of convenience, nothing more. He feels nothing."

I saw now where he was heading with this. "So if McGuane knew that Ken had become an informant—"

"Dead meat," he finished for me. "Your brother understood the risk. We were keeping tabs, but one night he just ran off."

"Because McGuane found out?"

"That's what we think, yes. He ended up at your house. We don't know why. Our theory is that he thought it was a safe place to hide, mostly because McGuane would never suspect he'd put his family in danger."

"And then?"

"By now you must have guessed that Asselta was working for McGuane too."

"If you say so," I said.

He ignored that. "Asselta had a lot to lose here too. You mentioned Laura Emerson, the other sorority sister who was killed. Your brother told us that Asselta murdered her. She was strangled, which is Asselta's favorite method of execution. According to Ken, Laura Emerson had found out about the drug trade at Haverton and was set to report it."

I made a face. "And they killed her for that?"

"Yeah, they killed her for that. What do you think they'd do, buy her an ice cream? These are monsters, Will. Get that through your thick head."

I remembered Phil McGuane coming over and playing Risk. He always won. He was quiet and observant, the sort of kid who makes you wonder about still waters and all that. He was class president, I think. I was impressed by him. The Ghost had been openly psychotic. I could see him doing anything. But McGuane?

"Somehow they learned where your brother was hiding. Maybe the Ghost followed Julie home from college, we don't know. Either way, he catches up to your brother at the Miller house. Our theory is that he tried to kill them both. You said you saw someone that night. We believe you. We also believe that the man you saw was probably Asselta. His fingerprints were found at the scene. Ken was wounded in the assault—that explains the blood—but somehow he got away. The Ghost was left with the body of Julie Miller. So what would be the natural thing to do? Make it look like Ken did it. What better way to discredit him or even scare him away?"

He stopped and started nibbling on another cookie. He would not look at me. I knew that he could be lying, but his words had the ring of truth. I tried to calm myself, let what he was telling me sink in. I kept my eyes on him. He kept his gaze on the cookie. Now it was my turn to fight back the rage.

"So all this time"—I stopped, swallowed, tried again—"so all this time, you knew that Ken didn't kill Julie."

"No, not at all."

"But you just said—"

"A theory, Will. It was just a theory. It's just as likely that he killed her."

"You don't believe that."

"Don't tell me what I believe."

"What could possibly be Ken's motive for killing Julie?"

"Your brother was a bad guy. Make no mistake about that."

"That's not a motive." I shook my head. "Why? If you knew Ken probably didn't kill her, why did you always insist he had?"

He chose not to reply. But maybe he didn't have to. The answer was suddenly obvious. I glanced at the snapshots on the refrigerator. They explained so much.

"Because you wanted Ken back at any cost," I said, answering my own question. "Ken was the only one who could give you McGuane. If he was hiding as a material witness, the world wouldn't really care. There would be no press coverage. There would be no major manhunt. But if Ken murdered a young woman in her family basement—the story of suburbia gone wrong—the media attention would be massive. And those headlines, you figured, would make it harder for him to hide."

He kept studying his hands.

"I'm right, aren't I?"

Pistillo slowly looked at me. "Your brother made a deal with us," he said coldly. "When he ran, he broke that deal."

"So that made it okay to lie?"

"It made it okay to track him down by any means necessary."

I was actually shaking. "And his family be damned?"

"Don't put that on me."

"Do you know what you did to us?"

"You know something, Will? I don't give a damn. You think you suffered? Look in my sister's eyes. Look at her sons."

"That doesn't make it right—"

He slammed his hand on the table. "Don't tell me about right and wrong. My sister was an innocent victim."

"So was my mother."

"No!" He pounded the table, this time with his fist, and pointed a finger at me. "There's a big difference between them, so get it straight. Vic was a murdered cop. He didn't have a choice. He couldn't stop his family's suffering. Your brother, on the other hand, chose to run. That was his decision. If that somehow hurt your family, blame him."

"But you made him run," I said. "Someone was trying to kill him—and you top that off by making him think he'll be arrested for murder. You forced his hand. You pushed him farther underground."

"That was his doing, not mine."

"You wanted to help your family, and in the process you sacrificed mine."

Pistillo snapped then, knocking the glass across the table. The iced tea splashed on me. The glass fell to the floor and shattered. He rose and looked down at me. "Don't you dare compare what your family went through with what my sister went through. Don't you dare."

I met his eye. Arguing with him would be useless—and I still did not know if he was telling the truth or twisting it for his own purposes. Either way, I wanted to learn more. Antagonizing him would do me no good. There was more to this story. He was not done yet. There was still too much unanswered.

The door opened. Claudia Fisher leaned her head in to check on the commotion. Pistillo put up a hand to tell her it was fine. He settled back into his chair. Fisher waited a beat and then left us alone.

Pistillo was still breathing heavily.

"So what happened next?" I asked him.

He looked up. "You haven't guessed?"

"No."

"It was a stroke of luck actually. One of our agents was vacationing in Stockholm. A fluke thing."

"What are you talking about?"

"Our agent," he said. "He spotted your brother on the street."

I blinked. "Wait a second. When was this?"

Pistillo did a quick calculation in his head. "Four months ago."

I was still confused. "And Ken got away?"

"Hell no. The agent didn't take any chances. He tackled your brother right then and there."

Pistillo folded his hands and leaned toward me. "We caught him," he said, his voice barely a whisper. "We caught your brother and brought him back."

45

Philip McGuane poured the brandy.

The body of the young lawyer Cromwell was gone now. Joshua Ford lay out like a bear rug. He was alive and even conscious, but he was not moving.

McGuane handed the Ghost a snifter. The two men sat together. McGuane took a deep sip. The Ghost cupped his glass and smiled.

"What?" McGuane asked.

"Fine brandy."

"Yes."

The Ghost stared at the liquor. "I was just remembering how we used to hang out in the woods behind Riker Hill and drink the cheapest beer we could find. Do you remember that, Philip?"

"Schlitz and Old Milwaukee," McGuane said.

"Yeah."

"Ken had that friend at Economy Wine and Liquor. He never ID'ed him."

"Good times," the Ghost said.

"This"—McGuane raised his glass—"is better."

"You think so?" The Ghost took a sip. He closed his eyes and swallowed. "Are you familiar with the philosophy that every choice you make splits the world into alternate universes?"

"I am."

"I often wonder if there are ones where we turn out differently—or, conversely, were we destined to be here no matter what?"

McGuane smirked. "You're not growing soft on me, are you, John?

"Not likely," the Ghost said. "But in moments of candor, I cannot help but wonder if it had to be this way."

"You like hurting people, John."

"I do."

"You've always enjoyed it."

The Ghost thought about that. "No, not always. But of course, the larger question is why?"

"Why do you like hurting people?"

"Not just hurting them. I enjoy killing them painfully. I choose strangulation because it is a horrible way to die. No quick bullet. No sudden knife slash. You literally gasp for your last breath. You feel the life-nourishing oxygen being denied you. I do that to them, up close, watching them struggle for a breath that never comes."

"My, my." McGuane put down his snifter. "You must be a barrel of laughs at parties, John."

"Oh indeed," he agreed. Then growing serious again, the Ghost said, "But why, Philip, do I get a rush from that? What happened to me, to my moral compass, that I feel my most alive while snuffing out someone's breath?"

"You're not going to blame your daddy, are you, John?"

"No, that would be too pat." He put down his drink and faced McGuane. "Would you have killed me, Philip? If I hadn't taken out the two men at the cemetery, would you have killed me?"

McGuane opted for the truth. "I don't know," he said. "Probably."

"And you're my best friend," the Ghost said.

"You're probably mine."

The Ghost smiled. "We were something, weren't we, Philip?"

McGuane did not reply.

"I met Ken when I was four," the Ghost continued. "All the kids in the neighborhood were warned to stay away from our house. The Asseltas were a bad influence—that's what they were told. You know the deal."

"I do," McGuane said.

"But for Ken, that was a draw. He used to love to explore our house. I remember when we found my old man's gun. We were six, I think. I remember holding it. The feeling of power. It mesmerized us. We used the gun to terrify Richard Werner—I don't think you know him, he moved away in the third grade. We kidnapped him once and tied him up. He cried and wet his pants."

"And you loved it."

The Ghost nodded slowly. "Perhaps."

"I have a question," McGuane said.

"I'm listening."

"If your father owned a gun, why use a kitchen knife on Daniel Skinner?"

The Ghost shook his head. "I don't want to talk about that."

"You never have."

"That's right."

"Why?"

He did not answer the question directly. "My old man found out about us playing with the gun," he said. "He beat me pretty good."

"He did that a lot."

"Yes."

"Have you ever sought revenge on him?" McGuane asked.

"On my father? No. He was too pitiful to hate. He never got over my mother walking out on us. He always thought she'd come back. He used to prepare for it. When he drank, he'd sit alone on the couch and talk to her and laugh with her and then he'd start sobbing. She broke his heart. I've hurt men, Philip. I've seen men beg to die. But I don't think I ever heard anything as pitiful as my father sobbing for my mother."

From the floor, Joshua Ford made a low groan. They both ignored him.

"Where is your father now?" McGuane asked.

"Cheyenne, Wyoming. He dried out. He found a good woman. He's a religious nut now. Traded alcohol for God—one addiction for another."

"You ever talk to him?

The Ghost's voice was soft. "No."

They drank in silence.

"What about you, Philip? You weren't poor. Your parents weren't abusive."

"Just parents," McGuane agreed.

"I know your uncle was mobbed up. He got you into the business. But you could have gone straight. Why didn't you?"

McGuane chuckled.

"What?"

"We're more different than I thought."

"How's that?"

"You regret it," McGuane said. "You do it, you get a thrill from it, you're good at it. But you see yourself as evil." He sat up suddenly. "My God."

"What?"

"You're more dangerous than I thought, John."

"How so?"

"You're not back for Ken," McGuane said. And then, his voice dropping: "You're back for that little girl, aren't you?"

The Ghost took a deep sip. He chose not to answer.

"Those choices and alternate universes you were talking about," McGuane went on. "You think if Ken died that night, it would all be different."

"It would indeed be an alternate universe," the Ghost said.

"But maybe not a better one," McGuane countered. Then he added, "So what now?"

"We'll need Will's cooperation. He's the only one who can draw Ken out."

"He won't help."

The Ghost frowned. "You, of all people, know better."

"His father?" McGuane asked.

"No."

"His sister?"

"She's too far away," the Ghost said.

"But you have an idea?"

"Think," the Ghost said.

McGuane did. And when he saw it, his face broke into a smile. "Katy Miller."

46

Pistillo kept his eyes on me, waiting for my reaction to his bombshell. But I recovered fast. Maybe this was beginning to make sense.

"You captured my brother?"

"Yes."

"And you extradited him back to the United States?"

"Yes."

"So how come it wasn't in the papers?" I asked.

"We kept it under wraps," Pistillo said.

"Because you were afraid McGuane would find out?"

"For the most part."

"What else?"

He shook his head.

"You still wanted McGuane," I said.

"Yes."

"And my brother could still deliver."

"He could help."

"So you cut another deal with him."

"We pretty much reinstated the old one."

I saw a clearing in the haze. "And you put him in the witness protection program?"

Pistillo nodded. "Originally we kept him in a hotel under protective custody. But by then a lot of what your brother had was old. He would still be a key witness—probably the most important we'd have—but we needed more time. We couldn't keep him in a hotel forever, and he didn't want to stay. Ken hired a big-time lawyer, and we worked out a deal. We found him a place in New Mexico. He had to report to one of our agents on a daily basis. We would call him to testify when we needed him. Any break in that deal, and the charges, including the murder charge from Julie Miller, could be reinstated."

"So what went wrong?"

"McGuane found out about it."

"How?"

"We don't know. A leak maybe. Whatever, McGuane sent out two goons to kill your brother."

"The two dead men at the house," I said.

"Yes."

"Who killed them?"

"We think your brother. They underestimated him. He killed them and ran again."

"And now you want Ken back again."

His gaze wandered over to the photographs on the refrigerator door. "Yes."

"But I don't know where he is."

"I know that now. Look, maybe we screwed up here. I don't know. But Ken needs to come in. We'll protect him, around-the-clock surveillance, a safe house, whatever he wants. That's the carrot. The stick is that his prison sentence is subject to his cooperation."

"So what do you want from me?"

"He'll reach out to you eventually."

"What makes you so sure?"

He sighed and stared at the glass.

"What makes you so sure?" I asked again.

"Because," Pistillo said, "Ken called you already."

A block of lead formed in my chest.

"There were two calls placed from a pay phone near your brother's house in Albuquerque to your apartment," he went on. "One was made about a week before the two goons were killed. The other, right after."

I should have been shocked, but I wasn't. Maybe it finally fit, only I didn't like how.

"You didn't know about the calls, did you, Will?"

I swallowed and thought about who, besides me, might answer the phone if Ken had indeed called.

Sheila.

"No," I said. "I didn't know about them."

He nodded. "We didn't know that when we first approached you. It was natural to figure you were the one who answered the phone."

I looked at him. "How does Sheila Rogers fit into this?"

"Her fingerprints were found at the murder scene."

"I know that."

"So let me ask you, Will. We knew your brother had called you. We knew your girlfriend had visited Ken's house in New Mexico. If you were us, what would you have concluded?"

"That I was somehow involved."

"Right. We figured that Sheila was your go-between or something, that you'd been helping your brother out. And when Ken ran off, we figured you two knew where he was."

"But now you know better."

"That's correct."

"So what do you suspect now?"

"The same thing you do, Will." His voice was soft, and—damn him—I heard pity in it. "That Sheila Rogers used you. That she worked for McGuane. That she's the one who tipped him off about your brother. And that when the hit went wrong, McGuane had her killed."

Sheila. Her betrayal pierced me deep, struck bone. To defend her now, to think I had been anything more to her than a dupe, would be to turn a blind eye in the worst way. You would have to be naïve beyond Pollyanna, to have rose-tinted glasses melded onto your face, to not be able to see the truth.

"I'm telling you all this, Will, because I was afraid you were about to do something stupid."

"Like talk to the press," I said.

"Yes—and because I want you to understand. Your brother had two choices. Either McGuane and the Ghost find him and kill him, or we find him and protect him."

"Right," I said. "And you guys have done a bang-up job of that so far."

"We're still his best option," he countered. "And don't think McGuane will stop with your brother. Do you really think that attack on Katy Miller was a coincidence? For all your sakes, we need your cooperation."

I said nothing. I could not trust him. I knew that. I could not trust anyone. That was all I had learned here. But Pistillo was especially dangerous. He had spent eleven years looking into his sister's shattered face. That kind of thing twists you. I knew about stuff like that, about wanting to the point of distortion. Pistillo had made it clear that he would stop at nothing to get McGuane. He would sacrifice my brother. He had jailed me. And most of all, he had destroyed my family. I thought about my sister running off to Seattle. I thought about my mom, the Sunny smile, and realized that the man sitting in front of me, this man who claimed to be my brother's salvation, had smothered it away. He had killed my mother—no one could convince me that the cancer was not somehow connected to what she went through, that her immune system had not been another victim of that horrible night—and now he wanted me to help him.

I did not know how much of this was a lie. But I decided to lie right back. "I'll help," I said.

"Good," he said. "I'll make sure the charges against you are dropped right away."

I did not say thank you.

"We'll drive you back if you'd like."

I wanted to refuse, but I did not want to raise any warning flags. He wanted to deceive, well, I could try that too. So I said that would be fine. When I rose, he said, "I understand that Sheila's funeral is coming up."

"Yes."

"Now that there are no charges against you, you're free to travel."

I said nothing.

"Are you going to attend?" he asked.

This time I told the truth. "I don't know."

47

I couldn't stay at home waiting for I-don't-know-what, so in the morning, I went to work. It was a funny thing. I expected to be fairly worthless, but that wasn't the case at all. Entering Covenant House—I can only compare the experience to an athlete strapping on his "game face" when he enters the arena. These kids, I reminded myself, deserve nothing less than my best. Cliché, sure, but I convinced myself and faded contentedly into my work.

Sure, people came up to me and offered their condolences. And yes, Sheila's spirit was everywhere. There were few spots in this dwelling that did not hold a memory of her. But I was able to play through it. This is not to say I forgot about it or no longer wanted to pursue where my brother was or who killed Sheila or the fate of her daughter, Carly. That was all still there. But today there was not much I could do. I had called Katy's hospital room, but the blockade was still in place. Squares had a detective agency running Sheila's Donna White pseudonym through the airline computers and thus far, they had not gotten a hit. So I waited.

I volunteered to work the outreach van that night. Squares joined me—I had already filled him in on everything—and together we disappeared into the dark. The children of the street were lit up in the blue of the night. Their faces were flat, no lines, sleek. You see an adult vagrant, a bag lady, a man with a shopping cart, someone lying in a box, someone begging for change with a diner paper coffee cup, and you know that they are homeless. But the thing about adolescents, about the fifteen- and sixteen-year-olds who run away from abuse, who embrace addiction or prostitution or insanity, is that they blend in better. With adolescents you cannot tell if they are homeless or just wandering.

Despite what you hear, it is not that easy to ignore the plight of the adult homeless. It is too in-your-face. You may divert your eyes and keep walking and remind yourself that if you gave in, if you tossed them a dollar or some quarters, they'd just buy booze or drugs or whatever rationale sails your boat, but what you did, the fact that you just hurried by a human being in need, still registers, still causes a pang. Our kids, however, are truly invisible. They are seamlessly sewn into the night. You can neglect and there are no aftereffects.

Music blared, something with a heavy Latin beat. Squares handed me a stack of phone cards to hand out. We hit a dive on Avenue A known for its heroin and started our familiar rap. We talked and cajoled and listened. I saw the gaunt eyes. I saw the way they scratched away at the imaginary bugs under their skin. I saw the needle marks and the sunken veins.

At four in the morning, Squares and I were back in the van. We had not spoken to each other much in the last few hours. He looked out the window. The children were still out there. More seemed to come out as though the bricks bled them.

"We should go to the funeral," Squares said.

I did not trust my voice.

"You ever see her out here?" he asked. "Her face when she worked with these kids?"

I had. And I knew what he meant.

"You don't fake that, Will."

"I wish I could believe that," I said.

"How did Sheila make you feel?"

"Like I was the luckiest man in the world," I said.

He nodded. "You don't fake that either," he said.

"So how do you explain it all?"

"I don't." Squares shifted into drive and pulled into the street. "But we're doing so much with our heads. Maybe we just need to remember the heart too."

I frowned. "That sounds good, Squares, but I'm not sure it makes any sense."

"How about this then: We go to pay our respects to the Sheila we knew."

"Even if that was just a lie?"

"Even if. But maybe we also go to learn. To understand what happened here."

"Weren't you the one who said we might not like what we find?"

"Hey, that's right." Squares wriggled his eyebrows. "Damn, I'm good."

I smiled.

"We owe it to her, Will. To her memory."

He had a point. It came back to closure. I needed answers. Maybe someone at the funeral could supply some—and maybe the funeral in and of itself, the act of burying my faux beloved, would help the healing process. I couldn't imagine it, but I was willing to give anything a shot.

"And there's still Carly to consider." Squares pointed out the window. "Saving kids. That's what we're all about, isn't it?"

I turned to him. "Yeah," I said. And then: "And speaking of children."

I waited. I could not see his eyes—he often, like the old Corey Hart song, wore his sunglasses at night—but his grip on the steering wheel tightened.

"Squares?"

His tone was clipped. "We're talking about you and Sheila here."

"That's the past. Whatever we learn, it won't change that."

"Let's concentrate on one thing at a time, okay?"

"Not okay," I said. "This friendship thing. It's supposed to be a two-way street."

He shook his head. He started the van and drove. We fell into silence. I kept my eyes on his pockmarked, unshaven face. The tattoo seemed to darken. He was biting his lower lip.

After some time he said, "I never told Wanda."

"About having a child?"

"A son," Squares said softly.

"Where is he now?"

He took one hand off the wheel and scratched at something on his face. The hand, I noticed, had a quake to it. "He was six feet under before he was four years old."

I closed my eyes.

"His name was Michael. I wanted nothing to do with him. I only saw him twice. I left him alone with his mother, a seventeen-year-old drug addict you wouldn't trust to watch a dog. When he was three years old, she got stoned and drove straight into a semi. Killed them both. I still don't know if it was suicide or not."

"I'm so sorry," I said weakly.

"Michael would be twenty-one now."

I fumbled for something to say. Nothing was working, but I tried anyway. "That was a long time ago," I said. "You were just a kid."

"Don't try to rationalize, Will."

"I'm not. I just mean"—I had no idea how to put it—"if I had a child, I'd ask you to be the godfather. I'd make you the guardian if anything happened to me. I wouldn't do that out of friendship or loyalty. I'd do that to be selfish. For the sake of my kid."

He kept driving. "There are some things you can never forgive."

"You didn't kill him, Squares."

"Sure, right, I'm totally blameless."

We hit a red light. He flipped on the radio. Talk station. One of those radio infomercials selling a miracle diet drug. He snapped it off. He leaned forward and rested his forearms on the top of the steering wheel.

"I see the kids out here. I try to rescue them. I keep thinking that if I save enough, I don't know, maybe it will change things for Michael. Maybe I can somehow save him." The sunglasses came off. His voice grew harder. "But what I know is—what I've always known—is that no matter what I do, I'm not worth saving."

I shook my head. I tried to think of something comforting or enlightening or at least distracting, but nothing broke through the filter. Every line I came up with sounded hackneyed and canned. Like most tragedies, it explained so much and yet told you nothing about the man.

In the end, all I said was "You're wrong."

He put the sunglasses back on and faced the road. I could see him shutting down.

I decided to push it. "You talk about going to this funeral because we owe Sheila something. But what about Wanda?"

"Will?"

"Yeah."

"I don't think I want to talk about this anymore."

48

The early morning flight to Boise was uneventful. We took off from LaGuardia, which could be a lousier airport but not without a serious act of God. I got my customary seat in economy class, the one behind a tiny old lady who insists on reclining her seat against my knees for the duration of the flight. Studying her gray follicles and pallid scalp—her head was practically in my lap—helped distract me.

Squares sat on my right. He was reading an article on himself in *Yoga Journal*. Every once in a while he would nod at something he read about himself and say, "True, too true, I am that." He did that to annoy me. That was why he was my best friend.

I was able to keep the block up until we saw the WELCOME TO MASON, IDAHO sign. Squares had rented a Buick Skylark. We got lost twice on the trip. Even here, out in the supposed sticks, the strip malls dominated. There were all the customary mega-stores—the Chef Central, the Home Depot, the Old Navy—the country uniting in bloated monotony.

The chapel was small and white and totally unspectacular. I spotted Edna Rogers. She stood outside by herself, smoking a cigarette. Squares pulled to a stop. I felt my stomach tighten. I stepped out of the car. The grass was burnt brown. Edna Rogers looked our way. With her eyes still on me, she let loose a long breath of smoke.

I started toward her. Squares stayed by my side. I felt hollow, far away. Sheila's funeral. We were here to bury Sheila. The thought spun like the horizontal on an old TV set.

Edna Rogers kept puffing on the cigarette, her eyes hard and dry. "I didn't know if you'd make it," she said to me.

"I'm here."

"Have you learned anything about Carly?"

"No," I said, which was not really true. "How about you?"

She shook her head. "The police aren't looking too hard. They say there is no record of Sheila having a child. I don't even think they believe she exists."

The rest was a fast-forward blur. Squares interrupted and offered his condolences. Other mourners approached. They were mostly men in business suits. Listening in, I realized that most worked with Sheila's father at a plant that made garage-door openers. That struck me as odd, but at the time I didn't know why. I shook more hands and forgot every name. Sheila's father was a tall, handsome man. He greeted me with a bear hug and moved toward his co-workers. Sheila had a brother and a sister, both younger, both surly and distracted.

We all stayed outside, almost as though we were afraid to begin the ceremony. People broke down into groups. The younger folks stayed with Sheila's brother and sister. Sheila's father stood in a semi-circle with the suited men, all nodding, with fat ties and hands in their pockets. The women clustered nearest the door.

Squares drew stares, but he was used to that. He still had on the dust-ridden jeans, but he also wore a blue blazer and gray tie. He would have worn a suit, he said with a smile, but then Sheila would have never recognized him.

Eventually the mourners started to filter into the small chapel. I was surprised by the large turnout, but everyone I'd met was there for the family, not Sheila. She had left them a long time ago. Edna Rogers slid next to me and put her arm through mine. She looked up and forced a brave smile. I still did not know what to make of her.

We entered the chapel last. There were whispers about how "good" Sheila looked, how "lifelike," a comment I always found creepy in the extreme. I am not a religious fellow, but I like the way we of the Hebrew faith handle our dead—that is, we get them in the ground fast. We do not have open caskets.

I don't like open caskets.

I don't like them for all the obvious reasons. Looking at a dead body, one that has been drained of both life force and fluids, embalmed, dressed nicely, painted up, looking either like something from Madame Tussaud's wax museum or worse, so "lifelike" you almost expect it to breathe or suddenly sit up, yeah, you bet that gives me the creeps. But more than that, what kind of lasting image did a corpse laid out like a lox leave on the bereaved? Did I want my final memory of Sheila to be here, lying with her eyes closed in a well-cushioned—why were caskets always so well-cushioned?—hermetically sealed box of fine mahogany? As I got on at the end of the line with Edna Rogers—we actually stood on line to view this hollow vessel—these thoughts became heavy, weighing me down.

But there was no way out either. Edna gripped my arm a little too tightly. As we got closer, her knees buckled. I helped her stay upright. She smiled at me again, and this time, there seemed to be genuine sweetness in it.

"I loved her," she whispered. "A mother never stops loving her child."

I nodded, afraid to speak. We took another step, the process not so different from boarding that damn airplane. I almost expected a voice-over to say "Mourners in rows twenty-five and higher may now view the body." Stupid thought, but I let my mind dodge and veer. Anything to get away from this.

Squares stood behind us, last in line. I kept my eyes diverted, but as we moved forward, there was that unreasonable hope again knocking at my chest. I don't think this is unusual. It happened even at my mother's funeral, the idea that it was all somehow a mistake, a cosmic blunder, that I would look down at the casket and it would be empty or it wouldn't be Sheila. Maybe that was why some people liked open caskets. Finality. You see, you accept. I was with my mother when she died. I watched her last breath. Yet I was still tempted to check the casket that day, just to make sure, just in case maybe God changed his mind.

Many bereaved, I think, go through something like that. Denial is part of the process. So you hope against hope. I was doing that now. I was making deals with an entity I don't really believe in, praying for a miracle—that somehow the fingerprints and the FBI and Mr. and Mrs. Rogers's ID and all these friends and family members, that somehow they were all wrong, that Sheila was alive, that she had not been murdered and dumped on the side of the road.

But that, of course, did not happen.

Not exactly anyway.

When Edna Rogers and I arrived at the casket, I made myself look down. And when I did, the floor beneath me fell away. I started plummeting.

"They did a nice job, don't you think?" Mrs. Rogers whispered.

She gripped my arm and started to cry. But that was somewhere else, somewhere far away. I was not with her. I was looking down. And that was when the truth dawned on me.

Sheila Rogers was indeed dead. No doubt about that.

But the woman I loved, the woman I'd lived with and held and wanted to marry, was not Sheila Rogers.

49

I did not black out, but I came close.

The room did indeed spin. My vision did one of those in-and-out, closer-and-farther things. I stumbled toward, almost landing in the casket with Sheila Rogers—a woman I had never seen before but knew too intimately. A hand shot out and gripped my forearm. Squares. I looked at him. His face was set. His color gone. Our eyes met and he gave me the slightest of nods.

It hadn't been my imagination or a mirage. Squares had seen it too.

We stayed for the funeral. What else really could we do? I sat there, unable to take my eyes off the stranger's corpse, unable to speak. I was overcome, my body quaking, but nobody paid any attention. I was, after all, at a funeral.

After the casket was lowered into the ground, Edna Rogers wanted us to come back to the house. We begged off, blaming the airlines for the tight flight schedule. We slipped into the rental car. Squares started it up. We waited until we were out of sight. Then Squares pulled over and let me lose it.

"Let me see if we're on the same page here," Squares said.

I nodded, quasi-composed now. Again I had to block, this time muffling the possible euphoria. I did not keep my eye on the prize or the big picture or any of that. I concentrated on the details, on the minutiae. I focused on one tree because there was no way I could handle seeing the whole forest.

"All that stuff we learned about Sheila," he said, "her running away, her years on the streets, her selling drugs, her rooming with your old girlfriend, her fingerprints at your brother's place—all that—"

"Applied to that stranger we just buried," I finished for him.

"So our Sheila, I mean, the lady we both thought of as Sheila—"

"Did none of those things. And she was none of those things."

Squares considered that. "Styling," he said.

I managed a smile. "Most definitely."

On the airplane, Squares said, "If our Sheila is not dead, then she's alive."

I looked at him.

"Hey," he said, "people pay big bucks to soak in this kind of wisdom."

"And to think I get it for free."

"So what do we do now?"

I crossed my arms. "Donna White."

"The pseudonym she bought from the Goldbergs?"

"Right. Your people only ran an airline check?"

He nodded. "We were trying to figure out how she got out west."

"Can you get the agency to widen their search now?"

"Sure, I guess."

The flight attendant gave us our "snack." My brain kept whirring. This flight was doing me a ton of good. It gave me time to think. Unfortunately, it was also giving me time to shift realities, to see the repercussions. I fought that off. I didn't want hope clouding my thinking. Not yet. Not when I still knew so little. But still.

"It explains a lot," I said.

"Like?"

"Her secrecy. Her not wanting her picture taken. Her having so few possessions. Her not wanting to talk about her past."

Squares nodded.

"One time, Sheila"—I stopped because that was probably not her name—"she slipped and mentioned growing up on a farm. But the real Sheila Rogers's father worked for a company that made garage-door openers. She was also terrified at the very idea of calling her parents—because, put simply, they weren't her parents. I took it all to mean a terribly abusive past."

"But it could just have easily have been someone in hiding."

"Right."

"So the real Sheila Rogers," Squares went on, his eyes looking up, "I mean, the one we just buried back there, she dated your brother?"

"So it seems."

"And her fingerprints were at the murder scene."

"Right."

"And your Sheila?"

I shrugged.

"Okay," Squares said, "So we assume the woman with Ken in New Mexico, the one the neighbors saw, that was the dead Sheila Rogers?"

"Yes."

"And they had a little girl with them," he went on.

Silence.

Squares looked at me. "Are you thinking the same thing I am?"

I nodded. "That the little girl was Carly. And that Ken might very well be her father."

"Yeah."

I sat back and closed my eyes. Squares opened his snack, checked the contents, cursed them.

"Will?"

"Yeah."

"The woman you loved. Any idea who she is?"

With my eyes still closed, I said, "None."

50

Squares went home. He promised to call me the moment they got anything on the Donna White pseudonym. I headed home, bleeding exhaustion. When I reached my apartment door, I put the key in the lock. A hand touched down on my shoulder. I jumped back, startled.

"It's okay," she said.

Katy Miller.

Her voice was hoarse. She wore a neck brace. Her face was swollen. Her eyes were bloodshot. Where the brace stopped under the chin, I could see the deep purple and yellow of bruising.

"Are you okay?" I asked.

She nodded.

I hugged her gingerly, too gingerly, using just my arms, keeping my distance for fear of hurting her further.

"I won't break," she said.

"When did you get out?" I asked.

"A few hours ago. I can't stay long. If my father knew where I was—"

I held up a hand. "Say no more."

We pushed open the door and stepped inside. She grimaced in pain as she moved. We made our way to the couch. I asked her if she wanted a drink or something to eat. She said no.

"Are you sure you should be out of the hospital?"

"They said it's okay, but I need to rest."

"How did you get away from your father?"

She tried a smile. "I'm headstrong."

"I see."

"And I lied."

"No doubt."

She looked off with just her eyes—she could not move her head—and her eyes welled up. "Thank you, Will."

I shook my head. "I can't help but feel it was my fault."

"That's crap," she said.

I shifted in my seat. "During the attack, you yelled out the name John. At least, I think that's what you said."

"The police told me."

"You don't remember?"

She shook her head.

"What do you remember?"

"The hands on my throat." She looked off. "I was sleeping. And then someone was squeezing my neck. I remember gasping for air." Her voice fell away.

"Do you know who John Asselta is?" I asked.

"Yeah. He was friends with Julie."

"Could you have meant him?"

"You mean when I yelled John?" She considered that. "I don't know, Will. Why?"

"I think"—I remembered my promise to Pistillo about keeping her out of it—"I think he may have had something to do with Julie's murder."

She took that without blinking. "When you say have something to do with—"

"That's all I can say right now."

"You sound like a cop."

"It's been a weird week," I said.

"So tell me what you got."

"I know you're curious, but I think you should listen to the doctors."

She looked at me hard. "What's that supposed to mean?"

"I think you need to rest."

"You want me to stay out of this?"

"Yes."

"You're afraid I'll get hurt again."

"Very much so, yes."

Her eyes caught fire. "I can take care of myself."

"No doubt. But we're on very dangerous ground right now."

"And what have we been on up to now?"

Touché. "Look, I need you to trust me here."

"Will?"

"Yeah."

"You're not getting rid of me that easy."

"I don't want to get rid of you," I said. "But I do need to protect you."

"You can't," she said softly. "You know that."

I said nothing.

Katy slid closer to me. "I need to see this through. You, more than anyone, should understand."

"I do."

"Then?"

"I promised I wouldn't say anything."

"Promised who?"

I shook my head. "Just trust me, okay?"

She stood up. "Not okay."

"I'm trying—"

"And if I told you to butt out, would you listen to me?"

I kept my head down. "I can't say anything."

She headed for the door.

"Wait a second," I said.

"I don't have time for this now," she said shortly. "My father will be wondering where I am."

I stood. "Call me, okay?" I gave her the cell phone number. I'd already memorized hers.

She slammed the door on her way out.

Katy Miller reached the street. Her neck hurt like hell. She was pushing too hard, she knew that, but that could not be helped. She was fuming. Had they gotten to Will? It hadn't seemed possible, but maybe he was just as bad as all the rest. Or maybe not. Maybe he really believed he was protecting her.

She would have to be even more careful now.

Her throat was dry. She craved a drink, but swallowing was still a painful chore. She wondered when this would all be over. Soon, she hoped. But she would see this through to the end. She had promised herself that. There was no going back, no end, not until Julie's murderer had been brought to justice one way or the other.

She headed south to 18th Street and then headed west into the meatpacking district. It was quiet now, in that lull between the daylight unloading and the perverse past-midnight nightlife. The city was like that, a theater that put on two different shows daily, changing props and sets and even actors. But day or night or even dusk, this street always had that rotted-meat smell. You could not get it out. Human or animal, Katy was not sure which.

The panic was back.

She stopped and tried to push it away. The feel of those hands clamped on her throat, toying with her, opening and closing her windpipe at will. Such power against such helplessness. He had stopped her breath. Think about that. He had squeezed her neck until she stopped breathing, until her life force began to ebb away.

Just like with Julie.

She was so lost in the horrible memory that she did not know he was there until he grabbed her elbow. She spun around. "What the—?"

The Ghost did not loosen his grip. "I understand you were calling for me," he said in that purr voice. Then smiling, he added, "Well, here I am."

51

I sat there. Katy had every right to be mad. But I could live with her anger. It was far preferable to another funeral. I rubbed my eyes. I put my feet up. I think I might have fallen asleep—I can't say for sure—but when the phone rang, I was surprised to see it was morning. I checked the caller ID. It was Squares. I fumbled for the receiver and put it to my ear.

"Hey," I said.

He skipped the pleasantries. "I think we found our Sheila."

Half an hour later, I entered the lobby of the Regina Hotel.

It was less than a mile from our apartment. We had thought she had run across the country, but Sheila . . . what else was I supposed to call her? . . . had stayed that close.

The detective agency Squares liked to use had little trouble tracking her down, especially since she'd gotten careless since her namesake's death. She had deposited money in First National and taken out a debit Visa card. You cannot stay in this city—hell, most anyplace—without a credit card. The days of signing into motels with a false name and paying cash are pretty much over. There are a few dives, dwellings not truly fit for human habitation, that might still look the other way, but almost everyplace else wants to, at the very least, take a credit card impression—in case you steal something or seriously damage your room. The transaction doesn't necessarily go through the system—like I said, they might just make an impression—but you still need the card.

She probably assumed that she was safe and that was understandable. The Goldbergs, a couple who survived by being discreet, had sold her an ID. No reason to believe that they would ever talk—the only reason they had was because of their friendship with Squares and Raquel, plus the fact that they in part blamed themselves for her theoretical murder. Add on to that the fact that now Sheila Rogers was "dead" and thus nobody would be tracking her down, well, it made sense that she would let down her guard just a bit.

The credit card had been used to withdraw funds from an ATM yesterday in Union Square. From there it was just a question of hitting the nearby hotels. Most detective work is done through sources and payoffs, which are really one and the same. The good detectives have paid sources at phone companies, the tax bureau, credit card companies, the DMV, whatever. If you think this is difficult—that it would be hard to find somebody who will provide confidential information for cash—you do not read the papers much.

But this was even easier. Just call the hotels and ask to speak with Donna White. You do that until one hotel says "Please hold" and connects you. And now, as I took the steps into the lobby of the Regina Hotel, I felt the jangle. She was alive. I couldn't let myself believe that—would not believe it—until I saw her with my own eyes. Hope does funny things to a brain. It can darken as well as lighten. Where before I had made myself believe that a miracle was possible, now I feared that it might all be taken away from me again, that this time, when I looked into that casket, my Sheila would be there.

Love you always.

That was what her note said. Always.

I approached the front desk. I'd told Squares that I wanted to handle this alone. He understood. The receptionist, a blond woman with a hesitant smile, was on the phone. She shot me the teeth and pointed to the phone to let me know that she would be off soon. I gave her a no-rush shrug and leaned against the desk, feigning relaxed.

A minute later, she replaced the receiver and gave me her undivided attention. "May I help you?"

"Yes," I said. My voice sounded unnatural, too modulated, as if I were hosting one of those lite-FM programs. "I'm here to see Donna White. Could you give me her room number?"

"I'm sorry, sir. We don't give out our guests' room numbers."

I almost slapped myself in the forehead. How stupid could I be? "Of course, my apologies. I'll call up first. Do you have a house phone?"

She pointed to the right. Three white phones, none with keypads, lined the wall. I picked one up and listened to the ring. An operator came on. I asked her to connect me to the room of Donna White. She said—and I noticed that this is the new all-purpose, hotel-employee catch phrase—"A pleasure," and then I heard the phone ring.

My heart crawled up my windpipe.

Two rings. Then three. On the sixth ring, I was transferred into the hotel's voice mail system. A mechanical voice told me that the guest was not available at this time and what to do if I wanted to leave a message. I hung up.

Now what?

Wait, I guess. What else was there? I bought a newspaper at the stand and found a spot in the corner of the lobby where I could see the door. I kept the newspaper up over my face, *Spy vs. Spy* style, and felt like a total idiot. My insides churned. I never thought of myself as the type for an ulcer, but over the past few days, a burning acidity had started clawing at my stomach lining.

I tried to read the paper—a totally futile act, of course. I couldn't concentrate. I couldn't muster up the energy to care about current events. I couldn't keep my place while glancing at the door every three seconds. I turned the pages. I looked at the pictures. I tried to give a damn about the box scores. I flipped to the comics, but even Beetle Bailey was too taxing.

The blond receptionist would flick her gaze in my direction every once in a while. When our eyes met, she'd smile in a patronizing way. Keeping her eye on me, no doubt. Or maybe that was more paranoid thinking. I was just a man reading a newspaper in the lobby. I had done nothing to arouse her suspicion.

An hour passed without incident. My cell phone rang. I put it to my ear.

"You see her yet?" Squares asked.

"She's not in her room. Or at least she's not answering the phone."

"Where are you now?"

"I'm staking out the lobby."

Squares made a sound.

"What?" I asked.

"Did you really say 'staking out'?"

"Give me a break, okay?"

"Look, why don't we just hire a couple of guys from the agency to do it right? They'll call us as soon as she gets in."

I considered that. "Not yet," I said.

And that was when she entered.

My eyes widened. My breathing started coming in deep swallows. My God. It was really my Sheila. She was alive. I fumbled the phone, almost dropping it.

"Will?"

"I have to go," I said.

"She there?"

"I'll call you back."

I clicked off the power. My Sheila—I'll call her that because I don't know how else to refer to her—had changed her hair. It was cut shorter, flipping up and under at the end of the swan neck. She had bangs now too. The color had been darkened to an Elvira black. But the effect . . . I saw her and it was like someone punched my chest with a giant fist.

Sheila kept moving. I started to rise. The dizziness made me pull up. She walked the way she always walked—no hesitation, head high, with purpose. The elevator door was already opened, and I realized that I might not make it in time.

She stepped inside. I was on my feet now. I hurried across the lobby without running. I did not want to make a scene. Whatever was happening here—whatever had made her vanish and change names and wear a disguise and Lord knows what else—needed to be somewhat finessed. I could not just yell out her name and sprint across the lobby.

My feet clacked on the marble. The sound echoed too loudly in my own ears. I was going to be late. I stopped and watched the elevator doors shut.

Damn.

I pressed the call button. Another elevator opened immediately. I started toward it but pulled up. Wait, what good would that do? I didn't even know what floor she was on. I checked the lights above my Sheila's elevator. They moved steadily. Floor five, then six.

Had Sheila been the only one in the elevator?

I thought so.

The elevator stopped on the ninth floor. Okay, fine. Now I pushed the call button. The same elevator was there. I hurried inside and pressed nine, hoping that I would get there before she entered her room. The door started closing. I leaned against the back. At the last second, a hand shot through. The doors banged against the hand and then opened. A sweaty man in a gray business suit sighed his way in, offering me a nod. He pressed eleven. The door closed again and we were on our way up.

"Hot out," he said to me.

"Yeah."

He sighed again. "Good hotel, don't you think?"

A tourist, I thought. I had been in a million New York City elevators before. New Yorkers understood the rules: You stare up at the flashing numbers. You do not engage anyone in conversation.

I told him that yes, it was nice, and as the doors opened, I dashed out. The corridor was long. I looked to my left. Nothing. I looked to my right and heard a door close. Like a hunting dog on point, I sprinted toward the sound. Right-hand side, I thought. End of the corridor.

I followed the audible scent, if you will, and deduced that the sound had come from either room 912 or 914. I looked at one door, then the other. I remembered an episode of *Batman* where Catwoman promises that one door will lead to her, the other to a live tiger. Batman chose wrong. Well, hell, this isn't *Batman*.

I knocked on both doors. I stood between them and waited.

Nothing.

I knocked again, harder this time. Movement. I was rewarded with some kind of movement emanating from room 912. I slid in front of the door. I adjusted my shirt collar. Now I could hear the security chain being slid to the side. I braced myself. The knob turned and the door began to swing open.

The man was burly and annoyed. He wore a V-neck undershirt and striped boxers. He barked, "What?"

"I'm sorry. I was looking for Donna White."

He put his fists on his hips. "Do I look like Donna White?"

Strange sounds emanated from the gruff man's room. I listened closer. Groans. Quasi-passionate groans of faux pleasure. The man met my eye, but he didn't look happy about it. I stepped back. Spectravision, I thought. In-room movies. The man was watching a skin flick. Porno interruptus.

"Uh, sorry," I said.

He slammed the door shut.

Okay, let's rule out room 912. At least, I hoped like hell I could. This was crazy. I raised my hand to knock on 914, when I heard a voice say, "Can I help you?"

I turned and at the end of the corridor, I saw a no-neck buzz cut wearing a blue blazer. The blazer had a small logo on his lapel and a patch on his upper arm. He puffed out his chest. Hotel security and proud of it.

"No, I'm fine," I said.

He frowned. "Are you a guest of the hotel?"

"Yes."

"What's your room number?"

"I don't have a room number."

"But you just said—"

I rapped the door hard. Buzz Cut hurried toward me. For a moment I thought he might make a diving tackle in order to protect the door, but at the last moment, he pulled up.

"Please come with me," he said.

I ignored him and knocked again. There was still no answer. Buzz Cut put his arm on mine. I shook it off, knocked again, and yelled, "I know you're not Sheila." That confused Buzz Cut. He frowned some more. We both stopped and watched the door. Nobody answered. Buzz Cut took my arm again, more gently this time. I did not put up a fight. He led me downstairs and through the lobby.

I was out on the sidewalk. I turned. Buzz Cut puffed his chest again and crossed his arms.

Now what?

Another New York City axiom: You cannot stand in one place on a sidewalk. Flow is essential. People hurry by and they don't expect to find something in their way. If they do, they may veer but they never stop.

I looked for a safe place. The secret was to stay as close to the actual building as possible—the shoulder of the sidewalk, if you will. I huddled near a plate glass window, took out the cell phone, called the hotel, and asked to be connected to Donna White's room. I got another "a pleasure" and was patched through.

There was no answer.

This time I left a simple message. I gave her my cell phone number and tried not to sound like I was begging when I asked her to call.

I slid the phone back into my pocket and again asked myself: Now what?

My Sheila was inside. The thought made me light-headed. Too much yearning. Too many possibilities and what-ifs. I made myself push it away.

Okay, fine, so what did that mean exactly? First off, was there another way out? A basement or back exit? Had she spotted me from behind those sunglasses? Was that why she hurried to the elevator? When I followed her, had I made a mistake about the room number? That could be. I knew that she was on the ninth floor. That was a start. Or did I? If she spotted me, could she have stopped at another floor as a decoy?

Do I stand out here?

I didn't know. I couldn't go home, that was for sure. I took a deep breath. I watched the pedestrians race by, so many of them, one bleary mass, separate entities making up a whole. And then, looking through the mass, I saw her.

My heart stopped.

She just stood there and stared at me. I was too overwhelmed to move. I felt something inside me give way. I put my hand to my mouth to stifle a cry. She moved toward me. Tears stung her eyes. I shook my head. She did not stop. She reached me and pulled me close.

"It's okay," she whispered.

I closed my eyes. For a long while we just held each other. We did not speak. We did not move. We just slipped away.

52

"My real name is Nora Spring."

We sat in the lower level of a Starbucks on Park Avenue South, in a corner near an emergency fire exit. No one else was down here. She kept her eyes on the stairs, worried I'd been followed. This Starbucks, like so many others, had earth tones, surreal swirling artwork, and large photographs of brown-skinned men too happily picking coffee beans. She held a venti iced latte between both hands. I went with the frappuccino.

The chairs were purple and oversize and just plush enough. We pushed them together. We held hands. I was confused, of course. I wanted answers. But beyond that, on a whole higher plane, the pure joy splashed through me. It was an amazing rush. It calmed me. I was happy. Whatever I was about to learn would not change that. The woman I loved was back. I would let nothing change that.

She sipped at the latte. "I'm sorry," she said.

I squeezed her hand.

"To run out like that. To let you think"—she stopped—"I can't even imagine what you must have thought." Her eyes found mine. "I never wanted to hurt you."

"I'm okay," I said.

"How did you learn I wasn't Sheila?"

"At her funeral. I saw the body."

"I wanted to tell you, especially after I heard she'd been murdered."

"Why didn't you?"

"Ken told me it might get you killed."

My brother's name jarred me. Nora turned away. I slid my hand up her arm and stopped at the shoulder. The tension had knotted her muscles. I gently kneaded them, a familiar moment for us. She closed her eyes and let my fingers work. For a long time neither of us spoke. I broke the silence. "How long have you known my brother?"

"Almost four years," she said.

I nodded through my shock, trying to encourage her to say more, but she still had her face turned away. I gently took hold of her chin and turned her to me. I kissed her lightly on the lips.

She said, "I love you so much."

I felt a soar that nearly lifted me off the chair. "I love you too."

"I'm scared, Will."

"I'll protect you," I said.

She held my gaze. "I've been lying to you. The whole time we've been together."

"I know."

"Do you really think we can survive that?"

"I lost you once," I said. "I'm not going to lose you again."

"You're that sure?"

"Love you," I said. "Always."

She studied my face. I don't know what she was looking for. "I'm married, Will."

I tried to keep my expression blank, but it was not easy. Her words wrapped around me and tightened, boa-constrictor-like. I almost pulled my hand away.

"Tell me," I said.

"Five years ago, I ran away from my husband, Cray. Cray was"—she closed her eyes—"incredibly abusive. I don't want to go into details. They're not important anyway. We lived in a town called Cramden. It's not far from Kansas City. One day, after Cray put me in the hospital, I ran away. That's all you need to know, okay?"

I nodded.

"I don't have any family. I had friends, but I really didn't want to get them involved. Cray is insane. He wouldn't let me go. He threatened . . ." Her voice trailed away. "Never mind what he threatened. But I couldn't put anyone at risk. So I found a shelter that helps battered women. They took me in. I told them I wanted to start over. I wanted to get out of there. But I was afraid of Cray. You see, Cray is a town cop. You have no idea . . . you live in terror for so long, you start to think that a man is omnipotent. It's impossible to explain."

I scooted a little closer, still holding her hand. I had seen the effects of abuse. I understood.

"The shelter helped me escape to Europe. I lived in Stockholm. It was hard. I got a job as a waitress. I was lonely all the time. I wanted to come back, but I was still so afraid of my husband, I didn't dare. After six months, I thought I'd lose my mind. I still had nightmares about Cray finding me. . . ."

Her voice broke off. I had no idea what to do. I tried to scoot my chair closer to hers. The armrests were already touching, but I think she appreciated the gesture.

"Anyway, I finally met a woman. She was an American living in the area. We started cautiously, but there was something about her. I guess we both had that on-the-run look. We were also lonely as hell, though she at least had her husband and daughter. They were in deep hiding too. I didn't know why at first."

"This woman," I said. "It was Sheila Rogers?"

"Yes."

"And the husband." I stopped, swallowed. "That was my brother."

She nodded. "They have a daughter named Carly."

It was beginning to make sense.

"Sheila and I became close friends, and while it took him a little longer to trust me, I grew close to Ken too. I moved in with them, started helping them take care of Carly. Your niece is a wonderful child, Will. Smart and beautiful and, not to get metaphysical, but there is such an aura around her."

My niece. Ken had a daughter. I had a niece I had never seen.

"Your brother talked about you all the time, Will. He might mention your mother or your father or even Melissa, but you were his world. He followed your career. He knew all about your working at Covenant House. Here he had been in hiding for what, seven years? He was lonely too, I guess. So once he trusted me, he talked to me a lot. And what he talked about most was you."

I blinked and looked down at the table. I studied the Starbucks brown napkin. There was some stupid poem about aroma and a promise on it. Made from recycled paper. The color was brown because they did not use bleach.

"Are you okay?" she asked.

"I'm fine," I said. I looked up. "So what happened next?"

"I got in touch with a friend back home. She told me that Cray had hired a private detective and that he knew I was in the Stockholm area. I panicked, but at the same time, I was ready to move on. Like I said, I had lived with Cray in Missouri. I figured that if I moved to New York, maybe I'd be safe. But I needed a deeper ID, in case Cray kept hunting. Sheila was in the same boat. Her fake ID was all surface, just a name change. And that was when we came up with a simple plan."

I nodded. This one I knew. "You switched identities."

"Right. She became Nora Spring and I became Sheila Rogers. This way, if my husband came after me, he'd only find her. And if the people searching for them found Sheila Rogers, well, you see, it adds another layer."

I considered that, but something still did not add up. "Okay, so that's how you became Sheila Rogers. You switched identities."

"Yes."

"And you ended up in New York City."

"Yes."

"And"—here was the part I was having trouble with—"somehow we happened to meet."

Nora smiled. "You're wondering about us, aren't you?"

"I guess I am."

"You're thinking it's a hell of a coincidence that I volunteered at the very place you work."

"It would seem unlikely," I agreed.

"Well, you're right. It wasn't a coincidence." She sat back and sighed. "I'm not sure how to explain this, Will."

I just held her hand and waited.

"Okay, you have to understand. I was so lonely overseas. All I had was your brother and Sheila and, of course, Carly. I spent all that time hearing your brother rave about you, and it was like . . . it was like you were so different from any man I'd ever known. The truth is, I think I was half in love with you before we ever met. So I told myself when I came to New York that

I'd just meet you, see what you were really like. Maybe if it seemed okay, I'd even tell you that your brother was alive and that he was innocent, though Ken warned me repeatedly about the danger of that. It wasn't a plan or anything. I just came to New York and one day I walked into Covenant House, and call it destiny or fate or whatever, but the moment I saw you, I knew that I would love you forever."

I was scared and confused and smiling.

"What?" she said.

"I love you."

She put her head on my shoulder. We grew quiet now. There was more. It would come in time. For now, we just enjoyed the silence of being with one another. When Nora was ready, she started up again.

"A few weeks ago, I was sitting at the hospital with your mother. She was in such pain, Will. She couldn't take it anymore, she told me. She wanted to die. She was in such discomfort, well, you know."

I nodded.

"I loved your mother. I think you know that."

"I do," I said.

"I couldn't stand just sitting there doing nothing. So I broke my promise to your brother. Before she died, I wanted her to know the truth. She deserved that. I wanted her to know that her son was alive and that he loved her and that he hadn't hurt anybody."

"You told her about Ken?"

"Yes. But even in her haze, she was skeptical. She needed proof, I think."

I froze and turned to her. I saw it now. What had started it all. The visit to the bedroom after the funeral. The picture hidden behind the frame. "So you gave my mother that photograph of Ken."

Nora nodded.

"She never saw him. Just the photograph."

"That's right."

Which explained why we never knew about it. "But you told her he was coming back."

"Yes."

"Were you lying?"

She thought about that. "Maybe I was engaging in hyperbole, but no, I don't think it was an outright lie. You see, Sheila contacted me when they captured him. Ken had always been very careful. He had all sorts of provisions set up for Sheila and Carly. So when they caught him, Sheila and Carly ran off. The police never knew about them. Sheila stayed overseas until Ken thought it was safe. Then she sneaked back in."

"And she called you when she arrived?"

"Yes."

It was all adding up. "From a pay phone in New Mexico."

"Yes."

That would be the first call Pistillo was talking about—the one from New Mexico to my apartment. "So then what happened?"

"It all started going wrong," she said. "I got a call from Ken. He was in a frenzy. Someone had found them. He and Carly had been out of the house when two men broke in. They tortured Sheila to find out where he'd gone. Ken came home during the attack. He shot them both. But Sheila was seriously wounded. He called and told me that I had to run now. The police would find Sheila's fingerprints. McGuane and his people would also learn that Sheila Rogers had been with him."

"They'd all be looking for Sheila," I said.

"Yes."

"And that was you now. So you had to disappear."

"I wanted to tell you, but Ken was insistent. If you didn't know anything, you'd be safer. And then he reminded me that there was Carly to consider. These people tortured and killed her mother. I couldn't live with myself if anything happened to Carly."

"How old is Carly?"

"She'd be close to twelve by now."

"So she was born before Ken ran away."

"I think she was six months old."

Another sore point. Ken had a child and never told me about her. I asked, "Why did he keep her a secret?"

"I don't know."

So far, I had been able to follow the logic, but I could not see how Carly fit into this. I mulled it over. Six months before he vanished. What had been going on in his life? It was right about the time the FBI had flipped him. Could it be connected to that? Was Ken afraid that his actions might put his infant daughter in danger? That made sense, I guess.

No, I was missing something.

I was about to ask a follow-up question, try to get more details, when my cell phone chirped. Squares probably. I glanced at the caller ID. Nope, not Squares. But I recognized the number instantly. Katy Miller. I pressed the answer button and put the phone to my ear.

"Katy?"

"Oooo, no, sorry, that's incorrect. Please try again."

The fear flooded back. Oh Christ. The Ghost. I closed my eyes. "If you hurt her, so help me—"

"Come, come, Will," the Ghost interrupted. "Impotent threats are beneath you."

"What do you want?"

"We need to chat, old boy."

"Where is she?"

"Who? Oh, you mean Katy? Why, she's right here."

"I want to talk to her."

"You don't believe me, Will? I'm wounded."

"I want to talk to her," I repeated.

"You want proof she's alive?"

"Something like that."

"How about this?" the Ghost began in his silkiest hush. "I can make her scream for you. Would that help?"

I closed my eyes again.

"Can't hear you, Will."

"No."

"You sure? It would be no problem. One piercing, nerve-shredding scream. What do you say?"

"Please don't hurt her," I said. "She has nothing to do with this."

"Where are you?"

"I'm on Park Avenue South."

"Be more specific."

I gave him a location two blocks away.

"I'll have a car there in five minutes. Get in it. Do you understand?"

"Yes."

"And, Will?"

"What?"

"Don't call anyone. Don't tell anyone. Katy Miller has a sore neck from a previous encounter. I can't tell you how tempting it would be to test it out." He stopped and whispered. "Still with me, old neighbor?"

"Yes."

"Hang tight then. This will all be over soon."

53

Claudia Fisher burst into the office of Joseph Pistillo.

Pistillo lifted his head. "What?"

"Raymond Cromwell didn't report in."

Cromwell was the undercover agent they'd assigned to Joshua Ford, Ken Klein's attorney. "I thought he was wired."

"They had an appointment at McGuane's. He couldn't wear a wire in there."

"And nobody's seen him since that appointment?"

Fisher nodded. "Same with Ford. Both are missing."

"Jesus Christ."

"So what do you want to do?"

Pistillo was already up and moving. "Get every available agent. We're raiding McGuane's office now."

To leave Nora alone like that—I had already gotten used to the name—was beyond heart-wrenching, but what choice did I have? The idea that Katy was alone with that sadistic psycho gnawed straight into my marrow. I remembered how it felt to be handcuffed to the bed, helpless while he attacked her. I closed my eyes and wished the image away.

Nora made an effort to stop me, but she understood. This was something I had to do. Our good-bye kiss was almost too tender. I pulled away. The tears were back in her eyes.

"Come back to me," she said.

I told her I would and hurried out.

The car was a black Ford Taurus with tinted windows. There was only the driver inside. I did not recognize him. He handed me an eyeshade, the kind they give out on airplanes, and told me to put it on and lie flat in the back. I did as he asked. He started up the car and pulled out. I used the time to think. I knew a lot now. Not all. Not enough. But a lot. And I was reasonably sure that the Ghost was right: It would all be over soon.

I ran it through in my mind and here was what I semi-concluded: Eleven years ago, Ken was involved in illegal activities with his old friends, McGuane and the Ghost. There was really no way around that anymore. Ken had done wrong. He might have been a hero to me, but my sister, Melissa, had pointed out that he was drawn to violence. I might amend that to say he craved action, the enticement of the edge. But that's just semantics.

Somewhere along the way, Ken was captured and agreed to help bring down McGuane. He risked his life. He went undercover. He wore a wire. Somehow McGuane and the Ghost found out. Ken ran. He came home, though I'm not sure why. I'm not sure how Julie fit in here either. By all accounts she had not been home in over a year. Was her return a coincidence? Was she there merely following Ken, perhaps as a lover, perhaps because he was her drug source? Did the Ghost follow her, knowing that she would eventually lead him to Ken?

I don't know any of that. Not yet anyhow.

Whatever, the Ghost found them, probably in a delicate moment. He attacked. Ken was injured, but he escaped. Julie was not so lucky. The Ghost wanted to put pressure on Ken, so he framed him for the murder. Terrified that he'd be killed or worse, Ken ran. He picked up his steady girlfriend, Sheila Rogers, and their infant daughter, Carly. The three of them disappeared.

My vision, even through my eyeshade, darkened. I heard a whooshing noise. We had entered a tunnel. Could be the Midtown, but my guess was that we were in the Lincoln, heading out toward New Jersey. I thought now about Pistillo and his role in all this. For him, it was the old ends-justify-means debate. Under certain circumstances, he might be a "means" guy, but this case was personal. It was easy to see his point of view. Ken was a crook. He had made a deal and no matter what the reason, he had reneged on it by running. Open season on him. Make him a fugitive and let the world comb through the muck and find his man.

Years pass. Ken and Sheila stay together. Their daughter, Carly, grows. Then one day, Ken is captured. He is brought back to the States, convinced, I imagine, that they'll hang him for the murder of Julie Miller. But the authorities have always known the truth. They don't want him for that. They want the head of the beast. McGuane. And Ken can still help deliver him.

So they strike a deal. Ken hides out in New Mexico. Once they believe it's safe, Sheila and Carly come back from Sweden to stay with him. But McGuane is a powerful nemesis. He learned where they were. He sent two men. Ken wasn't home, but they tortured Sheila to find out where he was. Ken surprises them, kills them, packs his injured lover and daughter in the car, and then he runs again. He warns Nora, who is using Sheila's ID, that the authorities and McGuane are going to be on her tail. She is forced to run too.

That pretty much covered what I knew.

The Ford Taurus came to a stop. I heard the driver shut off the engine. Enough with the passive, I thought. If I had any hope of getting out of this alive, I would have to be more assertive. I pulled the eyeshade off and checked my watch. We had been driving for an hour. Then I sat up.

We were in the middle of thick woods. The ground was blanketed with pine needles. The trees were lush and heavy with green. There was a watchtower of sorts, a small aluminum structure that sat on a platform about ten feet off the ground. It looked like an oversize toolshed, built strictly for function. Something both neglected and industrial. Rust licked the corners and door.

The driver turned around. "Get out."

I did as he asked. My eyes stayed on the structure. I saw the door open, and the Ghost stepped out. He was dressed entirely in black, as though he were on his way to reading poetry in the Village. He waved to me.

"Hi, Will."

"Where is she?" I asked.

"Who?"

"Don't start that crap."

The Ghost folded his arms. "My, my," he said, "aren't we just the bravest little soldier?"

"Where is she?"

"You mean Katy Miller?"

"You know I do."

The Ghost nodded. He had something in his hand. A rope of some kind. A lasso maybe. I froze. "She looks so much like her sister, don't you think? How could I resist? I mean, that neck. That beautiful swan neck. Already bruised . . ."

I tried to keep the quake from my voice. "Where is she?"

He blinked. "She's dead, Will."

My heart sank.

"I grew bored waiting and—" He started laughing then. The sound echoed in the stillness, ripping through the air, clawing at the leaves. I stood there, unmoving. He pointed and shouted, "Gotcha! Oh, I'm only joshing, Willie boy. Having a little fun. Katy is just fine." He waved me forward. "Come on and see."

I hurried toward the platform, my heart firmly lodged in my throat. There was a rusted ladder. I climbed it. The Ghost was still laughing. I pushed past him and opened the door to the aluminum shack. I turned to my right.

Katy was there.

The Ghost's laugh was still ringing in my ears. I hurried over to her. Her eyes were open, though several strands of hair blocked them. The bruises on her neck had turned into a jaundiced yellow. Her arms were tied to a chair, but she looked uninjured.

I bent down and pushed the hair away. "Are you okay?" I asked.

"I'm fine."

I could feel the rage building. "Did he hurt you?"

Katy Miller shook her head. Her voice quaked. "What does he want with us?"

"Please let me answer that one."

We turned as the Ghost entered. He kept the door opened. The floor was littered with broken beer bottles. There was an old file cabinet in the corner. A laptop computer sat closed in one corner. Three metal folding chairs, the kind used for school assemblies, were out. Katy sat in one. The Ghost took the second and signaled for me to take the one on his immediate left. I remained standing. The Ghost sighed and stood back up.

"I need your help, Will." He turned toward Katy. "And I thought having Miss Miller here join us, well"—he gave me the skin-crawling grin—"I thought she might work as something of an incentive."

I squared up. "If you hurt her, if you so much as lay a hand—"

The Ghost did not wind up. He did not rear back. He merely snapped his hand from his side and caught me under the chin. He connected with a knife strike. A choking sound blew past my lips. It felt like I'd swallowed my own throat. I staggered and turned away. The Ghost took his time. He bent low and used an uppercut. His knuckles landed flush against my kidney. I dropped to my knees, nearly paralyzed by the blow.

He looked down at me. "Your posturing is getting on my nerves, Willie boy."

I felt close to throwing up.

"We need to contact your brother," he went on. "That's why you're here."

I looked up. "I don't know where he is."

The Ghost slid away from me. He moved behind Katy's chair. He gently, almost too gently, put his hands on her shoulders. She winced at his touch. He reached with both index fingers and stroked the bruises on her neck.

"I'm telling the truth," I said.

"Oh, I believe you," he said.

"So what do you want?"

"I know how to reach Ken."

I was confused. "What?"

"Have you ever seen one of those old movies where the fugitive leaves messages in classified ads?"

"I guess."

The Ghost smiled as though pleased with my response. "Ken is taking that one step further. He uses an Internet newsgroup. More specifically, he leaves and receives messages on something called rec.music.elvis. It is, as you might expect, a board for Elvis fans. So, for example, if his attorney needed to contact him, he would leave a date and time and post with a code name. Ken would then know when to IM said attorney."

"IM?"

"Instant message. I assume you've used it before. It's like a private chat room. Totally untraceable."

"How do you know all this?" I asked.

He smiled again and moved his hands closer to Katy's neck. "Information gathering," he said. "It's something of my forté."

His hands slid off Katy. I realized that I'd been holding my breath. He reached into his pocket and took out the rope lasso again.

"So what do you need me for?" I asked.

"Your brother would not agree to meet his attorney," the Ghost said. "I believe he suspected a trap. We set up another IM appointment, though. We are very much hoping that you can persuade him to meet with us."

"And if I can't?"

He held up the rope. There was a handle attached to the end. "Do you know what this is?"

I did not reply.

"It's a Punjab lasso," he said as if beginning a lecture. "The Thuggees used it. They were known as the silent assassins. From India. Some people think they were all wiped out in the nineteenth century. Others, well, others are not so sure." He looked at Katy and held the primitive weapon up high. "Need I go on here, Will?"

I shook my head. "He'll know it's a trap," I said.

"It's your job to convince him otherwise. If you fail"—he looked up, smiling—"well, on the positive side, you'll be able to see firsthand how Julie suffered all those years ago."

I could feel the blood leaving my extremities. "You'll kill him," I said.

"Oh, not necessarily."

I knew it was a lie, but his face was frighteningly sincere.

"Your brother made tapes, gathered incriminating information," he said. "But he has not shown any of it to the feds yet. He's kept it hidden all these years. That's a good thing. It shows cooperation, that he is still the Ken we know and love. And"—he stopped, thinking—"he has something I want."

"What?" I asked.

He shook me off. "Here's the deal: If he gives it all up and promises to disappear again, we can all go on."

A lie. I knew that. He'll kill Ken. And he'll kill us all. I had no doubt about that. "And if I don't believe you?"

He dropped the lasso around Katy's neck. She let out a small cry. The Ghost smiled and looked straight at me. "Does it really matter?"

I swallowed. "I guess not."

"Guess?"

"I'll cooperate."

He let go of the lasso; it hung from her neck like the most perverse necklace. "Don't touch it," he said. "We have an hour. Spend the time staring at her neck, Will. And imagine."

54

McGuane had been caught off guard.

He watched the FBI storm inside. He had not foreseen this. Yes, Joshua Ford was important. Yes, his disappearance would raise eyebrows, though they had made Ford call his wife and tell her he'd been called out of town on a "delicate matter." But this forceful a reaction? It seemed like overkill.

No matter. McGuane was always prepared. The blood had been cleaned with a newly developed peroxide agent, so that even a blue-light test would reveal nothing. The hairs and fibers had been taken care of, but even if a few were found, so what? He would not deny that Ford and Cromwell were here. He would happily admit it. He would also admit that they had departed. And he could offer proof: His security people had already replaced the real surveillance tape with the digitally altered one that would show both Ford and Cromwell departing the premises on their own accord.

McGuane pressed a button that automatically erased and reformatted the computer files. Nothing would be found. McGuane automatically backed up via email. Every hour, the computer sent an email to a secret account. The files thus stayed safely in cyberspace. Only McGuane knew the address. He could retrieve the backup whenever he wanted.

He rose and straightened his tie as Pistillo burst through the door with Claudia Fisher and two other agents. Pistillo pointed his weapon at McGuane.

McGuane spread his hands. No fear. Never show fear. "What a pleasant surprise."

"Where are they?" Pistillo shouted.

"Who?"

"Joshua Ford and Special Agent Raymond Cromwell."

McGuane did not blink. Ah, that explained it. "Are you saying that Mr. Cromwell is a federal agent?"

"I am," Pistillo barked. "Now, where is he?"

"I'd like to file a complaint then."

"What?"

"Agent Cromwell presented himself as an attorney," McGuane went on, his voice even as could be. "I trusted that representation. I confided in him, assuming that I was protected by attorney-client privilege. Now you tell me that he is an undercover agent. I want to make sure that nothing I said is used against me."

Pistillo's face was red. "Where is he, McGuane?"

"I don't have the slightest idea. He left with Mr. Ford."

"What was the nature of your business with them?"

McGuane smiled. "You know better than that, Pistillo. Our meeting would fall under attorney-client privilege."

Pistillo wanted so very much to pull the trigger. He aimed at the center of McGuane's face. McGuane still showed nothing. Pistillo lowered the weapon. "Search the place," he barked. "Box and tag everything. Place him under arrest."

McGuane let them cuff him. He would not tell them about the surveillance tape. Let them find it on their own. It would have that much more impact that way. Still, as the agents dragged him out, he knew that this was not good. He did not mind being brazen—as mentioned earlier, this was not the first federal agent he'd had killed—but he could not help but wonder if he had missed something, if he had left himself somehow exposed, if, at long last, he had made a crucial mistake that would cost him everything.

55

The Ghost stepped into the woods, leaving Katy and me alone. I sat in my chair and stared at the lasso around her neck. It was having the desired effect. I would cooperate. I would not risk having that rope tighten around the neck of that frightened girl.

Katy looked at me and said, “He’s going to kill us.”

It was not a question. It was true, of course, but I still denied it. I promised her that she would be okay, that I would find a way out, but I don’t think I assuaged her worries. Little wonder. My throat was feeling better, but my kidney still ached from the punch. My eyes moved about the room.

Think, Will. And think fast.

I knew what was coming up. The Ghost would have me set up the meeting. Once Ken showed up, we were all dead. I thought about that. I would try to warn my brother. I would try to use some kind of code maybe. Our only hope was that Ken would smell a trap and surprise them. But I had to keep my options open. I had to look for a way out, any way out, even if it meant sacrificing myself to save Katy. There would be an opening, a mistake. I had to be ready to exploit it.

Katy whispered, “I know where we are.”

I turned to her. “Where?”

“We’re in the South Orange Water Reservation,” she said. “We used to come here and drink. We’re not far from Hobart Gap Road.”

“How far?” I asked.

“A mile maybe.”

“You know the way? I mean, if we make a run for it, would you be able to lead us out?”

“I think so,” she said. Then, with a nod: “Yeah. Yeah, I could lead us out.”

Okay, good. That was something. Not much maybe, but a start. I looked out the door. The driver leaned against the car. The Ghost stood with his hands behind his back. He bounced on his toes. His gaze was turned upward, as if bird-watching. The driver lit up a cigarette. The Ghost did not move.

I quickly scoured the floor and found what I was looking for—a big hunk of broken glass. I peeked out the door again. Neither man was looking. So I crept behind Katy’s chair.

“What are you doing?” she whispered.

“I’m going to cut you loose.”

“Are you out of your mind? If he sees you—”

“We have to try something,” I said.

"But"—Katy stopped. "Even if you cut me free, then what?"

"I don't know," I admitted. "But be ready. There'll be a chance to escape somewhere down the line. We have to take advantage of it."

I pressed the broken edge against the rope and started sawing back and forth. The rope began to fray. The work was slow. I hurried the pace. The rope started giving way, strand by strand.

I was about halfway through the rope when I felt the platform shake. I stopped. Someone was on the ladder. Katy made a whimpering sound. I rolled away from her and made it back to my seat just as the Ghost entered. He looked at me.

"You're out of breath, Willie boy."

I slid the broken glass to the back of my seat, almost sitting on it. The Ghost frowned at me. I said nothing. My pulse raced. The Ghost looked toward Katy. She tried to stare back defiantly. She was so damn brave. But when I looked toward her, the terror struck me again.

The frayed rope was in plain sight.

The Ghost narrowed his eyes.

"Hey, let's get on with this," I said.

It was enough of a distraction. The Ghost turned to me. Katy adjusted her hands, giving the frayed rope some cover. Not much if he looked closely. But maybe enough. The Ghost waited a beat and then he went for the laptop. For a second—for the briefest of seconds—he turned his back to me.

Now, I thought.

I would jump up, use the broken glass like a prison shiv, and jam it into the Ghost's neck. I calculated quickly. Was I too far away? Probably. And what about the driver? Was he armed? Did I dare—?

The Ghost spun back toward me. The moment, if there had ever been one, was over.

The computer was already on. The Ghost did some typing. He got online with a remote modem. He clacked some more keys and a textbox appeared. He smiled at me and said, "It's time to talk to Ken."

My stomach knotted. The Ghost hit the return button. On the screen, I saw what he had typed:

YOU THERE?

We waited. The answer came a moment later.

HERE.

The Ghost smiled. "Ah, Ken." He typed some more and hit the return.

IT'S WILL. I'M WITH FORD.

There was a long pause.

TELL ME THE NAME OF THE FIRST GIRL YOU MADE OUT WITH.

The Ghost turned to me. "As I expected, he wants proof it's really you."

I said nothing, but my mind raced.

"I know what you're thinking," he went on. "You want to warn him. You want to tell him an answer that's close to the truth." He moved over to Katy. He picked up the stick end of the lasso. He pulled just a little. The rope coiled against her neck.

"Here's the deal, Will. I want you to stand up. I want you to go over to the computer and type in the correct answer. I'll keep tightening the rope.

If you play any games—if I even suspect you tried to play any sort of game—I won't stop until she's dead. Do you understand?"

I nodded.

He tightened the lasso a little more. Katy made a noise. "Go," he said.

I hurried to the screen. Fear numbed my brain. He was right. I had been trying to come up with a decent lie, something to warn him. But I couldn't. Not now. I put my fingers on the keys and typed:

CINDI SHAPIRO

The Ghost smiled. "For real? Man, she was a little hottie, Will. I'm impressed."

He let go of the lasso. Katy released a gasp. He moved back over to the keyboard. I looked back over at my chair. The broken glass was in plain view. I moved quickly back to my seat. We waited for the response.

GO HOME, WILL.

The Ghost rubbed his face. "Interesting response," he said. He thought about it. "Where did you make out with her?"

"What?"

"Cindi Shapiro. Were you at her house, your house, where?"

"Eric Frankel's bar mitzvah."

"Does Ken know that?"

"Yes."

The Ghost smiled. He typed again.

YOU TESTED ME. NOW IT'S YOUR TURN. WHERE DID I MAKE OUT WITH CINDI?

Another long pause. I was on the edge of my seat too. It was a smart move by the Ghost, turning the momentum around a bit. But more important, we really didn't know if this was Ken or not. This answer would prove it one way or another.

Thirty seconds passed. Then:

GO HOME, WILL.

The Ghost typed some more.

I NEED TO KNOW IT'S YOU.

A longer pause. And then finally:

FRANKEL'S BAR MITZVAH. GO HOME NOW.

Another jolt. It was Ken. . . .

I looked over at Katy. Her eyes met mine. The Ghost typed again.

WE NEED TO MEET.

The answer came fast: *NO CAN DO.*

PLEASE. IMPORTANT.

GO HOME, WILL. NOT SAFE.

WHERE R U?

HOW DID YOU FIND FORD?

"Hmm," the Ghost said. He thought about that and typed: PISTILLO.

There was another long pause.

I HEARD ABOUT MOM. WAS IT VERY BAD?

The Ghost did not consult me for this one. YES.

HOW'S DAD?

NOT GOOD. WE NEED TO SEE YOU.

Another pause: *NO CAN DO.*

WE CAN HELP YOU.

BETTER TO STAY AWAY.

The Ghost looked at me. "Should we try to tempt him with his favorite vice?"

I had no idea what he meant, but I watched him type and hit the return key:

WE CAN GET YOU MONEY. DO YOU NEED SOME?

I WILL. BUT WE CAN DO IT THRU OVERSEAS TRANSFERS.

And then, as if reading my mind, the Ghost typed:

I REALLY NEED TO SEE YOU. PLEASE.

I LOVE YOU, WILL. GO HOME.

Again, as if he were inside my head, the Ghost typed:

WAIT.

SIGNING OFF NOW, BRO. DON'T WORRY.

The Ghost let out a deep breath. "This isn't working," he said out loud. He typed quickly.

SIGN OFF, KEN, AND YOUR BROTHER DIES.

A pause. Then: *WHO IS THIS?*

The Ghost smiled. ONE GUESS. HINT: CASPER THE FRIENDLY.

No pause this time.

LEAVE HIM ALONE, JOHN.

I THINK NOT.

HE HAS NOTHING TO DO WITH THIS.

YOU KNOW BETTER THAN TO PLAY WITH MY SYMPATHIES. YOU SHOW UP, YOU GIVE ME WHAT I WANT, I DON'T KILL HIM.

LET HIM GO FIRST. THEN I'LL GIVE YOU WHAT YOU WANT.

The Ghost laughed and clacked the keys:

OH PLEASE. THE YARD, KEN. YOU REMEMBER THE YARD, DON'T YOU. I'LL GIVE YOU THREE HOURS TO GET THERE.

IMPOSSIBLE. I'M NOT EVEN ON THE EAST COAST.

The Ghost muttered, "Bull." Then he typed frantically:

THEN YOU BETTER HURRY. THREE HOURS. IF YOU'RE NOT THERE, I CUT OFF A FINGER. I CUT OFF ANOTHER EVERY HALF HOUR. THEN I GO TO THE TOES. THEN I GET CREATIVE. THE YARD, KEN. THREE HOURS.

The Ghost disconnected the line. He slammed the laptop closed and stood.

"Well," he said with the smile, "I think that went rather well, don't you?"

56

Nora called Squares on his cell phone. She gave him an abbreviated version of the events surrounding her disappearance. Squares listened without interruption, driving toward her all the way. They met up in front of the Metropolitan Life building on Park Avenue.

She hopped into the van and hugged him. It felt nice to be back in the outreach van.

"We can't call the police," Squares said.

She nodded. "Will was firm on that one."

"So what the hell can we do?"

"I don't know. But I'm scared, Squares. Will's brother told me about these people. They'll kill him, for sure."

Squares mulled it over. "How do you and Ken communicate?"

"Via a computer newsgroup."

"Let's get him a message. Maybe he'll have an idea."

The Ghost kept his distance.

Time was growing short. I stayed alert. If there was an opening, any opening, I was going to risk it. I palmed the broken bottle and studied his neck. I rehearsed in my mind how it might go. I tried to calculate what defensive move the Ghost might make and how I could counter it. Where, I wondered, were his arteries located? Where was he most vulnerable, his flesh the softest?

I glanced at Katy. She was holding up well. I thought again about what Pistillo had said, how adamant he had been that I leave Katy Miller out of this. He was right. This was my fault. When she first asked to help, I should have refused. I had put her at risk. The fact that I was indeed trying to help her, that I understood better than most how much she craved closure, did little to ease my guilt.

I had to find a way to save her.

I looked back at the Ghost. He stared at me. I did not blink.

"Let her go," I said.

He faked a yawn.

"Her sister was good to you."

"So?"

"There's no reason to hurt her."

The Ghost raised his palms and in that hushed lisp, he said, "Who needs a reason?"

Katy closed her eyes. I stopped then. I was just making it worse. I checked the clock. Two hours to go. "The yard," a spot where pot smokers used to gather after a fun-filled day at Heritage Middle School, was no more than three miles from here. I knew why the Ghost had picked it. The site was easy to control. It was secluded, especially in the summer months. And once in, there would be little chance of getting out alive.

The Ghost's cell phone rang. He looked down at it as if he'd never heard the sound before. For the first time, I saw something that might have been confusion cross his face. I tensed, though I did not dare reach for the broken glass. Not yet. But I was ready.

He flicked on the cell and put it to his ear. "Go," he said.

He listened. I studied his colorless face. His expression remained calm, but something was happening here. He blinked more. He checked his watch. He did not speak for nearly two full minutes. Then he said, "I'm on my way."

He rose and walked toward me. He lowered his mouth toward my ear. "If you move from this chair," he said, "you'll beg me to kill her. Do you understand?"

I nodded.

The Ghost left, closing the door behind me. The room was dark. The light was starting to fade, shafts breaking through the leaves. There were no windows in the front, so I had no way of knowing what they were doing.

"What's going on?" Katy whispered.

I put a finger to my lips and listened. An engine turned over. A car started up. I thought about his warning. Do not leave this seat. The Ghost was someone you wanted to obey, but then again, he was going to kill us anyway. I bent at the waist and dropped off the chair. It was not the smoothest move. Rather spastic, in fact.

I looked over at Katy. Our eyes met and again I signaled her to remain silent. She nodded.

I stayed as low as possible and crawled carefully toward the door. I would have gone to my belly and done it commando-style, but the small shards of glass would have ripped right through me. I moved slowly, trying not to cut myself.

When I reached the door, I put my head against the floorboard and peeked through the crack at the bottom. I saw the car drive off. I tried to get a better angle, but it was tough. I sat up and pressed my eye against the side crack. It was harder to see here. The opening was barely a slit. I rose a little and bang, there he was.

The driver.

But where was the Ghost?

I did the quick calculation. Two men, one car. One car drives off. I am not much with math, but that meant that only one man could be left. I turned to Katy. "He's gone," I whispered.

"What?"

"The driver is still here. The Ghost drove off."

I moved back toward my chair and picked up the large piece of broken glass. Stepping as gently as possible, fearing that even the slightest weight change could shake the structure, I made my way back behind Katy's chair. I sawed at the rope.

"What are we going to do?" she whispered.

"You know a way out of here," I said. "We'll make a run for it."

"It's getting dark."

"That's why we do it now."

"The other guy," she said. "He could be armed."

"He probably is, but would you rather wait for the Ghost to come back?"

She shook her head. "How do you know he's not coming back right now?"

"I don't." The rope cut through. She was free. She rubbed her wrists as I said, "You with me?"

She looked at me and I thought maybe it was the same way I used to look at Ken, that mixture of hope and awe and confidence. I tried to look brave, but I've never been the hero type. She nodded.

There was one window in the back. My plan, as it were, was to open it, climb out, and crawl through the woods. We would try to keep quiet as possible, but if he heard us, we would break into a run. I was counting on the fact that the driver was either unarmed or not supposed to wound us too seriously. They'd have to figure that Ken would be careful. They'd want to keep us alive—well, me anyway—to bait their trap.

Or maybe not.

The window was stuck. I pulled and pushed against the frame. Nothing. It had been painted over a million years ago. No chance of opening it.

"Now what?" she asked.

Cornered. The feeling of a cornered rat. I looked at Katy. I thought about what the Ghost had said, how I had somehow not protected Julie. I would not let that happen again. Not to Katy.

"Only one way out of here," I said. I looked at the door.

"He'll see us."

"Maybe not."

I pressed my eye against the crack. The sunlight was fading. The shadows had picked up strength. I saw the driver. He sat on a tree stump. I saw the ember from the end of his cigarette, a steady marker in the dark.

His back was turned.

I put the broken-glass shiv in my pocket. I signaled with a lowering palm for Katy to bend down. I reached for the knob. It turned easily. The door creaked when it opened. I stopped and looked out. The driver was still not looking. I had to risk it. I pushed the door open more. The squeak quieted. I stopped the door after only a foot. Enough to squeeze through.

Katy looked up at me. I nodded. She crawled through the door. I bent down and followed. We were both outside now. We lay flat on the platform. Totally exposed. I closed the door.

He still had not turned around.

Okay, next step: how to get off the platform. We couldn't use the ladder. It was too out in the open. I gestured for Katy to follow me. We slid on our bellies toward the side. The platform was aluminum. That made it easier. No friction or splinters.

We reached the side of the shack. But when I turned the corner, I heard a noise not unlike a groan. And then something fell. I froze. A beam under the platform had given way. The whole structure swayed.

The driver said, "What the hell . . . ?"

We ducked low. I pulled Katy toward me, so that she was on the side of the shack too. He couldn't see us now. He'd heard the noise. He looked. He saw the door closed and the platform seemingly empty.

He shouted, "What the hell are you two doing in there?"

We both held our breath. I heard the crunch of leaves. I'd been prepared for this. I already had something of a plan in mind. I braced myself. And then he yelled again.

"What the hell are you two—?"

"Nothing," I shouted, pressing my mouth against the side of the shack, hoping my voice sounded muffled, as if it were coming from the inside. I had to risk this. If I didn't answer, he would definitely check it out. "This shack is a piece of crap," I said. "It keeps shifting on us."

Silence.

We both held our breaths. Katy pressed herself against me. I could feel her shivering. I patted her back. It would be all right. Sure, we were just fine. I strained my ears and tried to pick up the sound of his footsteps. But I heard nothing. I looked at her, urging her to crawl toward the back with my eyes. She hesitated but not for long.

My new plan, as it were, was to shimmy down the pole in the back corner. She would go first. If he heard her, a seemingly likely event, well, I had a plan of sorts for that too.

I pointed the way. She nodded, clear-eyed now, and moved toward the pole. She slid off and held on to the pole, firefighter-style. The platform lurched again. I stared helplessly as the platform wobbled some more. There was the groaning noise again, louder now. I saw a screw come loose.

"What the . . ."

But this time, the driver did not bother calling out. I could hear him moving toward us. Still holding on, Katy looked up at me.

"Jump down and run!" I shouted.

She let go and fell to the ground. The fall was not that far. After she landed, she looked back at me, waiting.

"Run!" I shouted again.

The man now: "Don't move or I'll shoot."

"Run, Katy!"

I threw my legs over the side and let go. My fall was somewhat longer. I landed hard. I remembered reading somewhere that you're supposed to land with knees bent and roll. I did that. I rolled into a tree. When I stood, I saw the man coming at us. He was maybe fifteen yards away. His face was twisted in rage.

"You don't stop, you're dead."

But he didn't have a gun in his hand.

"Run!" I shouted to Katy again.

"But—" she said.

"I'm right behind you! Go!"

She knew I was lying. I had accepted this as part of the plan. My job now was to slow down our adversary—slow him down enough so that Katy could escape. She hesitated, not liking the idea of my sacrifice.

He was almost on us.

"You can get help," I urged. "Go!"

She finally obeyed, leaping over the roots and high grass. I was already reaching into my pocket when the man leveled me with a tackle. The blow was bone-jarring, but I still managed to wrap my arms around him. We tumbled down together. This, too, I had learned someplace. Almost every fight ends up on the ground. In the movies, fighters punch and go down. In real life, people lower their heads and grab their opponents and end up in a grapple. I rolled with him, taking some hits, concentrating on the shiv in my hand.

I gave him a bear hug, squeezing him as tight as I could, though I knew I was not really hurting him. Didn't matter. It would slow him down. Every second counted. Katy would need the lead. I held on tight. He struggled. I would not let go.

That was when he landed the head butt.

He reared back and struck my face with his forehead. I have never been head-butted before, but it hurts like nothing else. It felt as though a wrecking ball had smashed into my face. My eyes watered up. My grip went slack. I fell away. He wound up for another blow, but something instinctive made me turn away, curl into a ball. He rose to his feet. He aimed a kick at my ribs.

But it was my turn now.

I prepared myself. I let the kick land and quickly trapped his foot against my stomach with one hand. With the other, I held the broken glass. I jammed it into the fat of his calf. He screamed as the glass sliced deep into his flesh. The sound echoed. Birds scattered. I pulled it out and stabbed again, this time in the hamstring area. I felt the warm gush of blood.

The man dropped and began to flail, fish-on-the-hook-style.

I was about to strike again when he said, "Please. Just go."

I looked at him. His leg hung useless. He would not be a threat to us. Not now anyway. I was not a killer. Not yet. And I was losing time. The Ghost might be back soon. We needed to get away before that.

So I turned and ran.

After twenty or thirty yards I looked behind me. The man was not pursuing me. He was struggling to a crawl. I started running again when I heard Katy's voice call, "Will, over here!"

I turned and spotted her.

"This way," she said.

We ran the rest of the way. Branches whipped our face. We stumbled on roots, but we never fell. Katy was good to her word. Fifteen minutes later, we headed out of the woods and onto Hobart Gap Road.

When Will and Katy emerged from the woods, the Ghost was there.

He watched from a distance. Then he smiled and stepped back into his car. He drove back and began the cleanup. There was blood. He had not expected that. Will Klein continued to surprise and, yes, impress him.

That was a good thing.

When he was done, the Ghost drove down South Livingston Avenue. There was no sign of Will or Katy. That was okay. He stopped at the mailbox on Northfield Avenue. He hesitated before dropping the package through the slot.

It was done.

The Ghost took Northfield Avenue to Route 280 and then the Garden State Parkway north. It would not be long now. He thought about how this had all begun, and how it should end. He thought about McGuane and Will and Katy and Julie and Ken.

But most of all, he thought about his vow and why he had come back in the first place.

57

A lot happened in the next five days.

After our escape, Katy and I naturally contacted the authorities. We led them to the site where we'd been held. No one was there. The shack was empty. A search found traces of blood near where I'd stabbed the guy in the leg. But there were no prints or hairs. No clues at all. Then again, I had not expected there to be. And I was not sure it mattered.

It was nearly over.

Philip McGuane was arrested for the murder of an undercover federal officer named Raymond Cromwell and a prominent attorney named Joshua Ford. This time, however, he was held without bail. When I met with Pistillo, he had the satisfied gleam in the eye of a man who had finally conquered his own Everest, unearthed his own special chalice, conquered his toughest personal demon, however you want to put it.

"It's all falling apart," Pistillo said with a little too much glee. "We got McGuane nailed on a murder charge. The whole operation is ripping at the seams."

I asked him how they finally caught him. Pistillo, for once, was only too happy to share.

"McGuane made up this phony surveillance tape showing our agent leaving his office. This was supposed to be his alibi, and let me tell you, the tape was flawless. That's not hard to do with digital technology—at least, that's what the lab guy told me."

"So what happened?"

Pistillo smiled. "We got another tape in the mail. Postmarked from Livingston, New Jersey, if you can believe it. The real tape. It shows two guys dragging the body into the private elevator. Both men have already flipped and turned state's evidence. There was a note, too, telling us where we could find the bodies. And to top it off, the package also had the tapes and evidence your brother gathered all those years ago."

I tried to figure that one out, but nothing came to me. "Do you know who sent it?"

"Nope," Pistillo said, and he did not seem to care very much.

"So what happens to John Asselta?" I asked.

"We have an APB out on him."

"You've always had an APB out on him."

He shrugged. "What else can we do?"

"He killed Julie Miller."

"Under orders. The Ghost was just hired muscle."

That was hardly comforting. "You don't think you'll get him, do you?"

"Look, Will, I'd love to nail the Ghost, but I'll be honest with you. It won't be easy. Asselta is out of the country already. We have reports of him overseas. He'll get work with some despot who will protect him. But in the end—and it's important to remember this—the Ghost is just a weapon. I want the guys who pull the trigger."

I did not agree but I did not argue either. I asked him what this all meant for Ken. He took a while before answering.

"You and Katy Miller haven't told us everything, have you?"

I shifted in my seat. We had told them about the kidnapping, but we decided not to tell them about communicating with Ken. We kept that to ourselves. I said, "Yes, we did."

Pistillo held my gaze and then shrugged again. "The truth is, I don't know if we need Ken anymore. But he's safe now, Will." He leaned forward. "I know you haven't been in touch with him"—and I could see in his face that this time he did not believe that—"but if you somehow manage to reach him, tell him to come in from the cold. It's never been safer. And okay, yes, we could use him to verify that old evidence."

Like I said, an active five days.

Aside from my meeting with Pistillo, I spent that time with Nora. We talked about her past but not very much. The lingering shadows kept crossing her face. The fear of her ex-husband remained enormous. It enraged me, of course. We would have to deal with this Mr. Cray Spring of Cramden, Missouri. I didn't know how. Not yet. But I would not let Nora live in fear for the rest of her life. No way.

Nora told me about my brother, how he'd had money stashed away in Switzerland, how he spent his days hiking, how he seemed to seek peace out there and how peace seemed to elude him. Nora talked about Sheila Rogers too, the wounded bird I'd learned so much about, who found nourishment in both the international chase and her daughter. But mostly, Nora told me about my niece, Carly, and when she did, her face lit up. Carly loved to run down hills with her eyes closed. She was a voracious reader and loved to do cartwheels. She had the most infectious laugh. At first, Carly had been lonely and shy with Nora—her parents, for obvious reasons, did not let her socialize much—but Nora had patiently worked past that. Abandoning the child (abandoning was the word she used, though I thought it was too harsh), taking away the only friend Carly had been allowed to have—had been the hardest part for Nora.

Katy Miller kept her distance. She had gone away—she didn't tell me where and I didn't push it—but she called almost every day. She knew the truth now, but in the end, I don't think it helped much. With the Ghost still out there, there would be no closure. With the Ghost still out there, we both looked over our shoulders more than we should.

We were all living in fear, I guess.

But for me, closure was drawing near. I just needed to see my brother, maybe now more than ever. I thought about his lonely years. I thought about those long hikes of his. That was not Ken. Ken would never be happy like that. Ken was in your face. Ken was not one for hiding in shadows.

I wanted to see my brother again for all the old reasons. I wanted to go to a ball game with him. I wanted to play one-on-one. I wanted to stay up late and watch old movies with him. But, of course, now there were new reasons too.

I mentioned earlier that Katy and I kept our contact with Ken a secret. That was so Ken and I could keep our lines of communication open. What we eventually arranged was an Internet newsgroup switch. I told Ken not to let death scare him, hoping he'd pick up the clue. He did. Again it harks back to our childhood. Don't Fear Death aka Ken's favorite song, Blue Oyster Cult's "Don't Fear the Reaper." We found a board that posted information on the old heavy metal band. There were not many posts, but we managed to set up times to IM each other.

Ken was still being cautious, but he wanted this to end too. I still had Dad and Melissa, and I had spent the last eleven years with our mother. I missed Ken like mad, but I think that maybe he missed us more.

Anyway, it took some preparation, but eventually Ken and I set up a reunion.

When I was twelve and Ken was fourteen, we went to a summer camp in Marshfield, Massachusetts, named Camp Millstone. The camp was advertised as being "On Cape Cod!" which, if true, made the cape take up nearly half the state. The cabins were all named for colleges. Ken bunked in Yale. I bunked in Duke. We loved our summer there. We played basketball and softball and participated in blue-gray color wars. We ate crappy food and that appealingly dubbed camp succor "bug juice." Our counselors were both fun and sadistic. Knowing what I know now, I would never in a million years send a kid of my own to sleep-away camp. But I loved it.

Does that make sense?

I took Squares to see Camp Millstone four years ago. The camp was in foreclosure, so Squares bought the property and turned it into an upscale yoga retreat. He built himself a farmhouse on what had been Camp Millstone's soccer field. There was only one path in and out, and the farmhouse was in the middle of the field, so you could see anyone approaching.

We agreed that it would be the perfect reunion spot.

Melissa flew in from Seattle. Because we were extra-paranoid, we had her land in Philadelphia. She, my father, and I met at the Vince Lombardi Rest Stop on the New Jersey Turnpike. The three of us drove up together. No one else knew about the reunion, except Nora, Katy, and Squares. The three of them were traveling up separately. They'd meet with us tomorrow because they, too, had an interest in closure.

But tonight, the first night, would be for the immediate family only.

I handled the driving duties. Dad sat in the passenger seat next to me. Melissa was in the back. No one did much talking. The tension pressed against our chests—mine, I think, most of all. I had learned not to assume anything. Until I saw Ken with my own eyes, until I hugged him and heard him speak, I would not let myself believe that it was finally okay.

I thought about Sheila and Nora. I thought about the Ghost and the high school class leader Philip McGuane and what he had become. It should have surprised me, but I'm not sure it did. We are always "shocked" when we hear about violence in the suburbs, as though a well-watered lawn, a split-level construction, Little League and soccer moms, piano lessons, Four Squares courts, and parent-teacher conferences, all worked as some sort of wolfsbane, warding off evil. If the Ghost and McGuane grew up just nine miles from Livingston—again, that was how far the heart of Newark was—no one would be "stunned" and "dismayed" by what they'd become.

I put in a CD of Springsteen's Summer 2000 concert in Madison Square Garden. It helped pass the time but not a lot. There was construction on Route 95—again, try to find a time when there isn't—and the ride took an agonizing five hours. We pulled up to the red farmhouse complete with fake silo. There were no other cars. That was to be expected. We were supposed to arrive first. Ken would follow.

Melissa got out of the car first. The sound of her door echoed across the field. When I stepped out, I could still visualize the old soccer field. The garage sat right where one goalpost used to be. The driveway ran across where the benches once were. I looked over at my father. He looked away.

For a moment, the three of us just stood there. I broke the spell, moving toward the farmhouse. Dad and Melissa trailed a few feet behind. We were all thinking about Mom. She should have been here. She should have had the chance to see her son one more time. That, we all realized, would have awakened the Sunny smile. Nora had given comfort to my mother by giving her a photograph. I cannot tell you how much that will always mean to me.

Ken, I knew, would be coming alone. Carly was someplace safe. I did not know where. We rarely mentioned her during our communications. Ken might risk himself by attending this reunion. He would not risk his daughter. I, of course, understood.

We paced about the house. Nobody wanted anything to drink. There was a spinning wheel in one corner. The grandfather clock's tick-tocking was maddeningly loud in the still room. Dad finally sat. Melissa moved toward me. She looked up with her big-sister eyes and whispered, "Why doesn't it feel like the nightmare is about to end?"

I didn't even want to consider that.

Five minutes later, we heard an approaching car.

We all rushed to the window. I pushed back the curtain and peered out. It was dusk now. I could see just fine. The car was a gray Honda Accord, a totally inconspicuous pick. My heart picked up a step. I wanted to rush out, but I stayed where I was.

The Honda came to a stop. For several seconds—seconds kept by that damn grandfather clock—nothing happened. Then the driver's door opened. My hand gripped the curtain so hard it nearly ripped. I saw a foot hit the ground. And then someone slid out of the car and stood.

It was Ken.

He smiled at me, the Ken smile, that confident, let's-kick-life's-ass smile. That was all I needed. I let out a yelp of joy and broke for the door. I threw it open, but Ken was already sprinting toward me. He burst into the house and tackled me. The years melted away. Just like that. We were on the floor, rolling across the carpet. I giggled like I was seven. I heard him laugh too.

The rest of it was a wonderful blur. Dad jumped on. Then Melissa. I see it now in fuzzy snapshots. Ken hugging Dad; Dad grabbing Ken around the neck and kissing the top of his head, holding the kiss, his eyes squeezed shut, tears streaming down his cheeks; Ken spinning Melissa in the air; Melissa crying, patting her brother as if to make sure he was really there.

Eleven years.

I don't know how long we acted like that, how long we were that marvelous, delirious mess. Somewhere along the way, we calmed down enough to sit on a couch. Ken kept me close. On several occasions, he put me in a headlock and gave me "nuggies." I never knew being hit on the top of the head could feel so good.

"You took on the Ghost and survived," Ken said, my head in his armpit. "Guess you don't need me covering your back anymore."

And pulling away, I said in a desperate plea, "No, I do."

Darkness fell. We all went outside. The night air felt wonderful in my lungs. Ken and I walked ahead. Melissa and Dad stayed ten yards or so back, perhaps sensing that was what we wanted. Ken had his arm around my shoulders. I remember once during that year at camp I missed a key foul shot. My bunk lost the game because of that. My friends started picking on me. No big deal. It's camp. It happens to everyone. Ken took me for a walk that day. His arm was around me then too.

I felt that same kind of safe again.

He started telling me the story. It pretty much matched what I already knew. He had done some bad things. He had made a deal with the feds. McGuane and Asselta had found out.

He skittered around the question of why he had returned home that night, and more to the point, why he had been at Julie's house. But I wanted it all out in the open. There had been too much deception already. So I asked him flat out: "Why did you and Julie come home?"

Ken took out a pack of cigarettes.

"You smoke now?" I said.

"Yeah, but I'll give it up." He looked at me and said, "Julie and I thought it would be a good place to meet up."

I remembered what Katy said. Like Ken, Julie had not been home in more than a year. I waited for him to go on. He stared at the cigarette, still not lighting it.

"I'm sorry," he said.

"It's okay."

"I knew you were still hung up on her, Will. But I was taking drugs back then. I was a total shit. Or maybe none of that mattered. Maybe I was just being selfish, I don't know."

"It doesn't matter," I said. And that was true. It didn't. "But I still don't understand. How was Julie involved?"

"She was helping me."

"Helping you how?"

Ken lit the cigarette. I could see the lines on his face now. His features were chiseled but weathered now, making him almost more handsome. His eyes were still pure ice. "She and Sheila had an apartment near Haverton. They were friends." He stopped, shook his head. "Look, Julie got hooked on the stuff. It's my fault. When Sheila came up to Haverton, I introduced them. Julie fell into the life. She started working for McGuane too."

I had guessed that it was something like that. "She was selling drugs?"

He nodded. "But when I got caught, when I agreed to go back in, I needed a friend—an accomplice to help me take down McGuane. We were terrified at first, but then we all saw it as a way out. A way to find redemption, you know what I mean?"

"I guess."

"Anyway, they were watching me closely. But not Julie. There was no reason to suspect her of anything. She helped me smuggle out incriminating documents. When I made tapes, I'd pass them on to her. That was why we met up that night. We finally had enough information. We were going to give it to the feds and end this whole mess."

"I don't understand," I said. "Why would you guys keep the stuff yourself? Why not just turn everything over to the feds as you got it?"

Ken smiled. "You met Pistillo?"

I nodded.

"You have to understand, Will. I'm not saying all cops are corrupt or anything. But some are. I mean, one of them told McGuane I was in New Mexico. But more than that, some of them, like Pistillo, are too damn ambitious. I needed a bargaining chip. I couldn't leave myself that exposed. I had to turn it over on my own terms."

That, I thought, made sense. "But then the Ghost found out where you were."

"Yes."

"How?"

We reached a fence post. Ken put his foot up. I looked behind me. Melissa and Dad were keeping their distance. "I don't know, Will. Look, Julie and I were both so scared. Maybe that was part of it. Anyway, we were reaching the endgame. I thought we were home free. We were in the basement, on that couch, and we started kissing. . . ." He looked off again.

"And?"

"Suddenly there was a rope around my neck." Ken took a deep drag. "I was on top of her, and the Ghost had sneaked up on us. Next thing I knew, my air was gone. I was being strangled. John pulled back hard. I thought my neck would snap. I'm not even sure what happened next. Julie hit him, I think. That's how I got loose. He punched her in the face. I pulled away and started backing up. The Ghost took out a gun and fired. The first shot hit my shoulder." He closed his eyes.

"I ran then. God help me, I just ran."

We both soaked in the night. I could hear the crickets, but they played softly. Ken worked on his cigarette some more. I knew what he was thinking. Ran away. And then she died.

"He had a gun," I said. "It's not your fault."

"Yeah, sure." But Ken did not appear convinced. "You can probably guess what happened from there. I ran back to Sheila. We grabbed Carly. I had money stored away from my days working with McGuane. We took off, figuring that McGuane and Asselta would be close behind. It wasn't until a few days later, when the papers started listing me as a suspect in Julie's murder, that it hit me that I was not just running from McGuane but the whole world."

I asked the question that had been bothering me from the start. "Why didn't you tell me about Carly?"

His head snapped away as if I'd connected with a right on his jaw.

"Ken?"

He would not face me. "Can we skip that for now, Will?"

"I'd like to know."

"It's no big secret." His voice was strange now. I could hear the confidence start coming back, but it was somehow different, a shade off maybe. "I was in a dangerous spot. The feds captured me not long before her birth. I was afraid for her. So I didn't tell anybody she even existed. No one. I visited a lot, but I didn't even live with them. Carly stayed with her mother and Julie. I didn't want her connected to me in any way. You understand?"

"Yeah, sure," I said. I waited for him to say more. He smiled.

"What?"

"Just remembering camp," he said.

I smiled too.

"I loved it here," he said.

"Me too," I agreed. "Ken?"

"What?"

"How did you manage to hide for so long?"

He chuckled softly. Then he said, "Carly."

"Carly helped you hide?"

"My not telling anyone about her. I think it saved my life."

"How's that?"

"Everyone was looking for a fugitive on the run. That meant a single man. Or maybe a man who hooked up with a girl. What no one was looking for—and what could travel from spot to spot and remain invisible to law enforcement—was a family of three."

Again it made sense.

"The feds were lucky to catch me. I got careless. Or, I don't know, sometimes I think that maybe I wanted to be caught. Living like we were, always in fear, never putting down solid roots . . . it wears on you, Will. I missed you all so much. You most of all. Maybe I did let my guard down. Or maybe I needed it to end."

"So they extradited you?"

"Yeah."

"And you cut another deal."

"I thought they were going to pin Julie's murder on me for sure. But when I met up with Pistillo, well, he still wanted McGuane so badly. Julie was almost an afterthought. And they knew I hadn't done it. So . . ." He shrugged.

Ken talked then about New Mexico, about how he had never told the feds about Carly and Sheila, still protecting them. "I didn't want them to come back that early," he said, his voice softer now. "But Sheila wouldn't listen."

Ken told me about how he and Carly had been out of the house when the two men came by, how he came home and found them torturing his beloved, how he killed both men, and once again, how he ran. He told me how he stopped at the same pay phone and called Nora at my apartment—that would be the second call the FBI knew about. "I knew that they would come after her. Sheila's fingerprints were all over the house. If the feds didn't find her, McGuane might. So I told her she had to hide. Just until it was over."

It took a couple of days for Ken to find a discreet doctor in Las Vegas. The doctor had done what he could, but it was too late. Sheila Rogers, his eleven-year companion, died the next day. Carly had been asleep in the back of the car when her mother drew her last breath. Not sure what else to do—and hoping it would take pressure off Nora—he put the body of his lover on the side of a road and drove away.

Melissa and Dad hovered closer now. We all let in a little silence.

"What then?" I asked softly.

"I dropped Carly off with a friend of Sheila's. A cousin actually. I knew she'd be safe there. Then I started making my way east."

And when he said that, when those words about making his way east left his mouth . . . that was when it all started to go wrong.

Have you ever had one of those moments? You are listening, you are nodding, you are paying attention. Everything seems to be making sense and following a logical course, and then you see something, something small, something seemingly irrelevant, something almost worth overlooking—and you realize with mounting dread that everything is terribly wrong.

"We buried Mom on a Tuesday," I said.

"What?"

"We buried Mom on Tuesday," I repeated.

"Right," Ken said.

"You were in Las Vegas that day, right?"

He thought about it. "That's right."

I played it over in my head.

"What is it?" Ken asked.

"I don't get something."

"What?"

"On the afternoon of the funeral"—I stopped, waited for him to face me, found his eyes—"you were at the other graveyard with Katy Miller."

Something flickered across his face. "What are you talking about?"

"Katy saw you at the cemetery. You were standing under a tree near Julie's tombstone. You told Katy you were innocent. You told her you were back to find the real killer. How did you do that if you were on the other side of the country?"

My brother did not respond then. We both stood there. I felt something inside me start shrinking even before I heard the voice that made my world teeter yet again.

"I lied about that."

We all turned as Katy Miller stepped out from behind the tree. I looked at her and said nothing. She moved closer.

Katy had a gun in her hand.

It was pointed at Ken's chest. My mouth dropped open. I heard Melissa gasp. I heard my father shout "No!" But that all seemed a light-year away. Katy looked directly at me, probing at me, trying to tell me something I could never understand.

I shook my head.

"I was only six years old," Katy said. "Easy enough to dismiss as a witness. What did I know anyway? Just a little kid, right? I saw your brother that night. But I saw John Asselta too. Maybe I mixed them up, the cops could say. How would a six-year-old know the difference between cries of passion and agony anyway? To a six-year-old, they're one and the same, aren't they? It was easy for Pistillo and his agents to finesse what I told them. They wanted McGuane. To them, my sister was just another suburban junkie."

"What are you talking about?" I said.

Her eyes turned to Ken. "I was there that night, Will. Hiding behind my father's old army trunk again. I saw everything." She looked at me again and I am not sure I ever saw such clear eyes.

"John Asselta didn't murder my sister," she said. "Ken did."

My support beams started giving way. I started shaking my head again. I looked at Melissa. Her face was white. I tried my father, but his head was down.

Ken said, "You saw us making love."

"No." Katy's voice was surprisingly steady. "You killed her, Ken. You chose strangulation because you wanted to pin it on the Ghost—the same way you strangled Laura Emerson because she threatened to report the drug selling at Haverton."

I stepped forward. Katy turned to me. I stopped.

"When McGuane failed to kill Ken in New Mexico, I got a call from Asselta," she began. Katy spoke as if she'd been rehearsing these lines for a long time, which, I suspect, she had. "He told me how they had already captured your brother in Sweden. I didn't believe him at first. I said, if they caught him, how come we didn't know about it? He told me how the FBI wanted to let Ken off because he could still deliver McGuane. I was in shock. After all this time, they were going to let Julie's murderer just walk away? I couldn't allow that. Not after what my family had been through. Asselta knew that, I guess. That was why he contacted me."

I was still shaking my head, but she pressed on.

"My job was to stay close because we figured that if Ken contacted anybody, it would be you. I made up that story about seeing him at the graveyard, so you would trust me."

I found my voice. "But you were attacked," I said. "In my apartment."

"Yes," she said.

"You even called out Asselta's name."

"Think about that, Will." Her voice was so even, so confident.

"Think about what?" I asked.

"Why were you cuffed to the bed like that?"

"Because he was going to set me up, the same way he set up—"

But now she was the one shaking her head. Katy gestured with the gun at Ken. "He cuffed you because he didn't want you to get hurt," she said.

I opened my mouth, but nothing came out.

"He needed to get me alone. He needed to find out what I'd told you—to see what I'd remembered—before he killed me. And yes, I called out John's name. Not because I thought it was him behind the mask. I called out to him for help. And you did save my life, Will. He would have killed me."

My eyes slowly slid toward my brother.

"She's lying," Ken said. "Why would I kill Julie? She was helping me."

"That's almost true," Katy said. "And you're right: Julie did see Ken's arrest as a chance for redemption, just like he told you. And yes, Julie had agreed to help bring McGuane down. But your brother took it a step too far."

"How?" I asked.

"Ken knew that he had to get rid of the Ghost too. No loose ends. And the way to do that was to frame Asselta for Laura Emerson. Ken figured that Julie would have no problem going along with that. But he was wrong. You remember how close Julie and John were?"

I managed a nod.

"There was a bond there. I don't pretend to know why. I don't think either of them could explain it either. But Julie cared about him. I think she was the only one who ever did. She would bring down McGuane. She would do that gladly. But she would never hurt John Asselta."

I couldn't speak.

"That's bull," Ken said. "Will?"

I did not look at him.

Katy continued. "When Julie found out what Ken was going to do, she called the Ghost to warn him. Ken came to our house to get the tapes and files. She tried to stall him. They had sex. Ken asked for the evidence, but Julie refused to give it to him. He grew livid. He demanded to know where she had hidden it. She wouldn't tell him. When he realized what was up, he snapped and strangled her. The Ghost arrived seconds too late. He shot Ken as he ran away. I think he would have gone after him, but when he saw Julie dead on the floor, he just lost it. He fell to the floor. He cradled her head and let out the most anguished, inhuman wail I've ever heard. It was like something inside of him broke that would never be fixed."

Katy closed the gap between us. She grabbed my gaze and would not let it go.

"Ken didn't run because he was afraid of McGuane or of being framed or any of that," she said. "He ran because he killed Julie."

I was tumbling down a deep shaft, reaching, trying to grab on to something. "But the Ghost," I said, flailing. "He kidnapped us. . . ."

"We set that up," she said. "He let us escape. What neither of us realized was that you'd be so willing and ready. That driver was only supposed to make it look good. We had no idea you'd hurt him so badly."

"But why?"

"Because the Ghost knew the truth."

"What truth?"

She again gestured toward Ken. "That your brother would never show just to save your life. He would never put himself in that danger. That something like this"—she lifted her free hand—"was the only way he'd ever agree to meet you."

I shook my head again.

"We had a man wait at the yard that night. Just in case. No one ever came."

I stumbled back. I looked at Melissa. I looked at my father. And I knew that it was all true. Every word that she said. It was true.

Ken had killed Julie.

"I never meant to hurt you," Katy said to me. "But my family needs closure. The FBI had set him free. I had no choice. I couldn't let him get away with what he did to my sister."

My father spoke for the first time. "So what are you going to do now, Katy? Are you just going to shoot him?"

Katy said, "Yes."

And that was when all hell broke loose again.

My father made the sacrifice. He let out a cry and dove toward Katy. She fired the gun. My father staggered and continued toward her. He knocked the weapon from her hands. He also went down, holding his leg.

But the distraction had been enough.

When I looked up, Ken had whipped out his own gun. His eyes—the ones I had described as pure ice—were focused on Katy. He was going to shoot her. There was no hesitation. He just had to aim and pull the trigger.

I jumped toward him. My hand hit his arm just as he pulled the trigger. The gun went off, but the shot was wild. I tackled my brother. We rolled on the ground again, but it was nothing like before. Not this time. He elbowed me in the stomach. It knocked the wind out of me. He rose. He pointed the gun at Katy.

"No," I said.

"I have to," Ken said.

I grabbed him. We wrestled. I told Katy to run. Ken quickly took the advantage. He flipped me over. Our eyes met.

"She's the last thread," he said.

"I won't let you kill her."

Ken put the barrel of the gun against my forehead. Our faces were no more than an inch apart. I heard Melissa scream. I told her to stay back. In the corner of my eye, I saw her take out a cell phone and start dialing.

"Go ahead," I said. "Pull the trigger."

"You think I won't?" he said.

"You're my brother."

"So?" And again I thought about evil, about the shapes it takes, how you are never truly safe from it. "Didn't you hear anything Katy said? Don't you understand what I'm capable of—how many people I've hurt and betrayed?"

"Not me," I said softly.

He laughed, his face still inches from mine, the gun still pressed against my forehead. "What did you say?"

"Not me," I repeated.

Ken threw his head back. His laugh grew, echoing in the stillness. The sound chilled me like no other. "Not you?" he said. He lowered his lips toward me.

"You," he whispered in my ear, "I've hurt and betrayed more than anyone."

His words hit me like cinder blocks. I looked up at him. His face tensed and I was sure he was going to pull the trigger. I closed my eyes and waited. There were shouts and commotion, but all of that seemed very far away. What I heard now—the only sound that really reached me—was Ken crying. I opened my eyes. The world faded away. There was just the two of us.

I can't say what happened exactly. Maybe it was the position I was in, on my back, helpless, and he, my brother, not my savior this time, not my protector, but looming over me, the cause of it all. Maybe Ken looked down and saw me vulnerable and something instinctive, something that had always needed to keep me safe, took over. Maybe that was what shook him. I don't know. But as our eyes met, his face began to soften, started shifting in degrees.

And then it all changed again.

I felt Ken's grip on me loosen, but he kept the gun against my forehead. "I want you to make me a promise, Will," he said.

"What?"

"It's about Carly."

"Your daughter."

Ken closed his eyes now, and I saw genuine anguish. "She loves Nora," he said. "I want you two to take care of her. You raise her. Promise me."

"But what about—?"

"Please," Ken said, his voice a desperate plea. "Please promise me."

"Okay, I promise."

"And promise me you'll never take her to see me."

"What?"

He was crying hard now. Tears ran down his cheeks, wetting both our faces. "Promise me, dammit. You never mention me to her. You raise her as your own. You never let her visit me in prison. Promise me that, Will. Promise me or I'll start firing."

"Give me the gun first," I said, "and I'll promise."

Ken looked down at me. He pushed the gun into my hand. And then he kissed me hard. I wrapped my arms around him. I held him, the murderer. I hugged him to me. He cried into my chest like a small child. We were like that for a long time, until we heard the sirens.

I tried to push him away. "Go," I whispered to him, pleading. "Please. Just run."

But Ken did not move. Not this time. I will never know why exactly. Maybe he had run enough. Maybe he was trying to reach through the evil. Maybe he just wanted to be held. I don't know. But Ken stayed in my arms. He held on to me until the police came over and pulled him away.

58

Four days later

Carly's plane was on time.

Squares dropped us off at the airport. He, Nora, and I headed toward Newark Airport's Terminal C together. Nora walked up ahead. She knew the child and was anxious and excited to see her again. Me, I was anxious and scared.

Squares said, "Wanda and I talked."

I looked at him.

"I told her everything."

"And?"

He stopped and shrugged. "Looks like we're both going to be fathers sooner than expected."

I hugged him, happy as hell for them both. I was not so sure about my own situation. I was about to raise a twelve-year-old girl I did not know. I would do my best, but despite what Squares had said, I could never be Carly's father. I had come to terms with a lot about Ken, including the possibility that he would probably spend the remainder of his life in prison, but his insistence on never seeing his daughter again gnawed at me. He wanted, I assume, to protect his child. He felt, again I assumed, that the girl was best off without him.

I say "assumed" because I could not ask him. Once in custody, Ken had refused to see me too. I did not know why, but his whispered words . . .

You I've hurt and betrayed more than anyone.

. . . kept echoing inside me, shredding with razor talons, inescapable.

Squares stayed outside. Nora and I rushed in. She was wearing the engagement ring. We were early, of course. We found the incoming gate and hurried down the corridor. Nora put her purse into the X-ray machine. I set the metal detector off, but it was just my watch. We rushed to the gate, though the plane was not due to touch down for another fifteen minutes.

We sat and held hands and waited. Melissa had decided to stay in town for a little while. She was nursing my father back to health. Yvonne Sterno had, as promised, gotten the exclusive story. I don't know what it will do for her career. I had not yet contacted Edna Rogers. I would soon, I guessed.

As for Katy, no charges had been filed following the shooting. I thought about how much she needed closure, and I wondered if that night had helped her or not. I think maybe it did.

Assistant Director in Charge Joe Pistillo had recently announced that he would retire at the end of the year. I now understood only too well why he was so eager for me to keep Katy Miller out of this—not just for her health but because of what she had seen. I don't know if Pistillo truly doubted the testimony of a six-year-old girl or if his sister's grieving face made him twist Katy's words to suit his purposes. I do know that the feds had kept Katy's old testimony under wraps, supposedly because they were trying to protect a little girl. But I have my doubts.

I had, of course, been crushed to learn the truth about my brother, and yet—this is going to sound odd—it was somehow okay. The ugliest truth, in the end, was still better than the prettiest of lies. My world was darker, but it was back on its axis.

Nora leaned over. "You okay?"

"Scared," I said.

"I love you," she said. "Carly will love you too."

We stared up at the arrivals monitor. It began to blink. The Continental Airlines gatekeeper picked up the microphone and announced that Flight 672 had landed. Carly's flight. I turned to Nora. She smiled and gave my hand another squeeze.

I let my eyes travel then. My gaze floated across the waiting passengers, the men in suits, the women with carry-ons, the families heading for vacation, the delayed, the frustrated, the worn. I casually swept over their faces and that was when I saw him looking at me. My heart stopped.

The Ghost.

A spasm ripped through me.

Nora said, "What?"

"Nothing."

The Ghost beckoned me toward him. I stood as though in a trance.

"Where are you going?"

"I'll be right back," I said.

"But she's going to be here."

"I just need to run to the bathroom."

I kissed the top of Nora's head gently. She looked concerned. She glanced across the gate, but the Ghost was no longer in sight. I knew better. If I walked, he would find me. Ignoring him would only make it worse. Running would be futile. He would ultimately find us.

I had to face him.

I started walking in the direction where he'd been. My legs felt rubbery, but I kept going. When I passed a long row of abandoned pay phones, I heard him.

"Will?"

I turned and he was there. He motioned for me to sit next to him. I did. We both faced the plate glass window rather than each other. The window magnified the rays. The heat was stifling. I squinted my eyes. So did he.

"I didn't come back for your brother," the Ghost said. "I came back for Carly."

His words turned me to stone. I said, "You can't have her."

He smiled. "You don't understand."

"Then tell me."

The Ghost shifted his body toward me. "You want people lined up, Will. You want the good guys on one side, the bad on the other. It doesn't work that way, does it? It is never that simple. Love, for example, leads to hate. I think that was what started it all. Primitive love."

"I don't know what you're talking about."

"Your father," he said. "He loved Ken too much. I look for the seed, Will. And that's where I find it. In your father's love."

"I still don't know what you're talking about."

"What I'm about to say," the Ghost continued, "I've only told one other person. Do you understand?"

I said that I did.

"You have to go back to when Ken and I were in the fourth grade," he said. "You see, I didn't stab Daniel Skinner. Ken did. But your father loved him so much that he protected him. He bought off my old man. Paid him five grand. Believe it or not, your father almost saw himself as charitable. My old man beat me all the time. Most people said I should be in foster care anyway. The way your father saw it, I would either get off on self-defense or end up getting therapy and three square meals a day."

I was stunned silent. I thought about our meeting up at the Little League field. My father's crippling fear, his icy silence when we got back, his telling Asselta, "You want someone, you take me." Once again it all made terrible sense.

"I only told one person the truth," he said. "Any guesses?"

Something else fell into place. "Julie," I said.

He nodded. The bond. It explained a lot about their strange bond.

"So why are you here?" I asked. "To take vengeance on Ken's daughter?"

"No," the Ghost said with a small laugh. "There is no easy way to tell you this, Will, but maybe science can help."

He handed me a folder. I looked down at it. "Open it," he said.

I did as he asked.

"It's the autopsy of the recently departed Sheila Rogers," he said.

I frowned. I didn't wonder how he got it. I was sure he had his sources. "What does this have to do with anything?"

"Look here." The Ghost pointed with a thin finger to an entry midway down. "You see down at the bottom? No scars on the pubic bone from the tears of the periosteum. No comments about pale striations over the breast and abdominal wall. Not unusual, of course. It wouldn't mean anything, unless you were looking for it."

"Looking for what?"

He closed the file. "Signs that the victim had given birth." He saw the look of confusion on my face and added, "Put simply, Sheila Rogers could not have been Carly's mother."

I was about to say something but the Ghost handed me another file. I looked at the name on it.

Julie Miller.

The cold spread inside me. He flipped it open and pointed to an entry and started reading, "Pubic scars, pale striations, changes in the microscopic architecture of the breast and uterine tissues," he said. "And the trauma was recent. See here? The scar from the episiotomy was still pronounced."

I stared at the words.

"Julie did not come home just to meet up with Ken. She was getting her act together after a very bad spell. She was finding herself again, Will. She wanted to tell you the truth."

"What truth?"

But he shook his head and continued. "She would have told you earlier, but she wasn't sure how you'd react. The way you so easily let her break up with you . . . that was what I meant when I said you were supposed to fight for her. You just let her go."

Our eyes locked.

"Julie had a baby six months before she died," the Ghost said. "She and the child, a girl, lived with Sheila Rogers in that apartment. I think Julie would have finally told you that night, but your brother took care of that. Sheila loved the child too. When Julie was murdered and your brother needed to escape, Sheila wanted to keep it as her own. And Ken, well, he saw how useful a baby could be to hide an international fugitive. He had no children. Neither did Sheila. It would be better than the best disguise."

Ken's whispered words came back to me. . . .

"Do you understand what I'm telling you, Will?"

You I've hurt and betrayed more than anyone.

The Ghost's voice cut through the haze. "You're not a substitute here. You're Carly's real father."

I don't think I was breathing anymore. I stared out at nothing. Hurt and betrayed. My brother. My brother had taken my child.

The Ghost stood. "I didn't come back for revenge or even justice," he continued. "But the truth is, Julie died protecting me. I failed her. I made a vow that I would save her child. It took me eleven years."

I stumbled to my feet. We stood side by side. Passengers were pouring off the plane. The Ghost jammed something in my pocket. A piece of paper. I ignored it.

"I sent that surveillance tape to Pistillo, so McGuane won't bother you. I found the evidence in the house that night and kept it all these years. You and Nora are safe now. I took care of everything."

More passengers disembarked. I stood and waited and listened.

"Remember that Katy is Carly's aunt, that the Millers are her grandparents. Let them be a part of her life. Do you hear me?"

I nodded, and that was when Carly came through the gate. Everything inside of me shut down. The girl walked out with such poise. Like . . . like her mother. Carly looked around and when she spotted Nora, her face broke into the most amazing smile. My heart broke. Right then and there, it shattered. The smile. That smile, you see, belonged to my mother. It was Sunny's smile, like an echo from the past, a sign that not all of my mother—nor all of Julie—had been extinguished.

I choked back a sob and felt a hand on my back.

"Go now," the Ghost whispered, gently pushing me toward my daughter.

I glanced back, but John Asselta was already gone. So I did the only thing I could. I made my way toward the woman I loved and my child.

Epilogue

Later that night, after I kissed Carly and helped her to bed, I found the piece of paper he'd jammed into my pocket. It was just the first few lines of a newspaper clipping:

KANSAS CITY HERALD

Man Found Dead in Car

Cramden, Mo.—Cray Spring, an off-duty police officer with the Cramden force, was found strangled in his car, apparently the victim of a robbery. His wallet was reportedly missing. Local police said his car was found in the parking lot behind a local bar. Police chief Evan Kraft said that there were no suspects at this time, and that the investigation was ongoing.